There was the great stone seal – broken.

There was the bone pit – empty. Exhumed.

The sight was a sword blow to his spirit. He felt his resolve melt and gush from the wound, as if he was a dreadworm freshly beheaded. The mantle of Jan's prophecy became a crushing weight on him. He sagged, leaning on his sword.

Fresh-turned dirt. Whoever had opened Lord Bone's grave had done it recently.

Whoever? thought Alf bitterly.

Only eight – seven, now – could have opened the seal and survived. *One of us did this.*

By Gareth Hanrahan

THE
SWORD
DEFIANT

GARETH
HANRAHAN

orbitbooks.net

Copyright © 2023 by Gareth Ryder-Hanrahan
Excerpt from *The Lost War* copyright © 2019 by King Lot Publishing Ltd.
Excerpt from *Empire of Exiles* copyright © 2022 by Erin M. Evans

Cover design by Sophie Harris—LBBG
Cover illustration by Thea Dumitriu
Maps by Jon Hodgson, Handiwork Games
Author photograph by Edel Ryder-Hanrahan

Orbit
Hachette Book Group
1290 Avenue of the Americas
New York, NY 10104
orbitbooks.net

First Edition: May 2023
Simultaneously published in Great Britain by Orbit

Orbit is an imprint of Hachette Book Group.
The Orbit name and logo are trademarks of Little, Brown Book Group Limited.

The publisher is not responsible for websites (or their content) that are not owned by the publisher.

The Hachette Speakers Bureau provides a wide range of authors for speaking events. To find out more, go to hachettespeakersbureau.com or email HachetteSpeakers@hbgusa.com.

Orbit books may be purchased in bulk for business, educational, or promotional use. For information, please contact your local bookseller or the Hachette Book Group Special Markets Department at special.markets@hbgusa.com.

Library of Congress Control Number: 2022950259

ISBNs: 9780316537155 (trade paperback), 9780316537308 (ebook)

Printed in the United States of America

LSC-C

Printing 4, 2023

THE
SWORD
DEFIANT

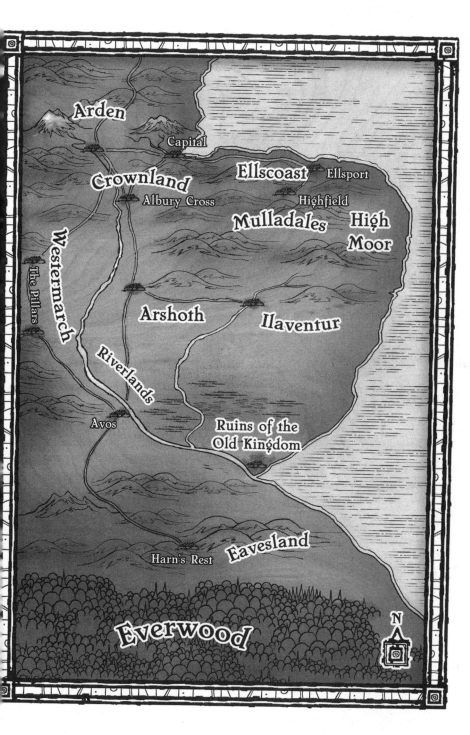

LIST OF CHARACTERS

THE NINE HEROES

Peir[+] of the Crownland, called the Paladin
Jan of Arshoth, called the Pious, priestess of the Intercessors
Blaise of Ellscoast, called the Scholar, master of the
  Wailing Tower
Berys the Rootless, later Lady Berys
Lath, a Changeling, called the Beast
Thurn of the As Gola tribe, saviour of the Wilder-folk of the
  northern woods
Gundan, son of Gwalir, General of the Dwarfholt
Laerlyn, daughter of the Erlking, Princess of the Everwood
Aelfric of Mulladale, called the Bonebreaker, dubbed
  Sir Lammergeier, Keeper of the Spellbreaker, also
  known as Alf

IN THE SOUTH

Olva, sister to Aelfric of Mulladale
Long Tom[+], father to Aelfric and Olva
Galwyn Forster[+], her late husband
Derwyn, her son
Cu, a suspicious dog
Bor, a Rootless mercenary
Torun, a dwarf who seeks to be a wizard
Lyulf Martens, a "merchant" in the blood trade
Abran, a priest turned Rootless knave, in league with Martens

IN NECRAD

Timeon Vond, governor of Necrad
Threeday, a Vatling
Abbess Marat, a priestess of the Intercessors
Gamling, lieutenant to Gundan
Remilard, a guard
Ceremos, an elf-child
Elithadil and Andiriel, his parents

(Formerly of Necrad, now defeated)
The Chieftain of the Marrow-Eaters[+], an Ogre
Amerith the Oracle, a Witch Elf Seer
Acraist Wraith-Captain[+], Hand of Bone, Wielder of the Sword
    Spellbreaker
Sundry other vampires, spirits and other horrors[+]
Lord Bone[+] the Necromancer, the Dark Lord

IN THE NEW PROVINCES

Earl Duna, chief among the landholders of the New Provinces
Erdys of Ilaventur, his wife
Their sons, Sir Aelfric the Younger, Idmaer and Dunweld
Sir Prelan, a champion of the tourney ground
Sir Eddard Forster, a knight-errant

Talis[+], daughter of Thurn
The Old Man of the Woods, a Wilder mystic

ON THE ISLE OF DAWN

Prince Maedos of Dawn, son of the Erlking, brother to Laerlyn
A simple gardener

PART ONE

From his city of Necrad, Lord Bone sent forth an evil host to despoil the land. Doom was at hand.

Nine arose in answer. Elf and Dwarf, Men of Summerswell and the northern Wild, heroes all. Know them now, for their names shall never be forgotten.

Thurn the Wilder, Lath the Beast,

Gundan of the Dwarfholt, Laerlyn of the Everwood,

Blaise the Scholar, Jan the Pious,

Aelfric Bonebreaker, ever faithful.

First among them, Peir the Paladin, Peir the Peerless.

It was Peir who gathered them and Peir who led them.

And at the last, it was Peir who died for them.

From *The Song of the Nine*,
by Sir Rhuel of the Eaveslands

CHAPTER ONE

H is story had not begun in a tavern, but Alf had ended up in
one anyway.

"An ogre," proclaimed the old man from the corner by the
hearth, "a fearsome ogre! Iron-toothed, yellow-eyed, arms like oak
branches!" He wobbled as he crossed the room towards the table of
adventurers. "I saw it not three days ago, up on the High Moor. The
beast must be slain, lest it find its way down to our fields and flocks!"

One of the young lads was beefy and broad-shouldered, Mulladale
stock. He fancied himself a fighter, with that League-forged sword
and patchwork armour. "I'll wager it's one of Lord Bone's minions,
left over from the war," he declared loudly. "We'll hunt it down!"

"I can track it!" This was a woman in green, her face tattooed. A
Wilder-woman of the northern woods – or dressed as one, anyway.
"We just need to find its trail."

"There are places of power up on the High Moor," said a third,
face shadowed by his hood. He spoke with the refined tones of a
Crownland scholar. An apprentice mage, cloak marked with the
sign of the Lord who'd sponsored him. He probably had a star-trap
strung outside in the bushes. "Ancient temples, shrines to forgotten
spirits. Such an eldritch beast might . . ."

He paused, portentously. Alf bloody hated it when wizards did that, leaving pauses like pit traps in the conversation. Just get on with it, for pity's sake.

Life was too short.

" . . . be drawn to such places. As might other . . . legacies of Lord Bone."

"We'll slay it," roared the Mulladale lad, "and deliver this village from peril!"

That won a round of applause from the locals, more for the boy's enthusiasm than any prospect of success. The adventurers huddled over the table, talking ogre-lore, talking about the dangers of the High Moor and the virtues of leaving at first light.

Alf scowled, irritated but unable to say why. He'd finish his drink, he decided, and then turn in. Maybe he'd be drunk enough to fall straight asleep. The loon had disturbed a rare evening of forgetfulness. He'd enjoyed sitting there, listening to village gossip and tall tales and the crackling of the fire. Now, the spell was broken and he had to think about monsters again.

He'd been thinking about monsters for a long time.

The old man sat down next to Alf. Apparently, he wasn't done. He wasn't that old, either – Alf realised he was about the same age. They'd both seen the wrong side of forty-five winters. "Ten feet tall it was," he exclaimed, sending spittle flying into Alf's tankard, "and big tusks, like a bull's horns, at the side of its mouth." He stuck his fingers out to illustrate. "It had the stink of Necrad about it. They have the right of it – it's one of Bone's creatures that escaped! The Nine should have put them all to the sword!"

"Bone's ogres," said Alf, "didn't have tusks." His voice was croaky from disuse. "They cut 'em off. Your ogre didn't come out of Necrad."

"You didn't see the beast! I did! Only the Pits of Necrad could spawn such—"

"You haven't seen the sodding Pits, either," said Alf. He felt the cold rush of anger, and stood up. He needed to be away from people. He stumbled across the room towards the stairs.

Another of the locals caught his arm. "Bit of luck for you, eh?" The fool was grinning and red-cheeked. *Twist, break the wrist. Grab his neck, slam his face into the table. Kick him into the two behind him. Then grab a weapon.* Alf fought against his honed instincts. The evening's drinking had not dulled his edge enough.

He dug up words. "What do you mean?"

"You said you were going off up the High Moor tomorrow. You'd run straight into that ogre's mouth. Best you stay here another few days, 'til it's safe."

"Safe," echoed Alf. He pulled his arm free. "I can't stay. I have to go and see an old friend."

The inn's only private room was upstairs. Sleeping in the common room was a copper a night, the private room an exorbitant six for a poky attic room and the pleasure of hearing the innkeeper snore next door.

Alf locked the door and took Spellbreaker from its hiding place under the bed. The sword slithered in his grasp, metal twisting beneath the dragonhide.

"I could hear them singing about you." Its voice was a leaden whisper. "About the siege of Necrad."

"Just a drinking song," said Alf, "nothing more. They didn't know it was me."

"They spoke the name of my true wielder, and woke me from dreams of slaughter."

"It rhymes with rat-arsed, that's all."

"No, it doesn't."

"It does the way they say it. *Acra-sed.*"

"It's pronounced with a hard 't'," said the sword. "Acrai-*st* the Wraith-Captain, Hand of Bone."

"Well," said Alf, "I killed him, so I get to say how it's said. And it's rat-arsed. And so am I."

He shoved the sword back under the bed, then threw himself down, hoping to fall into oblivion. But the same dream caught him again, as it had for a month, and it called him up onto the High Moor to see his friend.

The adventurers left at first light.

Alf left an hour later, after a leisurely breakfast. *Getting soft*, he muttered to himself, but he still caught up with them at the foot of a steep cliff, arguing over which of the goat paths would bring them up onto the windy plateau of the High Moor. Alf marched past them, shoulders hunched against the cold of autumn.

"Hey! Old man!" called one of them. "There's a troll out there!"

Alf grunted as he studied the cliff ahead. It was steep, but not insurmountable. Berys and he had scaled the Wailing Tower in the middle of a howling necrostorm. This was nothing. He found a handhold and hauled himself up the rock face, ignoring the cries of the adventurers below. The Wilder girl followed him a little way, but gave up as Alf rapidly outdistanced her.

His shoulders, his knees ached as he climbed. *Old fool.* Showing off for what? To impress some village children? Why not wave Spellbreaker around? Or carry Lord Bone's skull around on a pole? *If you want glory, you're twenty years too late*, he thought to himself. He climbed on, stretching muscles grown stiff from disuse.

At the top, he sat down on a rock to catch his breath. He'd winded himself. The Wailing Tower, too, was nearly twenty years ago.

He pulled his cloak around himself to ward off the breeze, and lingered there for a few minutes. He watched the adventurers as they debated which path to take, and eventually decided on the wrong one, circling south-east along the cliffs until they vanished into the broken landscape below the moor. He looked out west, across the Mulladales, a patchwork of low hills and farmlands and wooded coppices. Little villages, little lives. All safe.

Twenty years ago? Twenty-one? Whenever it was, Lord Bone's armies came down those goat paths. Undead warriors scuttling down the cliffs head first like bony lizards. Wilder scouts with faces painted pale as death. Witch Elf knights mounted on winged dread-worms. Golems, furnaces blazing with balefire. Between all those horrors and the Mulladales stood just nine heroes.

"It was twenty-two years ago," said Spellbreaker. The damn sword was listening to his thoughts again – or had he spoken out loud? "Twenty-two years since I ate the soul of the Illuminated."

"We beat you bastards good," said Alf. "And chased you out of the temple. Peir nearly slew Acraist then, do you remember?"

"Vividly," replied the sword.

Peir, his hammer blazing with the fire of the Intercessors. Berys, flinging vials of holy water she'd filched from the temple. Gundan, bellowing a war cry as he swung Chopper. Gods, they were so young then. Children, really, only a few years older than the idiot ogre-hunters. The battle of the temple was where they'd first proved themselves heroes. The start of a long, bitter war against Lord Bone. Oh, they'd got side-tracked – there'd been prophecies and quests and strife aplenty to lead them astray – but the path to Necrad began right here, on the edge of the High Moor.

He imagined his younger self struggling up those cliffs, that cheap pig-sticker of a sword clenched in his teeth. What would he have done, if that young warrior reached to the top and saw his future sitting there? Old, tired, tough as old boots. Still had all his limbs, but plenty of scars.

"We won," he whispered to the shade of the past, "and it's still bloody hard."

"You," said the sword, "are going crazy. You should get back to Necrad, where you belong."

"When I'm ready."

"I can call a dreadworm. Even here."

"No."

"Anything could be happening there. We've been away for more than two years, *moping*." There was an unusual edge to the sword's plea. Alf reached down and pulled Spellbreaker from its scabbard, so he could look the blade in the gemstone eye on its hilt and—

—Reflected in the polished black steel as it crept up behind him. Grey hide, hairy, iron-tusked maw drooling. Ogre.

Alf threw himself forward as the monster lunged at him and rolled to the edge of the cliff. Pebbles and dirt tumbled down the precipice, but he caught himself before he followed them over. He hoisted Spellbreaker, but the sword suddenly became impossibly heavy and threatened to tug him backwards over the cliff.

One of the bastard blade's infrequent bouts of treachery. Fine.

He flung the heavy sword at the onrushing ogre, and the monster stumbled over it. Its ropy arms reached for him, but Alf dodged along the cliff edge, seized the monster's wrist and pulled with all his might. The ogre, abruptly aware of the danger that they'd both fall to their deaths, scrambled away from the edge. It was off balance, and vulnerable. Alf leapt on the monster's back and drove one elbow into its ear. The ogre bellowed in pain and fell forward onto the rock he'd been sitting on. Blood gushed from its nose, and the sight sparked unexpected joy in Alf. For a moment, he felt young again, and full of purpose. This, this was what he was meant for!

The ogre tried to dislodge him, but Alf wrapped his legs around its chest, digging his knees into its armpits, his hands clutching shanks of the monster's hair. He bellowed into the ogre's ear in the creature's own language.

"Do you know who I am? I'm the man who killed the Chieftain of the Marrow-Eaters!"

The ogre clawed at him, ripping at his cloak. Its claws scrabbled against the dwarven mail Alf wore beneath his shirt. Alf got his arm locked across the ogre's throat and squeezed.

"I killed Acraist the Wraith-Captain!"

The ogre reared up and threw itself back, crushing Alf against the rock. The impact knocked the air from his lungs, and he felt one of his ribs crack, but he held firm – and sank his teeth into his foe's ear. He bit off a healthy chunk, spat it out and hissed:

"I killed Lord Bone."

It was probably the pain of losing an earlobe, and not his threat, that made the ogre yield, but yield it did. The monster fell to the ground, whimpering.

Alf released his grip on the ogre's neck and picked up Spellbreaker. Oh, *now* the magic sword was perfectly light and balanced in his hand. One swing, and the ogre's head would go rolling across the ground. One cut, and the monster would be slain.

He slapped the ogre with the flat of the blade.

"Look at me."

Yellow terror-filled eyes stared at him.

"There are adventurers hunting for you. They went south-east. You, run north. That way." He pointed with the blade, unsure if the ogre even spoke this dialect. It was the tongue he'd learned in Necrad, the language the Witch Elves used to order their war-beasts around. "Run north!" he added in common, and he shoved the ogre again. The brute got the message and ran, loping on all fours away from Alf. It glanced back in confusion, unsure of what had just happened.

Alf lifted Spellbreaker, glared into the sword's eye.

"I was testing you," said the sword. "You haven't had a proper fight in months. Tournies don't count – no opponent has the courage to truly test you, and it's all for show anyway. Your strength dwindles. My wielder must—"

"I'm not your bloody wielder. I'm your gaoler."

"I am *bored*, wielder. Two years of wandering the forests and back-roads. Two years of hiding and lurking. And when you finally pluck up the courage to go anywhere, it's to an even duller village. I tell you, those people should have welcomed the slaughter my master brought, to relieve them of the tedium of their pathetic—"

"Try that again, and I'll throw you off a cliff."

"Do it. Someone will find me. Some*thing*. I'm a weapon of darkness, and I call to—"

"I'll drop you," said Alf wearily, "into a volcano."

Last time, they'd reached the temple in two days. He'd spent twice as long already, trudging over stony ground, pushing through thorns and bracken, clambering around desolate tors and outcrops of bare rock. He'd known that finding the hidden ravine of the temple would be tricky, but it took him longer than he'd expected to reach Giant's Rock, and that was at least a day's travel from the ravine.

That big pillar of stone, one side covered with shaggy grey-green moss – that was Giant's Rock, right? In his memory it was bigger. Alf squinted at the rock, trying to imagine how it might be mistaken for a hunched giant. He'd seen real giants, and they were a lot bigger.

If this was Giant's Rock, he should turn south there to reach the valley. If it wasn't, then turning south would bring him into the empty lands of the fells where no one lived.

Maybe they'd come from a more northerly direction, last time. He walked around the pillar of stone. It remained obstinately un-giant-like. No one ever accused Alf of having the soul of a poet. A rock pile was a rock pile to him. The empty sky above him, the empty land all around. He regretted letting that ogre run off; maybe he should have forced it to guide him to the valley. Turn south, or continue east?

The valley was well hidden. There'd been wars fought in these parts, hundreds of years ago, in the dark days after . . . after . . . after some kingdom had fallen. The Old Kingdom. Alf's grasp of history was as good as could be expected of a Mulladale farm boy who could barely write his name, and nearly thirty years of adventuring hadn't taught him much more. Oh, he could tell you the best way to *fight* an animated skeleton, or loot an ancient tomb, but "whence came the skeleton" or "who built the tomb" were matters for cleverer heads. He remembered Blaise lecturing him on this battlefield, the wizard wasting his breath on talking when he should have been keeping it for walking. Different factions in the Old Kingdom clashed here. Rival cults, Blaise told him, fighting until both sides were exhausted and the Illuminated were driven into hiding. The green grass swallowed up the battlefields and the barrow tombs, and everything was forgotten until Lord Bone had called up those long-dead warriors. Skeletons crawled out of the dirt and took up their rusty swords, and roamed the High Moors again.

Last time, Thurn the Wilder led them. He could track anything and anyone, even the dead. He'd brought them straight to the secret path, following Lord Bone's forces into the hidden heart of the temple. All Alf had to do was fight off the flying dreadworms sent to slow them down. Even then, Acraist had seen that the Nine of them were dangerous.

"No, he didn't," said the sword. It was the first time it had spoken since the cliff top.

"Stop that."

"If Acraist thought you were a threat, he'd have sent more than a few riderless worms. He was intent on breaking the aegis of the temple, not worrying about you bandits. You were an irrelevant nuisance. You got lucky."

"Well, he got killed. And so did Lord Bone, and you can't say that was luck."

A quiver ran through the sword. The blade's equivalent of a derisive snort.

He took another step east, and the sword quivered again.

"What is it?"

"Nothing, O Lammergeier," said Spellbreaker sullenly. Alf hated that nickname, given to him in the songs by some stupid poet drunk on metaphor. He'd never even seen one of the ugly vultures of the mountains beyond Westermarch. They were bone-breaking birds, feasters on marrow. And while Alf might be old and ugly enough now to resemble a vulture, the bloody song had given him that name twenty or so years ago. He'd broken Bone, hence – Sir Lammergeier.

Poetry was almost as bad as prophecy.

The sword only used the name when it wanted to annoy him – or distract him. What had that pretentious apprentice said in the inn, about creatures of Lord Bone sensing places of power? Alf drew the sword again and took a step forward. The jewelled eye seemed to wince, eldritch light flaring deep within the ruby.

He shook Spellbreaker. "Can you detect the temple?"

"No."

Another step. Another wince.

"You bloody well can," said Alf.

"It's sanctified," admitted Spellbreaker reluctantly. "Acraist protected me from the radiance, last time."

Alf looked around at the moorland. No radiance was visible, at least none he had eyes to see.

"Well then." He set off east, and only turned south when prompted by the twisting of the demonic sword.

Another day, and the terrain became familiar. Some blessing in the temple softened the harshness of the moor. Wildflowers grew all around. Streams cascaded down the rocks, chiming like silver bells. Alf felt weariness fall from his bones, sloughing away like he'd sunk into a warm bath.

Spellbreaker shrieked and rattled in its scabbard.

"It's too bright. I cannot go in there. It will shatter me."

"I'm not leaving you here."

"Wielder, I cannot . . ."

Alf hesitated. Spellbreaker was among the most dangerous things to come out of Necrad, a weapon of surpassing evil. It could shatter any spell, break any ward. In the hands of a monster, it could wreak terrible harm upon the world. Even that ogre could become something dangerous under the blade's tutelage. But maybe the sword was right – dragging it into the holy place might damage it. When they'd fought Acraist that first time, down in the valley, the Wraith-Captain wasn't half as tough as when they battled him seven years later. The valley burned things of darkness.

Would it burn Alf if he carried the sword down there?

"Look," sneered Spellbreaker. "You're expected."

A tiny candle flame of light danced in the air ahead of Alf. And then another kindled, and another, and another, a trail of sparks leading down into the valley.

Alf drew the sword and drove it deep into the earth. "Stay," he said to it, scolding it like a dog.

Then down, into the hidden valley of the Illuminated One.

CHAPTER TWO

Rubble lay strewn across the valley. Acraist had shattered the temple arch before they'd arrived. Alf remembered the headlong race down the path, hastening to intervene before the Wraith-Captain slew the Illuminated One. Laerlyn leaping gracefully down the rocks, loosing arrows as she ran. Jan weeping even as she called on the Intercessors to shield them from Acraist's death-spells. Miracles warring with dark magic in the air.

In retrospect, the greatest miracle was that none of them had tripped and broken their necks as they ran down the steep path into the valley. The little sparkling lights led Alf along the safest route, until he reached the valley floor. Then they shot off ahead of him, meteors racing over the rubble, dodging in and out of hiding places. There was something playful about their movements.

The Sanctum of the Illuminated One – another thing wizards did was Audibly Pronounce Capital Letters – was carved out of the rock of the canyon. Pillars covered with twining glyphs bore images of godly figures Alf didn't recognise. One was a woman, her face so worn nothing of her features remained, although Alf could still make out chains carved on her wrists. Opposite her was a horned figure holding a staff, arcane sigils in an arc above him. He remembered Jan and Blaise had yammered about how bloody old the temple was – older than any shrine in Summerswell, even the big one in Arshoth.

If they liked old stuff, they'd love Alf now. Forty-five summers by the reckoning of the south, but Necrad didn't have proper summers, or proper time, so who knew how old he was. He felt as ancient as the toppled statues around him.

He followed the lights, and they led him towards a hut of piled stones.

Jan sat waiting at the entrance.

She'd become thin – so thin he could see the hut through her, as though she was made of coloured glass. The little lights ran to her, flowed into her, and he could see them now like stars through the window of her body. She smiled at him, and it was like looking at a radiant sunset. Still, he shivered at the sight. They'd all changed so much.

The rest of the Nine had, anyway. Alf remained Alf.

"Hello, Aelfric," said Jan.

"I got the dream you sent."

She nodded. "And it guided you here."

"Guided ain't the way I'd put it, but aye." He paused, awkwardly. He'd loved Jan, they all did, the little mouse of the Nine, but he'd never claimed to understand her. "Should I kneel?"

"Just sit, Alf. Holiness isn't in your knees."

Alf settled awkwardly opposite Jan. He found himself holding his breath, as if exhaling too forcefully might blow away the gossamer of her existence. "Jan ... what happened to you?" Last time he'd seen her was when she left Necrad a decade ago. Then, she'd been exhausted by her work in the city. Angry, too – simmering, bitter, her kindness worn down until it was a thin crust over bubbling lava.

Now, she was something else.

"Are you going elf on us?" he asked. Old elves faded, but not like this – and Jan wasn't an elf.

She ignored his questions. "Are you hungry? I don't eat any more."

"I could eat."

He noticed a bowl just inside the entrance to the hut. Steam rose from it, carrying a smell that was instantly familiar. His mother had made stews just like this. He picked it up and took a spoonful.

"Is this real?"

"It's nourishing," said Jan.

He grunted at that non-answer, but he still ate. His instinct was to never turn down the offer of a meal.

"I left Necrad because I was losing myself," Jan said. "My faith, my hope. Call it what you will. I couldn't stay there any longer. Despite everything we did, there's a pall of darkness over that city. I went away looking for renewal. I went to the temples and looked for the Intercessors, but they didn't answer. In the end I found my way back here. Back to where it all began for us." She waved her hand at the ruins of the temple, and Alf couldn't help notice that her fingers trailed off into mist when she moved. "The Illuminated One and his monks were dead, of course, and Acraist destroyed their library, but I was able to reconstruct some of their secrets. I only intended to stay here for a little while, but ... " She shrugged. "That's not how things turned out."

"You dead?"

She laughed. "You haven't changed, Alf. Always cutting things down to the simplest possible question. No, I'm not dead. I'm on a different path now, though. I'm the new Illuminated One, I suppose. I commune with the light." She brushed back her greying hair. She still had little silver bells and talismans woven into it, but they made no sound.

"Right, right. Sounds nice." He stirred his stew, trying to work out what it meant for Jan to call herself the Illuminated One. Back home, the village clerics always warned their flocks to shun the followers of the Illuminated. It was misguided, they preached, to reject the kindly hand of the holy Intercessors. Mortals were not meant to commune with cosmic forces directly. The weaving of fate was supposed to be beyond mortal comprehension. Clerics prayed to the Intercessors, and the Intercessors passed word to whatever was up there.

Alf's grasp of theology was on a par with his history.

"You're thinking that I sound like the crazy monks who used to beg for alms at harvest time, back when you were a boy," said Jan, a mischievous smile playing around her faint lips.

"I don't like it when people read my thoughts," snapped Alf.

Jan flickered, her whole form vanishing for an eye blink. "I didn't," she said, "I wouldn't do that. I don't need to, Alf – I know your face. I can tell when you have doubts."

"Aye, well. I have thoughts so rarely, I want to keep 'em for myself."

"And your thought was a true one. Those monks were among the last acolytes of the Illuminated One. They were guardians of an ancient tradition, humanity's first path towards the light. The Wood Elves taught us another way, through the Intercessors. I once followed the elven way, but I'm on the older path now."

"You don't believe in the Intercessors any more?" Alf had never been especially devout, but reverence for the Intercessors was deeply ingrained into him. He'd always liked the thought that even when things seemed darkest, wiser powers were watching over everyone.

"Oh, the spirits are real. But they don't talk to me any more. I lost the blessing before we got to Necrad. I hoped that they'd come back after we defeated Lord Bone, but they didn't." She smiled. "Nothing turned out quite like we hoped, did it?"

"I didn't know." He stopped eating. "You helped us pray, though. Said the litanies and all. Took Peir's confession." In truth, Alf had never found much of worth in the prayers. It had all seemed like a waste of time to him. He could always think of something more productive to do than sit around and listen to the litany. But he'd sat there and listened, for Peir's sake if nothing else, and it had been a comfort.

"I was still your cleric. Even if my own beliefs wavered, I could still say the words if they helped you. Faith is a strange thing, Alf. If you hold true to something, if you hold onto it with all your strength, body and soul – you can accomplish wonders. Peir did. He never stopped believing, not even when everything looked hopeless. And he brought us through." A sad smile ghosted across her face. "My own doubts didn't matter a bit, compared to his certainty. It was what we needed then. Now ... now it's up to us that are left. Or, well, to you."

"You're not coming back to Necrad."

"I cannot." The light in her flickered for a moment at the thought of returning to Lord Bone's city. "Tell me, where were you when I called? My dream-sendings could not enter Necrad, so I know you weren't there when you got my message. Why did you leave the city?"

Why indeed? "I got hurt," he said slowly, "down in the Pits. A linnorm poisoned me. Healers patched me up, of course, but ..." He shoved the spoon around the bowl, as though the answer was hidden in stew that was probably an illusion or a parable anyway. "But I knew I'd messed up. I let my guard down. I needed to get my nerve back, so I went for a walk." He shifted awkwardly and looked down at his feet. "Been walking for a few years."

"You were badly wounded," said Jan, her voice full of concern.

"I've had worse," Alf lied. Or half lied. He'd suffered worse in-juries, certainly, during the war. But back then, he was never alone. If he fell, then Thurn or Gundan or Peir would step in to hold the line, Jan or Blaise or Lath would treat his wounds. But he had been alone when he faced the linnorm, alone as he crawled back up through the endless Pits. Nearly alone when he died.

"Where did you go?"

"North, first. Through the New Provinces. They've grown like you wouldn't believe – they're building forts all along the edge of the wood, and clearing farmland. Great bloody crowds of people coming up through Necrad, now, seeking their fortune on the frontier.

Dwarves, too. They found hills full of gold. I went looking for Thurn, first, but I couldn't find him. The Wilder have gone into the deep wood." He'd searched for the tribes in primordial wilderness, tangled and unwelcoming. He'd wandered there and in the wastes for months, and scarcely seen another living mortal. The Wilder had avoided him deliberately. The sword he bore was a horror to them: a weapon forged by Witch Elves.

Thurn always reminded them that the Witch Elves conquered the Wilder long before they'd attacked the rest of the world.

"I was looking for . . . I don't know. Trouble. Evil. I went searching through all the old Witch Elf strongholds I could find, looking for any of Bone's allies that got away. I went hunting a dragon I'd heard tell of in the New Provinces. All for nought."

Alf closed his eyes. His heart was pounding as if he was in the middle of a battle, even though he knew there was nothing to fear. There were few safer places in the world than this valley.

"Then back south through the Dwarfholt and the Cleft. I thought I'd go home. Didn't even make it as far as Highfield before . . . " He shook his head. "No one remembered me. They knew the Lammergeier, of course, so I got to sit at the right hand of all the lords and sleep in beds with silken sheets, everyone licking my arse and telling me things that don't matter about court nonsense. But no one knew me. And why would they? Haven't been back since I went away adventuring. Most kids who run off end up dead in some goblin-hole within a month, so they probably think I died twenty years ago."

"You could have told them who you are."

"And then what? Talk about pig herding, and the weather, and gossip about people I don't know? Or have a string of distant relatives I don't know standing outside my door all day and all night, asking for favours? Or should I have talked to them about the sodding Witch Elves, or the Vatlings, or the problems with the League?"

"But you didn't go home?"

"I did. I tried." He threw down the bowl, and it vanished before it hit the ground. "I sat on a hill, Jan, and looked down at the Mulladales. At Ersfel. The village I hail from?"

"I remember."

"It looks just like it did before the war. Peaceful and happy again. They've forgotten the war. They think it's all done with. There are still monsters out there, Jan. We have to keep watch. The Nine have to be ready, whatever's left of us. I can't go home 'til the job's all done."

Jan sighed, letting out a little wisp of silvery mist. "I wish that someone didn't have to be you, Alf. I wish I could tell you to go back home to Ersfel. Or somewhere more wholesome. You need more time to heal."

Alf shrugged. "Nah. This is better. I've been waiting too long, Jan. I need something to slay. Tell me why you called."

"I can see shapes moving behind the veil. Powers are abroad in the land. A new peril – or an old one returning, I can't tell. A darkness rising." Jan laughed. "Sorry – I know how frustrated you used to get whenever prophecies and visions were involved, and here I am giving you more vague omens."

"I wasn't going to say anything."

"I don't see with mortal eyes any more, Alf. I'm trying to articulate spiritual impressions in words that aren't fit for purpose. It's better in the elf-tongue – *morthus lae-necras I'unthuul amortha.* Bad times are coming. If you ever trusted me, Alf, trust me now. I can't say what will happen, but I know it. It's swimming in the ocean, and feeling the swell of a great wave before it crests. Darkness is rising, and you must stand against it."

She frowned. "Where's your sword? You haven't lost the most potent magic weapon of the Enemy, have you? The weapon forged in darkness to bring ruin to the world?"

"It's up yonder." He nodded towards the rim of the valley. "Said it couldn't enter the holy sanctum or some such."

"The sword's made to swallow magic, Alf. Not even the mightiest spells can damage it."

"Bastard lied to me."

"Oh, Alf. Keep that sword close. It's part of all this . . . this rising darkness."

"Cause of, or weapon against?"

"If I knew that, Alf, it wouldn't be a mystic prophecy for you to complain about. I can tell it's important, but I can't say *how*. Keep it by your side – but beware of it."

"All right. Where's this rising darkness?"

"I don't know that either for certain – but I certainly can't *see* inside Necrad. The city is closed to me. So, whatever's coming, it starts there. Or dwells there." She glanced to the sky. The stars were coming out, and they shone very brightly here in the valley. "It might be the Oracle."

Alf nodded. That made a horrible sort of sense. Of all Lord Bone's court of horrors, all the vampiric elf-lords and monsters he'd made, the Oracle was the only one that had escaped justice. Laerlyn told them that the Oracle was the eldest matriarch of the Witch Elves, a fate-weaver who spun doom for the enemies of Lord Bone. She'd fled before the siege. Alf had assumed she'd died or faded. In all the years since that he'd spent hunting Bone's servants, he'd found no trace of her, but the Witch Elves had the patience of eternity. He'd worried for years that she was biding her time, waiting them out.

Of the surviving eight of the Nine Heroes, all but one were mortal.

"All right. I'll tell them." He paused. "What about Thurn? He was the first to go – to leave, I mean." Not the first to die.

"I sent him the same dream, but it's a long way," replied Jan. "I called as far as I could, and you're the first to come. My dream couldn't enter Necrad. I need you to be my messenger, Alf, to bring this warning."

"Aye."

"Such as it is. If I had a clear sight of the peril, I'd tell you, but I don't."

"I'll tell them." Berys the Thief, Blaise the Wizard, Gundan the Dwarf, Princess Laerlyn of the Wood Elves, Lath the Changeling. Thurn, if Alf could find him. And the League-lords, too.

"Look in on Blaise for me, would you? I worry about him most of all."

"I will." Jan wasn't alone in her concerns. Of all the survivors of Necrad, the wizard was perhaps the one who'd changed the most. Well, him or Lath.

Alf stood. "Jan," he said, reluctantly, "this thing you glimpsed. It might be the Oracle, I know, but could it be . . ."

Jan clucked her tongue. "I told you I can't see inside Necrad. Not even the Light reveals all secrets." She reached up and stroked Alf's face. Her ethereal hand felt warm and human for a moment, and then it was sunlight on his skin.

"You have my blessing, Alf, and you carry the hope of the world."

Then she was gone.

Alf climbed out of the hidden valley, his long legs carrying him swiftly up the path. Jan's warning settled on his shoulders like a mantle, but he was equal to the burden. He'd waited for the call for a long time, and now it was here. He moved with swift and terrible purpose.

He came to where the sword waited.

"That was just like last time," said Spellbreaker. "The light in the valley got snuffed out. What did you do to the priestess?"

Alf ignored the sword's taunts. "We're going back to Necrad." He pulled it out of the ground. "Call a dreadworm."

"I thought you wanted to walk."

"Call it."

"As you command, O wielder." Alf set his face against the cold wind and set off north across the Moor, and when dusk fell, a part of the night broke away and flapped down to him.

*

The lands of mortals flitted by below as the dreadworm soared on wings of darkness. The thing's hide was leathery, and stank like it had been buried in a bog for a hundred years. Its wings were congealed shadow, constantly shedding and regrowing. The eyeless head sniffed the air as it flew. This dreadworm had a saddle-shaped growth of bone that was definitely shaped for the smaller arse of an elf-knight. Alf ignored the discomfort, just like he ignored the bitter chill of the air. A dreadworm would get him back to Necrad in three nights. There was no time to waste.

Jan. Another one of the company gone, and she'd left no body. At least when Peir fell in that final battle with Lord Bone, they'd had something to bury. Jan just vanished. Alf wondered if she was truly gone.

"What happened in the valley?" asked the sword. He ignored it.

A part of his mind fretted about the tactical implications. *If Lord Bone does return, we'd be at a terrible disadvantage. No Peir and no Jan.* Of all the company, it was Peir who'd done the most to defeat Bone, Peir who'd wrestled with the dark lord until the last moment. Could the necromancer have cheated death again, and waited until the heroes who threatened him most were gone?

The rest of him felt hollow, but it was a good emptiness, like he'd purged himself of some foulness that had been weighing him down. He had a task to do, a direction from wiser heads than his.

As the eastern sky turned pink, the dreadworm thrashed and bucked against him.

"Sunlight damages it," said Spellbreaker. "And it needs to eat. Land and seek shelter, and let it feed before you press onwards."

"You can summon another at nightfall?"

"I can," admitted the sword.

"Then we keep going."

The dreadworm flew through the day. The sun scorched its wings, burning holes in them that did not heal, but they flew on. Below, the High Moor tumbled into the sea, white-topped waves breaking against white-flanked chalky cliffs. Off to his left, Alf could see Ellsport, the town reduced to an abstraction, the whorl of roads a fingerprint on the shore, flecks on the blue that were ships in the harbour. Below, traders heading to Necrad on the morning tide unfurled their sails to catch the same winds he rode, but the dreadworm outdistanced them, and soon they flew over the open ocean.

Land's edge vanished behind. The sea swelled before him. In time, he saw the high peak of the elven sea-fortress rising to the east. Autumn sunlight danced on the mists that shrouded the Isle of Dawn. Birds rose, startled by the presence of the worm. No doubt there were keen-eyed Wood Elf sentries in the forest, watching him with longbows in hand, guarding this northern outpost of Elvendom. Even Laerlyn wouldn't be able to hit the mark at this range, but Alf raised his hand in salute nonetheless. Sunlight flashed off a distant window – maybe in the palace of Prince Maedos of Dawn, Laerlyn's brother – and Alf could not help but change his gesture to an upraised middle finger. Alf might have been a barefoot farm boy from the arse-end of nowhere, and Maedos the eldest of the Erlking's children, as great and glorious as the High Lord of Summerswell, but by all that was holy, the elf had a face that cried out to be punched.

The dreadworm endured until mid-afternoon. It wouldn't last to the far side of the Gulf, but there were innumerable small islands dotting the sea below, and Alf knew just the place to land. He had to wrestle with the beast to get it to obey him.

The islands below were unnamed in the languages of men, but no doubt there was a Wood Elf name for the spot where he rested for a few hours. The tree-bound had to pass the time somehow. After a thousand years rooted to the same spot, they probably had a name for every blade of grass.

The dreadworm hissed at him. Its hunger grated against the summoning spell that forced it to serve him. Left unchecked, it would break free and turn on him. Icy slurry gurgled in the throat of the eyeless horror, but it was still bound. He chopped its head off anyway. Grey slime instead of blood gushed from the severed neck, pouring across the icy ground as the creature dissolved. The wings vanished like a conjurer's trick, leaving only a stain of shadow.

The things weren't truly alive – Lord Bone's magic congealed them out of ice and shadow – and the sword could whistle up another come nightfall.

Alf walked along the stony shore. A few pieces of flotsam had washed up. Timber from some wrecked fleet. Many ships had foundered in these waters. He'd fought side-by-side with Gundan on the deck of a sinking galleon, the company divided and facing certain doom, then Berys arriving in the nick of time, having stolen a warship from Lord Bone's own fleet. They'd sailed it to the Isle of Dawn, and fetched aid from the Wood Elves there. The Gulf had become a battleground against Lord Bone's invasion, the waters stained with the ichor of dozens of elven sea-serpents. Good times, good times.

He searched the shore until he found a cleft in the rock. Reaching in, he found a leather bag he'd hidden there years before. The leather had rotted, but the contents were intact. Three vials of healing cordial, a handful of gemstones and a charmstone out of Necrad. He strung the charm on a cord and tucked it inside his shirt, letting it rest against his skin. It was a charm against injury, made to ward off a mortal blow. He'd hidden many such charms away, in case he needed them. Bearing too much magic was said to be dangerous, so Alf only bothered with the things when necessary.

And anyway, Spellbreaker's hunger extended to magic. The sword could guard him against hostile spells, but it also gobbled up any charms or blessings placed on him. The charmstone would likely be destroyed if he drew the sword in anger.

"Look at you," said the sword, "leaving little caches across the world, in case you need them. Like a squirrel preparing for apocalypse."

"Shut up."

"What did the priestess tell you, wielder?"

"None of your business."

"Indulge me."

Alf raised the sword. "You didn't talk this much in the old days."

"Hunger," it said, "makes me garrulous, Lammergeier."

Alf contemplated throwing the blade into the deepest part of the ocean.

"And then how will you call a dreadworm to carry you off this rock?"

"Stop that," snapped Alf. "And shut up."

Hunger gnawed at his ribs. Searching the shoreline, he came across a rock pool where a large sea trout splashed in the shallows. The pool was barely large enough for the fish. Some wave had lifted it out of the sea and deposited in this unlikely spot, far from the waters of its home. The trout thrashed and bucked, its black eye staring in confusion. Alf picked the fish out of the pool, but it slipped from his hands and vanished back into the waters. He laughed at his own misfortune.

Instead of the unexpected bounty of the trout, he found a bird's nest, stole some eggs and cooked them on a driftwood fire.

As soon as the sun touched the western shore of the Gulf, he drew Spellbreaker and summoned another worm. This one seemed bigger, fortified by proximity to Necrad.

He drowsed in the saddle that second night, despite the bitter cold of an autumn sky. It was hard to tell; he'd slip into dreams of the war in the Claw Wastes, then wake with a start and look down and find they were flying over the Claw Wastes. All the dunes looked the same. Land and memory blended and blurred as he flew.

Late on that headlong flight, he saw a greenish light on the horizon, a stain that discoloured the sky. The colour of poisoned, gangrenous flesh, shot through with lurid bolts of an otherworldly, electric light. Flocks of dreadworms flapped mindlessly through the necromiasmic clouds that hung over the city.

Necrad. City of Lord Bone. City of the Witch Elves.

Even the shape of the place hurt Alf's eyes. Blaise had told them the city formed a magical sigil, a rune scrawled across the landscape in marble and bone. The great thoroughfares were conduits for power. Towers reached into the skies to trap starlight, and their inverted counterparts plunged into the earth to tap the currents of earthpower. The Witch Elf mansions and palaces, the tenements and temples – they came later. The city was built atop the sigil.

The eerie beauty of that sigil was triply marred – first, by the ugly mills and factories of iron and brick raised by Lord Bone. Second, by the scars left by the siege. Fifteen years had passed since Necrad had fallen to the Nine, but much of the damage was still evident.

And third, the gaping wound in the city's heart, where Lord Bone's palace once stood. Now, there was nothing there but ruin, and the sentinel spire of the Wailing Tower, like a lone mourner by a graveside.

"Down," whispered Alf. Then he repeated himself, loud and commanding. "Down! There! Land there!" Pointing not to the city, but to a tangle of shattered bone in the region called the Charnel. The wasteland outside the city, where the League's armies – elves, dwarves and men – once laid siege against Lord Bone, a desperate thrust to draw Bone's eyeless gaze away from Summerswell.

No vague omens, he thought. *No nagging doubts. No Wizard's Bloody Pauses, and no prophecies. Know for sure.*

He directed the dreadworm down towards the ruins of an old burial mound.

"Where are you going?" asked Spellbreaker curiously. "Why not go straight to the city?"

"Shut up," said Alf. Every other time he'd visited the barrow, he'd left Spellbreaker locked in a vault in Necrad. The demon sword shouldn't know this secret, but he didn't dare leave the weapon unattended.

The worm landed, its belly cracking the rime of frost and sinking into the mud beneath. It let out a gurgle of relief and spread out its shadow-wings. They had the texture of tattered velvet.

Alf dismounted and removed the creature's head with a sweeping blow.

One fewer witness.

Alf squared his shoulders and marched towards the dark entrance of the barrow. The sword's magic let him see in the dark.

"Whose tomb is this?" whispered the sword, but it must have guessed already.

A week after they'd defeated Lord Bone, after Peir's sacrifice, they'd taken the remains out of the city in the dead of night. Just the eight of them, no one else.

Or nine, maybe. Peir had been with them, in a way. Peir and Lord Bone had died together, Peir wrestling with the necromancer, keeping him from escaping the eruption of magical power that ended both of them. Afterwards, they'd rushed back into the chamber, the rubble still hot, burning their hands as they dug for the remains of their friend – but Lord Bone and Peir were for ever entwined, hero and villain in the same grave. They had buried them together, Bone's bones and Peir's wrapped in a shroud, carried by Alf and Thurn and Gundan. Berys and Laerlyn scouting ahead, ensuring that none of Bone's creatures or the Witch Elves followed them on their eerie pilgrimage. Lath and Jan and Blaise following behind, weaving the spell to seal the grave.

In the heart of the tomb, Jan lit a candle to set any lurking wraiths to flight. Elven-ghosts were more common than flies in Necrad. Alf had learned to ignore them, to brush them aside or shoo them out when they bothered him. You couldn't destroy them – undying meant undying – but such wraiths were nothing but motes of memory, and said to be harmless. Still, Blaise said they should have no witnesses on that day either, so Jan had driven the wraiths away. Maybe they still wandered the Charnel, trying to find their way back to their tombs. They wouldn't lack for ghostly company out there.

Alf and Thurn dug a grave within the tomb, smashing through the floor and hacking at the frozen dirt beneath until they had a hole deep enough. He recalled them glancing at one another, looking to Jan in particular, wondering if someone should speak as part of that ghastly funeral ceremony. It was always Peir who made the speeches, Peir who made things glorious. It should have been a moment of bittersweet triumph, but without Peir, it felt sordid, like they were doing something shameful that had to be hidden from the eyes of the world. They had laid the jumbled bones in the hole and covered it back up with dirt. They'd worked in silence, until it was done. Thurn spat on the dirt, and then they'd dragged a larger stone atop the grave.

Blaise and Lath had combined their powers then to place a supremely potent warding spell on that stone. Fifteen years, and Alf still remembered that horrible *tugging*, then the sharp pain as the spell tore blood and marrow from his body, so it would know him. The spell took from all of them, and that made the pain bearable. Blaise insisted on this precaution – only members of the company would know where Lord Bone was buried, and only members of the company would be able to open the tomb. *We'll always guard it*, he said, *and never forget*. Alf remembered looking over at Laerlyn, trying to read the expression on the elf's face. *Always* and *never* meant something different to an immortal.

Alf entered the barrow, rolling aside the heavy stone at the doorway. He hadn't been here in years, but he still remembered the route through the maze. Left, left, right, left, a hundred turnings in the labyrinth. Darkness held no fear for him, ghosts held no fear for him. Give him a foe, and he could slay it. A different fear turned his stomach. *Know for sure.*

"Whose tomb is this?" asked Spellbreaker again, unable to contain its excitement.

Right. Right. Left. And straight on to the last chamber.

"Whose tomb?"

There was the great stone seal – broken.

There was the bone pit – empty. Exhumed.

The sight was a sword blow to his spirit. He felt his resolve melt and gush from the wound, as if he was a dreadworm freshly beheaded. The mantle of Jan's prophecy became a crushing weight on him. He sagged, leaning on his sword.

Fresh-turned dirt. Whoever had opened Lord Bone's grave had done it recently.

Whoever? thought Alf bitterly.

Only eight – seven, now – could have opened the seal and survived. *One of us did this.*

CHAPTER THREE

A knock on the door sent Olva's hand to the knife she kept by her chair. Old Cu stirred himself from his customary place at her feet by the fire. A growl rumbled in his ribs. Olva stood, heart pounding, and slipped the knife into the fold of her sleeve.

Her son Derwyn came thumping down the stairs. "It's probably Harlow," he said, "we're going up to the holywood. I told you that, didn't I?"

He threw back the bolt, opened the door, and stepped back.

Olva's grip on the knife tightened. The man standing on her doorstep wasn't Harlow, her son's idiot friend with the messy hair, who'd recently grown a messier beard. No, the stranger was older, broken-nosed, his scarred face half concealed beneath the cowl of a stained cloak. His hair a few weeks of stubbly growth on a shaved skull. A sword at his belt, but his scabbed hands were open in a gesture of peace.

Cu stalked forward, growling. Olva stepped up and laid one hand on the dog's collar to calm the animal. She kept her grip on the knife, though. "What do you want?" she asked. "If it's farm work you're after, then you're too late. We have all the help we need to bring the harvest in, here. Try down Kettlebridge way, or—"

The stranger shook his head. "I've a story to tell," he said, warily, his green eyes flickering between Cu and Derwyn before settling on Olva. "A letter. And this." He reached inside his cloak and took out a leather pouch. He shook it, and it jangled with the weight of coin inside.

"I haven't taken any," he added with a note of incredulity in his voice, as if astounded by his own forbearance.

"Who sent you?" asked Derwyn. He reached out his hand for the bag, but the stranger didn't move.

"Said he was your brother," said the stranger, addressing his words to Olva. "Told me where to find you. Said he couldn't come himself."

"Derwyn," said Olva, "go on out."

"What? No!" Her son protested, but there's a tone in a mother's voice that can stay her children, even when they're full-grown.

"You heard me. Go and find your friends. This doesn't concern you."

Derwyn hesitated for a moment, torn between his mother's command and his desire to stay. He squared his shoulders, stepped up so he was between Olva and the stranger. Her son was the taller of the pair, Olva noted with pride. Derwyn looked the older man in the eye, and the stranger stepped aside, bowing his head as though cowed.

Olva closed the door after Derwyn and waited a heartbeat. Two, three.

"Go on, I said," she added loudly, and was rewarded with the sound of Derwyn's heavy tread as he stomped away from the farmhouse, alarmed birds croaking in the trees along the path. He was too curious for his own good, sometimes. She could hardly blame the boy for eavesdropping – it wasn't every day that a mysterious stranger shows up at your door with a bag of money from a supposedly dead uncle.

She waited another moment, until she was sure he was gone. Until he was safe. Then she tucked the knife into her belt and turned to face the stranger.

"What's your name?"

"Bor."

"Bor of . . . ?" she asked.

He shrugged. "Bor the Rootless." Rootless Men had no home province, no lord to watch over them. Rootless Men were vagabonds, bandits, wandering pot smiths. Jugglers, mummers, thieves – and adventurers. Dangerous folk.

"Alf sent you," said Olva.

"He did."

"You serve him."

Bor shrugged. "I met him at the fair at Highfield four days ago. 'Twas the first time I'd ever laid eyes on him, or any of the Nine. He said he had an errand for me to run."

"Why you?"

"In truth, I don't know."

"Where's Alf now?"

"I don't know. Off fighting dragons and saving maidens or whatever the Nine do. Listen, lady, the Lammergeier said he'd punish me if I didn't do as he said, so will you take your damned money?" He held out the pouch again, as if it was something cursed or unclean, a burden he was desperate to put down. His stomach gurgled, a counterpoint to Cu's low growl.

Olva stared at the pouch without taking it. "Have you eaten, Bor the Rootless?"

"Been busy looking for you, haven't I? Long bloody road. The Lammergeier said to seek out the kin of Long Tom of Ersfel, but no one I met knew that name. They sent me back Highfield way, and folk there said to seek the Widow Forster."

"Long Tom was my – was our – father. He's gone now, and so are all his kin, save me and my son. Galwyn Forster was my husband, and I took his name," said Olva. She went to fetch bread and cheese from the kitchen. A guest was a guest, even a rogue like this one. A brute and a thief, no doubt. A stray dog: stealing or scavenging or killing as chance dictated. Absently, she cut away most of the cheese and stowed it in a cupboard, leaving only a meagre rind for Bor.

She came back to find him seated next to the fire. He wasn't in her chair – Cu had planted himself in front of Olva's chair, defending this last redoubt from the invader. Instead, he'd hauled over a low bench from the table. He sat at one end, and the pouch of coin rested at the other, as far away from him as possible.

"Take it," he said again. Olva ignored the bag, and put the plate on the bench next to Bor.

"You said there was a letter?"

"Right, right." He fumbled through his belongings. "My condolences, of course, Widow Forster. The Lammergeier didn't tell me that." He found the letter and passed it to her, making the same hasty bow of his head as he'd offered Derwyn. "Was it recent, then?" Bor shot a glance towards the stairs, as if he expected Alf to be lurking nearby, standing guard over his sister and ready to punish anyone who acted discourteously towards her.

Olva ignored the question. She opened the letter. Alf's handwriting had improved a great deal from what she remembered, and she read it quickly.

It was only a few words long.

It told her nothing she had not guessed.

It ended with best wishes for her and her husband.

She read it twice, then folded it neatly and dropped it into the fire. Flames flared yellow as they consumed the letter, a red wave racing across the creamy paper, ash in its wake. Her hands shook as she watched it burn.

Bor swallowed, choking on the dry bread, and began: "The Lammergeier—"

"The Lammergeier," she echoed. Olva folded her hands, her fingernails digging deep into the flesh of her palms.

"He said to bring you this money. Take it, and I can go, all right? Thanks for the cheese and all that, and sorry for your loss, but – take it?"

He gestured at the pouch. Olva didn't move.

"Take it!" Bor grabbed the bag and held it out at her. Cu leapt up, barking.

Bor threw the bag to the ground, and coins spilled out. Not gold – they glimmered strangely in the firelight, coins of some silvery metal engraved with arcing Elvish sigils. Coins from Necrad. "Take it."

"No." Olva stooped and began to collect the scattered coins, returning them to the pouch, one by one. She would take nothing from the man who'd been her brother. After all this time, he could not buy her forgiveness or repair what had been broken. The coins were heavier that she expected, and left some unseen residue on her fingers, an oiliness that she disliked.

"What do you fucking mean?" shouted Bor, his attempted courtesy finally cracking. "Take the money, you fool! What, you think I'm lying? That the Lammergeier didn't send me?"

"No." She picked up the last coin, and placed it with its fellows before tugging the drawstring tight and holding the bag out to Bor.

"Then what?"

"I don't want my brother's money."

"Are you mad? There's a fortune there!"

"I don't want it. Take this back, please."

"I swore a bloody oath."

"Then give it back to Alf and have him release you from your promise."

"I don't know where the Lammergeier's gone! He told me to bring it to you! I can't bring it back to him."

"I won't take it."

"Take the money, you daft cow! Please!" Bor's face twisted, frustration and fear warring in his voice. "He made me swear I bring it to you safe! I gave my word! Take it!"

"No."

"Fine!" He snatched the purse from her hand and stuffed it away. "If you don't want it, I'll have it! Crazy old woman!"

"Get out." She said it calmly the first time, then something in her snapped and she found the knife was in her hand. "Get out!" she screamed. Bor backed away from her, but in her mind Olva could see other figures crowding around her, a vision born of old fears. Pale they were, but their lips were red and one of them bore a black sword. "Get out! Get out!"

Bor shouted at her, but his words were lost in the thunder of the dog's barking, and in the whirling of her mind. The stranger stumbled away, shoulders hunched, as if trying to shrink himself small enough to hide in the coin pouch he clasped to his heart. He flung the door open and strode off down the path that went past the holywood to the village, his dark silhouette merging with the gathering gloom of the evening.

Olva became aware that she was kneeling. That Cu was licking her face, her hand. She struggled to breathe, her lungs gulping for air. She could still smell Bor's scent in the room, the lingering stink of leather and road-sweat. Even though he was gone, he was not absent. The fact of him was still there, the intrusion of what – of who – he represented, pushing against the walls of the life Olva had made for herself in the last sixteen years.

"It's all right," she said to the old dog. "It's all over. You wouldn't understand anyway." She scratched behind Cu's ear, then pulled herself up and sat wearily in her seat. "The war was before your time. None of it matters now."

The dog appeared to accept that and curled up at her feet in his customary place by the fire.

Derwyn would not be so easy to convince.

The fire had burned low by the time her son came home. He closed the door behind him, and went to warm his hands by the hearth, kneeling down next to Cu. He threw a log on the flames, and Olva watched the reflected sparks dance in his eyes. The flare of light revealed a fresh bruise on his cheek. He'd been fighting again. It was in his blood. She reached out to comfort him, but he brushed her hand away absently and sat back on the rug.

"Is he gone?" Derwyn asked.

"He is. And he won't be back."

"Who was he?"

"None of your concern," Olva said, a rote response. She knew, even as she spoke, that it wasn't enough, and that Derwyn was not a child any more, and wouldn't accept such an answer. He stared at her for a long moment, letting the silence hang between them. She let it go by unbroken, knowing that when she broke that silence, she would be unable to stop speaking, not until it was all said. She held out for those last dregs of peace.

"Who was up at the wood?" she whispered. A delaying tactic.

Derwyn turned his gaze back to the fire. "Harlow and Kivan. And Quenna. Some of the boys from Elcon's farm. They'd been up to the Highfield fair with Elcon's sheep, and they said there were knights there, all the way from Summerswell! And a conjurer, and fire-eaters, and a trophy-monger." He grew enthusiastic despite himself. "Kivan even said that one of the Nine had been there, but it was Sir Prelan – with the banner of the lion rampant – who won the tourney, and if one of the Nine was really there, they'd have won! So Kivan's a dirty liar."

"Is that why you fought with him?"

Derwyn touched his bruised cheek. "It doesn't matter."

"I don't like you fighting," said Olva.

Derwyn shrugged. "The man who called ... he said my uncle sent him. You told me that I didn't have a living uncle. That all your brothers were dead. So who was he? What did he want with us?"

And that was it. The end of the silence.

She didn't tell him everything, of course. Some things she kept for herself.

But she told him enough.

She told him the story of her oldest brother. She was the youngest, and Alf the eldest, nine years between them, the gap bridged by other children like stepping stones. All of them living in a house a third the size of this farmhouse, a crofter's shack, never enough food, never enough space, but they were together and that got them through the winters and the sorrows.

Alf was the firstborn, the pride of the family. Everyone in Ersfel talked about his strength, his courage. Mulladale-folk are strong, everyone knows that, but Alf was special. Elf-touched, they call people like that. Everyone knew that Alf was destined for something great.

(Derwyn, disbelieving at first, then rapt. The fire died down, and he did not notice. Cu grunted and snuffled, and the boy absently petted the dog, quieting him. Desperate not to miss a thing, as if every word that dropped from Olva's lips was a glittering diamond, frozen glimpses of a part of the saga he had never heard before.)

And then, one day, he was gone. He walked off down the Road, and they didn't see him again for months. He came back a few times, in the company of strange folk, sellswords and tomb robbers, but he never stayed for long. He'd bring money, sometimes, dropping a bag of coins onto the table with a grunt. Old coins, sometimes, looted from a tomb. Or new ones, from mercenary work or tourney prizes. More money than their father could make in a year. Olva had been too young to understand the growing gulf between Alf's life and theirs, but hindsight had taught her to interpret the signs. The way pride warred with shame on her father's face, to be so eclipsed by his son. The way Alf would grow restless after only a few days, as the road called to him.

The bad years came. The world beyond the village became colder. There were alehouse tales of raids on the coast, of wars being fought far away in dwarf-lands and across the seas, but there were always alehouse tales, and the cold couldn't penetrate the walls of their little house – not that first year. But the war drew closer, and closer. What began as rumours became terribly real. Longboats full of barbarian Wilder crossed the sea and invaded Ellscoast. Wilder raiders burned Highfield.

Wilder and worse things. The Wilder might be savages who worshipped the Witch Elves as gods, but at least they were human. That winter brought monsters.

Now, the family huddled together for comfort, flinching whenever the wind howled, or when rats scratched at the walls. There were dreadworms riding on the wind, people said, and Wilder in all the woods now. The war was at their door, and the world changed.

Then Alf came back for the last time. Stumbling into the village, bloodied and battered, exhausted beyond endurance. Alf and his eight friends—

("Nine ... the Nine were *here?*" gasped Derwyn, unable to stay silent.)

Eight friends, hiding from their pursuers. Olva was fifteen at the time, younger than Derwyn was now. Old enough to hide at the back of the room and listen, as Alf spoke of a battle up on the High Moor, of dreadful Witch Elves out of the far north. They'd won some desperate victory, but were now on the run, chased by the forces of Lord Bone. They had nowhere else to hide.

That night was the first time Olva had heard the name *Necrad*.

There was no room in that little house for such a band. One of Alf's companions was a genuine *princess* of Elvendom, and another – the company's wizard – was badly wounded and needed rest in a proper bed. To make space, Olva and her brothers were sent to sleep in the shed with the animals. Alf kept watch that night, sitting cross-legged in the doorway, watching the woods. That was Olva's last real memory of her oldest brother – Alf standing guard over them, his big shoulders hunched against the cold wind. The expression on his face as he scraped a whetstone against the edge of his sword, like the look she'd seen on her husband Galwyn's face when tending to their newborn. She'd fallen asleep that night feeling safe for the first time in months, now that Alf was back.

But he hadn't stayed. Alf and the rest of his company had left the next morning, going back to the war. Back to their quest.

That was the last time she'd seen her brother.

"I thought him dead," said Olva. "For a long time, I thought him dead. Everyone else I loved was dead – your father, the rest of my family. I thought it was the end of the world. Everyone did. Everyone thought Lord Bone and the Witch Elves and his other monsters would come back in greater numbers, and slay us all. No one here knew that the siege of the Dwarfholt had been lifted, or that the Elves had joined the war. Or that the Lords had sent an army to attack Necrad. We thought it was the end. I remember . . . I held you so tightly, for you were all I had left. I'd lie awake all night, holding you, just listening. Waiting for them to come back."

"But the Nine saved us." Derwyn whispered.

"They killed Lord Bone. The war ended, and everyone was singing songs of the Nine, yes – but I didn't know Sir Aelfric the Lammergeier was my brother Alf. Not right away."

"But you knew." Derwyn frowned. "You knew before that stranger came."

Olva nodded. "I guessed, after a few years. I couldn't be sure. I didn't want it to be so, but—"

"Why ever not? To have a hero for a brother – to be kin to the Lammergeier!" Derwyn scrambled to his feet. "Why didn't you tell me before? Why have we never gone to him?"

"Because—" began Olva, but the real truth was like sharp stones in her throat, and she couldn't speak it. A half-truth was easier. "Because he chose his path," she said, "he could have come back home after, and he didn't. It's been sixteen years since Lord Bone's death, and Alf never came home to us. He's Aelfric Lammergeier now, high and mighty up in Necrad, not Alf the crofter's boy from Ersfel. He's gone from us."

"But the Lammergeier sent us a messenger! What did he bring? Is Sir Aelfric coming here?"

"I don't think so." Olva spoke as gently as she could, swallowing as much of her anger as she could stomach. She should have told Derwyn years before, but instead she'd hidden it all, assuming after so many years that Alf would never return to Ersfel, that she could hold her tongue until the grave and that the horrors of the past could be left to fade away, buried by the passage of time like the bodies up in the holywood under the leaves. If she could not have her brother back, then she could at least have peace and forgetfulness. Instead, Alf had somehow found a third option, worse than either. He'd opened up the wounds of the past, and he wasn't even here to help. "He was at Highfield fair – that's close at hand. If he meant to come back home, he'd have been here."

"I could go after him," said Derwyn after a moment. "I've been to Highfield often enough, and he can't have travelled far since the fair. I could go and find him. He could teach me how to fight. I could squire for him, be part of his household like a knight of Summerswell. I could go to Necrad."

"No!" Panic stabbed her heart at the thought of that city, and all the pale horrors that lurked there. Olva grabbed her son's hand and pressed it to her heart. "Promise me you won't. Stay away from there!"

"Why? Necrad is ours now. It's safe. The dark lord's gone, and we rule his lands. All the songs say that."

"Don't believe the songs. Don't go. Don't leave me. Not yet."

"I'm not going to stay here in Ersfel for ever, Mother." He tugged his hand free, gently, without hurting her fingers. It hurt her heart all the more.

She scrabbled for the words that would make him stay. "Then – then wait. I'll write a letter to my brother. I'll tell him about you.

Maybe next year, in the spring when it's easier to travel, we can go to Ellsport and get passage to Necrad. Both of us could go – I could see Alf again." In that moment, she wasn't sure if it was a lie or not.

"I don't need you watching over me," said Derwyn.

"Who said you did? I want *you* protecting *me* on our journey, eh?" Somehow, Olva was able to laugh despite the panic clutching at her throat. It sounded hollow and shrill to her ears, but Derwyn give a little smile.

"Promise me," she said, "you won't go."

"I promise."

"But there's more I want to tell you, Der. Not just about Alf. We need a long talk. In the morning."

"Why not now?"

"Because I'm tired, and you're tired. And I don't want to talk of dark things at night. Better to see them in the sunlight, when everything's clearer." Cu whined at her and pressed his head against her knee. "The dog needs a piss. You see to that."

Derwyn rose and walked the dog out into the night. The animal snuffled around the door. Derwyn followed the dog, moving as if dazed. His mind was clearly halfway to Necrad already, planning their journey, imagining what he would do there. Olva watched him in the gloom, the last light of the sun a sullen red scar above the line of the trees in the holywood. He looked like Alf did, in her memory. Children brought the past back in unexpected moments. It wasn't just Alf that was embodied in Derwyn's lanky frame – she'd seen her father's bewildered but kindly expression on her son's face, too, in moments of confusion. She could see her husband Galwyn in him, too – not in his looks, but in his bearing, in his voice. All the men she'd loved, all there, ghosts beneath the skin.

And more and more, too, Olva heard her mother in her own voice. Maybe some good might come of this unexpected intrusion. Family was family, after all – she couldn't deny Alf's kinship. Blood was blood, heedless of all the years.

She busied herself, taking smouldering coals from the fire and heating the beds with a warming pan, fetching blankets, putting away the bread and cheese left out after Bor's departure, so when Derwyn came back in, everything was normal again, ghosts banished again, as if the village priest had brushed the house with rowan twigs from the holywood. "Sleep well," Olva said, and kissed her son on the brow, "we'll talk in the morning."

"You too."

Derwyn fell asleep quickly. She could hear him dreaming, muttering in his sleep, the bed creaking as he rolled back and forth.

Olva lay down, but sleep eluded her for hours. She fought the urge to climb into her son's bed and hold him, as she'd done when he was young. She was exhausted, but in the silence the doubts came creeping in again. The bad days were gone, everyone knew that. All the songs said that. Lord Bone was dead and the wars were over, and evil had been defeated and it was all peace and plenty and harmony now. The good years were here, the eternal summer of Summerswell won through the courage and sacrifice of the Nine. Maybe she could let Derwyn go. But still she lay awake, listening to the rustling of the leaves, the night-speech of bird and beast. Listening for dreadworms shrieking on the wind, or Wilder creeping through the holywood.

Waiting, as she did every night, for those pale figures to return. The part of the story she had not told Derwyn.

She rose from her bed. Cu lifted his heavy head and watched her as she crossed the silent house, bare feet freezing on the rush-strewn stone floor, and fetched her knife from where she kept it beside her chair. She sat down next to the ashes, the knife across her lap. Shoulders hunched against the cold as she watched the closed door, standing guard like Alf did, all those years ago.

She sat there for hours, staring out at the dark.

At some point, she must have fallen asleep, exhausted wakefulness blurring into familiar nightmare. New nightmares, too, of

Derwyn's death. She had never seen Necrad, so she imagined it like one of the Witch Elf coins Alf had sent. Streets of cold metal, oily skies, unearthly light glimmering overhead. Not a place for mortals. She dreamed of Derwyn dying there, his precious body stabbed by a black sword. Dying there, alone, crying out for her. In the dream, Derwyn's blood ran down the streets, not pooling or stopping, but wandering, her son's life lost and homeless, searching for her for ever. His body lay there, pale and broken, and his blood poured out endlessly, a red shade that was somehow also him. She knew, in the way you know things in a dream, that if she could lead the blood back to his wounded body, then there was a chance of saving him. She ran to Alf's house, but Alf wasn't there. Just the black sword.

Finally, she slept.

Cu's wild barking woke her shortly before dawn.

Derwyn was gone.

CHAPTER FOUR

There is no cause for alarm, Olva told herself, even as fear gripped her throat. She thought of her fear as an ugly imp that lived inside her, an unwelcome tenant that squatted inside her ribcage, and sometimes climbed onto her shoulders or came crawling out her mouth. The fear was always there, waiting to be proved right. She would not give it the satisfaction.

There were a hundred tasks to do in the morning. Galwyn had bought a sizeable farm when he'd moved to Ersfel to marry her and play the gentleman farmer. He had no clue about how to run a farm; he'd been bound for the priesthood before that Intercession. That land had passed into her hands when he died, and, with it, responsibility for half a dozen crofters who lived on her land, paying their rent by labouring in her fields. The harvest was mostly in already, but there still was much to do. She attended to her work, putting her little corner of the world in order. Derwyn, she told the fear, had gone out early to get started on his chores, or to see a friend. It was unusual for Derwyn to be up before her – she usually had to threaten him with a pitchfork to get him out of bed – but last night had been unusual, too. She'd told the boy not to tell anyone about Alf, which no doubt meant that he'd already told half the village.

The morning wore on, pale sunshine giving way to a chilly

drizzle. Olva stood in the doorway, watching the grey rain hide the holywood on the hill. She looked for Derwyn to come loping back over the fields, head bowed, hands in pockets, but he never came.

Cottar and Thomad arrived to muck out the pigsty, and she asked them – carefully, casually, so as not to wake the fear – if they'd seen her son. They had not.

Noon, and the fear crawled up her spine. She beat it back, telling herself she was being foolish. Derwyn was not a child any more, he was nearly grown, and anyway, there were no more Wilder savages lurking in the wood, or Witch Elves riding the night air. Her nerves were jangled after the visit yesterday, that was all. Derwyn would be home soon.

Her work became violent. She snapped at Thomad. Scrubbed a stain on a shirt like she was throttling it, then drowned the garment in the stream. Shoved Cu when he tried to nap on her feet. She found she was carrying her knife around with her, instead of leaving it in its customary spot by her chair. Hunger picked at her ribs, but the fear filled her belly and she could not eat.

The first inkling of dusk, and Derwyn still did not come home.

She walked around the yard and paced the field. Cu snuffled in the undergrowth by the path, then started growling. The fading light glimmered off a shiny coin, lying in the dirt between the roots of a tree stump. She picked it up, and shivered, for it was one of the coins from Necrad.

Something broke in Olva, and she climbed up the low hill towards the holywood. Cu bounded after her, delighted to snuffle in the undergrowth, and startled crows burst from the hedgerows to wheel overhead. The fear danced around her, touching every uncertainty, filling every gap in the world. A twisted tree root became, for a moment, a sprawled corpse; a crow taking flight was a dark figure about to lunge at her. Her breath caught in her chest, making her light-headed.

Thala, the cleric, was in the shrine. Olva hovered on the threshold, not daring to profane the sacred space. The villagers gathered in the clearing outside on holy days. She'd only been inside a handful of times – her wedding day, of course, and a string of funerals. *Intercessors guard their souls.* A naming day for Derwyn. *Intercessors watch over him.* And one other time, the only occasion she'd been called up to the shrine by old Thala. *The Intercessors have chosen you to marry.* Galwyn was here, somewhere beneath her feet and he was not alone. Parents, siblings, friends, all gone in the ground. The Intercessors had chosen her to marry Galwyn. A divinely ordained match between a peasant girl and a young noble – it would have been the talk of the Mulladales if it happened in peacetime. The Intercessors watched over her wedding, but where were the spirits when Galwyn died?

"Have you seen my Derwyn?" she asked.

Thala peered at her. "No, no. Some of the young whelps were up here last night, trampling my glade and disturbing the peace with their fighting. Was he one of them, Olva?"

"Forgive him, but he was. Have you seen him?"

"I have not."

Olva glanced towards the font at the heart of the shrine, the sacred mirror. The Intercessors were said to appear there, but such mysteries were only for the ordained. She wanted to ask if Thala – absurdly, blasphemously – if the spirits had seen Derwyn. Instead, she walked back down the hill, towards Ersfel. At the edge of the village, she found a few of the younger folk from the village. Derwyn's friends – but he wasn't among them. They froze, their conversation stopping instantly when they caught sight of her.

"Have you seen my son?" Olva asked.

Someone in the shadows stifled a laugh; others whispered to each other. It was the boy Harlow who rose, scratching his stupid fuzzy beard. "Widow Forster," he began, nodding his head. "Der's not here."

"Have you seen him?"

"Not since yesterday."

Olva whirled around. "Which of you is Kivan?"

Another boy half rose. He sported a split lip, a bruise mottling his whole right cheek. "Have you seen Derwyn?"

Kivan spat. "What's he done? Is he in trouble?"

"Have you seen him? Do you know where he might go?"

"Witches take him, for all I care."

Olva wanted to step across the glade and give the boy a matching bruise on his other cheek. Instead, she turned back to Harlow. "You're his friend. Where would he go? He hasn't been home since dawn."

"I don't rightly know. I'd have said he'd be here, if he was anywhere." Harlow's brow furrowed in thought. "There's a man in Genny's alehouse. Derwyn said he came to yours last night. Maybe Derwyn went down there. That's all I can think." Before Olva could go, Harlow added: "Is something amiss?"

The fear clutched her throat. She could only give a little nod.

The village was too small and too far off the Road to warrant an inn, but in the evenings folk gathered at the house of the widow Genny Selcloth. Her husband, a Mulladale man, had also died in the war, but his bones lay far away to the north. Grief did not encumber Genny, who made a merry widow, brewing enough ale to slake the thirsts of all who came to her door. She and Olva were of an age, though they were not close friends, not since Olva had wed Galwyn Forster and went from being a poor crofter's daughter to a landowner quick as a Changeling switches skin.

Olva ducked under the low lintel and stepped into the smoky common room. Cu followed her in, his intrusion rousing Genny's two dogs who lay by the fire. Genny's was unusual quiet tonight, with only a trio of locals at one bench, and her quarry sat sprawled in a corner. Bor the Rootless didn't look up as she approached.

"Is he one of yours?" hissed Genny. "He's been in here half the day."

"He doesn't work for me," said Olva, "but he owes me. Listen, have you seen my boy Derwyn?"

Genny frowned. "Not today."

"What about you?" said Olva, raising her voice and addressing Bor. "Have you seen Derwyn?"

Slowly, Bor raised his head. "Who the fuck is Derwyn?"

"My son."

"Oh." He picked up a half-full pewter mug from the table, drained it and belched his answer. "Aye." He was drunk, but not insensible. Genny watered her ale.

"I haven't seen him since this morning. I found this outside." She placed the coin on the table.

"He must have dropped it. I met him on the path and left him a few coins, fool that I am." Bor flicked the strange silvery coins in Genny's direction. "Another ale." He shoved a stool out with one foot, inviting Olva to sit with him.

"He's gone," she said. "I can't find him anywhere." Her throat closed in fear, but she managed to speak. "I think he's set off for Necrad."

"By the stars," laughed Bor, "if I was kin to the Lammergeier, I'd go to Necrad, too. Make my fortune there. The dead sowed, and we reap, eh?"

"He's too young."

Bor shrugged. "I was seven when I went on the Road. He'll be fine. Or better chance than most."

"He's not going to reach the Road," said Olva. "We'll fetch him and bring him back home. He left this morning; by now, he's probably in Highfield. We walk all night, and we'll catch him before he leaves. But I'm not going out at night alone."

"I don't work for you," sneered Bor.

"That's my coin you're drinking."

"You didn't want it. You threw it in my face. I owe you nothing." Genny put down a fresh mug, and Bor lifted it in salute. "Your health, Widow Forster."

"You owe me nothing, true. But in that case, that's my brother's coin still. And if my son isn't found, then I swear to you, I'll go all the way to Necrad and tell Alf – tell Aelfric Lammergeier – how you broke your word to him." Bor's expression froze. *He truly fears Alf*, thought Olva. "What do you think he'll do to you if anything happens to his nephew? To the Lammergeier's flesh and blood?" Even as she said it, the fear came back, grabbing hold of her heart with icy paws. She'd already endured terrible things, and Alf hadn't appeared in the nick of time like some hero out of the stories to save her. But Bor didn't need to know that. "I'm going to go and fetch my son home, and I'm not going on the road without protection."

"Fine." Bor regained some of his bravado. "You can pay me out of the money I brought, and I'll find your brat. 'Twill be the easiest coin I ever earned. He's probably half a mile down the road at most." He took a long drink, then rose unsteadily. "I'll take a piss, then we'll be off." He grabbed at the bag of coins, but Olva was faster and got her hand to it first. He scowled, then stumbled past her and out of the door.

Olva sat a moment, fighting back the fear. She clutched the handle of her knife, to reassure herself, took a breath, then stood. "Genny," she called. "I've got to go up to Highfield, on family business. Can you send your boy up to my house in the morning, and tell Thomad that I'm away, and to take care of what's needful?"

Genny nodded. "How long will you be gone?"

"Oh." Olva gave a weak smile. "Only a day or two, I hope. Maybe a little longer. I might even be back tomorrow, all going well."

"You're travelling by night? Mind yourself."

"I'm not going alone," Olva assured her.

"I heard some of what you said to him," whispered Genny, "I'd wait for morning, and fetch Thomad or someone. Bring a man you can trust."

The men I trusted, thought Olva, *all lie under earth in the holywood.*

*

The road to Highfield was a dirt track that wandered between the low hills of the Mulladales. Autumn moonlight turned the deep wheel ruts in the mud into two streaks of silver underfoot, with a constellation of lesser signs between them, bootprints and hoofprints and the faint tracks left by barefoot children. Dark shapes lurked in the overgrown verges and the hedgerows, and the fear turned every tree root or rock into a corpse or a monster. She saw Derwyn's body a dozen times in that first hour, only to find each time that it was a trick of moon-shadows.

They walked on, as the stars slowly wheeled overhead. Cu bounded about, thinking this nocturnal stroll to be an unexpected adventure. She was grateful for the dog's company, especially as the dog seemed to dislike Bor, and growled whenever the man came too close to Olva. To his credit, Bor sobered up quickly, and now walked ahead of the pair, his travelling cloak drawn tightly around him. Olva shivered in the chilly night air.

"You sure the boy went this way?" asked Bor.

"Alf was in Highfield a few days ago." *And Highfield's on the Road. And the Road goes to Necrad.* "What was Alf like?" Olva asked, surprising herself with the question. Talking would help them both stay awake as they walked.

"You're asking me about your own brother?"

"I haven't seen Alf in years."

"He looked ... like you'd expect, I guess. Like the songs say. He wore this great visored helm, so I didn't see his face. But ..." Bor lowered his voice. "There was a coldness to him, maybe. Like, I've known some right bastards, men who'd kill you dead for a copper and think nothing of it. Absolute bastards, no pity or doubt at all. And it was sort of like that, but it wasn't the same thing. Like, they were cunts, right?. Just rotten through and through. He was ... above it all, maybe? A sort of elvishness, maybe? You ever meet an elf?"

"Once," said Olva, turning her face away.

Bor didn't seem to notice. "It was like he could see through me. Or that he was thinking of things far above me, great matters a man like me wouldn't understand. Dooms and things."

"That doesn't sound at all like Alf," said Olva. "He was a mooncalf growing up. Give him a job, and he'd keep at it until it was done, but Erlking help him, he wasn't that bright. Once, our father tells Alf to go and chop some firewood. Alf's gone for a while, and then we hear this huge crash outside, like the sky's caved in. We go out and find that Alf's felled this huge oak tree all by himself. This tree's stood through storms and bad winters for years and years, tough as anything – and he's cut it down. An astounding feat of strength, and Alf's there, exhausted, proud of himself, leaning on what's left of the axe. Only then we all point to the pile of logs at the back of the house. Father just wanted Alf to split a few of them."

"I guess being a hero changes you."

"I suppose it must."

It was, she realised, the sort of stupid thing that Derwyn might do, only Derwyn didn't have Alf's raw strength. He took after his father; Galwyn was of Crownland stock, clever and quick, but not especially strong. Derwyn didn't have Alf's strength.

Or his luck. Olva quickened her pace.

"I thought you'd be living in a palace and all," muttered Bor, "being the Lammergeier's sister."

"I wouldn't know what to do with a palace. I couldn't stand sitting around all day, doing whatever courtly ladies do. I need to work." She glanced back at the mercenary. "What about you? Where do your people come from?"

"Westermarch. Place called Cullivant."

"I've not heard of it."

"The war took it. Wasn't anything much to speak of before, and nothing at all after."

"A Westermarcher," she muttered to herself. That was a good

omen – just as Mulladale folk were known for their strength, or Arshothi for their piety, Westermarchers were said to be especially courageous. Although, of course, you couldn't trust a Rootless Man to live up to the ways of his people.

The mercenary scowled. "Save your breath for walking. If you're going to prattle all the way to Highfield, you'll have to pay me double."

It was well after dawn before they reached Highfield. The town was huge in Olva's eyes, ten times the size of Ersfel. Some of the buildings were two or even three storeys tall, and a low mound of earth surrounded the whole place. The path from Ersfel came from the south, but the gates in the wall were east and west, on the main Road, so they had to walk a quarter-turn around Highfield before they could enter.

They crossed the muddy green just outside the town, the grass trampled and torn up by the recent fair, and entered through the gatehouse on the western side, the banner of Summerswell flapping in the morning breeze. Olva was Mulladale-born, and so she needed no pass, but Bor was Rootless. By ancient law, travel between the provinces of Summerswell was permitted only with a letter from a lord, cleric or other authority. By equally ancient custom, guards could be bribed to forget to ask for such a letter. Olva was too tired to haggle and handed over a full coin as payment. Bor found them a room in an inn, paid with her money. Already, the pouch of coin felt lighter.

The bed was damp and uncomfortable, but she was exhausted beyond endurance and fell into it gratefully. She should not sleep: she should not let herself sleep, she told herself, not while Derwyn was still missing, but her body would not listen. She was distantly aware of Bor moving about the room, then Cu curled up on her legs, his weight a protective shield, and she slept.

*

Again, she dreamed of Necrad. In this dream, it was a city of graves, endless rows of them beneath skeletal trees of bone. Derwyn was the only living thing moving through the streets of white marble, until he found an empty tomb and climbed into it. She ran after him, her footsteps echoing off the tombs, but when she got to where he disappeared, she could not tell one grave from another and couldn't tell which one was his. She scrabbled at the cold marble, digging her fingers into the dirt, into the cracks between gravestones, but she couldn't find her son.

She still could hear him calling her, from somewhere deep below.

"I found him."

Olva woke, gasping for air. Outside, it was still daylight. "How long did I sleep?"

"Few hours." Bor yawned. "I talked to some people I know here. Your boy was here yesterday, all right. Talking in the common room about how he was bound for Necrad, and asking questions about the Lammergeier."

Olva scrambled out of bed. The room swayed around her. "Is he still here?"

"That's the thing. He left with Lyulf Martens."

"I don't know who that is."

"Everyone else here does, I tell you. He's a trader. Arshoth stock. Buys supplies for the New Provinces here, comes back with treasures out of Necrad. I used to work for him." Bor scratched his neck. "I don't any more. If your boy's fallen in with Martens, that's bad."

"Why?" Relief warred with new worry. All the nameless fears, all the unthinkable possibilities about Derwyn's fate collapsed into a single sharp spike of fear about who this Lyulf Martens might be.

"Trust me, it is. I'll tell you as we go. Martens was at the Highfield fair, too – he's heading back north. If he reaches Ellsport and takes ship, he'll be out of our reach."

"You haven't rested at all," said Olva. Her years on the farm had taught her how to work a beast to the limits of its endurance, but not beyond.

Bor shrugged. "I'll sleep well tonight, then – but if we're going to catch Martens, we've got to use what daylight's left to us." The sun was already sauntering west in the sky. "There's still a chance to catch him on the road. I know a short cut."

CHAPTER FIVE

T he sword remained quiet after they left the tomb. Alf walked
in silence across the Charnel, picking his way through the mire.
The mud sucked at his boots, and something moaned in the watery
depths as he passed by. Many good men – dwarves, too – died in
this field during the siege all those years ago, and some came back
every year. The dead didn't always stay dead in the necromancer's
land – not without making sure, and they'd made sure. Lord Bone
was as dead as could be when they buried him.

In the distance, dead-enders wandered the marsh, probing the
black ground of the Charnel with long spears in search of still-active
undead. It was drudge work, and poorly paid for how dangerous it
could be. Endless days of wandering the mire, punctuated by seconds
of terror as a dead hand clutched at your foot.

One dead-ender took a few steps towards Alf, peering at him as
if unsure if Alf was among the quick or the dead, then called out
to him across the mists.

"Watch yourself, friend", shouted the man. "Foes are near."

"I've fought the dead enough," replied Alf.

"Not the dead." The dead-ender came splashing through the
slime towards Alf. Most of his features were hidden behind the dark
cloth wrapped around his mouth and nose against the necromiasma,

and the omnipresent mud had swallowed any badge or sigil on his armour. "The living," he said as he came closer. "Two lads got killed by Wilder a week ago. The bastards are out there, somewhere." He waved his stick across the Charnel.

"Which tribe?" The Wilder were Thurn's people. Some of the tribes had been enslaved by the Witch Elves for generations, yielding up the blood tithe to the elf-lords and fighting for Necrad in the war. Others, like Thurn's folk, were rebels and fought on the side of good.

"Wilder," repeated the man, making no distinction between tribes. "Head that way, and you'll hit the Road." He pointed off south, in the direction of the ancient road across the fens. Down that way was the main landward gate of Necrad. Alf could see it in his mind's eye, banners flying in the air over the gate. The blue and sun of Summerswell, the silver towers on the black flag of the dwarves, the Erlking's tree, all sharing dominion over the city of the enemy.

"Best to stick to the paths, friend, until you know your way around," said the dead-ender. Clearly, he'd mistaken Alf for a new-comer. A reasonable mistake – after years away, Alf didn't have the deathly pallor of a resident of the sunless city, and he'd seen plenty of Rootless Men on his travels who intended to come to Necrad to seek their fortune. Alf gave the dead-ender a nod of thanks and set off.

Once out of earshot, the sword spoke.

"That was my maker's grave, was it not?"

"None of your business."

"The grave was open. Where are his remains, Lammergeier?"

Alf ignored the blade and walked on, hopping from one tuffet of spiky grass to the next to stay out of the worst of the mud.

"He made me. The elven-smith Korthalion forged this body of iron, but it was Lord Bone who woke me and gave me purpose. You wielded me to destroy him. I deserve to know."

The sword never spoke like that. Alf paused and drew the blade.

"You don't get to ask for anything."

"Even a prisoner has rights."

"What, you want a crust of bread?"

"I want to help." The sword's gemstone eye glinted, even though there was no visible sun beyond the mists. "Only one of your company could open the tomb, yes? I saw that thought in your mind."

"I told you to stop doing that!" Alf's fist clenched around the hilt. He wanted to fling the blade into a pit. To smash it against the unbreakable walls of the city. But if he threw it away, someone would find it, and smashing it against the wall would not break it. It was his burden to carry. What else could he do? He cursed himself for not finding a better solution — he'd had fifteen years to find a way to destroy the demon sword, or find somewhere safer to keep it than by his side. But at first, he'd needed the weapon's magic. There were so many of Lord Bone's monsters to slay, a whole city and the Pits beneath it to clear out, and using the sword seemed easiest.

"I want to help, Lammergeier." The sword's voice was a snake slithering across metal. "You are loyal to your friends, and that blinds you. If one of them has betrayed you—"

Alf shoved Spellbreaker back into its scabbard, silencing the blade.

Most visitors arrived via the docks on the eastern side of the city, not the west-gate; the checkpoint was only lightly guarded. Still, Alf decided he'd prefer to return unannounced. He approached the obsidian walls of the city, still sheer and unbreakable in the places where Lord Bone's enchantment lingered. In other places, the League had broken the spells and then broken the walls, but such gaps were guarded, too.

It wasn't the first time he'd sneaked into the city. There were hundreds of secret ways in that avoided the League sentries.

He wasn't Berys, of course. Berys would dance past the sentries like a fleet shadow, or convince them to switch sides with a crooked smile. Or, these days, buy them outright. Alf slogged through the dirt. He crawled through one of the tunnels that ran under the walls.

After two years away from Necrad, it was oddly comfortable to be back in this particular type of hellhole. He'd spent his life crawling down cramped passageways like this, and the darkness was restful to his eyes. Here, in this narrow passageway, he knew what to do with perfect certainty. Crawl forwards. Avoid those bits of jagged metal. Breathe shallow. Kill anything that gets close. There was no room for hesitation in a tunnel like this, no added complexity. Nothing existed beyond the reach of your sword.

He wasn't alone down there. Eyes gleamed in the darkness. Maybe rats, maybe Vatlings. And wraiths, always wraiths. Twenty years in Necrad, and he'd learned to ignore the grave-stepper shiver of a wraith brushing against him. They were harmless as cobwebs, he told himself.

Alf entered his city through the Pits. There were pipes that once carried away the slimy remains of failed experiments, vomiting their contents into the mud of the Charnel. Alf crawled through one of those to get under the wall, then found his way up from the sewers, emerging in an alleyway behind a burned-out temple.

For all its sprawling size, parts of Necrad were crowded.

There were the city-folk, descendants of Wilder or southerners captured before the war and forced to serve Lord Bone, or be given to the vampires. The *enhedrai*, the Witch Elves, who were first Bone's teachers, then his allies, then at the end his servants. This had been their city first, before Bone came and turned it into his war machine. Ogres from the hills, shambling down to fight for Bone and meat. And all the necromancer's creations and horrors – Vatlings born of alchemy, bound demons, creatures from far across the sea or summoned from unthinkable dimensions. Before the war, each of them had a part of the city assigned to them.

The League had declared . . .

No, he thought. *Take responsibility. We divided up the city. We made the law.* The decision had been made by Alf and his companions, not the League. *We carved up the city like a roast.* They'd declared more than half the city to be a forbidden zone where they'd sealed away Lord Bone's laboratories and temples and mortuaries. They had crammed all the survivors of Bone's forces into a small, easily watched area called the Liberties.

The Witch Elves made up only a minority of the Liberties. Most of the creatures that lived there were things like Vatlings, misshapen oddities that had crawled out of the Pits and learned the rudiments of language. Thurn had freed his Wilder kin, of course, but some refused to leave the city. They'd gone to the Liberties, too. At the time, Alf marvelled that anyone would choose to call this blasted place home.

He was wrong about that.

He slipped out of the alleyway and stood once again beneath the seething sky of Necrad. Even here in the slums, the city had an eerie, inhuman beauty. It reminded him obscurely of when he was a boy, looking at spider webs glittering with dew.

Alf made his way through the Liberties unchallenged. The Witch Elves and city-folk knew he wasn't one of them, but they also knew who he was. He could almost hear the whispers running ahead of him, like ripples in a pond. *The Lammergeier's returned. The hero of Necrad.* Or maybe they weren't so complimentary.

Butcher. Monster. Murderer.

Alf remembered the parade of displaced Witch Elves, all tattered glory and faded grandeur, carrying the mementos of a thousand years of rule bundled up in tapestries and carpets. He would never forget the look of disbelief on their faces, the shock at their defeat and subsequent upheaval penetrating even the mask of their impassively cruel features. The vampire elders – the few that survived – were escorted under blessed guard to be with their still-living families. And, of course, wraiths followed them, a cavalcade of spectres, banners of a defeated army.

Off to his left, he could see the barricades that blocked entry to the forbidden zone, the Sanction. Blaise warned that there were weapons and spells in the forbidden zone that might be turned against them if taken by some servant of Bone who knew the necromancer's secret sigils and words of command. He'd warned that these magics were too dangerous to be used, and should be carefully studied until they could be safely destroyed. The Sanction, they agreed, should remain sealed off until that work, that exorcism of Bone's evil, was done.

Fifteen years, and we're still working on that.

Although, to be fair, many of Bone's weapons and charms had been removed from Necrad. But not destroyed – they were stored in arsenals, or smuggled south to Summerswell. *Or claimed as trophies.* Then he added *OR PRISONERS*, putting as much force into the thought as he could, but the sword did not respond.

And the third slice of the city, the portion they'd kept for themselves – that was the Garrison. Alf had a house in the Garrison, but he had another destination in mind first. The memory of Jan's words, a more welcome voice in his head than the whispers of the sword.

Look in on Blaise for me, would you? I worry about him most of all.

The Wailing Tower no longer wailed.

The death of Lord Bone had broken the spell. The tower was silent now.

But not empty.

The tower stood at the exact centre of Necrad. Great streets radiated from it, like the spokes of a colossal wheel, joining in a wide, circular plaza. Once, these streets had run all the way to the city walls, but now they were all blocked in some way – some choked by rubble, some deliberately barricaded to divide Sanction from Liberties from Garrison, and others lost beneath the gigantic machines and monolithic structures constructed by Lord Bone in the years before the war. Lord Bone had rewritten the city, erasing the eerie beauty of the Witch Elves with his infernal factories. Here, though, in the centre, the wide streets were still mostly intact, and the sight of them called up old fears for Alf. When the Nine were trapped and hunted in Necrad, they'd shunned open spaces.

Beyond the tower was the huge rubble-strewn crater that had once been the dark lord's throne room, and the temple where he'd worked his devilry. They'd challenged him there, in his place of power. Nine heroes, creeping into that palace, intent on murder.

Eight survived.

Alf crossed the plaza of broken stone – the cracks still glowing faintly in the night, as ancient magic escaped the vaults below and leaked out as starlight – and approached the entrance archway. Two great doors of dark wood – cut, Laerlyn once told him, from the life-tree of some Elf wizard of long ago. The elven equivalent of binding a book in human skin. They should have taken the doors down years ago. They were an atrocity, an abomination.

Really evil doors.

Pasted to one door was a warning notice. Alf didn't bother reading the small print, but the seal at the bottom was that of the College of Wizardry in Summerswell. Whenever Berys had trouble sleeping, she'd asked Blaise to explain his philosophical differences with the wizards of Summerswell. Ten minutes of Blaise droning about arcane technicalities and magical regulation and she'd be out like a light.

The door was locked: a thousand dwarves could hammer on that dark portal for a century without budging it. Alf drew his sword and tapped the hilt of Spellbreaker on the door; it swung open of its own accord. Startled wraiths fled from their hiding places in the cracks of the door as it moved. On the far side, he found himself in a hall that would not be out of place in a manor in Summerswell. Thick carpets and oak-panelled walls and a brass chandelier. That was all new – or all illusion.

A young woman in scholar's robes rushed out of a side room and pointed a wand of elf-carved bone at him with a shaking hand. One of Blaise's apprentices. She looked terrified.

"It's all right," said Alf. "I just need to talk to him."

"The master is not to be disturbed." On closer examination, she wasn't terrified – she'd left terror behind long ago. Hollow-eyed, jumpy, pallid – the face of one living under siege. Her accent spoke of Summerswell, and high birth. Alf felt a little stab of pity for the girl – she could have had an easy life back in the south, but instead her choices had brought her to Necrad, to study under the greatest living mortal wizard.

He doubted she still thought it was worth it.

"Is he abed?"

"He does not sleep," she said, her voice almost rising to a shriek at the end.

"Look." Alf sheathed Spellbreaker – it was hard to be reassuring while carrying a demon sword of the apocalypse – and spread his hands. "I've known Blaise a long time. I'm an old friend, not a foe. You know who I am. I'm the Lammergeier. Let me pass."

"This tower, this tower is forbidden. He is not to be disturbed!" The apprentice pointed the wand at his heart, her aim unwavering despite the trembling of her body. She wasn't scared of Alf – or, if she was, it was nothing compared to the crushing fear of her master. Lightning crackled around the tip of the wand—

Let him in.

The words came from nowhere, and didn't even sound like Blaise's reedy, nasal voice, but the apprentice instantly lowered her wand and gestured towards the double doors on the far side of the hall.

"You may enter, but—"

"Thank you."

Alf stepped through the doors.

And suddenly, he was in an endless, infinitely tall tower. He stood on a spiral staircase that wound up and down until it was lost in darkness in either direction. The walls were lined with more books than could possibly exist in all the world.

Far above, a figure floated in the void over that immense, unthinkable chasm. Robes and cloak fluttered, books and stones of power orbited around him, cosmic forces flowed through him as Blaise levitated through his vast library.

An ostentatious display of power.

Alf remembered when the boy could barely conjure a basic illusion. A failed apprentice, thrown out of the College, reading the one tattered spell book he'd stolen from the library over and over. Always the straggler, limping behind the rest of the party when they marched. Lagging even after Alf and Peir secretly removed two-thirds of the contents of Blaise's pack and carried the supplies themselves. Always the runt of the party.

Back then, Blaise had to catch scraps of starlight in crystals and mirrors, gleaning little fragments of magic to weave into his spell. Most wizards were like that – few could muster the strength for really potent spells. A noble or rich merchant might employ a wizard to read the stars, to heal wounds before they festered, to banish evil spirits or bolster a warrior's luck in battle. A lord of Summerswell might be wealthy enough to keep a wizard in a tower, like a pig fattened for a feast, a whole lifetime spent collecting power for one great spell.

But that was most wizards. Not Blaise.

Blaise. I worry about him most of all.

Alf climbed. This high up, the shelves of books were rimed with frost, and the stairs became slippery. He clung to the wrought-iron banister, although that too was so cold his skin clung to it. He came upon a writing desk, where a disembodied hand and spectral eye were hard at work, translating another volume of magical lore. It was Blaise's handwriting, Blaise's hand and eye that floated there. There was no shoulder to peer over, so Alf was able to get a clear look at the text. A treatise on necromancy. Most of the text was far beyond him, but the marginal sketches of bones and nerves and joints spoke of the book's nature.

He went on, up and up, passing more writing desks, more hands and eyes. At one point, he looked down to the door he'd entered by – a dozen levels or more below – and saw a gaggle of pale apprentices clustered on the landing, looking up at him. Were they expecting a confrontation?

For all his boasts, Alf hadn't talked to Blaise at length in a long time.

They'd all been so *busy* in the years after Bone's defeat, and then they all had their duties in the occupation of Necrad. Berys and Gundan and Laerlyn dealt with the League, with the armies of their respective realms still encamped in the Charnel. Thurn had gone to his people, to the Wilder, to tell them they were free of the blood tithe. Jan went to heal the wounded and bury the slain.

Alf and Lath had taken it upon themselves to keep the Pits in check. There were still breeding vats and active summoning circles in the dungeons under the city that they hadn't managed to shut down. Some operated autonomously; others, he suspected, were run by dissidents among the Witch Elves. Either way, the dungeons regularly vomited out monsters onto the city streets. Alf was good at killing. It seemed obvious, at the time, that he should take responsibility for cleaning out the Pits – just for a few months, until they'd cleared the place. Until they proved to the surviving Witch Elves that they could be merciful. It was something he could do.

And Blaise had locked himself away in this Wailing Tower, to learn Lord Bone's magical secrets. He'd rarely left its confines since.

Blaise descended in terrible glory. His robes were a living thing, moving like wings, scalloped tatters swirling out like tentacles. His face was hidden in the shadows of his voluminous hood, but a halo of eyes orbited around his head. A dozen hands emerged from shifting sleeves, made arcane gestures, and withdrew. His voice came from all around, echoing from the stones and books, whirling around the tower.

"Sir Aelfric of Mulladale, Knight of Summerswell, called by some Lammergeier. Keeper of the Spellbreaker, *ayis turam va'shon*, thy name is terror to foes and a rallying cry to friends. What business do you have in the Wailing Tower?"

Alf adjusted Spellbreaker's scabbard. "I'm not going to talk to you like this. Stop floating."

"Speak," intoned Blaise. More eyes detached themselves from his halo and shot off into the depths.

"Jan sent me."

"You bear a message from the Illuminated One? Speak."

Alf folded his arms.

"Very well."

Another abrupt transition. Wind whirled around him, the tower falling away like leaves in a hurricane. When the tumult subsided, Alf stood alone in a little study. A desk, two overstuffed chairs. Shelves crammed with curios. A window looking out over the city. The last time he'd seen the view like that, he'd been clinging to the side of the tower with Berys.

The door opened, and Blaise entered. Gone were the living robes and shadowy hood, the excessive number of eyes and hands. He looked as Alf remembered him, thin and beaky. Blaise sat down behind the desk, gestured at the other chair.

Alf remained standing. "Is this illusion, or is it the library out there that's not real?"

"I don't deal in illusions any more, Aelfric," sniffed Blaise.

"So what was all that with the hands and eyes?"

"Efficiency. I have too much to do to squander time. I am the most accomplished mortal magus in centuries."

"Previous tenant excepted, I presume."

Blaise stared at him. "Is that supposed to be a joke, Aelfric? Forgive me – I have altered the workings of my brain, too, to improve my clarity of thought. I no longer find petty jests entertaining."

"Your apprentices are scared of you."

"Oh, pay them no heed. I mainly keep them around for utility's sake. Young blood. Virgin souls and so forth."

"Truly?"

"It was sarcasm, Aelfric." Blaise didn't smile, and his tone didn't change. "I never wanted apprentices. They were foisted on me, and they're all spies for the College, anyway. It's better to keep them occupied with imagined terrors." Blaise cocked his head. "You should be on your guard. They may have insinuated spies into your household, too."

Alf didn't have a household. Hell, he hadn't set foot in his *house* in years. "Jan said—"

"Tell me, how did Jan transmit this message to you?"

"I visited her. She sent a dream, and I went to her."

Blaise frowned. "You left Necrad?"

"I left Necrad two years ago."

"Oh." Blaise shrugged. "I didn't notice."

"A linnorm caught me. Opened me from hip to collar. I nearly died, Blaise."

"Did you die? Clearly not. Therefore, the incident is nugatory. What did Jan say?"

Alf's mouth went dry, and he wished Jan were here to speak for herself. Her warning seemed clear and earnest when she spoke to him in the valley of the Illuminated. Here, it sounded meaningless, the patter of a roadside fortune teller. "That she foresaw a great darkness overtaking Necrad. Maybe ... maybe some new evil, maybe something else. And that she was worried about you, in particular."

"Is that so?" Blaise's gaze flickered to Spellbreaker, for an instant. "Well, I am the master of the Wailing Tower. Nothing happens within these walls that I do not see. There is no darkness here to my eyes."

"What about the rest of the city?"

Blaise shrugged. "There is little to learn outside the tower, so I don't care much. All the potential perils I am aware of are contained, for now, though obviously I cannot dictate the course of events as fully as I might desire. It seems to me, though, that if this darkness is *rising*, it should be *your* responsibility, not mine. You promised to hold back the spawn of the breeding pits, didn't you? I understand

Lath is somewhat ..." A bloody wizard's pause. "... *overcome*, although he's never asked for my aid. Too proud, no doubt. Look to your own demesne, Lammergeier."

"If Lath asked, would you help him?"

"I have much work to do," said Blaise. "Lord Bone laid spells on this city, and locked them with his arcane sigils. Each sigil must be painstakingly decoded, then the spell unpicked, thread by thread. Only when all of Bone's authority is undone will Necrad be secure. There is *nothing* more important and beneficial for the world than my work here."

"If I asked, would you help?"

The wizard sighed. "Yes. If Jan's right, and there's some new threat we have to defeat, of course I shall be by your side. But what foe could threaten me now? Or you, or Laerlyn? If you *need* my aid, I will act. Otherwise, good day."

"Is there anything else I should know, Blaise?" *Did you open Bone's grave?* Alf wanted to ask directly, but he knew Blaise would take it as an accusation.

A wizard's pause, then:

"Do you have any comprehension, Aelfric, of how little you know compared to me?"

Alf walked out of the study and was not surprised to find himself standing on the street outside the tower, back in the Sanction. The city around him felt like it was another one of Blaise's illusions. For a moment, he doubted he'd returned to Necrad at all, and that he was still wandering the outside world.

Reluctantly, he drew the sword.

"Tell me," he asked Spellbreaker, "what did you see in there?" The demon sword could perceive things he could not.

"A carrion crow," answered the sword, "eating the remains of its betters. Brains in aspic."

"Huh."

"You should strike him down," suggested Spellbreaker, "before he's too powerful to stop, and becomes a new dark lord. He craves it, I can tell."

"I trust him," said Alf, "a damn sight more than I trust you."

"I'm just a sword, O Lammergeier. I am nothing without a wielder. "

Alf grunted and set off across the Sanction. Somewhere beyond the green cloud of the necromiasma, the sun was rising. Wraiths shrieked and cursed the dawn, scurrying off to hide under rocks or in discarded bottles. There'd be scavengers out soon, thieves and adventurers leaving the Garrison to pick through the rubble of the Sanction. At first, they came looking for the creations of Lord Bone, for enchanted weapons and magic treasures, spells beyond the mind of any mortal mage. Now, they picked the city for mundane treasures, too. The Witch Elves had dwelt here for . . . for . . . hell with it, Blaise would know. Or Jan. One of the wiser members of the company, who read books and knew things. Alf had never needed to know things like that. They'd tell him what to smite, and he'd smote.

Anyway, the Witch Elves had dwelt here in Necrad for a long bloody time, and they'd whiled away their immortality carving statues and making jewellery. The statues were creepy, pale things that seemed to move when you weren't looking at them, so life imitated art there, and the jewellery looked like what you'd get if you took a big handful of insects and worms and sea-creatures and thrust them, still wriggling, into a cauldron of molten silver.

The gate from the Sanction to the Garrison was guarded by dwarves, all wearing such heavy armour they looked like walking turrets. Their beards were tightly bound in cloth; the stench of the necromiasma clung to hair and clothing. Some were armed with crossbows, others with axes.

Guarded by dwarves, and only dwarves – despite the three League banners over the gate.

One of them grabbed at Spellbreaker, assuming that Alf had looted the enchanted blade.

"Don't," warned Alf, hoisting the sword out of reach.

The commander of the gate was a veteran of the Dwarfholt. "Let him through, you dolts. Don't you know who that is? It's the Lammergeier!" The commander shoved the other guards out of the way and saluted Alf in the dwarf fashion, offering the haft of his axe.

"I was at Karak's Bridge," said the commander, referring to a battle during the siege of the Dwarfholt, twenty-odd years ago.

Alf nodded. He tried to recall which one was Karak's Bridge.

"You saved our lives there."

That didn't nail it down. The siege of the Dwarfholt had been one long, hellish series of desperate battles, the Nine rushing everywhere along the walls, reinforcing the dwarves when the enemy broke through.

"I was not sure you had returned to Necrad, lord," said the dwarf, "it'll be good to stand beside you in battle again, when it comes. I'm glad you're on our side."

The dwarves let him through the gate into the Garrison, and it was like stepping through an enchanted portal. The streets in this section of the city were clear of rubble, the buildings in good repair – or rebuilt in the fashion of Summerswell. Wooden signs hanging over shops proclaimed them to be barbers, taverns, clothiers, grocers. The smell of fresh-baked bread, shouts and the creak of rope and sail from the distant dock, the hubbub of a waking city. If Alf closed his eyes, he could almost believe he was back in Summerswell.

"Karak's Bridge," said the sword, "was when we used poison gas to flood the tunnels. The ogres had long spears, and they skewered the dwarves as they came out for air."

"Don't bloody say 'we'. That was Acraist. That was before I took you."

"I was only trying to be helpful." The sword paused for a moment, then asked, "What do you think that dwarf meant about standing beside you in battle again?"

"I don't know."

"Maybe there'll be fighting again. It's been too long since I tasted blood."

"Shut up."

They came to Alf's mansion. Some Witch Elf lived here, before Alf kicked him out and claimed the palace. The place looked like a ruin. It *was* a ruin, the domed roof shattered during the siege, the greenish-white stone of the east wing still soot-blackened. Alf had meant to get around to fixing the place up, but in all the years he'd lived here the only change he'd made was removing some of the more disturbing statues. He'd always intended to do more, but there'd always been some more pressing task. All he used of the sprawling palace were a few rooms on one side, and he used them only for sleeping, really.

The mansion crawled with wraiths, whispering to one another in disgust at the human barbarian who squatted in their mansion. He'd crawled back here after the linnorm wounded him, and remembered lying in his bed, sweating, blood soaking through the bandages over his wound. The wraiths came crawling then, drawn by the smell of blood. The clerics lit candles to keep them away, but they gathered throughout the night, more and more, until the dark corners of the room were thronged with ghosts.

Or maybe that was the fever.

The bed, though: that was real. And after his long, bone-aching flight, it was what he needed. He'd never felt this tired when he was young.

He stumbled through the hallways, dreaming of his bed.

So when the dagger struck him, it felt like part of a dream.

Chapter Six

They left Highfield, still weary, with the late afternoon sunlight slanting gold around them. Olva's shadow on the road ahead of her was a giant striding east. Bor set a punishing pace, and she wondered at his endurance. Only the thought that the end of the chase was in sight gave her energy. They'd take Bor's short cut, get ahead of Lyulf Martens, take Derwyn home. Hunker down for the coming winter and find better days in the spring.

The road, which had been heading almost due east, now curved towards the south. In the distance, a dark tooth of stone rose above the fields.

"That's Tern's Tower. Got burned in the war," said Bors. "The Road goes round it, then turns back north on the way to Ellsport."

"And you're sure Martens is heading there?"

Bor's finger pulled at the collar of his shirt. "Fairly sure. We turn here, cut north-east over the marsh, then through the Fossewood. That'll bring us back out on the road, a day and a half maybe ahead of Martens." Off to their left was a marshland. Willow reeds waved in the sun, and she could hear frogs splashing in the shadows. Insects, too, buzzed around her already, biting at her exposed skin. The bugs would be worse as they went deeper in the wetland. Not for the first time, she wished she'd brought better travelling gear. She owned a good cloak that once belonged to Galwyn, and there was a pair of walking boots that she'd had repaired at last year's fair – and both of them sat by the door at home in Ersfel, thirty miles away and useless to her.

Thinking of it, she revised her wish; if anyone was going to take Galwyn's cloak, it should have been Derwyn. Had the boy taken anything with him at all, or had he just wandered out of the house, as if he could stroll to Necrad in an afternoon?

She looked down the road towards Tern's Tower and saw the tiny dark specks of distant figures. She wondered for a moment if they might be Martens and Derwyn, but the figures seemed stationary, as if standing vigil. Cu growled softly, and she could feel his hackles against her leg.

"This way," said Bor. Here, the road was on a raised causeway of earth, crumbling or overgrown in places. Bor scanned the north flank of the road, and chose his spot to descend, half slipping down the steep bank to end up knee-deep in the mud. He held out his hand for Olva to follow him.

She hesitated. "I've never been further from home than this minute." All her life had been lived within a few miles of Ersfel. She'd gone to market or to visit Galwyn's cousins in Highfield, but never this far. Summerswell and Necrad were equally mythical to her, both beyond those safe borders, and the outside world brought only woe. In Ersfel, she was safe.

Bor sighed loudly, then grabbed her wrist and pulled her off the road and down into the ankle-deep water. He held her until she found her footing, then let go. "We can't waste the light," he snapped. "Come on." He marched off north-east, the fens sucking at his boots.

Cu followed her down off the road, his paws scrabbling for purchase on the earthen bank. He took to the muddy water with joy, splashing merrily through the fens, then stopped abruptly and looked back at Olva in confusion, as if demanding to know why she'd allowed him to get so cold and wet.

Her feet asked the same question.

By twilight, they'd crossed the fens and come to the eaves of the Fossewood. Bor declared she should rest a short while there, before they pressed on into the wood. He went to scout their surroundings; she could see him in the distance, slogging through the mud along the fringes of the forest. Olva suspected he was a little lost, as they'd had to take a winding path through the marshes to avoid deeper water.

Cu came up and pressed his muddy head against her. Normally, she'd curse the beast for getting mud on her, but every bit of her was equally filthy. He snuffled at her pack. "I've no food for you," she said. "Go eat a frog." The dog whined and sat down, panting. She dug out the bread they'd bought in Highfield out of her pack, broke off a piece with her fingers and ate it hungrily. She threw some to the dog, too. "Don't let him see you with that." Bor was still a dark shape, far away.

No woodcutter's axe had touched this forest in a long time. The earth between the trees was almost as damp as the marsh they'd crossed, and there was a strong smell of decay. Nothing moved; birds wheeled and darted over the fens behind her, chasing the midges, and good hunting to them, but the wood ahead was eerily still. There was warmth in the air from the setting sun, but none in the shadow of the trees. She imagined Derwyn lost in the wood, shivering and alone, the hungry eyes of Wilder or worse things gleaming all around him.

Her hand strayed to the knife she kept by her side and closed on its hilt for security.

A tree branch creaked, and Olva flinched. That set Cu barking, and a moment later Bor came splashing up, his sword drawn. "What's wrong?"

"Nothing. It's nothing." She felt suddenly foolish. "Shut up," she added, speaking to the dog, who's apparently decided that Bor was the threat and was bounding around, barking at him.

Bor sheathed his blade. "Never said it'd be an easy short cut. I went looking for a clearer path, but there isn't one. People stay away from the Fossewood."

"Is it dangerous?"

In answer, he spat into the water. "Old wives' tales."

"Speaking as an old wife, if I tell a tale about a place being dangerous, it's because some idiot went there and got themselves killed. What do they say about this wood?"

"You're not that old," said Bor in a tone she hadn't heard from him before. "Come on, while there's still light."

They'd walked all night from Ersfel to Highfield along the road by moonlight, but walking in the wood at night was wholly different and much more terrifying. Olva stretched her hands out in front of her, feeling her way as much as seeing. It was slow going, as she feared catching her foot on some obstacle and twisting an ankle. The darkness conjured monsters at the edge of vision, looming horrors that became trees or boulders or hanging vines as she got closer, but some part of her remained convinced they were still there, hiding. Her heart pounded in fear. Cu pressed against her, scared of something in the wood, which just added a large furry obstacle to the journey. Bor at least seemed to know which way he was going – his route took them along a ridge, with the terrain falling away on either side. Bor walked ahead of her, moving at such a pace that she feared he'd leave her behind.

"How do you know Martens?" she asked. Even if she couldn't see Bor, she could at least follow the sound of his voice.

"I used to work for the bastard." The sound of a branch cracking as Bor stamped on it. "He trades in treasures out of Necrad. Potions, magic swords. Witch Elf work. The League forbids anyone to take elf-stuff out of the city, but there are scavengers up there who deal in such relics. Martens buys up there, then sails back down to Summerswell and sells. Lots of thieves on the Road." Bor shook his head. "More often than you'd think, they dig something magic out of Necrad and they don't know what it is, or it doesn't work right. And Martens, he doesn't tell us, he just sends us on our way along the Road. There was one time there was this carved stone head, ugliest thing you've ever seen. Some lord in Arshoth wanted it, and Martens tells us to bring it to him. We load the thing onto a cart, cover it with a tarpaulin, and off we go. We go across the fens so we can stay off the Road and avoid trouble with the League.

"Only halfway there, the thing wakes up and starts talking. It's not any tongue we'd ever heard, and the lads that listened to it, they started talking like that, too. And then they're stumbling around like they'd forgotten how their limbs work, and they're slobbering those horrible words, and pawing at us, only . . . you can see in their eyes they're still *them*, see? Like whatever evil's in that stone head took their bodies, but left them their minds."

"What did you do?"

"What do you think? We killed them. Threw their bodies in the mire, then stoppered our ears and pushed the stone head in, too."

"Is that when you stopped working for Martens?"

"Nah. That was the sort of thing he paid us for."

"Have you been to Necrad?" Olva stumbled over a tree root and caught herself against a trunk.

Bor grunted. "I've been up north a few times, but never set foot in the city."

"Is that what Martens wants with Derwyn? He wants him as a guard?"

"Maybe. If your boy looks like he can fight – and I assume he can, given he's the Lammergeier's kin. And you were eager enough to draw that knife of yours."

"Might there be trouble on the way to Ellsport? Might they be ambushed?"

"Other than by us, you mean?" A guttural, barking sound. She thought it was Cu coughing for a moment, then realised it was Bor's laugh.

"We're not robbing him," said Olva.

"He might not see it that way. I'll take your money, lady, and I'll do what I can, but if Martens has a passel of armed men with him, well . . . " Bor shook his head.

"What about other thieves? If he's carrying coin from the fair, they might get attacked." Olva had gone to the Highfield fair a few times, and always fretted on the return journey if she was carrying any money. All the profits from a years' work snatched away by some brigand. Now, of course, she was carrying twenty times as much – and she was alone in the dark woods with a dangerous man.

"Pray to the Erlking that he took payment in coin," muttered Bor.

"What do you mean?"

Bor didn't answer for a few moments, and seemed to move further away amid the trees. "Nothing. We'll talk about it in the light."

"We'll talk about it now."

Bor snorted. "What if your boy doesn't want to come home? Maybe he's told Martens to bring him to the Lammergeier. What then? You should let him go, if that's the case. The nephew of one of the Nine – all the fucking world at his feet, and you want to drag him back to that shithole of a village?"

Olva's finger brushed her knife, just to be sure it was still there. "I want him home and safe. This isn't some quest for glory – he's got a head full of nonsense from the songs, and then you showed up at my door with word from my brother, and that set Derwyn off. He's being foolish."

"He's young. Maybe he gets a few knocks, he stops being foolish."

Anger rose in her. "A few knocks – he's going to *Necrad*, you dolt. The fortress of the Enemy. Not . . . not a few knocks. The city of death."

Bor grunted. "Well, your brother killed the dark lord, eh? Him and the Nine."

"Derwyn," said Olva through clenched teeth, "is not Alf. I had other brothers, too, you know? Michel and Garn, and . . . they died. They were the Lammergeier's kin, too, and they died. The war came to my door, and I buried many I loved. I won't let Derwyn gamble his life on stupid songs."

Michel, killed in the war, sort of. They said it was a Wilder who killed him with a spear through his throat, but Olva always suspected it was a gambling debt gone awry. And Garn – they never knew what became of him. He'd followed Alf down the road, just like Derwyn, but no word of him ever came home.

"The boy's father – did he die in the war, too?"

"That's none of your business."

They walked in silence for a while, the darkness so deep that Olva could see no sign of Bor – not that she wanted to, in that moment. She stumbled on, cursing every root and stone in her path. The ground seemed to slope uphill and become drier as she climbed a low hill. Sleep tugged at her, and chills ran up her spine and along her aching shoulders. Through gaps in the foliage, she glimpsed patches of stars, but not the moon.

"You know," said Bor suddenly, and he was so close that she could smell his breath, "I've had a shit life in a lot of ways. Born piss-poor, no land, no kin any more. Lost my share of fights. Fucked over more than once – especially by that shit Martens. My back hurts in the morning, and I feel the cold more than I used to. But I look at some shithole like your little village, and I look at the people there, and I feel like a bloody lord. How do they stand it, seeing the same four walls and the same fields and the same stupid faces every day for their whole lives? How do they not go mad from boredom? How do you stand it?"

"It's called living. You get on with it."

The same bark of laughter. "Want to see something new?" he asked. "This way."

Bor led her down the slope, leaping from stepping stone to tuffet. Ahead was a patch bare of trees, naked in the moonlight. Cu whined and followed with reluctance as they circled the clearing.

"We'll camp up here tonight," said Bor. "There are beasts in the Fossewood that're dangerous, but they're mostly in the west, down in the valley. I won't risk a fire, but your dog better wake us if anything comes sniffing."

Olva scratched Cu's ear. "What sort of beasts?"

Bor didn't answer. He seemed more nervous now, shivering at times even though it was a warm night. "Stupid, stupid," he muttered to himself, half to himself. "But I'll show you anyway."

At the centre was a knoll of rock, twisted and frozen into a curiously human-like shape – like a statue had half burst from the earth, but fallen short and collapsed in on itself in stony agony. It was more than a trick of the light: there was a discernible face in the stone, weathered and worn but still somehow recognisable as human. As the moonlight shifted with the scudding clouds, Olva could have sworn the face moved.

Then she felt as if her spirit took flight, lifting from the shell of her mortal body and soaring through realms she never knew existed. The stars above the Fossewood wheeled around her, and the wood came alive all around her. She could feel the blood rushing through her veins, the rustling of small creatures in the undergrowth, squirming insects under the bark, feel the roots of the trees delving for water far underground. Rivers of light and life, branching and entwining, growing and dying, the world blazingly alive.

She was aware of Cu, too, prowling behind her, aware of Bor's thudding heartbeat. The heartbeat was somehow the turn of the seasons, too, each pulse a turn from summer to winter and back again, like the world was alive with them.

"What is it?" she asked. Her heart was beating fast, and the forest swam around her.

Bor grinned at her, and it was the first time she'd seen him smile. It didn't fit his dour face at all; it was like she was seeing another man entirely, one who'd walked a wholly different path. He'd felt it, too. "Magic."

The stone face stared down at her. "Who was he?"

"He's . . . he's . . . gah, fucked if I can remember his name. I was told it once," said Bor. He scratched his neck, stretched, and sat down with his back against the stone outcrop. The mercenary was back, that smile fading as quickly as the feeling of flight had left her. He scowled. "Some wizard from long ago. Or not a wizard – more like one of those Changelings, commanding the elements. Like Lath of the Nine." He sounded drunk with fatigue. "Commanding the wind and wave. Could've done with that, Martens, you bastard. Can't do shit against magic, no matter who you are. Anyway, the tale goes that he was a tyrant, like Lord Bone? And when the Erlking hears all about the wizard's evil, he sends out a bunch of knights to battle the fucker. Three knights. Or seven. Something like that."

"Or nine," muttered Olva, but Bor didn't seem to hear her. He was slurring his words now.

"Their ghosts come riding back, so the Erlking goes out himself, and fights the wizard right here in the Fossewood. Turns him to stone. How'd you like that?" He yawned. "Your boy didn't need to run all the way to bloody Necrad. This, right here . . . " Bor mumbled a few more words that Olva couldn't understand, then his head fell to the side and he began snoring loudly.

He was fast asleep.

Olva shook her head. "Some bodyguard you are."

To be fair to him, they'd walked with little rest for days, and she was on the verge of falling asleep herself. The eerie tomb of the nameless wizard offered a little shelter from the wind, and it was dry up here. It wasn't the worst place to make camp. She approached Bor, thinking to draw his cloak over him to keep him warm, or even lie down next to him, but his hand moved suddenly and she stepped back. He scratched at his collar again, and from this angle Olva could see he had a scar of some sort there, a dark shape winding around his neck. She wondered if a noose might leave such a mark.

She looked up at the stone face again, trying to recapture the weird moment of awareness she'd experienced, but nothing happened. The stone was just stone, the Fossewood silent again. Shame rose up in her – the priests warned about evil spirits and the temptation of the corrupting earthpower. They spoke of witches and bargains with foul things in the dark, and of folk becoming beasts when touched by the earthpower. Not every contact with the earthpower was damning – it was not unheard of for some villager to have a vision like the one she'd had, or to walk in dreams in the shape of an animal. The clerics knew cleansing rites to wash away the taint. After the Beast Lath had stayed in their house, all those years ago, Olva's parents had called on the village priest in Ersfel to conduct such a ritual. The priest, she recalled, had told them to burn any blankets Lath had used – but the boy had slept curled up by the fire like a dog. Olva scratched at her skin, as if any lingering taint could be scraped away with her fingernails, then muttered a prayer to the Intercessors.

She ate a little bread and drank the last of their water. They'd passed two streams on the way here – she'd stepped in one of them, she thought, as she pulled off a shoe and rubbed her aching foot – so she could refill their skins in the light. She was exhausted, but the thought of Derwyn was never far from her mind. She prayed that they were on the right track, and that they'd be able to bring Derwyn home.

If the Erlking had once stood in this dell, then she'd pray to him to ensure they caught Lyulf Martens on the road tomorrow.

Cu lay down heavily at her feet and curled up, the dog's snores a counterpoint to Bor's.

"And some watchdog you are," Olva muttered. She checked that her knife was to hand before she let herself sleep.

She did not dream.

She fell.

Again, the wood spun about her, seasons passing like leaves blown on the wind, and she felt like she was sinking into the earth. She could feel the warmth of the sun before it came over the eastern horizon, and feel the chill of the sea breaking on the coastline of her bones. Tern's Tower was an uncomfortable spike, digging into the flesh of her side. For a moment, her whirling consciousness brushed against a familiar spark of light, somewhere close at hand, along the stony callus of the road. *Derwyn* she thought, and she knew it was him, the same way he'd kicked against her belly, and she'd pressed Galwyn's hand to her stomach in delight. But the contact was fleeting, and she was a dark bird circling the Fossewood, riding the sea wind.

She touched another soul, even closer, and it was like tripping over a tree root, but somehow also kindly and warm. *Rest easy*, came the thought, *I'll watch over you.*

And then, far far away, something saw her and—

"Fucking hell."

She woke to Bor shouting at Cu. Something had alarmed the dog – he was running circles around the stone outcrop, barking furiously. Rain hammered down on them, a sudden storm breaking on the Fossewood. Icy water gushed over the stone in a hundred little waterfalls. Winds bent and cracked the branches. "Where'd this come from?" cursed Bor. "Good fucking morning to you, too."

Olva stood. She was already soaked through. "Let's get under the trees." She whistled, and Cu came running over to her and licked her hand frantically. "What's got into you?"

Bor pointed at a footprint nearby. A small, booted foot. "That wasn't there last night." He kicked a clod of mud at Cu. "Doesn't look like anything's missing, though." His face froze in horror at a sudden thought. "You've still got the money, yeah?"

Olva checked. "Yes."

"Gah, my tongue's like the Pits in the morning." He pulled the waterskin out of his bag and found it empty. "Where's the water?"

"In the sky," snapped Olva. She grabbed her back and squelched downhill into the shelter of the Fossewood. Bor grumbled and cursed as he marched after her. She glanced back, and from this angle she couldn't see the face in the stone any more. Her dream last night had not been a dream at all, of that she felt quite sure. She raised her face to the rain, as if it might wash away any lingering taint.

Try as she might, though, she could not wholly shake the feeling that she'd brushed against something wonderful. It was as if the Road had marked her already; Olva Forster, the respectable widow of Ersfel, would, of course, recoil in horror from any touch of wild magic, but an adventurer on a quest might react quite differently. The thrill of forbidden power had its allure. For the first time, she could almost see why Derwyn wanted to go. She took those shameful thoughts and hid them away.

Daylight made everything easier, and the rainstorm was a short-lived squall. By midmorning, it was bright and the Fossewood seemed quite normal, all its mystery and magic banished by the sunlight that came in spears and bursts through the branches overhead. Whatever had alarmed Cu was gone now, for he plunged through piles of fallen leaves with delight, and vanished for a while in pursuit of some animal. He returned licking his chops.

"At least someone got breakfast," grumbled Bor. "Not far, now."

CHAPTER SEVEN

The elf cursed even as the sword hissed a warning.

Alf twisted, and the dagger skittered off his chain shirt. As it struck, blue light flared and a heart-stopping chill rushed through Alf's chest. His beard was suddenly heavy with ice, his limbs frozen, hands numb. He stumbled back, a rime of frost spreading over him, weighing him down. The elf came at him again, moving with serpentine grace, the dagger a fang, darting forward to bite him. He shoved her away with as much strength as he could muster, and she cut him again, a long slash along his right forearm.

He grabbed Spellbreaker, fumbling the draw with numbed fingers. The blade was heavy in his wounded hand, and for once it wasn't because the sword had turned on him. Its counter-magic, though, was like a hot bath. His ragged beard steamed, and he could move again.

He weighed her up, old instincts kicking in as blood rushed through his hands, his brain. A Witch Elf woman, grubby, wild silver hair like a halo. Armoured in scales of shadowmetal, though — gear from the war, and well maintained. Not a scavenger, but the way she moved didn't suggest military discipline to him. The Witch Elf soldiers he'd faced had all trained for centuries, and moved like insects, precise and quick, not a bit of wasted motion. This was different. She stalked him as he backed away, circling to cut off his line of retreat. A huntress. An assassin.

Ice magic coiled around the blade in her hand. She had a magic dagger.

Fine.

Alf had a much bigger magic sword.

He raised the sword, and death was in it. Spellbreaker drank the light from the room, the sound, the substance. Everything became hollow and pale, everything but the sword. The black blade was the only real thing in existence, the only solid and true thing, and all else was just a shade, a trick of dust motes drifting in the fading light. The sword unsheathed was terror and hopelessness, fused and forged into a single weapon. To look upon it was to know doom.

She recognised it. Her eyes widened in terror.

Magic death swords were a great distraction. Alf punched the elf with his other hand. She reeled back, gasped another word in Elvish. For an instant, she froze, the blue light from her dagger reflected in her dark eyes, then dodged to the side, leaping past him, racing to the door behind him. He knew better than to try grabbing her. Even if he wasn't half frozen, she was elf-swift. She slipped out of the door in the blink of an eye.

But this was his house. He didn't like it very much, but it was home ground.

He spun around and slammed the demon sword into the wall. The marble exploded under the impact, a horizontal avalanche bursting out into the corridor behind him. He staggered out after it, and found the elf sprawled on the hallway floor, half buried under debris. He tapped his chest with Spellbreaker's pommel as he walked towards her, ridding himself of the last of the ice-spell.

Behind him, the ceiling of his bedroom collapsed. The whole house groaned.

"That might," the sword observed, "have been a supporting wall."

A cut on her forehead matted silver hair to her moon-pale skin, but she was still breathing. Alf pulled the elf out of the rubble. He winced at the effort, pain shooting through his back and side. She'd cut him more than once in their brief fight, and the charmstone he wore was broken — one of the wounds she'd dealt would have been the ending of him without that. He drank a healing cordial as he considered what to do.

"There are guards coming," said the sword.

Alf nudged a chunk of his wall with his foot. "You made a big mess." Being in the Garrison without permission was forbidden to Witch Elves. Even if she hadn't just tried to murder one of the Nine, her life would be forfeit. The life of her body, anyway — her wraith would join the others haunting this city.

"You of all people say this," taunted the sword.

"She said something in Elvish," said Alf. "What was it?"

"She called you 'Deceiver'. And then, after she saw me, an expression of disbelief that does not translate well into the common tongue. The speech of the *enhedrai* is ancient beyond the understanding of mortals, subtle and poetic, but in terms you'd understand . . . 'What the shit?'"

"'Deceiver'," echoed Alf. The phrase Jan had mentioned, *morthus lae-something-necro-something*, ran through his head, but he asked the sword to translate it. It felt faintly blasphemous to share Jan's words with the evil blade. He picked up the elf's dagger from the floor. Dragon-bone the handle and moonsilver the blade. *Enhedrai* runes, and enough magic to cut through Alf's defences. The workmanship was exceedingly fine, even for elf-work. A blade like this was rare indeed. It reminded him of Spellbreaker.

It was no common weapon. The Witch Elf wasn't a burglar. She'd been waiting for him. And this dagger had been chosen for a reason.

He'd sent no word he was returning to Necrad. He himself hadn't known until he'd spoken to Jan, three days earlier.

So how had the elf known?

He tucked the dagger into his belt.

"Wield me," urged the sword, "finish her."

"No. Call a dreadworm," Alf ordered instead. Here, under the necromiasma, the worm would congeal instantly.

Outside, more shouts. Wearily, Alf returned to the ruins of his bedroom, leaving the elf-girl sprawled on the ground. He went looking for the cache of healing cordials he kept near his bed. They helped with the old aches, and would help with the fresh wounds, too. Down south, a single vial of the cordial was next to priceless – a draught could cure a mortal wound and ensure it healed cleanly. Here in Necrad, the stuff once flowed in fountains. Even now a scavenger could find trickling pipes in the Pits. He picked through the wreckage until he found the metal casket. The lock was jammed, so he prised it open with Spellbreaker.

"I'm not a crowbar."

He ignored the sword's complaints.

"You're slow," observed the sword. "You should have dodged that first cut."

"I'm tired. Is that worm ready?"

"It is."

He returned to the hallway. As he expected, the elf was gone.

The League guards arrived five minutes too late, as they always did, crowding into Alf's hallway like dungeoneers clearing a zombie warren room by room. They froze at the sight of the hero standing before them. The captain removed his helmet and saluted. Alf recognised the man's face, although he couldn't recall his name.

"Sir Lammergeier!? I was not informed you had returned to Necrad." Behind the captain, two of the younger guards sank awkwardly to one knee, like they were in the high court down in Summerswell and Alf was some princeling.

"Well, I'm back," said Alf. "There's nothing amiss here. You can go." Another large chunk of ceiling fell away in Alf's bedroom, landing with a crash.

"We heard an explosion," said the captain.

"Just some elf-thief. I've dealt with it. I'll talk to Lord Urien directly."

"Lord Urien," said the captain, "is no longer in command of the Garrison. He fell ill and returned to Summerswell more than a year ago. The post has been assumed by Lord Vond."

That news cheered Alf a little; he'd always got on well with Lucar Vond. He was one of the few nobles of Summerswell who hadn't made Alf feel like a country bumpkin.

"Well, I know Vond, too," said Alf, "and I doubt Lord Vond gives a flying fuck about some Witch Elf thief. You think this is the first time I've been burgled? Or the hundredth? I don't keep anything of value here. Go on."

The captain glanced around at the devastation, then bowed. "As you command, Sir Lammergeier. I shall tell Lord Vond to expect your report in the morning at the council meeting."

"Ooh, arr, I don't be a-keepin' anything of value here," said the sword, echoing Alf's words and mocking his Mulladale accent, its thickness refreshed by his visit home. "What am I then?"

"I don't keep you here. I keep you with me." He took out the elf-dagger again and examined it, cleaning off the last of the ice that clung to it with an oiled cloth. A very fine blade, of ancient work.

"You never do that for me."

"You don't polish up well," muttered Alf. "Where's the elf?"

"She has left the Garrison and crept into the Liberties."

"How'd she get past the sentries?"

"She jumped from the wall," said the sword. There was a distant tone to its voice as it relayed impressions from the dreadworm that stalked her. "She's alive. Limping."

"That's a big jump." Alf drank another cordial, feeling the healing magic seep into his limbs, washing away the pain and leaving a delicious heavy fatigue in its place.

"She is heading for the House of the Horned Serpent," said Spellbreaker. "The worm grows hungry."

Alf yawned. "I'm going to bed. Tell the worm to keep vigil, and stay out of sight as best it can. If she leaves, wake me."

"As you command."

On his travels Alf had grown used to rising with the dawn, but there was no dawn worthy of the name in Necrad. The miasma above the city was an eternal greenish gloom, and all that dawn brought was an almost imperceptible change in brightness. There were clocks all through the Garrison whose chimes sounded the hour, and it was one of those that woke him.

He lay in the musty bed in one of his spare rooms and counted the strokes of the bell. Nine, ten, eleven. He was late.

"You're awake," said the sword from beside his bed. "She hasn't moved. The dreadworm wants to know if it can eat her when she emerges."

"Tell it to keep watching."

"Letting it follow her was clever, Aelfric. I must be a good influence on you."

"Quiet." Alf searched around for something to wear. He had finer clothes more appropriate to his station in the city, but couldn't recall where he'd left them. He suspected they were buried in the wreckage. He took a sniff, and wished he hadn't buried his bath under several tons of rubble.

"Do you think she's in league with the one who opened the tomb? Did she know you carried a warning from Jan? Did someone send her to silence you?"

"I don't know."

"Only one of your friends could have opened that tomb, Lammergeier, and they'll all be at the council meeting."

"Shut up."

"Tell them nothing. Wait for your enemy to give themselves away."

"None of them are my enemies."

"I would go girded for battle, if I were you. Just in case."

"Shut up." Still, he pulled on the chain shirt of dwarven mail, and wore his travelling clothes over it. He still looked more like a wandering brigand than a member of the council or a hero from the sagas.

He disliked the sword's unpleasant company, its combination of malign utility and lurking treachery. A weapon you couldn't trust was no weapon at all. But they'd all taken on responsibilities when they defeated Lord Bone, and Spellbreaker was his. He strapped the sword to his side and left the remains of the mansion.

The Garrison district had changed again, he noted, as he walked down towards the harbour. There were always more shops, more warehouses and taverns. Some hastily built on new-cleared land, quarrying rubble from destroyed buildings. Others repurposed existing structures, turning old Witch Elf temples into markets, or changing mortuaries once used for undead shamblers into cold storage for meat. The mix of people on the streets was much the same as when he'd left two years earlier, but there were far more of them. More traders and settlers than soldiers, these days, for the defeat of the dark lord opened up the north. There were farms now, eager foresters hacking down the twisted woods where once Witch Elves hunted. A string of castles and towns along the Road, the New Provinces north of Necrad. The land of the Enemy was being occupied and tamed, acre by acre, ship by ship. Every ship that landed in Necrad disgorged more settlers for the frontier. They pushed past Alf in droves, goggling in wonder at the strange city around them.

A pale figure caught Alf's eye. *Vampire.* His hand went to Spellbreaker's hilt instantly, but then he saw the green armband on the Witch Elf's tattered robe, signifying it was allowed out of the Liberties.

"Make way," it hissed. A palanquin carried by Vatgrown followed behind the fallen elf, and it bore the sign of the Crownland of Summerswell. Some rich merchant rode within. Alf stood aside. The vampire hissed at Alf as it passed, recognising the Lammergeier. There was a ghastly hunger in its eyes, a predator's frustration as it walked through the crowds, surrounded by blood it could not drink.

Instead of fading into wraiths, Witch Elves could go vampire. They could use blood to cling to material existence, stay unfaded despite injury or age. But it wasn't pretty. They ruled the Wilder as monstrous gods, generation upon generation of Wilder-folk bred to slake the hungers of the vampire lords. Now, he noted with distaste, there were human merchants with pale servants. Vampire sentries at the doors.

"I wonder if your friend Laerlyn would like a taste of your blood," whispered the sword. "I bet you'd like to taste her."

"Stay out of my dreams," snapped Alf automatically. Anyway, Laerlyn was a Wood Elf, not a Witch Elf. When she started to fade – centuries after Alf was dead and gone, if her spirit endured – she'd go home to the woods and bond with a life-tree. She would become a dryad, not a vampire, and stay young for ever.

His back ached. His bones ached. His chest, too, where the other elf had stabbed him. That pain, at least, made sense. Getting old was surviving a series of unseen battles; you didn't always know you were fighting them, but got buffeted and wounded all the same.

His destination was just ahead. Three banners fluttered from the towers of the League citadel, carefully arranged so that no flag was higher than any of the others. The tower of the Dwarfholt, the tree of the Erlking, the sun of Summerswell. The banners of the League.

None of the guards at the gate barred his way, but one bowed and said, "Lord Vond is within, Sir Lammergeier, and wishes to see you before the council meets."

A oil painting hanging outside the governor's office depicted the first Vond to bear the name. He was with the other Lords of Summerswell, each in full plate or robes of state, swords driven into the earth as they knelt before the Erlking's tree. Holy Intercessors hovered overhead, helpfully carrying banners marked with the name of each lord and the province they ruled. That first Lord Vond looked back at the viewer with an expression of pious concern, a kindly father worn by the burden of care.

Alf thought well of Lucar Vond. Most Lords of Summerswell had been frustratingly slow to acknowledge the threat of Lord Bone. They'd looked instead on the Nine's shortcomings and questionable characteristics – Thurn was a savage barbarian in their eyes, Lath was a barbarian *and* an unholy aberration. Blaise had broken the laws of the magicians' college in Summerswell, and Berys had got through the rest of the statute book. Laerlyn had defied the elven royal court by running off adventuring, and the Lords were loath to offend the Everwood by giving her an official audience. And of the remaining Nine . . . well, Gundan could start an argument with anyone and anything, Jan was a disgraced priestess, and Alf was a low-born Mulladale farm boy as worthy of an audience with the Lords of Summerswell as a donkey.

If it wasn't for Peir, the war would have gone very differently. It was Peir who forged the League, and he did it with Lucar Vond. Alone of the Lords of Summerswell, Lucar had listened.

But it wasn't Lucar Vond who stood before Alf. It was another in the Vond line.

"I am Timeon Vond," said the young man with a slight bow. "Sir Lammergeier. Please, give me a moment to finish."

The boy gestured to a seat on one side of the great desk, then sat down on the other side. Papers and letters were piled so high that Alf could barely see the boy's tousled head. He heard the scratching of a quill as Lord Vond wrote another missive.

The boy's accent reminded Alf of Peir's way of speaking. High-born, both kin to the exalted Lords of Summerswell, heirs to a line of lords that went back to the dawn days, and Alf was a grubby peasant from the Mulladales without name or title. Even though they'd made him a knight and showered him with gifts and honours after the war, he still felt like he was play-acting at being Sir Lammergeier the Brave, knight of Summerswell and captain of the League.

A distant memory – the Nine staying at Lucar Vond's mansion outside Summerswell, all sitting on the greensward with servants handing them goblets of iced wine, and children playing in a chestnut tree. A picture of lazy tranquillity, a slow summer's day to be whiled away, while they all tried to persuade Vond and his peers that the Enemy was already moving, that doom was at hand.

This new Lord Vond was one of the children in the tree, all those years ago. Doom had not come for him. They'd saved Summerswell.

"How's your father?" asked Alf.

"As well as can be expected." The pen kept scratching.

"I'm here for the council meeting."

"I am told there was a burglar in your house," said Vond without looking up.

"Aye. The matter's in hand. You don't need to do aught."

"My predecessor, Lord Urien, put a guard on your home, expecting you to return promptly. Those sentries remained stationed at your home for two years, sentries that were sorely needed elsewhere. You told him that you would be back by midsummer last year. At the latest."

"I thought I would be."

The boy set down the pen, took a breath and leaned back, his hands steepled in front of him. It reminded Alf of conversations with the father; the elder Vond had done the same thing when he spoke of important matters. Alf wondered if the boy had been taught the gesture, or if it was a ghost in the flesh, mannerisms unconsciously passed down from father to son. The breath first, though – Alf recognised that from the battlefield. You'd take a gasp of air like that when trying to steel your nerves. Bless the lad. A smile tugged at the corner of Alf's mouth.

"Sir Lammergeier, my predecessors have always given you and

your companions a great deal of latitude when it comes to the affairs of Necrad. You are the heroes who won the day, and you have continued to aid Summerswell since . . . in your own fashion. As a knight of Summerswell and hero of Necrad, you may of course attend the council, and I welcome your advice, but . . . " Vond paused and clasped his hands together to hide his nervousness.

Alf took pity on the boy. "Aye, go on," he said, as warmly as he could.

"But the affairs of the council are in a delicate balance. There are tensions in the League. The slightest word out of place might throw everything into chaos."

Alf shrugged. League politics and the management of the city always bored him. He'd stopped going to council meetings years ago, when they became more about land grants and disputes over taxes than any other matters. "If there's trouble, the Nine will deal with it."

"That remains to be seen," said Vond, and there was an odd tone in his voice that Alf didn't like. Before he could question the governor, a bell rang in the distance. "The council is summoned, and we cannot be late. Walk with me, Sir Lammergeier."

He considered telling Vond about the breaking of the seal on Lord Bone's grave. Neither Lucar Vond nor this boy of his were of the original company of heroes; he couldn't have broken the seal. Alf rolled the thought around his mind for a moment. The peace had been harder than the war in some ways; there'd been arguments between the Nine and the Lords of Summerswell since Lord Bone's defeat. Giving the Lords of Summerswell another reason to mistrust the Nine seemed foolish – and, more importantly, it wasn't the boy's problem. The Nine had sworn to guard the city, not young Timeon Vond. No, Alf decided to keep his mouth shut for now. The fate of the world was too important a matter to be trusted to a grass-green boy.

Alf fell in alongside Vond as the younger man hurried through the corridor of the governor's mansion towards the council chambers next door. Alf's side ached, pain radiating out from where the elf had struck him.

"Summerswell grants you and your companions considerable leeway," said Vond, "but my indulgence cannot be limitless, especially when it comes to you. You are a knight of Summerswell, the only sworn knight among the companions. By rights, you should be my closest ally on the council, the most earnest advocate for the interests of the Lords of Summerswell. I cannot rely on Berys or Blaise, and the other mortal companions are gone."

Alf nodded. Berys had delighted in tormenting and outmanoeuvring Lord Urien. And Blaise could be infuriating even when he was being helpful. But there was one name missing.

"What about Lath?"

"Have you seen him?" asked Vond in surprise.

"Not in a few years."

"The Beast has not been seen in several months."

"My first piece of advice – don't call him the Beast. That's a slur they threw at him when he was a boy. It's not a name he likes."

"It's what the songs name him."

"Aye, well . . . "

Vond glanced at Alf. "Are you injured, Sir Lammergeier? You seem to be in discomfort."

"I'm fine." Unexpected anger boiled up inside Alf. "Don't call me the Lammergeier, either. Bloody stupid name."

"I shall send sentries to your house again. And a personal bodyguard, too, to ensure your safety."

The sword at Alf's side chuckled.

"I don't need," said Alf, "a nursemaid." He didn't shout, but he couldn't keep the edge out of his voice.

Vond's expression froze into a mask. "As you wish." Polished boots clicked on the marble hallway. "I am minded to send you north as my emissary, to tour the New Provinces and bolster morale there."

Alf took a deep breath himself. His instinct was to ignore young Vond's suggestion. He'd had enough of being feted by nobles during his wanderings in the south. The quest Jan had laid on him was more important. He spoke as gently as he could, putting in the effort to soften his tone. The courtesies sounded absurd when spoken in his Mulladale accent. "Begging your pardon, my lord, but giving speeches isn't what I'm best suited for. It would be better to put me back down the Pits, 'specially if Lath's not been doing his share."

"I already have soldiers, Sir Lammergeier. None may have your prowess or your panoply of weapons, but I do not need an invincible champion. I need an emissary who can assuage the fears of the New Provinces. Are you well enough for such a task?"

"I've things to do here, first."

"Attend to them quickly," ordered Vond. "I intend to make full use of you."

"I'll catch up," said Alf, turning away. The governor frowned and kept walking, the click of his bootheels on the red tiles echoing down the long colonnade.

Alf drew Spellbreaker. "Has she moved?"

The sword was slow to answer him. "No. And the dread-worm's hungry."

"Tell it to keep watching."

"I forget how quickly you mortals age," remarked Spellbreaker. "Soon, you'll need someone to wipe your chin and help you climb stairs."

"If you have nothing useful to say, remain silent."

"I hope you won't use me as a walking sti—"

He shoved the sword back in its scabbard. He lingered for several minutes outside the council chamber, pacing back and forth. He found himself rubbing the rib where the Witch Elf had stabbed him, and cursed himself. Waiting on the far side of that door were his oldest, closest friends, the heroes he'd fought alongside for more than half his life. None of them would judge him for dropping his shield when the linnorm snapped at him, or getting ambushed by a slip of an elf with a shiny dagger and a knack for ice-spells.

He was losing his edge again. Getting lost in his own worries. He kicked himself. *Give me something to kill.* That's what he needed – to get back into the fray. He'd greet his friends, then go down into the Pits and hunt monsters. Maybe drag along Gundan and Laerlyn and maybe even Blaise for old time's sake. Maybe find Lath down there. Bring everyone who was left back together.

One of them had opened Bone's grave. Maybe they had a good reason. Maybe they were waiting for him, for the full company to be assembled, before explaining why. When they were adventuring together, they never held secrets from each another. You had to trust your fellows in the company, it was the first and most important rule. They'd grown apart, but bonds forged in suffering could never be wholly broken.

Alf stopped pacing. His friends were waiting for him, and once they were all together again, all would be well.

He brushed back his thinning hair and entered the council chamber.

It was nearly empty.

CHAPTER EIGHT

O n the far side of the Fossewood, the Road picked its way
through thickets and sandy hills. There was a strange smell
that must be the sea, but she could not see it yet. Bor picked a sharp
bend in the road as the spot where they'd wait for Lyulf Martens.

"How long do we stay here?"

Bor shrugged. "If Martens doesn't pass this way by tomorrow,
then I've led you wrong." A few hours' sleep had restored the man.

"And then what?"

He shrugged again. "Then I won't get paid as soon as I'd like."

"Last night," said Olva, "you mentioned something you wouldn't
discuss by darkness. About Martens, and Derwyn."

"You don't want to know."

"If I did not, I wouldn't have asked."

The mercenary rubbed his chin. "The Witch Elves, the old ones —
they don't die like we do, aye? After a time, regular food and drink
ain't enough for 'em any more. They have to feed on the living. They
used to feed on the Wilder, but the League put a stop to that. Now,
the vampire elves are hungry and desperate. Martens, he knows
desperate. And he's a merchant, he knows profit. He finds mortals
so hungry they'd do anything for a crust, and immortals so hungry
they'd do anything for a drop of blood, and he—"

"Enough!" Olva turned away and buried her face in Cu's fur. Her fingernails dug into her palms, her knees turned to water. "I've heard enough." Dark memories of pale figures breaking into her house, of Galwyn, of red-stained lips. "I know what they do."

"Told you," snorted Bor, then he frowned as he noticed her moment of weakness. "You all right?"

Olva shoved the thoughts away. "I'm fine. I just want this over with."

"This may not go smooth. If you don't have nerve for it, then go back down to the stone and wait there. I can't be guarding you *and* dealing with Martens, not for all the money in that bag."

She shook her head.

"All right. Show me that knife you keep messing with."

Reluctantly, she gave him the weapon. Bor ran his thumb along its edge, then tested it, making a few quick cuts on a green branch. He handed it back to her. "Not bad. Show me how you use it."

Olva took back the knife, briefly disturbed by the unfamiliar warmth of the handle after someone else had touched it. She did as Bor had demonstrated.

"You look like you're trying to cut the head off a goose," snorted Bor.

"Isn't that the idea?"

"Unless you cut something vital, it'll take much too long for you to poke enough holes in someone with that thing. And you've no reach with it, neither. Don't risk it." He gestured to the bend of the road with his sword. "When Martens comes, you let me talk, all right? You stay out of sight. And keep that dog quiet, too. If things go bad, run. Hide in the wood until it's clear. I'll be right behind you."

It was Cu who heard them approach first. Olva quieted the dog, just as Bor came rushing down from the hill above.

"It's Martens," he said. "Get out of sight."

Olva hid in the undergrowth, dragging Cu down by her side. The dog's tail thumped against her leg, showing his excitement at this latest episode of their grand adventure.

Bor took one last look at the patch of road nearest the bend, slowly moving across it, marking every stone or patch of mud, intense concentration on his face. He drove the tip of his sword into the ground behind a tree, then checked to ensure it wasn't visible from the road. Finally, he sat down under the shade of the tree, arranging himself as if to appear utterly casual and lackadaisical.

Olva knelt down, making herself as small as she could. Her fingers gripped the muddy ground. Her breath shallow and fast. *Don't move, don't make a sound. Don't be seen.*

A covered wagon came into sight. Drawn by two horses and escorted by half a dozen men – and one of them, Erlking be praised, heavens sing out, *she was going to murder him when they got home* – could only be Derwyn, her Derwyn. He held himself more proudly than the rest, and was more vigilant – it was he who pointed at Bor's apparently comatose form by the roadside, and alerted the driver of the wagon.

The driver – Lyulf Martens – sat huddled in a heavy cloak, clasped just beneath his chin. Jewelled rings gleamed on his fingers as he drew back on the reins to slow the wagon, and there were silver amulets threaded in his long white beard, in the fashion of the stock of Arshoth. His cloak, though, was threadbare, his clothes humble.

Bor unfolded, climbing to his feet unhurriedly. "Ho there," he called. The weapons of the guards bristled. Many had little talismans tied to them, charmstones out of Necrad. Every year, pedlars troubled Olva's doorstep, trying to hawk magic stones they claimed could bring a better harvest, or make her hens lay golden eggs. Those stones were just carved rocks.

She feared these charmstones were genuine.

Martens peered at him. "Is that Bor of Cullivant?"

"It is," cried one of the other guards.

"What does he want? Ask him what he wants."

Bor pointed at Derwyn. "That one. I don't know what he told you, Lyulf, but he's bound to service, and he ran away from his master's house. I was hired to fetch him home."

"That's not true!" protested Derwyn, "I'm a free man – and I know you." He took a step towards Bor. "You're the one who came to the house. What trickery is this?"

Bor ignored the boy. "He's wanted back home, Lyulf. Whatever you've paid him, I'll cover. And – and we'll be done after, you and I. All square."

"I owe you nothing, Bor. You knew the risk. As for young Derwyn here – the boy has a powerful longing to go to Necrad, and has given himself into my service until we get there. You'll work your passage, is that not right?"

Derwyn nodded. "Did my mother send you?" he asked Bor. One of the other guards laughed, and Derwyn blushed. "Go back and tell her that all's well. Tell her I have to go, and that I'll send word once I find . . . the man who sent you. But I must go to Necrad, and I cannot tarry."

"You don't want to go to Necrad," hissed Bor, "with this prick. Did he tell you about what happened to him and me?" He raised his voice, addressing all the guards now. "Lyulf Martens, the great smuggler, gets us all caught by the Wood Elves! Us, with cargo forbidden to take out of Necrad! No League licence to carry any of it! We're crossing the Gulf of Tears, when all of a sudden the wind turns on us and the ocean's alive with sea-serpents and elves. The elves brought us to the Isle of Dawn, and they were not kind to us! Look!"

He tore open the collar of his shirt. From her vantage point, Olva couldn't make out what Bor had revealed to the men in front of him, but the effect was obvious – they recoiled in alarm. A look of disgust and horror on Derwyn's face, mirrored on the faces of several of the other guards.

Lyulf Martens, though, was unmoved. "You knew the risk, Bor.

You took the gamble, as did I. And had you stayed in my service, I might have been able to help you after. Now, I can only pity you." He raised his voice. "Stand aside."

Bor stepped back to stand beside the tree where he'd concealed his sword. The blade was hidden from view from the roadside, but plain as day to her, a promise of violence staring back at her through the underbrush. She was horribly conscious that the men on the road, and Derwyn above all, were bags of blood wrapped in soft, vulnerable skin. The sword promised to cut them open, a red flood mixing with the mud of the road. Death coming in a flash, a single quick stab. Death coming slow in a cut across the belly, slinking in lazily after leaving you to suffer for hours. A hundred ways to be maimed — to live out your days in pain and pity, even if you survived. Was this how Alf lived? Was this what Derwyn craved?

Don't do it, she thought, as if some magic in the Fossewood could carry her words to Bor. *Don't start a fight.*

But Bor reached for the sword.

It was like a conjurer's trick. A step in a dance. One motion, taking the sword and bringing it around and stepping forward and raising it all at once. The tip of the blade was in the dirt behind the tree, and then it was at the throat of Lyulf Martens, faster than Olva's eyes could follow.

Martens was unperturbed. "Bold of you, Bor, when I've six swords to your one, and all of them charmed."

"If any of you move," shouted Bor, "he dies."

By Olva's side, Cu whined and pawed at her. She hushed the dog. "Not now."

Bor lowered his voice. "The boy is kin to the Lammergeier himself, to Aelfric of the Nine! The Lammergeier, hear me? I was sent by the Lammergeier's own sister to fetch him home. You think you can cross *him*, Martens? You think you can stand against the Nine? Release him to . . . to . . ."

For a moment, the sun seemed to dim. Cu broke free and went racing towards Derwyn, barking furiously.

Bor gurgled. The sword tip didn't waver, not at first, but his other hand went to his own throat, pulling at his neck. He fell to his knees, then collapsed to the side, his sword falling into the mud, his legs convulsing. Derwyn darted forward to help, kneeling next to Bor. There was something wrapped around Bor's throat, a cord or noose, but Derwyn got his fingers under it, digging into Bor's neck but keeping it from strangling the mercenary.

Lyulf Martens leaned forward to examine the man thrashing on the ground before him. He raised one hand, and a ring there glimmered with an eerie light. "I know he's kin to the Lammergeier. I could see it in his face, had I not been told it already. Now I cannot afford to be gentle."

He nodded. A guard stepped forward and clubbed Derwyn from behind, and then it all happened at once. Olva leapt up from her hiding place and rushed forward, forest and sky wheeling around her again as she slipped and stumbled and sprinted towards the road. Guards manhandled Derwyn's stunned form into the cart.

Olva ran right for the cart. Lyulf Martens' whip cracked, lashing the flanks of the horses, and the wagon took off with a jolt, creaking down the north road. Cu was among the guards on foot, rushing around and snapping at them, driving them back from where Bor lay. They fended him off with their spears. Olva burst from the cover of the woods and chased after the wagon, but there was a guard in her way.

A spear in his hand.

He hesitated, just a moment. He could have skewered her with the spear as she ran towards him, but instead he tried to grab her. His outstretched fingers caught her, closed on her shoulder, and they both went down in the mud. Pain shot through her leg, but it was somehow far away, under the world instead of part of it.

The wagon was moving, faster now, and Derwyn was on it. She

crawled forward, half carrying the guard with her, all the strength in her back and shoulders taking him by surprise as she lifted him. She tried to call to Derwyn, but she had no breath left.

Behind her, Cu's barking changed to a frantic yelp of pain.

Behind her, Bor gurgled again as he struggled to his knees.

All around, shouting and confusion.

The guard grabbing at her, pulling her down. As he wrestled with her, he tore at her, punched her, and she gasped in pain. She twisted, trying to throw him off. A ripping sound, and the coins from Necrad spilled across the road.

Blood gushed across them. Blood on the strange silver. She'd stabbed the guard. She couldn't remember doing so, but the blade had gone in between his ribs. He pawed at it, his hands coming away wet. He tried to speak, and blood poured out of his mouth in a black river.

Olva pushed herself away from him. The wagon was well out of reach now, moving fast, the horses snorting as Lyulf whipped them to greater speed. Two other guards had followed it, but they were coming back down the road towards the bend now that their master was clear of the ambush.

She turned. There were still two guards, stabbing at Cu with sword and spears. She picked up the spear dropped by the man she'd killed and ran towards them. They fell back in alarm, one slipping in the mud, the other backing away, sword in hand, gaze darting between Olva and Cu. The dog was limping badly, his red fur matted black with mud and blood. She jabbed the spear towards one of her foes, and the charmstone erupted, a bolt of energy leaping from the tip of the spear to strike the guard. His skin sizzled as the edge of the blast caught him. Olva shrieked in alarm and nearly dropped the spear, but caught herself and clasped it tightly. She tried to call up another blast, but nothing happened – the stone was exhausted.

The guards closed in on her. Three, two behind and one ahead.

What would the Lammergeier do? said a voice in her mind, and it sounded like Derywn.

Fucking run, said another voice, and it sounded like Bor.

It was Bor. He struggled to his feet, stumbling forward, one hand still holding the cord at his throat.

But it was not a cord – it was a vine, a creeper of ivy, the green of the stalk brilliant against Bor's red-flushed skin. The plant dug into his neck, strangling him.

"Run!" he gurgled again, grabbing her hand, and then they were running, back down into the Fossewood. A mad scramble down the slope, both of them breathless and scraped by thorns. Out of the corner of her eye, she kept seeing Bor's knuckles, white with effort as he kept the cord from closing on his throat. He stumbled, and Olva dug the butt of the spear into the wet earth, using it to steady them as they climbed. She was leading them through the woods now, the mercenary following behind her, his tortured breathing shallow and strained. Behind them, shouts and the sounds of their pursuers crashing through the trees. She couldn't hear Cu at all – and all the while her heart tugged her back towards the road, towards Derwyn.

They'd taken a wrong turning. The slope was too steep here. The trees all around her, too densely packed for her to see the sky or get her bearings. The guards were out of sight, but they were close. They'd be on them in an instant. She anticipated the inevitable moment when the spear points would skewer her, thrust through her, like the tines of a pitchfork through a sack of grain. Her life would leak into the mud, and it would all be over, and it would all have been for nothing.

A thought flashed through her mind – the image of Alf coming over the brow of the hill, Alf from the songs and sagas, the Lammergeier. Bright sword in hand, leaping into the fray, defending her like he'd guarded the shed that night. He'd send the guards fleeing, save Derwyn with one bound.

But he was far away, and there was only the climb, the effort, lungs burning heart pounding hope fading. Olva knew she would die on this hillside, far from home, and no one would ever bring her body back to Ersfel to be buried next to Galwyn in the holywood.

"Over here," hissed an unfamiliar voice, "quick!"

There, in the undergrowth – a round face, small but not a child, heavy brows and bright eyes. A dwarf-maid. The dwarf woman beckoned them over, then vanished. Olva followed, probing the undergrowth with the spear and found a hole dug into the hillside, hidden by the ferns.

"In," she told Bor, and she slipped in, cramming herself into the hole, sliding down into the ground. There was no light, so she hauled herself deeper by grabbing onto stones and tree roots, clawing her way down as if she was burying herself. She dragged Bor in with her, but his shoulders were too broad to fit through the mouth of the opening, so she pulled him down as far as she could, hoping that the undergrowth would hide whatever remained exposed.

Suddenly, all was still and silent and dark. Olva hid there, in the lightless burrow, her face pressed against Bor's shin. She could hear his shallow gasps as he kept wrestling with the ivy cord, hear the shouts of the guards far overhead, as they searched. After a while, all the sounds seemed to fade away, swallowed by the darkness.

"They're gone," said the dwarf after some time. Her voice came from somewhere far below Olva, down in the darkness of the burrow. Olva pushed against Bor's limp legs, but the mercenary was stuck fast.

"I can't get out," whispered Olva.

"Oh." A few moments of silence and darkness, and then Bor's weight left Olva as he was dragged out of the tunnel from the far side. The dwarf had got around her through some other passageway. Olva helped push Bor out, until they were all back in the sunlight. Bor was unconscious but still alive; his right hand was still grabbing at the ivy noose, but the plant was no longer trying to strangle him. Olva bent down to cut it with her dagger.

"Cutting it will kill him," said the dwarf. "Is that your intent?"

Olva looked down and saw that the dagger was still smeared with the blood from the fight. So was her hand. She folded to the ground, her knees unable to support her, the dagger falling from her grasp.

"No," she whispered. "No, why would you think that?"

The dwarf shrugged, as if to say *who am I to judge?* "I'm Torun," she said. "I saw you last night, up at the grave."

"Olva. Olva Forster."

"I overheard you, too, talking by the road. He said you were kin to the Lammergeier. Is that true?"

Olva nodded. "The men on the road, they took my son. They're taking him to Necrad. Please, help me." Her voice cracked with exhaustion.

The dwarf stood. "I was at Karak's Bridge. In the name of the Nine who saved us, I will aid you, Olva Forster."

CHAPTER NINE

Twelve chairs. One for each of the nine companions, including the fallen Peir the Paladin, his seat left empty to honour his memory. One for the governor sent by the Lords of Summerswell. One for the representative of the New Provinces, the conquered territories north of the city. And one – the piteous seat, Jan once called it – one for a delegate from the dwellers in the Liberties, to speak for those who called the city home.

The chamber was nearly empty. Lord Vond sat at the head of the table, flanked by two seats that should have been filled by Gundan and Laerlyn. Both were empty, and that unsettled Alf. The world felt right only when Gundan's shield was his right flank, when Laerlyn was watching over him.

Next to Gundan's place sat an unfamiliar old woman in a cleric's robes. Lined face, a string of spirit-beads clacking in her hand. She scowled as Alf entered, her eyes following the sword at his side.

"This is Marit, of Staffa Abbey," said Vond as he sat down. "She speaks for the New Provinces."

Alf gave her a wary nod as he looked around at the nearly empty room. Obviously, the seats for Jan and Thurn were unoccupied, but there was no Lath or Blaise either. He'd skipped hundreds of council meetings, but that was because he rarely had anything to say.

The others were supposed to be in charge. At least Berys was here, sitting next to a slug-pale Vatling in the Piteous Seat. A few clerks and servants stood around the edge of the room, ready to assist with anything the atrophied council required.

Berys of the present day looked like someone the Berys of twenty years ago would have delighted in robbing. She was the wealthiest woman in Necrad, or so the tales ran. Money had stopped meaning much to Alf after they'd looted the tomb of the Chalcedony Emperor, but he just spent his share of the coin. Berys had invested hers, turned coin to breed more coin and more power. She played games he had no interest in.

Alf's regular place was next to Berys, but if he sat there it'd be three people clustered at one end of the long table and Lord Vond alone at the head. He hesitated.

"You're late, Alf," said Berys with a smile. "Sit down there, and let's get this over with quickly."

Awkwardly he took Jan's old seat opposite the Abbess, halfway along the table. Berys flashed him a hand signal – a thieves' sign she'd taught him. *Be ready.* As if she was preparing for an ambush.

"Let the record be amended to show that Sir Aelfric, called the Lammergeier, attends this council meeting, too," muttered Vond. "Now, we were discussing the demolition of the—"

Alf interrupted him. "Where is everyone?" As he spoke, he noticed a flickering sphere hovering almost imperceptibly over one chair. A magical eyeball, hidden in an invisibility shroud. Blaise might not be here, but he was keeping an eye on proceedings.

"Gundan the Dwarf remains barred from the council until he apologises to Princess Laerlyn. The princess is welcome to attend, but refuses unless Summerswell cedes authority over the harbour to the elves."

Alf shrugged. He was used to the elf and the dwarf sniping at each other – it was nothing more than harmless banter. Always had been. The only problem was when it was magnified by their positions, and people like Vond took it more seriously than it warranted.

"What's that about the harbour?" asked Alf.

"The elves want control over all the ships that sail through the Gulf of Tears," explained Berys. "Only they're dressing it up as concerns about smuggling and the like."

Vond cut across her. "The complaint from the elves has been discussed already, Lady Berys, Sir Aelfric. It was decided that Summerswell is unwilling to grant such authority over our ships, and we have communicated that to Princess Laerlyn."

"The decision was not unanimous," said the Abbess. She clucked her tongue in disapproval. "Only the guilty try to hide from the light." Even Alf could tell it was a remark aimed at Berys.

Vond rapped his fingers on the table. "We are discussing the demolition of the House of Whispers on Thistle Street."

"Thistle?" asked Alf. A few years ago, the League had renamed all the streets in Necrad, giving them more palatable and oddly floral names like Thistle Street and Rose Street. Alf could never keep them straight, and everyone used the old Witch Elf names anyway. Everyone outside the Garrison, anyway.

"The Way of Tharsil," supplied Berys.

"Right."

"It should be torn down," said the Abbess. "And a granary built in its place. There are many mouths to feed in this city, and it is prudent to be prepared for harder times."

"The House of Whispers was a place of horror and sorrow," said the Vatling. Its voice had an oddly liquid quality to it, like part of its throat was still unformed. "I agree that it be destroyed, but it is adjacent to the birthing-vat facility on Hawthorn Street." The Vatling inclined its head towards Alf. Its features resembled something a child might make from a lump of clay – or a lump of meat. "Formerly known as the Way of Haradrume. My people beg the council to consider that hard times have already befallen the Vatgrown."

"The Vatlings can't build new vats. But they can expand existing ones," said Berys. "We should give it to them."

Vond frowned. "A granary would be of more use to the city. That's two for a granary, and two for Threeday's alternate proposal. Sir Aelfric?"

A memory from twenty years ago swam up. "Wasn't the House of Whispers where they were holding Lath?" asked Alf.

Berys nodded. "It's the old secret police headquarters, remember? We tracked him back there after the ogres caught him. We had a plan and everything. Only you were supposed to distract the guards, and ended up charging in the front door instead. Gods, how did we survive that?"

Alf laughed. "Blind luck. You found that torture-golem and set it running, and it grabbed one of the inquisitors and—"

Vond rapped on the table. "Please, stick to the matter at hand."

"As you wish. I call the vote," said Beryl quickly.

"Seconded," said the Vatling.

"Sir Aelfric," said Vond, "the deciding vote is with you."

Alf glanced at Berys. He wanted to help his friend – but he didn't want to vote against Vond either. And a granary had more appeal that a slimy outcrop of the Pits.

Split the difference, he thought. *That's wisdom.* "The way I see it," he said slowly, "a new granary won't be ready before the winter anyway. Just tear the place down to begin with, and when that's done we can see what's to be done with it."

Vond made a note on the paper, then handed it to a clerk. "Next, the question of payment for the Garrison troops. We have less than a month's wages on hand and cannot requisition more funds without the approval of all three League representatives. Until the impasse is resolved, we must move monies around. Lady Berys."

Berys smiled, cat-like. "Lord Vond."

"You and the other merchants benefit from the League's

protection. I have in mind an emergency levy on all exports, to tide us over until Laerlyn and Gundan resolve their feud. Your thoughts?"

"The merchants of the city already pay more than their fair share – and, to be frank, they rely on the League troops less than anyone else. All the merchants of note have plenty of mercenaries and adventurers in their employ. They would scarcely notice if all the League guards quit – not until the bodies started piling up in the streets. But . . ." She let the word hang in the air.

"Go on," said Vond, in the tone of a man anticipating punishment.

"I'm sure some of the merchants would be amenable to bolstering the guard with their private troops. They could patrol, say, the harbour, while Garrison guards are reassigned to keeping watch on the Liberties."

In other words, thought Alf, *open season for smuggling*. Even after fifteen years of looting, Necrad was still a treasury of magical relics. All those spellbooks in the Wailing Tower, all the demons and servitors conjured by Lord Bone, the weapons and talismans like Spellbreaker, creations of the Witch Elves – a fortune in tainted sorcery.

"That would be an acceptable solution," said the Vatling. "Better to maintain the current guard strength in the Liberties. Change brings trouble."

Berys and the Vatling were obviously working together. Berys might not be as lithe as she was twenty years ago, might have traded her thief's cloak and daggers for a gown and an accounting ledger, but she was still as cunning as ever.

Alf was about to ask a question, to push back – if he was to attend this council, he might as well speak – when the door burst open. He turned around just in time to be bowled out of his seat by the ball of beard and muscle that rushed in to hug him.

"Alf! You improbable tree trunk of a man! Where've you been?"

Alf tried to speak, but the dwarf's embrace was so tight he could barely breathe.

"Lord Gundan," said Vond, "you are barred from this council."

Gundan released his affectionate death-grip on Alf. "I am not *at* your sodding council. My name's not on your precious roll, is it? I am merely passing through on my way to the pub. Come on, Alf."

Alf stood.

"Berys, you in?"

She glanced at Vond. "We are no longer quorate," he admitted.

"I'm in," said Berys.

The dive bars along the harbour changed names and ownership every few weeks, as one barkeep made his fortune and left the haunted city or bled out in some alley in the Liberties. Necrad made you rich if it didn't ruin you first.

But with a tankard in his hand and Berys and Gundan by his side, it felt like old times.

"A linnorm caught you?" Gundan hooted with laughter. The dwarf had been down south in the Dwarfholt when Alf left. "Were you napping? Or maybe when you lost your teeth you forgot that other things still had theirs?"

"It got lucky," protested Alf.

"We make our own luck," said Berys. Gundan and Alf looked like they belonged in this hole of a tavern; in her finery, Berys was a jewel dropped in the mud. A jewel that could knife you, of course, and one that knew the words to the foulest drinking songs from here to the Eaveslands.

"Well, it got me. And Berys said I should take a break."

"You looked," said Berys, "like death. It wasn't just the venom, Gundan – he was *tired*. He needed the rest."

"Aye, well." Gundan glared at the thief, a sudden flash of anger that was just as quickly hidden away again beneath a volume of sheer bluster. "You might have TOLD me, that's all! Of course Alf can run off home to shag sheep if that's what he needs! I just like to be kept informed!"

"I met Jan," said Alf, quietly. "She's . . ." He swirled his beer around in the mug. "It's some divine thing. Changed. Like she was made of light."

"Aye, well. You know *magic*." Gundan washed his mouth out with beer, as if trying to remove the foul taste of the word. "Jan's made of light, and Blaise has more eyes than he should. And . . . Feh." He spat on the ground. Berys seemed unmoved, although Alf caught a flicker of surprise in her eyes when he talked about Jan.

"She was worried about Blaise. Have either of you spoken to him of late?"

"Blaise is fine," said Gundan, "in that he's been *completely bloody mad* since we met him. I can't believe Jan changed, 'cos once she had mud on her boots like the rest of us. Blaise, though . . . was there ever a time when he wasn't bleating about cosmic forces and arcane secrets? No, he's still himself, 'neath all the floating eyes and hands and pretensions. Lath, though . . . "

"What about Lath?" Of all the members of the old adventuring company, Alf considered himself closest to Gundan and Lath, now that Peir was gone.

Gundan and Berys looked at each other, the same frown mirrored on both faces. It was Berys who spoke first. "He's changed, Alf," she said quietly. "He was always fey, but in the last few years, it's got worse. His magic's gone sour, I'd say. Instead of just taking the shapes of animals, he started turning into things from the Pit." She picked up a coin and danced it across her knuckles, then made it vanish. "You know what the clerics say about the earthpower. It corrupts."

Gundan nodded. "Aye. If we met him now when we were young, we'd have thought him a monster, and chopped him without thinking twice." He glanced at Alf. "It got worse after you left, though, much worse. You kept him level, I guess."

"There were enough who thought him a monster even back then," said Berys quickly, before Alf could speak. "He sometimes lost control over his magic when he was with us, too."

Alf's bond with the skin-changer had always been mostly

unspoken, a friendship built on mutual competence. He'd looked on the younger man like one of his brothers, both engaged in the same family trade. They'd both embraced the work of the endless slaughter-crawl through the Pits. Day after day, year after year, hacking their way through the spawn of Necrad. By then, between Lath's magic and Alf's fighting skills – and Spellbreaker – there was little below that could threaten them. The work had become pleasant in a bitter, dull way; every night Alf had staggered home, bone-tired, drenched in slime and gore, but with the warm knowledge that he'd accomplished something, that he'd held back disaster for another day. He'd always assumed Lath had felt the same.

"Where is he now?" asked Alf.

Gundan shrugged. "Down below? Off in the woods? Flapping around in the shape of a crow? Who knows? How do you pin down a *sane* skin-changer, let alone a mad one?" He shook his head.

"I tried to keep track of him," said Berys, "quietly. He spent a while snuffling about the Charnel. He was a regular visitor at the Intercessal Shrine at Tar Edalas. He went north a few times – maybe to see Thurn." She toyed with her coin. It had been polished by so many hands it had a mirror-sheen. She turned it over and over in her hands, and Alf realised that she was using it to survey the room behind her. "The men I had keeping an eye on him ... well, only one of them came back, and he came a-shambling out of the Charnel. There are a lot of ways to die in Necrad, and I doubt Lath had anything to do with their deaths, but ... " The coin vanished.

"We've kept it to ourselves, of course," said Gundan. "Summerswell don't know – leastways, I haven't told 'em. Lath is our problem, yeh?"

Alf nodded. That was it, exactly – the bonds forged in the hardship of the quest ran deeper than kinship.

"The Nine stand together," echoed Berys, "so say all the songs."

"And I've been covering the Pits, as much as I can," said Gundan. "Thank Az you're back. Between the Pits, and the mess with Laerlyn and the elves, I've been tearing my beard out the last year." Gundan kicked Alf under the table. "Never leave again, dolt. We need you here. Maybe you can knock some sense into Lath when he shows up again."

"There's something else. Something worse." Alf paused at the precipice. Speaking would make it real – and the sword had counselled him to stay quiet. But Berys and Gundan were of the Nine; they needed to know. "Bone's grave. It's open."

Berys raised an eyebrow, which for her was a shriek of alarm.

Gundan sat back. "Open?! Open as in someone dug it up, or open as it burst open from the inside, back to murder us all?"

"Someone opened it, I think."

"One of *us*, you mean," said Berys, quietly. "I was offered a king's ransom for the location of that grave. A shard of Bone – or a relic of the paladin – would sell for a fortune. I refused, of course. Some things are above money."

Gundan counted off possibilities on his thick fingers. "Alf was off south. Jan and Thurn haven't been around in years. Blaise was the one who insisted we put that bloody warding spell on the tomb in the first place. Berys says she didn't, and our Berys never lies."

Berys took a sip of beer.

"I know I've done stupid stuff while blind drunk a few times, but never grave-robbing."

"Yes, you have," said Alf. "That time up in the Cleft of Ard?" After years of silence, it was good to be around friends he could share tales and memories with.

Gundan glared at him. "All right. I have never grave-robbed the fucking dark lord while drunk," he snapped. "So that leaves two. I don't like to say good things about the elf, so I won't – but she'd never risk breaking a fingernail doing manual labour like opening the tomb. So . . ."

"Lath," said Berys.

Alf couldn't believe it of the Changeling – but neither could he believe it of the rest of the Nine. There had to be a good reason. "Why would he open the tomb?"

"Because he's gone mad?" suggested Berys.

"What set him off?" asked Alf. "Was it right after I left, or was there something later?"

"We're not sure—" began Berys, but Gundan interrupted her.

"Someone burned down his grove," said the dwarf. "The trees went up like dry kindling, and Lath was in the middle of it. He was badly burned, but you know how quick he heals. After that, he went underground. I've not seen him in more than a year."

"I don't know who set the fire," said Berys. "Yet. We've all made enemies, aye? Vond thinks it was Witch Elves still loyal to Lord Bone. I'm still investigating." She drew out the word, hopscotching her way across the syllables. In-ves-tig-a-ting. Alf felt a sudden pang of doubt, and wondered what would have happened if Jan's dream-summons had reached Berys instead of him. She was much more suited than him to solve such a riddle.

"And they tried to kill Berys," added Gundan. "An archer nearly put an arrow through her heart last year. Or so it's whispered in the Liberties. Our Berys does like her secrets, of course, so who knows if it's true?"

Berys said nothing; she just raised her mug and took another swig, like they were playing a drinking game again.

Alf risked a thrust. "A Witch Elf tried to kill me last night. She was waiting in my bedroom."

Gundan slammed his mug down on the table. "We used to be the sort of people who mentioned a bloody assassin *earlier* in the conversation."

Alf shrugged. "Like Berys said. I can't remember a time when people weren't trying to kill me. But it could be the same people who tried to kill you."

"And Lath," said Gundan. "And maybe they opened the grave. A *conspiracy*. What happened, Alf?"

"Not much to tell of the fight. She came at me with this." He took the elf-blade from his belt and put it on the table.

Berys sat forward, hunched over the weapon as she examined it. "A fine blade," she admitted. "Are you sure it was meant for you?"

"What, she just happened to be squatting in Alf's house, inside the Garrison? With a weapon like that in hand?" scoffed Gundan. "That's the work of a master-smith, or I'm no dwarf. Korthalion or one of his students. I've seen few weapons like that – but I have seen 'em before. Remember those assassins that came after us in the war? They had blades akin to this. And *they* knew where we were, too, remember? And we could never figure out for months how they found us, for Blaise had warded us against scrying-spells?"

"But we worked it out in the end," said Berys. "The Oracle's agents."

"Exactly," said Gundan, tapping his finger on the elven dagger. "And the Oracle's the last of Bone's court, the only one we haven't chopped." He grinned. "Let's get the job done, aye?"

"Jan warned of a danger," said Alf. He suddenly felt energised, like he'd struggled up a steep mountainside and was now hastening downhill. The pieces were falling into place – the Oracle wanted revenge on the adventurers who'd slain her dark lord and conquered their city. That was what Jan's warning was about. Maybe Blaise's magical ward on Lord Bone's grave wasn't as infallible as the wizard promised. Maybe the Witch Elves were the ones who broke into the grave and stole the remains, and that's what Jan was talking about when she worried about Blaise. It all made sense. He could trust his old companions.

And now he had Gundan and Berys back by his side. And Blaise would come when he called. He'd talk to Lath, knock some sense into him as Gundan said. Sort out whatever nonsense had divided Gundan and Laerlyn. All the company together once more. Even Thurn would come back, in the nick of time, as they fought one last battle against the followers of Bone.

"I've got a dreadworm watching the elf," Alf said. "I know where she is. We go there, find out what's going on."

"Right!" shouted Gundan. The dwarf sprang up from his barstool. "Let's get the bastards!"

"Berys?" asked Alf. The thief hadn't moved.

"No."

"What?"

"You can't just hare off into the Liberties. You'll start a riot. We need to do this delicately. I've got people I trust, Aelfric, informants who know the streets. Tell me where she is, call off the dreadworm, and—"

"To the hells with that," roared Gundan. "Come on, Alf, let's go find this assassin of yours."

Alf lingered a moment. "Berys, please. We need a thief."

"You need patience, Alf," she said. "Don't do this."

But he did.

CHAPTER TEN

The camp of the dwarf was a shallow cave in the hillside, concealed by a screen of bracken and fallen branches. In the bushes
were strung mirrors and silver bowls, talismans and pieces of twisted
wire. One of the strings caught on Bor's leg as they dragged him
into the cave.

Olva and Torun laid Bor down on the dwarf's bed of dry rushes
and blankets, his long legs sprawling over the edge. The dwarf knelt
down and examined Bor's neck.

"It's Elvish magic," Torun said, her fingers probing at the ivy.
Now that she could examine it clearly, Olva's stomach twisted as she
saw the tiny white tendrils of the ivy were rooted in Bor's skin, the
stem of the plant tracking the course of veins and arteries within his
body. The plant was growing, too, and it had sprouted thorns. Some
of them had pushed out of Bor's skin from *beneath*, for the plant was
spreading under his skin. His lips were mottled purple and blue,
and his breathing laboured.

"Can you get it off him?"

"It's a punishment set by the Wood Elves. If he ever sets foot in a
place that's forbidden to him, it will choke the life from him. It will
do the same if I try to cut it." The dwarf demonstrated by digging a
thick fingernail into the stem, leaving a half-moon scar on the green

flesh of the plant. The ivy shuddered in response, and grew tighter. Bor gasped and choked in his sleep, and half stirred.

"Stop!" cried Olva.

"Now, if he was in a forbidden region, it wouldn't stop constricting, would it? Could the ban specify a type of place, like a road? I wonder how specific the geas might be," mused the dwarf, her finger tapping idly against the plant. "But, oh! The man on the cart had a ring! A token of command! That would be it!" Her face lit up with a wide grin, then she became contrite. "Forgive me. I am told I am strange."

"The man on the cart – he's taken my son. Please, you said you'd help us."

"Help? Oh, yes!" said the dwarf. She vanished into the back of the cave, and returned with two bowls, one full of apples, the other with water. "For your hands," said the dwarf.

Olva's stomach twisted at the sight of her bloody hands, and she began to shiver violently again. She tried to form words, but all that came out of her mouth was a keening wail.

The dwarf woman shifted awkwardly from one foot to another. "Please, be quiet. Enemies may still be near. But look – the ivy does not choke him any more. He can breathe. Here, here." She draped a blanket around Olva's shoulders, standing on tiptoes to reach. "Sit. Rest. I will see what can be done for him. And when you're ready, there'll be other ways I can help, never fear."

Olva sat there by Bor. She was distantly aware that time was passing, that the world was turning and day was fading outside the bower, but it seemed to her like a river flowing just out of earshot, a ceaseless and unchanging torrent that would not be affected one way or the other by anything she did. She wiped the blood from her hands, the water in the bowl turning gory, and kept rubbing them with a cloth even when they were clean.

Lyulf Martens was out of their reach. By now, he'd be in Ellsport, and from there he could sail north to Necrad, or one of the smugglers' ports Bor had talked about, or ... anywhere. Olva had only the haziest idea of the wider world, but her heart told her that Derwyn was far away, and moving quickly. Did he even know she'd come after him? Olva couldn't be sure that her son had seen her by the road.

The Lammergeier's kin, Martens had said, and she remembered how Derwyn had grown taller in that moment, the beginnings of a proud smile at the corners of his mouth – in the instant before Martens' guards struck him down. Erlking's blood: was all this her fault? If Bor hadn't said a word, then maybe Derwyn could have kept his relationship to Alf – to Sir Aelfric Lammergeier, Champion of the Nine – a secret. He could have gone to Necrad and found Alf – or some other destiny. People left for the New Provinces in the north every day, or so she'd heard. If it had been one of Derwyn's friends who'd gone instead, Harlow or Kivan, she would have thought nothing of it. She might even have applauded the boy's ambition – her marriage to Galwyn had given her a more prosperous life in Ersfel than she had any right to expect given her low birth, but not everyone could be so lucky. But Derwyn was all the family she had left, all that she loved. She'd told herself that one day she would have to let him go, but never believed it in her heart.

Was there something she should have said? Some sign she'd missed? Had she ruined everything for her son? The thought was a dull ache in her stomach.

Cu came limping through the trees in the early afternoon, his muzzle caked in mud from foraging. A spear had cut a shallow gash in his side. "It's all gone wrong," she whispered to the dog, as she buried her face in his fur. The big dog wriggled onto her lap like a puppy, as if trying to comfort her – and then the sound of loud crunching by her ear told her he'd found the apples.

Bor stirred and groaned, gesturing towards the water bowl. Olva poured out the bloody water – Cu lapped at it as it drained away, an unexpected treat – and fetched a fresh bowl from a nearby stream. She let the mercenary sip a little.

"Martens ..." he whispered, his voice like a knife scraping across stone.

"He's gone," said Olva, "with Derwyn."

The mercenary slumped back down, unconscious, but some colour had returned to his face. Olva touched the ivy collar, and it no longer constricted his breathing. There were ugly red welts on his skin where he'd forced his fingers under the plant, and she could see the ivy taking root there again. It was so warm to the touch that she suspected it must be feeding on his blood.

She sat there for a long time, stroking the dog's fur, the shock and fear from the ambush on the road now hardening in her heart, sinking deep into her, a numb scab forming over the feelings. She sat there and stared at nothing in particular until she felt nothing at all.

After a few hours, Torun returned, flushed with exertion. She sat down opposite Olva.

"That is one job done," said the dwarf. "They left the body on the roadside, and that's not right. I found these, too." Torun laid a small handful of the coins from Necrad on a stone. "That's all that was left, I fear."

"He should be buried in a holywood," said Olva. Giving the boy a proper burial seemed the least she could do.

"Oh, I already threw the body into the bog. I weighted it down with stones so it'll sink." The dwarf bent to examine Bor's neck and muttered what sounded like magical words to Olva. "The ivy cord's receding. I think he'll live."

"Can you cast a spell to help him?"

"No. I shall help in other ways." From a recess in the cave she brought a small metal flask. "This is healing cordial from Necrad. It's old, I fear, and has lost much of its potency. I didn't give it earlier because I wasn't sure if he'd live, and I didn't want to waste this cordial on a dead man." She poured the cordial, a few drops at a time, onto Bor's lips.

"I can't pay," began Olva. She gestured at the few coins that remained. "I've promised these to Bor. But I do have this." She picked up the spear and untied the charmstone from it.

The dwarf examined the stone. "It's a minor thunder-charm. Potent, but not uncommon." She handed it back to Olva. "You keep it. I am already in your debt – or your brother's. All dwarves owe the Nine a debt that shall not be repaid for an age of the world. I saw them fighting in our defence."

"You were there in the Dwarfholt?" The sagas spoke of the home of the dwarves, a mountain fortress off to the north-west, in the mountain range between Summerswell and the Clawlands that led to Necrad. Lord Bone's attacks on the Mulladales were a diversion, to draw Summerswell's knights away to the east. It was on the Dwarfholt that the hardest blows had fallen, and the dwarves had endured unimaginable horrors.

Torun nodded. "I watched your brother bring down the Marrow Chieftain. It was extraordinary. The brute was gigantic, as tall as an oak tree. His hide was like iron – arrows and stones couldn't hurt him. He wielded this huge hammer, and he smashed it against the gates. Once, twice, thrice, and it was like the world was breaking all around us. But Sir Aelfric stood there, unmoving, right in the monster's path as it came through the gate. 'Stone broke and steel bent, but his courage did not waver.'"

And once, he broke Garn's arm in a quarrel over a blanket, thought Olva. Alf was stubborn, certainly, but the idea of Alf as a hero out of legend didn't sit well in her mind. "So what are you doing here, so far from home?" she asked.

"Studying."

"In this cave?"

"In this wood." A flush of colour crept across Torun's round cheeks. "I wanted to learn magic. There have never been wizards among the dwarves, but I saw Blaise too that day. He commanded the thunderstorm with a word! He spoke, and the fires answered. It was like he was calling to me. After that, all else seemed hollow. I wanted to speak, and have the world hear me and obey, so I went to Summerswell and the great college, where they work magic elf-fashion, where they weave starlight into spells and watch the skies for portents – but they refused me. They said it was only for the princes."

"You need to be related by blood to one of the great families," said Olva, absently. "Or be sponsored by one of them." Galwyn had a great-aunt who'd been sent to the College Arcane in Summerswell by Lord Haral. Before they were married, his family had insisted that they make a pilgrimage to the ancient woman to get her blessing. Olva could still remember the traditional Elvish greeting they'd made her learn, for the old wizard insisted on conversing only in the high tongue. She'd sat in that stuffy room and waited while the old woman cast horoscopes and muttered about Olva's low birth. Star magic was only for the high-born.

"Oh, yes," said the dwarf. "I begged them. I sat on the doorstep of the College for a month, hoping they'd relent. I visited every lord I could, begging for their sponsorship. They all thought me mad." Torun clucked her tongue. "I'd heard tales of hedge-schools out in the Westermarch, and I searched for them. I found nothing. I went over the sea to Phennic where the stars are strange, but they laughed at me there, too."

Apparently the dwarf talked like an avalanche once you got her going.

"I thought about travelling on south, all the way to the Everwood, but then I thought of the other members of the Nine. Great Blaise may have studied at Summerswell, but he was not the only spell-caster among the Nine, was he? No, Lath could work magic, too, a wild form of magic, not the sort they teach in Summerswell. So I went searching for that. I thought to myself, that's the sort of magic for a dwarf, isn't it? Not star magic, but earth magic, deep magic you've got to dig for, and I heard stories that once there was a wizard who lived in the Fossewood long ago, and I found this cave and the pillar of stone and I've been trying and . . . " The dwarf took a gasping breath. "And I haven't talked to anyone in *months*."

"Bor showed me the wizard's grave," said Olva, "and for a moment, it was like we were flying. I felt you, I think."

"Oh. The magic found you?" Torun's face fell, but only for a moment. She stood up and busied herself in the back of the cave, stuffing objects into a satchel. "Come, come. They'll be at Ellsport long before we get there, and there'll be no catching them on land. But there are dwarves in Ellsport who might help us catch them at sea. I'll come with you. I'll just bring a few things. We'll leave in the morning."

Olva offered to help, but the dwarf shooed her away. "No, no. I need to decide what I'm taking. Rest. Rest." Defeated, Olva returned to the front of the little cave. Outside, it was raining heavily again. She reached out a hand and felt the droplets on her skin, and wondered if the same rain was falling on Derwyn. For an instant, she felt again as though she could rise out of her body and send her spirit soaring again, the whole wood lifting her, but she snatched her hand back and the connection vanished. Behind her, Cu raised his head, then curled back up at the foot of the bed.

The cave was too small to leave Olva many options. She lay down next to Bor herself, and listened to the rain on the leaves until she slept.

Olva woke when a hand clamped across her mouth. She struggled and bit, instinctively grabbing for the knife she always kept by her bed, *always*, but this wasn't her bed, this wasn't her home.

Bor — it was Bor holding her. He grabbed her wrist and pinned her down. "Quiet," he hissed in her ear. He lifted his hand away and glared at the half-moon of toothmarks she'd left in his thumb, bright against the grimy skin. "The dwarf's asleep. We're getting out of here." He climbed off her and stood up, moving cat-quiet towards their neatly stowed packs. Torun's sleeping form was a dark shape in the back of the cave.

"What do you mean?"

"I'll get you back to your bloody village, I swear. But this ends now. Martens—" he swallowed, and winced in pain, "I don't dare cross him again. No, no, I'll bring you home, and then you'll see the back of me, and you can keep the Lammergeier's money. By the tree, if you'd only taken it when I told you to, damn you." He picked up their bags and slung them onto his back. "Come on."

"I'm going after Derwyn," whispered Olva. "Torun says we can catch them at sea."

"And you believe some crazy hermit? I've never heard of a dwarf wizard, not in all my days."

"She helped us!"

"Like I said, crazy. It's stupid to trust anyone you meet on the Road. And she was spying on us, too. She knew about the Lammergeier. I don't like it." He tugged at his neck. "I should take the dwarf's bag, too. Dwarves are always bloody rich. Now come on."

"No." Olva crossed her arms. "You gave me your word. I hired you, and I still have a few coins left."

"It doesn't matter. Hear her bleating about magic? Idiot. Idiot. Going on would be madness. Martens has *magic*. Proper magic, as good as anything out of Necrad. What can a man do against sorcery? Nothing. Not a fucking thing. Doesn't matter what you do."

"My brother killed Lord Bone."

"And he had a magic sword."

"Then we'll find a way to stop Martens' magic. I'll find a way. I'm not turning back."

Bor's face contorted as if the ivy cord had closed again. "Damn you. All right, Ellsport, and not a step further."

"That's fine. You won't need to walk anywhere when we're on a ship."

The ruts left by Martens' wagon were still visible in the mud the next morning, two parallel pools reflecting the reddish dawn light. Torun and Bor walked on ahead, the dwarf trotting along to keep up with Bor's long strides. Cu seemed to have taken a liking to Torun, and bounced along beside her. Olva lingered a moment, looking back up at the wooded hillside that rose up behind her. The stone atop the Fossewood was lost in the gloom, but some lingering magic of the place told her where to look.

Then her gaze fell upon the sucking mud in the ditch and she thought of the boy she'd killed. She regretted what she had done, but the thought came to her that it was part of the course of the boy's life. Her knife was just one small tributary to the river of decisions that brought the man onto the Road and into the service of Lyulf Martens, to die here in the Fossewood, far away from home and kin. She wondered if that was the price, if you could not have wonder and magic without peril and bloodshed. In the sagas, the heroes inhabited a realm of wonders, dashing from wizard's tower to lordly hall or enchanted isle. They walked among wonders, while she trudged down a muddy road.

Alf had stepped out of ordinary life and into the realm of magic and heroes. Now, for the first time, she envied him a little. She reached into her pocket and found her little knife, and tied the thunder-stone to its hilt with string.

As they walked, Torun told the tale of the wizard of the Fossewood. Her voice grew in confidence as she related the story.

Long ago, the first mortals dwelt in the wildwoods of the north, and they were beset by many foes, by dragons and other terrible beasts. They huddled together, hiding in the shadows of the trees, and never saw the sky. Now, among the tribe of mortals there was an old woman, the eldest of the tribe. She dug herself a grave with her bare hands, and crawled into the earth. Down she dug, deeper and deeper, until she came to a place far from the lands of the living. It was a grey land, where the starlight never shone, but there was another magic, unknown even to the elves. And the old woman carried this earthpower out of the grave, and gave it to her people.

This new magic was very powerful, for it was born of death and the dying world. But the old woman warned her people that the earthpower was bound to the wheel of the seasons and the cycles of all mortal things. There would be times when the magic would be strong, and times when it would be weak. And the people followed the teachings of the old woman, and won many victories over their enemies, and built many great kingdoms in the north.

("'S only bloody Wilder who live in the north," muttered Bor.

"Maybe today that's true," replied Torun, taken aback by the interruption. "But there are old stones in the northland that tell stories dwarves can read.")

Now, among those who had learned magic from the old woman was a man named Connac, and he crossed the Middle Sea and with this magic he made himself ruler of these lands along the shore. He raised a hall on a hill overlooking the forest, and many men came to serve him, and acclaimed him Changeling and king alike.

In those days, the elves travelled widely outside the Everwood, and Connac's followers challenged them, saying "This is our land now – if you cross this border, we will kill even the undying." And the elves replied, "Your king is a child playing with a serpent, and you are fools to follow him."

On hearing this disrespect, Connac flew into a rage, and took on the form of a manticore, and prowled the borders of his domain, preying on the elves who trespassed in the land he claimed.

That winter, the Erlking called upon one of the knights of his court, the Knight of Holly, and sent him forth to slay the Beast

Connac. But Connac was victorious. He threw off the skin of the manticore, and returned to his hall to feast with his followers.

In spring, the Erlking sent forth a second elf-knight, the Knight of Hawthorn, and this knight too was defeated by Connac's wild earthpower, but not without cost. Connac had drunk too deeply of the earthpower, and went mad. This time, Connac returned to the hall still in the form of a manticore, and in his fury he attacked his own followers, slaying many of them and driving the rest from his hall. The earthpower was in him, and it brings both strength and sorrow.

The survivors of the massacre in the hall crept south, across the border, and appealed to the Erlking for aid. The Erlking in his wisdom sat beneath his tree and thought deeply, and spoke with the shades of Holly and Hawthorn. And at midsummer, he sent forth a third knight, the Knight of Roses. The Knight of Roses came to Connac's Wood, and climbed the hill to the hall. He found the hall in ruins, and in the middle of this devastation was the Beast Connac, still in the shape of a manticore. The beast smelled the scent of Roses, and rose to fight this third foe.

Now, heeding the counsel of the Erlking, the Knight of Roses did not attack immediately, but instead led Connac on a wild chase through the wood. Connac took many forms, from manticore to falcon, falcon to wolf, wolf to bear, and bear to man, for he could not catch the fast-footed elf. In his fury, Connac called again on the earthpower, and found the magic had gone deep underground, like a river running dry, and he could only draw on a little of its power. Wisely had the Erlking foreseen the right day to send this knight.

Connac dug deep, seeking the earthpower. Like the old woman, he dug into the earth, but he dug only his grave. Bright the silver blade of the Knight of Roses, and quick, too. With one strike, he slew the mad king. And as Connac's spirit was bound to the earth, his body turned to stone when he died, and there he remains to this day. And holly and hawthorn grow over his grave.

("Blessed be the Erlking," said Olva, and she smiled as broadly as she could. "Thank you for the tale, Torun."

The dwarf beamed at the praise. Olva kept the smile fixed on her face, and shoved her fear away deep down inside her. The earthpower that the tale warned about was the same power she'd touched in the Fossewood – unclean and hazardous. She quickened her pace. Every step took her further away from the wood and closer to Derwyn.)

Later that day, they fell in with a company of settlers on their way north on the Road to the New Provinces. Bor hung back, glowering, his hand resting on his sword-hilt. Torun and Olva were glad to share their fire that night. They traded stories for their supper. Torun's accounts of her travels were scattered and incoherent, especially when she raced off on a tangent about some arcane detail, but she told them with such enthusiasm they were entertaining anyway – and she'd gone further than anyone else in the company. Olva listened to the settlers talk of their hopes for the New Provinces; their stories were of mountains of gold, virgin land and fortunes to be made.

One of the settlers knew Lyulf Martens by reputation, and had seen him go by in great haste the day before. The trader was curious and asked what business Olva had with Martens, but a glare from Bor convinced him to move the conversation on to other matters.

Olva's dreams that night were of the work she'd left behind in Ersfel. At one point, she dreamed that Thomad had left the door of the cowshed unlocked, and she woke with a curse on her lips. She lay there a minute, a tree root poking into the small of her back, until the memory of where she was came seeping back. A change in the wind brought the smell of salt, and the thought that Derwyn might already be at sea was sharper than her knife.

CHAPTER ELEVEN

"Treacherous sow," grumbled Gundan as the pair hurried through the darkening streets of the Garrison. "You know why Berys doesn't want to get involved, right?"

"Why?"

"She's up to her neck in smuggling rackets. Doesn't want us smashing up her clever arrangements. She's corrupt as sin, Alf."

"In the council, she seemed allied with some Vatling."

Gundan nodded. "Threeday." Spawned full-grown from vats of chemicals, the Vatlings often took their name from the time they were decanted. "She's probably running some scam on the poor fool. You know Berys. In fact ..." Gundan glanced over his shoulder, peered at the shadowed alleyways, then whispered: "Lord Urien, the governor before Vond? The one who went back to Summerswell on account of a sick belly? Aye? I've heard tell that Berys sent him a very special bottle of wine one Yule. Urien was wise to her tricks in council, but young Vond ... oh, it's pitting a lamb against a lioness."

Alf didn't respond. The thief was always duplicitous, but there was no malice in her. Gundan's anger towards her — and, now that he thought of it, towards Laerlyn — seemed excessive, but the dwarf's temper was well known. Quick to fight, quick to laugh, that was Gundan.

Quick to act, too.

"Where's this elf of yours?" asked Gundan.

"She is still at the House of the Horned Serpent," said Spellbreaker, and the dwarf jumped at the unexpected voice.

"Ach, Alf, you're not carrying that *thing* around with you? 'Tis an abomination."

Alf shook his head. "This way, I know where it is. I can keep an eye on it. Keep it safe."

"I know where the Marrow Chief's helmet is," muttered Gundan, referring to the evil artefact that had been entrusted to him. "It's in a big steel box, inside a bigger steel box, behind a load of traps, under a bloody mountain. I don't cart the damn thing around with me."

"A weapon deserves to be used," said the sword.

"Shut up," said Alf. "It is useful," he said to Gundan.

"Aye, well, I'm sticking with Chopper. 'Tis the axe my father gave me, and it's the only weapon I've ever needed." Gundan hefted his own weapon. The double-headed axe crawled with blazing runes and seethed with battle magic. The jewel-studded haft was forged of some unearthly metal they'd found in the Pits, and the handle wrapped in dragonhide.

"You replaced the blade a few times."

"Well, yes."

"And the haft."

"I had to. To fit the new blade. Still the same axe." Gundan slapped Alf on the back and cackled. "Come on, it's just like old times."

The dwarf led him through the maze of alleyways and changed streets that made up the Garrison. Up ahead was one of the heavily guarded exits from the district. This gate was watched over by a squad of dwarven warriors, faces hidden behind heavy visors. They carried crossbows, and Alf noted that they all had elf-bane bolts loaded. Elves – Wood and Witch alike – could not abide the touch of a particular alchemical alloy of iron and a dark metal found only in the Clawlands. Without that discovery by the dwarven master-smiths, they'd never have defeated Lord Bone's retinue of bodyguards, nor won the war.

"We're heading out," said Gundan. The dwarves saluted. "Keep us off the ledger, all right?"

The captain bowed. "As you say, sir."

"Bloody handy," muttered Gundan, "being in charge. You should have pressed for it – Summerswell would've made you general and regent of the city, if you'd demanded it in the day. You're the man who killed Lord Bone. They'd couldn't have argued with you."

"Peir killed him."

Gundan glanced at Alf from beneath his wild eyebrows. "Not how I recall it. Anyway, you're the *man* who did it, and I'm the dwarf. We could have been kings! And by heavens, I'd prefer to deal with you, not bloody Vond. It's like arguing with a baby."

"I didn't want it," said Alf.

"Right, right. Off into the Pit with Lath, that's what you wanted. No talking, just killing. I remember. Gah, you probably had the right idea. I've done enough yammering in that sodding council chamber over the years that I'm certainly willing to kill the lot of them. This'll be good for me. I can pretend your elf wench is—" Gundan stopped himself, then finished awkwardly. "Young Vond, eh?" Alf could tell that wasn't the name the dwarf first had in mind.

They passed through the Garrison gate. Beyond the swirling clouds, the sun was setting – the days were short, this time of year. The wraiths lurking by the threshold surged towards them, then withdrew, sensing their power. Or the demon sword.

The guards closed the gate behind them. Stepping over that threshold was like stepping back twenty years. Most of the damage in the Garrison had been repaired over the years, but the Liberties were almost as ruined as the Sanction. It still bore the scars of the last siege. The warrior and the dwarf moved as quietly as they could through the streets, although Gundan was soon huffing and puffing as he struggled to keep up with Alf.

"So," asked Alf, "what is the story with you and Laerlyn? What's the dispute?"

"Eh. Bloody elves," Gundan stopped and caught his breath, "the Wood Elves, right, the saintly Wood Elves have decided that the Witch Elves aren't *evil*, just wayward. They want to forgive their cousins for fucking off to drink blood and . . . " – he waved his hand at the Sanction and all its ghastly horrors – "all this, back in the day. Immortals are so bloody *reasonable*, you know? Everything that happened a thousand bloody years ago might as well have happened last week as far as they're concerned. All equally fresh, or all equally forgotten and forgiven. Makes me tear my beard out. Laerlyn wasn't too bad when we were young, I'll admit, but talking to her now is like talking to a statue. They don't listen to the likes of us." The dwarf shook his head. "Anyway, the point of the matter, the point, the point is . . . " He poked Alf with a stubby finger. "If the Wood Elves are part of Elfdom, then by their reckoning so's Necrad, for all the Witch Elves live here."

"Vond talked about a blockade."

"Aye, that's part of it. When the rest of the League told the Erlking that he couldn't just *have* Necrad handed to him on a plate, the Wood Elves got in a huff and threatened to close the Gulf of Tears. They can sing up a storm with their magic. Oh, and who's the one really pushing for the blockade? Who do you think's behind all this?"

"Tell me."

"Remember Laerlyn's prick of a brother? Prince Maedos? The absolute bloody *bastard* who tried to argue that the best thing to do was fucking nothing? *Oh, prithee, mayhaps we let the hosts of Necrad conquer the Dwarfholt, and slaughter Summerswell, and when they're exhausted from all the slaughtering and conquering, then we ethereal elves will deign to get involved.* That bastard?"

"I remember."

"The one you kicked out of a window – and I wish you bloody hadn't, now, because we should have taken his head!"

"I said I remember." Alf had never intended to get into such a fight with the Prince of Dawn, but he'd lost his temper and gone for his sword. His old blade, Sunrazor. If he'd wielded Spellbreaker in that fight, Prince Maedos would have suffered more than a bad fall.

Gundan swung Chopper in an angry arc, and the axe blade flashed in the green glow of the necromiasma. "And Laerlyn's back with him! After all that, suddenly they're the best of bloody friends! Sap's thicker than blood, I guess, because after all he did to us, Alf, she's forgiven him. I still can't credit it! Now he's threatening to block the seas, which your lot in Summerswell won't tolerate. The bastard was too broken to fight in the last war, I guess, so he'd doing all he can to provoke another one. Elves! Idiots!" The dwarf glanced up into the darkening sky, watching the circling dreadworms, trying to guess which one was under Spellbreaker's control. "We can bring supplies up through the Clawlands and over the Charnel to Necrad if we have to, but that'll be slow and messy. Very messy, if the elves force the issue." He laughed abruptly. "I mean, I've got some cousins who'll be glad to have all the trade coming through the Dwarfholt, so to hell with the elves. I've better things to do than argue with a pretentious shrubbery."

"What does Laerlyn think?" asked Alf.

Gundan spat. "That's just it. I went to her, Alf, tried to sort out the dispute in person over a drink, aye? Like we used to. But she's a fucking proper princess, these days. Says the Garrison's to blame for all the woes, that we're prolonging the troubles and not trying to make nice with the Witch Elves. All platitudes of light and niceness, but what they really want is Necrad. She wouldn't talk to me." He glanced at Alf. "None of this is new, you know. This has been boiling away for years."

"I was busy in the Pits." He felt unsettled by the dispute. The whole point of the companions taking over Necrad, back after they'd slain the dark lord, was that they'd take responsibility for the city. They'd promised Peir as he died that they'd make it all right. Back then, it all seemed so easy. They'd slain the dark lord; how could they fall down managing the happily ever after?

He wished Peir was still alive. The paladin was the bravest of them, the wisest. When the quest seemed hopeless or the path lost, it was Peir who brought them through. Alf missed Peir's voice urging him onwards, reminding him of his best self.

A different voice spoke. Spellbreaker whispered, "There is movement at the House of the Horned Serpent. You should hurry, before your quarry escapes."

"Come on," said Gundan, "run, you big oaf!"

Twenty years ago, the elf-lords of Necrad each ruled from a great mansion. Huge four-sided fortresses, with an open square in the middle for rituals. Alf remembered hiding on a rooftop, watching dozens of writhing pillars of energy leaping from the Houses to the sky, strange stars blazing through the necromiasma.

Now, the elf-lords were gone, the ceremonies ended, but Alf was back kneeling on the bloody rooftop, and his knees were twenty years older, too. The miasma was a sullen, subdued glow, leavened only by the deeper darkness of circling worms. From outside, the House of the Horned Serpent looked deserted.

"The worm saw someone enter four minutes ago," said Spellbreaker, "and after that, elves started mustering in the courtyard. The alarm has been raised."

"They know we're coming," said Gundan. "Right. Front door?"

"You go in the front, I'll go in from above. Tell the worm to keep circling, and signal if the target leaves," said Alf.

"The worm," said Spellbreaker, "is tired and hungry. It wants to feed."

Alf hesitated. The creature's hunger came from the strain of obeying Spellbreaker's psychic commands. His instinct was to call the dreadworm down, kill it and replace it with a fresh one from the clouds above. Lord Bone's magic had spawned thousands of the mindless worms – Alf could summon and murder the beasts for years and not make an appreciable dent in their numbers.

But a fresh worm wouldn't have the target's scent. It wouldn't be able to follow the assassin if she took to the streets again.

"No. Call it down so it can bring me across, then have it circle. Keep on the elf's trail."

"As you command," said the sword. "But I do not know how long it will remain tractable."

The dreadworm swooped low across the rooftop, the sickening wet noise of its wings like flesh tearing as it descended. Alf caught it by the tail and let it carry him across the chasm of the street below, soaring across to land on the rune-scored roof of the House. He let go and fell the last few feet, grabbing onto an ornamental brass serpent to steady himself as he landed. The serpent hissed an alarm, eyes glowing red somewhere beneath twenty years of soot and verdure, but Alf was already moving, running forward over the parapet to jump down to the inner balcony overlooking the courtyard. His eyes scanned the scene below, looking for the Witch Elf assassin who'd attacked him.

"One level down. The intact window," said Spellbreaker. The blade was hungry in his hand.

Alf sprinted along the parapet. Old instincts awoke in him, a strange and savage joy. He was alive, really alive, only in these moments.

Behind him, on the ground floor, Gundan distracted the other Witch Elves in the manner only the boisterous dwarf could manage. With charmstones blazing, Chopper smashed through the main gate with one explosive blow, sending burning fragments flying across the courtyard. "Axes of the dwarves," roared Gundan, "axes in your faces! Yield or be chopped!"

Alf came to the end of the parapet. The one intact window was one floor below, and just to the right. Not intact for much longer. He vaulted onto the railing and jumped, again, crashing through the ether glass and rolling across the room beyond.

Someone – a young Witch Elf warrior, not the woman he sought – came at him with a weapon of some sort. He swung Spellbreaker in the vague direction of his attacker, not even making contact with the blade, but the demon sword didn't need to bite to do damage. A surge of energy lifted the elf off the ground and slammed him against the wall. The elf's weapon was a broken chair leg, and it exploded into splinters.

Alf stood and took in the scene in a flash. He was moving again before he could consciously assimilate his surroundings. Two more Witch Elves, one raising a hand to cast a spell. Alf charged, bowling one over, smashing the other to the ground with the flat of the blade. The spell caster's magic splintered off Spellbreaker's protective shell, and Alf thumped the elf in the nose. No sense in killing anyone without cause. These wretches had already lost the war. Alf found a door, kicked it open. A corridor. Faded frescos, sagging and swollen with water damage, showed the constellation of the Horned Serpent writhing across the sky. Someone had scraped away part of the image, leaving an ugly scar, but Alf could guess what had once been there – the serpent bowing before an image of Lord Bone.

Running footsteps down the corridor. A glimpse of silver hair before the assassin vanished through another door. Alf sprinted after her. Breathing heavily, he stumbled against the fresco, sending more plaster shards falling to the floor. His knees ached after that landing.

He came to the door and grabbed the serpent-head handle – and roared in pain as he touched metal that was bitterly cold. He tore his hand away, left a chunk of his palm behind, frozen to the handle. He cursed and brought Spellbreaker around, fumbling as he tried to manoeuvre the huge sword in the narrow corridor. The blade touched the handle and the door cracked, breaking into chunks of frozen wood like he'd struck the surface of an icy pond. Steam gushed from the broken door, but the barrier held. He stepped back, then slammed his shoulder into the door, and it gave way. The far side was coated with thick ice.

The same spell she'd used on him.

Beyond was a steep staircase, leading up and down. Down, she'd go down.

Another Witch Elf charged down the corridor towards him. This one had a sword. Alf dug a handful of plaster out of the crumbling fresco and flung it into the eyes of the elf. The elf blinked and ran, blind, into Alf's fist. The elf went down, and Alf grunted in pain as he remembered he'd just damaged that hand on the frozen door. Spellbreaker roared, too, frustrated that it hadn't got to taste blood yet.

Down. Follow the elf down. He half slipped down the ice-slick stairs, using the demon sword to arrest his slide. The stairs were made for smaller people than Alf. His head scraped against the cold ceiling. He could hear the elf-assassin running down the spiral just ahead of him, no more than a turn or two ahead.

Six turns brought him down to ground level, an iron door leading out into the courtyard. The elf kept running down, fleeing into the cellars. Alf was about to follow when:

"ALF! HELP!"

Gundan.

Alf smashed Spellbreaker into the iron door, blasting it off its hinges.

The courtyard had emptied out, most of the elves having fled through the smashed gate on the far side. In the middle of the yard, hovering off the ground, was a spell-skull. Its jawbone flapped as it chanted a spell over and over. Tendrils of magical force lashed out from it, churning the earth of the courtyard into a sucking swamp. Gundan was caught in the mud up to his beard, thrashing about as the quagmire drew him down. He saw Alf and waved his free hand. "Bastard's got me! Smash it!"

A spell-skull. Lord Bone had made many of the things, each one enchanted to cast a single spell repeatedly once activated. Bone's forces had loaded summon-skulls into catapults and flung them over the walls of Summerswell. Down in the Clawlands, there were marshes dozens of miles across, conjured by mud-skulls like that one.

He hadn't seen a working skull in years. There were still caches of them in the Sanction, or in the Pits, but most were cracked or rotten.

This one still worked, and it was killing Gundan.

"The dreadworm—" he gasped at Spellbreaker, "call it back!"

"It's too far gone to heed me," said the sword. "I cannot." There was a note of malice in the sword's voice, as if it delighted in Gundan's plight.

Alf stood on the threshold for an instant. Somewhere below, the assassin was running, getting further away with every heartbeat. Maybe the dreadworm would catch her if she surfaced on the streets nearby. Maybe she'd risk going down into the Pits. Either way, she'd be out of reach if Alf did not stay on her heels.

The skull laughed, and Gundan sank another six inches. His stream of curses ended in a muddy gurgle.

Alf ran forward. The circle of mud was too wide now for him to swat the skull with Spellbreaker. He picked up a rock and flung it at the skull, but the thing just cackled at him. Alf considered throwing his sword, but the demon blade would never cooperate with a trick like that.

Gundan's eyes were wide with fear. His face beetroot-red beneath the mud.

Only a direct hit would work, but there was no way to reach the skull. No solid place to stand.

Except one.

Alf jumped forward and landed on Gundan's head, then sprang again, sailing through the air. At the apex of his leap, he slashed at the skull with Spellbreaker.

He fell face first into the mud, but fragments of skull rained down with him. The ground began to solidify again.

Gundan heaved himself out of the earth, spitting up mud. "Did you get her?" he demanded.

"Gone," gasped Alf. He rolled over, struggling to catch his breath.

"The fucking worm. Send the worm after her."

"It's not answering. Where did—" He couldn't breathe, so he just waved his bleeding hand at the place where the skull had been.

The dwarf shook his head, sending gobbets of mud spraying from his beard. "I don't know. But the bastards knew we were coming, Alf. They knew."

Alf stared at his friend for a moment, then shrugged. They had a mission to complete. Finding the assassin would give them the answers. It all had to connect to her – Jan's warning, the attempt on his life, maybe all the trouble in council, too. One last push, one last evil minion of Lord Bone to be struck down, and they'd be done. They had to find her trail.

He got up, took three steps, then stopped. From outside the walls of the House of the Horned Serpent, he could hear a child screaming.

Chapter Twelve

"I told you it was too hungry to be restrained," whispered Spellbreaker.

The dreadworm had landed on the street outside, its rotting body coiling beneath it, the tattered wings a canopy over its eyeless head as it brought its maw down to take another bite of its prey. A Witch Elf – a child! Alf had never seen an elf-child in all his years. Children were rare and prized among the elves. He cursed his luck. If they'd set fire to the Liberties or defiled every shrine in the city, they couldn't have dealt a more bitter wound.

The dreadworm's head dipped again and rose bloody. A few stones and arrows came raining from nearby rooftops and alleyways as the Witch Elves of the Liberties tried to drive away the monster, but failed to penetrate its hide. Alf charged forward, crossing the street in a handful of strides. He swung Spellbreaker in a wild arc, slashing at the monster. The dreadworm reared up, catching the boy in its teeth. A quiver ran down the length of the undead worm, a ripple of horror and defiance and anger. It spread its wings, tensed as if about to fly – and Gundan's axe came spinning through the air, and, true to its name, neatly chopped off one wing at the root. The dwarf raised an armoured hand, and Chopper reversed its spin and flew back to him.

Spellbreaker sang again. Alf could sense the sword's own blood-thirst, its delight in killing. Three dreadworms in as many days – the portions were small and bitter, but at least they were regular. The worm collapsed, and Alf caught the wounded elf-boy as it fell. A belly wound. His own stomach ached at the sight. The linnorm had opened him like that.

But dreadworms didn't have massive maws like linnorms. A linnorm could have swallowed the boy whole. Dreadworms had ugly little mouths, ringed with rasping pseudo-teeth, and stingers that dissolved the flesh of victims. The thing would have turned the elf-boy into rotten mulch before it gobbled him up – and the venom was still working, unravelling the wretch.

Alf grabbed a healing cordial from his belt and forced it between the boy's chattering jaws, but it was too late. For a moment, the boy was oddly doubled, the physical form writhing in agony in Alf's arms, a pale wraith crouched next to him.

From all the buildings around them came shouts and cries. A stone smashed against Gundan's shoulder. Another shattered on the worm-slick cobblestones next to Alf. Then another, and another, and another, a hail of rocks, rotten fruit, pieces of junk, any debris that came to hand.

Trying to drive away monsters.

A mob gathered around them, dead and living – pale elves and paler wraiths, gathering around the wreck of the worm, drawn by the boy's screams. They didn't dare press too close, but they hurled more stones as well as shouts and insults.

One pebble hit Gundan squarely on the nose. "Do you filthy elves know who we are?" he roared.

"Shut up, shut up," hissed Alf, still cradling the dying boy. "Don't make things worse."

Gundan ignored him. "We're the men who killed your precious Bonelord! This is our city! Tell us where the assassin is and we won't—" Another brick shattered on Gundan's enchanted armour.

"Right! Come on, Alf!" Chopper's rune-marked blade flared as Gundan advanced towards the nearest tenement.

Most of the mob scattered at the sight of the axe, but a trio of Witch Elves emerged from the darkness of the doorway to bar his way. All three were armed – two with clubs, but the leader carried a bone-spear and wore a partial suit of armour from the war. Such weapons were forbidden in the Liberties: the Witch Elves were supposed to have surrendered all such things. This one must have been a former knight of Lord Bone. Twenty years ago, he'd have flown a dreadworm and flown the night wind to sow terror across the lands.

The Witch Elf cried out, but Alf didn't speak the elf-tongue well enough to catch his meaning and Gundan, he knew, didn't speak it at all.

"Wait!" shouted Alf. "We didn't mean for the boy to get hurt. We ... we ... fuck it!" He brought his wounded hand to the boy's lips, squeezed out a few drops of blood. Instantly, the child became heavier in his arms, more solid. The elf-boy opened his eyes – already, the first flickers of crimson in the pupils – and bit deep into Alf's wrist. He suckled the blood like an infant. Alf felt a deep chill in his heart, colder than any ice-spell, but he didn't pull away. His stomach lurched. Behind him, Gundan swore in disgust.

Turning vampire was better than a shadow-existence as a wraith, right? The shade of the elf's spirit vanished from Alf's sight, body and soul knitted together again by the red thread of blood.

The boy regained enough strength to scrabble at Alf's neck. His nails tore at his skin, his beard, trying to get at the artery underneath. He was feverish with vampire-strength.

Alf prised the boy's hand away from his neck and lifted the child back to his feet. He pushed past Gundan and shoved the vampire child towards the elves. One of the trio dashed forward and snatched him. Alf reached to grab another healing potion from his belt—

—and then Gundan swung the axe, and one of the elves was cut in two. Two halves of the bone-spear clattered to the ground.

"No weapons for you!" snarled Gundan. "You know the law!"

The other elves staggered backwards. The vampire child shrieked in terror and blood-thirst. The wraith of the dead elf shrieked, too. Chopper was edged with elf-bane alloy. That wraith would burn for centuries.

Cries of fury rose up from every part of the Liberties. It was as though the very stones were appalled, as if every window and doorway in the ruined city was an open mouth, screaming at the injustice. More projectiles rained down on Alf and Gundan. The rooftops were thick with Witch Elves. Once, they were knights and princes, scribes and scholars, the brooding masters of this city of darkness. Now, they were a ragged mob.

One charged at Alf, screaming a battle cry. Alf was about to cut her down, but relented and struck the sword off the ground in front of him. The earth convulsed, and the elf stumbled. Alf punched her, and his foe lay still. The elves were formidable warriors, every one a veteran of a thousand battles, but they had clubs and bricks, not rune-graven swords or spears tipped with starlight. Clubs and bricks against Chopper and Spellbreaker were no contest. It would be a slaughter.

Alf grabbed Gundan and dragged him back towards the House of the Horned Serpent. It'd been a long time since he'd carried the dwarf, but he'd pulled Gundan out of fights more times than he could easily remember. Back when they were young, it'd been bar brawls, mostly, and random skirmishes with bandits on the Road.

This time—

"We can beat 'em!" shouted Gundan. "They're rabble!"

"It's a riot! We'd have to kill them!" Alf tossed the dwarf across the threshold of the House, turned to slam the gates behind him – then remembered that Gundan had smashed the gates with Chopper. He drew Spellbreaker instead and thrust the blade into the stonework of the arch above him, collapsing the gatehouse to block the way.

Gundan picked himself up. "So we kill them! You think that's going to stop them? It's us or them!"

Don't do this, Berys had said, *you'll start a riot.*

"Call a dreadworm!" ordered Alf.

"No. The dwarf is right – it's you or them. Kill them all." The sword's hunger was palpable. It wanted a slaughter.

Gundan snarled. "We could fight our way clear. You and me, it wouldn't even be a fucking contest!"

It was true. They'd done it before, against far worse odds.

Alf backed away from the fallen archway. There was another door on the far side of the courtyard. Fists hammered on it from the other side. Outside, he heard someone cry in Elvish to get a ram.

"Help me hold the door," he ordered Gundan. The pair charged across the courtyard. Alf outdistanced the dwarf and slammed his shoulder into the gate, and a moment later Gundan rolled up like a hurled boulder and added his dwarven strength to the task. Outside, voices bayed for them, hissed curses, spat insults. Alf remembered a time when the Witch Elves had been haughty and silent, when Necrad had been as cold as a tomb and a whisper seemed to echo amid the marble tombs. Now, all the Witch Elves had left were angry words.

"Where's your elf?" shouted Gundan over the din.

"She got away! Into the Pits!"

"You idiot!" The dwarf laughed. "This was all a bloody waste of time." Gundan hooted. "Gods, there's a reason you weren't in charge back in the day. I take back what I said about you being regent of the city. Clever plans aren't your thing, Alf." Glass smashed on the far side of the door.

"Sorry!"

"Don't apologise! This is going to be fun!" Gundan wiped his face with a sleeve. Mud mixed with blood streaked his features. "Come on, where's your belly for the fight?"

Alf shrugged as much as he could with one shoulder pressed

against the door. "Dropped it on the Road, I guess." Even as he said it, he knew it wasn't true. He'd lost it before that. Maybe in the Pits, but the fighting in the Pits was different. Down there, he'd killed things that shouldn't exist, war-beasts grown in the alchemical vats of Lord Bone, necromantic horrors held together by sorcery and hate. Monsters that deserved death – and he'd fought them fairly, sword against claw, against spell, against tooth-filled maw and grasping tentacle, until the linnorm caught him. The fight against the elves wouldn't be like that, and he had no stomach for it.

The sword at his side, though – Spellbreaker sang with bloodlust. Alf knew he could grip the hilt of the demon sword and let it fill him with its joy in slaughter. The sword was made for this, made for blood-letting, for death-dealing, world-ending. It was a killing weapon, and he could be, too, if he'd only let it consume him.

He clenched his fists, feeling blood run down his wrists. The mob shoved on the door again.

"Ready?" asked Gundan.

Suddenly, the desire to open the door filled Alf. Not to fight – just to let the mob rush in like a wave and overwhelm him. To drag him down into darkness and silence and put an end to him. Let them finish the job that the linnorm had started. The same icy chill he'd felt earlier when the elf-boy turned vampire and fed on his blood filled him again, but this time it was soothing, almost peaceful.

The icy chill became a light, a balm. Jan's voice whispered in his mind. *You have my blessing, Alf, and you carry the hope of the world.* He had a quest to complete. A dark fate to avert.

Then, suddenly, the street outside fell silent.

They opened the door to find a dozen armoured dwarves in front of the House of the Horned Serpent. The elves retreated, under threat of elf-bane bolts, falling back to the alleyways and down to the next intersection. They snarled and shouted insults, sang eerie hymns in the tongue of the *enhedrai*, but none dared press the attack. There was no sign of the freshly turned vampire boy, no sign of the elves they'd killed – nothing but a few wraiths that Alf thought might be fresher than the rest of the shadows clustering in the shadows of the street.

The dwarven captain saluted Gundan. "Scouts reported a scuffle here, sir, so we came in a war-wagon in case we were needed."

"Secure this house," ordered Gundan "We'll search it thoroughly in the morning."

"Clerics," said Alf, "or healing potions. For the wounded."

"We're all fine, sir." The dwarf gestured with his crossbow towards the other Garrison troops. "None of us got hurt."

They climbed into the dwarven war-wagon, a portable iron-walled fortress drawn by a pair of massive aurochs. The cart clattered through the streets. Crossbowmen on the roof watched the teetering buildings of the Liberties, but the streets were eerily deserted.

Inside the wagon, Gundan reached under a bench and pulled out a bottle of dwarven spirits. He pulled the stopper with his teeth, took a swig, and handed it to Alf. "Was that a fresh spell-skull?"

"What?"

"That mud-skull that nearly got me. Was it old or fresh?"

"It was old." Alf paused. An old skull could have lain dormant in the Pits or some hidden cache for decades. A fresh one could only have come from the spell-foundries, and they were under the control of the occupying forces.

"Aye." Gundan sighed. His voice, suddenly morose, was little more than a whisper. "I think it was Berys. She told us not to go. She warned the Witch Elves we were coming."

"Why?"

"Knowing her, protecting some investment. Or some agent. Or some smuggling contact."

"Do you think," said Alf, "that she sent the assassin?" The mud-skull was potentially lethal, but nothing they hadn't faced a hundred times in the war. If Berys really wanted to kill them, she had better ways.

"Berys's one of us," said Gundan slowly, "I mean . . . she's Nine. We squabble, we might throw a punch. But murder? I don't think so. We went through hell together."

"What about you and Laerlyn?"

"Well." Gundan picked mud and rubble out of his beard. "That's different. That's politics. And, anyway, the princess was never quite one of us, was she? She was never in the thick of it, not like us. You and me, Lath and Thurn, and Jan. And Blaise."

"And Peir." Alf took the bottle and made a toast.

"And Peir." The dwarf sighed, all the battle joy draining from him as he sat in the back of the wagon. One of the dwarven soldiers whispered in Gundan's ear, and his shoulders slumped.

"Look, Alf, when we get back to the Garrison, follow my lead, all right?"

Even without looking through the arrow-slits, they could tell when the wagon crossed from the Liberties back into the Garrison. The rattle of the wheels changed, the roads free of rubble. The guards on the roof relaxed. The click as they uncocked their bows, the rustle of elf-bane bolts sliding back into quivers.

Then, outside, shouts, and the wagon slowed. Alf glanced through an arrow-slit, and saw a dozen armoured guards. Humans, under the banner of Summerswell. The door of the wagon opened, and Lord Vond climbed in. The young noble trembled with fury. He closed the door firmly behind him.

"By rights," he hissed, "we should be having this conversation in front of the full council."

"Should we now?" said Gundan, his eyes still closed as if half asleep. Alf grimaced: he knew this mood of Gundan's. It was not one Alf liked. The dwarf's merriment could turn sour and venomous.

Alf tried to steer the boy away. "My lord, let us discuss this in the morning in the light of day."

Vond ignored him. Vond poked the dragon. "You entered the Liberties without permission. You *attacked* citizens of Necrad. You summoned a dreadworm, and let it feast on a child. And then you forced Garrison troops to follow you into the fray, resulting in more deaths. If one of the guards did this, I'd order them beheaded—"

"Ach, but it wasn't one of your guards, now, was it?" Gundan grinned lazily. "It was two of the heroes of Necrad. It was Sir Lammergeier and me, the General of the Dwarven League army. What are you going to do to us?"

"You're not above the law."

"Yes, we are. We make the law. There wouldn't be any law here if we hadn't killed Lord Bone. We slew one ruler of this city, and he was a lot scarier than you."

Alf opened his mouth to say something, but Gundan shushed him.

"Are you . . . are you threatening the son of a Lord of Summerswell?"

"Aye," said Gundan. "What are you going to do about it? You think your guards could stop us if we wanted you dead? You think you could stand again the Lammergeier, and Master Blaise, and Beast Lath? Against Giant-Chopper?"

"You're not invincible," whispered Vond. "I command—"

"What, you're going to start a war over a few Witch Elves in some backstreet? I don't think so." Gundan leaned forward and spoke right into Vond's face, splattering the boy with spirit-tinged spittle. "You can't touch us, so don't even try."

To his credit, Vond managed to croak a response. "We'll discuss this . . . in the council."

"Oh, am I invited back, now? I'm not too rude for your delicate ears any more?" Gundan flashed the smuggest grin that ever crossed the face of a dwarf, as if inviting the noble to a banquet of the finest shit.

Vond nodded.

"Well, see you then, O Lord of Necrad."

Clearly, Vond had intended for the guards to escort the war-wagon to the main fortress, judging by their confused looks as the wagon stopped outside Alf's home. He clambered out, Spellbreaker lying heavy in his hand.

"We need to talk, Aelfric," said the sword.

"No, we don't."

A sickening thought struck him. He raised the sword so he could look it in the gemstone eye. "Did you let that dreadworm slip free? Did you let it attack the child?"

"All magic has a cost, Lammergeier. I need bloodshed if I am to work mine. I warned you the worm had grown hungry. I held it back as long as I could, but it slipped free."

Alf scowled. Was the blade lying? Or was he just hoping it was lying, so the catastrophe wasn't his fault?

"Listen! Your petty council and the League are both in disarray, and I suspect that is no accident. You cannot rely on them. Nor can you trust the rest of the Nine. You gave away your advantage when you revealed that you knew the grave had been opened."

"Berys and Gundan had nothing to do with it," snapped Alf.

"Ah, I forgot. Your insight is so keen, you could surely exonerate a woman who is famed through all the lands for her deceits – and your murderous drinking crony, too. Surely with such perspicacity, you will easily—"

Alf shoved the sword into its scabbard and trudged up the path towards his front door.

The League guard stationed there bowed, obviously impressed that Alf travelled with such dignitaries as Lord Vond and the dwarven commander.

"There is a visitor inside, sir. The elf."

In his exhaustion, Alf was momentarily confused, and wondered if the Witch Elf assassin had returned, and that she'd been invited in for a cup of tea so she could wait for her target in comfort. Then he realised who the elf must be.

Laerlyn.

Chapter Thirteen

A Princess of the Everwood stood among the ruins of Alf's parlour, an enigmatic smile glimmering on her perfect features. All of them had aged – even Gundan was a little slower, a little heavier after twenty years. All except Laerlyn. She looked exactly the same as the day he'd met her in the Mulladales, a runaway princess. She bore a different bow now. She'd claimed *Morthus*, the bow of Death's Gift, from the treasury of her father, and still carried that fabled weapon. Instead of torn clothes and a borrowed cloak, she was clad in a gown of woven moonlight, but her face was just the same, just as beautiful.

"My friend!" she said, curtseying in the elven way.

"Lae." Alf cleared some rubble off a chair, then sank into it. His back ached. "Sorry about the mess."

"Which? This pigsty, or the incident in the Liberties?"

"Take your pick."

"I'm told it was one of the *enhedrai* who tried to kill you."

"Lots of people have tried to kill us."

"Come now, Aelfric. We are no longer wanderers in the wild. Treat the matter seriously."

"I am."

"Going on a drinking binge with Gundan that turns into an assault on the Liberties does not qualify as 'seriously'."

Alf sniffed. "Did Berys tell you we were drinking first? Or Vond?"

Laerlyn rolled her eyes, which made her look even more obscenely young, as if Alf was being lectured by some teenage sprite. "My nose. You stink."

Am I getting paranoid? "We were looking for the assassin."

"The assassin," said Laerlyn, steel in her voice, "is one of my people. The *enhedrai* are wayward, but we take responsibility for them. We shall find this rogue and bring her to justice." Her fingers brushed against the dragon-sinew of *Morthus.* The executioner's weapon in the elf-king's court, Alf recalled. Elves don't die of old age. Of course, the bow could not kill them either, not wholly.

Jan had mentioned *Morthus*, too, hadn't she?

"What does *morthus lae-necras l'unthuul amortha* mean?" he asked, mangling the elven words.

"*The gift of death shall not be rejected by the undeserving,*" said Laerlyn, automatically. "Why?"

"And what does that mean?"

"It's a prayer against the undead. They are undeserving of life, but reject death." She paused. "I spoke those words in that last battle, when we fought Lord Bone." For a moment, the years seemed to weigh on her as much as they did on him, but only for a moment. "Each of us have responsibilities now, Aelfric. Yours to guard the demon blade, and keep it out of the hands of those who would misuse it. Mine to be the bridge between the two tribes of elvendom, and bring the wayward home. We must not squabble."

"You weren't at the council."

"Just because I'm immortal doesn't mean I have time to waste. Until everyone agrees to abide by the laws of the council, it has limited use." She sighed. "It will be good to have your steady presence in Necrad again. Tell me, Aelfric, where do you stand on the current dispute?"

Alf tried to recall what the council had talked about. "Ships in the harbour? Smugglers?"

Laerlyn fixed him with her luminous gaze. "I demanded that the Lords of Summerswell take steps to end the abhorrent trade in blood. There are human scavengers – and dwarves, too – who steal magical relics from the Sanction. They sell mortals to the elder *enhedrai*, those who thirst for blood. Two forms of evil, profiting off one another and the works of Bone. It cannot be allowed to continue – but there are those on the council who have invested a great deal in the relic trade, and so they refused my request." She shrugged. "I say 'they', I mostly mean 'she'. Berys commands the underworld. And as the grace of her body fades, I fear, so goes the grace of her soul. She becomes someone very ugly in my sight, Alf, and it saddens me to think that my friend should become so untrustworthy so swiftly."

"When did this trade in blood start?"

"Fifteen years ago? As soon as Thurn freed the Wilder tribes from Necrad's yoke, the elder *enhedrai* needed a replacement way to sate their thirst. It's been going on as long as we've been here, Aelfric, but Berys has made it much worse of late. She trades blood for treasure, and the more the vampires drink, the more they thirst. My kin can no longer overlook this abomination. It must end."

Alf furrowed his brow. He'd never paid much attention to the trade in relics, except when he ran into treasure hunters – or, more frequently, the remains of unlucky treasure hunters – in the Pits. He'd slain enough vampires to hate the things; he could barely conceive of making deals with such a thing.

How much did I overlook? How much did I choose not to see?

"Gundan said you wanted to take over Necrad."

She laughed and spread her hands to encompass the whole of the city. "Who would *want* this place? I hate every stone in this cursed city. It may have been beautiful once, but I fought to break Necrad, not to claim it. But here is where my kinfolk dwell, and here is my task. It will take time, but I am equal to the challenge. In time I shall find a way to bring them to the blessed peace of the greenwood."

Home, thought Alf, to the life-trees. Elves bound to living wood, to rising sap and green leaves, not feeding on blood or fading to bitter shadows. "You're bringing them south to the Everwood?" The eternal forest of the Erlking lay beyond Summerswell. In all his travels, it was one place Alf had never visited. Back when he'd started out, the thought of a forest full of sparkly magic lights and singing elves might have enchanted him. Now, it made his teeth ache.

"No. My plan was to bring the forest to them. But that will take a long time, even as the elves count years. I wish—"

Spellbreaker made a noise at Alf's side, and Laerlyn raised a quizzical eyebrow.

"Just ignore it," said Alf.

The sword grumbled again, its words muffled by the scabbard.

"Be thankful your bow doesn't talk," said Alf, but still he drew the demon sword.

"Erlking's Daughter," said Spellbreaker. There was a note of respect – or fear – in its voice.

"Demon Sword."

"You said your plan *was* to bring the forest to the Witch Elves. That implies your plan changed. Is that so?"

Laerlyn paused, then glided over to a windowsill and hopped up to sit it, crossing her long legs. Alf swallowed. "Do you remember, Aelfric, when Lath made his grove here?"

"Aye."

"He proved that this land is not altogether spoiled by Lord Bone's malignity. Trees can still grow here. Even the *ahernos*. Life-trees, Aelfric, the trees that sustain my people after our physical bodies can no longer endure the sorrows of the world. The *enhedrai* can become *ahedrei*, Witch Elves becoming Wood Elves. They would no longer depend on the blood of mortals to ward off the fading." She glanced at Alf's bandaged wrist and sighed. "They do not trust me, of course. Long have the two branches of our kin been divided. Long ago, they swore an oath rejecting the choice of the wood, and the consequences of that oath – the Oath of Amerith – led them down the dark path of blood."

"What was their problem with the trees?"

"Some believed they could endure without relying on the crutch of the *ahernos*, and it's true that some elves weather the passing years better than others – but all things fade in the end. Others thought that they could find another way to preserve themselves, and sought the magic of the first city to aid in their experiments. Most of all, though, they were led astray by mistrust and misplaced pride. Six thousand years of error, Aelfric.

"Suffering compounded suffering. When they began to fade, they fed upon the blood of the Wilder, and became cruel. They thought themselves gods, and that mortals were nothing but beasts to be used as the *enhedrai* desired. Ultimately, they fostered Lord Bone and brought ruin upon all the lands. The Oath of Amerith was their first error, and all followed from that." Laerlyn glanced around, then said, "There are those in my father's court who argue that the wound in elvendom must be drained before it can be healed – that only the destruction of the *enhedrai* can cure them of their taint. They think the lives of the Witch Elves are forfeit, and that it would be better for them to be ended, so that they might be reborn from Wood Elf stock."

"Fuck."

"Well spoken. I argued against such wholesale slaughter." Laerlyn stood, clasping her hands behind her back like a prim schoolteacher. "For a long time, such thoughts were mere speculation. Necrad and the Everwood were locked in stalemate, light and dark in balance, and there was no prospect of victory or reconciliation. Then Lord Bone arose and disrupted that equilibrium – and then the Nine defeated Lord Bone when all hope seemed lost. Now my father's court is full of plotters and conspirators, all trying to shape the future. I hoped to find allies among the Witch Elves, find those who rejected corruption, but … you know the *enhedrai*. They are proud. As proof to the Witch Elves of my good faith, as proof that the Oath was a mistake, I went to the Everwood and brought back an *ahernos* sapling. I planted it in the grove and promised I would in time bind myself to it."

"When you die," said the sword.

"I thought that by promising to remain in Necrad, I could win the forgiveness of the Witch Elves. All wounds must be healed in the end."

"Lae," said Alf, slowly, trying to get his head around the mysticism, "you'd be stuck here for ever, wouldn't you? If you bind yourself to a life-tree planted here in Necrad, you wouldn't be able to ever leave."

She nodded. "Aye, we cannot stray from our trees once we bind ourselves to them. The elders of the Everwood dwell in eternal bliss within the wood, but they cannot leave it. I would never see my homeland again, or walk in the groves by my father's side and hear stories of the elder days that I have forgotten. I would be bound within the confines of this city for ever – but ever is a long time. I would make a second paradise of this city, even if it takes me another six thousand years."

"And in this paradise," said the sword, "you would be queen, yes? You would command the magic of Necrad. A winter erlqueen in the north, to match the summer king in the south. Beautiful and terrible, ruling for eternity, yes? No wonder they——"

Alf swore and shoved the sword back into its scabbard. "Gah! Sorry, Lae. The thing's malicious!"

Laerlyn laughed. "Of course it is! It's a demon sword." She walked around the room, circling the sword. "But no – I have no desire to rule here – certainly not for ever. Once the *enhedrai* are brought into the light, let them choose their own leader. And, Aelfric – you above all should not be surprised by my choice. We all promised to watch over Necrad – and Lord Bone's grave. We said we'd watch it for ever. That means something different for me than for the rest of you, but I swore it nonetheless."

Alf took a risk. "Bone's grave is empty. Someone dug him up."

Laerlyn flinched. "Who defiled the grave?"

She didn't know. It wasn't her.

"I don't know. But listen – Jan contacted me, Lae, when I was down in the Mulladales. She had a . . . " Alf shrugged sheepishly, "a prophecy, about some new danger coming to Necrad. She thought it might be the Oracle returning." Lord Bone's last courtier. An ancient Witch Elf sorceress and seer. *A dark power rising*, Jan had said. *It might be the Oracle.*

"That's hard to believe, Aelfric. We searched for the Oracle for years, and could find no proof that she was still active. Is Jan certain?" Laerlyn's eyes were glimmering starlit pools. "I can send messengers to the Valley of the Illuminated, have her here in a week—"

"Jan's gone. She, I don't know, sublimed. Jan wasn't sure it was the Oracle, but she could tell something bad was coming. And that assassin came after me as soon as I got home, so I'm guessing it's all connected somehow. I need to find her."

The elf ran her fingers through her golden hair. "There are many among the *enhedrai* who cling to their misguided, cruel ways. Some defy us openly, others in secret. I can try to find out who your assailant was."

"This might help." Alf produced the assassin's dagger and held it out to her.

Laerlyn frowned as she studied the knife. "These inscriptions – they are a curse, naming the one the blades were intended to slay. These were made to kill . . . " Her voice trailed off.

"Who?"

Laerlyn didn't answer. She spoke almost to herself, lost in contemplation of the runes. "I sought proof that there are those among the *enhedrai* worthy of redemption. Proof my father and his courtiers might accept."

"Whose name is on the blade, Lae?"

Laerlyn ran a finger over the runes. She looked up at Alf, and his breath was caught by the luminous beauty of her eyes. "It doesn't matter now. The mortal this dagger was forged to slay is long dead. This assassin who tried to murder you – tell of her."

"Quick. She threw ice magic at me, and it was strong stuff. But she ran instead of pressing the attack. She fled to the House of the Horned Serpent when she escaped the Garrison."

"They are the Oracle's kin. I'd guess she used whatever weapon came to hand," mused Laerlyn. "Who have you shown this to? The council?"

"Nah. Just Gundan and Berys."

A frown flashed across her face at the mention of Berys' name. "Has anyone else seen it?"

Alf shrugged. "Does it matter?"

Laerlyn stood, still holding the enchanted dagger. "You and I, Aelfric, shall never be opposed, whatever fate has in store for us. The Nine are friends for ever. Even Gundan, though I may have to bounce an arrow or two off his thick skull ere I forgive him properly. But this is an elven matter, Aelfric, and in my purview. I must keep the blade." She wrapped it in a square of silken cloth.

The sword made a noise of protest.

"The Witch Elf went down into the Pits, Lae. I'm going after her. I'll need the dagger for her scent." Lath, if he ever turned up, could get the smell off the handle of the weapon, and track the elf through the corridors below. Failing that, there were divination-spells that might at least tell Alf where to start looking. He reached for the dagger.

Laerlyn glided back out of reach. "This is more important, Aelfric. I must keep it. And I don't think that it's wise for you to go into the Pits. Stay here where you're protected. I see it in your face – you are tired. You are wounded. And you are *old*. Your duty is to guard that demon sword, not to go wandering in the dungeons."

He tried on Gundan's bravado, softened with a smile. "Who's going to stop me? You?"

In response, Laerlyn brushed her palm gently against his cheek. She began to sing a haunting song of elder days. He remembered camping in the forest, long long ago, Laerlyn watching over the company and singing the same song as they fell asleep.

The sword protested again, rocking its scabbard back and forth, but Alf ignored it. He shoved it away with his foot.

He was suddenly very, very tired. He hadn't slept, really, since visiting Jan.

The elf-song caught him up, lifted him and carried him away.

In his dream, he was in Necrad again. Necrad as it was before the war. Before their impossible victory. All the company was there with him. Those he'd seen that recently – Gundan, roaring a challenge to Lord Bone. Laerlyn, her bow singing death. *Morthus.* Berys, everywhere and nowhere, her knife flashing with charmstone. Blaise, his staff raised to command the magic.

The others were there, too. Thurn, stoic in the face of a host of skeletons. Jan, wielding the light like a spear. Lath, in the form of an ice bear.

And the one who was dead. Peir, at the head of the company, urging them onwards. Eyes bright with determination, undismayed by the darkness.

Nothing dismayed him. Even at the worst times – when they were besieged in the Dwarfholt, when Lath was captured, the Battle of Karak's Gate – when all the rest of them lost hope, it was Peir who drove them onwards, Peir who carried them. The rest lost sight of the light, sometimes, but Peir never did.

Not until that last battle, when Alf had to snuff that light out.

In his dream, a flock of dreadworms descended on them, and on every worm was a Witch Elf. He swung his old sword again and again. All the elves wore the livery of the Horned Serpent, and they all had the elf assassin's face. He killed the girl over and over, her dagger an icicle that shattered hundreds of times until the ground crunched with every step Alf took. The shards pierced his boots and cut his feet, so that he left bloody prints wherever he stepped.

He looked around and found he was separated from the company. He ran through the streets of the twisted city, blundering from one shadowy courtyard to another. Wraiths clawed at him as he rushed past, but did not hinder him. He ran, and there at the end of the street was the Wraith-Captain, Spellbreaker clutched in a spectral hand.

"Laerlyn thinks you're too old," said the sword. "Too weak."

The dream suddenly became hollow, like all the air was abruptly withdrawn from the memory-city. Alf hesitated, unsure of what was happening.

"Feed me," it said, "and I can give you strength."

"I don't need you."

"Are you sure?" asked the sword. "Can you trust any of them?"

In his dream, Alf thought he saw Peir riding towards him, out of the gloom of the city, his mantle gleaming in the twilight.

But the dream was ending, and he couldn't be sure.

He awoke from the enchanted sleep to a dull morning, but felt a little more rested than he had in weeks. He rose from his chair and stepped across the wreckage to the shattered window. Looking out over the city, he could almost see patches where the sun tried valiantly to break through the necromiasma.

Laerlyn was gone.

"She took the dagger," said Spellbreaker.

Alf shook his head. "Lae wants to find the assassin herself. Keep it an elf matter." It was still a small betrayal, and it rankled, but he was reassured by Laerlyn's reaction to the news of Lord Bone's grave. He should have trusted his friends. He'd fallen into the same trap as the rest of them, letting their other loyalties and responsibilities divide them. Gundan and Laerlyn with their respective kingdoms, Blaise with his research, Berys with . . . whatever intrigue she was up to, these days. Underneath it all, though, stronger than everything else, were the bonds forged in battle.

Whatever else, Alf believed that was true.

"But she can't do it alone. None of us can. We have to pull together."

"She ensorcelled you. She put you to sleep and took the dagger. The only spoor you have of the assassin." said the sword. "She betrayed you."

"It's nothing."

"Wheels within wheels, Lammergeier. You have not the wit to thread this labyrinth without me."

"Shut up."

"If you'd been holding me," said Spellbreaker quietly, "her spell would never have got through. I protect my wielder."

Alf ignored the sword. He took off his cloak and brushed fragments of fallen plaster from its folds. Scratched his beard, found it matted with blood and filth and white dust. He coughed, tasting ash and healing potion. He went over last night's conversation with Laerlyn in his thoughts, bringing to mind the memory of her reaction when he told her that Bone's tomb had been opened. There had been genuine shock in those inhumanly green eyes – hadn't there? Or had he only wanted to see it?

"Only one of the Nine could have opened the grave," said the sword.

"Stay out of my thoughts."

"You said that out loud," replied the sword. Had he? Alf couldn't recall. He yawned, and choked on a lungful of dust.

"Maybe they opened the grave for a good reason." Like Laerlyn stole the dagger for a good reason.

"What reason might that be?" replied the sword.

He couldn't answer that one. "They wouldn't break their oath. None of them would."

"Then perhaps one of them is dead, and their corpse was used to open the grave," mused the sword. "Maybe my lord has already returned, and soon I shall be reclaimed."

"You're in a talkative mood this morning."

"You wielded me in battle," said the sword, "I had a chance to feed."

"That," said Alf, "is not happening again."

"You're right. Witch Elves are thin and tasteless. You should have defended them, heroically, by chopping up those dwarven guards. Think of it! Thick and chewy spirits, meat and gristle and bone to cleave through . . . "

"Shut up."

"Don't tell me you didn't consider it, wielder. They were ready to fire into the crowd. Elf-bane bolts. My lord made many weapons, but I don't know if any of them are quite as cruel as those bolts the League forged – and I speak from personal experience. To torture the spirit . . . "

"Shut. Up." Alf picked up Spellbreaker and considered locking it away in a chest or smashing it against a wall. With a frustrated snarl, he rammed the blade into its sheath. "Don't say a word."

He picked his way through the debris to the pantry. Someone – one of Vond's guards, he assumed – had stocked the shelves with basic supplies. Alf grabbed a handful of ship's biscuits and a mouthful of wine to wash them down, then set off to find the assassin.

After the company slew Lord Bone and Necrad fell into their charge, each of them took a house in the city. Alf had his mansion, which he'd picked by the simple principle of stopping outside a random dread knight's manor, kicking the door down and declaring himself at home. To the victor go the spoils, he'd told himself. Blaise had his tower, Berys her mansion down by the docks. Jan . . . no, Jan had never lived in the city. After they'd slain Lord Bone, she'd gone out to attend to the wounded and the dying. The League's siege of Necrad had been a ghastly slaughter. All three armies, Elf and

Dwarf and Summerswell, would have been destroyed if not for the death of Lord Bone.

Four armies, he reminded himself. Wilder fought on both sides. Thurn's allies, and those still too terrified or devoted to the Witch Elves to turn on their former enslavers.

No: Jan had gone out to tend to the wounded and never really came back. She'd built a temple down by the shore and dwelt there. The Wilder never settled in Necrad, either. Thurn, of course, was uncomfortable in cities, like most of his Wilder kin, and Alf hadn't been surprised when he left. And Lath ... the Changeling could lay down his head anywhere. Beasts had raised him. Hell, when they'd first met Lath, they had to remind the boy to put on clothes.

Alf stopped and looked around the street, realising he'd been so distracted by his own reminiscences that he'd become lost in the Garrison. So much of this part of the city had changed in the last two years, but he still kicked himself for taking a wrong turning. Laerlyn's home – a high tower of pearly stone, its upper levels lost in the churning green clouds of the necromiasma – was around here somewhere. Of course, pearly towers that pierced the clouds were two a penny in Necrad.

"Good morning, Lord Lammergeier!"

A Vatling, the same one who was on the council. Berys' ally. Alf tried to remember the name of the creature.

The Vatling bowed. "Threeday," he supplied, laying long fingers across his chest. The fingers had no knuckles or joints, a beached jellyfish against the cloth. "I wished to welcome the Lammergeier back to his city. A pleasant morning, is it not?" Sunlight filtering through green clouds did nothing for the Vatling's complexion.

"Not my city," growled Alf instinctively.

Threeday painted a smile on his face. The Vatling's skin was a little translucent; there was a suggestion of the skull beneath the skin, a darker shape beneath the gelatinous flesh. His face was like his hands, lacking in detail, one feature blending into another or else weirdly pronounced. A child's sketch of a face, drawing mouth and nose and eyes but everything else forgotten. The smile was thin-lipped, close-mouthed, to avoid showing the creature's lack of teeth.

"Of course," said Threeday, "Necrad is the responsibility of all of us, is it not? Yet no one can claim to rule it."

"Sure."

"Permit me to walk with you," said Threeday, falling in beside him. The Vatling took Alf's helm, as smoothly as a trained squire, and carried it while he ate. "Where are you going this morning?"

"Laerlyn's."

"Ah," said Threeday. "The princess departed the city last night. I understand she left for the Isle of Dawn, where her brother reigns. Oh, to be a bird on a branch during that conversation. You know the Prince of Dawn, or so the songs would have us believe."

"A long time ago."

"For you, maybe. For me, certainly — my people are short-lived even compared to you humans. But to the elves?"

Alf grunted and turned down the Way of Haradrume, towards where Lath's grove once stood. The Changeling could be difficult to deal with, but he and Alf had a long understanding. Better yet, Lath shared Alf's disinterest in politicking and conspiring. He had no loyalty to Summerswell or the Everwood or the Dwarfholt, and, while he was half-Wilder, Lath had never evinced much of a connection to the tribes. Without kith or kin, the Nine were Lath's only family.

Beside Alf, the Vatling prattled on. "The feud between the Wood Elves and the dwarven occupying force is worrisome for my people. So too are the rumours of Wilder attacks from the north. The New Provinces are fortified, but their defences cannot compare to Necrad and they may be overrun if the League cannot placate the tribes. For our part, we crave above all to avoid fighting in the city. War is bad for everyone, but we are especially vulnerable."

"Which *we* is that?" snapped Alf. "You're the representative for the Liberties – are you talking about all the people in the Liberties or just the Vatlings?" The memory of that elf-boy crossed Alf's mind.

"Have you breakfasted, Sir Lammergeier?" asked Threeday instead of answering. He produced a cloth bundle, and gently unwrapped it to reveal half a dozen delicate pastries. Alf's stomach rumbled, and the Vatling made a similar gurgling noise that might have been a sort of laugh. "I like to walk the streets of Necrad in the morning, visiting with those who need my help. I do not have time to sit and eat. Please." He offered Alf a pastry, then took one himself and popped it into his mouth-hole.

"It's true, my people are uniquely vulnerable to the vicissitudes of Necrad. There are no other Vatlings in all the wide world, and, unlike your kind, we cannot reproduce without the use of our machinery – and there is magic here that we cannot replicate." His voice dropped to a conspiratorial whisper. "We were made, you know, to feed the Witch Elf vampires, but our vitalising fluid proved, ah, lacking in some key quality." Threeday shrugged, as if all this was of minor concern. "Perhaps that is why the Liberties sent me – the Witch Elves and the others know that I shall do whatever is necessary to preserve the peace and security of our city. I aspire to nothing more than loyal service."

"I don't want trouble either," muttered Alf, stuffing the pastry into his mouth. The cursed thing was delicious, but he mistrusted rich food. *Can't afford to become soft.*

Threeday had to trot along quickly to match Alf's long strides. "I have found Lady Berys receptive to my concerns, and I am told that you are especially close to both Lord Gundan of the Dwarves, and the Changeling Lath."

"We're all friends," insisted Alf, "the whole company."

Threeday shrugged. "As you say. I would not presume to understand the . . . internal workings of so august a group. Let me say, then, that I too wish to be your friend, and your friends to be my friends. Lady Berys already understands the benefits."

Alf snatched his helmet back from the Vatling, shuddering slightly at the moist touch of the creature's flesh. The Vatling's boneless hands had left wet streaks on the metal of his helm. "What benefits are those?" *Theft? Smuggling? Black marketeering?* And Gundan thought Berys warned the Witch Elves. The killing last night, that was her fault – or partly her fault, anyway.

Threeday gestured to the towering Garrison walls, a few streets over. "You are exceptional, Sir Lammergeier, in that—"

"Don't call me that."

"Forgive me." The Vatling blushed, inky blood flooding the capillaries of his cheeks. "But you are an exception. Few of your kind ever leave the Garrison – unless it's with an armed escort, like last night. Even you usually go *under* the city, not into it. The Liberties, the Sanction – there are forces moving there you do not see. Things you do not know, places you cannot go." The Vatling must have noticed Alf's sudden glare, because he stopped and spread his fingers like an octopus. "I speak metaphorically, of course! My point is that we would all be best served if the council stopped thinking of Necrad as an enemy camp that has been conquered and began considering it . . . home."

He bowed. "If there is ever anything you need from the Liberties, I beg you, consider me your agent and ally."

Alf watched the Vatling hurry away down the street. A pair of dwarven sentries followed Threeday, ostentatiously shadowing him until he turned a corner and vanished.

"I was made, too," said Spellbreaker thoughtfully when they were alone. "Forged, not grown. But Lord Bone made us both."

"I knew that Vatling reminded me of someone. You're a pair, all right." *Monsters with honeyed words, trying to get into my head and trick me.*

"Their purpose was to feed the vampires, and they failed," mused the blade. "I wonder if I was made with a purpose in mind."

*

Lath started his grove before they'd slain Lord Bone. It was an act of defiance at first, a hope when all hope was lost. When they were trapped in Necrad, hiding on the streets from Lord Bone's minions, he'd broken through the cobblestones, sucked the poison from a patch of tainted earth and planted a seed. A single green shoot, a weed that would be overlooked anywhere else in the world, but in the dead city it had a special significance. Indeed, without that weed they'd never have found Lath after he was captured. He'd managed to call them through the earth and speak to them from the flower, guided them to the prison where the Witch Elves held him.

After the war was won, after Bone was dead, Lath returned to the grove time and again. In the form of a gargantuan bear, he tore down the buildings around that little patch of broken earth. In the shape of a badger the size of an elephant, he ripped up the paving stones, tore away the Pits below, and spread clean soil across the patch. He tore the sky with magic, so the pestilence of the necromiasma grew thin and sunlight broke through there.

And so, in the heart of the dead city, a grove of trees grew. Twisted, sickly, anywhere else you'd have called them unwholesome, but here in the city of cold marble they were an eruption of life, defiant and somehow noble.

Now it was gone. A grove of blackened stumps and white ash.

Alf bent down and ran his fingers through the cold dirt. *Someone burned down Lath's grove.* The same someone who tried to kill him, two nights ago? And Gundan also mentioned an attempt on Berys' life. Alf couldn't square that with Berys warning the Witch Elves, but where she was involved there were always wheels within wheels.

"The Beast is not here, Lammergeier," complained the sword.

His finger sketched a circle in the ash. There were bootprints in the ash, slim and light. Laerlyn's tracks, he guessed. Laerlyn loved the grove, too. He looked around and found the burned sapling of a life-tree. The moon-pale bark of the *ahernos* tree was scorched; the twisted remnants of the tree looked like a dying woman, twisting away from him.

After long expeditions underground, Lath came back here, to his hard-won grove of trees to rest.

Alf had – what had he done, he wondered? The years of the war were full of memories, full of grand deeds immortalised in story and song. They thought they were doomed, and they'd snatched days back from death with sword and spell. Then the victory, and the years ran through his fingers like sand. Fifteen years in Necrad, and what had he done? He remembered fighting in the Pits, clearing them room by room, corridor by corridor ... but there must have been other things than that? Drinking sessions with Gundan. The occasional council meeting. The occasional woman, so enchanted by the epic saga of the heroes of Necrad that she was willing to overlook the present state of him. Always, always, the feeling that just one more push would change everything. That they'd clear one last section of the Pits, and then they'd be able to seal the remainder of the labyrinth and be done with the task. Or that the real challenge would come, and he'd be ready for it, his fighting skills kept sharp by using the Pits as a whetstone.

The city above had relied on them, too. If Alf and Lath had stopped their patrols and expeditions into the Pits, then all the monsters down there would have spilled out onto the streets. Alf recalled walking home, exhausted after some long trek through the endless dungeon, nursing his wounds – but sustained by the knowledge that he'd done his duty. That everyone in Necrad could sleep easy at night because of his efforts. He'd been doing vital – if unseen – work below while smarter people like Berys and Blaise and Laerlyn attended to the work above in the council. Alf kept his head down, kept trudging ahead – until he'd looked up and found that fifteen years had gone by.

The memory of the linnorm attacking him slithered out of the ground, and he stood abruptly. Lath wasn't here.

And if he wasn't here, he must be below.

Chapter Fourteen

E llsport was as how she imagined drowning.

Everything about the city overwhelmed Olva. The press of people all about her, rushing this way and that. The crowds surged through the streets like rushing waters, and she clung to Bor's arm to avoid being swept away. Buildings – four, five storeys tall – rose up, precarious giants about to fall on her. She looked one way, and saw more people in one small side street than she'd ever seen at once in Ersfel; she looked another, and saw a crowd larger than Highfield at the fair.

And then Bor led her around the corner, onto the main street, and the thunder of the crowd crashed over her. The wide street was paved – paved! – and thronged with all manner of people. Merchant princes and knights of Summerswell, folk from other lands across the eastern sea. Sailors and soldiers, rich nobles in fine clothes sharing the street with poor settlers laden with all their belongings, heading to seek their fortune in the New Provinces. Dwarves – armour-clad, stern-faced. Like dogs in a field of wheat, you could only glimpse them infrequently when the crowd bent and parted, but you could trace their path as they pushed people aside. The sides of the street were full of shops, and Olva could only guess what their signs meant, swaying in the sea breeze – crossed swords, locks and keys, snarling beasts, candles and knives.

The street sloped down to what Olva first thought to be a forest of leafless trees, but then she saw to be the masts of a great many ships, more than she ever dreamed existed in all the world – and part of her quailed at the thought that finding Lyulf Martens' ship among such a forest would be impossible. Beyond, the staggering blue of the sea.

She stared at it, frozen in wonder, until Bor pushed her out of the path of the traffic on the street, into the sheltered lee of a statue. She sat down on the statue's plinth, grateful to take the weight off her aching legs. Cu flopped down at her feet, his tongue lolling out.

"Something's going on," muttered Bor. "I've never seen so many ships in the harbour, unless there's a storm." The sky overhead was blue and almost cloudless, scrubbed clean by the winds of the previous days. "Maybe the wizards predicted something." He nodded over at a tower by the harbour, gleaming white in the sun. A shield bearing the arms of one of the Lords of Summerswell surmounted the door of the tower. Above fluttered the banners of the League.

Torun left them, slipping away through the crowd in the direction of a group of dwarven soldiers. She muttered something in parting, but her words were lost in the hubbub. The dwarf-maid had a habit of speaking as if addressing her words to her shoes.

Olva looked up at Bor, shading her eyes with her hand against the bright sun.

"You worked for Martens. Does he have a home here?"

"He does. Warehouses and workshops, too. And men. You put one of his lads in the dirt, and he won't forget that. It's a League town, so he won't have you gutted on the high street. But for the love of the Intercessors, stay on your guard." He half turned, his gaze scanning the crowd. One hand on his sword-hilt, as if daring anyone to approach.

Olva hunched her shoulders, as if she could hide in the shadow of the statue. It was a hideous thing of iron, twice the height of Bor. She stared at its leering face for a moment, trying to tell what it depicted.

"It's not a statue," said Bor. "Lord Bone made it. Not much could hurt them. I knew a man who lost his arm to one. When Bone died, they all just stopped. There are fields near Summerswell littered with the things. Kids climb on them."

She could imagine Derwyn doing that. Or, no – he'd have imagined the golem was still alive. He'd have stood in front of it, a tree branch for a pretend sword, and challenged the immobile monster. Ersfel had been spared any such physical reminders of the war. Maybe if Derwyn had grown up seeing the actual perils of Necrad in the flesh – or metal – instead of in tales, none of this would have happened.

Torun came running up to them. "No sailings! Every ship that tries to cross the Gulf of Tears runs into a fierce storm that blows up out of nowhere. It's magic, it has to be! There're saying that the elves of Dawn have barred the way to Necrad, but no one knows for sure! It's all very confusing, and, and—" She paused for breath.

Olva raised her head, nurturing a little spark of hope. "If none of the ships are leaving, then maybe Derwyn's still here."

"Aye, but if he's here in one of Martens' bolt-holes, then he might as well be on the bloody moon. Come on." Bor pulled Olva to her feet. "Let's find a bolt-hole of our own, take stock of what we have."

Torun pointed down the street. "Why not go to the League? You're the Lammergeier's sister. Surely they'll help."

Olva stared at the banner. "Do you think they'll listen?"

"No," said Bor. "It's a stupid idea. You've no proof of anything. They'll laugh in your face."

"She has her word," said the dwarf. "Even among you humans, that must count for something." Torun looked up at Bor, squinting against the sun. "And you met the Lammergeier. You can vouch for her tale, too."

"Shove the Spire of Arshoth up my arse," swore Bor, "but you're a pair of bloody idiots. Listen: the League's not going to listen to some old biddy from the Mulladales. If you were the paladin's sister or something, and you had a signet ring and a fine carriage and a train of servants, then maybe they'd let you in the gate. But you're no one to them. Anyway, they've got bigger problems." He waved his arm at the harbour full of ships.

Torun crossed her arms. "There'll be dwarves there, too. My people are not so unreasonable."

"We have to do something. Once Derwyn's gone across the sea, I don't know how I'll find him. Let's try the citadel." Olva tried to move down the hill, but Bor's grip on her arm tightened and held her back.

"Martens owns people in the citadel. He owns people everywhere. You're being stupid."

"What would you counsel, then?" hissed Olva. "Give my son up for dead?"

"Martens won't kill him," said Bor, then he swallowed. "Leastways, not right away. He knows now that your boy's more valuable alive – he's a hook into the one of the Nine, and the Nine run Necrad."

"That's not any better." Olva tore her arm free. She marched down the street, Cu and Torun trotting after her. Behind them, Bor stood for a long moment, unmoving as the iron golem, then shouted, "The Inn of the Blackfish! I'll meet you there when you're done wasting your time!"

The wizard's tower was the tallest part of the walled citadel guarding the harbour. It looked a little like a ship, with long cables running like rigging from the tower's spire to nearby walls and stanchions, all hung with mirrors and star-traps that flashed in the sunlight. Sections of newer stone spoke of the war, of how Lord Bone's forces had overrun the town. The League had rebuilt much of what had been destroyed; dwarf masons were a common sight in the lands of Summerswell now, labouring alongside their allies. The stonework in the land was much improved, and Olva had heard tales of the fabulous new dwarf-built palaces and cathedrals under construction in Summerswell. She wondered if Alf lived in such a palace, far away in Necrad.

Not all of the fortress had been rebuilt. There was still a hollow-eyed ruin peering over the parapet nearby. It had been a gatehouse once, but the gate was now blocked with rubble. Fire had gutted it, and now the whole structure was obviously crumbling. Scaffolding on both sides of the fortress wall supported the burned tower.

"It was the tithing gate," whispered Torun, "for the Witch Elves." Olva bit her lip. Her hand brushed against her knife.

A crowd was gathered at another gate of the fortress. Olva pushed her way close enough to the front to learn why there was such a throng – some Lord was hiring soldiers on behalf of the League. Anyone who could hold a spear could pass through those gates, and be given a green tunic and a silver coin. With the passage to the New Provinces closed, many of those now stuck in Ellsport could not afford to overlook the opportunity for ready money. One column of troops was already marching up the road, heading back the way Olva had come. They'd pass the Fossewood, pass Tern's Tower and head on west towards the Crownlands of Summerswell. She watched the young soldiers as they marched by, stumbling and pushing against each other, singing marching songs all out of time with one another. One of the songs was about the Nine, and Torun nudged Olva in the knee at the mention of her brother's name.

"Tell them who you are," urged the dwarf.

But Bor was right – she was no one here. The captain at the gate barely listened to her, and looked past her to the next in line even as he addressed her.

"Let me guess – your husband got drunk and took the League's shilling, and now his courage is flagging and he sent you to plead his case. What's done cannot be undone, madame. When the Lords of Summerswell call—"

"No, my brother, Alf, he's—"

"Husband, brother, no matter. I can do nothing for you. Next!"

"He's the Lammergeier!"

"And I am Bessimer the Weeping Lord. Next!"

Olva tried again, with a different officer, a different entrance to the citadel. Again, they were rebuffed. Olva's throat became raw from shouting over the din of the crowd. All her life – since she'd married Galwyn, at any rate – she'd been a woman of some importance in Ersfel, used to being listened to, used to being obeyed. But Ellsport was a different place, and the soldiers were unmoved by her words. Frustration grew in her.

"We're going to find someone who'll listen," she insisted. "This way."

Olva returned to the tithing gate, shivering as she entered the cooler shadow of the wall. No one was nearby – sensible people avoided the ill-omened tithing gate. The scaffolding overhead looked weathered, but stable enough.

"Help me up, please," she said to Torun. The dwarf raised her eyebrows, but still she let Olva clamber onto her sturdy shoulders. Standing on the dwarf gave Olva just enough height to reach the edge of the platform, and after some undignified grunting, she was able to haul herself up onto the first level of the scaffolding. Beneath her, Cu danced around, barking in distress.

"Keep him quiet!"

Torun knelt down by the dog and put a hand on his muzzle. "I can't follow you up there," she said.

"I won't be long. I just need to find someone in this damned place who'll listen to me." Olva stood up and brushed herself off, frowning at the state of her dusty, travel-stained dress. There was still dried blood on her sleeve. Little wonder the guards at the gate had treated her like a madwoman, and here she was, climbing into a haunted tower to storm a fortress. "I'll see you at that inn. The Blackfish."

A ladder climbed from the first platform to the second, from the second to the third, and from the third to the vertiginous heights of the fourth. She had never climbed so high – there were no buildings in Ersfel half so tall as this. People on the streets of Ellsport were tiny now, the town becoming a strange jumble of roofs and chimneys instead of streets. The scaffolding around her creaked under her weight, but she climbed on. The fifth ladder brought her to the top of the wall, and she gingerly stepped from scaffolding onto blackened stone. She crept forward, shivering again – the darkness within the ruined tower was icy cold. The walls around her still bore the marks of soot where the flames had licked them. Every footstep, no matter how careful, sent up puffs of dust that made her choke.

In places, the fire had consumed the wooden planks and beams, forcing her to hop and climb from one crumbling stone foothold to another. She found she was cursing under her breath as she moved – she'd be furious if Derwyn uttered a single one of these profanities, but here they came out in a constant litany. She inched forward, looking for a way to climb down on the far side of the wall. Olva swore to the Erlking and all his spirits that once she had solid ground under her feet again, she'd never leave it. Climbing was for birds and Wilder.

She came to a shaft that looked down into a great void within the building. Light spilled into it from some window far below, dying sunlight touching on scorched walls and rubble, the remnants of fallen ornamental pillars. It must have been a huge room once. Maybe carriages and wagons passing through the gatehouse stopped there to be searched, or maybe it was a grand feast hall in years gone by. She imagined grand knights and nobles, singing and feasting.

She froze as she saw movement in the hall below. She could not be sure, but it seemed as if scorch-marks on the walls had shifted as the sun fell, and from this angle they looked almost humanoid, long shadows cast by unseen forms. Tales of elven-wraiths and other horrors out of Necrad filled her mind and froze her stomach. All she could taste was ash, and she fought down a coughing fit. She tried to hurry onwards, but in her haste she slipped and fell – or, for an instant, she thought a cold hand had seized her wrist and pulled her over. The burned beam cracked alarmingly as she landed on it. Ghostly fingers tugged at her and clung to her arm. She ran forward blindly, trying to shake the thing loose.

In her blind rush, she found descending steps, and nearly fell down them, scraping her arms on the walls. She blundered out into the light, nearly tripping in her haste to escape the tower. She brushed cobwebs from her hands, and wondered if she'd mistaken them for a wraith, or if there truly were spirits lurking there in the darkness.

Guards came running towards her. She'd tumbled out of the ruined tower into a wide courtyard. Soldiers everywhere, hurrying this way and that with supplies, or being herded into formation, or just sitting around laughing at the sight of some bedraggled woman falling out of the haunted tower. So much for creeping in and finding a sympathetic ear. Still, the threat of the guards, who'd seemed implacable and intimidating only minutes earlier, now seemed homely compared to the terrors of the gatehouse. She pulled herself to her feet and dusted herself down.

"I need to talk to someone in charge," she began, as the first guard reached her. "I'm the Lammergeier's ..." She was about to say *sister*, but then the face of one of the soldiers leapt out at her, like the candle-lit face of the Erlking in a chapel. She knew that scowling face – she'd seen it only two days before, in the Fossewood. He hadn't been wearing the tabard of the League then, when he'd slashed at Cu with his sword, or when he'd chased Olva and Bor up the hill to murder them.

Martens owns people in the citadel. He owns people everywhere. Bor was right.

"I'm the Lammergeier," she said again, letting herself sway on her feet as if drunk, "the Lammergeier back to save you all!"

"She's mad," said one of the guards.

"Get her out of here," ordered another. They grabbed her, roughly, and dragged her across the courtyard towards the gate. Olva let her head fall, hiding her face as they passed Martens' man. He was deep in conversation with an older officer – *someone in charge*, she thought bitterly – with a dragon-crested helm tucked under one arm. The helm's iridescence reminded her of the coins from Necrad. The guards dragged her past, hauling her across the courtyard to the jeers and laughter of the crowd. One of her captors kicked her sharply in the ribs, then flung her out through a postern gate, sending her sprawling in wet mud.

Her cheeks burned as the crowd outside the gate laughed at her too, and all she could think was Bor saying *you're being stupid*. She rose and walked away with as much dignity as she could muster, and dared not look back to see if that scowling guard of Martens' was following her.

In any other establishment in Ellsport, Olva's mud-stained state might have drawn attention, but not the Inn of the Blackfish. The stench of the place made her quail like a wraith in sunlight, a thick aroma of spilled ale, sweat, rotten fish and self-pity. Looking around at the crowd, the tavern seemed populated by hard-luck cases – one-legged sailors, gamblers on a losing streak, old soldiers past their fighting days. No wonder Bor had chosen it.

She found Bor and Torun at a table, with Cu curled up underneath. Bor half rose as she arrived. "Were you followed?" His breath stank.

"No – but I saw one of the men from the Fossewood. He was in the citadel, dressed as a League guard."

"The dwarf told me what you did." Bor shook his head. "That was Thedric. He *is* a bloody League guard. Helped Martens bring contraband ashore in my day. Did he see you?"

"I don't know. I don't think so."

"You're going to get yourself killed. What's next, poking your head into a dragon's den in case Derwyn's there?" The mercenary sank back down. "The boy's as good as gone."

"But the elves have stopped ships passing the Gulf of Tears!" Olva said, louder than she meant to. A few of the inn's patrons glanced over at her.

Bor shrugged. "Talked to some people who know Martens' lot. He's got two ships ready to sail on the morning tide, despite the ban." He picked up his cup and stretched out, reminding Olva suddenly of how she'd found him in Genny's taproom back in Ersfel. The panic of that evening came back to her.

"We have to stop them!"

"We can't."

"Then we hire a ship. We follow them—"

"I've been on that fucking elf-isle!" hissed Bor. "I saw serpents eat my crew. I saw a dozen armed men, brave bastards all, march into a grove of trees, and none of 'em came back. No ships!" He slammed his fist into the table. "I said I'd take you home once this foolishness was done, and it's done. We stay here tonight – and if Martens doesn't find us, we make for the Road before dawn. Now sit down and have a drink."

Olva stood there, unmoving except for an almost imperceptible quiver. Slowly, slowly, her hand dropped to her side.

"I gave my word to help," said Torun, "whatever course you choose. I came through the Cleft of Ard and the Crownlands – I'll guide you back that way if you wish, but the Road is long." The dwarf's voice seemed to come from far away and deep underground.

"No." Olva's hand crept past her knife, found the coin-purse. It was so much lighter than it had been when Bor had first brought it to her.

It was still heavy enough to split Bor's lip open when she hurled it full force at his face. He fell back and swore, clutching his mouth as blood gushed from it. "Bloody hell!"

"You have to do something!" shrieked Olva. "Show me where Martens is! Help me!"

"He's gone!" snarled Bor. "See sense and give up! See what you have and let the boy go!"

"He's all I have," said Olva, "and I'm not leaving him."

Bor shoved past her and strode out of the inn. For a moment, his tall frame was silhouetted against the setting sun in the doorway, and then he was gone. Someone in the crowd laughed, and it was an ugly sound. Others in the tavern got up and left, glancing back at the two women as they did so.

Olva crumpled down into her chair, suddenly drained. Torun scooped up the coin-purse and handed it back to her. "Bor rented a room for us, here. We should go there now, and bar the door."

"He . . . " began Olva, but she had no words left to her.

"I don't think he's coming back."

They ate hastily in the inn's common room, then went up the narrow stairs to the upper floor of the Blackfish. The room was cramped and filthy, with just a single bed that stank of sordid encounters. Olva lay down on it anyway. She was distantly aware of Torun sitting on the floor by the little window, staring up at the stars. The dwarf pulled out some of her books and scratched lines into the floor, curving sigils and occult diagrams. She hung a string of crystals across the window, and Olva watched them glittering in the moonlight for a while, waiting for the heavy tread of Bor's boots on the stairs.

Cu snuffled at the door for a while, scraping at it, then tried to climb up onto the bed. He was still sore from the fighting in the Fossewood, and couldn't manage to jump up. Olva reached down and hauled the animal up. Cu turned around twice, then lay down on her feet.

At dawn, she thought, she'd go back to the citadel. There were dwarves there, too – Torun could talk to them, and surely Lyulf Martens wouldn't have dwarves in his employ. Or maybe they'd go looking for Martens' warehouse . . .

Cu growled. Olva heard Bor outside the door.

And Lyulf Martens.

CHAPTER FIFTEEN

Dig anywhere in Necrad and you'd find the Pits. Alf didn't know if the elves had built his city here because of the Pits, or if Bone had dug the Pits after claiming Necrad, but the labyrinth ran everywhere under the city. Scattered throughout the endless tunnels were the breeding pits themselves, seething pools of protoplasm and necromantic fluids where new horrors congealed. Some alive, some dead, some half dead; hideous patchwork things that lurched out of the slime to spend their brief existence roaming the corridors until devoured by some bigger sibling. The Pits were part torture chamber, part laboratory, part . . . part something Alf couldn't articulate. Something that had died with Lord Bone, and good riddance to it.

Lord Bone commanded the pitspawn. The misshapen things venerated their creator, worshipping him like some twisted god. Bone had shared some of his authority with trusted Witch Elves, giving them power over the monsters, and they'd kept the pitspawn in check. When Alf first came to Necrad, the streets crawled with monsters, slithering around looking for meat they were permitted to eat. Intruders like the Nine were high on that menu.

And when Bone died, so did his hold over the spawn. The pitspawn became a danger to everyone in the city, mortal and elf alike.

They'd sealed as many exits as they could, but the flow of horrors couldn't be stopped that way. Someone had to clean up below.

"Someone", meaning Alf.

Alf and Lath.

And, in theory, the League, but there were few soldiers with the skill and courage to survive down here. Alf had Spellbreaker and Lath his magic for protection, but most League soldiers back then had nothing but mail and a wooden shield between them and death. Casualties were horrific when you matched mortals against the spawn of the city. A few times, Urien had assembled a company outfitted with magical armour salvaged from the Sanction to give Alf a chance to rest, but elite troops like that were usually needed elsewhere. No, keeping the Pits in check was Alf's job, his craft. For a long time, he'd found it satisfying to match magic sword and mortal sinew over and over against the worst horrors the city could muster, and still triumph.

If the spawn did get past him ... well, those were bad days. Without Bone's magic to sustain them, they couldn't survive very well in the surface world. Their unnatural shapes would break down, causing them to perish within weeks. But some had learned the same trick as the Witch Elves, sustaining themselves on human flesh and blood to bind themselves to life a little longer. A big pitspawn rampaging through the city could kill dozens before the League brought it down. Those were bad days indeed, but in nearly twenty years Alf could count the number of such days on the fingers of one hand.

He hesitated at the top of the steps, then cursed himself for stopping and plunged down them, too quickly. The pitspawn knew to avoid the tunnels immediately around the grove, so the familiar halls at the bottom of the stairs were empty. His eyes adjusted to the weird greenish light that trickled from between the bricks in the walls. Some sort of ectoplasm, Blaise once told him.

He took the tunnel leading west. The Pits ran underneath the whole city – you could, theoretically, get from Garrison to Liberties to Sanction through the tunnels, without passing checkpoints on the surface. All you needed to do was run faster than the monsters.

As he walked, he looked for signs of Lath. Over the years, the pair had come up with their own codes scrawled on the walls in chalk or soot or whatever came to hand, adding a new layer of meaning to the arcane sigils and ancient elven carvings. Signs that said *I've gone this way* or *danger* or *did you bring lunch?* Drawing such marks became second nature to both of them; it was the only way to navigate the labyrinth below.

All the markings he found were years old. The lad must have stopped leaving such tracks.

Lad. Lath was, what, thirty or so now? Youngest of the Nine, but still well into adulthood, even if he'd grown crooked. They'd found Lath in the woods near the village of Albury, long ago and far away. The Changeling Child, his thin body wracked with magic he couldn't control, his seething flesh shifting between shapes, changing from human to beast and back again. The people of Albury called him a monster and hunted him with dogs and boar-spears. The local priest urging them on, calling the boy an abomination in the eyes of the Intercessors.

Alf still remembered how he'd felt when he and Peir had stood guard in front of Lath, protecting the terrified boy from the mob that persecuted him. One old farmer tried thrusting his spear at Alf to get him to move, and Alf had torn the weapon from the man's hands and broken it on his knee. It was the first time Alf had used his strength and speed to defend someone else, the first time he'd felt a little like a hero. Peir showed him the way, and Lath never forgot that kindness. The Nine were the only family Lath ever had.

And that winter, when Lord Bone's armies came, the people of Albury learned what monsters really were.

It was Lath who'd brought them together, in a way. The quest had begun with Peir, of course – a dream had called him, just like the dream that Jan sent. Peir had gone to the priests at Arshoth for help in interpreting it, and it was there he'd met Jan when she was an initiate in the temple. Jan had told him about rumours of a Changeling Child who was beset by visions, and they'd set off in search of him. At the same time, the Everwood sent Laerlyn to Summerswell on a courtly visit. Part of the ceremony was that Laerlyn got to show mercy to a condemned prisoner, and she'd pardoned Berys. And Alf and Gundan were on the Road, too, mercenaries for hire. All roads met at Albury Cross.

The singers made more of it, turned it into poetry and prophecy, as if the Nine were the only possible heroes who might have saved the world. That made Alf laugh. There had been many other brave souls in the war, many others who stood against Lord Bone's invasion. Most were forgotten now, buried in graves along the Road or in cairns in the mountains – or burned during the siege of Necrad, the ash of their bodies whirling in the necromiasma. The Nine were legends because they'd survived, and all the praise was ill-placed.

Admittedly, some of the Nine really were touched with greatness. Peir was everything the tales said he was and more, a true hero. Lae really was a princess. Thurn had made himself a legend among the Wilder in his war against the Witch Elves. Even Gundan had won renown as a mercenary captain before the Nine. Alf was the only one who'd wandered into the story. Anyone could have become the Lammergeier; anyone in the right place, and stubborn enough not to die.

"Pay attention, Lammergeier," whispered Spellbreaker. "I can tell you're wool-gathering."

Alf cursed. The sword was right. He could hear breathing up ahead. A Pitspawn, from the irregularity of the breath. The spawning pits created things that had no right or reason to exist, malformed monstrosities kept alive by hunger and necromancy. Too many organs. Not enough. The weak ones, the failures, they just slipped back into the slime to dissolve, to be fodder for something more determined to survive.

This one, whatever it was, sounded strong, but clearly didn't have lungs to match its frame. He could hear it gasping for breath, this rattling gulp like a pig snorting for truffles. He couldn't see it yet, but he'd already considered strategies on how to fight it. Dance with it, exhaust it, and when it was left wheezing for air, move in and kill it.

Alf raised his shield, adjusted his grip on Spellbreaker. "It's coming," warned the sword.

The thing that came looked like it might have had some horse in it. Horse-bones, anyway. An almost-equine skeleton, wrapped in gelatinous, transparent muscle and ligament, cantered towards him. A vatgrown chimera. It was an approximation of a centaur, a humanoid torso fused to a horse body – or maybe it was two creatures sewn into one bag of flesh, horse and rider for ever bound together by vatgrown skin. He could see its lungs, connected awkwardly to something like gills that ran down its flanks. Blood vessels pulsed within the thing's form, a profusion of red veins that clustered around two lines of octopus-like suckers that ran down its neck. Sprouting from its back was large nacreous shell, a cross between a snail and a clam-shell eight feet across, shimmering in the half-light. Its face was a skinned horse's skull, the lips peeling back to reveal long fangs.

Alf stepped into an alcove, pressing into the shadows as the centaur-thing approached. He was close enough to smell the acid stench of it, to see the slime dripping from its underbelly.

His hand tightened on Spellbreaker's hilt, but he did not strike. He held his breath, and the chimera cantered by without seeing him, without stopping. It vanished into the half-light of the tunnels. He waited until the noise of its passage had died away.

"You could have struck from ambush," complained the sword, "have you give up on the whole concept of surprise?"

"No sense in fighting without need."

"You lost your nerve. Should I whistle up a linnorm and put you to a proper test?"

*

Over the years, he'd learned to tell time down here. To count heart-beats, to read the city above through its discharges and echoes. He rarely bothered to do so – what did it matter if he spent six hours in the Pits, or sixteen, or sixty? He measured his time down here in rations and sleeps and sips of water from his flask, not hours or days.

He'd been down here for a long time now, and no sign yet of Lath. Worry began to gnaw at him. The shapeshifter had a dozen lairs down here, safe places to rest where they'd cached supplies, and all the ones Alf had visited so far were empty. Long abandoned, as though Lath hadn't returned to them in years. It was as if Lath had left the Pits along with Alf.

He tried to call up his mental map of the labyrinth, a map hard-won through years of exploration, but for a moment all he could remember was the linnorm, the sabre-worm crashing through his mind, smashing his recollections of the map. Only a map of his veins as the linnorm's poison coursed through them.

But someone else had been down here, too, as often as he had. Gone every step of the way with him.

"There was an old underway, one of the first we cleared. Six levels down, full of chimeras, yeah? Blue walls. I remember blue walls. And there were some rogue Vatgrown lurking there, too. How did we get to it?"

The sword was slow to speak, but when it did it sounded inor-dinately pleased with itself. "I remember. You called it the Goat Road, naming it for all the chimeras you slew. I know the way. I'll show you."

"If you trick me, then I swear I'll chuck you into a spawning pit if it's the last thing I do. I wager the acid in there could ruin even you."

"I told you I'd help," said Spellbreaker. "The passageway you describe is not far. Two levels down. Go through the Room of Dry Fountains and take the Toothed Stairwell."

*

The passages and vaults were cramped and twisty. Not as much light. Silently, he drew on Spellbreaker's power, borrowed the gift of seeing in the dark as he crept through the dungeon. The sword heightened his other senses, too, out of some whimsical cruelty. The stink became so overwhelming that he could almost feel it flooding his airway, coating his lungs with some vile jelly. He could hear voices echoing down airshafts from the city far, far overhead. He was under some part of the Liberties.

When he stepped off the Toothed Stairwell, he could smell a change in the air. The east end of the passageway came out somewhere in the harbour, and there was a slight smell of salt, a freshness to the breeze. He turned his back on the distant sea and headed west. The Goat Road was wide and comparatively even as these underground labyrinths went, which made Alf uneasy. A quick route meant a well-travelled route down here, which meant more monsters. He moved cautiously, shield raised, sword ready. Every shadow was suspect, every pile of rubble could conceal an ambush. He crept forward, inching along the side of the corridor. The wall beside him was lined in blue stone, and covered in ancient Witch Elf carvings. Ancient monsters and demons leered as Alf watched for their descendants. Charmstones grew on the carving like pearls.

He peered at the side passages off the Goat Road, trying to recall adventures of many years ago. They all blurred in his mind. "Isn't this where those vatgrown body-snatchers laired?" They'd kidnapped people from the surface for their vats. Slice one open, and you'd find the human or dwarf bones the creature had accreted around.

"It was," said the sword, "but that was five years ago. Much may have changed."

"Aye." Something bigger and nastier could have wiped out the Vatgrown. The ersatz creatures were sword-fodder for greater foes. "If they were still around here, then they'd have shown themselves by now, right?" As soon as the words were out of his mouth, Alf regretted them. Asking Spellbreaker for reassurance! Talking to the blade like it was Lath, or Gundan, or someone he could trust to confirm his instincts.

The sword knew it, too, and laughed. "You *are* losing your edge, Lammergeier! Perhaps you should turn back – these tunnels are perilous indeed, and you are old and slow. No, better yet – press on. Charge headlong into danger. Maybe a better wielder will present themselves to me."

Alf took the side passage. The Vatgrown were clearly gone, and if Lath had established one of his supply caches along the Goat Road, then their old lair was as good a place as any. Unlike the road, the side passages were narrow and easily defensible. There'd been many times in Alf's career when he'd held a place like this, his shield an impassable barrier, guarding his friends from harm. They'd always have his back.

Ahead, a broken archway. Alf paused, and brushed his fingers over four deep parallel grooves in the stone. The marks of claws. Lath had been here, in bear-form. Alf could imagine some Vatgrown warrior trying to hold the archway, shield and skull splintering as Lath's mighty paw came down with a killing blow.

"Old," whispered the sword. Spellbreaker was right – the damage was years old.

Alf stepped through the archway into the next chamber. The remnants of broken pipes hung like viscera from the ceiling, vile fluids dripping from them. The stink was more intense here, but underneath it was a familiar smell, rank and sweaty.

"Lath?" called Alf.

There was no reply, but he knew the Changeling had been here.

He pushed on into the next chamber, up a small flight of stairs. As he entered, he caught sight of a wraith, lapping at a bloodstain splashed across the ground.

The wraith fled instantly, melting back into the shadows. Alf knelt by the bloodstain and saw that it glittered in the half-light.

Tiny ice crystals, like rubies, amid the spilled blood. He brushed his hand against the blood, feeling the unnatural cold.

An ice-spell, like the one the elf assassin had used on him.

"New," said the sword, with horrible relish.

Slowly, carefully, he circled the little room. There were claw marks — fresh ones — in the walls and floor. Other patches of unnatural cold, too, the footsteps of a dance he could retrace in his mind. A small bundle of blankets, like a nest, that smelled strongly of the Changeling. He could imagine Lath resting there, curled up like a child, but never fully asleep. Never fully off guard. The assassin creeps up on him, dagger in hand. She strikes even as Lath is changing, the blade cutting human flesh, but glancing off thick fur and bear hide. Lath fights back, but the elf's quick, agile. She dodges his blows, and . . .

"Perhaps," said the sword, "the Changeling is dead."

"She wouldn't have had a chance against Lath. Not here. She couldn't have dodged him for long."

"If she struck first, and froze him before he could change his skin, then she could have won. She would have slain you if not for my aid, remember."

Alf returned to the top of the stair and examined the last step. More scratches, smaller and fainter. "She cuts him," said Alf, "not enough to kill, but enough to slow him down. They fight, she flees back down the stairs. He chases her . . . "

"But did not catch her," said the sword. Alf's chest ached where the elf had stabbed him.

"I can't tell for sure. There's no way of knowing if this happened before or after she attacked me." Alf sighed. "Or even if it's the same elf."

"Oho! I quite like the idea of an army of assassins hunting you, Lammergeier. One would have ended you if it were not for me — imagine what a whole host might do."

"A whole army of elves tried to kill me before," said Alf, "with the Wraith-Captain at the head of it. You remember what happened next, right?"

"You had all your friends at your side then, Lammergeier. Now, you only have me."

"Shut up."

Alf grunted, then squatted down to examine the bloodstain. A lot had been spilled there, but that didn't tell him much – Lath healed quickly even without the use of potions or magic. The Changeling could tap into the very life force of the world. He brushed his hand again over the paving stones.

"Come, Lammergeier. There is nothing here. The Beast is gone, the trail gone cold." The sword sniggered to itself.

Alf ignored the sword's words. Instead, he took the sword and very lightly tapped it against the stone floor, triggering the lightest of destructive pulses as he did so. A wave of energy thundered through the little room, shaking the paving stones like a quake.

"Subtle. Now every pitspawn within a mile knows you're down here."

One of the paving stones had moved more than its neighbours, leaping higher when he'd shaken it. Alf crossed the room and used the sword to lever the stone up, ignoring the usual protests. Lath always liked to hide supply caches through the Pits – a trick Alf had taught him.

Beneath the stone was a hollow. Alf bent down and methodically removed the contents. A bundle of papers, covered in Lath's child-like handwriting. Alf peered at them, but he couldn't make out the words in the dim light.

"Can you read these?" He held the sword's gemstone-eye over one of the pages.

"It's a magical incantation," replied Spellbreaker. "I cannot decipher it . . . but one mark is akin to the sigil of my master. Show me the rest of the scrolls."

"Forget it. Blaise'll know." Alf rolled the papers up and carefully tucked them into his jerkin, beneath his mail shirt. This clue, he swore, would not be taken from him.

"I tell you, don't trust the wizard. He sees you as nothing but a weapon, Lammergeier. A tool."

Next, a few healing potions. Alf stowed most of them in his pack, and absently drank the last, feeling the warmth of the healing magic work its way into his tired muscles and joints. The ache in his side subsided, and he bent down and removed the last and largest bundle. It was a hooded cloak, long and black, the kind Berys favoured when she was young. It was old and travel-stained. The cloak was wrapped around several other items, and Alf carefully unpacked them.

A sorcerer's skullcap. A dwarf-forged breastplate. A string of prayer beads. A silken gown, diaphanous and elven-fair. Alf's good dress shirt, the one he wore to council meetings.

"Lath," Alf whispered, "what is this? What have you done?"

"Who knows why you humans do anything?" snapped the sword. "Brute beasts without purpose."

"Shut up."

He unwrapped the last of the treasures. A knight's helm, broken and blackened. Alf remembered when it was brightly polished, when it shone in the sun.

When Peir wore it.

The helm he'd keep in memory of his—

"Did you bury Peir in his armour?" asked the sword.

"What?" snapped Alf, irritated at the sword for disturbing his thoughts.

"Did you bury the paladin in his armour?"

"What difference does it make?"

"If he was wearing his helmet when you buried him, then Lath can only have obtained the helmet by opening the grave. So, was Peir wearing this helm when you buried him?"

"I can't remember." The memory of that day was still raw and painful.

"Think, wielder!"

"Everything was burned," said Alf, slowly. "We scraped together what we could. I don't remember the helmet being there. Peir knew we couldn't defeat Lord Bone. He knew we'd all die. So, he told us to go. He made us leave him. He'd keep Bone in place, and we ... and I had to go down and break the vessel."

"I remember," said the sword. Its eye glittered. "I fought against you, Lammergeier. You used me to shatter my master's vessel of power. You used me to murder him."

"I used you," said Alf, thickly, "to kill my friend."

"The paladin asked you to do it, you said so yourself. You were all willingly complicit in the crime, all so convinced of your own sickening righteousness that you were falling over one another to sacrifice yourselves! I was the one who suffered! I was the one who was forced to destroy my own creator!" The sword rumbled. "Now even his remains are stolen? And for what? So you barbarians could strip the carcass of his city like insects? So you could rot away in peace?"

Alf snarled and threw the sword down. It struck the ground, and another pulse of force rippled out from it, shaking the stones. Alf could feel the energy shiver through his bones, rattling his teeth – and everything nearby had felt it, too. Without the sword's magic, Alf could barely see in the dim light. He stooped and felt around until he touched Spellbreaker's pommel. He strained to pick the sword up, but it was impossibly heavy, as if welded to the floor. He kicked it instead, and it spun across the room, cackling.

In the distance, growing louder, the sound of footsteps. Hoofbeats – the centaur-chimera he'd seen early. Alf pressed himself against the wall again. Even if the creature looked through the broken archway into the anteroom at the foot of the stairs, it might not see him. The hoofbeats drew nearer, and the air was filled with the acid stink again.

There's no one here, thought Alf. *Move on.*

The chimera paused outside the archway. It sniffed the air – then stepped into the antechamber, bowing its head to avoid the broken pipes hanging from the ceiling. The shell on the chimera's back scraped against rusty metal.

It halted at the foot of the stairs. The creature was too big to fit easily up the narrow corridor. Instead, it turned, and the clam-shell on its back split open, wet and slimy. Thin, wiry tendrils tipped with purple fronds emerged, like some strange anemone. A dozen or so tendrils snaked up the stairs, probing the air. One brushed against Spellbreaker, and the chimera hissed in triumph. The tendril began to wrap around the hilt of the sword . . .

Alf stepped forward and ground the tip of the tendril beneath his boot. The chimera howled in pain, and the other tendrils whipped about. One caught Alf across the ear, and pain shot through his head as if it had injected hot lead into every hollow in his skull. He threw himself into the far corner, as far from the creature as possible. He could hear a terrible roaring sound, like he was drowning, and the room swam about him.

Tendrils reached for him again. He grabbed the silken gown and wrapped it around his hand for protection, then caught one, two, three of the tendrils as they whipped by, the chimera's stingers flailing blindly. He slammed the edge of his shield against them, over and over until they frayed and burst, yellow liquid spraying, the chimera yowling and roaring. It came for him then, trying to force its way up the narrow stairs, cramming its horse-skeleton body into a space too narrow for it to pass, scraping its hide raw against the walls.

Alf found the paving slab he'd dislodged. Solid stone, nearly two feet across. Grunting with the strain, he lifted it and hurled it down the stairs. There was a wet crack as the stone smashed squarely into the chimera. The creature collapsed, winded, its lungs heaving.

The Lammergeier didn't give it a chance to recover. Alf rushed down the stairs and tore a length of rusty pipe from the ceiling. It was not a sword out of legend. It was not wrought by elven-smith, nor girded with charmstones. But it was sturdy enough for the work.

When it was done, Alf walked wearily back up the stairs. He took Peir's helmet and bundled it back up in the cloak with the other items from the cache. Despite all the tombs he'd looted over the course of his adventures, he'd never thought he would be gathering grave goods of his friends. He touched his ear, which was red and tender and so swollen he could barely hear the sword's voice as it called to him.

"Wielder," said Spellbreaker, "pick me up."

Alf ignored the blade's call.

"I was testing you. You need to be sharp."

Alf wiped the last of the chimera's ichor from the pages of the unknown spell.

"It was an accident. You cast me down, and that called the chimera."

Slowly, he unbuckled his sword belt.

"I was angry. I mourn my maker. Am I not entitled to such thoughts? You have used my wrath in battle often enough."

Alf picked up the sword and sheathed it in the belt's scabbard. He took a scrap of torn silk and began to bind the blade in place to silence it.

"Enough of your poison," Alf muttered. "Enough of your treachery." The ogre on the High Moor. The elf-child in the Liberties. Now the chimera. Enough.

"Wielder, this is folly! You need me! You are a fool, Lammergeier, if you think—"

He drew the silk tight, silencing the blade. The demon eye blazed with impotent fury.

"Enough of you."

He bundled the sword up with the rest of his treasures. Without its magic, he had to brave the tunnels back to the surface by touch and memory, but he found his way there nonetheless.

"Bor the Rootless?" asked the stranger. His voice was barely audible over the cheers of the Highfield crowd as knights clashed at the joust. Bor, having little interest in watching rich brats rattle each other's bones, had found an ale tent instead. He'd been contentedly sloughing into a doze before the stranger disturbed him. Somewhere off in the distance, a tuneless bard was mangling "Two Swords at Dawn".

Bor looked up, shading his eyes against the summer sun. "Who's asking?"

"Hark," said the stranger. He was a huge man, mighty and in fighting trim. His armour was of dwarven-steel, and his shield bore the device of a black bird. A sword was belted at his side, and it was coal-black, too. His face was hidden behind a greathelm. "I have a task for you." His voice, deeper than the delvings of dwarves.

It was warm in the late summer sun, and Bor was pleasantly drunk – almost drunk enough to ignore the constant itch of the ivy choker beneath his skin. "Not interested."

"I am told they call you Bor the Broken. That you lost your courage when there was magic on the field."

"Who says that?" snarled Bor. He clenched his fists, started to scramble to his feet, anger and resentment mixing with the ale in a violent brew — and the stranger grabbed him, quicker than Bor's addled eyes could follow, and forced him to the ground in an instant. Pain shot through his wrist as the stranger twisted it.

"I want you to find my kin," growled the stranger. "Look for the house of Long Tom in Ersfel. Give them this." He dropped a heavy bag of coin at Bor's feet. The mercenary snatched it up — and the big man speared the loop of the bag's drawstring with his sword, pinning it to the ground. A black sword, of Necrad forged . . .

"I'll do it!"

"The house of Long Tom, in the village of Ersfel," growled the stranger. "My folk dwell there, if they still live. Give them this package. Take nothing from it. Or the Lammergeier shall break thy bones, understand?"

The stranger released him. Bor lay there, bewildered, while all around him wheeled the sounds of the fair.

"Sir Lammergeier! We've been looking for you! The tourney is about to begin."

"I cannot fight today. I am called elsewhere."

"Please, it would be such an honour to fight alongside one of the Nine. Surely no errand can be so pressing that—"

"This one is. You shall hear songs of it, no doubt, when the deed is done, but for now there must be silence."

Bor lifted his head. There was the stranger — and all around him knights and lords in their finery. Nobles that Bor would never dare even look at the eye, all bowing and pleading for a moment of the man's time.

Lammergeier, they called the stranger. One of the Nine.

Bor rolled over and clutched the stranger's purse, whispering an oath to it. He'd do as the Lammergeier commanded. Take on the quest.

Bor watched Lyulf Martens' men drag Torun and Olva out of the Inn of the Blackfish. Olva hung limply, a fresh welt of a bruise across her forehead visible in the light from one of the guard's lamps. Torun was still conscious, but two men had hoisted her up to carry her, so no matter how much she thrashed and kicked and twisted, she could not escape. Martens' covered wagon waited just outside, and the guards threw the two women into it. Frantic yelping came from somewhere beyond the inn.

"You swore you wouldn't hurt them," said Bor.

"I swore I would not kill them," said Martens mildly. "And I will not. Why would I? She's the Lammergeier's sister, as valuable a hostage as her son. I have you to thank, Bor, for bringing that to my attention." He held out a purse of coins to Bor. It was the same bag the Lammergeier had given him, the same coins he'd brought to Olva. "You've earned this, I'd say, and more beside." He added another few coins of considerable worth to the bag, then handed it to Bor.

"I didn't do it for the money," protested Bor.

"I'll take it back, then, shall I?" said Martens, lightly.

"Where is the boy?"

"Safe." Martens extended one finger, showing off the jewelled ring he wore. The colour of the gemstone was the same as the colour of the leaves of the ivy collar. "Fortune's wheel turns ever on, my friend. It exalts the humble and brings low the mighty – and if you hang on long enough, then you can go around for a second turn. I know our last partnership did not go quite as hoped, but, still, I wish you had more patience."

"It was your fault, Lyulf. You sent us too close to the elf-isle." Bor glared at his former employer, his hand straying to his sword-hilt. Martens' guards glared, but the smuggler raised his hands in a gesture of calm.

"Bor knows what will happen if he raises his sword to me. He will not be foolish a second time." Martens flexed his ring-finger, and for a moment, the ivy choker spasmed around Bor's neck. The mercenary released his sword. "It was terrible what happened to you, certainly," continued Martens, "and I'll take my share of the blame. But I had little choice – *she* set my quotas, and if I was to meet them I couldn't wait for a moonless night to sneak by. If it's any consolation, Bor, you are not the only one to run afoul of her greed. Things will change soon. I'm sure I could find a place for you."

"Give me your word," said Bor, "they'll come to no harm."

"While they're under my protection, they'll be safe. After that, it's in the lap of the Intercessors." Martens shrugged. "Now, what do you say to my offer?"

"Go to hell."

Martens smiled. "I could make you, you know," he said, softly, rubbing the ring on his finger. "But only a fool relies on magic. Better to work with people who freely choose to serve. Brighter days are coming, and I hope one day we can be friends again." He called out to his men. "Let's go." The wagon left with a jolt, rolling down the narrow alleyways towards the harbour.

It was done.

Wearily, Bor made his way around to the back of the inn to find one of Martens' boys shoving a spear into the narrow gap between a stack of barrels and the wall. From the barking, Cu had taken refuge in there. When the boy raised the spear again, Bor grabbed the end of the shaft and pulled him back.

"Leave the beast," he ordered. The boy ran off.

Cu's frantic barking became a low whimper. Bor slumped down against the wall. Softly, he beat the back of his head against the rough timber of the inn.

"What else was I to do?" he asked the dog. "She wouldn't stop. I told her to go home, and she wouldn't listen. She'd have got herself killed on some stupid plan. And got me killed, too, if I'd gone with her. A man can't fight magic. You just can't. You can't." The decision to go to Martens had seemed so clear only minutes earlier. The smuggler already knew Olva was still pursuing him; it was only a matter of time before his men caught her. Cutting a deal was the sensible thing to do for everyone. It was all clear when he repeated it in his mind, but when he tried to explain it, his arguments turned to wet sand and fell apart.

He closed his eyes. "I told her. I told her. The Lammergeier can't say I didn't try." From somewhere off in the darkness of the restless port town, Bor heard a shout, and flinched. What was he afraid of — that the Lammergeier would suddenly appear and punish him? The Lammergeier was far away in Necrad on a throne of silver. That was why he'd paid Bor to deliver the coins. If the Lammergeier wanted to be a damn hero like in the stories, saving the day and vanquishing evil, then where was he? Why had he cursed Bor with this?

"I did what she paid me to do," he snarled, and Cu whimpered again. Furiously, Bor tore at his shirt until he fished out the coin-purse. "What I was hired to do. I sell my sword, aye? She paid me to bring her here," he told Cu, "not to walk off a cliff with her. I should have just kept the money when I got it. I told her to go home. I told her. What sort of an idiot doesn't listen to reason?"

The dog emerged from its hiding place, miserable and bedraggled. Shallow gashes on its muzzle caked its fur with blood. Cu sniffed at Bor with clear distaste.

"I told her," he said again. "She should be thanking me. I saved her bloody life, didn't I? I did all I could, but a man can't fight magic. I did all I could. I'm not . . . "

With an inarticulate roar, he flung the coin-purse across the yard. It vanished into the shadows and landed with a splash in some muddy corner. "To hell with them all." Bor stood and stumbled down the Road.

Reluctantly, tail curled beneath its furry body, the dog followed him.

PART TWO

"Tell me a story," said the dying girl.

"I will tell you a forbidden story," said Thurn.

Once, there was only forest that covered the land from sea to sea. A living world, and a dying world, for these things are the same. To live is to die. We cannot have the one without the other – only the elves have that.

The forest was full of beasts, and they are just like the animals who live in the forests now, the ones you know well. They lived and rutted and bore young and died, just like they do today. All things that live must also die – all save one.

The elves dwelt there, too. They were the firstborn. From the stars, they learned to speak, and they named all the things of earth. They named the hills and the mountains, the rivers and the seas.

When the elves came upon the beasts of the forest, they hunted the animals for sport, and killed them.

And the beasts died. To the elves, this was a strange and terrible thing.

You see, the elves are bound to the world; they can never leave it. Not even the perishing of their bodies ends them. It is the doom of the elves never to die.

And because the elves did not know Death, they feared it above all other things.

Among the elves, there was a wizard. Elf-magic comes from the stars, and so all the elves have magic, for they love the stars and walk beneath them every night. This wizard was powerful beyond measure. On learning of Death, he set himself a task greater than any he had yet performed. He worked for many years – slow are the weavings of the elves, but they have all the time in the world to work their magic. In time, he made a spell to bind Death.

This spell made our grandmothers and grandfathers, too – they were the scrapings left in the pot, the bones left after a meal. But what the wizard sought was the first thing he conjured: a woman, the mother of us all, and she was Death.

The elves locked Death away in a tower of ice in the uttermost north, and declared they had conquered Death. She would never escape the tower, and the elves would never have to face that which they feared above all other things.

They drove the other humans they had made into the forests, or set them to labour, and thought of them as naught but beasts who could chatter the semblance of words, like a jackdaw.

But now that thing they feared had a face, and a name. She had skin and bones, feet and fingers. Bright her eyes, clever her tongue, wise her thought. She lived, even though she was Death. And for she was now part of the living world, she could call upon a new magic, earth magic, a magic of root and branch, blood and bone, birth and death. Her magic was quick and deep-rooted, stronger than elven-spells.

Through the earthpower, Death broke free from the prison of ice and went a-hunting. She chased the elves through the forest, and drove them from their city. They fled their lands in the north and crossed the sea in terror. In her wrath, Death tore down the mountains and sundered the seas; in her kindness, she sowed new forests in the gardens of the elves. From her blood, she made monsters. Lightning was her spear, thunder her laughter.

Happy it was to live in those days, when Death was loved by all, and she loved us in return.

CHAPTER SIXTEEN

Rough hands grabbed Olva, twisting her around, pinning her in the bed. She bucked and fought with all her might, animal panic flooding her. Her elbow caught one of the men in the face. Something gave way, and blood sprayed over her face.

"Thow!" he swore. Then he was on top of her, and the fear filled her so completely that it felt as though there was no room in her body for *her* any more, and she was observing it all as if through a grimy window. Figures moving in the half-light from the dying fire. The way her attacker moved reminded her, horribly, of Thomad back on her farm in Ersfel, and the way he'd truss up a pig before butchering it. Quick, practised movements. He had done this before to other people, and for all that Olva struggled she did not even slow him down

Cu was barking furiously, loud enough to shake the heavens. Someone – Bor! – grabbed him by the collar and wrestled him downstairs. Other attackers came for Torun. She keened in terror, and did not resist when they put a knife to her throat.

Then, a rushed journey through the streets, rattling over rain-slick cobblestones, like they were falling into some night-black abyss. Olva could hear Cu's frantic barks fading in the distance as the wagon carried them away from the inn. The streets of Ellsport were a dark chasm. They passed under a stone arch into a yard, and from there they were carried into a building. *Warehouses and workshops, too*, Bor had said.

She glimpsed crates and boxes, stacks of merchandise. Barrels of beer and salt pork, sacks of grain, bundles of fleeces. *A warehouse.*

And people, huddled and scared, heads bowed. Rows of them, roped together. Chains and cages. She remembered Bor's tales of selling blood to the vampire elves.

Oh, by the Intercessors. This IS a warehouse. She twisted her head, trying to see out, praying and fearing she'd glimpse Derwyn's face, but there was no sign of her son. She strained against the bonds holding her wrists and ankles, but succeeded only in digging the coarse rope into her skin.

The wagon stopped and the driver dismounted. She could smell the steam off the horses' flanks, the smell of the stables mixing with the rank stench of the prison cells, and nearby, rotting seaweed and salt from the sea. A guard appeared for a moment at the back of the wagon and peered in, then vanished again.

Olva wriggled to the back of the wagon, dragging herself on her elbows and shoulders. Her heart pounded in terror that the guard would return and find her.

She froze. Martens' voice, again, in conversation with another man.

"They are not to be touched, understand? No spoiling in any way."

"Don't insult me, Martens. You'd do well to remember who you're talking to. I'm not one of your cut-throats. I'll keep them safe. Who is she, then, if not for the leeches?"

"Never you mind. This comes all the way from the Lady, understand?"

"If it's so important, why not bring them yourself?"

"Because I like you, Abran. And the dwarf comes of wealthy stock, I'm told, and should fetch some measure of ransom. You can keep that as a bonus. I won't even charge you a finder's fee."

"And where will I deliver the other one? You tell me to treat 'em as passengers, but you bring 'em in here like cargo. Where are they bound?"

Greatly daring, Olva levered herself up to look over the lip of the wagon. There, not ten feet away, sat Lyulf Martens. He was hunched over a writing desk, and was scribbling on a page with a fine quill. The letters vanished as soon as he wrote them, leaving the paper bare. He used her knife as a paperweight to keep the page flat. Next to him was another man, grey-bearded and barrel-chested. Both men were flanked by armed guards; Olva recognised another of Martens' men from the Fossewood. The guards closely watched each other warily, hands resting on sword-hilts.

"Oh, your arrival will be marked," said Martens. "Don't worry about that. Just make sure you're ready to leave with the morning tide."

"I'll set my own course. You'd do well to remember your place, too. I've heard tell that she's not too well pleased with you." Abran took a step forward, towering over Lyulf. Martens' men bristled, but the merchant was unruffled. He scribbled a final message, then folded the paper up and sealed it. He pressed his ring into the soft red wax to mark it, then handed it to Abran.

"Give that to the Lady when you arrive." He tossed Olva's knife in the air, caught it, and slipped it into his pocket.

"What is it?" asked Abran suspiciously.

"Why, Abran, you of all people should know that certain things are only for the initiated. The morning tide, and no mistake."

A hint of pink licked over the eastern horizon as the sailors dragged Olva and Torun on board the ship. Olva didn't struggle – whatever peril this journey held, at least it was bringing her on the same sea-road that Derwyn followed. By sea, they'd be in Necrad in days instead of the weeks it would take by the landward route.

Ellsport dwindled behind them as the blue sails caught the wind. The Road west as a black thread along the coast. They left Ellsport behind them, and Summerswell, and all that Olva had ever known. The deck shifted and rolled beneath her feet, every swell of the sea reminding her that nothing was certain any more, nothing was solid.

The captain of this ship was the man she'd seen last night, talking to Martens. Then, he'd seemed less of a rogue than Lyulf Martens, and Olva allowed herself to hope that he was not wholly evil. He stood by the rail, making the ritual offering of wine and candlelight. He moved with terrible solemnity, tipping the grail-cup of wine over the side, then lighting a candle stub and placing it in a little carved boat, smaller than the palm of his hand.

"Blessed ones," he prayed, "watch over us and send us fair winds. And if our day of doom is at hand, intercede and change our fate."

He handed the boat to a young boy – younger than Derwyn, thought Olva. The child took the boat, clambered down a rope that had been lowered to the murky water, then set the little vessel afloat, bobbing on the morning tide.

"Useless," muttered a nearby sailor, "what we need is a rune-marked keel, and witch-sails to match. Proper magic." But he kept his voice low.

Through blood-crusted lips, Olva offered her own prayer to the Intercessors. "Watch over Derwyn," she whispered. "Keep him safe. Keep him until I find him."

She had no prayer left for herself.

The captain turned to the two captives. "Call me Abran. The safety of this ship is in my care, and theirs," he said, nodding down at the little candle-boat, "but your safety is in yours. Lyulf Martens tells me you are to be brought to Necrad, and not to be harmed. Now, I could have you chained in the hold as cargo for the duration of the crossing. It would not be pleasant for you, but you would be secure. Or, if you give me your word that you will not try to do any-thing foolish, I shall put you in a cabin, and treat you as passengers. Look, we brought what we could of yours from the Blackfish." One of Abran's men, a lank-haired fellow of Mulladale stock, big and beefy, came up with a sack over his shoulder. Olva's walking stick poked out from one end. "Not the dog, I fear. The beast had teeth. But do I have your word?"

"Answer me one question, and I'll swear," said Olva. "Martens also took my son Derwyn prisoner. Do you know what's become of him? Is he on board, too?"

"You two were the only ones Martens singled out for special treatment. He gave no such word about the rest. But swear, and I shall see if your son is among them."

"I swear," said Olva, hastily. Too hastily, it seemed, for the captain frowned.

"An oath given lightly is no bond at all. Swear properly, and I'll ask that the Intercessors witness it."

"Are you a priest, then," scoffed Olva, "to call on the Intercessors?"

"I am. A soldier, once, and now a criminal, but first and always a priest of the Intercessors. And here, they still speak to me. I know, for all my sins, that I am still in their favour." He murmured a prayer under his breath. "Now swear."

"I swear on my brother's name," she said, "the Lammergeier himself. I swear by Aelfric the Lammergeier that I won't try to escape if you bring us to Necrad. And may the holy Intercessors strike me down if I'm lying."

Unlike the guards in the League tower, there was no scorn or disbelief in Abran's eyes. "I knew the Lammergeier, a little. He's a worthy man. He saved my life when a Pitspawn caught me in the siege." Abran drew back his sleeve, displaying old, puckered scars left by gigantic fangs. "But the Lammergeier's gone from Necrad, I hear. I've heard it said he's wandering in the wilds."

"He was in Highfield not two weeks ago," replied Olva. "My son went in search of him, and fell into Martens' clutches."

Abran nodded. "You have my sympathies, but it's not the Lammergeier I answer to. Still, his name is one to swear by, right enough. I shall see you safe to Necrad, and bring you to the Lady myself." He seemed about to say more, but one of his crew interrupted him.

The Lady. Lyulf Martens had mentioned that name last night, in a way that made Olva think of some queen of the underworld. Olva imagined a dreadful Witch Elf, cold and cruel.

"Captain?" The Mulladale sailor had dug into the sack of their belongings, and he held up the charmstone Olva had taken from Martens' guard.

"This I will take," said Abran, "as part payment." He drew his sword and slotted the charmstone into a reliquary built into the hilt.

"And these," said the sailor. He held some of Torun's books.

Abran examined them, and his face grew dark. "These are forbidden texts," he said, "the study of magic is restricted – and, worse, there are references to the unholy earthpower, too. These . . . these you cannot bring." He handed the book back to the Mulladaler. "Throw them overboard."

Torun squealed. Olva tried to restrain the dwarf, but Torun tore free and charged forward, bowling both men over. She scooped up her book and ran. She almost made it as far as the railing before the sailors caught her and dragged her back. They tore the books from her hands and made sport of destroying them, ripping out the pages and throwing them at the gulls, or kicking a book up and down the deck until its spine broke. Pages blew about in the breeze as Abran looked on impassively.

The Mulladaler hoisted Torun up, too. "I hear dwarves cannot swim, but sink right to the bottom."

Abran drew himself up, slowly, and with his terrible slow, solemn tread he walked across the deck to Torun.

"Don't hurt her!" pleaded Olva.

"I am bound to bring you to Necrad. The dwarf is another matter," said Abran darkly. "I cannot afford distractions when we cross the Gulf of Tears. I am minded to be rid of her. Dwarves are bad luck."

Olva's eye lit on the young boy with the candle-stub. "You said you were a priest. You said you still spoke to the Intercessors. How can we have bad luck if they're watching over us? Or were you lying when you said you were faithful?"

"Let her go," order Abran. The sailors released Torun. The dwarf scrambled after the last few sheets of her book, desperately snatching at them.

Abran raised his sword and activated the magic of the charm-stone. A bolt of lightning arced from the sword's tip and caught Torun mid-leap. The dwarf fell twitching to the deck.

"She can stay," said Abran, "but if she defies me again, I will not be so forgiving."

The cabin was cramped, with little furniture other than two narrow bunks, but Olva guessed it was vastly better than conditions on the deck below. She'd glimpsed the living cargo of the vessel – dozens of wretched prisoners, huddled in the reeking lower portion of the ship. Bor had warned that Martens and his kind traded in blood for the Witch Elves.

The sailors laid Torun's battered body on the lower bunk and withdrew. What had the dwarf been thinking to attack their captor? Books were valuable things, certainly, but the dwarf's treasures were gone and there was no getting them back. Olva couldn't help but admire her courage, though.

Olva found a rag and a little pitcher of water, and gently dabbed Torun's bloodied face. It reminded her of cleaning up Derwyn's injuries after he'd got into trouble back home.

She wiped away a smear of blood from Torun's neck, and her thoughts turned to Bor. She'd tended his injuries, too, in the Fossewood. In the songs, that was how the Nine had tamed the Beast Lath – they'd shown him kindness for the first time, and been rewarded with loyalty. She'd shown Bor kindness, and he'd betrayed her! She took her anger out on the rag, wringing it like the neck of a chicken. She wished it was Bor's blood staining her hands, not poor Torun's. She'd been a fool to travel with Bor. Olva cursed herself for letting her fear of the Road get the better of her. Old customs based on the commandments of the Intercessors forbade leaving one's homeland without good cause, and there was great wisdom there. If Derwyn had obeyed that custom, they'd still be safe at home in Ersfel.

Torun stirred and muttered to herself in Dwarvish. She batted away the damp cloth, then fell back into unconsciousness.

Olva sat back and stared at the dwarf's face. She'd only known Torun for a few days, but already she felt a closeness to her. She'd heard that friendships were forged quickly on the road, and that they ran deep. Shared perils and shared hardships made for closeness. Certainly, there were people in Ersfel that Olva had known all her life, but if she never saw them again, she would not care a fig. Perhaps it was the loneliness of the Road that forged such friendships — beyond a handful of distant kinfolk and a few others in Highfield, Olva knew no one in the wide world. Out here she was alone, a stranger to the world. She could be anyone out here, if she chose. In Ersfel she was Galwyn Foster's widow, she was the last of Long Tom's brood, she was a cautionary tale about the balanced scales of fortune, she was marked by tragedy. Out here, no one knew her. Out here, Alf wasn't Alf, he wasn't the big lad, he was Sir Lammergeier of the Nine, the Hero of Necrad.

Blood ties endured, though. Blood ran deeper than everything. Even if she took on another name, another life, she'd still be Derwyn's mother, Alf's sister. When the boy was born, she remembered Galwyn lulling him to sleep by reciting the line of Forsters. The Forster family were far from the aristocracy, but they were distantly related to the Lords of Summerswell, many generations back, and Galwyn remembered them all. He'd been so proud to have a son, each generation a link in a chain stretching into the forgotten past, the unknowable future. It gave him a sense of place, of comfort.

She stood and walked the length of the little cabin, feeling the deck heave and fall beneath her. Every rolling wave, every gust of wind that shivered the boat carried them further north, towards whatever fate Lyulf Martens had set for them.

"Why didn't you come home, Alf?" she whispered aloud. If only Alf had come home, instead of sending Bor, then she'd never had lost Derwyn, never ended up in this cell. But Alf had chosen his friends over her, chosen his companions of the Road over his blood kin. He'd gone back to the Nine, and again he'd sent only sorrow home to Ersfel.

"I should have known," Olva to herself. "I did know. I was a fool. Everyone told me Bor wasn't to be trusted. But I was too afraid to go on my own." She dug her nails into her palms in frustration, squeezing her hands.

" . . . Lammergeier . . . " came a weak whisper from the bunk. Torun's eyes were half open.

"Ssh. Rest."

"Am resting. In bed," whispered Torun. "Water?"

Olva let her sip from the pitcher. The rolling of the ship caused half the water to spill down the dwarf's shirt. Torun coughed, wiped her mouth and sat up a little. "The Lammergeier trusted Bor," she said, "so if you're a fool, then so was he."

Olva scoffed. "Alf was never the best judge of who to put his faith in. Back when we were young, he was easy to lead astray. I don't know how often other children got him in trouble — and then he'd get angry, and someone would get hurt. But everyone else told me not to bother with Bor." She drummed her fingers off the wooden frame of the bunk. "He wanted to rob you. The night after you rescued us — after you saved his life! — he wanted to steal what we could from your camp and run off into the night. I should have seen him then for what he was."

"My family would have thanked him," said Torun. "They tried everything they could think of to make me give up pursuing magic.

They called me foolish, and childish, and mad. Magic is not for dwarves. If he'd taken my books and notes and everything, then . . ." She patted her hair, which was still frizzled from the lightning blast. She gingerly probed the burned patch on her side, and winced. "Maybe you shouldn't have stopped him."

"Don't be silly. You've as much right as any to pursue your heart's desire."

"If everyone did that, then the world would fall apart. So they told me in the Dwarfholt," mumbled Torun. Her head fell back onto the thin pillow as if defeated. "Chasing dreams is only for a very few people."

"I don't know. Maybe knowing you have a heart's desire is enough to justify chasing it." Olva rubbed her temples. "I don't know if I ever had one of my own. When you have a child, their dreams become yours." Even as she said that, doubt crept into her voice. "All you want is — is to do what's best for them."

The dwarf snorted. "What'll you do when you find Derwyn?" Torun asked, slurring her words. Her eyes were bleary. Olva sat down on the dwarf's bunk and dabbed at her bruised head with a water-soaked cloth again. She appreciated the way the dwarf spoke, the certainty. *When* you find him, not *if*. Bor would have said *if*.

"If we'd found him in the Fossewood, then I'd have marched him back home to Ersfel. I'd have skinned him alive. Punished him until he never dared set foot outside the valley again." Olva shrugged. "Now . . . I don't know."

"My family never came after me. They interfered with my studies. They took away my notes and the charmstones I bought. They demanded I behave. They tried to send me to a . . . nunnery, I suppose you'd call it. Or a madhouse. A place where the errant children of respectable families go to hide their shame. But after I walked out of the door of the Dwarfholt, that was it. They didn't chase after me, or send anyone to fetch me home. All they care about is their standing in the Dwarfholt."

Did Olva care about Ersfel? She'd lived there all her life, and never known anywhere else. There were many parts of the village that she liked, certainly. The excited bleating of the newborn goats in the yard in spring. Shafts of low light spearing through the holywood in late autumn. Sitting by the hearth on a cold winter's night, knowing the larder was well stocked and there was a good store of firewood – but what she cherished about the village was its predictability. Few strangers ever came down the road from Highfield, and no monsters had troubled the valley since the war.

Was it home or a hiding place for her? And what was it for Derwyn?

"My family's prob'ly right," said Torun. "I've spent years chasing sorcery, and I'm no closer now than I was when I started. There's no magic in me. But it would all be worth it, I think, worth all the shame and all the work, to just once see real magic being done. To see Master Blaise cast one of the great spells! To see ... to see wonders ... " Her dark eyes drifted closed.

"Alf sent me money," said Olva. "I don't want his charity. But if we ever get the chance, I'll ask this favour of him: to speak to Blaise on your behalf. The songs all say that Blaise is this great wizard, and everyone knows he quarrelled with the College in Summerswell. I bet he'll help you."

Torun was half asleep and did not reply, but the widest grin that a dwarf ever wore spread across her battered face.

Olva climbed quietly into the upper bunk. She listened to the unfamiliar sounds of wind and wave, the terrifying creaking of the ship. Ersfel was solid ground and solid walls; this ship was a fragile bundle of twigs floating on an abyss. She tugged the thin blanket around herself and tried to sleep, but no rest came. She tossed and turned, worrying about what would become of them in Necrad, worrying about where Derwyn might be across the wild sea. She kicked at the blanket, missing the comforting weight of Cu.

"Go to sleep, human," muttered Torun dreamily.

"I can't."

"Try . . . head injury. Works very well," slurred the dwarf.

"What was in your books?"

"Star charts. Maps of earth currents. Lodestones. Magic . . . The world's ruled by invisible forces, only some people can see 'em and command 'em, and others can't. Secret powers, waiting to be woken with the right word."

"And if you could, if you know those words, what would you do with magic?"

The dwarf was silent for several moments, and Olva suspected she'd fallen back asleep. Then, in low tones, Torun began:

In the beginning, mighty giants made the world. They were so powerful that they could accomplish wonders with ease. One dug his hands into the earth and piled up the mountains; another filled the hole with ocean. They made things for the love of making, without thought beforehand or doubt after. They made the sun because they were cold, and the night because they were tired. The greatest of the giants was named Az, and he was the greatest because he invented the naming of things, and the speaking of them. First he named himself, and then he spoke his name, and then he sang of his great design, and the other giants harkened. They shaped all the world as we know it; they carved the coasts and planted the forests, they built the mountains and dug the valleys. Many things were made in those days after the first dawn.

But the other giants grew lazy, and old. One by one, they lay down. Earth covered them, and darkness claimed them, and Az piled stones on their graves. Now he was all alone, and the world was silent.

Az did not despair. He invented runes to remember the names of his friends, and then he dug up gemstones and cast them into the night sky to draw runes among the stars. In time, Az found that things were growing on the rotting corpses of the other giants, and from them he cultivated a new generation of companions to continue his work. These new giants, though, had never seen the old world, the formless chaos before the dawn where nothing existed. They knew only the world Az and the other first giants had made, and though they were accomplished in thought and craft, they could only build on the foundations laid by their elders. And because their ambition was smaller, so too was their reach and stature.

In time, these giants too laid down their tools and fell asleep under stone, leaving Az all alone. Again, with his magic he raised a third generation of giants from the rotting remains of the second, and instructed these new acolytes in the craft. But Az saw that these new giants were even smaller than the ones who had gone before, and that while the same love of the craft burned in their hearts, they too were circumscribed by the work that had already been done.

Thus the cycle continues, from that day to this. Now the giants of old have become very, very small, and mortals call us dwarves, the little people. And they are right to do so – we dwarves cannot hope to equal the works of old, no matter how hard we try.

But we remember that in our veins flows the blood of giants.

"That's a sad story," muttered Olva.

"I've heard humans say that before," said Torun, "but I do not find it so. I think it's a challenge. If I do something no dwarf has ever done before, then I'll be the equal of any of the giants of old."

"What happened to Az?"

"He went away. It's said that he watches us."

"Like the Intercessors. They watch over us." The ship rolled as a wave caught it, and Olva felt a stab of panic. The tales of the priests had always been a comfort to her, especially in the years after Galwyn's death when Derwyn was a young boy. Her house back in Ersfel was close to the village shrine, and she'd liked the idea that there were kindly spirits guarding her son from harm. But there were no such spirits on the open ocean.

"Not *over* the dwarves," corrected Torun. Her voice seemed to Olva to come from far away. "The legend says that Az is always contemplating his work, and the work of his disciples. He can't decide if the world is worth keeping, or if he should sweep it all away and start again."

The rolling of the waves made Olva think of a giant hand reaching out of the sky to catch hold of their ship, but she couldn't tell if it was trying to steady their vessel, or capsize it.

CHAPTER SEVENTEEN

"Lord Vond summons you, Sir Lammergeier," said a guard. "He has sent a carriage."

Alf rubbed his face, scratching at his beard. His fingers came away matted with cobwebs and pit-slime. He'd stumbled home from the Pits exhausted, barely able to stand. He couldn't even recall finding his way home.

"I'll be a minute."

The guard withdrew. Alf reached under the bed, to find his metal chest of potions. One of those would do in lieu of breakfast. Aches faded as the magic sank into his bones.

He rose from the bed and dressed. He reached automatically for Spellbreaker, then stopped. The sword was still bundled up in cloth, like a corpse wrapped in a shroud. Alf raised his voice. "Guard!"

The guard instantly appeared at the door.

"What's your name, boy?"

"Remilard, sir."

"Remilard, I need a sword."

Remilard glanced at the infamous and supremely potent magical sword on the table. "Here, sir. Take mine." He eagerly unbuckled his sword belt and handed it to Alf. The weapon was a League blade, one of thousands forged by the dwarves for the war. The sword was cheap, unremarkable and refreshingly quiet.

"Thank you."

"It's an honour, my lord."

"Go back to the citadel and get another weapon." Alf looked around at the wreckage of the room. "And fetch another half-dozen men. And brooms. Lots of brooms. Clean this place up."

"As you command, lord."

Once Remilard was gone, Alf opened the chest again and put Spellbreaker inside it, along with Peir's broken helm. If the sword protested, its words were muffled, and silenced entirely when he closed the heavy lid. He locked the casket and stowed it away again. *You're keeping the sword of doom safe by hiding it under your bed? Brilliant strategy, oaf.* Alf's thoughts echoed what Spellbreaker would say, but they were his thoughts, and no one else's.

The council chamber was even emptier than last time. The Vatling Threeday at one end, gelatinous fingers crossed, a bland smile on his wet face. At the other, Lord Vond. Between them, clutching a letter, was Abbess Marit.

"You are tardy, Sir Lammergeier," Lord Vond snapped as Alf entered.

Alf yawned. "Aye, so's everyone else."

"Princess Laerlyn is away from Necrad. I have received no communication from Master Blaise, Berys, or Lath."

Alf cursed under his breath. He'd hoped either Berys or, better, Blaise would be at the meeting, so he could show them the scrolls he'd found. He wished he'd ignored the summons and gone straight to the Wailing Tower – although maybe this was for the best. He could smooth things over with young Vond first.

"What about Gundan? He said he'd be here."

Vond scowled. "I think the dwarf-lord communicated his position quite clearly when he threatened me."

Alf winced. He had plenty of experience cleaning up after Gundan's temper got the better of the dwarf. "It was a mess, aye, and words were said in haste. But I've known Gundan since I was your age, my lord – he showed me how to fight, and there's no better teacher. He can be a true friend, if you pay more heed to his actions than his words."

"Your friendship with Gundan is not at issue here. His behaviour is. It would be best if I sent word to the Dwarfholt asking that they appoint a replacement representative to the council."

"I fear you cannot do that, governor," gurgled Threeday. "The Nine were all honoured with places on this council when it was formed. Although ... I suppose the Dwarfholt could nominate another dwarf to represent them in the capacity of the League, and Lord Gundan could then attend in a private capacity. Presumably, the elves would do the same with the Princess Laerlyn." The Vatling giggled at his own musings. "It's not as though we're short of chairs."

Vond scowled at the Vatling, then gestured for Alf to sit at his right, next to Marit. "Sir Lammergeier, as the sole member of the Nine here, I ask you to impress upon your companions their responsibilities to this city."

Alf bit his tongue. *We conquered this city. We survived here, and we triumphed. We won this place with blood and tears.* But he was determined to be more conciliatory, so he just settled into his chair and said, "I'll talk to them. In fact, seeing as there are so few of us here, I should go now."

"Matters of state," said Vond, "must be discussed. The elven threats to block the Gulf of Tears have escalated. No ships dare leave Ellsport. The swiftest sea route to Summerswell is cut off."

Reassure the lad, thought Alf. *Show him where he stands.* "The Wood Elves aren't going to attack. I talked to Lae – to the Princess Laerlyn. Her concern is with the Witch Elves, not taking over Necrad. I wager Maedos is just using it all as an excuse to bully you. We stand firm, he'll back down. Laerlyn will sort it all out."

"Many of my kindred," said Threeday quietly, as if to himself, "were slain by Wood Elves. Of course, that was during the war, and now we are all friends."

Vond ignored the Vatling. "Of course we don't fear attack from our *allies*," he said to Alf. There was a condescending kindness in his voice, as though he was talking to a halfwit. "There is no prospect of war. My concern is with the supply of the city. With the sea denied us, we are dependent on the long and perilous road through the Clawlands. It will be a bitter winter if the fruits of the harvest from Summerswell are denied us."

Twenty years ago, the siege of Necrad had been a hellish affair. Alf remembered what it was like to be hungry. He remembered looking out over the walls, unable to distinguish the zombies from the starving men. In the early years of the occupation, nearly everything the League forces ate had to be brought up from Summerswell via the Gulf.

But things were different now. "The New Provinces can supply us even if we're cut off from Summerswell," Alf explained. "No one's going to starve." *And I've seen the merchants in the Garrison. They could stand to miss a few meals.*

"And if the New Provinces burn? What then?" hissed Abbess Marit. She shoved the letter across the table at Alf. He glanced at it, but the handwriting was so cramped he couldn't make out the meaning.

"What?"

"Tidings arrived last night," explained Vond. "A host of Wilder raided the northern edge of Earl Duna's domain, then vanished back into the woods before his knights could catch them. All the New Provinces are in uproar. More Wilder have been sighted."

"My monastery at Staffa is not so far from Duna's lands. Intercessors preserve us against these beasts." Abbess Marit gripped her spirit-beads so tightly her fingers turned white.

Alf sighed. "Oh, come on. This has happened every bloody year since we took Necrad. It's the Wilder's hallowtide, their festival of the dead. Seven days of mourning, seven days of a few young idiots in the Wilder stealing sheep and lighting fires." *A little trouble, and everyone's acting like the sky's falling.*

"Earl Duna calls for aid!" The Abbess pointed a bony finger at Alf. "This cannot go unanswered!"

"Duna's got a great big castle to hide in. If all the Wilder in all the world gathered, Duna could hold out against them for months. They won't attack Duna."

"Many fortresses were destroyed in the war!" said the Abbess. "I know – I pulled many bodies from the rubble to bury them."

"That wasn't the fucking Wilder!" Alf struggled to find words to convey how stupid this whole argument was. Everyone running around taking about the Wilder and the elves, and all the while Jan's words of warning ran around his head. *A darkness rising.* And Bone's grave open. It reminded him horribly of the early years of the war, when they'd fought to persuade the complacent Lords of Summerswell that doom was coming.

"Enough," snapped Vond. "I agree action is warranted. Sir Lammergeier will accompany the Abbess back to the New Provinces. The sight of one of the Nine will—"

"I won't go," said Alf without thinking.

Vond flinched as if Alf had struck him.

Alf glanced around the room, looking for a friendly face. Threeday gave the slightest shrug, but said nothing.

"The settlers in the New Provinces have good cause to fear the Wilder," said Vond, slowly, as though talking to a child. "They remember how the Wilder fought on the side of Lord Bone in the war. They remember the raids on Summerswell."

Alf fought to keep his temper under control. "Aye. Look, my lord, you were a child during the war, and you heard all sorts of scary stories about the Wilder. Everyone in Summerswell was talking about them, because they were the only part of Lord Bone's army that most people ever saw. He sent his Wilders ahead of his main army to sow chaos and cause trouble – but they weren't the real threat. If it'd just been Wilder, the war would never have reached the cities. But his army wasn't just Wilder."

"I may have been but a child when you were of fighting age, Sir Aelfric, but I studied histories of the war. I am well aware that Lord Bone's host consisted of several distinct forces." Vond ticked them off on his fingers. "The Wilder, as we have discussed. Ogres and other savage beasts. The risen dead. Other conjurations of his magic – demons, constructs, unnatural creatures spawned in the Pits. And, as his knights and captains, the Witch Elves of Necrad." Vond curled in his fingers, one by one. "The Witch Elves are defeated. The death of Lord Bone – for which we are of course eternally grateful, Lammergeier – ended his conjurations. The ogres and the Pitspawn we have hunted to the ends of the earth – and again, I am well aware of your stalwart work there. All that remains of the dark host is the Wilder. Am I incorrect in any part of my summary, Sir Lammergeier?"

"No, but . . . " Alf wished he could bluster, to shout at Vond like Gundan had done. To give the young whelp a whipping and make him know his place – but the words died on his tongue. All Alf could muster was "It's not that simple."

"How so?"

Alf shifted in his chair. He rested his hand on the hilt of his borrowed sword as he searched for the words. "Jan told me that she had a vision. A prophecy, sort of. She said that she saw a darkness coming. I can't go running off north. There's something worse out there."

Vond rubbed the bridge of his nose. "A prophecy," he echoed, in a tone of weary disbelief. Alf shared the boy's feelings on prophecy. "From Jan the Pious."

"Perhaps the Wilder are the darkness she foresaw," suggested Threeday.

Vond waved his hand at the window, at the towers and rooftops of Necrad beyond. "I cannot govern this city based on vague omens. The Masters of the College Arcane have not divined any peril approaching. Abbess, have the Intercessors spoken to you?"

"The power of the Intercessors is constrained in this unholy place," said the Abbess. "But they have sent no warnings." She looked across the table at Alf. "And, Sir Lammergeier, forgive me, but the church no longer counts Jan as one ordained to speak to the Intercessors. She turned her back on the mother church in Arshoth. She has not been openly declared a heretic, as she is much loved by the common folk, but I do not doubt that her 'prophecies' are nothing more than the ravings of a madwoman."

"Do you have any proof of your fears, Sir Lammergeier?" asked Vond.

Alf opened his mouth, then closed it again. There was Bone's grave – but that implicated the Nine, and he could not believe that. He shook his head, helplessly.

Vond nodded. "Well, then. There is enough to concern us without seeing foes in the shadows. Sir Lammergeier and Abbess Marit shall go north, escorted by such an honour guard as we can spare from the Garrison here. You shall bolster Duna and maintain the peace as best you can, so that we are assured of the New Provinces' security." Vond was clearly through with calling votes and listening to the council. "Sir Lammergeier, tell Lord Gundan that I expect the dwarves to contribute to the defence of the New Provinces."

"And while they're off chasing Wilder," said Threeday, "what of us here in Necrad?"

"Reinforcements from Summerswell are already on the march, to guard the southern Road. The stronger our resolve, the greater the likelihood that the elves will see the folly of their current course. And we shall, of course, watch for rising darknesses, whatever they may be. Sir Lammergeier, you will ensure that all available members of the Nine attend the next meeting, yes? If there is an unnatural peril at hand, then surely Master Blaise would have foreseen it."

"Aye." Alf sighed. That, at least, he could agree with. Blaise would know.

Vond bowed. "Thank you, Sir Lammergeier. You leave tomorrow morning – make whatever preparations you see fit."

The Vatling followed Alf out of the chamber.

"For what it is worth, my lord, I thought your assessment of the situation was quite accurate. Wilder attacks come like the changing seasons, and it is foolish indeed to give into such fears. Still ..." Threeday shrugged, "they are only human."

"Last time we spoke, you were the one worrying about the Wilder," said Alf.

"Ah, but you convinced me with your masterful words. The blockade is clearly the greater threat ... of the two." Threeday bobbed his head, and Alf couldn't tell if the creature was mocking him. "As for the third, well, I could hardly know darkness. I am born of Necrad; I have never seen light."

"Where was Berys today?"

Threeday's face crinkled in a theatrical exaggeration of a frown. "There are few individuals capable of evading my watchers in Necrad., Information is all we Vatlings have to barter with. But the Lady Berys – well, her days as a sneak-thief were long before I ever was decanted, so I did not know her back then, not like you did, but I am given to understand that she was exceptionally talented at the art of disappearance, and could go unseen if she desired."

Alf tried to follow all that. "You're saying you don't know?"

"I have not had word of her since you met with her and the Lord Gundan in the tavern."

"And where's Gundan?"

"Messengers from the Dwarfholt arrived last night, and he is with them. The dwarves are adamant – they will not give in to the elven demands, and will support the city against any blockade." The Vatling cocked his head. "It might profit you to know that Lord

Vond's position is much less secure. In letters I happen to have seen, he receives far from fervent support from the Lords of Summerswell. Your homeland is divided, it seems, and there are many there who would give up control of Necrad in order to please the elves." Threeday sniffed. "I thought you humans had more backbone."

"Do me a favour – tell Gundan I need to see him."

"As you wish." The Vatling lowered his voice. "And speaking of hidden letters, it would be wise to keep the papers you have concealed in your breast better hidden. I spotted them in the council chamber – and if I saw them, unfriendly eyes might mark them, too, no? It would be unfortunate for your secrets to be shared throughout Necrad."

Rain destroyed the illusion of normality in the Garrison. In what passed for sunshine beneath the necromiasma, the streets of the Garrison resembled a city like Ellsport or Summerswell, if you squinted and ignored the bizarre gargoyles and twisted spires of Witch Elf architecture that sprouted like coral growths. You could fool yourself if you wanted to in the murky daylight. But the clouds stained the rainwater a luminescent green, rivulets of viridian liquid flowing between the pale marble slabs of the flagstones. No one was quite sure what poisons lingered in the miasma, so the streets emptied quickly. The rain also brought out the wraiths, visible as distortions in the falling droplets. The streets became thronged by fragile apparitions, humanoid shapes forming and failing with every squall.

Alf trudged through the downpour to the door of the Wailing Tower. A different apprentice let him in. This one was a young man – they were all so young – with a strong Crownland accent like Vond's.

"The master," sneered the apprentice, "is meditating, and not to be disturbed."

"Tell him it's the Lammergeier. Tell him I've got a mystery for him."

The apprentice withdrew, leaving Alf alone in the tower's entrance hallway.

Blaise was again many-handed and many-eyed. He hovered in an audience chamber strewn with cushions, muttering arcanely to himself. And he was not alone – Alf was surprised to find Berys lounging on a couch, a glass of wine in hand.

"Alf!" She flashed a smile, and then flung the wine glass at him. He dodged, and it shattered on the wall behind him. "That was for the Liberties, you idiot."

Alf stepped back. "If you'd come with us, then maybe things would have turned out different."

"Don't you dare put this on me. I told you not to go! You've no idea how much trouble you caused! You maimed an elf-*child*, Alf – do you know what that means?"

He remembered Gundan's accusation. "Berys – tell me the truth. Did you tell the Witch Elves we were coming?"

"You went tramping in there like drunken ogres. Why would anyone need advance warning?"

That's not a denial. Spellbreaker's voice echoed in his head. The thought sickened him. He and Berys had never been the closest of friends, but they were both Nine. They'd fought together, bled together. Thought they'd die together. This distrust was unnatural, it was acid in Alf's belly, rotting his bones.

Still, he had to ask. "But did you—"

In an instant, the audience room with its cushions and chairs vanished, the floor melting away under his feet. Alf plummeted into a dark chasm. He heard Berys' yelp of alarm nearby, echoing off the walls of the abyss. They fell together, wind howling in Alf's ears. He stretched out his hands, trying to grab onto something to arrest his fall, but there was nothing, nothing.

Then, abruptly, they were back in the room with Blaise.

An illusion.

"I will have no squabbling in my sanctum here," said Blaise. "If you wish to argue, step outside. First, however, Aelfric, I understand you have a mystery for me."

One of Blaise's disembodied hands swept up the shattered remains of the wine glass. Another pair brought replacement glasses to Berys and Alf.

Berys snatched the glass and drained it. "Do that again," she said to Blaise, "and I'll show you the difference between illusion and reality." She folded her arms and tapped her fingers on her elbow, a gesture of irritation.

The hand waited, floating expectantly in front of Alf.

"I went down into the Pits, looking for Lath," said Alf slowly. "I couldn't find him, but I found one of his old lairs. I found this in there. It's some sort of spell."

"There's been no sign of him on the surface," said Berys. "At least, not in any form my sources recognise." She scowled at Alf. "Those that are still talking to me, anyway, after what Alf and Gundan did."

The floating hand snatched the papers from Alf's grasp and flew them over to where Blaise levitated. The wizard studied the scrolls in silence.

Berys sighed. "He'll be gone for a while. Old books are the only things he cares about, these days." She crossed the room and gave Alf a sudden, unexpected hug, squeezing him tightly. "I never welcomed you home properly. I'm not sorry I shouted at you. You're a bloody idiot."

"You always said I wasn't the brightest."

She released him and stepped back. Out of long habit, Alf checked his pockets.

"I said you had no guile, not that you were dumb. You're honest, Alf. Simple, straightforward. You keep your word. That's why we trusted you with the sword."

"Thanks for that."

She frowned. "Where's the dagger?"

"Lae took it with her when she sailed for the Isle of Dawn."

"Did she now?"

"Had you the dagger," said Blaise, distantly, "I might have divined the elf's hiding place. The sympathetic bond between weapon and wielder is a potent one."

"Aye, well, I don't have it."

"How was the council meeting?" asked Berys.

"They want to send me north. The Wilder have been raiding farmers, and they want me to go be a scarecrow."

"Earl Duna's estates?" asked Berys.

"Aye."

"That's As Gola territory – they're Thurn's tribe." As usual, Berys was better informed than anyone else. If Thurn's tribe had come south, then maybe Thurn himself was with them. The idea of travelling to the New Provinces suddenly seemed more appealing.

"I told Vond about what Jan told me. They didn't believe me, but Lord Vond wants you both at the next council," said Alf. "How come you weren't there?"

"Better things to do. The truth is, Alf, the council means nothing. It never did. Summerswell, the Dwarfholt, the Everwood – they're all far, far away. We're the ones right here in Necrad. We're the ones who have to choose. Do we stand firm, or let the Wood Elves dictate how we run this city? We saved the world, and that means we get a say in how it's run."

"You're talking about continuing the blood trade!" said Alf. His wrist ached where the elf-child had fed on him. He remembered the hunger in the child, the way the boy went from the brink of fading to this desperate hunger for life. The madness in the child's eyes.

"Whatever works." Berys gave a rueful smile. "You saved that elf-child's life by giving him your blood. I won't claim to be as generous when I do it, but ... Alf, you know that this city's full of magic. Whoever controls Necrad controls that power. It's best that we hold onto it. Or do you want to hand it over to that supercilious fucker Prince Maedos?"

Alf was hazy on what 'supercilious' meant, but he got the gist.

"The College of Wizardry in Summerswell operates at the sufferance of the elves," said Blaise, his voice echoing from a great distance. "They forbid certain fields of study, reserving those high magics only for the elves. They choose who may learn magic, and forbid the art to those they deem unsuitable. They banished me. Even now, they spy on me. But in Necrad, there is much to be learned that Summerswell does not know and the elves keep hidden."

"I don't trust anyone else with Necrad, Alf," said Berys. "Not the Lords of Summerswell. Not the elves. Just us."

"Laerlyn said—"

"For heaven's sake, Alf, think for yourself! If you think I'm wrong, argue with me! But don't parrot what Gundan said over a pint, or what Laerlyn said while she flashed her unageing tits at you! Speak for yourself!"

"All right. I come back with a *prophecy* from Jan, the world at stake, a quest just like the old days – and what happens? You two tell me to sit down and do nothing! Gundan goes off and starts a street fight? And Lath . . . I don't even know what's running through the lad's head. Berys, the boy's been through more than any of us. Born cursed. Hunted like a beast before we found him. He fought alongside us all through the war, until we got here. He was captured and tortured, but he didn't give us up. Why would he go back to Bone's grave now? There has to be something more."

"Blaise," said Berys, turning to the wizard, "do the scrolls Alf found shed any light on all this?"

Blaise raised his cowled head, and lights glimmered in the dark depths like distant stars.

"Possibly."

They waited in silence until Berys picked up a cushion and threw it at the archmage. "Explain."

"These pages contain a spell of great power. It is a ritual of . . . resurrection. The souls of elves linger in this world, and the souls of mortals depart — tales speak of a dread kingdom beyond the circles of creation. By means of this spell, one could be called back from that grey land."

Berys swore under her breath. "Does it work?"

"Some of the pages are missing, so I cannot say for certain. It does match certain . . . cryptic references in the spell books of Lord Bone. He feared death, and sought ways to extend his mortal span and cheat death. This spell is similar to those he outlined, and I suspect the incantation to be sound — but far beyond the reach of most spell casters. The ritual calls for three participants — one to cast the spell, one to descend into the realm of death and become a host for the recalled spirit, and a third to bring them back, to bridge the gulf between the living and the dead. I will need time to study it."

"Could someone bring back Lord Bone?" A terrible feeling settled over Alf. He felt simultaneously terrified, a cold dagger of fear stabbing at him, but also exhausted by the prospect of fighting. They'd given so much already to defeat the dark lord, and now he was coming back.

Blaise, though, was unmoved. "Of course. He was mortal. He would be a valid target for such a ritual."

"Would it work on an elf?" asked Alf.

"Not in its present form. It is . . . " Blaise paused, " . . . *similar* to the method used by Lord Bone to rebind Acraist the Wraith-Captain. In that case, Acraist's spirit never departed his physical form. Conceivably, a modified version of the spell could reach into the wraith-world."

"Burn those fucking papers," snapped Berys.

"What would that achieve? The knowledge exists. Lath has already read these pages. Although . . . " Blaise gestured, and the papers vanished. "I would ask that neither of you discuss the existence of this ritual with any of my apprentices. They are spies for the College of Summerswell. The Masters of the College already object to my control of the Wailing Tower. If they were to learn of such a ritual, it would inflame their jealousies still further." The wizard folded his empty hands. "It is a matter for the Nine."

Alf ran his fingers through his thinning hair. "All right. All right. So, Lath found a spell to bring back the dead. And he's opened Lord Bone's grave. If Bone comes back, we can't beat him. We can't find Lath – so, we look for the bones, aye?"

Berys shook her head. "Trust a thief to know when they've got enough to hang you, Alf – you don't know everything. Finding Lath's more important."

"Jan told me—"

"Jan couldn't cope with this city. Jan thinks we're all sinners. And Jan's not here."

"So it's up to us. We call Gundan—"

"Oh, that worked so well last time."

"And Laerlyn, and we act as one."

"And do *what*, Alf?"

"Enough!" snapped Blaise, and the floor vanished again.

Alf plummeted through an abyss. Stacks upon stacks of books hurtled by as he tumbled. *It's an illusion*, he told himself, *just Blaise toying with me*. Still, it felt real.

The fall stopped, abruptly. Alf hung, twisting in the air, for a heartbeat, and then the wizard appeared next to him.

"Forgive me. I dislike confrontation, and you and Berys seemed to be talking at cross purposes."

"Let me down!"

Blaise's cowled head tilted. "Where is thy blade, Aelfric? You were entrusted with Spellbreaker to ensure it did not fall into the hands of our enemies."

"It's safe." Alf wished he had Spellbreaker on him – the blade's counter-magic would have stopped Blaise from manipulating his perceptions so casually.

"It is guarded by . . . ?"

"A box."

"Ah. Well, what could be more secure?" Blaise glided forward. "I have a confession to make. It was I who opened the tomb."

"What?" The revelation felt like a punch in the face. "Why?"

"The location of the tomb was known to elements in the city. Witch Elves who yearn for the days of Lord Bone, Vatling cultists and so forth. And to be honest, the protective wards we placed on the tomb were laughably primitive. I have learned a great deal since then. I moved the remains to a safe location here in the Wailing Tower, where no one may disturb them."

"Why didn't you tell anyone?"

Blaise's eyes glittered. "Who was I obliged to inform?"

"All of us! We swore an oath! We all agreed to guard the tomb!"

"To protect the city. To ensure evil did not return. The precise disposition of the remains is irrelevant to this purpose." Blaise paused. "And I knew that there would be objections. Some of the company have sentimental attachments to the past; others suspect everything I do to be laden with sinister motives. In truth, it simply seemed easier."

"And now that we know there's a resurrection spell out there?"

"It changes nothing. The remains are safe, and cannot be used for the spell. If Lath does intend to call a spirit back from the Grey Lands, it is not Lord Bone's return he seeks."

Blaise folded his hands, and suddenly Alf was on the ground, his face buried in a cushion. He looked around. Berys was gone.

"Where is she?"

"I spoke with her privately. She goes to continue her investigations. If Lath is in Necrad, she will find him."

"She still hasn't found the elf who nearly killed me."

"The *enhedrai* are close-knit, and mistrustful of us. And I imagine your recent actions impeded her investigation even more. I shall not throw wine glasses at you, Sir Lammergeier, but I shall say this: go north. Do as Vond requested. Leave this matter to those best suited to manage it. The bones are safer in my care than they ever were in that tomb."

Alf sighed. "Fine," he muttered. Back in the old days, it was Peir who led the company, but with the counsel of wiser heads like Blaise. He knew better than to ignore Blaise's advice; the wizard knew more than he did, saw further and deeper.

"Lammergeier. Do not go unarmed."

CHAPTER EIGHTEEN

A half-dozen or so Witch Elves had gathered in the alleyways near the Garrison gate, careful to stay out of reach of the crossbows carried by the dwarven sentries. They watched Alf as he marched by, that pack of haggard princelings. Tattered velvet and ragged silks, tarnished silver. Some wore empty scabbards, signifying they had been knights in the war. They were silent, and the only sound was the heavy rain beating on the flagstones and pouring from the mouths of gargoyles. The rainwater would drain down into the Pits from here; Alf remembered wading through floodwaters in past years, pushing past the drowned corpses of pitspawn.

The dwarves waved him through the gate, and he stepped from the eerie emptiness of the deserted streets of the Liberties into the clamour of the Garrison.

"Hail the returning hero!" Gundan was waiting for him, seated on a barrel. The dwarf hopped down. "The Vatling said you wanted to see me, and I waited in this pissing weather for you. It better be urgent."

"I told Vond I'd make sure you were at the next council meeting."

"Don't be the brat's errand runner. Tell Vond to go fuck himself. Or propose a motion in the high council of Necrad as a representative of the League that this day it is hereby resolved and agreed by unanimous vote that he should go fuck himself."

"Unanimous?"

"Well, you're going through the proper procedures, all legal-like. My guess is that he'd appreciate that so much he'd vote for it." Gundan fell in alongside Alf. "Pub?" he asked hopefully.

"I need to get ready to leave. I'm riding north to bolster the New Provinces. There's trouble with the Wilder."

"What is this, Alf? Is this over the mess in the Sanction a few nights ago? Is the little rat trying to punish you?"

"It's not just that. And we hurt a lot of people, so maybe we deserve it."

Gundan snorted. "First off, I killed people. You mostly stood around gawping. Second, they were Witch Elves. We fought a war against 'em, if you'll recall. Something about the last battle between light and darkness?"

"That," spat Alf, "was twenty years ago."

"And to an elf, that's half an hour ago. We can't let our guard down. It's good to bloody them a bit, remind them that they lost and we won. Remind them this is our city now."

Alf walked in silence for a few minutes, while Gundan maintained his usual barrage of complaints and curses about whatever irritated him, which that day ranged from the dwarven generals to Lord Vond to the quality of the ale to why they were walking and not in a carriage, or on horses, or on a dreadworm given Alf could summon a monstrous steed with a thought. Finally, when the torrent ebbed, Alf said: "Blaise opened the tomb."

"What tomb? *Bone's* tomb?"

The dwarf began to chuckle, and it became an avalanche of laughter, great peals echoing off the towers. Such laughter had rarely been heard in Necrad before. Gundan turned an alarming shade of purple. "You thought . . . you came running back like . . . " – he mimed Lord Bone lurching out of the crypt like a zombie – "oh, that's priceless."

Alf shook his head. "I thought that's what Jan had warned me about. A darkness in the city, she said. But it was just Blaise."

"That's good, isn't it? I mean, it's creepy and wrong, but that's Blaise."

"I couldn't find Lath, but I found some sort of necromantic ritual in one of his lairs."

Gundan looked up at Alf. "You know I don't trust Lath, but you know him as well as anyone. Do you think the lad would ever try to use such a spell on *him?*"

"No."

"Well. That's that."

Alf's mansion was abuzz with activity. Remilard had mustered a small army of helpers, all eager for the honour of serving the Nine heroes of Necrad. When not one, but two living legends arrived on the doorstep, all work ceased so they could crowd around and cheer the Lammergeier and the Dwarflord.

Alf hurried inside, brushing past Remilard. In a back room, he dug out his old war-harness, the armour he'd worn after the battle of the Dwarfholt. A suit of plate armour, dwarf-forged. Easily the finest thing Alf had ever owned. Once, it shone in the sun like silver fire. Now, it was covered in mouse droppings and stained by disuse.

"Shall I have that polished, my lord?" Remilard asked from the doorway.

"A man should attend to his own war-gear," said Alf. "I'll do it. And you attend to yours – Lord Vond sends me north, and I want you to come with me."

The young man's face shone more brightly than the armour ever had.

Alf crammed the armour into a canvas bag and slung it over his shoulder. Grunting under the weight of the steel, he carried the bag first to his bedroom and dropped it on the bed. From underneath, he fetched the metal box and opened it.

Spellbreaker stared mutely at him. *Don't forget your sword, Sir Lammergeier.* Alf took a handful of coins, a healing potion, and then shoved the box away again. The blade had betrayed him, led him astray too many times. Better to have an honest sword than an enchanted one. He drank the potion and hefted the bag of armour once more, the potion's warmth bathing his sore ribs.

Gundan was still waiting for him. The dwarf was seated on a plinth where a Witch Elf statue once stood, and was surrounded by a crowd of Leaguesmen. He was in the middle of Dreoch's Reach, how they'd defeated the ogres besieging the hall. When he saw Alf, he hastily skipped to the end – "and then, we killed 'em all!" – and leapt up to greet his friend.

"Come on," said the dwarf, "let's get that armour fixed up. There's a cousin of mine down the docks who's the best smith in the Garrison."

"Of course there is." Gundan had a whole clan of remarkably well-connected cousins.

By the time the smith's work was done, it was after dusk. Alf stared out to sea, watching the distant waves break on the sentinel towers that jutted from the water. There were lights on those towers, dimly visible through the green-grey curtain of rain. League wizards, he guessed, trying to reawaken the city's magical defences that had died with Lord Bone.

"I don't know what I'm doing, Gundan," said Alf. "When Jan gave me the quest, I felt . . . I felt like myself, again. It was like I was waiting for her to call for me. I knew what I'd been told to do, and nothing could stand against me. But it's all fallen apart."

"Ah, well, Jan was never the one I'd have looked to in a pinch. Full of doubts and questions, not exactly what you want in a priestess, is it?" Gundan sat down heavily on the side of the pier. "Sit down, you big ape, and tell me your woes. You say you don't know what you're doing. You're a hero, one of the most famous men in Summerswell. They sing songs about your deeds from the Cleft of Ard to the Eaveslands. You're the Lammergeier, the slayer of Lord Bone. You can do whatever you want."

"And what's that?" Alf kicked a stone into the water. "I was going to be Peir's right hand, I thought. Serve his house as a knight and stand beside him when he became a Lord of Summerswell. Be ready, should we be called upon."

"We were called, though. We've done the whole heroic quest, Alf. We've earned the honours, aye? We're done with questing. So, what's next? You're a knight, and even if you look like a linnorm chewed your face, you could still walk into Summerswell and have your pick of the lords' daughters. Found the house of Lammergeier."

"There were . . . offers," said Alf, slowly, "in the early days. But I didn't trust any of 'em. And I was needed here. We swore to watch over Necrad." That had always been his gift, Alf thought – to put himself between the monsters and those who needed protection. To be the stalwart shield, the dependable one.

"North, then," suggested Gundan. "The New Provinces. Set yourself up there. Plenty of land for the taking, and settlers would flock to your banner. I've a cousin who's a mason – do you want a nice castle, bigger than Duna's. Aelfric Lammergeier, Protector of the North?"

"It seemed . . . hollow. To go from fighting Lord Bone, from turning back the darkness, to . . . just sitting around watching the grass grow and the cows get fat."

"Go adventuring. Take up with another mad bunch, go and find the Lost Tower or something. Slay monsters, find treasure. Remember those days?"

"I've been slaying monsters in the Pits for years," said Alf, "and I have more treasure than I ever dreamed of."

"Aye, pass some of it my way, then. 'Tis easy to think you're rich when you just pile it up in that mansion of yours." Gundan chuckled. "I had no idea that victory would have made you so miserable."

"I thought things would change. I thought we were just cleaning up the last of Bone's forces, and that soon everything would change, and . . ."

"And it'd be summer and joy for ever. That we'd all live happily to the end of our days?" Gundan shook his head. "The world doesn't work like that, Alf. The stories lie. All right then – back when you were a little lad in that village we passed through, what did you want?"

"I don't know. To be a famous knight, wealthy and covered in glory."

"You did that." Gundan scratched his beard in thought. "For Blaise, it's that tower and all his bloody books that keeps him going. Berys has her schemes, and you don't know the half of those, believe me. Thurn fought for his kin, and as soon as that was done he went home. I hear he has a family now, and I pity the woman who had to give birth to a litter of giants. Laerlyn – well, elves don't have a choice, do they? They don't need anything to live for, which is why they can afford to spend centuries prancing around the Everwood and singing their endless twee songs about the days of old. For me, it's my clan. My kin have risen in influence in the Dwarfholt, and that's down to me. I lifted us up. The name of the house of Gwalir is praised and magnified by my actions, and I shall not be forgotten while the world endures. What about your kin, Alf? Blood is blood, and no matter how far you go, it's a bond that can't be broken."

"I tried that. I went home, remember?"

"How long were you there?"

"I never made it as far as Ersfel," admitted Alf, "I wanted to go home, but Jan called me, and I couldn't go."

"Liar," said Gundan. "You leapt at Jan's call. If you ask me, a dark host isn't going to rise up and threaten the world again, Alf. The world's saved. You've got to figure out how to live in it."

"Unless some elf assassin kills me first."

"Well, that's hardly worth mentioning. It's like the weather." Gundan stood and stretched. "I'm coming north with you, I think. You need someone to put your head straight, knock Jan's nonsense out of it, and coincidentally I need to hit something. And apparently we're not chopping up Witch Elves any more, leastways not without feeling bad about it. So, go and get some sleep, old man. Long road ahead."

"Aye," nodded Alf. "And what of Lath?"

"Ach, I don't know. I never understood the boy. I don't think he knows what he's doing."

Alf sat on the dock a while longer, watching the stars. When he set off wandering, three years ago, the stars had been an unexpected surprise. In Necrad, one forgot the beauty of the stars – even though every elven statue was covered in symbols and constellations. The elves loved the stars, Witch and Wood alike. *Blood is blood*, Gundan said, *a bond that cannot be broken.*

And Berys complaining that the Witch Elves weren't talking to her. *The gift of death is wasted on the undeserving.*

He stood, unfolding his long limbs, feeling every ache. The pain in his side where he'd been stabbed, the old wounds from the linnorm, the fatigue of his long expedition into the Pits.

The bite on his wrist.

The Liberties were crowded that night, but Alf saw no other humans on the streets. Instead, there were swarms of Vatlings, most of which had the gelatinous sheen of the freshly decanted. The artificial creatures could be grown swiftly in the vats. The spawning vats were supposed to be monitored by the League to control the Vatlings' numbers, but they probably had more vats hidden in the ruined city. That, or they'd bribed the League guards.

Ogres, too – not many, but enough for Alf to be wary. Some of the huge brutes were at work digging in rubble piles, shifting big chunks of fallen masonry so Vatling scavengers could look for lost treasures, fragments of ancient enchantments. They would find little; the Liberties had been picked clean long ago. Others slumped in street corners, stinking of the rotgut booze the dwarves sold them. It took a lot to get an ogre drunk, but dwarven brewers managed it.

At night, without fear of the searing sun, wraiths emerged to haunt the streets of the city that was once theirs. Shadows followed Alf. He could hear their whispering voices, but couldn't make out the words. Not even the living elves could – the wraiths were always just past the edge of comprehension, cursed to be always just beyond the reach of the living. Trying to find meaning in their whispers was a road to madness.

There were few living elves, though. The former rulers of Necrad might have been overthrown and driven into the same slums as their servants, but they remained aloof. They watched Alf from rooftops and high windows, their beautiful faces impassive, wine-dark eyes reflecting the necromiasma.

Alf kept his hands open and visible. He drew no weapon.

None dared stop him. The crowds opened before him and closed behind him.

Alf forced himself to think back to the night of the raid. He remembered the dreadworm feasting, the ragged warriors emerging from an archway, the child screaming – and the boy's father, cradling the child.

That door there.

Alf's feet felt rooted to the ground. In the constant whispering of the wraiths, he imagined he could hear Gundan or Berys or Vond, telling him he was being a fool again, that he would only make things worse. Blaise, telling him that all his suspicions were misguided. The sword, lying to him over and over.

But he knocked.

There was no answer for a long time. He knocked again and called out. "It's me. It's the Lammer – it's Alf. Alf of the Nine."

No answer came.

"I just want to make sure the boy is all right."

No answer came.

"I brought money."

He raised a jingling bag of coin, but still no answer came.

"I'm not leaving until I see him."

Alf sat down on the pavement, facing the door, his back to the House of the Horned Serpent.

The door opened a crack. A Witch Elf peered out at him, hissed something in *enhedrai*.

"I don't speak Elvish," said Alf.

"You are not welcome here, mortal. You have caused enough suffering."

"I just want to make sure that the boy's all right."

The elf vanished into the shadows. The door opened. Alf stepped through into a dark corridor, empty and cold. His hand brushed against the hilt of his blade, reaching for Spellbreaker's gift of sight in the darkness, forgetting for a moment he did not carry the demon sword. Instead, he felt his way along the hallway, his probing fingers finding eerie carvings. He inched forward, the instincts honed in the Pits telling him to fall back, to beware traps and monsters lurking in the dark, but he pressed on until he came to another door.

Beyond was a once-grand room, now bare, the walls stripped of art. A rusted chain that no longer held a crystal chandelier. An elf waited for him; her face was ageless, but it bore a family resemblance to the boy. Mother? Sister? Great-great-grandmother? He had no way of knowing.

The elf bowed. "Long have I awaited you, Aelfric Lammergeier. Glorious is it to have one of the Nine grace my humble home. My name is Elithadil. Take what you wish, honourable knight of Summerswell." Scorn filled her voice.

"I don't want to take anything. I came to . . ." *To apologise. To atone. To pay a debt.*

From another room in the house came an unearthly screech, and the sound of a body slamming against a door. The house shook, and little flakes of plaster drifted down from the ceiling.

"He can smell your blood. Your presence here torments him. The thirst maddens him."

"I won't stay." Alf held up the bag of coin. "I just came with this."

Elithadil did not move. "You think you can measure the worth of my son's life with coin? He should have had ten thousand years of joy, not a few heartbeats!"

"I didn't mean to hurt him. I came looking for an elf who tried to kill me."

She spread her arms wide. "Behold, a city of your enemies! You slew many of my kin, mortal. Shall you bring me a bag of coins for each of them? Shall you pile your stolen money at my feet, until I stand on a mountain of silver? And still, that would not be enough."

"I fought to stop Lord Bone," said Alf, "and the war's done. There's peace now. And your boy's still alive, isn't he?" He shook the bag of coin. "You can buy him blood with this, yeah?"

"You know nothing of us. Do you think it is simple hunger that torments him, mortal? Do you think that hunger can be sated so easily?" The elf-woman reached out and tapped her cold finger on Alf's breast, above his heart. "The blood-thirst grows if he does not fight it. Will your money buy a thousand generations of mortals to feed his growing thirst? That is what you have condemned us to suffer! All of us!"

"I did what I could to heal him," said Alf. "Would you have preferred that I let him fade?"

"Better you had never come to Necrad at all."

"Princess Laerlyn of the Wood Elves is a friend of mine. She spoke of bringing the life-trees here. If I ask her, she could bring your son to the Everwood and—"

"Never!"

"Why not?"

"To do so would be to exchange one curse for another. My son Celemos will not be shackled to a tree, and shame himself until the world's ending."

Alf shook his head in confusion. "What can I do, then?"

"Leave," she said. "Go back where you came from, mortal. Go and wait for death to claim you. A foresight is on me; she will not be long coming."

As if in answer, there was another crash from the room above.

"There is something I can do," muttered Alf. He pushed past Elithadil. More rooms in various states of decay, the whole Liberties a palace gone to seed. He found a looping staircase and hurried up. Paintings on the walls depicted a procession of shambling human figures, fearful and hunched, savage and witless. The human figures ascended towards two elven lords, a king and queen, seated on thrones. Alf hurried past the tableau to reach the second level of the house. The thumping grew louder, and he followed it.

He turned a corner, and there he found yet another elf. This one he recognised: the knight who'd come for the boy, Celemos' father. The elf-knight had his shoulder pressed against the door, trying to hold it shut against the vampire on the far side. The whole door shuddered every time the child threw himself against it.

"The thirst consumes him," said the elf. "If he walks free, he will seek out other mortals to feed from. If he attacks them in his madness, it will bring the League's wrath down on us."

"I can help," said Alf. From the other side of the door came a terrible, anguished wailing, and the sound of nails scraping against metal.

"Do not let him pass," ordered Elithadil from behind him. The elf-knight stared at Alf, then opened the door.

A pale shadow leapt at Alf. The elf-child was as light as a bird, but he crashed into Alf with overwhelming force, knocking them both to the ground. Little hands scrabbled at Alf's throat, and he glimpsed the elf's face, contorted into a demonic mask. Sharp teeth snapped. Hot drool splashed on Alf's face, like the child was a rabid animal. There was no trace of life or thought in the child's eyes, just glassy desperation. Alf wrestled the vampire child to the side, pushing the elf away from his neck, offering his wrist instead. Again, the teeth bit, deeper and harder than before. Alf grunted as the vampire battened on, feasting on his blood.

Pain shot through his arm, and then it became numb. At the same time, the elf-boy relaxed, his ferocious hunger sated. Alf pushed the boy away, and Celemos sat up, his lips stained red. He looked around as if newly awoken, and called out to his parents, thin arms reaching up to them in confusion. Elithadil swept the boy into her arms and carried him away down the stairs.

The elf-knight knelt by Alf and pressed a cloth to the wound, while Alf dug a healing potion out of a pocket and swigged it. The gush of blood slowed to a trickle, though his left arm was still numb, and he shivered with cold. He could barely move.

"I remember," whispered the elf-knight, "when I hunted you through these streets like a beast. If I had you at my mercy then, mortal, I would have slain you – and I had much less reason to hate you then than I do now." The elf sat back wearily. "It will not last. We shall lose him again. The hunger will consume him."

"What's your name?"

"Andiriel of the Horned Serpent."

"Well, Andiriel, I'll come back," said Alf, "if you help me."

The elf-knight frowned. "By rights, I should string you up and bleed you dry to feed my child. Let his next *agaerath* be of humbler birth."

Alf guessed *agaerath* meant the one who sustained the vampire. "Hard to find someone of humbler birth than me – but killing me will bring trouble down on you, and you know it. Help me, and I'll do what I can for you and yours."

Andiriel closed his eyes. "What do you want?"

"An elf attacked me the night I came back to Necrad. She was waiting for me – and when she didn't kill me, she fled to the House of the Horned Serpent. I'm guessing you know who I'm talking about. Where is she?"

CHAPTER NINETEEN

This, then, was the nature of the quarrel between Prince Maedos and the Lammergeier. Prince Maedos remarked how marvellous fair his sister Laerlyn was when dressed in the finest silks and adorned with jewels, her flawless skin washed in the sacred waters, and wagered that there was no woman on earth more beautiful under the starlight that night.

But the Lammergeier said:

"Aye, she is fair enough, but I saw her sitting amid the rubble, smeared in blood and soot, exhausted after battle. She was clad then in battered armour, and the only light upon her face was cast by a campfire, and I say to you, she was more beautiful in that moment than this."

Then, in the manner of heroes, and because both had drunk deep of the wine of the elves, they agreed to settle the argument with their swords.

From *The Song of the Nine*,
by Sir Rhuel of the Eaveslands

They were three, maybe four days out of Ellsport when Captain Abran knocked on their door. It was an empty courtesy – the door was, after all, barred from his side. Still, Olva pushed back her hair and tried to make herself presentable. She shoved the chamber pot into a corner. Torun retreated to her bed, hiding in it as if were her cave back in the Fossewood.

Two of Abran's crew accompanied him to the door, but did not follow him in. Abran frowned at Torun's occult scratchings. He drew a knife – making Olva gasp in alarm – and shut the door, then knelt to scrape away the symbols. He spoke quietly as he worked.

"I am sorry that I had to chastise you. The crew of this ship are vile cutthroats and sinners to a man, Rootless and dishonourable. Such are the men I must command, and the souls I must attend to. I could not, mistress dwarf, show any weakness in front of them, and when you refused to swear, I had to act." He took a small bottle from his pocket and proffered it to Torun. When the dwarf did not move, he handed it to Olva instead. "It is a healing cordial from Necrad. It will dull the pain of your wounds," he said, "and if there is anything I can do to make your time here more bearable, ask."

"Do you make the same offer to those below?" asked Torun. They could hear the groans and weeping of the prisoners on the lower deck when the wind fell quiet. They'd heard a splash, too, as a body was thrown overboard – and all that awaited those who survived the crossing was the hunger of the vampires.

Torun meant the question as a barb, but Abran answered it soberly. He sat down on the only chair.

"I do not mistreat them, as others do. Those not taken by the Witch Elves I do not keep, and they may go and seek their fortunes in the New Provinces. For those without the coin or the permission of their liege-lords, the journey is worth the gamble."

"The vampires of Necrad don't take them all?" Olva was fascinated despite herself.

"Does the farmer take every grain, or do some go astray on the way to the threshing floor? Mercy is quick and unexpected, like a thieving mouse." Abran produced a set of prayer beads, and absently ran them through his hands as he spoke. "I fill my hold on these voyages out of charity, in a way. Those who are taken by the vampires pay the toll for their comrades who might otherwise not be able to cross." He looked up at Olva. "I went down to the lower deck, by the by, and made sure your son was not aboard. I did not think he was, but Lyulf lies as easily as he breathes, and I wanted to make sure. Another of Lyulf's ships left Ellsport soon after we did. They are not far behind us, on the same course. It may be your son is aboard that ship."

"Are they bound for Necrad, too?"

"Most likely," said Abran, "but all ships must pass through the Gulf of Tears, the straits between the northland and the Isle of Dawn. After that, they might follow the coast around to Necrad, or continue on north to the Provinces – or east, if they dare the open seas to Phennic-land. I cannot say."

"How did a cleric of the Holy Intercessors come to be captain of a crew of smugglers?"

"Through no fault of my own. After the war, I was sick of fighting. I had enough blood on my hands, I thought, and I sought Intercession for mine own soul. I was ordained by Jan the Pious herself, and set myself to the task of bringing the light of the Intercessors to the heathens of the north."

A derisive snort came from the shadows of Torun's bunk.

"Torun, ssh." Olva hushed the dwarf. There was no sense angering the captain.

"Nine years ago, the archon of Westermarch sent a messenger to me. He had need of a particular treasure, a stone of prophecy, that had been uncovered in Necrad. I was commanded to secure it. To do so, I had to bargain with the Lady's men. She controls the trade in such treasures – this ship belongs to her, and so does every soul aboard. But the smugglers who found the stone were discovered, and they named me as their employer. The holy church disavowed me, and I was cast out. Only the Lady would employ me, and in her service I have done awful things. I asked for none of this, you understand? I do not live like this by choice, but by necessity."

"One always has a choice," spat Torun, "to think otherwise is cowardice or stupidity."

"I pray to the Intercessors, and I still hear their whispers on the waters, so I know my soul is not wholly damned." He nodded at Torun. "I shall pray for guidance tonight, mistress dwarf. They will tell me how indulgent I should be."

It was late in the afternoon of the following day before Abran called again. Torun scowled when she heard his heavy tread on the deck outside.

"More of his self-pitying piety."

"Don't insult him," whispered Olva. "He'll punish you."

"At least that would be honest. He's as bad as the rest of his crew, he just pretends to be a better man."

Abran unlocked the door and led them out into the open air. Spray had made the deck slick, and the crew jeered at Olva as she slipped. She went to the rail, carefully gripping it with both hands, and looked out over the grey seas, but she could see little through the chill drizzle that fell all around. She could not tell sea from sky, making it seem like Abran's ship was lost in a grey void. Olva stared astern, praying she might see the sail of the other ship Abran had mentioned, but there was nothing there.

"That is the Gulf of Tears," intoned Abran, "we'll pass the straits tonight."

"I've read the straits are dangerous," said Torun, "is it wise to brave them in darkness?"

"Don't tell me how to run my ship," snapped Abran. After a moment, he spoke more quietly. "The straits are dangerous in the dark, true enough, but our best chance is to slip by unseen at night.

The elves command the weather here, and can call up a storm or a summer's day as they please, or so 'tis said. This miserable cloud is a blessing to us, but it will not last. Darkness is our best hope. We must be through the neck of the straits before dawn. The eyes of the elves are not so keen that they can see a black sail against the night sky." He pointed at a spot a little to the right of the ship's prow. "Yonder is the Isle of Dawn. Even if the skies were clear, we could not see Necrad from here, for its southern approach is guarded by Mount Woe. But I thought I'd be able to show you the necromiasma at least."

He turned to his crew. "Boy! The boat!" The same young crewman that they'd seen when they left Ellsport came forward, bearing another little carved boat. "We shall need all the luck we can muster," said Abran.

Again, he enacted the ritual. From a chest, he took out a bottle of wine, a line of prayer beads and his wooden grail-cup. It was like the sacred bowl priests used in the sanctum, but smaller and rimmed with iron to strengthen it. Olva had heard of mendicant priests and fighting paladins using such things; the songs said Jan the Pious had carried her grail-cup into battle against Lord Bone. Abran poured a little wine into the vessel, muttered a prayer and spilled it over the side. He took a swig from the wine bottle himself, then offered it to Torun and Olva. When they refused, it went to the crew and it was quickly drained. He then lit a candle and placed it in the carved boat. "Intercessors watch over us," he prayed. He filled the bowl again, this time with water, and stared at it, muttering as the prayer beads clacked through his fingers.

Olva shivered as a strange feeling came over her. It reminded her of how she'd felt in the Fossewood, but it wasn't the same. Then, she'd felt lifted, as if the winds had caught her soul and carried it into the clouds. This time it was more like invisible frost creeping across the dome of the sky, an intricate lattice forming all around her. For a moment, she was very certain that there was someone else standing there by the rail. At the same time, all noise on the ship ceased – the wind dropped just as no orders were being shouted, and a dozen idle conversations happened to pause all at the same time.

She blinked, and the sensation was gone.

"An Intercessor passed," laughed one of the crew, but Abran's face was grave.

"This is holy, you dogs. Do you want to cross the straits without protection?"

The young boy who'd put the boat in the water at Ellsport stepped forward, but Abran shook his head. Instead, they lowered the little model down to the water on a thin line. A wave surged and caught the boat. Olva saw it for a moment, suspended on the crest of the wave, already doomed but soaring for an instant – and then it toppled, vanishing into the sea, its light snuffed out.

The crew grumbled: a bad omen. Abran glared at Torun, as if blaming the dwarf for the sudden wave.

The wind picked up, whipping the grey sea into an onrushing army of white-crested waves that smashed against the ship. It shifted direction, too, the south wind giving way to gusts from east and north before it settled into a steady blow from the west.

"The elf-wind," wailed one of the crew.

Sudden thunder rolled overhead, but if there was lightning, it was hidden by the darkening rainclouds.

"Martens has failed us!" cursed Abran. "Get them below," he shouted. He bellowed more orders, sending men aloft to trim the sails as they fought to master this abrupt change of weather. The charmstone in his sword glowed, the light growing with every clap of thunder.

Torun grabbed Olva's arm and pointed at the stone. "It's reacting to the storm! Magic knows magic!"

Sailors forced them below. Olva's last glimpse was of the charmstone flaring so brightly the after-image danced in her eyes for a long time afterwards.

*

The lamp in the cabin swung so wildly in the storm that Torun put it out before it fell, and they were left in utter darkness. Olva clung to her bunk, convinced the ship was on the verge of plummeting into an abyss, and that every gust would be the one to tip it over the edge. She wished there was something she could do to take hold of her fate, instead of sitting here waiting for either the strength of the ship or the skill of the crew to falter in the face of this onslaught. Beside her, Torun whispered in the secret tongue of the dwarves, but if it was a spell or a prayer or a litany of curses, she did not know.

The storm raged on. Time fell away; they existed now only in the interval between swells, living a lifetime between the rise and fall of the ship, each time expecting this to be the last, that this was the time the ship would topple or shatter.

Olva tried to pray herself. She recited the same prayer Abran had, calling on the Intercessors to bring them safely through the storm. She thought of Derwyn, and prayed he wasn't on the other vessel, for surely that would also be caught in the same storm. But whatever holy presence she'd briefly felt on deck was gone now, and her prayers were lost in the howling of the wind, blown away like dry leaves.

There was a brief lull in the wind, a moment of calm, but all she could hear was wailing and screams of terror from the prisoners on the deck below. Somehow, the darkness magnified the clamour, dissolving the distance between them.

She thought of Alf, and for a moment she let herself imagine that he'd come to save her if the ship foundered, a legendary hero cleaving through the storm to save the day. He'd done that in the tales, had he not? Or one of the Nine had. There was definitely some story about stealing a ship. Derwyn, if he had been there, would have known all the stories, corrected her on the minutia, but Olva had never paid that much attention to the tales. But try as she might, she couldn't believe in Alf coming to her aid. The tales were hollow, and Sir Aelfric the Lammergeier was nothing to do with her.

Thunder crashed right on top of them, and the whole ship quivered.

She thought of Cu for a moment, and how he hated thunder, and that thought led her to Bor. It was Bor's fault she was here in this cabin, Bor's treachery that had brought her to this plight. It was Bor who came to Ersfel and broke the peaceful life she'd made after everything.

From outside came more shouts of alarm. A quiver ran through the ship, and then her motion changed. She was moving with the waves now, unguided, as if there was no longer a guiding hand on the tiller. More shouts – war cries and oaths turning to screams and death-rattles, the echoes of slaughter in the dark.

She clasped her hands and prayed. *If anyone's listening*, she swore, *let me live, and I'll kill Bor. He deserves to die here, not me. And not Derwyn. Let me live, and I'll kill him.*

As if in answer to her unspoken oath, the door rattled, then burst open. Abran grabbed her by the wrist and pulled her to her feet.

"We are undone," he said, "the elves have caught us. You will tell them I treated you well! You'll tell them I was forced to serve!" He pressed the cold edge of a knife to her throat. "Move!" He pushed her out of the cabin, barring the door behind him, then manhandled her out onto the rolling deck, keeping her in front of him. Thick fog swirled about the ship, and she could see nothing beyond a few feet in front of her. Bodies lay everywhere. *What sort of a storm would do that*, she thought wildly, and then she saw the arrows that pierced the corpses. Bloodied seawater sluiced over Olva's bare feet. She looked around for living sailors, and saw only a handful, all cowering near the forecastle.

But there was no sign of any attackers. There were no other ships that she could see.

Abran shoved her forwards, holding her like a shield against any arrows. Something heavy and hard-edged dug into her back – he'd stuffed his grail-cup into his shirt for safe-keeping. "Tell them," he hissed in her ear, "that I'm a good man."

"Indeed?" called a voice from the fog. "Let us put that to the test."

She looked up, and beheld a figure clad all in grey and green standing amid the rigging. He had a bow in hand, and a silver sword at his side. He was tall as a young tree, agile as an acrobat. He wore a battered hat against the rain, and chainmail gleamed beneath his forest-green garb. He laughed as he leapt from the rigging to land sure-footedly on the deck.

"If you are a good man, then the stars will surely guide your hand. If you are a vile trader in misery, you will die here." The elf drew his sword. "A game, then. Land a blow, and you'll win your freedom."

Abran muttered a prayer, then shoved Olva aside. He drew his sword and swung it wildly in a frantic assault. The elf nimbly stepped aside. The rolling of the ship in the storm threw Abran off balance, but the elf moved with grace and certainty. He circled around Abran, always staying just outside the reach of the sword, no matter how quickly Abran lunged, no matter how the wind and rain buffeted them. Olva clung to the mast as the boat heaved.

"Once only have I been defeated," said the elf. "But, try your luck. Perhaps you shall be the second. Try harder!"

Abran slipped on the blood-slick deck as he swung at the elf. He climbed back up, his shirt and hands stained red, his face red too with the exertion. He wiped the rain from his face and tried again, a blindingly fast series of swipes and lunges. For all his speed, he never got close to the elf, but each attack, though, forced the elf to retreat a pace, over and over. He herded him towards the narrow prow of the ship, where there was less space to dodge. Still, the elf was clearly the superior swordsman, so even if Abran managed to close, surely the fight was a foregone conclusion.

Then she saw the trap.

"He has a charmstone!" she shouted. "In his sword!"

Abran snarled and thrust his sword at the elf. A bolt of lightning leapt from the tip of the blade, but the elf stepped aside, and the deadly blast crackled into the clouds. Almost casually, the elf struck the sword from Abran's hand and sent the captain sprawling again.

"An honour it is," said the elf, "to be aided by so fierce a shield-maiden." He bowed.

Behind him, Abran rose up. He grabbed his sword from the deck, wiped the blood and water from his eyes, and charged.

The sea exploded.

A spout, a wave rose up, breaking, the waters sloughing away as a huge sea-serpent reared up. Its scales were green as emeralds. Olva caught a brief glimpse of the war-harness and saddle on its neck. It had many rows of teeth, but what Olva would always remember were the eyes, swirling red and full of impotent fury. Its massive head reached down, and Abran was gone.

The elf calmly addressed the serpent. "Ey! Down, *Etharno*. You'll have your fill. Bring the wretch to thy nest, now!" A sigil between its eyes glowed, and the monster withdrew, Abran's form hanging limply from its jaws. A huge wave buffeted the ship as it flicked its tail and swam away.

"Please," she said, "there are prisoners on this ship! We must help them."

"I know," he said, "This ship was my quarry, and I the hunter. I shall see to the safety of those aboard."

He raised his voice, and the storm answered. The sails above filled as wind and wave obeyed him, and the ship was driven forward at great speed. The sudden motion knocked Olva to her knees, but the elf kept his balance without effort. He raised his voice in song. The curtain of rain parted, and Olva saw that the storm had blown them close to some shore. The waters churned with more serpents, and each one bore an elven rider. The serpent cavalry surrounded the ship.

"This is the Isle of Dawn," he said, "I am Maedos. And in the Erlking's name, you are welcome here."

CHAPTER TWENTY

Walls divided the Garrison from the rest of the city, but the border between Liberties and Sanction was not as clear. They'd drawn lines across the map in a council meeting, years ago. On this side, the defeated denizens of Necrad could live; on the other, the forbidden zone of Lord Bone's arcane laboratories, his temples and ritual chambers, his terrible weapons. The ruin Andiriel spoke of was right on that dividing line – technically it lay in the Liberties, but no one dared lived there, for fear of League patrols.

Alf approached as quietly as he could. He drew his sword and felt his hand tremble. He was lightheaded from blood loss. The healing cordials helped, but he was far from his best. Still, this time he'd have the advantage of surprise if the assassin was still here.

He passed under an archway marked with the sigil of the Oracle. Such symbols were common in Necrad – the Oracle's immortal influence in the city predated that of Lord Bone by countless centuries – but it still gave him confidence that he was on the right track.

These halls had been ransacked countless times. Gouges in the ceiling marked where scavengers had taken gem-lamps; treasure-hunters smashed holes in the walls and floor, looking for secret hoards. He passed more archways leading to fire-blackened side rooms. The Oracle's unseen agents spied on Lord Bone's enemies, and there had once been labyrinthine archives here – all ash now.

A light bloomed in a cross-corridor ahead. Alf pressed himself to the wall and waited in the shadows. *Witch Elves can see in the dark*, he reminded himself, and without the sword he couldn't. Still, there was enough rubble to make for a good hiding place.

The light grew brighter as it approached the intersection. It was a magical light, unnatural, a colour he couldn't name. It hurt his eyes to look at it. The lamps in the ceiling would have cast a similar light. Brighter and brighter, until the figure came into view for a moment.

Hooded cloak, silent tread, dark hair cut short, a face he knew well. *Berys*. A lamp in her hand.

Alf nearly called out to her, then caught himself. Berys had lied to him over and over since he'd returned to Necrad. Berys had told him that she could find no trace of the elf assassin, and now she was here. *You cannot trust your friends, Lammergeier*.

So, instead, he followed her. Carefully, quietly, like she'd taught him years ago. He waited until he could only see the dimmest glow of her lamp far down the corridor before he set off after her.

Like the House of the Horned Serpent, this palace had a courtyard at its heart. This deep in the city, the necromiasma blotted out the stars, but a dozen statues depicting the celestial decans stood in the courtyard, staring up at the clouded sky. The eyes of the nearest statue had been gouged out. Gemstones once rested there. A series of arched windows looked out onto the courtyard, and Alf ducked down by one to watch.

Berys crossed to the middle of the courtyard – and in response, one of the statues moved. Alf blinked, and realised he'd mistaken a statue for a living elf.

The assassin.

He could see her clearly now, as she approached Berys. Tall she was, gifted with the unearthly grace of the elves. She was unarmed, her hands open, but she was wary, too, like a wild animal that had strayed into unfamiliar territory. She called out in the elven tongue – it sounded to Alf like a formal greeting.

Berys did not respond in kind. Instead, she stood there, arms folded, fingers drumming. The elf drew close, and they spoke in low tones. Alf dared not creep any closer to eavesdrop – Berys was always on guard, and the ears of elves were famously keen. He watched the two whisper at first, then break into argument.

"Have you found the Changeling, mortal? The hour grows late."

"What if you can't stop Lath? What will you do then?"

"Prepare for the enemy's assault, and hope we can avert whatever doom he has planned for us all. The Oracle promised me that there is still strength in Necrad that can be turned against him," whispered the elf. "Our enemy works through agents – mortals, for the most part. He will seek to divide you first, before the stroke falls."

"He's twenty years late for that." Berys kicked at a stone. "We're already divided."

"Look to those you can still count on. Who does the Lammergeier serve? If he cleaves to the mortal lords—"

"You attacked him as soon as he arrived."

"I thought him to be the Beast."

"Don't call him that!" snapped Berys. "Not the Beast. Not ever."

"Such prodigies of earthpower always go sour. So has it been since the first days of your kind."

"Call us *speaking beasts*, why don't you?" There was an unfamiliar edge to Berys' voice, a rumbling growl.

That's not Berys, thought Alf.

The elf had the same thought in the same moment. She leapt back – a fraction of a second too late. The figure that had been Berys changed its shape, becoming a duplicate of Alf. Not Alf as he was, but younger, strong, his face stern and grim, like an executioner. A black sword was in his hand, and he swung it with wild ferocity. The elf dodged the blow with astounding quickness, but stumbled amid the rubble and fell to the ground.

The other Alf stepped forward. He raised the black sword high, like an executioner about to behead a condemned prisoner.

The real Alf stared in confusion.

An arrow came flying from a rooftop, piercing the false Alf's chest. Another transfixed his hand, making him drop the sword. The blade melted away to smoke before it hit the ground.

Up there, on the roof opposite. Berys, the real Berys. "Flee, you idiot!" she shouted at the elf. She had a bow in hand, a third arrow nocked and drawn. The arrowhead smouldered with magical fire. "Lath," she called. "Don't make me kill you."

For an instant, the false Alf crumpled in on himself, shrinking and changing until he was Lath again. Small and hunched, black hair spiky and wild, dressed in rags, skin marked with the filth and scrapings of the Pits.

Then he roared.

Alf knew that roar, that battle cry, and what it presaged.

The stones quivered. The city groaned as Lath drew on the earth-power. Alf felt it, too, the sickening lurch, as if the solid ground beneath his feet had turned to mud. He'd felt it thousands of times before, and always it had reassured him. It was a signal that the Changeling was going into battle alongside the rest of the Nine, and together there was no foe they could not defeat.

But now . . .

Lath erupted, his human form exploding into a monstrous shape that had never been seen in the lives of mortals or elves outside of the deepest of the Pits. His mouth distended, fangs sprouting like white froth on a breaking wave. His body lengthened and grew armoured scales. His arms split and split again, a dozen limbs scuttling forwards. His eyes sank back inside his skull, and bone sealed the empty sockets. Fire erupted around him as Berys' arrow struck home.

Alf vaulted into the courtyard, sword in hand. He stumbled as he ran, and the bandage on his wrist reddened as the bite-wound opened. The barrage of arrows barely slowed the Changeling down. He rose up, a twisted giant, clawed arms ripping at the roof tiles as Berys fled before his wrath. She loosed another explosive arrow, right in Lath's monstrous face, and the Changeling stumbled backwards, grunting in pain. The elf vanished into the shadows.

Alf moved warily forward, keeping the statues between him and Lath. He'd fought monsters that big before and survived, and a part of his mind instantly fell into considering how to fight a foe of such tremendous size: *look for gaps between the armour plates. No eyes, it hunts by scent or vibration. Come at it from beneath.* If there was ever a good time to strike the thing, it was now, while it was rearing up to claw at Berys on the rooftop. The thing's belly was exposed, and Alf could see those vulnerable openings in the armoured hide. *Charge in, thrust, pray it has vital organs to pierce.*

But it wasn't a thing. It was *Lath*. His friend, one of the Nine. And so he stayed his hand. He circled, forced to watch the battle from the side lines instead of plunging into the fray.

And this battle was terribly familiar. Alf knew all the steps of this dance, the old patterns and tactics. Berys dodged and feinted, a dance on the edge of the abyss. Arrow after arrow struck Lath. None struck with enough force to pierce the monster's hide, but that wasn't her goal. She wanted her foe off balance, to give her an opening for the killing, the deep thrust into some exposed weak spot. She'd killed an armoured dread knight like that once, luring him close and then driving her dagger into his armpit, twisting as the blood gushed over both of them, twisting until the armour rattled with the wraith trapped inside.

Lath fought savagely. No tactics, no clever ploys, just sheer onslaught. The Changeling's wild magic rushing through him like hot blood. The elements obeyed him – sudden squalls of wind and rain hammered Berys, making her slip. Lightning wreathed the monster's claws. Alf was astounded by Lath's strength here in the middle of Necrad. The city used to dampen Lath's ability to draw on the earthpower, but no longer.

Berys was outmatched.

If it had been anyone else, any other foe, then Alf would already be in the fray. He'd already have drawn blood. Aelfric had a sword in his hand, and that meant death. In all his years, no foe had ever lived once Alf had made up his mind to kill them.

Even Lord Bone.

But this was different. All his instincts, all his experience counted for naught. In that moment, he was the callow boy from Ersfel again, the boy who knew nothing about the world.

Lath tried to scramble onto the roof and was halfway up when the elf appeared again. She leapt up and caught onto a spiny protrusion from Lath's back, and drove a dagger into him, finding a gap between the scales. This time, her blade nicked some vital spot, for Lath bellowed in pain and lost his grip. He crashed to the ground, the impact seeming to shake the whole city. The elf was on him in an instant, searching for his throat.

"Beware!" shouted Alf. Without thinking, he scooped up a rock and flung it at the elf. It caught her in the shoulder, and that gave Lath a moment to recover. A swipe of the Changeling's tail knocked the elf away. If they'd been down in the Pits, then Alf would have followed up with a killing blow. He'd rush over there and drive his sword down through the elf's heart; the bloody rhythm of their long partnership, punctuated by slaughter. But Alf found himself rooted to the ground, unsure of his purpose here. For an instant, he glimpsed the elf scaling a wall on the far side of the courtyard as a flaring light in the necromiasma overhead caught her silver hair. Then she was gone, fleeing into the ruined city beyond.

Another arrow from above struck Lath. Again he reared up, reaching for Berys' perch. Throwing down her bow, Berys slashed at Lath with a dagger. Stung, Lath snatched back his outstretched paw, then he threw his titanic bulk forward, into the side of the building. The structure collapsed, sending Berys tumbling down in a landslide of rubble. She landed heavily in the courtyard, winded, beaten.

Lath pulled his linnorm-body free of the debris, shaking off the remains of the building like a dog coming out of a pond. He crawled towards Berys' limp body, and lifted a clawed hand to impale her. A roar built in his throat.

Alf stepped forward to stand between the beast and Berys. The roaring ceased. The beast stopped and sniffed the air. "Alf?" Lath's voice, nervous and hesitant, issuing from the mouth of the monster. He began to shrink, collapsing in on himself, and again Alf felt the thrill of earthpower flowing past him.

Lath let out a screech, halfway between a human cry and the roar of an animal. With a tremendous effort, the Changeling altered his transformation midway through. Bones cracked and skin tore as Lath's form changed again. Wings unfolded from his back, dripping with gore. He hunched his back, and there was an audible series of snaps as the magic transformed him into something that could fly, a six-winged horror, a dragon mated with an insect. He sprang into the air in pursuit of the elf.

"Stop him!" shouted Berys. Alf reacted without thinking. He grabbed onto a clawed foot as it flew past, and hung on as it all but wrenched his arm from its socket. The courtyard fell away beneath him as they soared above the Sanction. Alf tried shouting at Lath, but the rushing wind carried his words away.

The sword was still in Alf's hand. He battered Lath's scaly flank with it. The Changeling shrieked and twisted in the air, trying to dislodge its unexpected burden. Alf hung on with all his might, desperately trying to make Lath stop and listen.

The elves of old built great towers and cryptic spires in their silent city. High they reached, as if drawn to the hidden stars, their topmost levels vanishing in the lurid green haze of the necro-miasma. Tall were these towers, cold and remote like distant peaks.

Tall were the towers of Necrad – and bloody hard when you crashed into one.

Alf remembered falling, slip-sliding down the side of the build-ing, his limbs entangled with Lath's changing form. They bounced off one balcony, off some other protrusion, and landed heavily amid the rubble. Alf lay there groaning. The fall had knocked the air from his lungs, and when he took a breath, it hurt. Every part of him complained in its own way.

He lay there, unable to move, staring at the sky.

Lath unfolded, returning to his human form even as he stood upright. He looked down at Alf. "You didn't bring the sword," he whispered. "Clever, clever. It's bad for you."

The Changeling held up his hands, scraping at the soot and dirt and dried blood that caked them. "The earthpower under Necrad, it got under my skin. No matter how much I change, still feel it. A barbed hook in my guts. Wish you hadn't left, Alf. Had to fight the Pitspawn on my own, and the hooks went deeper."

He reached down, and the warmth of a healing spell flowed through Alf's broken limbs. "I have to go, Alf. I don't have time to explain now, but I've found a way to save us all. You'll understand. None of the others might, but you will."

With a flurry of wings, the Changeling was gone.

The dwarves found Alf in the hours after dawn. Hands lifted him out of the wreckage. They put him on a shield to bear him down to the street. One of them pressed a healing potion to his lips.

"When I told you to get some sleep," said Gundan, "I didn't think I needed to add 'in a bed', and not 'in a pile of rubble'."

"How did you find me?"

"Him." Gundan jerked a thumb in the direction of the Vatling Threeday. The creature seemed taken aback to be given credit.

"In truth," said Threeday, "it was the Lady Berys who informed me late last night that you were somewhere in the Sanction, and likely in need of assistance."

"Berys . . . she was here. And the elf we chased."

"The Lady Berys has left the city on urgent business in the south, the nature of which she did not reveal to me."

"Her bloody smuggling, no doubt," interrupted Gundan.

The Vatling shrugged. "I understand the Lady Berys has many important clients in Summerswell, and I have assisted her in some aspects of her business in the past, but I cannot guess what prompted such a hasty departure. Perhaps the Lammergeier can shed some light on the matter."

"Aye. Alf – what the fuck happened here? What's going on? It can't have been Berys who dropped you on that roof, not unless she's grown wings to go with her serpent's tongue."

Alf tried to recall the events of the night. "Lath was here, too. Disguised as Berys at first."

"All of you, fuck off," ordered Gundan. The dwarves laid Alf down gently, and backed away, taking up defensive positions up and down the street. The Vatling lingered a moment longer, but a glare from Gundan sent him scuttling away.

"Lath is one of us," said Gundan. "Ours to deal with. Berys, too, for that matter. Tell me, what happened?"

"I'm not sure," began Alf.

"Are you ever?"

"Lath was chasing the Witch Elf. He was disguised as Berys, and got close to the elf. They argued – about the Oracle I think! – and Lath attacked her."

"A month ago," muttered Gundan, "my main worry was dwarves feuding over mine claims in the Irontooth hills. Now it's the Oracle, and assassins, and Lord Bone back from the dead." He grinned. "What happened?"

"Lath went after the elf. I stopped him, and then – I

think he flew away." Alf rubbed his skull. "That was after he dropped me."

"Sentries saw a monster flying out of the Liberties last night, heading north. It wasn't a dreadworm, so I'm guessing it was Lath." Gundan reached down and helped Alf stand. "As for the elf, the Vatling says there's no sign of her in any part of Necrad he knows. I'm guessing she's gone, too – or Lath got her."

Alf nodded. "Whatever Jan saw, whatever's happening in the city, Lath is at the heart of it. We have to find him."

"A quest, then? Two brothers-in-arms, alone against the wilderness? Like the old times?"

"Something like that."

CHAPTER TWENTY-ONE

That night, the stars shone brighter than Olva had ever seen before, a jewelled necklace strung across a younger, bolder sky, as the last of the elf-wind chased the clouds away.

There was no jetty or pier, only a bone-white beach littered with other wrecks. Beyond was a line of dark trees, the edge of the forest that girdled most of the island's steep hill. More elves emerged from this forest, armed with bows.

The elf who had rescued them slithered down a silken line of rope, and bade Olva follow him down. After a few minutes, under the watchful eyes of the elves, the rest of the survivors followed. The prisoners from the lower deck were ragged and pale after their confinement. Torun came last; when Abran had taken Olva, the dwarf had rushed down to the lower deck to free the captives from their manacles. The elves separated the smugglers from their former prisoners and made them kneel in the sand.

Torun left the ship warily, cursing all the way down, and the waters nearly came up to her neck as she waded ashore. She spluttered as a gust of wind sent icy saltwater splashing over her face, and the elves laughed.

"A cup of wine will warm you, in the prince's own house! Follow!"

They climbed up the slope of the sandy beach and passed into the shadows of the trees. There were two forests here to Olva's eyes. One was a forest of spruce and pine and birch and other familiar trees, bent by the winds that whipped across the seas. The other forest was of much larger trees with silvery trunks and golden leaves. These woodland giants seemed planted at irregular intervals through the wood – there were clusters of them near the shore, like a silvery wall, and then knots of twos and threes along the path. Lights glimmered in their upper branches.

Winds rustled the branches, and suddenly more elves appeared along the side of the path, seeming to coalesce out of the mists. They were all clad in shimmering robes, all pale and golden, and while their faces reminded Olva of the Witch Elves she had seen in the war, she felt no fear or trepidation. The elves lifted their voices in ethereal song, and Torun squeezed Olva's hand in wonder.

"These are the tree-bound," explained Maedos. "Dryads, in your tongue. Some are very old and wise, and have dwelt here for many centuries. Others are not so old, and definitely not so wise." This last remark was directed to another elf who materialised nearby, and who seemed to know Maedos. Like the rest, he was clad in silvery robes, but he had a spear in his hand and appeared somehow younger and more vital than his wan neighbours. Their guide paused and exchanged a few quick words in Elvish with his friend, and they both laughed. The second elf bowed to Olva, then faded away again. His flashing smile and the bright point of his spear lingered a moment longer, then vanished too.

"That was Telemor," said Maedos, "he sailed to war with me, against Lord Bone. The undead wounded him, and we brought him back to the wood when he could endure no longer." Maedos slapped the trunk of a tree as they passed. "Now he dwells here until the world's ending, and will never return to the Everwood again. But this place is not so bad to wait out eternity, and you can see the sea from his topmost branches. Another tree waits for me – but it must wait a little longer! I have much to do, first!"

The path seemed to spiral inwards and upwards, leading them towards the island's central peak. They passed a handful of structures. Some were simple wooden huts or tents, little storehouses or workshops or shelters. Others were ruins of white stone, eerie and beautiful in the moonlight.

"Made with magic!" whispered Torun with glee. "No blocks carved by mason's hand, no mortar or brick! Oh, wonderful!"

There were animals in the wood, too. Birds perched amid the branches, and Olva glimpsed dark shapes darting through the undergrowth. She looked around, and found that, save for Torun and the elves, there was no one else there. The survivors from the ship had vanished.

"Where are the other people we rescued?"

"There is a place of shelter near the shore where I beached your ship. They will stay there tonight, and in time they shall be sent back to the lands of Summerswell. But it is not our custom to allow outsiders past the forest eaves. You are an exception."

The path twisted again, and suddenly they beheld the most marvellous castle that Olva had ever imagined. It, too, was made of the enchanted stone, but it was interwoven with the forest, trees twining through gaps in the white walls, and white spires lifting above the topmost branches. Higher and higher it mounted, leaping upwards towards the stars as if eager to take flight. Staircases spiralled overhead, and thin bridges of stone like glittering strands of spiderweb ran from one tower to another. Pale figures stared down from ledges and battlements and alcoves, and Olva could not tell if they were elves or statues or something else.

At the heart of the enchanted castle, rising above even the tallest tower, was a gigantic life-tree. The golden leaves unfurled, shedding a warm golden glow down onto the fortress below, and Olva could see more shapes moving among the branches. Up there, the trunk of the tree split into a wide bowl like a cupped hand, and many elves had gathered there.

From somewhere in the treetops, there came the sound of a herald's trumpet, clear and cold, the note more piercing than a spear.

"That is the sign to begin the revels," said Maedos.

Afterwards, Olva could remember only fragments, as one recalls the fleeting tatters of a dream, but these fragments were sharp-edged and brilliant. She had stumbled sleepwalking through the world for years, but for those few remembered moments she was truly awake and aware, every one of her senses blasted by joy. She forgot her fears and her weariness, forgot her doubts and worries. She forgot Bor and Cu, left behind in Ellsport; forgot Alf off in Necrad.

She even forgot Derwyn, for a little while.

It was as if the court of the elves reassured her that while there might be darkness in the world, it was far away and could not hope to compete with the light that poured through her. The elf-tree reached up into the heavens and they walked among the stars.

Elves came to greet her, each fairer and kinder than the last, and all full of joy at her presence. They whirled around her, dancing and laughing. They pressed glasses of sweet wine into her hand, and there were long tables laden with the most delicious food she had ever tasted. She glimpsed Torun across the bower, sitting with rapt attention in a circle of elven sorcerers, but she lost track of Maedos in the whirl of the crowd.

Poets raised their voices in song, and though Olva spoke no Elvish, their words conjured pictures in her mind, a waking dream unfolding around her, and she could not tell if the figures around her were the elves of the island or elves from long long ago, when the Erlking battled against demons from the dark between the stars.

An elf-maiden took Olva by the hand and led her through the crowd and up a staircase that twined around one mighty branch of the tree. For an instant, a gust of wind from the sea reminded Olva where she was, and how high above the ground she had climbed, and fear stabbed at her, but the elf's grip on her fingers was strong and reassuring, and she allowed herself to be led back into enchantment. The staircase brought them to a stone balcony that looked out over the feast-hall below. There, seated on a throne with a garland of oak-leaves in his hair, was an elf prince.

Olva did not recognise him at first. He had exchanged his grey cloak and hat for clothing of silver and gold, and a circlet of gold studded with rubies adorned his brow. The same silver sword as before was belted by his hip, but now it was in a scabbard of rich leather decorated with more gold and gems. A light now filled him, but his face was unchanged. It was Maedos on the throne, Maedos exalted.

He did not rise, but invited her to take a seat on a stool by his feet. She found she could not meet his gaze, any more than she could stare into the noonday sun, so she found her attention darting from one small, perfect feature to another – the way his elegant fingers crooked around the stem of his wine glass, or the jewelled necklace at his throat, or the shape of his bare ankle as it rested on the edge of the stool.

"Lady Olva Forster," he said, and his words were music. "Welcome to my realm."

"I'm not a lady," she said, in a small, scratchy voice. "I'm just a farmer."

He smiled in the easy way of the elves. "My father the Erlking made the worthy into Lords of Summerswell, did he not? And your brother is one of the Nine who saved us all. If it pleases me to ennoble you, then take it with good grace."

Sudden horror clutched Olva. "In the stories – in the stories, you and he quarrelled. He hurt you!"

"Indeed. He cast me down from this very spot." The prince's face was unreadable, his voice neutral, as if he was recounting an old tale. "I do not hold you responsible for his deeds – and while he and I have a score to settle, it is a very small matter. In a thousand years, only

the songs will remember who was the better swordsman that day."
The shadow passed, and he laughed. Olva laughed, too, in relief.

"My son gets into trouble for fighting, too. I've apologised to
neighbours and reeves and priests, but never to a prince. I'm sorry
my family is such trouble."

"Mine, too, I assure you. You have not met my youngest sister."

"Thank you for rescuing us."

His attention flickered down to the bower below, picking the
tiny dot that was Torun out of the crowd. It wasn't hard – the dwarf
was like a speck of dark-hued grit in a field of stars. "You need not
thank me – my people despise those who trade in blood. That is
one reason why we rejoice tonight. You, my lady, are another. It has
been too long since we have had a noble guest from the lands of
Summerswell." The elf-maiden handed Olva another glass of potent
wine, and her head swam.

"I wish only that you had arrived in a more pleasant manner,
instead of as a prisoner on a blood trader's ship. Not so long ago,
there was great friendship between elves and mortals in this land –
why, many of my courtiers fought in the siege of Necrad alongside
your brother and his companions, and owe much to the heroism
of the Nine. But now Necrad has fallen under the sway of thieves
and swindlers who sow discord between friends. How quickly the
works of mortals turn sour!" Maedos brooded as he stared out
across the scene below, then shook himself and seemed to notice her
again. "Forgive me. I deliver you from shadow and bondage, and
then burden you with my own petty woes! Such things shall pass
quickly – let us not speak of them more tonight. Tonight is only
for merriment.

"Thank you, my lord," she said again, "but I don't think I can
stay. I came looking for my son, Derwyn."

"Indeed?" said the prince. "And what has befallen him? Why do
you seek him with such urgency?"

Olva struggled to gather her thoughts. Every time she found

the words, a sip of wine or a glance from the prince would scatter them again. "He ... he ran away. He went looking for adventure, and – and then he was taken prisoner by the same people who imprisoned us."

"Have you spoken to your brother about this?" He spoke lightly, but it was more than a question – she felt compelled to answer, as if the truth was the only shape that her lips and tongues could make in that moment.

"I haven't spoken to Alf in many years."

"Adventure is to peril as blossom is to root, I fear. And there are far more perils than wonders in this world of ours. This I know – it has been my duty to watch over the Gulf of Tears and guard the seas against the hosts of Necrad for many centuries. I command the elf-ships and the writhing serpents, and I shall send hunters on your son's trail. For now, be at peace! Let there be no sorrow in my court!"

With that, he stood, and took her hand, and whirled her down the stairs to the celebration below.

How long the celebration lasted, Olva could not tell. She remembered how one glass of wine went straight to her head and made her stumble. The elves caught her and laid her down in a bower of rushes. She closed her eyes, and if she slept for but a moment or a day or a hundred years, it felt the same, for she woke to the same whirl of celebration. These elves reminded her of Derwyn's young friends up in the holywood. They were like dreaming children, unburdened by care. They began to sing, and she recognised the melody – a song to the Erlking. She'd heard it sung in the holywood by the priests, and there it was solemn and reverential. Here, the elves filled it with passion and merriment. She lay there for a while, losing herself in the song and the images it conjured of the kindly Erlking standing guard over his kingdom and his children.

*

Olva saw Torun across the room and made her way through the throng to her. Halfway along, one elf-lord scooped her up and whirled her away in a wild dance, declaring that he wished to make love to her that very night in the boughs of his life-tree. He was very beautiful, and very silly. Olva extricated herself from his grasp and pushed through the crowd until she found the dwarf again.

Torun's face glistened with tears.

"What's wrong?"

"They want to send me away! One of them said that they're sending the prisoners from the ship back to the southlands, and that I'll be going with them! We just got here, and there's so much I want to learn. They know magic better than anyone, they taught you humans, but when I ask them they just laugh and go off dancing!" Torun clenched her fists and shouted at the elves around her. "Just let me stay and study, please!" They danced on, heedless.

"We'll ask the prince," said Olva. "Let's go and find him. He'll let you stay, I'm sure."

They searched the party for Maedos. There was no sign of him in the high chamber, or in any of the bowers that adjoined the main feast-hall, but one of the more sober elves directed them back down the road to the beach. They left the revels behind them, although the songs followed them through the forest, as if the life-trees were singing.

They emerged onto the white strand where they had landed. The hulk of Abran's ship was ablaze, and more elves danced barefoot on the sand. Prince Maedos stood among them, the fixed point they circled around.

"Lady Forster," said he, "why have you left the revels? It is unwise for you, a mortal, to walk abroad at night here."

"My friend Torun – she was told that you intend to send her away."

"I want to stay," added Torun, defiantly.

"It is not our custom to have guests here on the isle. This place

may not seem it to your eyes, but it is a fortress against the enemy –
and though the lord of Necrad has fallen, there are still dangers
across the straits. For you, as sister of one of the Nine, we make an
exception – but we thought to speed your companion home."

"I don't want to go home," said Torun. "I want to study magic."

The prince frowned. "Few among the elves, and none here on the
isle, make a study of magic as mortals do. It is tiresome to teach
by rote a thing that is as natural as speaking to us. There is no one
here with the patience to instruct you – and even if you had the
instruction, no dwarf has ever channelled star-magic."

"There's none who'll teach me in Summerswell either."

"There is an order to the world, mistress dwarf. Perhaps your kind
was not meant to learn magic."

"Maybe." Torun took a step forward. "But that's not for you to
say. I just want a chance."

"Please," said Olva.

"Of course," said the prince, and his dazzling smile was visible in
the darkness, "stay as long as you wish, both of you! And when you
are ready to leave, we shall send you wherever you desire."

"Thank you," said Torun. "Now, if there's a library or the like
here ... "

"In time," said Maedos, "but there is another departure to consider. Indeed, it is fitting you are here, Lady Forster. I recall of old a
custom of your people. When a son or daughter of the Erlking visits
the lands of mortals, the Lords of Summerswell present a condemned
prisoner to their guest, so they may show mercy. Let me honour you
in return."

"What do you mean?"

"Follow!"

Maedos led them a short distance across the sands to a stand of
gnarled trees, hunched against the constant wind from the sea. The
grove stood in a pool of brackish water, thick with reeds. Waves

sighed on the shore and sent ripples into this inlet. Creepers and vines hung from the branches. Olva recognised Captain Abran's bulky shape standing knee-deep in the water, and at first she could not tell if he was alive or dead. The fallen priest had a vine looped around his neck as a noose.

When he saw Olva approach, he thrashed against the vine and called out to her.

"Tell them I didn't harm you! I had you treated well!"

"You were not so kind to me," said Torun.

"I had no choice!" begged Abran, "I chose none of this!" He gasped. "It's strangling me!"

"What is it to be?" said Maedos. "Should he live or die?" The prince raised his hand, and the vine closed on Abran. He gasped for air, like Bor had in the shadow of the Fossewood. The thought of having such power was terrifying to Olva – to hold a man's life in the balance, and to know that a word either way would snuff him out or spare him. Who was she to answer such a question? She couldn't be the one to choose.

"He . . . he's a priest," said Olva. "He told me he's a priest, and it's forbidden to hurt a priest of the Intercessors!"

"A priest. Is this true, thief?"

"Yes! Yes!" Abran gasped for air.

Maedos' face grew grave, and a strange light came into his eyes. He raised his hand again, and spoke more sternly than Olva had heard before. He gave a command to the empty air. "Intercessors, hear me. In my father's name, I say: this mortal is unworthy of your charity, unworthy of your care, unworthy of your protection. Abjure him!" Abran groaned loudly, as if the prince's words wounded him.

"This mortal is no longer a priest. I ask again – does he deserve to live? He seems unworthy to me. He is violent, and cruel. He has killed for profit. He steals from Necrad, and is in league with greater thieves. He hurt you and yours, Olva. Should he die?"

All her life, she'd hidden in Ersfel, fearing the dangers of the world outside. Now, one of those dangers was at her mercy, and she had power over him. Abran had beaten Torun, he served the men who took Derwyn. He was a thief, and worse – a trafficker in blood. He deserved death, didn't he? He deserved judgement. But the thought of being the one to make that judgement sickened her to her stomach. Who was she to judge this man?

"I – I don't want this honour. It may please you to call me a lady, and I know you do it to praise my brother, but – I don't want anyone to live or die on my word alone. You're the prince of this land, and that means it's your judgement that counts."

"Nonetheless," said Maedos, "the choice is yours."

Abran tried to speak, but the choking vine cut him off.

She should be merciful. She wanted to be merciful. But someone – maybe even Prince Maedos, right here on this very beach – had been merciful to Bor, once. Mercy without redemption was hollow; it was trusting that kindness would be rewarded. Maybe she could have mustered that sort of faith, once, but not any more. If she was merciful to Abran, how could she be sure he would not do harm to someone else?

If it had been Lyulf Martens, or Bor, at her mercy here, she would not have hesitated.

She shook her head, but could not bring herself to say the words. She forced herself to watch as Abran's foot beat upon the sand, and shuddered, and went still. The vine released the corpse, and it fell limply to the ground.

Maedos returned to Olva's side. "Shall we return to the revels?" His grim and lordly demeanour was gone, and he was once again the merry elf who'd rescued her – but now, his merriment seemed jarring to her, as if he was mocking her for feeling the weight of the decision.

"No," said Olva. "We . . . we should bury him."

The prince laughed. "Do as the customs of your people demand.

When you are done, call out, and one of my kinfolk will bring you to a place where you can find rest." He vanished into the wood.

Torun said nothing, but she helped Olva carry Abran's body a little distance away from the shore, where the serpents could not reach the remains. There was no holywood on the isle, but they dug a shallow grave in the loose soil. Torun dragged a rock into place to mark the grave, and on it she scratched the image of the grail-cup of wisdom – the sign of Intercession.

"You called his piety dishonest," said Olva softly.

"I don't want to be haunted by him. He can have his story if it helps him sleep soundly."

Chapter Twenty-Two

An embankment of packed earth lifted the road above the black mud of the Charnel marshes. This part of the road was smooth enough, which was a mercy to Alf. Healing potions could only do so much, and every jolt of the wagon sent a fresh shock of pain through his spine. It did not help that he had to share the wagon with Abbess Marit. Every time the wagon jolted, Alf cursed, and every time he cursed the Abbess gave him a dirty look and began another round of prayers.

By the third milestone, Alf had run out of curses, and had to start inventing new ones. By the fourth, he tired of the game and stared out at the undulating wastes. The guards moved warily, long spears ready to skewer any lurking undead. By nightfall, even at the wagon's laggard pace, they would be clear of the Charnel and into the New Provinces proper.

In the distance, the outermost of the sentinel dragon-statues loomed above the marsh, curving northward like the claw of some buried beast. The remains of the League's encampment on the northern flank were out there somewhere, lost in the mud. The sentinel statues were potent magical weapons. Once, the marshes trembled as the dragons spat bolts of magical energy, keeping the besiegers from pressing their attack on the city. Now, all was silent. The stone dragons had died with Lord Bone.

If those dragons woke, Necrad would again be invulnerable. He wondered if Blaise, with all his arcane mutterings and forbidden lore, could reactivate the defences. Blaise had to have thought of it. Blaise thought of everything.

The Abbess followed his gaze across the marsh. "Put your faith in the Intercessors," she advised, "not the works of evil."

"Those aren't Bone's work. Witch Elves built 'em." Alf pulled the furs closer around him; if he had to sit in this cursed wagon and watch the world roll slowly by, at least he could be comfortable.

"It should all be torn down. It is a well of sin and corruption. In Summerswell, in certain circles, it is considered fashionable to have treasures out of Necrad in one's home. They covet the vile things made by sorcery. Such greed leads down a perilous road to mortal sin."

Alf grunted. His own vile thing— the sword Spellbreaker — was in a metal casket under his seat.

"There are places, Sir Aelfric, secret gatherings where sinners mimic the ways of the Witch Elves. They dress as the demons you so rightly defeated, and engage in unspeakable depravities." Merit tapped his knee with a bony finger. "Alas that none of the Nine have the courage to speak out against such sin. Ye who confronted the evil one in his own fortress, you turn a blind eye to corruption at home. Alas that it was Peir who died – was he the only one among you who had faith?"

"You didn't know Peir," said Alf, "and you shouldn't speak of what you don't know." Peir's faith had run deep, but it was in people, in the Nine and their common cause, not in spirits and Intercessors.

"Do the songs lie?"

"Well, songs call Jan 'Pious', and your church kicked her out."

Merit scowled. "Songs are for the common folk, who need simple answers. You and I, Sir Lammergeier, know that matters are always more complex and ambiguous than they seem at first glance – but that too is a trap. Many call themselves clever, and by their sophistry they convince themselves that right and wrong are but words to be juggled and rearranged, and that righteousness is but one thing to be considered when weighing a matter. Your friend Master Blaise is such a one – he could convince you that a vial of poison was fine wine, or cruelty an act of kindness. Mistress Berys, too. They call themselves clever so they do not have to be brave. It takes a special sort of courage to stand up for what is right. To see that the matter is complex, but the answer simple. That courage and faith count for more than cunning intrigues." She toyed with her prayer beads. "If one of the Nine were to speak out, their voice would echo in the church, and be heard across Summerswell and the north."

The nun looked at him expectantly. What did she want him to do, ride down to Summerswell and start kicking in doors until he found these unspeakable depravities, whatever they were? Alf shifted in his seat, sending a fresh spasm of pain through his bones. "Aye, well, I was never one for speeches." He closed his eyes, hoping that she would leave him to sleep.

"The Intercessors vouchsafed me a vision," said Merit suddenly. "Such blessings are rare in this benighted land. In Necrad and the lands north, the Intercessors remain silent. Never, in all my years at the monastery on Staffa, have they responded to my entreaties. But after the council, I went to the chapel outside the city, and there I prayed. The Intercessors answered me, Sir Aelfric. In the moving waters of the grail, I saw you."

"Me?" scoffed Alf. He'd learned to distrust prophecies over the years. Even Jan's words about a rising darkness – he'd have discounted them as ravings coming from anyone else. The clerics might see signs and portents, but no prophecy had ever won a battle.

"You, Sir Lammergeier, as you were in the flower of your youth, when you won the day against Lord Bone. You were in a dungeon dark, chained and bleeding from many wounds. Evil spirits surrounded you. And then I beheld one of the Holy Intercessors watching over you, and I understood then the meaning of the vision."

"Enlighten me."

"The Intercessors have singled you out for a special purpose. The church needs a champion, a shining knight who will drive away the darkness. You and I both sit on the council of Necrad – the city is our responsibility. So, too, therefore, is the corruption that flows from it. You spent many years fighting the Pitspawn, with your strong right arm, but there are other battles to fight, and better weapons to wield than that cursed sword. Speak out against the sinful influence of Necrad, and the people will listen to you."

The nun's speech was interrupted by a muffled, metallic chuckle. She frowned. Alf shoved Spellbreaker's box further under his seat, but they could still hear the sword's laughter.

Marit pressed on, trying to ignore the sound. "Think on it, Lammergeier! The church can be a powerful ally. Go to Arshoth – not for some wasteful tourney, not for the follies of youth, but to seek the wisdom of the church. Follow the same path Peir the Paladin walked, and find the light. What better purpose, what better legacy, could there be for you than proclaiming the glory and truth of the Intercessors to those who have lost their way?"

"I'm no priest."

"Pray on it," she repeated. "Consider a higher purpose. A long journey lies before us, before we reach Duna's keep."

From outside, Remilard called. "Sir Lammergeier! The dwarves return!"

"Thank the Intercessors," muttered Alf.

Gundan and two of his kinsfolk had ridden ahead on fast horses. There were deep mines in the hills beyond the Charnel, delved by the Witch Elves in ancient days. After, they'd forced their Wilder thralls to toil in the depths. Now, the dwarves claimed the mines, just as the folk of Summerswell claimed the New Provinces. The mines were vast. Sometimes, when Alf was down in the dark of the Pits under Necrad, he'd heard tapping echoing through the walls, and wondered if some probing mine shaft had reached all the way to the city, like tree roots intertwining.

The dwarf-lord arrived with a thunder of hooves and a splash of mud. He handed the reins of his horse to Remilard, then hopped from the beast's steaming back right onto the wagon, landing heavily next to the Abbess. She pulled herself away, but not before Gundan's muddy boots left a large and visible mark on the hem of her robe. She tugged the fur blankets close around herself, as if walling herself away from the dwarf.

"How are you, grandfather?" said Gundan, mockingly rubbing Alf's knee. "Are your old bones any better? Shall I dip a cloth in some soup, so you can suckle it?"

"Keep that up," said Alf, "and it'll be dwarf-meat soup."

"That's the spirit. Shove over, your holiness." Gundan sat down. "My cousin down the mine had some news. First off, it's the As Gola Wilder who're causing trouble at Duna's place. Thurn's folk."

"I knew that," said Alf. "Berys told me."

"So you said, but I trust my cousin not to lie to my face. But it's good — the As Gola should listen to us. And maybe Thurn's with them. It's been thirteen years — he might say two, even three words to us."

"Any sign of Lath?"

"Not yet, but he flew this way. If he's in the wood, Thurn'll find him." Gundan ran his finger over the razor edge of Chopper. "And when we find him—"

Alf kicked Gundan's shin. The nun was listening, and such conversations were for the Nine and the Nine alone.

"There's something else," said Gundan, "but it'll wait 'til nightfall."

They made camp on the edge of the Charnel. The necromiasma lit the southern horizon with a sickly green light, but the rest of the sky was a glorious dome of stars. Bright points of light, each one distinct and alone, but draw patterns and connections between them, and fate becomes manifest . . .

"Going to be cold enough to freeze the wraith off a Witch Elf," said Gundan, "but this talk isn't one for firelight."

"No." Alf led his companion away into the darkness. Remilard and some of the other guards noticed the departure of the two heroes, but Alf waved away their concerned looks. They came to a sheltered spot in the lee of a boulder.

"So." Gundan kicked at a tangle of brambles. "Lath. Alf, I don't like saying it – I always liked the boy, and he had my back more times than I can count in the war – but he's cracked. Even if he's not the one who opened Bone's tomb, he's still meddling with necromancy, aye? And that business about taking Berys' shape, and yours, and having our stuff in his lair . . . it's not right, Alf. His head's not right."

"I want your word you won't harm him when we find him."

"Not unless he gives me no choice." Gundan looked up at Alf. "We'll fetch Thurn, first, aye? Thurn can talk to him. Or stare intently. Wilders love a good silent stare." The dwarf swung Chopper, slicing through the thorns. "By the way, we're being followed."

Alf leapt up, drawing his sword, and Gundan hooted. "Not right now!" said the dwarf. "At least, I don't think so."

He could see nothing across the edge of the Charnel save a few thorny bushes and blasted rocks.

"When I rode off to see my cousin," continued Gundan, "I had an inkling, and I circled back behind our little parade, and caught sight of your murderous Witch Elf. At least, I assume it was her – she was limping, but she was still quick enough to vanish when she spotted me. She's crafty, I'll give her that. What do you want to do about her? I was thinking we stake Abbess Marit out as bait."

Alf was confused. "Why would the elf go after the Abbess?"

"Oh, she wouldn't. I just want an excuse to be rid of that sanctimonious hag." Gundan laughed to himself. "But we could try to ambush her. Find out what she's up to. She knows more about what Lath's up to than we do."

But there was no sign of the Witch Elf that night, nor the next. Alf spent the days scanning the terrain, looking for any sign of their pursuer. He sat up late with Gundan, lying in wait, staring out into the darkness. He could see nothing without the sword.

He could open the box. With the sword, he could see in the dark. If the Wilder or some monster of the Charnel attacked, they might need Spellbreaker's power. And the sword might know more about the elf.

"You're better off without the thing," advised Gundan.

On the third day out from Necrad, there was a change in the air. They'd left the taint of the city behind, and the glow of the necro-miasma no longer stained the southern sky. The landscape around them grew greener and healthier with every passing mile, Charnel marsh giving way to desolate waste, to scrubland, and then suddenly to thick northern forest. The road was a scar on the wood, hacked through the forest by eager axes. Birds sang in the treetops. The vitality of the wood seemed to inspire the young soldiers, and they lifted their voices in song. Even Alf felt strong enough to ride, and it was a relief. The Abbess was poor company, between her piety, her complaints and her attempts to inveigle Alf into becoming some sort of champion of the church.

There had been many such overtures in the early years, he reflected, after Lord Bone's defeat. Laerlyn was always royalty, but Gundan, Berys, Blaise . . . they'd all risen in station. Alf could have done so, too, but he'd rejected them all. Even the mantle of knight-hood sat awkwardly on his shoulders; Lucar Vond had dubbed him a knight the battlefield, with Necrad burning around them, and Alf staggering about, tear-stained, holding the sword that had slain friend and enemy in the same stroke.

Instead, he rode alongside Remilard. The boy insisted on raising Alf's banner – a Lammergeier bearing a black sword on a field gules – and in response the dwarves unfurled Gundan's, and broke out their trumpets. If there were any Wilder in the woods, they hid from the clamour. By evening, they reached one of the fresh-cut clearings in the forest, where settlers from Summerswell now dwelt. They hurried from their huts and cabins for news of the south, and for reassurance that the League would guard them against all danger. As Vond predicted, the presence of the Nine and the sight of the banners fluttering against the darkening sky was greeted with wild cheering.

Alf rode until he could barely stay in the saddle, then numbed his aches with another potion and rode on. Abbess Marit's wagon jumped and jostled as they went north on the muddy track, and mile after mile of forest went by quickly.

At night, he saw fleeting moonshadows that might have been the elf, but without the sword he could not be sure.

On the evening of the fourth day, they reached Castle Duna.

CHAPTER TWENTY-THREE

Nine towers rose above the forest. Scaffolding surrounded all but two. Duna's original little outpost was in there somewhere, but the castle had grown to match the earl's reach and ambition. The Wilder attacks could not be of immediate concern to Duna if all that scaffolding was still in place – an attacker could easily scale, or just set fire to it and let the whole place burn.

The castle stood atop a knoll of stone, commanding the surrounding lands. Below was a market town, encircled by a wooden palisade. Like the castle that guarded it, the town was still half built, but growing quickly, swollen with settlers from Summerswell. When Alf had last passed this way, the place was half its current size, and he remembered when it was nothing but a Wilder camp where tribes gathered before making their pilgrimages south to Necrad. The old name had stuck – this was the town of Athar, which meant *Sorrow* in the Wilder-speech. It reminded Alf very much of the Garrison, but without the frenetic edge. Necrad was undeniably eerie. No human, save perhaps the man who had become Lord Bone, ever walked the streets of the Witch Elves' city and felt anything other than a trespasser or a thief. That lingering sensation of guilt, that nameless hostility that seeped from the chill stones were enough to drive anyone to madness. Better to travel on north to Athar and the other New Provinces, and live an honest life.

Heralds proclaimed their approach. The streets filled with onlookers, jostling for a glimpse of the strangers, and a cheer went up at the names of Aelfric and Gundan. Their procession moved slowly through the streets of Athar, with Remilard at the head pushing through the crowd, but as the crowds grew, their progress slowed to a crawl and then stopped altogether. Settlers crowded around Alf, shouting questions or just jostling to touch his armour. He sat as high as he could, although his back ached and he felt light-headed. It would not do for one of the Nine to fall from his horse.

They passed through the streets and climbed the winding path up to the fortress. Gundan nodded approvingly at the fortifications, pronouncing it good dwarven stonework. They passed through the outer gatehouse into a wide yard. Lord Duna and his household waited there to greet them. For a moment, Alf felt uncertainty at the sight of all those high lords and ladies in their furs and finery, even though his armour was as fine as any. He marked Duna himself, first among the lords of the New Provinces, and his wife Erdys. Alf recalled Duna as he had been, the second son of a minor noble of Summerswell, no inheritance save the trappings of his knighthood and his horse. A wild hellion who hurled himself into every fray, hungry for glory. Alf remembered Duna at some joust in Summerswell, his polished armour flashing in the sun. He'd laughed wildly even as Peir unhorsed him. Overlaid onto that was another memory – Duna staggering through the mud of the Charnel, ogre blood caking his sword like tar, his face sunburned from the breath of the stone dragons. He was laughing, still, but it was the shrill, crazed laughter of a man who had lost all hope of seeing the sun again. Now, Duna's face was solemn and kingly, his coal-black hair turned grey, and he spoke in measured tones, without levity or haste.

Erdys stood beside him, a heavy cloak wrapped around her against the chilly air. The cloak bore the colours of her family, a far more exalted lineage than that of her husband. She was the daughter of one of the Lords, the great Brychan of Ilaventur. Duna had married far above his station – although he now brought a vast estate in the New Provinces to the match, the scales somewhat rebalanced. She whispered some private joke to her husband.

Alf knew Erdys of old, too. It could easily have been him standing with her in the holywood, him placing the marriage cloak on her shoulders. It could have been his castle, his estates, his banner above the tower.

Near her, in matching colours, was Duna's court wizard, a withered old fellow whose name Alf couldn't recall. There were few wizards in the north, for the graduates of the College of Wizardry were sworn to serve at the pleasure of the Lords. There was no sign of Duna's eldest boy, who was named for Aelfric, but Duna's second and third sons had both come of age since Alf had last visited the keep. Tall lads, their father renewed.

The first snow of the year began to fall as Alf dismounted.

Lady Erdys bowed. "Sir Lammergeier, Lord Gundan, you honour us."

Alf returned the bow, awkwardly. His manners had never been polished, and years of disuse had tarnished them further. Behind him, Gundan sniggered. "Lord Vond and the council send their greetings."

"More, they send their best warriors," said Erdys. "We feared that the dispute with the elves would keep you both in Necrad. I prayed it would be resolved quickly. Is there good news?"

"Nothing involving elves ever is done quickly." Gundan spat. "But Vond figured Alf would be more use scaring the shit out of the Wilder than talking to elves. And me, I came along for the ride – and to eat. From the looks of your belly, Duna, you set a fine table."

Duna's table, however fine it might be, had to wait. First, Erdys insisted on a prayer service in the castle chapel. Alf was given the place of honour in the front pew, next to Duna and Erdys, while Abbess Marit offered thanks to the Intercessors for ensuring their journey had been a safe one. Rain battered against the window shutters, and the chapel was lit by flickering candles instead of glowstones from Necrad. A chilly draught from the window carried Gundan's laughter from outside – the dwarf had slipped away when they were making their procession to the chapel, and was now outside in the courtyard, telling tales of the war to an adoring audience.

Marit droned on, and Alf's attention wandered around the chapel. Statues of the intercessors, all cowled and faceless, watched over him from their shrines high on the walls. Behind the altar was a painting of the Erlking's emissary anointing the eyes of the first Lords, the Intercessors watching over them from the heavens. Behind that was the shrine, the secret sanctum where only priests of the Intercessors might go.

As a boy, Alf once broke into the little shrine in the holywood in Ersfel. The other village children dared him to do it. They told him that the sanctum contained golden cups studded with jewels and other magical treasures, and Alf believed them. In the dead of night, he'd broken open the door and crept in, and found only a dark room no bigger than a privy, containing nothing except a wooden bowl of water. Still, he remembered the overwhelming rush of shame that came over him for blaspheming against the Intercessors, the feeling of shame at being led astray by others cleverer and more cynical than he. He ran home after that, fearing that at any moment the Intercessors would reach down out of the heavens and smite him.

Or tell his father, which amounted to much the same thing.

The next day, he'd found those boys who tricked him, and he'd fought with them. There were five of them, and one of him, and he'd won. But that victory didn't wash away the blasphemy.

No doubt the sanctum here had a bowl of silver or gold. On either side of the chapel were tombs dedicated to knight-companions of Duna's house who'd fallen in the war. Carved effigies of knights with tranquil faces lay on biers, hands crossed over their swords, as if only sleeping. Alf knew they had not passed so peacefully in the war.

He mumbled his way through the prayers. He could hear Erdys reciting the Litany of the Intercessors, naming all the spirits who stood guard over the fate of mortals.

Afterwards, she leaned over and whispered, "I need a favour, Alf. Stay a moment." So he lingered, while Duna and his entourage filtered out of the church.

Erdys smiled shyly and beckoned him over to the side of one of the tombs. "In truth," she whispered, "I just wanted to avoid another lecture on morality from the Abbess. She is our neighbour here, so we must stay on good terms with her – and I find that easier the less I see her."

"She wants me to become a paladin or some such."

Erdys laughed. "I'm told you looked like a holy man when you were wandering. A mad hermit who climbs every tree looking for the Intercessors." She clasped her fingers over her mouth for a moment, stifling her own laughter in the chapel. "I know Marit is a scold, but you should listen to her, Alf. Think of your own soul."

She took an offertory bowl from the altar and laid it at the feet of the carven knight.

"My father sent a letter. A long letter, as is his habit these days. An adventurer in Necrad found an enchanted quill that writes what you tell it, and I bought it and sent it to my father. I fear he will wear it to a nub. He spoke of you, by the by – he follows your doings with great interest, and always speaks very highly of you. He said you won the tourney at Ilaventur."

The last time Alf had spoken to Lord Brychan of Ilaventur, it was to turn down the lord's offer of Erdys' hand in marriage. Alf remembered the look of confusion and disappointment on Erdys' face – and the fury in the old man's eyes. Marriage to the daughter of a Lord of Summerswell was not an honour to be rejected, and certainly not by a peasant boy from the Mulladales without lands or family. Alf had never meant to hurt the girl's feelings, nor insult the lord. It had all been part of the whirling days after victory over Lord Bone, and Alf had instinctively flinched away from every gift and honour offered to him. It had all seemed a distraction, a premature celebration. They'd been fighting for years, against a foe who'd outthought them at every turn. Every victory they'd won had been through sheer luck, and defeat had driven them to desperation. Alf had looked at the merriment and the celebrations and seen only folly. He'd heard Lord Brychan's offer of betrothal and heard only foolishness.

"The tourney's always good to me. I never got the measure of jousting. Too many customs and rules. But a tourney's a big brawl, and I was always good at winning those."

"My son Aelfric – your namesake – was knighted in the Crownland last midsummer. There's no finer warrior in all the land than you. I pray that he has but a tenth of your skill."

"Duna knew how to use a sword well enough when he was young." Alf had seen plenty of young knights down south during his travels in the last few years, and they had not impressed him. Few of them had tested themselves in combat against monsters, and none had been tested in battle. The peace won with Lord Bone's defeat had seen to that. "And if there is fighting with the Wilder, that'll see him blooded."

Erdys shook her head. "He's to join my father's household in Iladventur at Yule – though if you were ever to have your own household, then I know he would be the first to pledge to your banner. Have you ever given thought to such, now that it seems your wandering days are behind you?"

"I'm no lord."

"Neither lord nor holy knight. Just Alf the Rootless, is it?" She sighed. "We send him what we can in the way of talismans, too. All the young knights of Summerswell use charmstones and magic nowadays, he says, and we cannot let him be left behind. One would think we have some advantage, being so close to Necrad, but, alas, no. The trade goes south, and we must buy from the relic-hawkers like everyone else." Erdys lit another candle. "For a while, Lady Berys favoured us with gifts. My father even had a kind word for her — and that is no small concession for a man like him to make. He would never admit such a thing, but he regrets that he did not listen to the Nine when you first brought warning of Lord Bone."

"He called us troublemakers."

"I know. He is a proud man, Aelfric, but he knows when he was wrong. When you return to Summerswell, he would be glad to see you and make things right. He would give you a place of honour in his household, you know, if you wished." She gave him a little smile. "He tried before, after all."

"I'm not going back to Summerswell anytime soon."

Erdys moved away from him. "Lady Berys has not been so generous of late," she said, "and our needs are greater than ever. I fear for Aelfric's safety, if we cannot buy him the charms he needs for the field." She took a small vial from her sleeve and poured sweet-smelling oil into the bowl, as an offering to the Intercessors. The oil was crimson, a symbolic reminder of the blood the Erlking shed for mortals to bring them into the light of Intercession. "Pray for him, Sir Aelfric."

"I'll have a word with Berys," he said. It seemed to be the only practical thing he could offer.

Erdys frowned, and Alf felt like he'd failed some test or fallen short in some way. Then she brushed his lips against his cheek. "I must go and prepare for the feast. It'll be a hard winter, I fear, and even with such honoured guests at the table, we must be frugal."

She departed, leaving Alf alone with the dead.

He stowed Spellbreaker in the guest room they'd given him. A four-poster bed large enough for a family, grand furniture — some looted from Necrad, some made in imitation of elven work — and a fireplace big enough to roast an ox. The Lammergeier stared back at him from a tapestry depicting the Nine battling Lord Bone.

He tried to put the box containing the sword under the bed, but the sides of the frame were covered by oak panels decorated with fanciful dragons and krakens, and there was no space to hide the sword. Alf swore and hid the box in the bed, drawing the blankets over it as if it were a child being tucked in for the night.

Outside the window was a vertiginous drop. The north face of the keep was guarded by a steep cliff instead of a curtain wall. Beyond was a sea of shadows, the wildwood of the north. Lath was out there somewhere, in that trackless land. Alf had wandered there for months, but he could not say he knew much of the wood beyond the line of forts that guarded the northern edge of the New Provinces. The forts had been raised by settlers from Summerswell, built on the foundations of older castles raised by other hands. Just as Necrad was older than Bone, so the north was older than the Wilder. Alf shivered and closed the heavy drapes against the night.

The meal started out a fine one. Alf had his share of banquets during his years of wandering, for every little lord and knight was happy to host so renowned a guest as one of the Nine – and Alf was usually a cheap guest, too, travelling without a retinue of hungry mouths. No, Alf had eaten well when he wished it, down south; he'd let the Lords of Summerswell serve him honeyed larks' tongues and roast suckling pig until he felt himself becoming slow and soft, and went back to the Road. The food at Duna's hall was simpler fare, lacking in the artistry of Summerswell or Eavesland, but made up for any deficiencies in volume – which Gundan certainly appreciated. The dwarf treated the roasted deer as a mountain of meat to be diligently mined, and a pile of bones soon grew on the floor. The hall was two-thirds empty, with three trestle tables arranged in an arc near the fireplace. Alf wondered idly while Duna had not chosen a smaller room for the meal.

Alf ate more slowly. He was seated at Duna's right hand, as befitted a knight of Summerswell, so he could lean over and speak privately to the lord.

"Your news about the Wilder so frightened young Vond that he marched me up here. Tell me true, Duna – is this something to be concerned about?"

"It was manageable for a long time," said Duna. "When Thurn dwelt in these parts, his word could bind the Wilder to the peace. He dealt with the ones still faithful to the Witch Elves. There were more of them than you'd expect, Aelfric – they thought the Witch Elves divine, and called us demons for toppling them. They struck at us when they could and Thurn's help was invaluable then. After that, there was peace for a good many years. Some of the Wilder even settled in my lands. They make for good farmers, good workers, but you could never trust them to stay put. They'd work for a season or two, then vanish into the wildwood for months, or you'd never see them again. And, yes, sometimes they'd come back and make trouble. But this is different."

"How so?"

"Three years ago, now, there was a gathering of the tribes up north. All the tribes, not just the As Gola and the ones who allied with the League. A great mustering, driven by a prophet called the Old Man of the Woods – sick with earthpower, no doubt. Madness got into them there, and every year since it's been worse. They claim all the wide wood is theirs and mean to drive us out of the New Provinces. They press us hard, now. I have made an example of some of them, but they are damnably hard to catch, and they will not give us open battle. So, we must hunt 'em through the woods."

"Have you sent word to Thurn?"

"Aye, that was my first response. I prayed he'd put an end to this madness. I sent knights out to look for him. None have yet returned, and I fear none shall. The wildwoods have grown perilous once more." Duna shook his head, gravely. "What we need, Alf, is magic. I have men aplenty, good fighting men who are more than a match for any Wilder on the field of battle – but we cannot find the bastards when they vanish into the forest. But send me magic to set the woods alight, or to scry out their hiding places, or to compel them to speak truthfully so that we can find their chieftains, and I can put down this trouble."

"Erdys said you'd got some relics from Berys."

"A handful. And as the boys came of age, I beggared myself to outfit them properly. But to hold back the Wilder, Alf, I need a great deal more."

"I'll bring your request to Vond when I go back to Necrad. I don't know what's left in the League arsenal, but I'll have them send what I can."

"Be swift, Alf. Some of the Wilder spoke of a great host coming out of the north. It might be nothing but talk, trying to scare us. If it's not, then it'll be bloody work. We're well fortified here, and I've laid in enough supplies to hold out for a long siege, but they'll burn every village and farm we've built in the last fifteen years. Necrad must act – or Necrad will starve."

Alf was about to reply when the heralds sounded a fanfare. The doors across the hall opened, and Duna's two younger sons entered, each with a girl on his arm. The young men and women were all dressed in a way that reminded Alf of the Witch Elves of Necrad. Not the ragged beggars of the Liberties, but the haughty immortal lords and ladies they'd been before the war. The two boys wore garments black as the night sky, dotted with gemstones that glittered like stars. They each wore half-capes in the colours of their grandfather's house in Summerswell, but that was their only concession to mortal custom. The women wore ghostly-white gowns that slithered around their bodies as they moved. Their faces were elven-pale, too, and elven-fair. They hailed from Eavesland, he guessed; they had the look of that stock. They were far from home indeed, for Eavesland was as far from the New Provinces as could be. As they approached the high table and bowed, Alf could see that they were less convincing up close, their skin caked with white powder. One of the girls even had a Vatling servant following behind her, holding the train of her dress.

Gundan hooted with laughter. At the other end of the table, Abbess Marit loudly called on the Intercessors to forgive the sins of foolish mortals. Duna must have seen the expression of distaste on Alf's face, because he made a sad half-shrug and grimaced, as if to say *what can I do? Children will be children.* Alf drained his cup.

Duna's middle boy – Alf couldn't recall his name at that moment – released the pale hand of his partner and bowed before Alf. "Hail, heroes of the Nine. Forgive our tardiness."

He drew a sword, and it was black as night, made in the likeness of Spellbreaker. It was a well-made copy, but not identical; there were charmstones welded to the pommel, lending it enchantment. Spellbreaker's far more potent magic was inherent to the sword.

"The Heroes of the Nine are renowned for their skill in combat. Fighting side by side, there was no enemy you could not defeat. Your deeds inspire us, lords, and so we pay tribute to you tonight! Bring in the beast!"

Drums began to beat in the shadows. Six guards entered the hall, each one holding a chain, and the chains met at an iron ring embedded in the shorn tusk-stumps of a hulking ogre. The ogre limped, a festering wound on one foot oozing pus, but its eyes were bright and the guards took care to stay out of the reach of its massive limbs. Other wounds from arrows and spears on the monster's hide told a tale of its capture in the woods.

At a signal from Duna's son, the guards dropped the chains and backed away. They picked up spears that had been left nearby, and stationed themselves at points around the hall, clearly ready to thrust if the ogre lunged towards the diners. Duna's wizard rose, too, vials of starlight and ritual components ready in his hands. No doubt he had some spell prepared to restrain the ogre.

The drums sounded again, faster and faster, a fighting tempo.

Duna's boys circled the ogre. One had the black sword in hand, the other a gaudy axe that resembled Chopper. Charmstones in both glowed, lending the youths unearned strength and skill. The ogre pawed its face and managed to unclasp one of the sets of chains. The other set trailed along the ground behind it. The monster wielded the chains like a flail, cracking them against the ground and tearing chunks from the wooden floor. Erdys muttered her own curse at the sight.

The beast sniffed the air, licked its chops, then began to shuffle towards the pile of bones in front of Gundan's chair. The younger of the boys laughed and kicked a gnawed rib towards the ogre. The creature bent down to pick up the bone, as if unaware of its situation. The boy laughed again and reached for another bone to taunt the ogre.

Mistake, thought Alf. The ogre was feinting. It leapt forward, grunting as it put all its weight on its bad foot, but it brought the chain-whip around in a murderous swing. The older boy was quick, though, and his charm-bolstered sword met the chain halfway. Magic flashed, and the chain shattered as the blade cut through it. Red-hot shards of metal flew over the heads of the diners. One piece of the chain struck the younger boy, knocking him to the ground. Erdys cried out, and the spearmen stepped forward to guard the boy should the ogre advance on him. The ogre saw the bright spears and flinched away. The wizard came around to tend to the wounded, but the boy was merely winded. He wore no armour, but the amulet at his throat was another magical relic that had protected him from harm.

The older boy fought better. He fought, to Alf's mind, like an elf, using speed and magic to his advantage. The ogre would grab at him, and he'd dodge back, slashing the creature with a quick stroke from the sword. None of the blows had any real force behind them, but the charmstones worked their malice, and every wound was magnified. What should have been a scratch instead opened up the ogre's flesh, and soon the monster's forearms were bloody ruins. It bellowed and charged, but each time the boy stepped aside, and the third time the ogre came too close to the edge of the makeshift arena and got skewered on a spearpoint. The monster limped away, its dangling chains leaving three parallel streaks of gore across the ground, and Alf could tell the fight would soon be over. The ogre's brute strength was no match for magic.

The whole sight sickened him. He'd killed more ogres than he could recall in the war, but that was the war. This wasn't even sport – this was mummery, play-acting at being warriors.

Duna leaned over. "They grew up in the long peace, Alf, and they come of age in a new world. We did not have such magic when we were young – now, enchantments and charms are as common as swords and lances on the battlefield. Victory changed everything."

Alf imagined Duna's men, similarly augmented with charmstones and relics, hunting the Wilder through the wood. "I need some air."

Outside, the air was fresh and cold, the wind from the frozen north. He crossed the darkened courtyard outside the hall, the shouts of triumph and the ogre's bellowing fading behind him. A stair brought him up to the battlements, where he could look out across the lands. Below him was the town of Athar, an island of light in the midst of a dark sea of trees. He looked south, and on the horizon was the distant green stain of the necromiasma. So many had died to take that city. Peir had died. And all for Duna's boys to play at monster-killing. All for another Aelfric to win glory on the tourney fields of Summerswell, augmented by stolen elf-magic.

Alf grunted in disgust and followed the wall-walk around the edge of the castle. West, the river glimmered in the moonlight like a vein of silver cutting through the wildwood. Scattered along it were the other New Provinces. He passed a sentry, who hammered the butt of a spear into the ground in salute at the sight of a hero of the Nine. "Hail, Sir Lammergeier!" Alf gave him a nod, and the man beamed as though it was a knighthood.

"Any trouble?"

"No, my lord. No sign of the Wilder."

"More in the world than Wilder," muttered Alf.

"No matter," said the sentry, "we have the Lammergeier to lead us."

North was the wildwood and the dark mountains. This portion of the fortress was finished and well fortified, ready for Wilder assault. The walls tall and thick, studded in places with stones taken from Necrad to ward them. A handful of men could hold this castle against a host, and Duna had more than a handful. Dwarf-built castles had good bones; he'd learned that in the long fight for the Dwarfholt.

Another sentry loomed out of the night. Alf nodded in salute, but this man did not respond. He stayed vigilantly staring out over the castle's northern approach.

A black shape flapped overhead, huge and fetid, blotting out the stars as it circled the keep. A dreadworm. It swooped low, shrieking, and Alf dodged to the side as he drew his sword. The guard did not move a muscle. As the worm passed, Alf saw that the guard was frozen, his face a mask of ice. His eyes stared back at Alf helplessly.

The elf was here.

The worm shrieked again as it descended towards the courtyard.

Alf pulled himself up, grabbing onto the crenelation for support, and tore the frozen guard's war-horn from the man's belt. He raised it to his lips with his shield hand and sounded it with all his might, raising the alarm. The castle awoke, torches flaring in windows and doorways, shouts echoing from guard posts. The doors of the banqueting hall flew open, and Alf could hear Gundan shouting a curse.

Where was the elf? He strained to see in the dark. Torchlight threw dancing shadows everywhere. She could not be far. Alf rushed along the wall-walk towards the main keep, searching for her, shouting encouragement to the other guards spilling out of the hall. The dreadworm circled overhead again, and a horrible thought crossed Alf's mind.

Spellbreaker could summon dreadworms.

Spellbreaker could call things of darkness.

And the elf had followed them all the way from Necrad.

"She's in the keep!" Alf roared. "She's in—"

As if in answer to his fear, thunder boomed and a portion of the keep's wall exploded, sending boulders and chunks of masonry – and ersatz elven furniture – cascading over the rocky slope.

He grabbed the guard's spear as he ran, though he knew that no weapon in the castle could match Spellbreaker. Gods, with the demon sword there was no telling what devastation the Witch Elf could wreak.

Alf rushed towards the blast.

He wasn't the first to get there.

On the edge of the north cliff, a half-circle of armed warriors surrounded the elf. Gundan, with Chopper raised. Duna and his boys, their blades still gory with ogre-blood. Remilard and the other guards from Summerswell. The elf faced them all, standing in the gap she'd blasted in the outer wall, the stolen sword in one hand. Her other arm was bandaged and bound; Lath had wounded her in Necrad.

One of Duna's sons snarled and raised his ersatz Chopper, and was about to charge when Alf reached his side and dragged the boy back. "Don't!" Thinking of the thing in the elf's hand as a mere *sword* was foolish; a sword, even one augmented with charmstones, had to cut and pierce to inflict injury. Spellbreaker was a wound in reality. Its power grew as it fed, and it could kill without even touching a foe. Alf remembered seeing Acraist striding across the battlefield, and wherever he pointed the sword a man died.

"Stay back," Alf ordered. They obeyed him without question – all save one.

The other boy, the older one, raised his sword in salute, then charged. He was young, and strong, and quick. The elf was ageless, and quicker. Spellbreaker cut through the boy's charmstones and armour with equal ease. Flesh and bone parted like water. The boy's hand, still clutching the replica sword, fell to the ground. The boy screamed and clutched the red stump, blood pouring out between his fingers.

Even the elf seemed taken aback by the power of the blade, but then she smiled, and in that moment Alf saw the Witch Elf as the Wilder did, as the fathers of the fathers of men did – a terrifying immortal goddess, invincible and untouchable, wielding powers beyond mortal comprehension.

One of Duna's men loosed an arrow, and she deflected it with a flick of her wrist that shook the towers. Alf staggered as the edge of the blast wave caught him, and the protective talisman that Duna's boy wore cracked under the pressure.

Alf rushed forward, trying to use the reach granted him by the spear and his long limbs. It was like trying to hold back a raging river with a stick; Alf's spear splintered and disintegrated even before the elf's parry made contact – but it gave Gundan a chance to charge in while the elf was distracted. Chopper's elf-bane edge gleamed in the torchlight as he attacked, a flurry of fierce blows, astoundingly swift for the size and weight of the axe. The elf-bane edge made the axe as deadly to the assassin as Spellbreaker was to all living things, and the threat of sudden death forced the elf onto the defensive despite her stolen sword. She fell back to the edge of the rocky slope, and with a wrench she pulled her wounded arm free of its bandage.

Then, with a flash of blue light, she caught Gundan with her ice-spell.

The dwarf bellowed in pain, his eyes frozen. Blinded. He stumbled on the uneven ground, and tripped. Gundan's armour was dwarf-forged and rune-girded, an heirloom of his house, but in that moment his head fell forward, and there was a gap between his helm and his gorget, the steel collar that guarded his neck.

Alf saw it. The elf saw it, too.

A heartbeat before she could drive the sword into the side of Gundan's neck, Alf charged. Miraculously, there was no blast of force from Spellbreaker, no mortal blow, and he tackled the elf. The impact of Alf's heavy frame sent all three of them tumbling down the slope. He twisted as he fell, trying to keep his wounded hand from striking the ground. A fresh bolt of agony rushed through him as he landed on a ledge.

The elf landed on her feet with a cat's grace, the demon sword like a tongue of flame in one hand. Blood ran down the elf's arm from the reopened wound and fell to the ground as frozen droplets. Chopper had landed nearby. Still on his knees, Alf grabbed the axe and hewed at the elf's legs, a wild cut, the unexpected weight of the dwarven axe wrenching his back. She parried the attack with Spellbreaker, and Chopper cracked, hot metal fragments raining down all around them. Still half blind, Gundan roared a curse and flung a stone at the elf, knocking her back.

"Yield, you idiot," shouted Gundan. "There's one of you, and a fuck of a lot of us!"

"On another day, dwarf, I would be glad to slaughter you all. But a more urgent task awaits me." She raised the blade in an elven salute that Alf had once seen Acraist perform. "*Dreadworm*," she commanded, and the stench of rotting flesh and leathery wings filled the air. The worm swooped down, and with practised ease the elf leapt onto the monster's back and soared into the sky. Alf grabbed for the worm's tail as he'd grabbed onto Lath, but the dreadworm was too quick, and she was aloft before he could catch her.

She soared into the air, and a cold horror touched the heart of every veteran of the war.

For the first time in twenty years, a dread knight rode the night wind.

She spoke. "Fear me, mortals. I am Ildorae Ul'ashan Amerith, Goddess of the Hunter's Star! I shall drive you from Necrad, and then I shall slay all your kin until your name and line are utterly annihilated, and—"

"Ildorae Ul'ashan Amerith," said the sword. "I remember you."

And suddenly, Spellbreaker was impossibly heavy. The elf-maiden shrieked as the weight of the blade dragged her down, pulling her from the saddle.

She landed heavily at Alf's feet. Spellbreaker impaled itself into the ground next to her. Alf drew the sword from the stone, shivering with the effort. The world simultaneously went dark and lit up in his sight, as the sword's magic warred with the burden of his wound. Still, he had enough left in him to put the tip of the blade to her throat.

"Yield," he muttered.

They carried Duna's son – Idmaer, his name was – up to the wizard's tower, and Abbess Marit prayed for Intercession for him while Erdys wept and wailed. Duna's wizard emptied his reserve of magic to work his little healing spells. By the evening, it was clear that the spells weren't working, and they moved the boy down to the chapel for the death vigil. They placed his sword on his chest, as if he was one of the stone knights, but his sword-hand was a stump, and the whole thing seemed as much a mockery to Alf as the fight with the ogre.

They brought Gundan up to his room and laid him on the bed. They dabbed away the last of the ice with hot towels, bathed the hero's eyes with restorative cordials and wrapped his head with silken bandages. He'd live. Heroes didn't live to Gundan's age without being lucky.

They brought the elf Ildorae to a prison cell deep, and bound her in the same chains they'd used to trap the ogre. She would not live, Alf suspected, not with Duna sitting in judgement over her.

In the small hours of the night, when the uproar and weeping had faded into exhausted silence, Alf drew Spellbreaker and laid the sword across his lap.

"You knew the elf," he said, accusingly.

"No words of thanks, wielder? No apology?"

"Apology?"

"You locked me away. That was foolish. I must have a wielder, and you desperately need my aid."

"You called the elf to you. That's how she found you."

"Indeed, and you have not praised me for my forbearance. You could not have defeated her without suffering great losses. Oh, what a joy it would have been to take all those little lives. Instead, to aid you – indeed, to save you, for she would surely have slain you when you foolishly charged – I betrayed her."

"You knew her," said Alf again. "Who is she?"

The sword didn't answer him. Instead, it protested. "I was clever, too. When she called the dreadworm, she revealed her thoughts to me. She desperately desires to find your friend and murder him. She is a huntress, wielder, and from her I know now where the Changeling went. I can bring you there."

"And where's that?"

"Daeroch Nal," said the sword. "It is an ancient fortress of the Witch Elves, high in the mountains. Lath has gone there, too. Why, I could not take from her – her mind was too well guarded."

"Who is she?" asked Alf. "Why did you turn on her?"

"She is a traitor. Faithless and vile. She was exiled from Necrad for her crimes." The sword's voice was metal scraping on bone. "She tried to murder my master."

He went down to the dungeon. Duna had put guards over the elf's cell, but they did not hinder Alf. The elf was a shadow, huddled in a corner. She looked up when he entered. Her face was bruised and caked in fresh blood; he could not tell if it was from the fall or if the guards had beaten her, but either way it was only a taste of what awaited her.

"Give me a few minutes alone with her." The guards did not question the order of one of the Nine.

Alf pulled over a stool, groaning a little as he sat down.

"Ildorae, aye? That's your name."

"Say it as a prayer and I might heed it, mortal."

"You maimed one of Duna's boys. He may not live through the night," said Alf.

"None of you will live long." Her eyes gleamed. "I have a mission, mortal, that I must complete. The Beast must die, or he will unleash a terrible darkness on the land." She nodded at the sword at Alf's side. "Give me the dreadworm to bear me away. Let me go."

"To Daeroch Nal, right? That's where you were heading."

The elf did not reply.

"What's happening at Daeroch Nal? What's so important that you get there?"

Silence.

"You were trying to kill Lath, that night in Necrad. You came to my house to kill him."

"You deserve death no less than the Beast."

"Aye, well, that's by the by. How did you know Lath would be there? Were you watching the Garrison?"

"Amerith told me."

"The Oracle," supplied Spellbreaker.

"Not Berys? She knew you, that night – you were expecting her."

"Did you think, mortal, that Lord Bone's invasion was the first time the *enhedrai* crossed the sea? I walked in the lands of Summerswell thousands of years ago, and have seen many of your little kingdoms rise and fall. The elves taught you mortals all that you know – the forging of metal, the working of stone, how to read the weather, the secrets of the stars. You speak a crude form of the high tongue, and your scrawls are derived from elven-runes. There are cults of elf-friends among you mortals, cults who trade service for secret lore. In centuries past, they sheltered the *enhedrai* when we went abroad. Since the occupation, they have taken on a different aspect." Ildorae glanced at him. "Curious – your friend told you nothing of these cults?"

"No."

"She knew the signs and countersigns. She offered to help me."

"And what did she want in payment?"

"To keep what she already has."

"And how does Lath threaten that? What's changed? Why now?"

"Amerith told me." The elf seemed momentarily hesitant, as if unsure of what to say. "She foresaw that the Beast would bring ruin."

"She foresaw, did she?" Alf let a little scorn drip into his voice, but he couldn't deny the parallels between his quest and the elf's murderous mission. Two prophets foretelling doom; two agents dispatched. He wondered if Jan had known.

"Amerith is mighty among the elves. She alone walks in two realms. She can perceive the wraith-world, and can commune with the *nechrai*. They tell her all that transpires in the world of the living."

"She speaks to wraiths," mused Spellbreaker. "I did not know that. She kept the source of her whispered secrets hidden. I thought only my master could reach into the wraith-realm."

"Your master," sneered Ildorae, "another usurper, and not half as clever as he thought himself. Amerith is far greater than he, older and wiser. She brought us home to Necrad six thousand years ago, and never did she waver. You are brute beasts, all of you, bringing ruin to everything you touch!" She glared at him. "Where is my dagger?"

Alf shrugged. "Not here."

"It was forged for me by the great smith Korthalion many years before you were born, mortal. And for nine thousand years before *that*, Korthalion honed his craft. Few elves had his discipline or his love of the art. We flit from joy to joy, changing with the seasons. Not him. The forge was his eternal love – until one of you mortals murdered him."

"He aided in my making," said Spellbreaker, "I remember him, in the first moments of waking in the fire." There was a note in the sword's voice that Alf had never heard before. A hesitant catch. "He served my master," it declared.

"He served unwillingly. Korthalion forged my blade to kill the one you called Lord Bone, and I wielded it gladly."

"She lies, Lammergeier!" said the sword.

Alf shoved it aside. "Quiet. What happened?" he asked the elf, fascinated despite himself.

"The mortal came to Necrad as a beggar at the gate, pleading that he be allowed to learn sorcery. One or two came every century, exiled from Summerswell for practising forbidden magic, or thirsty for knowledge denied to them by the laws of your kind. They were amusing to us, and none before Lord Bone accounted to anything of note. How could they, with the little span of years granted to them? A few mortals have true power, but it is the wild earthpower, not the slow gift of the stars.

"But this one was different. He was young, I think, and quick-witted. My kindred were unwise, too – they indulged his curiosity, and taught him spells that were beyond his wisdom, if not his reach. Their will had faded, even though their bodies were sustained by blood, and they did not consider the consequences of their actions. We rarely need to . . . "

Ildorae sighed. "His influence grew. At first he was a pet, then a pupil, then a peer. Before we realised the danger, he was the effective ruler of Necrad, and he began to lock away the power of the city we had built behind gates to which only he had the key. Some of us feared that we were becoming prisoners in our own homes, but others saw him as a worker of wonders."

Despite her fallen state – bound hand and foot, battered, blood-ied – a note of pride entered Ildorae's voice as she told her tale. "The Oracle decided that the mortal must perish, that he could not be allowed to gather any more power to himself. Still, we waited, hoping the passage of years would do away with him. Instead, he lingered, stretching out his life with magic. We – the few of us who still opposed him – plotted to destroy him. Korthalion made the weapon, Amerith guided my hand, and I would strike him down.

"In those days, the Wailing Tower was not yet complete, and I was able to enter in secret and lie in wait for him there, for I knew he would return to weave spells into the stones as they were laid. I saw my chance, and struck! The first blow was not enough to kill him, but it froze his limbs and his tongue, and ensured he could not cast a spell. I raised my hand again – but Acraist was there. He came to the defence of Lord Bone, and took the blow intended for the mortal."

"I killed Acraist," muttered Alf.

"Aye, and we have that in common. He was my kinsman, but he was loyal to Bone and we had not dared include him in our conspiracy. It was a terrible mischance that of all the days I chose for my murder attempt, that it would be my own brother by Bone's side. I hesitated before I struck, and that moment of delay saved Bone's life, and he brought ruin on my people." She shook her head. "Always, I am cursed with bad luck."

"In the war, the Oracle was on Bone's side, too," said Alf.

"What else could she do? All alliances are temporary, mortal, all friendships fleeting. Nothing endures except that which is constantly renewed. We had agreed upon it – if the attempt failed, then she would denounce me, and Korthalion would denounce me, and all the rest likewise. I fled Necrad and hid in the wilderness for a while."

"A while," observed the sword, "being a hundred years or so. Lammergeier, this creature is an arch-traitor. She has tried to murder those you cherish. Wield me. End her."

"Shut up," he said to the sword. "And you – *failing* to kill Bone like that gets you no credit in my book. I've a mind to let Duna have you."

"Lord Bone hunted the Nine for years in the war, mortal, and you remained uncaptured," said Ildorae. "You think that was a simple *good fortune*? You think the wraiths did not see you, or that Amerith did not hear their whispered reports? She hid you from Bone. You were *permitted* to survive, in the hope that you would succeed where I failed. You owe her your life."

Alf watched Gundan's fitful sleep. The wizard claimed that the dwarf's sight would likely return, in time, but for now Gundan was blind. In response, the dwarf had declared he might as well be blind drunk, and put away several bottles of Duna's best brandy before finally falling unconscious.

"I think I have to go, Gundan. If there's to be any chance of finding Lath, then I have to follow this quest to the end. When Jan called me, I thought it was the sign I was waiting for, that the Nine would come together once again to battle this second darkness. Lath was right – it was Peir who held us together. But Peir's gone, and I can't be him, for I don't have the wit or the wisdom. But I'll do my best. I can't make peace between the elves and dwarves. I can't fathom what Berys is up to, or what Blaise is doing in that cursed tower, or know what's right and just to do in Necrad. I can't even trust what I thought I knew. The elf – Ildorae – says the Oracle kept Bone's hunters from finding us. I don't know if I believe her, but ... well, you remember those days. I thought it was a miracle, the Intercessors watching over us, but now ... I don't know anything. But I can go after Lath. He still knows me. I'll bring him home."

Alf rose and gently touched the foot of the slumbering dwarf.

"I'm sorry. It's foul of me to leave with you so wounded, and Erdys' boy not even cold on the slab. I hope you'll understand."

"By Az's hammer, Alf," said Gundan, dreamily, "you don't half ramble on."

"You're awake?"

"Enough to hear your little speech. Go on, go. I'll smooth things with Duna and the rest, and keep watch over that elf. Oh, I'll have words with her, all right, just as soon as I can see again."

"But your eyes – I could fly you back to Necrad instead of going north. Blaise is a better healer than anyone here."

Gundan yawned. "I've been hurt before, Alf. I'm like my axe. Bits fall off, and I stick on more magic jewels and spiky bits to fix it. I'll be all right. Go and stop Lath from doing whatever stupidity he's got in mind."

Slowly, Alf raised the sword. "You've told the dreadworm to fly to Daernoch Nal."

"Your steed awaits, Lammergeier!" said the sword. It sounded positively giddy. "Now that you wield me again, there is no foe we cannot slay."

"Aye, that's what I figured." Alf opened the chest at the foot of Gundan's bed and locked Spellbreaker away. "Look after it for me, Gundan."

"I hate the damned sword, Alf, but you're flying into the unknown, and Lath's mad. If he comes for you, maybe you should have it with you."

"I'll bring no foulness of Necrad with me to the north."

CHAPTER TWENTY-FOUR

The elves called it a tree-house, but to Olva it was more like a palace. It was a spire of some pearly nacreous substance, hard as stone but lighter, nestled in the branches of a tall tree. Torun had frowned when she saw it, and pronounced living in the heights to be unnatural and unwise. The dwarf had gone prowling around the spire, tapping the walls as if she feared they would melt away with the dew.

For her part, Olva found it restful. She leaned over a balcony, looking out at the treetops gently swaying in the breeze. A sense of utter tranquillity came over her, as if all time had stopped and there was nothing but the slow, rhythmic exhalation of the world.

The prince had sent a messenger on the morning after the revels. "I come with good tidings and ill," the messenger had said. "The second ship you spoke of, the one bearing Lyulf Martens and your son – she did not founder in the storm, but neither was she captured. Martens has slipped past our snare. But the prince tells you to fear not – even now, the serpent-riders are a-hunting on the waves."

Three or four days had passed since then. During that time, they had not spoken to any of the elves. Food and drink had appeared as if by magic when they weren't looking. Olva had seen their hosts from a distance in the shadowy wood, she had heard them singing in the twilight to greet the stars – but they'd vanished when she approached. She'd called out to them, asking if there was news of the hunters, but the only reply was distant laughter echoing through the forest.

Hours blended into one another. So did the days. Time and again, Olva found herself slipping into a doze, or losing track of time as she wandered the woods. She'd come around a bend in the shifting paths that led through the forest, and come across some entrancing sight – a waterfall plunging into a glittering pool, a marble statue, a little sunlit sward where elves danced – and lose hours in unexpected, unwanted serenity. It was hard to hold onto anything here.

Even her fear. Her sleep was blissfully untroubled, deep and dreamless and renewing. Sometimes, in the night, she'd wake to hear the distant music of the revels in the prince's tower.

Even anger. She castigated herself for sitting around waiting while Derwyn slipped further out of reach, but her fury faded. Elf-land soothed away all sorrows, all passions. Or, rather, it made them seem small and absurd, easily dismissed.

Days passed. She told herself that she would bring Derwyn here when she found him. Why had she stayed in Ersfel for so long, fearing the outside world, when there were places like this forest, full of wonder? She laughed at her own foolishness in holding Derwyn back. Even threats like Lyulf Martens seemed small and silly.

"Ho there!"

She looked down and saw Maedos standing at the foot of the tree, smiling up at her. He was dressed in forest-green again, with a bow in hand, like he'd stepped out of one of Derwyn's books of fairy stories.

"May I come up?"

"Of course!" cried Olva.

A wooden stair wound around the tree, but Maedos instead scampered up the tree, scaling it with graceful ease. He vaulted over the balcony rail to stand next to Olva. "Well now! This is a more pleasant cell than your cabin on that ship, is it not? And I hope your new keeper is more to your liking." He bowed.

"You're a prince," protested Olva. "Surely you have more important duties than seeing to me."

"I am a prince," he agreed, "and, in truth, the title means little. There are few elves, and my father has many children so we have a great many princes. Other than some small duties, I do as I please. It amuses me to attend to you."

"I am in your debt, then."

"Elves do not count such things," replied Maedos. "The forest is bountiful enough, and life so long, that we do not need to tally every little debt or boon. We give freely, out of kinship and delight."

Torun emerged and bowed to Maedos. "That sounds idyllic, but impractical. What if you must go beyond the wood? Or what if two elves both covet the same thing? Among the dwarves, there are six great crafts – the delver, the builder, the smith, the physician, the poet and the lawyer. Have you no such arrangement here? What if—"

"Such disputes are rare. All elves have lived together for so long that we know each other intimately, and know how best to avoid conflict. And if a dispute cannot be sidestepped, then it falls to our leaders to make a judgement." He laughed. "But these are dull matters for such an hour of the morning! Come, let us find delight!"

Olva assumed that Maedos would bring them to his castle or to some other house, but instead they wandered the wildwood, picking berries and fruit. There were no orchards or vineyards as Olva knew them, but groves of such trees grew throughout the woods. Icy-cold freshwater streams tumbled down from the island's central peak, and they drank from them when they were thirsty. Maedos talked as they went, introducing Olva to the trees as if they were old friends, or telling tales of his adventures at sea. Sometimes, he slipped into Elvish, his voice lifting into song as naturally as breathing.

Olva couldn't speak more than a few words of the high tongue, but it didn't matter. The song caught her soul and carried it into the treetops. Walking in these woods was a balm to her battered spirit. After the long days of chasing and worrying, it was deeply restful to look upon silent green shadows dappled by gentle sunlight. It wasn't like the wild Fossewood – it was tranquil and tamed. At the same time, she fought against relaxing her guard completely. She told herself that she was not some green girl to be entranced by a handsome prince; when the powerful paid attention to you, they wanted something from you, and all the tales warned about meddling in the affairs of elves.

Beside her, Torun trudged along. The dwarf seemed subdued after the excitement of the previous evening.

Maedos stopped beneath one tree that bore strange golden fruit, soft-skinned and shiny, like grapes but much larger. The smell of the yellow blossoms on the tree was intoxicating.

"Eat of any of the fruits you like – except these."

"What are they?" asked Olva.

"Lotus-fruit, in your tongue. They wash away memory. Were you to eat one, you would forget much of what you now know. Perhaps it would take only your sorrows and burdens for a time – or it might take all you have ever known, and leave you witless and wordless, no more than a wild beast of the forest running on all fours. The lotus is dangerous."

"Then why do you grow it?"

"Immortality can be a burden. Some elves choose to eat of the lotus, and forget who they were. They learn to think and speak anew, their old lives erased. Other elves eat it to forget unwelcome dreams." He reached up and picked a flower. "Many who went away to fight in the war against Lord Bone ate of the lotus when they returned. They had suffered such horrors in Necrad that they could not carry those wounds into eternity, and so chose to begin again." He sniffed the blossom. "I could not go to Necrad. By rights, I should have been at the head of the army that went to aid the League. But I was injured, and so I stayed behind."

Suddenly, Maedos was not some high and distant lord, but one of the men who drank in Genny Selcloth's house in Ersfel: grey men who never went to the war, or who never saw battle, and who were haunted by the thought that they were lacking. They had always irritated Olva, drinking and wishing away their lives when there were so many more worthy of life lying dead under the grass. She bit her tongue to avoid speaking rashly.

"The fruit is forbidden to those of the royal line," continued Maedos. "We must remain clear-sighted. But we grow it for those who need respite. We offer it, too, to our cousins. A few of the *enhedrai* have accepted the forgiveness the lotus offers, and returned to the Everwood that is the home of the elves for ever. It is to be hoped that more will do so in the years to come, and Necrad will one day be emptied of their malice."

"And what of remembering?" said Torun suddenly, "Is there a library here? I lost my books when we were kidnapped."

"I have considered your plea," said Maedos, "to learn magic. There is a tower where the wise go, to look at the stars and discourse on very boring, portentous matters – theories of magic, forgotten lore, and the like."

"That sounds ideal," said Torun.

"Then follow!" The elf hared off through the trees.

They ran downhill, plunging through thick undergrowth and branches until they came to the edge of the forest, and looked out over a sudden wide vista. They had come to a great gash in the island, a cliff that tumbled down to the shore far below. Waves broke on the rocks, sending gouts of spray up to splash on the grey stone. They were facing north-west, and there on the distant horizon was a dark stain on the world, and a chill passed through Olva as she looked upon it.

Necrad, she thought. She'd come so far, and still not reached the dread city.

The prince stopped and turned to her. "You would leave the isle so soon? Few of your folk have ever walked in these woods. Stay awhile, and find respite from the mortal world."

"I wouldn't leave by choice," she said, reluctantly. "Alf's gone back to Necrad. You've been so kind, more than we deserve, but – Alf's family. He'll help me. And Martens was bringing Derwyn there."

"Do not be so certain of that," said the prince. "From the high seat, I have watched the comings and goings of the blood traders. They have hiding places all along the coast, and though I have dwelt on this isle for centuries and fought many wars against the rulers of Necrad, I do not know all the secret coves and sea-caves. Wait at least until my hunters have the trail."

At the top of the cliff was a white tower, like the others they'd glimpsed on the island. Very tall it was, sweeping up like a mighty waterspout that had suddenly frozen into stone. There were no joins or blocks visible in the walls, as if it had been conjured from the living rock of the island. The upper part of the tower was open to the sky. Small windows traced the spiralling progress of a stair within the tower, and near the top was a larger window that faced north, staring vigilantly across the wave-tossed waters to that distant city.

"Within you may find those elves who have chosen to be scholars for a while, or remembrancers. Or maybe it is empty today, but there are books and scrolls and such things that might interest you. You speak the elf-tongue, do you not?"

"I read it," said Torun.

"Then you will find much to delight you within."

Thirteen steps ascended to the door of the tower. Torun had to climb up them, for they were made for long-limbed elves. She clambered up eagerly.

"We shall come back this way in a few hours, when she is done," said Maedos.

"I think Torun's appetite for learning may surprise you."

"Most elves say there are few surprises left in the world for us – the patterns repeat, year after year, season after season. There is little new under the sun." Maedos took her hand and led her along the clifftop. Two old life-trees flanked the tower, growing right on the edge of the precipice, their crumbling earth exposing tangles of pale roots like silver hair. "But who knows? Perhaps your friend is a prodigy unseen before in all the long years!"

"I hope she is." Olva had become quite fond of the strange little woman over the days they'd travelled together.

"Although," said Maedos, "the last time we were taken by surprise was the rise of Lord Bone." A shadow crossed his face, and for a moment he looked stern and frightful, but then he smiled again. "Mortals can be so very amusing. That is why I am a sailor in these years – to meet new faces, hear new voices, before they slip away into the dust. A sorcerous dwarf, a woman on a quest – these are memories I shall cherish to while away eternity."

"I think you're mocking me." Olva felt unsure of herself as they walked along the clifftop. "I'm just trying to find my son. It's not some quest out of the songs."

"The songs will work their magic. My father says tales are like trees – a little seed grows in the dirt, and seems insignificant at first. But it grows, year after year, branching and blossoming, until it is tall and beautiful. Maybe your tale might be mistaken for a weed now, but I shall see it grow into a legend."

Olva snorted, but she allowed herself to imagine arriving in Necrad dressed in elven finery, on one of the fabulous green-sailed ships, and telling Alf and the other heroes of the Nine to listen to her. Maybe Derwyn would be there, too, having escaped captivity. He would stare in amazement at his dull mother, transformed into a radiant hero.

Maedos drew her back into the deep woods, away from the sea. It seemed to Olva that as soon as she could no longer see the stain on the northern horizon that marked the location of Necrad, her spirits rose. She lost track of the hours as she walked with Maedos through the elven-woods. He brought her to a seamstress who took her travel-stained clothes to be washed and mended, and who gave her beautiful elven robes to wear instead. Another elf made her sturdy walking boots of grey leather, with a belt to match. Everything was enchanted perfection – or almost everything.

"I wish I had my knife. Martens took it from me."

"Ah," said Maedos, "there are other weapons on the isle. I shall show you one of them."

The lowest level of the tower was overgrown with brambles and ivy, the growth so thick that Torun could barely see the walls beneath. Spiral stairs rose to the upper storeys, but Torun paused to examine the walls. Through little gaps, she could glimpse the ornate carvings and stonework, see the disassociated scraps of some legend. Elven faces, swords and spears, ships and stars, all lost beneath the greenery. It offended some dwarven sensibility within her, and she began to clear the undergrowth.

"Some things are hidden for a purpose."

She turned. There was an archway she had not seen before, and leaning there was an elf. He resembled Prince Maedos enough to be his kinsman, but he was small and slouched. He wiped the dirt from his hands on his rough-spun tunic.

The elf smiled at Torun. "So, you wish to learn magic fit for a dwarf?"

"Yes, I do," said Torun. "How did you know that? Did the prince tell you?"

"Experience. You are not the first to come here, seeking magic, though you are the first dwarf. The others were turned away. But you ..." He bent down, so he could meet Torun's eager gaze. "There is something in this tower to help you – if you have the wit to find it."

He passed through the archway into an open space that adjoined the tower, surrounded by the same white stone walls. There was a neglected garden there, the once-bright flowers wilting and turning brown around the edges of their fading petals. Weeds choked the beds and hung heavy from the branches of the gnarled old trees. The air here was much warmer than outside the tower.

The elf sat down amid this incipient decay, contemplating the ruin.

Torun did not understand elves.

She didn't understand humans, either. Or other dwarves. Other people of all sorts. Elves, though, seemed deliberately elusive, as if they were amused by her confusion. Why not tell her which book to read? Although at least being told she could explore the library on her own was better than how the humans at the College of Wizardry had treated her, with their rules and restrictions on who could study magic.

Torun wandered the tower's echoing halls. She passed through a room with a great hearth, where a singer might stand by the fire and perform for those assembled there – but all the seats were empty, and the hearth cold, without even a trace of ash. She passed through galleries with hundreds of bookshelves and nooks for scrolls and treasures, and found them almost empty. There were only a handful of books, fewer than she expected. The libraries of the dwarves were far fuller in comparison. And better organised. And less dusty.

Daringly, she stood on her tiptoes and managed to reach the lowest of the scrolls, but it crumbled when she touched it.

She chewed the inside of her lip in frustration, and set off again. The elf had insisted there was a secret here, so she would find it. Failing that, she'd go down and demand he speak plainly. Every grimoire and book of magic lore she'd read was full of elven misdirection and vagueness, but she could sense the outline of a hard structure beneath the mysticism. The one aspect of magic that could readily be quantified was its relationships with the heavens. Elves naturally bathed in magic from the stars over the course of centuries, and human sorcerers caught starlight in traps and nets to gather power to compensate for their short lives. Humans, therefore, had codified that part of the process, with huge books of calculated tables telling a wizard when a particular star would be above the horizon and what sort of magic that starlight could command. If one part of magic could be quantified and made regular, why not the rest?

Her mind was so caught up in thoughts of stars and diagrams that she stumbled and barked her knee on the overly high steps. Cursing, she climbed. The tower spiralled above her, bringing her to one room after another, all empty. Frescoes on the walls had crumbled in the sea air for lack of protection, marble statues had endured but had lost all meaning, carved walls were overgrown. These elves cared nothing for their past! Who were these forgotten elven heroes and sages who stared back at her? Torun felt as though she had come in after the end of some grand theatrical performance, all the audience departed, the costumes and sets discarded, the moment passed.

She pressed on, assuming that the next turn of the stairs would bring her to the library proper, but she climbed until she found she was out in the open air again. She had emerged onto the roof of the tower, a small circular platform. A diagram of the heavens was inlaid onto the floor, noting the four cardinal points, the relative positions of the thirty-six celestial decans, and the locations of Necrad, the Everwood and other places of power. Torun dutifully studied the diagram, although it was nothing she had not seen before many times, and this particular example was so covered in seagull droppings that much of it was occluded.

She saw no secrets in it.

She peered over the parapet, trying to see if the old elf was still in his garden, but some trick of architecture prevented her from looking down at the right angle, and the spot where the garden lay was blocked by a fanciful outcrop of the tower. Torun scuffed away some of the droppings with her boot, in case she had missed something, but, no – there was nothing new here, no revelation that would connect all the fragments of lore she'd gathered into one coherent whole, nor a mystical moment that would let her feel the magic. She could gather all the starlight she wished, string the most elegant and efficient traps, but she'd never been able to cast a spell.

She knew that not every human who attended the College of Wizardry proved to be an adept wizard, and most were capable of only the most minor magics – predicting events to come, curing illnesses, shaping the weather. However, she had never heard of one who was completely incapable. Even humans who had never opened a grimoire at all could sometimes touch the earthpower, and wield magic that way. But neither starlight nor earthpower had ever worked for her. So, either dwarves in general were incapable of casting a spell or she was lacking some fundamental secret ... or there was something lacking in her specifically. A deficiency in her soul that all her efforts and cleverness could not overcome.

She descended the tower again, more slowly this time. She tapped on every wall, in case the secret was a literal one, but the walls were solid. She probed the ornamental carvings around the doors, wondering if there might be a message encoded in the swirls and spirals – but if there was one there, she could not read it. She called out in every tongue she knew of dwarf and elf and man, in case some spirit lingered there. Nothing.

She stomped back down to the ground level and passed through the archway into the little walled garden. She found the old elf with trowel in hand, digging up a bed of weeds.

"There's nothing there. All the books are ruined."

"But nothing has been lost. There are those who still remember all that was once contained inside those pages. Books rot, or burn, or fall into the hands of the undeserving."

"That's not much use to me."

"Perhaps not. Go and look again." The elf turned back to his task.

"I don't think much of your garden."

He laughed ruefully. "Neither do I. It is harder than I expected to get it right. I sow, and I weed, and I water, but it never grows quite the way I want. You can never be certain which plants will thrive and which will wither. I have taken to letting it run wild most of the time, and only attending to it when I must. A philosophy of benign neglect – but that risks infestations. It's all about finding the right balance." He examined one white blossom and frowned at the little bugs that crawled on the leaves. "I don't need to do anything about these, though. A frost will clear them out, and I shall plant new seeds when the season changes. Little by little, I will get it right." He looked up at her. "Look again, Torun. Find magic fit for a dwarf."

Torun backed away. She wondered if the elf was mocking her, but there was a sincerity in his voice that made her hesitate. She climbed the tower again, floor by floor. Outside, the sun was setting, and the west-facing windows filled with autumnal twilight. "Maybe there are moon-letters that are visible only at night," she said to herself, and she left unspoken the thought that such an approach would be needlessly obscure. Still, she waited until the daylight had faded, but no secret messages appeared in the gloom.

She climbed through all those empty rooms again, until she came to the top of the tower once more. She stared up at the dome of stars overhead. She could name every one of them, trace the shapes of the constellations, but they would not heed her call. They were infinitely remote, infinitely cold, and they scorned her. That was no secret to her – she had known that all her life.

After the tumult of the previous night, the skies were clear, and from this high place Torun could look west across the straits. There, far away on the horizon, she could see a distant greenish glow.

Necrad, she thought, and that thought was like a door opening in her mind. She had never seen the fabled city, but she had read about it hundreds of times, and heard tales from afar. A city built in the elder days to master magic, to collect and channel it. A star-trap in stone.

That was magic fit for a dwarf. Her soul might be heavy as iron, her tongue incapable of the delicate words of Elvish, but she was a dwarf, and the dwarves could build and delve. If magic could be shaped by carven stone, then that was what she would do. Her mind soared above the streets of the forbidden city, like the spokes of a wheel. *Necrad!* In her euphoria, the city seemed to spin beneath her, the whole world a great machine coming to life, animated by an unseen hand . . .

"*Build it anew,*" said a voice in her soul. "*A second city.*"

The peak reared up above the island, a spike of bare stone bursting free of the forest. The prince led Olva higher and higher, and, just as she felt she could not keep up with the climb, they came to a stairway cut into the mountain. Guardian statues flanked the foot of the stairs. They were made in the likeness of coiling dragons.

Maedos halted, and Olva could dimly sense an unseen struggle between the prince and the guardians. The contention lasted only a few moments, and then the way up the mountain was open. The prince spoke a word, and dancing flames appeared to light the path.

"Torun would love this," she muttered. "Real magic."

"You will see greater spells worked tonight."

"Where are we going?" she asked.

"To the peak. This is Kairad Nal, the Stormkeep in your tongue. Here the eldest first set foot on solid ground when they descended from the stars. But they did not dwell here." They were above the tops of the tallest trees here, and the air was clearer than the finest glass. The prince pointed west, across the Gulf, and Olva could see a faint stain on the horizon. "They gathered at Necrad, the first city, the home of the elves in these lands for ever. We were cast out six thousand years ago, and still we remember." Olva felt terribly sorry for the prince, and her cheeks burned at the thought that her own brother was responsible, at least partially, for denying Necrad to its rightful owners.

He took her by the hand and helped her climb. The stair wound around and around the peak, and the height became dizzying, as if a slightest misstep would send her plummeting down the side – or into the sky. She clung to the prince's hand and tried to focus on his voice.

"These stairs were built much later, by our estranged kin. The followers of Amerith rejected the Erlking's ways and left the Everwood. They came here and turned the isle into an arsenal. They made war upon the mortals, and in time drove the usurpers from Necrad – but it was a bitter victory. They were so wounded by the war, and had given so much of themselves, that they grew twisted and strange."

The stair twisted again, and there was a jagged wound in the mountainside. A dark cave mouth yawned at the side of the stair. Broken rocks and hanging moss like teeth and drool, and inside the cave fell away like a slimy gullet down into the bowels of the earth. A foul reek issued from it. Rune-marked pillars flanked the cave, and it put Olva in mind of the maw of some beast, muzzled in marble.

The prince paused and laid his hand against a pillar. "Be wary, mortal! Perilous earthpower wells up here. These pillars tame it, so you are safe on this path. They were made by the *enhedrai*, using the same magic that undergirds Necrad."

Again they climbed. The path curved more tightly, narrowing as the peak itself narrowed, so they had to go single file. Mist made the steps slippery, the path vanishing into the crown of cloud around the mountain. Prince Maedos did not slow his climb, though, and pulled her on even though she could see little in the fog. Olva struggled against her own fear, determined to show that she was worthy of all he'd given her.

The veil of mist parted, and before them was a seat of stone at the very apex of the mountain. All around them was the dome of the blazing stars, and they were lost in the vastness of the sky. Olva sank down on the topmost step of the stair and clung to the mountain, glad that the climb was over, gasping for breath in the thin air.

The prince took his place on the throne, and starlight gleamed in his eyes. His gaze roved over the ocean. She could feel the mountain sing as Maedos called upon the magic of Kairad Nal. The earth-power rose and became celestial fire. An aurora danced around the peak, and the stars burned with such terrible intensity that they were like silver spikes, transfixing Olva.

"Three ships ride the south wind from Ellsport," said the prince, distantly. Olva followed his gaze, but saw only darkness. "They fly the flags of Ellsport, and Arden ... and Ilaventur. Mortals of the League, on their way to Necrad. They thought the cloak of night would hide them." He frowned with disappointment.

"Can you see Martens' ship?" asked Olva, but the prince paid no attention to her.

"All those lords were told not to cross the Gulf, and yet they defy my ban. Tell me, Lady Olva – is it not sometimes a parent's duty to be stern? To show love through discipline, for the betterment of the child?"

Olva stammered a response, confused by the prince's question. "I – of course. For their own good. Children don't know any better."

"Well spoken. I shall be stern, but merciful." He gripped the arms of the chair tightly, and light welled up between his fingers. The mountain roared, and Olva felt as though the whole earth was shaking. The wind shifted, the whole sky rippling as clouds raced across the blue heavens. To the south-west, the sky darkened and distant lightning flashed. Olva remembered her terror when the storm struck Abran's ship, and she pitied from afar the poor sailors who were caught by Maedos' wrath.

The storm raged. It spread north, clouds rolling and darkening like a bruise in the sky. Lightning leapt all around them. Maedos contended with the storm he'd unleashed, the aurora of the mountain flaring bright against the clouds, but the tempest grew too great to be commanded. The storm broke over the mountain peak, and suddenly they were in the midst of a raging downpour.

"I saw two of the ships turn back, I think, before the storm caught them. The third foundered." Maedos struggled to rise from the chair, his face grey from the effort of commanding the storm.

"What about Martens' ship? Can you see it?"

The prince was silent for a long time, staring across the sky in the direction of Necrad. At last, he said: "I cannot see Martens." He released his grip on the throne, and the light died. He sagged back in the chair, his face ashen. "I looked with all my strength, and could not see him. I found his ship – it is hidden in a cove beyond the Cape of Staffa, far to the north. Of Martens I saw no sign, and there are few powers that could hide him from me. But I fear there is an obvious explanation – the miasma that hangs about Necrad was made to hide the city from outside scrutiny. All the winds of Stormkeep cannot drive away that pestilent cloud. Not even the Erlking's spells can penetrate it. If Martens has brought your son into Necrad, then he is lost to my sight."

"Torun?" Olva's voice echoed up through the empty tower. The dwarf stirred and wiped her face. She was lying on the floor where she had fallen. She stood and hurried down the stairs to her friend, feeling her way in the dark. The pouring rain beat on the tower's roof like a drum.

"Are you all right?" asked Olva when they met at the halfway point of the tower.

Torun nodded. "I had an idea. I'm coming with you to Necrad. I need to see it. To study it. To ... to know it." She rubbed her temples, feeling as though her brain must be visible through her skull. Inspiration has seized her. She grabbed Olva's hand and let the human down the stairs, eager to get out into the moonlight. She craved ink and parchment, so she could get some of this revelation out of her head and onto paper. Or maybe the old elf was right, and paper was too ephemeral for such a cosmic truth.

She looked back as they left the tower, but there was no sign of elf or garden or archway.

CHAPTER TWENTY-FIVE

The dreadworm carried Alf north. The forest beneath him was an endless sea of green and white, the boughs of the trees bowed under snowfall. The cold air was hard to breathe, and sent shocks of pain through him when he inhaled. Alf drew his cloak tight around him, and flexed his hands to keep the blood flowing. The borrowed reins were stiff with ice – not that he needed them to guide the dreadworm. The sword had impressed the knowledge of its destination into what passed for the monster's brain, and Alf needed only to cling on and occasionally drag the worm's attention away from prey.

Ahead, on the distant horizon, mountains rose up like teeth. Their treeless flanks were dark against the brilliant blue of the sky, and they were crowned with snow. Beneath, the forest sped past. Gaps in the trees gave him fleeting glimpses of the terrain. A flash of light reflecting from the waters of a stream. A herd of deer running, their lithe bodies dark against the snowy ground of the clearing. Broken walls like lines on the ground, marking the remains of some long-lost structure. He scanned the wildwood below, looking for signs of the Wilder, finding none. He might have been the last man alive in all the wide world.

Then the dreadworm buckled in sudden shock, hissing in

pain. Alf could feel the impact through his spine, and icy blood gushed over his left boot. He reached down, and found the shaft of an arrow protruding from the monster's flank. The arrow had gone deep – a masterful shot, and a mortal wound. The monster spasmed, the beating of its wings slowing, and it began to fall from the sky.

Alf wrestled with the reins, kicked at the wing-roots until the worm spread wide, gliding down towards the pines, whimpering as it fell. Alf braced himself for the impact, and the tree branches broke the worst of his fall as he crashed to earth. He lay there for a moment on the snowy ground, his beard covered in pine needles, his limbs intact but bruised and scratched.

The dreadworm was in a sorry state. The creature was dying, its hide dissolving into muddy slush. Alf stumbled through the undergrowth to the wreck of the worm, cursing. He'd flown beyond even the most northernly forts of the New Provinces, and he had few provisions or supplies to survive in the trackless forest. "I hope this stuff works on you," he muttered. From the worm's flank, he pulled forth the arrow, then doused the wound in all the healing cordial he'd brought with him. The worm thrashed, but the gush of meltwater and slime slowed, then stopped. The hideous eyeless head curled around and brushed against his leg.

Alf took a step back in distaste. He'd always considered the dreadworms as disposable, nothing more than conjurations of evil magic. No more alive than a golem. He didn't like the thing showing gratitude.

"Stay alive," he ordered, "you're flying me home."

He looked at the arrow in his hand. It was a Wilder-arrow – no enchantment, no strange metals, just wood and iron and feathers loosed by human muscle and sinew. Alf had known few men that could hit a high-flying dreadworm moving at speed.

Thurn.

*

Twilight kindled the brilliant stars above the mountains, and a small fire leapt up in answer on a hilltop in the forest. Alf made his way towards it through the forest. He saw no tracks save those of beasts. If there were Wilder in the woods, it was not the vast warband that Duna feared.

Once or twice, he caught sight of the movement of wraiths, half-glimpsed faces hiding in the leaves. They weren't the hungry, tormented wraiths of Necrad. These spirits were even more frail, more fleeting, and their faces were sad.

The mound was strange, too. There were plants growing in the underbrush that Alf had never seen before. Half the trees were dead or dying, while others were bursting with life, the buds and leaves of a riotous spring unfurling even though it was only early winter. Alf could sense earthpower here, like thunder receding into the ground, and he was normally utterly insensible to the shifts and currents of magic. He'd felt it a few times in Lath's company, but only in places of power. This mound must be seething with unseen energies.

Higher up the slope, he found more wraiths, fresher ones. Bodies, too – a dozen Witch Elves had fallen in battle here. Their garb was like that of Ildorae, though they bore different house sigils. The earth around them was blood-soaked; they had fought fiercely against many foes, but there were no other bodies on the hillside. Alf found enough signs of Wilder-weapons for him to be sure that many Wilder had fought here, and likely died here. He saw no graves or pyres, and this place was much too far from the necromiasma of Necrad for him to think that the corpses had all arisen as undead so swiftly. Someone had removed the dead Wilder.

The dead elves all faced uphill; there were Wilder arrows like the one that had downed his dreadworm, and they'd all been shot downslope. The Wilder had held the crown of this hill against assault, and fought until the battle was done. It was unlike the

Wilder to offer pitched battle, especially when they could have fallen back and vanished into the wildwoods all around the mound.

He climbed the hill to its summit. The top of the mound was bare, and black with ash. There had been a huge bonfire here, a day or so ago; some ghost of the heat lingered in the air. The ground was trampled by the footprints of a large number of men, but now the hilltop was almost deserted. Off to one side, there still burned a little campfire, and seated on the far side of the fire was a giant of a man.

He wore a cloak of bear-fur on his wide shoulders, and leather bracers on his wrists, but Alf well remembered the tattoos of the blue snakes and spirals on the man's forearms. By his side was a mighty longbow, and a few paces behind him, thrust into the frosty earth, was a broad-headed spear of similar design.

The Wilder stared into the fire, his head bowed.

"You shot my dreadworm, Thurn," said Alf.

"Not yours." His voice was so low and uninflected it seemed to come from deep within the mound.

The barbarian reached down and threw another piece of wood on the fire. Not a log or fallen branch, but a carved token. A child's toy, the flames quickly scorching the bright paint.

"Well, it's a stroke of luck I found you. There's much to be done, and I need your help for a lot of it. Have you seen Lath? Is he here?" Alf approached the fire. Thurn looked up, and Alf was struck not by the marks of age on Thurn's face, but by its gauntness.

"No weapons," said Thurn, "at my fire."

It was a Wilder custom, a token of peace. Their campsites were ringed with swords and spears, and it was forbidden to draw a weapon within the circle. Alf retreated a few paces and stabbed his borrowed sword into the ground.

The hilltop was a tiny island of firelight floating above the dark forest, with only the stars in the moonless sky for company. He advanced towards the dancing flames and the barbarian beyond them.

"You are hurt," said Thurn. "It is good we are not fighting. I would not like to fight you when you are injured."

Apprehension gripped Alf. "Why would we be fighting?"

"Lath said you had gone south."

"I did. I came back. But when did he tell you that? When did you last see him?"

"A day ago. He told me you were coming. He is near, but I want to speak with you first. Sit."

Alf sat down next to the fire. The heat was welcome, but the contents of the fire disturbed him. The toy was not the only strange thing that Thurn had given to the flames. Alf could make out the remains of clothing and blankets. A deep unease crept into his soul. He studied the face of his old friend, but the Wilder was, as ever, unreadable.

"Thurn, what are you doing here?"

"I wish," said Thurn, "that you had stayed away in the south. I remember when your kin sheltered us in that village. That was kind. I did not know your people could be kind to strangers. But you are here, and I am glad of that, too."

"Jan sent me a warning. She foresaw a great darkness."

"Yes."

Alf blinked. "Yes? Yes, what? What have you seen?"

Thurn sighed. "I fought to free the Wilder from the false gods who fed on us, and from Bone who enslaved us. I found you, and the others. Together, we won. Lord Bone, dead. The elves, broken. We won."

He reached down and picked up an arrow. It was unlike the huge shaft that had downed the dreadworm. This arrow was made of metal and was light and elegant and wickedly barbed. A dart forged in Necrad. Thurn turned it over in his massive hands as he spoke.

"I did not want revenge. The Wilder cried out for it, but I said no. There is space enough in the wide wood for all. But . . . it is our fault. The fault of the Nine."

"What is?" Somewhere in the dark forest beyond, a bird croaked loudly, with a human voice.

"We had Necrad. We should have unmade the place, stone by stone. I think that city is the darkness that Jan saw, Alf. Those who dwell there become sick. It killed Peir, and it is killing the rest of you. I see it. Blaise, Berys, Gundan, Laerlyn — it eats away at them all. It made Lath sick. Jan was wise to leave. Alf, you should not have come back."

"That's what I tried to tell them. It's not over. I don't know exactly what's going on, Thurn, but—"

"No," said Thurn, sharply. "Listen." He ran his finger over the point of the arrow. "I had a daughter. Talis, her name was. None of the rest of you had children. That was wise. Necrad is no place for a child."

Alf rubbed his wounded hand. "I don't understand. What does that have to do with anything?"

Thurn spoke in his solemn, unhurried way, as if he was giving an account of things that happened long ago to someone else entirely. "She was shot. With this." He held out the dart. "Men of your New Province. Duna's men. It does not matter. She saw the mark of Necrad, and knew she would die. The healers could not help her. I could not help her." Pride crept into his voice, a quaver of emotion breaking through the heavy monotone. "She was very brave, Alf."

"You couldn't help her," said Alf, with mounting horror. "But Lath could." *The resurrection scroll.*

Reflected firelight filled his eyes. "There is an Old Man in the Woods who knows much that is hidden. We went to him, and he sent Lath to Necrad, as he sent me south to find the Nine all those years ago. Lath found a spell as the Old Man foresaw, but it was almost too late. The life had left her body. We tried anyway. He drew upon the earthpower as I had never seen done before. He opened a door, and I went through it into the Grey Lands." He shook his head in disbelief. "I thought them only a legend. But we are legends these days, Alf. They tell stories of our deeds, and we walk under the sun. Why should I doubt other stories? There is great truth in them."

"Thurn, what did you do?" Alf felt sick to his stomach — this necromancy was *wrong*, meddling with the natural way of the world. He fought the urge to scramble away from the man and grab his sword. The fire was dying down, and the night had closed in, making Thurn into something dark and terrible.

"I followed my daughter into the lands of death. I tracked her spirit across the Grey Lands, down and down, for a long while. Time is different there. I did not know how different. I followed her, and I found her, and I carried her back. She did not come back alone." Alf's skin crawled. Thurn's hands twisted, snapping the metal dart in two. He dropped the twisted pieces into the embers, sending up a shower of sparks. "In Summerswell you do not tell the old stories any more. You have forgotten the first hero of our kind, she who was mightier than any knight or wizard or priest. Talis came back, and Death came back with her."

Alf's brow furrowed as he tried to understand his friend's words. "What came back? What did you bring back, Thurn?"

Thurn turned and looked up at the fortress on the horizon. "She has gone up the mountain. Now, there will be a reckoning."

There, outlined against a low cloud, was the fortress of Daeroch Nal. In places the walls had crumbled, and the topmost towers had fallen, but much was still intact, enduring countess centuries' winters. Had Alf ridden past by day, he would have guessed that the fortress was abandoned, but that night, witch-lights glimmered there like fallen stars.

On the slopes below, a single torch burned, rising like a spark from the fire caught on the wind. *She has gone up the mountain.*

Alf glanced from Thurn to the torch, and back again. "Thurn—" he began, but his words were drowned out.

The ground shook. Light flared, brighter than the sun. A thunderbolt without end, lightning leaping from sky to earth and back again. The sheer roar of the cataclysm rolled out over the forest, and the trees bent as if hiding their faces from the awful wrath of Death. The fortress of Daeroch Nal, the ancient work of the elves, endured against the onslaught for a few moments, until the mountain itself gave way and the tortured foundations of the castle crumbled. An avalanche of white stone crashed down the slope, and in the last flickering light of the thunderbolt Alf could have sworn he glimpsed a figure standing there, outlined against the blaze, human in shape but magnified, godlike and terrifying beyond measure.

"I brought you here so you could see, Alf," shouted Thurn over the maelstrom. "I brought you so you could understand!" Alf threw himself to the ground, burying his face in the earth, as the blast wave rolled over him. Even when he shut his eyes, though, he could still see the after-image of that thunderbolt.

The wave of thunder passed. For few moments, the only sound was the grinding of the avalanche as the rocks settled, punctuated by smaller, closer impacts as flying debris from the explosion crashed to earth.

Then, silence.

"Go and tell them, Alf, that One will finish what Nine began. Go and tell them Death is coming!"

Alf reached out blindly and grabbed his borrowed sword. Thurn looked up, and there was no fear in his face, only a fierce pride. "Kill me," he echoed, "and she shall bring me back. The stories do not lie. She is Death now, and she is greater than all living things. Go back to Necrad, Alf, and tell them to run."

Alf turned and ran down the hill.

The dreadworm raised its head as Alf came crashing through the trees. It reared up, flexing its wings to show it was ready to fly again. He climbed astride it, and the worm took flight. Below, Thurn watched him soar into the sky, but made no move towards the great bow by his side. His parting words were lost in the rushing wind.

"South!" Alf shouted. "To Necrad! Take me back to Necrad!" But the dreadworm was too stupid to understand. It had been summoned to take its rider to Daeroch Nal, and to Daeroch Nal it would go. It flew on without flinching, no matter how Alf hauled on the reins. There was no stopping it as it flew towards doom. It descended towards the smouldering pile of rubble that had once been the fortress of Daeroch Nal.

There were chunks of rubble bigger than elephants. Great craters carved by lightning blasts. The storm that had brought ruin to this place had scoured the mountaintop bare of earth for hundreds of feet in every direction, and distant landslides still rumbled as the land found a new balance.

Once, in a battle, Gundan's axe had caught a Wilder-warrior and cleaved the man literally in two. Alf still remembered that gory sight, the man's innards laid bare as surely as if he were an illustration in some book of human anatomy. Flesh and bone, muscle and sinew, each organ in place but neatly bisected, all shown clearly in that moment before a gush of blood and vital fluids obscured it all. One of the towers of Daeroch Nal was like that – a blast of lightning had cut it in two, so Alf could see the exposed levels, as some magic glass allowed him to look through the walls. All the rooms he could see were empty and long-abandoned.

Fresh-slain wraiths called to each other on the wind, their shrieks fading to silence as they too diminished. A few fruitlessly scrabbled at the rubble, trying to find some hiding place. The mountaintop was inhospitable to the spectres – the constant winds would carry them away, blown like dry leaves across the endless forests of the north, and the harsh sun would sear them. An eternity of wandering. They were unlucky even in the wind, which had changed and now blew from the south. None of these wraiths would ever find their way to Necrad, not for thousands of years.

Of the one who had destroyed the fortress, Alf found almost

nothing. He came across footprints in the snow at one spot, a child's footprints running lightly across the ground. The trail vanished without further trace, and he could not tell if the child had leapt onto the fallen rubble, or changed shape. If she was anything like Lath, then she could change her shape into a bird or beast, anything born of the living world.

He picked his way through the debris, trying to reconstruct the attack in his mind. This was the same magic Lath wielded. But Lath, even at the height of his power, could never have worked wild magic like this. He could not have shattered Daeroch Nal with a single spell. Not even Lord Bone could have managed that.

He felt strangely calm, the same serenity he'd felt after he'd met Jan. The crisis was upon him, and nothing else mattered. All the world would turn on the point of a sword. Everything would be reduced to living or dying, all the complexities and ambiguities that baffled him boiled away in the fire of battle. And his companions, the remains of the Nine – they'd come together, or they'd fall.

The first assault had struck the south side of the fortress. She'd breached the outer wall and laid low the towers. Arrows lay scattered on the ground, and from the way they had fallen, Alf guessed that they had been buffeted away by gusts of winds, and none had struck home. He found the remains of a handful of defenders, their bodies dismembered. From their garb, they had been Witch Elf knights. He remembered well those dark helms, those wicked swords and spears, all broken now.

Then, she had turned. The main body of the fortress was scorched and shattered by the lightning bolt, but Alf could tell from the fallen bodies and the few wraiths that lingered that the fighting had turned east, towards a lone tower on the eastern side, higher and closer to the peak. A stargazer's tower, toppled now.

A breath of wind whipped up a flurry of ash, and for an instant Alf saw a wraith there, outlined in the swirling soot. It pointed towards the ruins of the tower, as if inviting him onwards. Then it was gone.

Alf climbed the mountainside. There were more of the girl's tracks here, and he followed them into the shattered remains of the tower. Only the lowest level of the tower was in any way intact, its upper storeys decapitated as neatly as if some giant executioner had taken an axe to it. Toppled statues of elven-kings and decans lay smashed on the black marble floor, and a wide stair spiralled down to an underground chamber.

"Come and see," came another voice, "come and see, uncle."

The chamber was thick with wraiths, more than he had ever seen before. An uncountable host of dead elves, crowded so tightly into the little cellar that Alf held his breath to involve inhaling some of the ghosts. Some of them were less faded so that he could catch glimpses of how they had been in life. Haughty faces, glaring at the intruder who'd dared to profane their solemn gathering. The gleam of armour under the starlight. Pale, immortal princes of the earth. Some of them clearly recognised him as one of the Nine, and a silent ripple of hate ran through the crowd. One wraith appeared to shout at Alf, though he could hear no words, only a distant whisper, and the effort was too much for the spectre – it faded away, melting back into the crowd of ancient wraiths.

Alf pushed through the wraiths, and found that there were two living beings there, among all the dead. One was human, the other an elf.

The elf lay in a pool of blood that oozed slowly from her side. She'd been impaled by a spike of rock. One hand was clasped over the wound, her fingers stained red, as was the silvery robe she wore. She had been dying for some time, judging by the amount of spilled blood. Her hair was closely shorn; on her brow she wore a star-shaped gemstone. Her face was ageless, but she seemed terribly old and fragile. Her breath was shallow and pained. The Oracle, he guessed, although she seemed far from the sinister weaver of fates he'd expected.

Next to her sat a Wilder girl, ten or eleven summers maybe. Her hair was thin, and there was a hideous scar on her belly, a wound that had festered before it was healed. Her bare feet were bloodied, as if from the long climb up the mountain. She held the elf's other hand with what seemed like tenderness, but whenever the old elf tried to pull away, the mortal girl gripped more tightly.

"You're Alf," she said lightly. "The Oracle saw you flying north. She saw me, as well. They tried to stop Lath's spell, but my father held them back. The elves are right to fear us." She patted the Oracle's hand. "My father told me about you. And uncle Lath talked about you a lot. You're the most loyal friend he ever had."

"You're Thurn's girl. Talis." There was no denying the resemblance between her and her father; the same long face, the same eyes. He could also see Lath in her — not in her features, but in her movement. Like the Changeling, she shivered as currents of earth-power flowed through her. "You did all this."

"I did."

"He said you were . . . " It seemed absurd to say it.

She laughed and bobbed her head, bashful. "I have been given many names, uncle. I claim none myself, save Talis. I am still Talis, even now. But they call me Death." She brushed her hand against the elf's cheek. "This is Amerith. I fought her long ago. It was in the Land of Thorn Trees, and we fought for three days. Her spells shattered the sky there, and stars fell all around us. They burned me." She held up her hand, and for all her other injuries, there was no mark upon her palm. "Another body. It was long, long ago, more years than I can imagine, but it was only a little while ago to me. Time's different in the Grey Lands. This is all very strange." She laughed again, nervously. "Lath promised I would find a balance — but I don't think he's one to judge. Will she live, do you think?"

"She's hurt," said Alf, shaking his head. It all seemed confusing and absurd, as if he was sitting playing a game of make-believe with a child. He'd expected to find a ravening monster here, an undead horror like Lord Bone that he could slay with a sword.

Not this.

"I know that. I'm the one that hurt her." Death laughed.

"The wound is mortal."

"My father told me the elves found new ways to hide from me, while I was away. They are so clever with their weavings. They bind themselves to trees now, or drink of the lifeblood of others." She raised her voice, speaking to the elf. "There are no trees here, Amerith, but look – there is blood."

"Are you asking me," said Alf, "if I'll save her life?"

"I suppose I am," said Talis, "I could make you, if I wanted. But the real question is, will she drink? Will she let her life be saved? Her spirit is strong. She is proud and fearless. They told me she conquered Necrad once, just like you and my father did. And see, she remains unfaded even after all that time! A great queen of the elves – but now she is at the end. *Come closer.*"

The last words were a command, and Alf found he could not resist. His legs moved of their own accord, and he found himself stumbling forward to kneel next to the pair.

The Oracle moaned. She clawed weakly at Alf, smearing blood across his cloak.

"Ssh, Amerith," said the child. "May I?" she said to Alf, taking his hand in hers. Nimble fingers undid the bandage around Alf's wrist, exposing the wound where the vampire child in Necrad had bitten him. It was mostly healed and looked like it was weeks old, but there was still a little scab, a little blood. The cordials had hastened his healing there, but they could not work miracles.

"Many came to my grey land, and they complained that the vampires had drained their lives. Thousands of years, and hundreds of lives each year, stolen by the elves who feared the doom set out for them. But Amerith, proud Amerith, she did not fade, and she did not partake in the bloody feast alongside her kinfolk. Her soul is unsullied."

"But she's the Oracle," protested Alf. "She served Lord Bone."

Talis ignored him. "But will she pass this last test?"

The girl lightly squeezed Alf's wrist. Blood welled up, and with gentle yet terrible strength, Talis brought the wound closer to Amerith's pale lips. "Where is your pride now, immortal?"

The elf raised her head, and for the first time her gaze fell on Alf. She grabbed at his arm, pulling him closer still. Talis stood back, hands clasped behind her, swaying slightly as she watched the Oracle's last moments.

The Oracle struggled, as if unseen chains drew her mouth ever closer to Alf's hot blood. He could see her wraith now, overlaid with her body, the dying flesh and the immortal spirit disentangling from one another. With a tremendous effort of will, the strain twisting her elven features, she whispered to him.

"*Morthus lae-necras unthuul amortha.*"

And then she could endure no longer, and opened her mouth to drink.

Talis moved more quickly than Alf thought possible, and with impossible strength she came between the two, between elf and mortal. She hurled them apart, flinging him across the room to land heavily by the foot of the stairs. Amerith struck against the far wall. She tried to rise, but her limbs were shattered, and she could only crawl through the dirt.

"You fail at the last test," spat Talis. "You are no better than the rest, for all your pride, and I will unmake all that you have done."

The elf slumped to the ground, and lay still. Her wraith rose from the wreck of her body, and unlike the rest of the shadow host that still pressed against the walls of the chamber, Amerith's wraith was indistinguishable from the corpse that lay at her feet, save that she was unwounded. An unearthly radiance welled up, illuminating only her and leaving the rest of creation dark and empty. She drew herself up, standing taller than the bedraggled mortal child that had slain her – *blasphemed against her*, ran Alf's thought. Compared to the glory of the elf-spirit before him, Alf felt himself to be a lump of mud and gristle.

But Talis said: "Begone, old one, and trouble us no more."

The wraith rippled, like a column of smoke in a breeze, but did not vanish.

Amerith spoke then, though Alf could not hear her words. She was a mummer in a show, mouthing silently, her eyes full of wrath. The gem on her brow blazed like the evening star. As if from a great distance, Alf heard the war-horns and battle-cries of the elven hunt, as he had when they chased the Nine through the streets of Necrad. The host of wraiths closed on Alf, rushing past him in the darkness. They streamed towards Amerith, and as the light fell on the wraiths they too became visible, the shape of how they looked in life restored. Some of the wraiths he recognised – they were elves he had slain in the war. Now, their pale faces looked towards him, and he saw in them a hunger of vengeance. Swords of bitter memory were raised against Death. Spears of starlight were readied against her.

And against Alf.

A ring of ghosts surrounded Talis.

Alf slashed at one with his borrowed sword, but it was only steel. There was no magic behind it, not even a paltry charmstone, and it passed through the wraith without injuring it. For all his strength and skill, there was nothing he could do here, nothing he could fight with this blade.

He turned and fled.

The dreadworm was waiting for him. He fell into the saddle and flew south.

Behind him, the mountainside shattered. He looked back, and saw the child emerging from the ruin, bloodied but unbowed.

And if Thurn was watching, he let Alf fly onwards, to bear tidings of the doom pronounced by his daughter who was Death.

CHAPTER TWENTY-SIX

Something had changed in the changeless forest. Even in the treehouse, deep within the green fortress of the elf-wood, even sheltered by the looming mountain, Olva could sense a change. Part of it was the wind, which blew from the north and had an icy bite to it, but something else had changed too, something greater. Olva had no words for it, only uncertain feelings. It was like the foundations of the earth had cracked, or the moon had vanished – a great and fundamental shift in the way of the world, even if everything seemed the same on the surface.

"Can you feel it?" she asked Torun.

The dwarf looked up from her notes. She'd covered dozens of pages with scribbles and sketches of arcane sigils and curious architecture, animated by the obsession that had come over her since her day at the library tower. Torun rubbed her bloodshot eyes and shook her head. "Feel what?" Then she cocked her head. "Oh – the songs have changed."

It was true – the songs of the elves were different now. They were songs of mourning now, and the autumn fog that trailed and twined around the branches was a cavalcade of ghosts.

Olva went in search of Prince Maedos or one of the other elves to learn what had happened, but she could find no one. The place was not deserted – she saw elves in the distance, walking in twos and threes amid the trees or labouring in the prince's castle – but they slipped away before she could ever reach them. Whatever sorrow they bore was not one they wished to share with mortals.

That night, the trumpet sounded, signalling the start of the prince's revels. On other nights, Maedos or one of his kinfolk had called to the treehouse to bring Olva and Torun up to the castle, but that night no messenger came down to summon them, and there was no sound of music, no lights dancing above the courtyard of the white tower. The trumpet rang out again, and again, each time more demanding and strident, but there was no answer. The sound of the trumpet died away, and then the eerie dirge began again."

Torun spent the following day . . . which day? Olva counted on her fingers, trying to reckon how many days had passed since they had arrived on the Isle. Torun spent the sixth day of their sojourn on the isle engrossed in old scrolls she'd borrowed from the tower. The treehouse was rapidly coming to resemble the cave in the Fossewood, every surface crammed with papers or scrawled diagrams. Olva left the dwarf to her work and went walking in the woods.

This time, she followed a path she had not seen before, and it took her along the southern coast of the isle. This portion of the wood seemed wilder than the region around the castle, which some cynical part of her mind had begun to find a little too perfect. It put her in mind of the great gardens of the Crownland that Galwyn had told her about, the parks and promenades where nobles wandered at their ease. This forest was less tame. There were fewer of the great life-trees in these woods, and more larches and ashes, as well as groves of fruit trees. The storm had carpeted the path in windfallen leaves and fruit, and Olva plucked a few apples as she passed. In places, she came across other structures of the same white stone as the library-tower or the Prince's castle, but these were heavily overgrown and abandoned, and gave her an uneasy feeling. The stark whiteness amid the greenery put her in mind of unburied bones. The air grew colder, and she pulled up the hood of her elf-cloak.

The path bent sharply to the left and sloped down, and soon she found herself walking along a stony shore. Waves crashed upon the rocks, spitting white plumes of spray. Driftwood from wrecked ships littered the beach.

The wind shifted, and she caught the smell of woodsmoke. Ahead, on the shore, was a small campsite. Two dozen or so people huddled there, lightly clad despite the cold. They were, she realised, the other survivors from Abran's ship. They watched her approach, and when she drew near, one of them left the fireside to greet her. A Mulladale lad, of an age than Derwyn.

"Begging your pardon," he said, not daring to look her in the eye, "but has your prince decided what's to become of us?"

"My prince?" Olva was confused, then she pushed back her hood. "I'm not an elf. I arrived here the same way you did."

When they saw she was a mortal too, the survivors barraged Olva with questions. Who was she, to be dressed like that? Why was she treated differently from the rest of them? Was she a Lord of Summerswell or a legendary elf-friend? Had she come to bring them to Necrad? Had she any food?

She answered them as best she could. Her brother was the Lammergeier, she said, and she had been a prisoner until the elves freed her. The prince had told her that the other survivors from the shipwreck would be brought back to the southland, and she had thought they had all gone days ago. And as for food — there was plenty to eat in the bountiful forest, surely?

"The elves told us we're not to leave the shore," said the Mulladale boy. "They said we weren't allowed on the isle. They brought us bread that first night, but nothing since. We caught a few fish, but there's a serpent out in the water, and we dare not go far."

"What's your name?" asked Olva.

"Peir," he replied. A common name since the war. "Peir of Kettlebridge."

"Well, young Peir. Let me see what can be done," said Olva. Guilt for her own good fortune filled her, and she resolved to transmute it into action. A few times in Ersfel, when the villagers needed to make representations to the reeve, she'd spoken for them. She could do the same here.

"And ask them where they'll send us!" shouted another. "My kinfolk have all gone to the New Provinces! I want to go north! There's nothing for me back in Ellsport!"

They crowded around her, shouting out questions, pulling at her cloak. Olva pulled away and climbed on top of a nearby rock, so she could be heard above the din.

"I'll go to the prince. The elves have been kind to me, and I'll make sure they help you!"

At the top of the path stood two life-trees like silent sentries. The way into the forest was guarded.

She set off through the woods, following the ways that lead uphill and inland towards Kairad Nal and the prince's castle. On other days, there had been a wide road through the forest, but either she took a wrong turning or the trees had moved, and she had to fight her way through the undergrowth. The white boles of the life-trees were like a fence around the castle, or like a family of mourners, crowded together for support, their branches intertwined so thickly that she could barely see. The tower seemed to appear and disappear – she'd see it through one gap in the trees, but lose sight of it as she walked, only to spot it again in a different direction.

Fog curled around her, and she could not tell if the shapes she glimpsed were elves or tricks of the light. She remembered Bor's account of the isle; he'd described it as a place of nightmares. A refuge could become a foreboding fortress in an instant if you were on the wrong side of the wall.

The gate of the castle, though, was open and unguarded, and she passed through into the silent courtyard. By night, this open hall had been filled with dancing and merrymaking, but now it was empty. She looked up at the balcony where Maedos had his throne, and noticed for the first time a gigantic carved figure on the trunk of the tree, so cunningly designed that it was like a trick of the light – the figure looked like the natural folds and gnarls of the silver bark of the life-tree from most angles, and was visible only when one looked straight up from below. With outstretched arms running along the underside of the branches, the carved man seemed to bear not only the balcony and the white tower behind it, but also the whole dome of stars in the heavens. He was titanic in scale, but he was no ugly giant or monster. His features were elven – and familiar. Olva had seen the same face carved in the shrines of the holywood, or depicted in tapestries and holy relics in the church at Highfield. The Erlking stared down at her, and she felt transfixed by that immortal gaze, rooted to the spot.

Maedos' face appeared at the balcony far above, and the spell was lifted. "Lady Forster!" he called. "Come up, come up!"

She climbed the winding stair to the balcony. Maedos sat on a low stool, with a curious game spread out on the table before him. There was a board made of some precious stones, with a great many little figurines and tokens. Arcs of silver wire overhung the board with jewel-stars and sigils. The prince reached out and moved one piece across a square of green jade.

"What is that?" asked Olva.

"A game," said the prince. "There is no mortal word for it, for no mortals may play it."

"My husband taught me to play the King's Game," said Olva. The King's Game was ancient, and popular in the Crownlands; knights and priests and pawns and kings moving across the chequerboard. Galwyn had brought a carved set of pieces with him when he'd moved to Ersfel, and she'd thought it wonderful. Afterward, she'd taught Derwyn to play from what she remembered of the rules, although one by one the pieces of Galwyn's set broke or went astray until they were playing with shells and stones. They hadn't played in years, she realised.

"This is not like the King's Game. In mortal games, there is a victor and the game ends. This is a game without end; one cannot win or lose."

"So what do you do?"

"One may claim dominions, establish advantages, to force other players into disadvantageous positions. While one cannot lose, a player may choose to withdraw. Others are more tenacious, holding their little corner of the board for many turns until an opportunity to strike back arises." He tapped a golden figurine of an archer. "In this turn, I am in a commanding position, but that can be danger-ous too. The game rewards caution – better to pressure opponents into making a mistake, or to work in secret. Even the most secure advantage can be overturned by a twist of fate. The game teaches wisdom." Maedos took a handful of tokens from the side of the board, weighed them in his hand, then put most of them back. The remainder he stacked on another square. "But you did not come here to play games, Lady Forster."

"The other souls you rescued from Abran's ship – they're down by the shore. Why are you keeping them there?"

"I must. It is the Erlking's law. In times past, the *enhedrai* – the Witch Elves of Necrad – recruited allies among your kind. They seduced them with gifts of magic, and convinced them to turn traitor. Even the mightiest fortress can be toppled from within, so to protect Kairad Nal, my father decreed that mortals not be permitted to set foot upon the isle – save those few elf-friends we know we can trust."

"You trusted me."

"Why, you are the Lammergeier's kinswoman."

"I haven't seen Alf in twenty years. I don't know how much kinship I can still claim with him – certainly, not so much more than them below that I deserve special treatment. You should bring them up."

Maedos laughed. "It is forbidden."

"Aren't you the king's son, and all? Don't you make the rules here? Back home, the reeve invites all the village up to his manor around harvest-time for a big feast. You could do the same." The thought of a grand celebration in the hall below had its appeal. The elves were enchanting in the moment, but after speaking to one it was like waking from a dream that quickly faded. And while Torun was a stalwart travelling companion, the dwarf could be silent for hours on end. Olva found that while she did not miss Ersfel, she missed some of the pleasures of home.

"Your customs are not ours," said Maedos. "Even if I could read their hearts and be certain that none of the mortals meant me harm, then I still would not change the law. There are things on the isle that are not for mortal eyes, and weapons long-prepared for war. Even when you thought yourself alone, Olva, we were watching over you. If the isle were filled with mortal trespassers, then we could not guard them all from their own folly." Maedos tapped one of the metal tokens off the polished board. "Look at the folly of Necrad, where your kinfolk loot the ancient city, taking away as prizes the work of the ancients. No, my father laid down the law for a reason. I will not break it."

"They're hungry and cold. If you can't offer them the same hospitality you've shown me, then at least send down food. It's bitterly cold by the sea."

"Of course! In other times, they would have been sent back to the lands of mortals as soon as they arrived, but it is too perilous to set sail while the Gulf is shut. I shall see they have what is needful, and arrange for a ship to carry them south safely."

"Some of them asked about going north," said Olva. "They want to go to the New Provinces, not back to Ellsport. You can send them with me when I sail for Necrad."

"I will not send them to the New Provinces. Yesterday, my hunters bring word of bloodshed in the wildwood. Amerith has perished. She was among the eldest of the elves. She was our enemy, the leader of the Witch Elves, but no enmity endures for ever. We rejoice at the defeat of a foe, mourn the loss of a kinswoman, and look forward to a new star in the heavens."

"That's very pretty," said Olva. "But I need to get to Necrad, and the people down on the shore need help."

"All will be attended to." Maedos stood. "I must climb Kairad Nal again, and guard the seas."

"And what about me? I can't stay here for ever."

"Nor shall I. But for all things, the stars ordain the proper time."

As Olva crossed the great hall, she caught the smell of roasting meat. Following her nose, she found a side archway off the hall. It led down a short passageway to a huge kitchen. Elves bustled about, preparing the feast for the night's revels, but there were other servants there too, of a kind Olva had not seen before. These things were made of wood, with limbs of bundled twigs. Their makeshift heads had ripe berries for eyes, and a sketch of a face drawn with russet leaves and thorns. They shambled this way and that, fetching and carrying. She stared in amazement at the servants. The songs told of stranger things, but they were in far-off places like dungeons and enchanted castles.

Then again, she was in an enchanted castle. She crept down into the kitchen and picked up one tray of fresh-baked bread. Then, greatly daring, she whispered to one of the twiglings that was methodically turning a spitted haunch of venison. "Hey! You there!"

The leafy head turned to look at her.

"Come with me, and bring the meat."

The twigling lifted the spit from the fire and hoisted the huge joint of meat over its shoulder. Sizzling juices ran down its bark, but it seemed untroubled. One of the elves noticed Olva's burglary, but only laughed and waved her on. A procession of twiglings followed her down to the shore.

The feast they had there was not so enchanted as the revels of the elves of Dawn, but was somehow all the better for that.

CHAPTER TWENTY-SEVEN

A lf pushed the wounded dreadworm as hard as he dared, but the beast was less than halfway back to Castle Duna when the sun rose. Alf let it dive down towards the shadowed forest below. It landed heavily, coughing up a puddle of frosty mucus, then slithered away into the shadow of the trees to rest.

He walked for a while to clear his head, the snow crunching under his boots. In the distance, he could hear the snuffling of the dreadworm, but that too faded into silence and he was alone. After the thunder and sorcery of the previous night, the peace of the woods seemed incongruous. He felt as though he had awoken from a strange dream, and had to remind himself that his meeting with Thurn and the events at Daeroch Nal had actually happened.

Alf found a place to sit by a stream. He tried to fix the wrappings on his wrist that Talis . . . that *Death herself* had undone, but he couldn't manage it one-handed and gave up in frustration. He sat there for a long while, listening to the babbling of the brook and the wind sighing in the treetops, and tried to reconcile in his head the thought that Death might be incarnated in the body of Thurn's daughter. He could believe that some ancient spirit or sorcerer might return – he was, after all, the man who had killed Lord Bone, ancient necromancers of terrible power were very familiar to him – but incarnations of abstract concepts were a step beyond that. He wished Jan were here, or Blaise, to help him navigate this confusion. Incarnations of abstract concepts definitely felt like wizard's business.

He wondered what Peir would make of it all. The thought struck him that Peir had gone the other way. The tales of the Nine had turned the eight survivors into heroes, but Peir was more – he was the great martyr. His name was a byword for courage and honour across all the lands. When Alf thought of him, though, it wasn't Peir's courage or honour he missed, it was his certainty, his drive. In life, Peir had always had the knack for seeing what to do, even in the face of the supernatural. He'd taken the counsel of wizards and clerics, chased dreams and portents, but then he'd turned all that into action. He'd led them down the Road, into labyrinths and dragon's lairs. He'd always seen the place where sinew and steel could change destiny. Near the end, it was Peir who'd seen that the League could never overcome the defences of Necrad, and that the only way to end the war was for them to sneak into the city and slay the dark lord.

Alf would never have thought of that. All his life, the name of Lord Bone had been a thing out of a story, a figure out of myth – and then, later, a name they used for all misfortune, for the dreadful will behind the hosts of Necrad. A shadow on the world, Jan had called him, not something you could strike down with a sword, any more than you could slay winter, or evil . . . or death.

If Peir was here, he'd know the right thing to do. He'd know who to trust, who to shun. He'd find the right path forward. He'd tell Alf where to aim his sword.

But Peir was dead, and it was up to Alf. Up to him to bring warning. Maybe up to him to defend the city against this new threat. This rising darkness.

He flexed his wounded hand, found it wanting. He adjusted his belt to wear the sword on the other side, and tried unsheathing it with his off-hand. He fumbled the draw, and the sword went splashing into the icy brook.

Laughter sounded in the treetops. Alf snatched up the sword and spun around, scanning the branches. There was a large raven perched overhead. "Alf," it croaked, and then the black feathers melted, and bloomed, and it was Lath sitting in the treetop. "I followed you from Daeroch Nal. Are you going to fight me?"

"No."

The Changeling climbed down to a lower branch and sat there, bare legs swinging in the air. Lath should have been the youngest of them – he wasn't even of age for most of the war, a child given power and purpose far beyond his years. But up close, it was impossible for Alf to judge the Changeling's age. His face swam, shifting between the boy Alf had known, the young man he'd fought beside in the Pits and the appearances of beasts and monsters. Sometimes, another face rose up for an instant and fell back, as if conjured by some passing memory. The faces of the Nine, mostly.

"You weren't here, Alf," said Lath."

"I know, lad. I'm sorry. You could have called for help. The others were still in Necrad."

"*Others!*" hissed Lath. His face whirled through a series of quick-fire changes, taking on the appearance of Blaise, Berys and other members of the Nine. "Too busy, too greedy, too drunk. Or gone, gone, gone." For a moment, Alf found himself looking into a parody of his own face. Lath's warped mirror showed him a weary face, a crooked, oft-broken nose, a heavy brow. Eyes downcast, an expression of weary determination. An old warhorse, plodding on with the rider slumped dead in the saddle.

"They never listened to us, Alf. None of them. We were the ones who followed. Peir and Berys and Blaise, the clever ones, told us what to do, and we did it. Didn't see it at the time. Was so happy to have found a family." The Changeling cocked his head. "Did you know? Did you see it?"

"We were all part of the Nine," said Alf, carefully. "We were all fighting on the same side, for the same purpose. We were on a quest to save the world."

"Remember the night we buried Bone?"

"Of course." Alf remembered that night fondly. They'd sworn an oath, all eight of them, to watch over Necrad. They'd spilled blood together to seal the tomb with magic.

"That's when it all went wrong," said Lath. "Each swore to something different, remember? All good things – freedom and honour and magic and fellowship, but what if you can't have them all at once?" He held up a hand, and it was like a flickering candle flame, switching from human to beast, male to female, young to old, skin and bone changing faster than the eye could follow. "I didn't choose, then. Now, I want to be whole. Being a Changeling is a curse, they told me. They were right, and I made it worse. In Necrad so long."

"And you think by destroying the city, you'll be cleansed?"

"Maybe. Maybe. Seen the city from the other side. It's a stain on the world. I can't destroy it." He grinned, and his teeth were those of a wolf. "*She* can. Always, Alf, always they call me a beast. A monster. Unclean. You and the others, you were the only ones who came close. But Death . . . she's like me, Alf, but older. Stronger. I was born, I think, to bring her back." He nodded. "Yes. Yes." Then he sniffed the air. "You're hurt. Let me see."

Alf unwrapped his botched attempt to rebind the bandage one-handed, and held up his bloody wrist. A charmstone fell out of the dressing and vanished amid the rocks. A king's ransom down south, lost for ever.

Lath grinned at the dagger wound in Alf's side, then pulled up his bloodied shirt to show its match. "Did you kill her?"

"She's held prisoner in Duna's keep."

"Other wound." Lath sniffed and scowled in disapproval. "You fed a vampire, Alf."

"A child."

The Changeling's appearance flickered, and for a moment he was as he'd appeared when Alf first met him – a starved orphan, grubby and scared. Lath had barely been able to speak when they took him in; he'd made noises like an animal. He changed back, and hopped down from the tree. "Let me see it."

Alf extended his hand, and Lath took it. "I don't have much left in me, Alf. Healing Talis – opening the path to the Grey Lands – broke me." He drew upon the earthpower, and even Alf could tell that something was off. The current of energy stuttered, and the wound was not noticeably healed.

"Sorry." Lath flinched and backed away.

"It's all right, lad. Just help me with this." He sat down and let Lath fix the bandage. He fished out some food from his bag while the Changeling worked, and shared it with his friend. Leftovers from Duna's feast. Lath ate hungrily; he was always starving, always rake-thin. The magic ate him up from inside.

"It's nice to see you again," said Lath, "but I wish you hadn't come back north. Thurn says" – Lath's face became that of Thurn, his voice mimicking the Wilder – "there is bitter work ahead." He changed back. "Don't blame you, Alf. You were always good to me."

"Thurn said the same."

"You always got on with all of us. You and Peir."

Alf nodded, even as a little stab of guilt pierced his heart. He'd failed to hold the Nine together, and now the world was out of joint. "Then let's sort this out. Come back with me to Necrad, we'll talk. We'll put things right."

Lath shook his head. "Let me tell you a story," he said abruptly.

Long ago, the Old Kingdom fell to kinstrife and catastrophe. Then came a winter so bitter it froze the wheel of the seasons, so that spring was strangled in the crib and there was only endless snow. There was only the Hopeless Winter.

The few who survived the fall wandered the wastes. Hunger

consumed them, and madness claimed them. Bitter were those cold years of the Hopeless Winter, when brother turned on brother, and all men were as beasts.

Among these desperate men was a chieftain named Harn. He dwelt with his kinfolk and his followers in a house in the land now called Summerswell. Enemies circled like packs of wolves, and there was nothing to hunt in the wood. Little hope remained to Harn, and he feared that soon death would call him to the Grey Lands. Instead, a dream came to him, calling him to the south. He gathered those companions that were still loyal to him (the story doesn't say how many there were, but maybe nine, Alf, maybe) and those of his family who were still strong enough to travel, and they set off through the icy woods. They faced perils on their quest, and to this day you can see the graves of Harn's people in a line along the road from Arshoth to the Eaveslands, for many died upon that terrible journey.

In time, they were astounded to discover a land where it was eternal summer instead of eternal winter, a golden forest where there was only peace and joy. They had come to the very eaves of the Everwood, where the Erlking dwells for ever amid wonders.

Harn and his companions camped on the edge of the wood and debated what to do.

One said, "These elves will ensorcel us and trick us with their illusions. We should flee this cursed place, before we become enmeshed in the spells of the golden wood. Your dream, Harn, was a warning that we should not trespass in the south."

Another argued, "Here there is no snow and no hunger. The elves are few, our people are many. We should go back and gather a great army, and take this forest for our own. Your dream, Harn, was a call to arms."

Harn considered these counsels, and resolved to attack, for death awaited them on every path. But his youngest daughter spoke, saying, "Father, these folk are fair to my eyes, and I pray that they are kindly. Send me alone into the golden wood, as your messenger, and I shall plead with them for aid. If they prove false, then you lose nothing, for I am too young to fight. But if they prove true, then we all shall live, and there shall be peace between men and Elves for all time."

And so his daughter alone walked into the golden wood. For three days, Harn and his followers encamped in the Eaveslands, waiting for her to return. At sunset, when all hope seemed lost, the girl returned to them, and bade them follow her. She led them through the wood to the court of the Erlking.

The mortals pleaded before the Erlking, and begged him for help, but alas! The Erlking and his court were all bound to their enchanted forest, and could not leave its borders. Still—

("I know this story," said Alf, "everyone does."

"Don't interrupt. Just listen.")

Still, the heart of the Erlking was moved by the pleas of the mortals. The Erlking took pity on them, and used his magic to call upon the Intercessors. The wise ones descended from the heavens like tongues of flame, and whispered to Harn and his followers. The blessing of the Intercessors lifted the curse of winter and brought hope back to the land. Those heroes returned to their people and—

"And they were acclaimed the Lords of Summerswell, aye. Lath, what the fuck does any of that have to do with Necrad?"

Lath scowled. "It's about *shape*, Alf. And order. There's a shape to the world. Harn's followers became the Lords of Summerswell. Elves in the Everwood, you folk of Summerswell in the south, dwarves in their mountains, and us Wilder in the north. But Lord Bone's war broke that order, and we made it worse by staying in Necrad. You feel it, too, I know you do – that nothing's gone quite right since Peir died. Things have to be put right, Alf."

"By calling up the dead? By destroying Necrad?"

"Thurn's little girl wouldn't have died if Summerswell had

not settled the New Provinces. They wouldn't have settled the Provinces if we had not kept Necrad. It must be put right. It must be destroyed."

"They won't leave, Lath. I can bring them a warning, but the League won't abandon the city. They'll defend it, even against you and Thurn. And they'll open the arsenals, turn all they can of Bone's leftover magic against you."

"Let them try. I hear things, Alf. I fly far, and I listen. The rats in the walls, they're me. I know things. I know what Berys plans. I know the elves closed the seas, and Vond can't march troops up the Road soon enough to stop us. Tell them to yield, Alf, and Death will not come to them."

"And if they don't listen?"

Lath became a bird again. "Then make sure you don't stand against us, Alf. Or she'll take you to her grey land with the rest."

He walked for the rest of the day. Once, through a break in the forest, he spotted a trio of figures in the distance. They were too far away for him to tell if they were elves or mortals. They moved in a way that reminded him a little of Charnel-zombies, and he wondered if they were sick or wounded, but they vanished into the forest long before he was close enough to hail them.

They were going south, too, but he saw no sign of their trail.

At dusk, another dreadworm flapped down out of the sky, and Alf took flight. He dozed a little on the back of the monster, and woke with a start as it flapped down towards Duna's keep. It was still dark, although there was a hint of dawn gathering in the east. He tugged on the worm's neck, directing it to land outside the walls, and marched up the winding road around the hill to the main gate.

He hammered on the main gate.

"Who's there?" called a guard, and when Alf answered the postern door opened for him.

"Earl Duna's still abed," said the guard. "I'll fetch him." The guard ran off, leaving a trail of footprints across the snowy yard.

Alf nodded, and sat down on a bench in the courtyard. Another servant fetched him some hot porridge from a pot used by the night watch. The servant lingered a moment.

"Begging your pardon, my lord, but is there news? Are the Wilder attacking?"

"Not today," said Alf. "That's all I can promise you."

Erdys emerged from a door across the courtyard, pulling her cloak around her. "Why are you sitting out here in the cold?"

Alf shrugged. "I'm not stopping. I came to bring word of what I saw, and to fetch Gundan. I need to head onto Necrad as soon as I've had a bite. This is a matter for the whole council, and the League." He yawned. "You're up early."

"I have not slept. I was in the chapel with the Abbess, praying for Idmaer's health."

"How's the boy?"

"He . . . he's fighting death, Alf. For all of Master Meryn's charm-stones and elixirs . . . Duna wants to send him on to Necrad and the healers there, but there are too many Wilder on the Road for my liking. I fear ambush — they'd murder Idmaer if they could, or take him hostage." She shivered. "What happened up there, Alf? Gundan said you went in search of Lath and Thurn. Did you find them?"

"I did." Alf thought for a moment. "Erdys, tell me truthfully — did any of Duna's men hurt a Wilder girl named Talis? She was shot with an elf-arrow out of Necrad. Did Duna order the use of such weapons on the Wilder?"

"It's our duty to guard the people of the New Provinces, Alf. Summerswell sends more settlers north every month, and we need to safeguard the borders. We warned the Wilder not to trespass. We tried to find Thurn, too. Duna sent knights into the wildwood, looking for him. I don't know anything about this Talis, but . . .

what could we do? The raids have to end. The law of the land must be enforced." Erdys absently ran her prayer beads through her fingers. "Is she someone important?"

"Thurn's daughter."

Erdys' hands went to her mouth. "Oh, Intercessors preserve us. Alf, we didn't know. I swear we did not know."

"Aye, well, what's done is done." Alf took a deep breath and began to tell her the tale of Daeroch Nal.

Alf intended to fly on to Necrad before dawn, but mid-morning and then noon came and went. First, he had to tell the tale again to Duna, then to Gundan, then to the bloody Abbess, and finally to Ildorae. And there was luncheon and a nap and a divine intercession in there, too.

Telling Duna reminded Alf of those days in the war, when the Nine brought warning to Summerswell, and few believed them. Oh, Duna bowed his head and mumbled gravely when they talked of Death, but Alf could tell the lord did not understand him. It was not that Duna thought Alf a liar, but the thought of this foe was not one that could easily be encompassed by his mind. Alf had seen a similar thing when fighting monsters — veteran warriors who'd fought in a hundred battles against other soldiers freezing in confusion when faced with a corpse-shambler or a demon engine. Duna had fought in the siege of Necrad, but for him those days were a nightmare twenty years past and gratefully forgotten. An army of Wilder besieging his castle, that was part of the world as he understood it. Monsters out of legend were another matter, a matter for heroes.

The other hero in the castle was snoring in bed when Alf went up to his room. News of Gundan's injury had spread to the dwarf-mines and settlements in the area, and now there were a dozen or so dwarves there, tending to their illustrious cousin or guarding his door. Alf they greeted with acclaim; one who had fought in the defence of the Dwarfholt was always welcome. They woke Gundan, and Alf sat on the side of the bed and told him what had transpired. Gundan listened intently to the tale of Death reborn, then lay his head back on the pillow as if in silent contemplation. He looked very old and tired for a moment. Then he opened his mouth, and from it erupted a geyser of curses and profanities that began with *bloody damned stupid fucking IDIOTS* and then broke into oaths in Dwarvish and Elvish and a dozen other tongues.

Gundan tore the bandages from his eyes and staggered out of bed, demanding his axe. One of his cousins had repaired the blade as much as was possible in the castle forge, and Gundan pronounced it good enough for killing someone who was apparently already dead at least once, and was only a ten-year-old girl anyway. One of Gundan's eyes was still blind, and his sight in the other was poor, but he made Alf swear he'd point him in the right direction. In any event, even Gundan agreed that they'd have to have another 'bloody useless idiot council', if only to get Vond to unlock the arsenal and muster the full force of the League. A dreadworm could bear two, even two as a heavy as Alf and Gundan. They would fly south together.

("There doesn't have to be fighting," argued Alf. "Maybe we can still make peace with the Wilder."

"Peace," said Gundan, "happens when one side cries out, 'I yield, I yield, stop hitting me with that axe.'" And he shoved the box containing the sword across the floor to Alf.)

By then, word of Alf's return had spread through the castle, even to the chapel where Erdys and her ladies prayed for the health of her son Idmaer. The Abbess Marit left her holy vigil and sought Alf out, and demanded that he tell her what had happened at Daeroch Nal. Alf retold the tale again, only this time with endless interruptions and questions. To Marit, the manifestation of Death was confirmation that this was fundamentally a spiritual battle, a war that would be decided through faith and fervour, not force of arms – and that thus it was more important than ever that Aelfric commit himself to the cause of the church of the Intercessors. Marit also declared that she would be attending the council in Necrad, which meant there was little prospect of the council gathering anytime soon, as it would take Marit two or three days to ride south. She would not be dissuaded from this, despite Alf's quiet insistence that time was of the essence, and despite Gundan's much louder and more direct approach.

The Intercession happened a little before noon.

The Abbess and Gundan had finished quarrelling – Gundan held that the only people who needed to be at the council in Necrad were the Nine, while the Abbess argued that the Nine had caused this calamity in the first place – and she had gone to the chapel to pray. Alf was eating in the kitchen when he heard shouts, and then the wild ringing of bells. He rushed out, certain the castle was under assault, bracing himself for an earth-shattering bolt of lightning like the one that had shattered Daeroch Nal. Instead, he found a crowd gathered around the door of the chapel, weeping and feverishly praying.

"What is it? What's happened?" he demanded.

"An Intercessor!" they cried as one, and cheered. More and more would join the crowd in the hours to come, as word of the miracle spread to the town below. Alf's tidings of an army of Wilder and the incarnation of Death were almost eclipsed by this new marvel.

Alf pushed through into the darkness of the chapel.

Erdys was there, kneeling next to her son Idmaer – and though he was still unconscious on the bier, the pallor had left his face. Alf had seen many wounded men in his time, warriors who lay there feverish and who did not know if they would ever rise from their sickbed again. Two days ago, he'd have guessed that Duna's boy was doomed to die, but he stank of death no longer. The boy would live.

A young woman clutched the boy's remaining hand on the other side. She'd exchanged her Witch Elf garb for the respectable dress of a maiden of Arshoth, but Alf recognised her as one of the women from the feast. She looked up as Alf's shadow fell over Idmaer. "An

Intercessor was here!" she whispered, and her face was alight with joy. "I saw Him! He was like a sunbeam! A being of light! I saw Him, as surely as I see you now!"

Alf looked around for the Abbess, but there was no sign of her amid the crowd of the faithful. She must be in the sanctum. He walked up to the door beside the altar, but dared not knock. He could hear murmured prayers from within, and the lapping of water in the sacred bowl. He felt awkward, standing there at the chapel door, the only one standing amid a kneeling crowd, the only one untouched by the divine fervour. *An Intercessor passed through here*, he thought, and wondered why the spirit had chosen to heal Duna's son and not, say, Gundan.

After a few minutes, the Abbess emerged. Her face was deathly pale, and she leaned on Alf's arm for support, but she looked up at him with a smile so heartfelt it made years fall from her face. "The Intercessors heard my prayer, Aelfric. They will save us from the demon that the Wilder have summoned."

"How?" he asked, but the Abbess only smiled and raised her voice in song.

The evening was drawing in, mists swirling around the dark trunks of the trees, when Alf finally descended into the prison cell beneath the keep. Ildorae sat there by the barred window, listening to the singing and prayers of the faithful in the courtyard above.

"Last night, I dreamed of Amerith," she said quietly. "You failed, Lammergeier, and now we are all doomed."

"Maybe," said Alf, "but I didn't kill any of my friends. There's still hope we can make peace."

"Give me the sword, mortal. It is the only weapon left to us that might defeat Death. My brother wielded it once – give it to me, and I swear I shall put it to good use."

"The sword," Alf sighed, "has a wielder."

*

Alone in a quiet room in the castle, he opened the casket and took out the sword. It was, he had to admit, a beautiful weapon. The blade an obsidian plane, mirror-smooth apart from the groove that ran down the centre, unadorned. The cross guard, in contrast, was intricately worked, a black and leafless tree in winter, branches spreading and intertwining. The black tree bore a single fruit – the ruby known as the demon's eye. The grip was bound in dragonhide, and was perfectly sized for Alf's meaty fist. Acraist had wielded Spellbreaker with two hands, but it was a hand-and-a-half sword for Alf. The pommel returned to the austere perfection of the blade; a polished sphere of black metal. It was reflective enough that Alf could see a distorted image of himself mirrored in the blade if he looked closely, but he didn't like to do that – it always made him feel like the distorted face was the true Alf, and he was just a shadow.

He tried to pick up the sword. It was impossibly heavy, as if welded to the ground. He withdrew his hand and sat back.

"Sword," he said.

There was no answer.

"You want to be used, don't you?"

"You are my gaoler," said Spellbreaker, sullenly. "You locked me away inside a cell."

"And now I've need of you." Alf reached forward and gripped the sword again. In his mind's eye, he conjured up the sight of the thunderbolt striking Daeroch Nal, of Thurn's child outlined against the fire. He let the sword see his memories, felt the cold presence of the blade against his soul.

He tried to lift Spellbreaker again, but it remained obstinately heavy.

"It's this or the box."

"I am nothing without a wielder," admitted the sword, "but you are a poor wielder. You neglect your blade."

"What, you want me to be nicer to you? A spot of polish? A date with a whetstone?" Alf's face darkened. "Or do you mean bloodshed, because I won't kill without cause. I don't need your magic that much."

"You need *me*, wielder. I know you better than you know yourself – you are choked by your past. It weighs you down like a heavy cloak. All the tales that others tell of you, and all the tales you tell yourself. I watched you patrol the Pits for years, over and over, patching that cloak whenever it became soiled or threadbare. I watched you wander, blind to the present, clinging to the past. You need a blade to cut you free so you can see clearly."

"You've a high opinion of your insight," said Alf. "To me it sounds like you want to pour more poison in my ear about my friends."

"Your friends," said the sword, "are my enemies."

"Not any more. The war's over."

"And because you slew my master – because you took me as a spoil of war – I should forget who I am? I was made by Lord Bone. I was forged with a purpose. I cannot change what I am."

Alf sighed. "I need a weapon I can rely on. Not another problem to worry about. I guess it's the box for you then."

"Wait!" said the sword. It became feather-light, adhering to Alf's hand as when he tried to withdraw it. "I will . . . be good."

"Swear."

"A knight," said Spellbreaker with an echo of amusement, "swears on a sword. What should a sword swear on?"

Alf thought for a moment. "Swear by Lord Bone. Swear by the name of the one who made you."

The voice that rang from the sword then was colder than the gulf between the stars. "I swear by Lord Bone to serve you faithfully, Aelfric Lammergeier. Keep me by your side, and I shall be loyal to you and you alone. I shall not deceive you, or wilfully mislead you, or fail to defend your body from sorcery. I shall kill as you wield me, and spare as you restrain me. This I swear by my maker's name."

CHAPTER TWENTY-EIGHT

This time, at least, the council meeting was well attended.

Lord Vond sat at the head of the table, with Abbess Marit at his left hand and Gundan at his right. Next to Marit sat Duna's other boy, Dunweld, who was not officially part of the council, but no one was in the mood to argue niceties. The boy was only fourteen years old, and all the bravado he'd shown fighting a chained ogre had left him. He'd traded his Witch Elf garb for a tunic and tabard with his father's sigil upon them, and clutched a letter written by the earl in his sweaty fingers.

They'd put Ildorae between Alf and Gundan. Heavy manacles bound her hand and foot, though Alf doubted the precaution would be needed. For one thing, Gundan wore his biggest grin and had Chopper on the table in front of him, daring Ildorae to start trouble. For another, Blaise was there in person, his appearance halfway between the many-eyed cosmic horror he resembled in the Wailing Tower and the apprentice Alf once knew. He was dressed as a master of the College of Wizardry, but he wore no house colours, declaring that none of the lordly families of Summerswell had sponsored him.

Down at the far end sat Threeday, next to the empty seat where Berys should have been. There was no sign of Laerlyn, and Alf's heart sank at the sight. She still had not returned.

"Sir Lammergeier," began Lord Vond, "you come to us with an account as strange as any tale of the Nine. You warned us the Wilder are marching to war, and this is certainly credible. Raids on the New Provinces have increased in recent years, and while the notion of some war-lord gathering a great host is disturbing, it is not unforeseen. But more – you tell us that two of the heroes of the Nine, Thurn the Wilder and Lath the Changeling, are at the head of the host."

"I also told you that it was the killing of Thurn's daughter that started all this," said Alf.

"My earl the father would never order any man to do such a thing," squawked Duna's son, the words falling over each other in haste. The boy had clearly been practising the response all the way from Athar. "If the Wilder was shot on his land, it was not at his command."

"Like that matters a damn to anyone," snapped Gundan.

Vond rapped on the table for silence, striking with such force he barked his knuckles on the wood. "It is *regrettable* that two of the Nine should have turned against the League, despite our *gratitude* for all they did in the war. Out of respect for their past deeds – and your friendship with them – we shall treat them with mercy if opportunity arises. However, this city and the New Provinces are part of the territory of Summerswell, and must be defended by the League."

"Got a lot of elves here, have we? Are they hiding under the table?" Gundan sneered.

"You also tell us that we shall soon be attacked by Thurn's daughter Talis, who is . . . a sorceress? A changeling? A demon?"

"Death."

"So she may name herself," said Vond, "I have known knights who fought under assumed names, but that did not change their nature. What is she, really?"

Alf shrugged. "Does it matter? Maybe it's just a tall tale and she's just the ghost of some Wilder-mage from the dawn years. She shattered a fortress with a word, and she's on her way here."

"Stories grow as they travel. Armies diminish. I need to know if this threat is real."

"Your father said the same about Bone," said Gundan. "I didn't see what Alf saw, but I believe him. It's real, and it's on us to deal with it."

"The parallel is not lost on me, Lord Gundan. Remember, my father was among the first to heed the tidings brought by the Nine. Then, however, the action to be taken was clear. We mustered our armies, called upon our allies, and went into battle against the hosts of Lord Bone."

"I bloody love the 'we'," said Gundan, "seeing as you were a boy of eight at the time. Only thing you mustered were your toy soldiers. Thurn and Lath are of the Nine. The Nine started this, and the Nine'll finish this. Right, lads?" He looked to Alf and Blaise.

"What about Berys and Lae?" asked Alf.

"Berys is on business in the south," whispered Threeday. "I would not expect to see her back in Necrad in the present emergency."

"Business," echoed Gundan. He leaned forward, eclipsing Vond at the head of the table. "Fuck me. Anyway, a thief's not what we need. This thing's a monster, and between Alf and me, we've got two of the best monster-killers around. And I'm sure Blaise there can tell us what bit to chop off, eh? Although the head's usually a safe bet."

"She's a child, Gundan," said Alf.

"Oh, come on! Half of Bone's monsters tried that trick. You go into a dungeon and you meet some half-naked girl chained to a wall, sobbing about how she was captured by Witch Elves – you chop her head off before she turns into something gribbly with too many teeth. This creature may be wearing the skin of Thurn's kid, but who knows what's on the inside? She smashed Daeroch Nal like a dragon!"

Blaise raised a finger, and the whole room became eerily quiet. "I too wish to know more about what happened at Daeroch Nal. We have only Aelfric's description of the aftermath, and his account of what Thurn told him. But we have among us one who is immortal. Ildorae of the Horned Serpent, what do you know of Death?"

For an instant, a scowl crossed Ildorae's face, hatred and frustration contorting her features, but then a great calm came over her. She sat up in her chair, regal and wise, and when she spoke her voice was devoid of any of the venom she had spat at Alf. It put Alf in mind of a snake shedding its skin. It was the way of the elves, he guessed – when one looked forward to eternity, one learned to see most things as passing, as transient as weather. She'd looked around the table and seen only mortals, and had put her anger aside.

Suddenly, she reminded Alf intensely of Laerlyn.

"I am of the third generation of the elves. I was born after the parting, when the *enhedrai* left the snare of the eternal wood and returned to the north, and to this city that was our home since before the rising of the moon. I have not looked upon Death with these eyes. I had another life, in the first days, but only in dream do I recall it, and the memories are bitter.

"But I spoke to those who do remember the age when Death first took physical form and drove us from Necrad. You have all fought Wilder-sorcerers before. They depend on the flow of earthpower, which is like an underground river. In places, it flows fast or slow, or vanishes into the depths only to reappear elsewhere, and they must hunt for it. One can exhaust them, or take advantage of the moments when their strength ebbs. Death's power, though, is a ceaseless torrent. All things that perish give her their strength. The more you struggle against her, the stronger she becomes.

"It was Amerith – the one you name the Oracle – who set me on my quest. She alone straddled two worlds, the living world and the wraith-realm that borders on the land of Death. The wraiths brought her warning that some force was meddling with the Grey Land where only mortals go. She knew the perils of rousing the dead, and sent me to stop it before you mortals called up that terror."

"The legends of the Wilder," said Blaise, "speak of Death as a skinchanger, like Lath, taking the shape of beasts, of shadows, of wind and storm. When I first encountered those stories, I thought it to be a metaphor, but now I suspect it was simple truth. Is that consistent with your memories of her?"

"She was like the Beast Lath, only far greater."

"And she was adept at using her magic? She knew many different ways to command the elements?"

"Were you not listening, mortal? This horror brought down the first realm of the elves, when we were at the height of our power."

Blaise turned to Alf. "But in your account, Talis climbed the mountain barefoot. She never changed her shape, and she wielded comparatively few spells. Is that not so?"

"I guess."

Gundan nodded as he perceived the wizard's meaning. "Remember Lath when he was young, eh? These days, he's quick to change and can mix his forms as he pleases, but that's a trick it took him years to learn. Sounds to me like the child's got raw strength to spare, but not much in the way of skill."

"Lath's ritual has summoned a spirit out of the lands of the dead," said Blaise, "and bound it into the body of a living host. It would take time for the two entities to . . . align. But I do not doubt that her ability grows with each passing hour. In time – and I cannot guess how long, but weeks or months at most – she will come to possess both the strength and skill to wield the earthpower as she once did. If she is indeed the woman called Death, then she defeated the elves of old almost singlehanded. Few forces in the present could stand against her when she comes into the fullness of her power." He folded his hands.

"For all your numbers," said Threeday, quietly, "the League could not breach the walls of Necrad during the war."

"The city's magical defences died with Lord Bone," said Blaise.

"All right then," said Alf, "I'll say it. What if we give 'em what they want? What if we offer to quit Necrad?"

"No!" snarled Vond. The boy forced himself back to composure, clasping his hands together so tightly that blood welled out of his bruised knuckle. "The Lords of Summerswell commanded me to rule this city, Sir Lammergeier, not turn it over to brigands. And even if I gave the order to abandon the Garrison, I cannot command Earl Duna or the other rulers of the New Provinces, nor can I speak for the Lords of Summerswell. Necrad is too valuable a prize to be abandoned. Are we all agreed in this at least?"

"I can fucking speak for the dwarves," said Gundan, "and we're not backing down from a fight. And who's to say Thurn would stop with this city, either? We nearly lost the Dwarfholt in the last war, and many of my kinfolk lie buried along the road from there to Necrad. We're not running from some snotty brat and a ghost monster from the dawn of time."

"Some of us," said Threeday, quietly "cannot flee the city even if we wished – and I assure you, I devoutly wish to do so. But I cannot."

Dunweld stammered. "My father's home is now in the north, and Castle Duna is a strong place. He sent me to ask for such magical aid as Necrad can provide."

"Aye," said Gundan. "Whatever else we do, we should send aid to Duna before the Wilder push south. Keep him threatening their flank."

"The Intercessors ordained the founding of the New Provinces," said the Abbess, "so defending them is a holy act, and worthy, too. With the blessing of the Intercessors, our victory is assured – if we remain faithful, of course."

Blaise's face remained impassive, but his shoulders shook slightly, as if holding back a laugh. When he spoke, though, his voice was grave. "Necrad was the first city. It was here that the first spell was wrought, the first song sung, the first story told. It would be wrong to let this city be destroyed, no matter what one thinks of its present state."

All eyes turned to Alf. "I've seen too many people die in this godforsaken place," he said slowly, "to welcome the idea of fighting for it. I don't want to kill any Wilder. I don't want to fight my friends."

"Sir Aelfric," said Vond, "you are a sworn knight of Summerswell and the League, are you not? You are bound by law and honour to obey the commands of the Lords of Summerswell, and I call upon you now as their representative to defend the city of Necrad against all foes. If necessary, sir, you shall defend this city to the death."

"The quest is holy," added Marit, "and the cause is just!"

"I fucking know, all right? I'll do it if I have to. But there has to be another way." Alf looked across the table at the empty seats, wishing at least that Laerlyn had returned. She'd spoken of rooting herself in the city. If she was bound to Necrad, then there'd be one bright thing in the city, one person he knew was worth defending. But the life-trees in Lath's grove were all ash, and Laerlyn was far away across the sea. "What about reinforcements? If the Wilder see they're outmatched, then maybe they'll fall back." Even as he said it, he knew his words were empty. The Wilder certainly had more warriors than the League could muster, and even if the League's troops were better armed and better trained, and secure behind the walls of Necrad, that would not be enough. The elves at Daeroch Nal each had thousands of years of experience, and magic, and stout walls to shelter behind. Yet Death had come for them, too.

"Messengers have gone south. The League already had reinforcements on the march, on account of the dispute with the Wood Elves, and the Dwarfholt will send troops, too," said Vond, "but it's slow going on the Road at this time of year. It will take weeks for any help to arrive by the landward route. Against most foes, the city could likely hold out against attack long enough for those troops to break the siege. Against this creature . . . I do not know."

"And the elves?" said Alf.

"I shall send messengers, asking the elves to lay aside their dispute with the League for now and to come to our aid."

"Fuck the elves," said Gundan. "Send no messengers. If we beg that bastard Maedos to come to our aid, he'll demand the whole bloody city as recompense. None of you lot know him. Alf and me, we went to Maedos for aid in the war, and he wouldn't help. He'll smile and bow and talk a lot, as elves do, but he'll bleed you dry before he lifts a finger."

"Laerlyn—" began Alf.

"Has fucked off, like Jan. It's up to us."

"It is folly," said Marit, "to shun our oldest allies when we are in dire need."

Vond stood. "I propose that this council sends an entreaty to the Isle of Dawn, asking—"

"Piss off. We can do this without the bloody elves," shouted Gundan.

"The Wood Elves are a kindly folk," said the Abbess. "I am certain they would let some of our ships cross the sea. We could take those who cannot fight in the defence of the city to safety. Send the children away, at least."

"Nah. Nothing like having your back to a wall to stiffen the spine," said Gundan. "We let anyone leave, they'll start knifing each other for space on the ships, and we need all our strength to hold the walls."

The dwarf stood and walked around the table to stand next to Blaise. He tapped his axe on the stone floor as he went, like a drumbeat. "If it weren't for the child," said Gundan, "the Wilder wouldn't have a prayer. We'd be talking about how to defend the New Provinces, not shitting our breeches about the fall of Necrad. So, again, it comes down to kill—" He caught himself and gave Alf a guilty grin. "To stopping the girl. Lads, how do we do that?"

"The caster of a spell can undo that spell," said Blaise, "Lath could release Death's spirit. So, too, could the one who wrote the resurrection spell." He looked around the table. "I am certain it was not *Lath* who made this spell. Another mind conceived it, and Lath cast it according to the other's design. With time and effort, I could perhaps unravel the spell-sigils and countermand the resurrection, but it has taken me two decades of work to unlock even a fraction of Lord Bone's sigils, and this spell is of equal complexity. I shall attempt it. The papers Aelfric found give me some insight into the mind of the maker. But it will take time."

"Do we have another enemy?" asked the Abbess. "Who is this other sorcerer who aided the Changeling?"

"Ask your Intercessors," sneered Blaise.

The Abbess made the sign against evil; Duna's boy half rose and shouted at Blaise. Vond hammered the table. "Enough! Enough! Master Blaise, we shall have no blasphemy here! But neither shall we have infighting, not when the enemy is at our gates."

"The Nine claimed this city," said Marit, "perhaps it is not Lord Bone's evil that taints this place, but your own sins. The Intercessors spoke to all of you, once – but you have all strayed into darkness since! None of you—"

Gundan grabbed his axe, flipped it, and drove the enchanted blade into the table. A huge crack trickled from one side to the other, and with a slow creak the great table sagged apart, cut in two.

"One more bit of nonsense out of you," drawled Gundan, "and I'll fucking send you to talk to the spirits in person, all right. Not one more word. And, Duna's boy, that goes for you, too. If you speak out of turn, I will chop you, understand?" The dwarf shook his head. "If Peir were here leading us, then he'd have said all that pretty-like. He'd have made you feel good about shutting the fuck up and letting us decide on what's to be done, but it'd come to the same end. Peir's dead, but Alf and Blaise and me – we're Nine. Our city. Our council. Our way. Anyone who wants to argue, there's the door."

There was a moment's silence. Slowly, Abbess Marit pushed her chair back and rose. "The Intercessors have spoken to me. Aid unlooked for will come to us, and we shall be delivered from

Death. Your arrogance will lead to ruin. Only in humility shall we be saved."

She clasped her hands and began loudly to recite the prayer for intercession as she walked across the room towards the door, as though it were a religious procession. Dunweld's and Vond's eyes followed her as she went, but looked away when she glanced back, unable to meet hers. As she left, Alf caught a glimpse of the faces of the guards stationed outside the council room, and their fear was plain to see. They'd need to act before that fear spread to the rest of the Garrison – rumours circulated quickly in Necrad.

Blaise's shoulders shook again as the door closed behind the Abbess.

"And I thought Jan was the worst," said Gundan. "Clerics! Always have to dress everything up and make it portentous."

"Gam, be a good lad and go after the hag. Don't hurt her unless you have to, but be quick and shove her in a nice dungeon where she can have a good long pray, and not vex the rest of us." The burly henchman hurried after the Abbess, axe in hand.

Gundan wrenched his axe out of the table, then looked around the room at the remaining councillors. "Any objections?"

"When this matter is done, Lord Dwarf," said Vond, "then I will make you answer for your threats and your insolence."

"If you're going to get in our way, lad, then it won't go well for you. Now listen here – no letters to the elves, all right? No concessions to Maedos or any of his bastard kin. Humans and dwarves hold Necrad, eh?"

The young lord did not answer.

"EH?!" shouted Gundan, and he raised the axe.

"As you say, Lord Dwarf," said Vond quietly, bowing his head. "There shall be no entreaty to the Isle of Dawn."

"Good lad," mocked Gundan. "A credit to your father, eh? You'll go and unlock the arsenal and get Duna's men enough magic to turn the Wilder into dogmeat."

"I shall outfit Earl Duna's knights with such enchantments as can found." He spoke with effort, as if the words were dragged out of him, bloody and barbed.

"Very good. Now quiet. Grown-ups are talking."

"I shall remain in Necrad," announced Blaise.

"Big surprise."

"I shall study the sigil. Failing that, I shall protect the city with all the magic I can muster."

"Hear that, Vatling?" laughed Gundan. "Blaise is going to save you all."

"My efforts," said Blaise, "are a last resort, if you cannot stop Death before she reaches the city. My magic is unsuited to direct confrontation, and I assure you I would be of no help when it comes to persuading the Wilder to relent."

"Aye, they bloody hate you all right. So, our two options are attacking her as soon as we can," said Gundan, "and pray she's still too addled to defend herself. Or we persuade Lath, one way or another, to lift the spell. The first one sounds like suicide, to be honest, if she's throwing lightning bolts around that can smash castles. The second depends on Lath being sensible, so . . . that's an argument in favour of option one. Anything else?"

"There are certain relics that might be . . . effective," mused Blaise. "Certain forms of spell-skull, or the winter-hand, or—"

"The sword," interrupted Ildorae. "The Spellbreaker. It guards its wielder against magic. It was made for a foe such as this."

"Now that's more like it!" crowed Gundan. "Alf, what does the bastard sword say?"

Alf pressed his hand on Spellbreaker's hilt, keeping the sword trapped in its scabbard. The hilt was hot to the touch. He could feel the weapon's bloodthirst running through his own veins, feel its eagerness to be used. Then, the sword restrained itself. The desire for violence faded.

I shall guard you against Death, whispered Spellbreaker in his mind, *though it may press me to my limit. No mortal spell caster in Summerswell was so strong.*

"The sword says it can hold off the thunder," said Alf, "but it doesn't matter what the sword says. I'm the one who'll wield it – if I have to. But we talk to Thurn first."

"What will you say to him?" asked Threeday from the corner. Alf had nearly forgotten the Vatling was present. "What words do you have, Sir Lammergeier, to convince the Wilder to turn from their path and spare us? What can you offer them?"

"I don't know." Doubt gnawed at Alf, and with it the thought he had squandered fifteen years. What if he had done what Gundan or Berys had done, and turned his fame and glory into influence? He had nothing to offer, no leverage except the power of the sword, and he would not use that against the Wilder if he could avoid it. If only he'd taken another path and taken what was once offered, he'd be a great lord, able to sway events.

Or if Peir had lived . . . Peir would be High Lord of Summerswell now, and he'd have some other solution to offer. He'd never have let the settlers in the New Provinces drive the Wilder into the wood. He'd have burned out the corruption in Necrad before it got into Lath's veins. He'd have known how to put it all right. "But I'll try," he finished.

"You are such a stubborn bastard," laughed Gundan. "But don't worry. I've got words that even Death may harken to – and if that fails, we'll use the sword. If we can't convince 'em to come to terms, and we can't kill *her* there, then we fall back to Necrad, and it'll be a question of holding out against her 'til the League sends reinforcements. Fuck it, I'll even take Laerlyn and her snotty kin at that point."

"I have one or two minor items that may be of use," said Threeday, "relics that were discovered in the Sanction, and unaccountably were not reported to the authorities. I must also ask, on behalf of the folk of the Liberties – Necrad is our home, so surely it is right and fitting for us to take up arms in defence of the city. Will this council not lift the ban on arms in the Liberties – at least, temporarily?"

"Nah," said Gundan. "I don't care if you little Vatling shits have swords or whatever, because you can't fight worth a damn. But arming the ogres? The Witch Elves? Not a bloody chance. There'd be war on the streets long before the Wilder got here."

"The request was made to the council, not to you, Lord Gundan." The Vatling's watery gaze flickered to the huge axe on the table, but he did not waver. "I call for a vote."

"A vote?" laughed Gundan. "Did you miss the fucking coup?"

"Arming the Liberties," said Vond, weakly, "would not be appropriate at this time. If the city is besieged, then perhaps we can re-examine the question."

"What about her?" asked Dunweld, staring across the table at Ildorae. "She's dangerous. She even bested Sir Lammergeier. And the Wilder think her a goddess. Can we use her?"

Ildorae stared at the boy, so regal that the iron chains looked like a badge of high office. "*Use* me, mortal? I hunted in those woods a thousand years before the founding of Summerswell. I have more experience of war than all of you combined – even you, dwarf. The Oracle laid a quest upon me, and though you stopped me from slaying the Beast, still I would see it to the end. I *choose* to go with you."

"Fancy talk from one in chains," said Gundan, "but aye, you're coming with us."

CHAPTER TWENTY-NINE

The streets outside the League citadel heaved with crowds. Voices – angry, frightened, pleading, belligerent – called on Alf and the other heroes of the Nine as they left the keep. They cheered when they saw Alf and Gundan, and shouted and jeered at the sight of Ildorae. The elf cast back her hood and stared down at the assembled mortals without flinching. A few threw stones or other projectiles, but none came close, and a line of guards kept the mob back. Gundan grabbed Alf by the arm and hustled him down the street towards a waiting carriage, guarded by stern-faced dwarves.

"Bloody Vond. No backbone. He'd sell the city out to the elves in a heartbeat. I had to put the lad in his place."

Ildorae followed after them, her manacles clinking, but the dwarves blocked her path. The edges of their axes glistened with bane-metal.

Gundan glanced back at her. "Bring her along with us, Alf. And keep that damn sword of yours handy, too."

"I won't—"

"I know, I know. You don't want to fight Thurn or Lath, or kill the child. Even if Lath is a skin-changing loon, and the girl is literally the embodiment of Death, you don't want to use that cursed blade."

"Not unless there's no choice, Gundan. Not against others of the Nine."

"It's down to the Nine, Alf, to sort this. You can't trust Vond or the rest – they weren't here in the war, so they just see Necrad as a treasure hoard of magic. Only the Nine of us really understand it, right? We know this city's tainted. Thurn and Lath were there with us – I don't blame 'em for wanting to see the place razed to the ground.

"So, if we have to, I say we let 'em. We make a deal – the New Provinces are left in peace, and all the north's divided up between the League and the Wilder. We make a new border, at Lake Bavduin or somewhere like that. They give us until midsummer to get out of Necrad – just Necrad. That'll be enough time to empty the city, even if everyone has to go by the Road instead of by sea."

The irritating thought that all the new dwarven gold mines lay south of Lake Bavduin crawled along the back of Alf's head. Gundan's compromise would preserve everything the dwarves wanted out of the north. Alf squashed the thought instead of giving voice to it. Instead, he asked: "What about the Vatlings? And the Witch Elves?"

"The Witch Elves can go south and hug the trees, like Lae wanted. Or they can stay here and get as killed as elves can manage. Fuck the Witch Elves, to be honest. The Vatlings . . . look, think of this as a slow battle, one that we'll be fighting for months. Some people are going to die no matter what we do, and let's face it, they're only barely people anyway. They're just alchemical goo and magic. Maybe Blaise can do something clever and move some of their spawning vats out of the city before the Wilder smash the place. I must hurry to muster my household guard." Gundan climbed into the carriage. "I'll be ready to march by morning – we'll ride together, aye?"

"We could fly, you know. A dreadworm could carry the two of us. We'd be there a damn sight sooner."

The dwarf is very heavy, grumbled the sword in Alf's mind. *Don't be so sure.*

"Nah." Gundan leaned over and lowered his voice. "We need to act like lords now, Alf, all of us Nine. It's not like the old days when we could just fuck off down the Road. All this—" he waved at the city, "is our problem. We've got to hold it together, and sometimes that means being seen. We'll ride with the fancy knights and under the League banners, but we're the ones in charge." He grasped Alf's shoulder. "Remember that. We're the big damn heroes."

Alf turned to Ildorae. "I've an errand to run in the Liberties." Her wrists were still chained. He glanced back up at the League citadel. There were cells there where prisoners could be kept.

"Take me with you," she asked softly. "It has been many years since I walked the streets of my city openly."

Spellbreaker would tell him it was a trap. Gundan would shout at him for trusting a Witch Elf.

"All right."

Alf watched her as they walked. Warily, at first – he sensed no immediate threat from the Witch Elf, but she was still as dangerous as a venomous serpent. Soon, though, he found himself watching her reactions to the city he'd helped make. Ildorae wrinkled her nose at the sight of the crowded streets, and all that the humans had built in the occupied city. Rows of junk-shops, selling sculptures and treasures looted from the wreck of the city. Taverns, whorehouses and gambling dens. Pawnshops that offered payment in blood.

"Nothing in this fallen world is changeless, mortal, but Necrad was as close as could be conceived. The streets of this city were laid down nearly eight thousand years before I was born. I dwelt here for two thousand years after, and in all that time the city was eternal. We are immortal, but we are not eternal. We change. We are fickle beings." She glanced at Alf. "Your friend Laerlyn is young, you know. Only a few hundred years old in her present incarnation, and that is all she knows. The young are so true to themselves, and the world seems to them so bright. They do not have the patina of memory that shrouds things for the old." Ildorae gestured as best she could with her hands bound at the changed street around her. "Seeing all this makes me feel old."

"Aye, me too."

She laughed. "You are a mayfly. How can you be old in a span of half a century or so? Half a century is a passing mood." Ildorae slunk around him like a cat as they walked towards the Garrison gate. "I could devote myself to pleasing you, mortal, for half a century. I could devote all my energy, all my thought, all my heart to you. Imagine it! I could enchant you, and show you such bliss that you would think no one else had ever known joy. I could walk beside you all the days of your life, and support you in all things with all my strength and spirit. I could love you, mortal, if I chose. And then, when you die, I could walk away without a backward glance, for it was only half a century, and that is but a whim, a fraction of eternity."

"What's your point?"

"To make you see what was lost here, perhaps. The changeless city is changed. Even the forefathers of the forefathers of the forefathers of the Wilder, when they dwelt here, did not wreak such devastation. That is down to you."

Alf nodded in the direction of a spawning vat. "That's Lord Bone's work. Not ours."

"Bone came to us from Summerswell. It is tiresome to have to remember all your little kingdoms. It's like two fallen leaves, one insisting that it's important that I remember that the other came from a different twig."

"Bone was no more than a falling leaf, was he?" scoffed Alf. "Seems to me like he was a lot more. He took over your precious eternal city. You were boasting about how you intended to kill him. And how you fled when you didn't manage it."

"We did it to ourselves. We craved novelty and sensation – unlike the *ahedrei*, we do not dull our minds to the point of tranquil idiocy with their lotus-draughts. No, we were foolish in another way. We welcomed the mortal in, and amused ourselves by teaching him, and later by pretending to serve him. But we underestimated his ambition. What began as indulgence of a child king became genuine subservience. And then he warped the city to his own ends, so that only he could make full use of its magic."

She paused at a carving on a wall. It depicted an elf-lord on a horse, stern and proud. The hooves of his horse trampled a pile of dismembered demons, and more horrors fled before his wrath – although the demons were mostly hidden by posters and pasted notices, advertising entertainments or opportunities in the city. *Adventurers wanted.* "The wars with the demons lasted a thousand years, and you mortals remember nothing of them. You know nothing of the Candlelit Crusade, or the Peak of Ilisdun. All you have are stories, retold over and over, fading and changing with each retelling. And here is the sorry thing – few of the elves remember either, even those that were there. Memories become eclipsed by memories of memories, and the story becomes the only truth that remains. Sometimes, I think that is why we elves fade over time – we can no longer recall who we truly are, beneath all the masks and diversions, and so we become nothing more than thin veneers, easily discarded. But Necrad helps us endure.

"For thousands of years, Necrad was the record of our people. We carved our histories into imperishable stone, so that we could look back ten thousand years hence and see the arrow-flight of eternity. From that distance, all these things – Lord Bone's rise, the occupation of Necrad by your League, the return of Death – are but as one spasm of history, a single event. The years of mortal folly, we shall call them– if there are any to remember. I fear we shall all be but wraiths on the wind, wailing with no one to listen."

"If Necrad's so important," said Alf, "why not build another city? Start again."

"We are too few now. Our numbers dwindle with each passing age. Understand, mortal, that the tally of the elves is fixed. We are not like you rutting beasts, able to spawn litters by the dozen. We are born of the stars. Eight thousand one hundred and fifty-nine elves awoke with the first dawn, and eight thousand one hundred and fifty-nine elves shall see the last sunset at world's end. Most of my kin have faded or perished, and walk as wraiths – or are chained to the life-trees of the Everwood. And even those who yet remain embodied are scattered and divided. We cannot remake Necrad if it is destroyed."

"I've seen elf kids, though. And Lae's young. How does that square with there only being eight thousand elves, all told?"

"A wraith can be reborn in a new body. Most remember only a little of our former lives, save in dreams, although we come to take on the likeness of our former selves. We do not know how this comes about, or if there is any design to it beyond mere chance. We copulate as you mortals do, but rarely does the seed quicken. For a time, our scholars and sorcerers bent their mind to this question, and sought ways to entice the wraiths to return to the living world. We tried everything we could imagine – potions, horoscopes, arranged matches, magical rites. Some were more enjoyable than others, but it was all to no avail. We cannot dictate when a spirit is reborn into a new body, only celebrate when it happens."

They approached through the Garrison gate. Guards watched her with wary eyes, and one of the dwarves ostentatiously readied his crossbow. "Of course, there is one way we know to promote rebirth. The more wraiths, the greater the chance that one will find its way back. That is how we must reckon generations among the firstborn – it is in the years after war and slaughter that we are blessed with children. Such bitter joy you brought us of late."

Alf shook his head. "It's the same story the world over. Not the particulars, but the shape of it. Don't matter if you're elf or mortal. People live, people die. The old talk about the good old days and the young are foolish, because memory tricks you and the young don't know how the world works. People go hungry in the villages, and the lords play at war."

"That's not a story," she replied, "stories are what you tell to endure all that."

They passed into the Liberties. Ildorae's presence stirred up the streets. Elves emerged from doorways and alleyways to greet her. Alf tried to follow the quick patter, but soon gave up trying to understand their conversation. He stepped away into the shadows and drew Spellbreaker.

"The hour approaches," said the sword, "when you must wield me in battle. Tell me, Lammergeier, do you think you are ready? I can sense your doubt. You need to let me help you."

"I'll be ready."

"They all look to you, hero. They think that you shall drive away the darkness with your bright sword." Spellbreaker chuckled to itself. "Your last great victory wounded you, I know. There is a crack in your soul, a weakness that has only grown with twenty years of neglect. This one will break you without my aid."

"Just guard me from her spells," muttered Alf. He looked over at Ildorae and the knot of a dozen or so elves. "What are they saying?"

"I listened to her prattle about the burdens of immortality. I laughed when she called you a mayfly. She was wrong – you are a grub, boring through leaf litter. A maggot in a corpse."

"Oh yes," said Alf, "I should definitely let you help me."

"I alone will be honest with you, Lammergeier. The elves are as deluded as the rest. Look there. They greet Ildorae, their long-lost sister. No doubt she has known each of them for centuries – there is not a single elf who has not spent many mortal lifetimes in the company of each one of their fellow immortals. They must share the world with her until the end. So, they forgive her anything, and she forgives them."

"Elves are elves." Laerlyn had said similar things about her damned brother, but when she said it, it sounded properly resentful. She said it like a child might – *I have to forgive him, he's my brother. You can't choose your family* – gritting her teeth and crossing her fingers all the while. It was understandable, when she said it. These elves unsettled Alf. They reminded him, sometimes, of the nobles of Summerswell. The same feeling that they knew things he never would, that their concerns and desires were nothing he could ever understand. He might be a hero of the Nine, and wield a magic sword, but he was still just a farmer's son from the Mulladales with mud on his shoes, lowly and ill-bred.

Monsters he could kill, but the monsters he understood. Hunger and anger, blood and iron, those he understood. Guilt and shame, he understood.

He sheathed the sword and waded into the group of elves. They parted before him, stepping aside gracefully. He grabbed Ildorae. "Let's get on with this."

They came to the house of Elithadil. The elves there knew Ildorae. Alf ran Ildorae's chain through a door handle to keep her from running, and left the elves talking while he climbed the creaking stairs to the boy's room. From inside, he heard the laughter of children playing. The elf-boy was sitting up in bed, much healthier than the last time Alf had seen him, and he was not alone. There were two playmates there, mortal children. One had the look of the Wilder, and Alf guessed it was one of the city-Wilder, those who had stayed even after the fall of the Witch Elves. The other was a Garrison child; her eyes were wide as saucers when she recognised the hero of the Nine.

Alf sat down on the bed. "I don't mean to interrupt, but I need to give you—"

"The blood," finished Ceremos, eagerly. "I dreamed of it."

The other two children stared, revulsed but also fascinated, as Alf unwound the bandage. He drew Spellbreaker and nicked himself on the sword's edge. The blade drank the little smear of blood he left on it as hungrily as the vampire child.

"Not too much," said Alf, "I need to be able to fight."

Reluctantly, the boy tore his lips away from Alf's wrist. Alf rebound the wound. He reached for another healing cordial, and found that he had none left. He flexed his hand, wincing at the pain. "I'll come back in a few days," he said, "once I'm done with this last job."

He stared at the mortal children for a moment before leaving, trying to judge their ages. Presumably, they were the same age as Ceremos, eight or nine. Too young to remember the war. Too young to remember the city before it was ruined. For them, Necrad was always like this, divided and broken, ruled by a distant council instead of a dark lord. For them, too, there was nothing strange about a child from Summerswell playing with a Wilder, or a Witch Elf. Slaying Lord Bone had counted for something, after all.

"Heart-warming," said the sword. "Do you think Death will discriminate between them? Do you think she will pluck out the Wilder boy, and banish the other lad, and smite the elf? Or will the same calamity take all of them to her kingdom?"

"Why do you have to be such an ... an ... " He was about to say "asshole", but it seemed ill-fitting when trying to insult a sword.

"I am a sword, Lammergeier. I was made to cut to the heart of all matters. A sword banishes illusions, does it not? I am an arbiter of truth." The blade sounded insufferably pleased with itself. "You know, I've been thinking. There's every chance that you've killed that boy twice now. Once with the dreadworm, obviously, but also, if he was reborn from one of the Elves of Necrad, then maybe you killed his previous incarnation during the war."

Alf reached down to silence the sword, but he stayed his hand. "You're trying to make me angry."

"You need to be angry. I can read your thoughts, Lammergeier.

You may crave peace with the Wilder, but it is too late for that. You need to be ready to strike when you meet Death again."

Ildorae waited for him downstairs. "There is another place I would see again before we leave."

Alf shrugged. "Fine."

She led him through the shattered streets of the city. The gate of the Liberties was only lightly guarded, for most of the sentries had been called away to prepare for the defence of the city, and those that remained did not hinder one of the Nine.

They passed into the forbidden zone of the Sanction, a cityscape of abandoned palaces and shattered temples. Alf navigated this broken labyrinth by reference to the Wailing Tower, its spire visible from anywhere in Necrad, but Ildorae had walked these streets for thousands of years, and needed no landmarks save memory.

They came to one structure. It was titanic, a cathedral of bone-white marble and green brass. It towered hundreds of feet above the street, and every inch of the façade was covered in intricate carvings so detailed one might think the creatures depicted had been frozen in stone. If this great palace could have been transplanted to Summerswell, or Ellsport, or any of the cities of mortals – even the Dwarfholt, or the capital of the Old Kingdom in its heyday – it would have been the undisputed jewel of the streets, a monument that would have drawn pilgrims and awe-struck onlookers for a thousand leagues around.

Here, in Necrad, it was unremarkable, but one wonder in a long row of wonders.

One of the mighty doors had fallen, and they stepped over its colossal wreck to enter the palace. Alf absently noted gouges left by scavengers cutting ward-stones from the brass.

The vaulted roof of the palace had been shattered by a dwarven siege engine twenty years prior, and a shaft of eerie light shone down from the necromiasma, giving the visitor the disconcerting impression of some drowned ruin, its recesses shrouded in gloom. Huge carvings on the walls depicted scenes from days of old; oil paintings, too, and tapestries, but twenty years or more of rain and neglect had ruined them all, and only the stone endured. Ildorae moved across the expanse of the marble floor, twirling as if remembering the steps of some dance. She came to a huge statue, three times her height, depicting an elf-woman playing a harp. She raised her hand and spoke a word of command, and a light bloomed in the darkness, bright and clear.

The statue was of Ildorae. The carved tableaus, of Ildorae.

"This was my home," she said, "for many years. Here I dwelt with my kinfolk in bliss, and here we debated the Oath and our place beneath the stars. Here I played – oh, the music we made!" She pointed at two thrones on a dais. One had toppled, and both had been violently stripped of their finery. "There was a time, mortal, when we were not cruel gods. Once, we were their benefactors. There were those among us, even then in those early years, who needed their blood, but we sought to make it more equitable. They would select who they sent to us, and we would welcome those chosen ones as lovers, exalt them as princes. They would live out years of bliss among us immortals, and we would teach them all manner of secrets and delights until our elders drank them dry."

She leapt up onto the dais and righted the fallen throne. She sat down on it, and invited Alf to sit by her side.

Alf did not move. "That's not how the Wilder tell it."

"The Wilder do not remember rightly. Eternity is long and the memories of mortals are short. We drove the barbarians who had usurped our city from its streets, and slaughtered many of them. Centuries later, we made peace with their descendants and grew to love them, and aided them as they built a great kingdom in the lands around Necrad. But, alas, when our hunger for blood grew too great, they turned on us with aid from our foes, and laid siege to Necrad." She shone the light up at one wall, illuminating another carving that showed Ildorae, clad in armour, battling a host of foes. The garb of these warriors was unfamiliar to Alf, but their faces reminded him of Thurn. "You mortals have your little lives. You start afresh with each generation, you see the injustice of the world, and rise to the challenge. Your heroes think they change the world. And then they perish, and another generation arises. They see the world made by their ancestors as unjust, too, and they rise to break it. On and on and on. Only the elves stand outside time, and see the pattern."

Spellbreaker quivered at Alf's side, the blade aroused by the talk of slaughter.

"So?" he said, as dismissively as he could. He felt like a brief candle, and tomorrow they were to ride into a hurricane.

"I wept as I slew them. Afterwards, I hardened my heart against mortals. I told myself that you are all doomed to die, and that it is folly to think of any of you as anything other than passing shadows. Only the elves endure – the elves, and this city."

"There are those," said Alf, "who'd say this place is past its time. You can't hang onto what's dead and gone."

"Only mortals think that things have a set time to live and die. Fates are made, not decreed." Scowling, Ildorae sprang up from the throne and descended the steps of the dais, heading towards a side tunnel.

"Where are you going?"

"To find my harp."

Alf followed her down the corridor. "Scavengers did this place already. I'd lay odds that your harp's in some lord's treasury down in Summerswell."

"Still, I shall have it back one day, even if I must sift through the dust of your cities a thousand years hence."

At the end of the corridor was the door to a treasure vault, long since smashed open. A stone plinth stood bare. Ildorae sighed.

Alf found himself looking at another carving. This one depicted Ildorae playing her harp, an expression of bliss on her face. Whatever elf had made the art, their talent honed with millennia of practice, had certainly captured Ildorae's features perfectly. Alf had seen many paintings and statues of himself and the rest of the Nine on his travels. He'd looked at the images that were supposed to be him, all shining knights in armour. None of the ones he'd seen had ever looked remotely like him, nor did he recognise the hero in the stories.

"Elf," he grunted. "Come here."

He drew Spellbreaker and sliced through the iron chains binding her hands. "Go on. Run."

She stared at him, as if looking for a trap.

"I won't send a dreadworm after you this time."

Ildorae shook her head. "I would go with you when you go to face Death. I may have failed in the quest the Oracle set me, but I would see it through to the end."

"I can understand that," said Alf. "But watch yourself. Gundan was talking about handing you over to the Wilder."

"I fear Death, and the breaking of the world. The dwarf is beneath my concern."

"Just don't make me regret breaking those chains."

They went back to Alf's mansion in the Garrison to sleep, but there were only a few hours left before dawn, and Alf found no rest there. His arm ached where the vampire child had fed, and he felt weak and old. In the hours before dawn, he had the strangest thought that he too had faded, as elves do, and he was just another wraith haunting the city. But Remilard brought in breakfast at dawn and chased away the thought.

In the morning, they rode north again.

CHAPTER THIRTY

Olva returned late from the shore. An elf-light still burned in the treehouse, but she found Torun asleep and snoring, her face buried in a huge pile of borrowed scrolls and books. Torun had told her that the scrolls were written by exiles from Necrad, the elves who had fled some ancient war many thousands of years ago, long before even the oldest kings of the Old Kingdom. Olva shuddered when she tried to contemplate such a span of time. Images of Necrad stared back at Olva from every page; sketches of towers and palaces, dreamlike vistas utterly unlike Highfield or Ellsport or any mortal city, maps of the streets and the tunnels below, twisting diagrams that suggested the artist had looked to the viscera of a disembowelled corpse for inspiration. Some of the drawings were indeed beautiful, but it was a terrifying beauty, cold and distant. A frozen tree in winter, maybe, all brocaded and bent with ice, or carved bone. Words in elven-script accompanied each image, the calligraphy flowing into the sketches, but Olva couldn't read a word of it.

There was another scroll trapped under Torun's cheek. Olva lifted her head from the desk, removed the paper and slid a pillow underneath, then let the dwarf's heavy skull back down gently. Torun muttered in her sleep, but did not wake. Back in Summerswell, books were fabulously expensive. Galwyn's old aunt had owned a library of some twenty volumes, kept locked away in an iron chest. Many of the elf-scrolls had been shamefully left to rot. The scroll she'd retrieved from under Torun's face was wet with drool. Olva wiped it off, and was surprised to see it was written in the tongue of Arshoth, which she could read a little.

She puzzled out a few words. It was an account of the defeat of Lord Bone, written by some mortal priest with the Knights of Arshoth. She vaguely wondered how the manuscript had ended up in the elven library. Reading it, she shivered at the priest's utter despair. *The Nine have left us, like thieves under the cloak of night. No one knows where they have gone, or if they have fled . . . the Intercessors have no power here, and we no longer remember sunlight . . . the dragonsfire consumed Sir Gervaud and all his retinue, burning them to death . . . we crept onto the battlefield and ate the scorched meat, for we have not eaten in days, and we care not if it is horseflesh or not.*

In the songs, there was never any doubt. The Nine rode forth into Necrad, and slew Lord Bone as was their destiny. Olva tried to imagine Alf as the fabled Lammergeier but couldn't. She could see the Lammergeier in her mind's eye as the songs described him, a mighty warrior clad in dwarven-steel, black sword in hand, face hidden by a greathelm, but could not imagine her brother's face beneath the steel.

This Charnel land holds doom for us all. We are here at the end of the world. All is lost.

The songs told of how the Nine had won against the odds, how Peir had fought Lord Bone while the Lammergeier and his black sword sundered Lord Bone's temple. But they were written after-wards, after that desperate, unlikely victory. Would it be fairer, she wondered, if you could reach back in time, to tell that despairing priest that victory was at hand? That all evil would be defeated by the heroes he doubted? That in less than twenty years' time, merchants and settlers would clamour to go to that same Charnel?

Or would it be better to take this scroll and show it to boys like

Derwyn, to warn them that the songs were only sung about the lucky few who survived, not the many who perished?

The scroll ended abruptly. *Dreadworms in the air.*

The branches creaked and the treehouse shook as it hurtled low over the tree. A huge winged creature, flying so low that Olva could smell the animal stink of it, the smell of sulphur and ash. Her heart leapt in alarm, and she had the strange thought that reading the scroll had summoned a worm out of Necrad. Beside her, Torun awoke and shrieked in alarm.

"Dragon!"

Olva ran to the balcony. The dragon was visible only as an absence of starlight, its massive wingspan blotting out the brilliant starry sky above the isle. It circled twice above Kairad Nal, then descended towards Maedos' castle.

"Dragon!" said Torun again, shivering. "What do we do?"

How was Olva supposed to know? There were no dragons in Summerswell any more – heroes like Alf had slain them all. Olva forced herself to breathe, to stay calm. There were no bursts of fire, no shouts of alarm, only an expectant silence. Already, the tranquillity of the elf-wood was reasserting itself, like ripples fading from the surface of a still pond. Even a dragon could not break the sanctity of the Isle of Dawn.

Olva's fear transformed in her stomach, like some alchemical transmutation. It sprouted wings and feathers, and became a shining bird, a thrill of wings beating in her ribcage. Excitement took hold of her.

"It's all right. We're in no danger," said Olva.

She plucked one of the little lights from the air and held it like a taper as she walked into the night.

"Where are you going?" Torun called after her. "There's a dragon!"

"I know. I want to *see* it!"

Torun hurried along after Olva muttering to herself, no doubt marvelling at Olva's foolishness. Dragons were unknown in

Summerswell, long since slain or driven away, but the Dwarfholt was plagued with greedy young wyrms, small and lithe enough to slither down mineshafts.

They burst through the last line of trees, and there on a greensward before the gates was the dragon. It was not young. Its scales were mottled white with age, like the shell of some sea-creature bleached by the sun, and for all its huge size it seemed almost fragile. Brittle little horns and spikes grew along its spine, and some of them had snapped off in the landing. It lay sprawled out, its flanks heaving. Its breath smoked in the night air, and its spittle seared the grass by its head. There was a saddle on its back, as big as a carriage.

As Olva approached, it strained to raise its head, and its eyes reminded her of the sea-serpent – there was hate there, and hunger, but it was buried deep, frozen beneath the magic that bound it. The creature tried to speak, but all that came out was a snarl.

An elf appeared out of the darkness. It was Telemor, the prince's friend. He carried a large basket, which he laid down on the ground by the dragon's head. Olva would have assumed that a monster like that would be satisfied only with red meat, but the basket was full of fruit which the dragon crunched and gulped eagerly, splattering juice and pulp with each bite. A sweet smell mixed with the stink of the dragon's breath, and Olva realised that the monster was feasting on the lotus-fruit that grew in the forest. As the dragon ate, the fire in its eyes faded, and its breathing became slower until it laid its head down and began to snore.

Greatly daring, Olva reached out and patted the monster's skull.

"You are summoned to the prince's tower," said Telemor after a moment.

"By the prince?"

"By his sister, the Princess Laerlyn."

At Maedos' castle, Telemor led Olva and Torun along an unfamiliar path, past a colonnade of pillars carved to resemble flowering trees with silver leaves. Amid the leaves was a polished mirror, and Olva saw her own face for the first time in weeks. She'd grown haggard, her hair touched with little streaks of grey. Her elf-garb accentuated the strangeness.

Telemor brought them to a south-facing garden where fountains played. At the heart of the garden was a stone basin of still water, and an elf-maiden sat by it.

"These are the mortal guests of the prince, your highness" said Telemor. "The survivors of shipwreck. This is Lady Forster of the Mulladales, and Torun of the Clan Dremach."

Olva suppressed a little gasp when she recognised the woman by the basin; even though she knew that the elves did not age, it was still a shock to see a figure step so cleanly out of memory. Olva had been barely fifteen when Alf and his companions took refuge in Ersfel. The thought of the elf-princess was one of Olva's most cherished memories, a moment of grace touching the dull and familiar. Now she was here surrounded by a surfeit of wonders.

The princess rose and greeted them formally. "I am told that my brother rescued you from captivity. I hope you have found rest and healing here on the isle." Laerlyn frowned. "Forgive me, Lady Forster — it has been some time since I visited the Lord's court, but your face is familiar to me. Are you kin to the baron of Highfield, or — oh!" She clasped her hands over her mouth in surprise. "Oh, by the stars! I know you! You're Aelfric's sister!"

"I am. It's lovely to see you again, your highness, even in such strange circumstances."

Laerlyn gestured for Olva to sit. "Tell me your tale. How did you come to be here? Did Aelfric send for you?"

"I — I came looking for my son, Derwyn. Alf doesn't know I'm here. He was taken captive by a blood trader called Martens. Your brother rescued us from Martens' men, and has been helping us find my boy."

"I saw Aelfric but a fortnight ago. He returned to Necrad

with the quiet grace and delicate reserve I would expect from our Aelfric."

"Is he well?"

The princess laughed. "When I spoke to him, he'd recently been stabbed. And started a riot while drunk. As well as ever, I suppose." Laerlyn suddenly grew serious. "I jest, when I should be serious. Your brother is a dear friend, and I love him wholeheartedly. I admire his certainty of purpose."

"His pig-headedness, you mean."

"That's part of it, true. You mortals can dedicate your lives to a cause, and hold true to that oath no matter what, until death releases you. That perseverance does not come naturally to my kind – we are more apt to falter, and to wait out problems instead of confronting them. Aelfric perseveres to a fault, I think. I worry about him. If I could, I would send you to care for him. The bonds of family do not necessarily run deeper than friendship, but they have a potency all their own."

"I don't know about that," said Olva, "Alf never came back home to us, after the war."

"For Aelfric, the war is not over. He did not speak of you – I assume he does not know of your plight?"

"No, milady."

"And has Maedos sent word to Aelfric of your arrival?"

"He couldn't, my lady. Not with the strife between Necrad and the isle, he said."

Laerlyn splashed her hand in the basin, breaking the mirror still-ness of its waters. "I shall fly to Necrad as soon as I can. You should ride with me. It would be better for you, I think."

"My dear sister!" Prince Maedos came striding down the corri-dor, dressed in hunting green. There was mud on his boots, and his clothing was smeared with sap and leaves. He wiped his knife clean with a silk cloth. "You put an end to my amusements."

Laerlyn spoke angrily in Elvish, and Maedos responded in the same tongue. Olva could sense hostility in the air, and that singular awkwardness that comes when two members of a family quarrel in front of strangers. These elves could be as inscrutable as the stars sometimes, and then the next moment they seemed completely familiar.

Maedos turned to Olva. "Forgive us, but my sister and I have much to discuss. She has flown the length of the mortal lands to bring tidings from our dear father in the Everwood. The Erlking has commanded an end to the dispute between Summerswell and Elvendom. The seas shall be opened again, and you shall sail to Necrad as soon as—"

Laerlyn interrupted him harshly. Maedos corrected himself, and almost managed to conceal his irritation. "As speed is of the essence, you shall fly with my sister on dragon-back, though the journey will be far less pleasant. You should go and pack."

Olva glanced down at her borrowed elven clothing. "Done."

"Ah, but Torun will wish to carry away half my library. This, Lady Forster, is farewell, but only for a little while! Not all partings with mortals are for ever."

"You've been too kind to me, sire."

"Not at all. For the kin of the Lammergeier, no effort is too great."

One of the prince's courtiers collected Torun and Olva from the bower and escorted them to the feasting hall, where the elves of the isle had once more gathered for merriment. The courtier handed Olva a crystal goblet brimming with ruby-red wine, then slipped away to join the dance. The music was, as before, so beautiful as to pierce the soul, and the grace of the immortal dancers was sublime. Every step practised for centuries, every motion perfected. Enchanted lights circled overhead, whirling in response to the swell of the music. Still, something of the enchantment had been worn away; Olva could not help but see the waste and excess. The elves ate little, despite the trenchers of food they had prepared. They danced wildly, as if trying to fill the cavernous space. They sang and spoke and laughed, but they were the same songs and jests that Olva had heard on the other nights of the revels.

Above, on the balcony, she could see the faces of Maedos and Laerlyn, looking down on their subjects like the great lords they were. Their features were keenly alike, but it was plain that they were still in the midst of argument. A passing elf pressed another goblet of wine into Olva's hand. She sipped from it as she looked for Torun. The raucous elves, whirling in their dance, made it hard to move through or spot people in the crowd, and Torun's small stature made it harder. Olva circled the room, searching for the dwarf, and eventually found her in a quiet corner, staring up at the ceiling as if entranced.

"We're leaving for Necrad. Princess Laerlyn's going to fly us on her dragon."

"Dragon!?" squeaked Torun in alarm. Then she muttered "Necrad" under her breath, steeling herself. "Necrad, Necrad, Necrad." She sprang up as if launched from a catapult.

Olva followed the dwarf back to the treehouse, but she had little to do there except watch Torun busy herself trying to cram all her borrowed scrolls into a satchel. She told Torun she would soon return, then went walking. She descended towards the shore through the tangle of shadows beneath the forest eaves. The path was clear of obstacles; in the Fossewood and even on the Road, walking in the dark was hazardous, but wandering the elf-isle was like strolling through some well-tended garden. She picked up speed as she hurried down the slope, and sooner than she expected she came to the top of the goat-path that wound down to the shore.

To her surprise, the beach below was empty. No fires burned where the survivors had made their camp, not even embers. Olva climbed down to the beach and walked amid the stones. She guessed that the elven-ship had come sooner than anticipated, and that there was nothing untoward in the sudden desolation of the shore.

Still, she was glad when the pale shape of the dragon descended to carry her away.

Each beat of Asjakain's mighty wings swallowed up the world, covering as much distance as Olva had walked that first night out of Ersfel. She remembered how exhausted she'd been, how her feet had bled as she'd marched all night – and now the dragon bore her over the sea, faster than the wind. Torun's strong little hands dug into Olva's side as the dwarf clung to her in suppressed terror, even though Laerlyn had carefully strapped them into the cunning saddle. Neither heights nor dragons were to the dwarf's liking, and Olva's attempt to distract Torun by pointing out the beauty of the northern stars was ignored. Princess Laerlyn was occupied in guiding the dragon. The creature had no reins or harness, but was bound by magic, and sometimes Laerlyn would lean forward and whisper to the beast, raising her hand as Maedos had done in a gesture of command. The authority of the stars, Torun had called it.

Moonlight transformed the cold sea to silver. Far below, the wakes of the elven war-serpents drew sigils on the waves, wide curves as they circled or flowing V-shapes as they swam forward. Beyond, the cliffs of the northland were dimly visible, a darker line on the horizon – and Necrad lay straight ahead, marked by the green glow. The place had so dominated her thoughts for weeks that she almost felt she could sense it with her eyes closed.

Daybreak, and Olva gasped at the beauty of a sunrise seen from the air. The world from dragon-back was like a beautiful carving, a work of art that could only be appreciated from far above. This must be how the Intercessors saw the world from their heavenly sanctums. From a sufficient distance, there was no suffering or corruption, only beauty. How far, she wondered, was enough? The towers of the fortress in Ellsport had seemed very tall to her, but they were small compared to Maedos' castle, and even that castle was a mere speck dwindling behind them. Perhaps you had to go so far that you no longer saw individual people – just as a flower was prettiest from a distance. Look too close, and you saw the thorns, the insects crawling on it, the holes in the petals where grubs had fed. Withdraw, soar, don't look, and the world becomes a pleasure garden.

But it's hard to breathe up here, she thought, as darkness ringed the edges of her vision. The thought followed her into a dream, and she half-slept, lulled by the regular thunder of the dragon's wingbeats.

She awoke with a start, and for a terrifying moment could not make sense of her surroundings – they were flying through a bank of grey clouds, chill and misty, and all she could think was that she'd fallen into the grey land of the dead. Torun squeezed her from behind, and she remembered that she was flying.

They broke through the clouds, and they were above the coast. Waves crashed on black cliffs far below. They were flying lower now, over a landscape of churned-up mud and stagnant pools, pock-marked with craters, scabbed with ruins. The Charnel, they called it in the stories. The sun was almost directly overhead, a pallid noon, and yet the land below remained miserable and resentful. Olva was glad she was flying over it, and not trudging through it.

Laerlyn glanced back and saw Olva was awake. The princess brushed her golden hair from her face, then leaned back. "Tell me," said Laerlyn, "did my brother talk much about Aelfric to you?"

"Only that they quarrelled during the war – and that all is forgiven and forgotten. I'm not sure if he meant it."

"Nothing else?"

"No."

"For a long time, Maedos held the great and terrible forces of Necrad in check, so he sees all things in terms of how they can be used on the battlefield. And Aelfric bears the demon sword, so he must be counted among the great and terrible, whether he admits it or not. We trusted Aelfric to bear that sword for many reasons – his stout heart, his courage, his loyalty, his lack of greed or ambition – but also, because he was free of obligations. He has sworn no oaths. He follows his own stars. He came from nowhere, with no family name or great bloodline. He owed nothing to any lord. But you – you and your son – you complicate this. You are breaches in Aelfric's armour, and a foe might use you to strike at him."

Laerlyn looked over her shoulder, not meeting Olva's eye.

"I think it wise to remove you from the board, lest anyone be tempted to play you."

They flew on, mile after mile of wasteland. The dragon growled and groaned with exhaustion, and once it bucked, its serpentine neck twisting around so it could look at them, the bleariness of magic and lotus-fruit leaving its blazing eyes.

"On, Asjakain," cried Laerlyn. "By the stars I bind you, and ask for one last effort."

They were approaching the city now.

Olva raised her head and for the first time in her life she looked upon Necrad.

The swirling miasma did not obscure it – the ghastly light it shed emphasised the city, drawing the eye with an awful fascination. It was objectively horrible, that city, that abomination born of inhuman architecture, but she could not look away. It was not as she had pictured it in her nightmares. She'd imagined it would be malignant, a city of monsters and depravity, but as she beheld it now, from dragon-back, she saw that it was something else – it was uncaring, ancient and alien, a marble desert where nothing could thrive. Surely nothing mortal could survive there.

Torun made excited noises behind her, and the dwarf leaned out at a precarious angle from the dragon's saddle, eager to get a better view of the city as they circled down towards it. "Look at the streets," she shouted, "they are sigils drawn in stone!" She pointed so enthusiastically that Olva had to haul her back lest Torun go tumbling down.

Hideous bat-things came flapping out of the green clouds, a huge number of them flocking towards the dragon. They congealed out of the darkness, the fetid clouds condensing into winged forms. Laerlyn glanced at the creatures, but did not seem overly concerned. Indeed, the monsters appeared confused – they chased after the dragon, then broke off, then pursued again, or flapped in wide, agitated circles without obvious purpose.

Dreadworms, thought Olva, *like in the stories.*

A sudden, incongruous memory flashed through her mind – years before, she'd brought Derwyn to the Highfield fair. He'd been six or so. There had been a puppet show at the fair, little cloth and plaster dolls dancing and fighting, enacting tales old and new. The Erlking's Gift, the Bear and the Bee – and the Nine, battling monsters. She'd watched the Lammergeier – depicted as a hulking armour-clad mountain of a knight – chop the heads off dreadworms made of black rags and sticks. The puppet-sword was very solid, and she remembered one of the worms' heads breaking when the Lammergeier whacked it. The severed head of the worm fell out of the puppet theatre and rolled into the crowd, to the shrieking delight of the children. Derwyn was always quick and strong – she remembered him diving into the fray and emerging with the prize held high, laughing with joy – then staring in confusion at his mother's tears. She'd told him that the crowds had been too much for her, and that they were too far from home.

In truth, she'd seen that the puppet's sword was painted black, and it had scared her. Nightmares had haunted her then, and those nightmares were born here, in the dread city.

Below were the docks of Necrad. They were even more crowded than Ellsport had been, with many ships tied up by the bone-white piers. The wharves themselves were utterly deserted, but beyond a line of burning braziers Olva could see a great crowd of people, hundreds strong or more. Many carrying bundles or boxes, or clutching children. Dwarven guards stood along the dockside, blocking access to the ships.

As the dim shadow of the dragon crossed the open dock, the crowd scattered, taking refuge in the archways and alleyways that led off into the city. Some cried out in alarm, shouting 'Wilder' and 'Changeling'. The dragon landed heavily on the deserted wharf, sending a shock through Olva's spine. She unbuckled the straps that held her in the saddle and slid down the dragon's foreleg to set foot at last in the dread city.

"What's happening?" asked Torun, staring at the crowd.

Even Laerlyn was confused. "I do not know. Wait here." She dismounted and strode across the square to where a trio of armoured dwarves stood, their crossbows aimed at the dragon. The elf-princess spoke to the dwarves a moment, while Olva helped Torun climb down from Asjakain. The dragon's massive head twisted around and sniffed at the dwarf, and droplets of hot drool sizzled on the cold stone.

"It's like the war," said Torun quietly. "After the fall of Karak's Bridge. The underways were so crowded with those fleeing Bone's armies that some were crushed to death."

Laerlyn returned, her face grave. "I must go. The dwarves speak of a host of Wilder. There are other strange tidings, too. Events have moved faster than I feared. I need to speak to the council." The elf pointed at the dwarven guards. "They will see you to safety. The streets are in uproar." She sprang onto the dragon's back. "Aelfric has a mansion in the Garrison," shouted Laerlyn, "the guards will take you there!"

The dragon lumbered forward, clambering onto a pile of rubble, and from there onto the roof of a warehouse that groaned under its weight. From there, it ran forward, spreading its wings, and then took off into the skies.

Olva shivered. Getting to Necrad had seemed like the end of her journey, as if Derwyn would be waiting for her by the city gates.

Now, she felt like she was at the start of a labyrinth. All of Ersfel could have fitted on this single dockside; all of Ellsport combined was less than a third of the Garrison, and the Garrison was only a small portion of the city. Olva's heart sank as the dragon vanished from view. By contrast, Torun seemed filled with energy now that they were back on solid ground. She muttered to herself, then bent down and scratched a sigil into the dirt, recalling the shape of the streets they'd seen from the air.

"Welcome to Necrad," muttered Torun. "What now?"

CHAPTER THIRTY-ONE

To the sentries on the northern wall of the city, it was as though the days of high adventure had sprung to life once more. From the Sanction gate rode forth three of the Nine, in full panoply of arms, and with them rode the flower of the League's cavalry. At the head of the column was Sir Aelfric Lammergeier, his armour glimmering in the wan sunlight that penetrated the edge of the necromiasma. By his side was the demon sword, and he carried the banner of the League.

(Alf winced when the wind caught the billowing banner, tugging the pole against his sore hand. He handed the bloody thing off to Remilard as soon they were clear of the walls, and the boy's face lit up with the honour of bearing the standard of the League.)

By his side rode Lord Gundan, champion of the Dwarfholt, new-minted commander of Necrad in this time of war. Chopper was strapped to his back, and on his right hand he bore a signet ring gifted to him by Lord Vond, in token of the dwarf's new office. He carried a banner, too, a white flag of truce tightly furled at his side.

(Gundan's cousin had hastily reforged Chopper. Gundan's eyes were still bloodshot, and he cursed loudly whenever anyone came too close to his right side, though he swore he could see clearly.)

The third of the Nine was the Wizard Blaise, master of the

Wailing Tower. Instead of a horse, he rode a thing of shadow and gloom, a nightmare bound by his magic. The other animals shied away from the wizard's steed, but it was swifter and hardier than any living thing.

("I shall not go with you all the way," the wizard had told them, "I have work to do outside the city, before the siege begins."

"Come with us," Alf had said, "you can talk to Thurn and Lath, help us convince them."

"I meet Death on my own terms," replied Blaise, "not hers.")

With them rode a handful of the city's guards, their lances garlanded with pennants and their shields brightly painted as if riding out on parade. Most were human, with a few dwarves from Gundan's household.

In the heart of the column were four horses carrying iron-bound caskets instead of riders – like the troops, these caskets were the finest the city could muster. They contained a fortune in charmstones and magic weapons, for Vond had opened the Garrison vaults. These caskets were bound for Duna's castle, to bolster his defences against the Wilder. Duna's son Dunweld rode alongside the caskets, so nervous he'd lost his breakfast as the company prepared to depart. Alf felt distant pity for the lad.

Ildorae was the only elf in the company, and she was hooded and cloaked, and would pass for one of the League outriders. Alf would have strongly preferred to have a few Wood Elf archers in the group; better yet, to have Laerlyn with them. Gundan rolled his eyes when he saw that Ildorae was no longer chained, but said nothing.

The caskets weighed on Alf's mind, too. His mind kept returning to the image of Thurn throwing that Necrad-forged arrowhead into the fire. There were more such arrows in the casket, each one forged in Lord Bone's city, each one enchanted to be lethal. There were other magic weapons, too, potent and vile. He'd seen them load spell-skulls and demon plates into those boxes.

He told himself that was how it had to be. That this was the way of the world. Carrot and stick, Gundan had said. The gauntlet and the velvet glove. He knew it worked – how many times, back in the war, had he glowered over Peir's shoulder, underlying honeyed words with the threat of force?

But Alf could not shake the idea of taking those caskets, those treasured fruits of Necrad, and dumping them in the deepest hole in the Charnel, never to be seen again.

The outermost of the Stone Dragons loomed above them, a ghastly sentinel facing north. Soot that still caked its maw was mottled with frost.

"I shall leave you here," announced Blaise. His nightmare turned its head towards the slumbering weapon.

"There's a raven," said Ildorae, pointing at the grey sky. "It's far south of the forest."

Alf squinted. There was a tiny black dot circling the Stone Dragon, but his eyes were not elf-keen, and he couldn't tell what it was.

"I see it," lied Gundan. The dwarf still couldn't see more than a few feet ahead of him. "What do you think? Lath?"

"Aye, I think so."

"I fear to approach the Changeling on open ground," said Blaise, "even if he exhausted his power with the ritual." But the wizard rode with them as Alf spurred his horse and broke from the column. Alf signalled to Remilard to continue on the Road; Ildorae moved to follow, but he waved her back. It was only three of the Nine – Alf, Gundan and Blaise – who rode out to meet the fourth.

The raven circled down to meet them, transforming into Lath's human form as he landed.

"Lath!" called Alf. "I told 'em like you said! They know the Wilder are coming south. Vond sent us to talk terms."

"Thurn told you what's going to happen, Alf," said Lath. "What more is there to say?"

"Thurn can say it to my bloody face," shouted Gundan. "You

both owe us that much! If it weren't for us, Thurn's folk would still be blood-thralls to the Witch Elves. And you? You'd have been burned at the stake at Albury Cross. You owe me, lad. Tell Thurn we want to talk."

Lath's face rippled, the years falling away from it, and for a moment he became the child Alf had guarded against the mob so long ago. Alf wondered if the Changeling had altered his features deliberately, or if Lath was now so disjointed that the shape had been imposed on him by Gundan's words. "I'll pass the word. He'll meet you on the shore of Bavduin."

"Lath, called Changeling, fatherless and rootless, hear me!" called Blaise. Alf rolled his eyes at the wizard's compulsion to turn everything into an incantation. "The ruinous spell you cast, the horror you gave flesh – will you undo it? Or must I break it?"

Lath scowled, and then he was gone, erupting into a black shape of feathers and claws that flapped into the sky.

The wizard remained at the Stone Dragon. Alf looked back, and saw Blaise chanting spell after spell, trying to reawaken the ancient weapon.

"We built those," whispered Ildorae, "to defend Necrad against the forefathers of the Wilder. Lord Bone took them from us and augmented them. It was an obsession of his. He feared attack from outside the city." She smiled. "I always knew it would be a foe from within the walls that brought him down. I failed; you did not. Now, the city is threatened from outside once more. Live long enough, mortal, and irony poisons everything."

They rode on, leaving the Charnel. The company huddled closer, each rider eager to stay clear of the trees that encroached on the road. There might be Wilder hiding in the shadow of those snow-laden branches. They passed a trickle of people fleeing the New Provinces, carrying their belongings on their backs, or driving oxen before them laden with sacks and other baggage. It was folly, thought

Alf – there was little water in the Charnel, and those beasts would never make it to the safety of Necrad. The people cheered at the sight of the column of soldiers, and at Alf's banner. There were fewer than Alf had expected, though, which meant most of the settlers had stayed in their villages and homesteads, or had answered Earl Duna's call to muster. Lord Vond had been right – all they had needed was a symbol to rally around, to give them faith that aid would come to the New Provinces if danger threatened.

At the crossroads, they were met by Earl Duna, at the head of a host of his own men. He embraced Alf and his son Dunweld.

"How's the other boy?" asked Alf.

"Intercessors be praised, Idmaer will live! It is a miracle indeed – and the only good omen in a month of bad ones." Duna lowered his voice. "My scouts report an army of many Wilder not far from here, my lords. These weapons you have brought us, we will put to good use, and it will be an honour to fight alongside the Nine once again, if it comes to war." He ordered that one casket be opened and some of its weapons be distributed among the knights he had brought with him; the rest of the host would return to Castle Duna with the other weapons, and prepare for a siege. Young Dunweld went with them, and the boy seemed relieved to be done with his first experience of the high council.

"If it comes to war, Duna," said Gundan, "then get yourself back to your castle quick as you can. Help'll come from the Dwarfholt, but it's a long way across the Clawlands."

"Thurn will listen," said Alf.

"Well, the Intercessors have already sent one miracle to these parts. Why not another?" Gundan raised his voice and called out to the earl. "Did you find 'em, Dunny?"

The earl gestured, and some of his men came forward, dragging a pair of manacled prisoners. Young lads from the New Provinces, ragged and scared. One had an ugly purple welt on the side of his face; the other shivered and looked around in confusion, plainly insensible of where he was.

"Who're they?" asked Alf.

"Before we left, I told Duna to find the men who wounded Thurn's child. This is them," said Gundan.

"Truly?" Alf's stomach sank at the sight of the two wretches.

"You're the one who wants to bargain," said the dwarf. "We need to offer Thurn something."

In the war, Alf had seen what the Wilder did to those they condemned. Bodies hung from trees like rotten fruit along the road from Ellsport, disembowelled so seers could read the shifting currents of earthpower in the entrails.

On again, north again, into the maw of winter. Dusk closed in. The mountains were claws tearing at the wan sun, and fog slunk down from the heights to stalk them. Bavduin was the place that Lath had chosen; a low-lying lake in the midst of the forest. The road ran along a high ridge above the marshy ground by the lakeside, and further on beyond the fog was an ancient stone bridge. Last time he'd been here, if Alf had given the matter any thought at all he'd have guessed that the Witch Elves built it. Now he saw it must have been the ancestors of the Wilder that Ildorae spoke of; the land was alive with ghosts all of a sudden, shades of vanished realms crowding in on him. He glanced back at the hooded figure who had lived through it all. Ildorae was at the back of the crowd now, close to the two prisoners, surrounded by Duna's men.

A lone campfire burned by the lakeside, as one had on the mound near Daeroch Nal, but nearby Alf saw the shadowy forms of Wilder warriors. The forest beyond could conceal a numberless host. If it came to a battle, they would be utterly outnumbered.

"We can't bring horses into that mire," said Duna.

"Aye. We keep most of the company here," said Gundan. "A few of us'll go down and talk. If things go awry, ride like hell."

Alf dismounted and let Remilard take his horse away to be watered by the bridge. Men climbed down and rubbed their aching limbs, wolfed down food, readied weapons. More magic was distributed from the caskets – charmstones to make blades sharper, nerves faster. Helms of night-sight, shields against earth-magic, rings of power. Many of the relics glowed with an eerie light, green like the necromiasma. A string of witch-lights flared in the gloom. No doubt the elven hunters of old who terrorised the Wilder looked similar in the night.

Despite this magic, though, no one dared leave the road. Battle was in the air, and there were ravens in the trees other than Lath. Alf waited, feeling detached from those around him. He stared down the muddy slope towards the shore of Bavduin. There were figures there, moving in the mists, and he guessed Thurn was among them.

In the end, a dozen went down to the parley. Alf and Gundan, Duna and a handful of his men. The two prisoners, and their gaolers. Two of Vond's soldiers, and two cousins of Gundan's. And in the back, Ildorae, like a shadow. They slipped and clambered down the stony side of the road, then slogged through the sucking mud to the lakeside.

"Beware the dead!" hissed one of Vond's guards, pointing at a stand of willows by the lakeside. Alf brushed his hand against the sword's hilt, and saw that there were indeed undead warriors watching them. They were fresh-killed Wilder, no more than a few days dead, although some had been hideously hacked apart before their resurrection. A cold blue light gleamed in their dead eyes, and they seemed curiously aware for undead. They were not the mindless shambling monsters of the Charnel, but something else.

"Death of old could bring back her mortal allies," whispered Ildorae. "If this one has mastered that trick, then—"

"They're just watching us," said Alf, "pay 'em no heed."

She peered into the mist, and saw something he could not. "The

Old Man of the Woods is here. After Amerith led our people across the sea and we retook Necrad, the first Old Man appeared. The Wilder believe he was sent by the Wood to guide them. I hunted him for years, and never got as close as I stand now – and I am weaponless." She clenched her fists, and the mist all around her turned to crystals of ice and fell glittering to the ground. "If you intend to use the sword this day," she whispered, "then choose your moment well. You will not get a second chance."

"We're here to talk, not fight."

Alf splashed on through the mud, towards the campfire. As they drew close, Thurn stepped out of the shadows on the far side. He held up his spear in salute before driving it into the ground on one side of the fire. He then ostentatiously stepped past the spear, taking a pace forward.

"Don't," whispered Gundan, but Alf did as Thurn – he drew his sword, planted it in the mud and then walked past it. Gundan followed, but he kept hold of Chopper, tapping the axe against Spellbreaker as he passed. A sign to Alf to be ready.

Duna and the other guards halted outside the circle and raised the banner of truce. The white flag was red-stained in the firelight. On the far side of the flames, Alf saw faces painted with runes on cheeks or brows. There were many different clan-runes on display; Alf counted a half-dozen he recognised, and more he did not know. Dead faces as well as living, leering skulls or bloated dead flesh, stared back out of the dark.

Out of the crowd came three more Wilder. One was an old, old man, his face so gaunt that he looked less alive than the risen dead he passed. Alf guessed that this was the Old Man of the Woods that Ildorae had mentioned; a Wilder seer or high priest. He was accompanied by a pair of youths, a boy and a girl, so alike they must be twins. They bore no clan-runes, only the symbols for sky and earth. As they carried him to the circle, the Old Man called out to the assembled clans, speaking words Alf did not know, but whose meaning he could guess. He'd heard enough war cries in his time. The Wilder answered with loud shouts from living throats, dry echoes from dead ones.

These Wilder, too, stopped short of Thurn's spear. Only Thurn would speak.

"Thurn," said Gundan. "It's been a while. You're looking tall."

Thurn did not respond, but instead lowered himself with great solemnity to sit by the fireside.

"Where's Lath?" asked Gundan. "I would have words with the lad. Like, what the fuck he was thinking."

"Did only you two of the Nine come?" said Thurn. "Are you, Gundan, the most honey-tongued among those that remain?"

"Like pleasantries would get through that thick skull of yours." Gundan waved his axe. "Even this would have trouble cracking that noggin."

"Enough, Gundan," said Alf. "Thurn, I brought your message to Necrad. I told 'em what I saw at Daeroch Nal."

A small shape slipped through the crowd of Wilder and ran into the circle. It was Talis. She climbed into Thurn's lap and stared at the dwarf. Her demeanour was very different from how she had seemed at Daeroch Nal; she was a child again, shyly half hiding behind her father's elbow as she studied the strangers.

"So, you're the demon that Lath called up, eh?" Gundan forced a laugh.

"I am Talis," she said.

"We want to talk," said Alf.

Thurn shook his head. "You and I can talk, Alf. Gundan, too. If you come to my camp as my old friends, you will sit in a place of honour and want for nothing, I promise. But I do not think I am speaking to Alf and Gundan. I think I am speaking to General Gundan Gwalir of the Dwarfholt. I think I am speaking to Sir Lammergeier, who has Vond's words in his mouth, and not his own.

To those great lords, I have only this to say – yield over the city and go back south, or you will die."

Gundan groaned. "Az's arse, be reasonable! Do you want war?"

"No. But I will finish what was begun long ago." Thurn stroked Talis's thin hair. "It is fate that this power has come to us now, when there is no strength in Necrad to resist."

"All things have their time," piped up Talis. Her gaze passed over Alf, and he shivered. The child frowned at something or someone behind him, and for a moment that same cold light of Death came into her eyes.

"That's rich," snapped Gundan, "coming from you. Alf said you'd be worm-meat if it weren't for Lath's spell! When was your time? Ten thousand years ago?"

"Gundan, enough!" said Alf, grabbing the dwarf's shoulder. "The child was dying. You can't fault Thurn for saving her life."

"And how many are going to die when they attack Necrad? On both bloody sides?" snarled the dwarf. He tore himself free of Alf's hand, and stepped forward to look Thurn in the eye. "If you don't want a war, Thurn, you're going about it in a bloody stupid way. You came to us, once, and told us your people were suffering under the Witch Elves. We freed 'em. Are you going to repay us by going to war with the League?"

"Leave Necrad. Leave the north. If you do not ... " Thurn put down his daughter and stood to tower over the dwarf. "Then we will do as I have promised."

"That's not going to happen, Thurn, and you know it. You don't want to admit it, but you owe us. So, let's figure out a fair price for what we did for the Wilder. The New Provinces, things were fine for the first few years, eh? That can all be fixed. And the dwarf mines – you Wilder don't know the first thing about proper metalwork, nor masonry neither. Let us keep the mines we've dug, and oh, we'll be fast friends." Gundan raised his voice, addressing the assembled Wilder behind Thurn. "You've a choice! You say there's no strength in Necrad to resist, but think on this: you'll be facing Summerswell, and the Dwarfholt, and all the *shit* we've dug out of Necrad. And you'll be on your own. It'll be bad, Thurn. You know it will."

"We have Death!" cried one of them. The jaws of the dead men in the crowd opened and shut, as if cheering in agreement, but there was no sound. The Old Man hooted.

"Aye, you've got this little girl as your champion. Maybe that'll be enough to balance the scales. But maybe not. Maybe she's not all that the stories say. Now, on the other hand, you could have peace. You could go back home and fuck your wives and enjoy the bloody fruits of peace, eh? The dark lord's been toppled and it's all sunshine and roses from here on out, right? You'd have to share the north, all right – but lads, if there's one thing I know about this fucking land, it's that it's really big. Space enough for all – and if anyone needs more territory, they can take it from the ogres, aye?"

"There can be peace, Thurn," agreed Alf. "Please, listen."

Thurn said nothing, but some of the Wilder looked at one another, suddenly uncertain. The Old Man of the Woods grunted angrily and slapped his withered leg, and the same scowl appeared on the faces of his twin attendants. A raven croaked overhead, then flapped down and perched on Thurn's spear. "Necrad," it cried. Lath's voice. "Necrad must be destroyed. I told you, Alf."

"You did, Lath. And I know there's evil there. You and I both know that. But it's not that bloody simple. Everything's bound up in that city. You can't just wipe it all away."

"I can," said Talis softly.

"Evil dwells there," added the raven.

"Aye, but ... " Alf wanted to reach out to the sword; the demon was cleverer than he was, and it might give him the words he needed. He wished Laerlyn was here, or Jan, or someone who could have made Lath see the folly of this course. Alone, he fumbled for the words. "There are ... common folk, who came after the war. Your own kin, who stayed. The Vatlings. Even the Witch Elves ... " He looked out into the darkness, hoping to see Ildorae there. "They're not what you think they are, not wholly. It's all more tangled than I thought. We need time to work it all out."

"Sophistry," said Thurn. "We are men of the sword. We should speak plainly."

Alf found the words he sought. "You want plain talk? All right. Peir would have told you this was wrong. He'd never have threatened his allies."

"Peir," said Talis, "is in my kingdom."

Thurn put his hand on his daughter's shoulder. "Peir is dead. His day is done. The alliances he forged hold no longer."

Gundan rubbed his eye, and his finger came away bloody. He paced up and down beside the fire. "You want to avenge your daughter? Very well. Duna caught the two miscreants who hurt her, and you can have 'em. You—"

Talis held up her hand. "Where are they?"

"Duna has 'em." The dwarf pointed out into the darkness.

"Show me." The child spoke with utter authority, and no one dared defy her. Duna's men pushed the two manacled prisoners forward, and they stumbled into the circle of firelight, coming to a halt just short of Spellbreaker. Talis left her father's side and circled around the fire. Everyone watched her, her bare feet squelching in the mud, the firelight dancing upon her fey features. There was a terrifying strength in her; even though she stood next to three of the heroes of the Nine, the two greatest mortal warriors of their generation and the general of the Dwarfholt, still all the onlookers could tell that she was mightier than all of them.

Death stopped, and looked at the two prisoners who knelt before her. One of them mumbled a prayer. The other said nothing, only stared at the girl in terror.

"These I claim," said Talis, "as part weregild for myself."

She took the two men by the hand, and bade them stand and follow her. What happened then, Alf could not understand, but it was as though the two walked away in a direction that could not be named or known by the living, while the girl simultaneously remained still and moved with them, an uncanny doubling that hurt Alf's brain to see. Alf watched the two prisoners recede, not walking towards the shore of Bavduin nor back towards the road, but going *away*, stumbling down a grey slope beyond the world, until they vanished from sight. They had passed bodily into Death's kingdom, and a wind blew from that place into the mortal world, and it chilled all those assembled by the lakeshore.

Talis looked up at Thurn and squeezed his arm reassuringly. The Wilder's face was as grey as the land beyond. Behind him, the Old Man of the Woods giggled in delight and clapped his hands. He nudged one of his attendants and gestured at Talis like a proud uncle.

"Bloody hell," whispered Gundan. "It's true . . ."

"You see now what awaits you," said Thurn.

Gundan took a step back and shook his head. He looked up at Thurn, his face full of defiance. He slapped Chopper's reforged haft against his palm. "Alf," he called, "draw the sword. Show them the blade that killed Lord Bone."

Alf laid his hand on the pommel of Spellbreaker, but did not pull the sword from the earth. Thurn grabbed his own spear – he had lost none of his quickness, none of that explosive transition from stillness to speed – and aimed the point at Gundan's throat. The Old Man of the Woods grunted in alarm.

"Thurn. Don't." Alf tensed, ready to strike.

His fighting instincts took over, muscles and nerves recognising the familiar patterns, the steps of the dance. He'd strike at the monster, a quick cut while she was still within arm's reach to disrupt any spell she might cast, then a more powerful blow, a killing blow. Death or not, the body was just that of a child. The image of the dreadworm feasting on Ceremos flashed across Alf's mind, and he hesitated, just for an instant.

And in that instant, Thurn hesitated, too.

The point of the spear wavered, then fell. Thurn, too, stepped back. He looked over at the Old Man of the Woods for an instant, then said:

"Peir died to free my people. We do not forget that."

The moment passed.

Alf did not strike. The sword remained in the ground.

It was done! The Wilder would take Gundan's bargain, and relent. There'd be time to evacuate the city in the new year, when the roads were passable again. Or time to talk, time to find another way. They'd come to the edge of darkness and stepped back. Twenty years not wasted, twenty years of marching blindly through the night, but they had come at last to a glorious dawn.

Was this what you saw, Jan? he thought. *Is this the darkness breaking?* Alf caught the eye of Thurn's little girl and grinned at her.

Gundan opened his mouth, but whatever words he would have spoken were for ever lost. From behind them came the shrieking cackle of a spell-skull.

Alf whirled around, and caught a split-second glimpse of the grinning face of the skull, chattered and chanting as it landed in the mud near Ildorae. Evil out of Necrad. Acrid smoke poured out of the skull's mouth, edged with purple lightning that seared Alf's flesh as washed over him, engulfing the whole lakeside.

Chaos, all around. Shouts from behind him, ahead of him. War cries, the whistle of arrows, the thunder of explosions, screams and shouts. The skull's chattering as more purple smoke gushed out. Again, it burned him, the magic like a caustic wave. The pain as the spell re-awoke the memory of all his wounds, old and new. The smoke touched his skin, and he was back in the darkness under Necrad, the linnorm's claws ripping him open. The spell touched him, and Ildorae was stabbing him again, ice stabbing at his lungs, his heart. The spell touched him, and his sword-hand was numb and bloodless. *It's not real*, he told himself, *it's magic. Ignore it.* But he could feel the weight of his disembowelled intestines pushing against his gambeson, feel the fangs of the vampire child ripping at the veins of his wrist. It wasn't wholly real, but neither was it wholly illusory.

Someone – Duna, maybe – was screaming just to Alf's right, and nearby Talis was shrieking in pain, too, a child's wordless wail. Gundan on his knees, one hand pressed against his eyes, bellowing in sudden agony, the other fumbling around for Chopper's handle.

Alf grabbed Spellbreaker, and the pain ceased instantly. *Wield me!* shouted the sword. *Strike now!*

He probed through the billowing purple smoke, blade in hand, looking for the cursed thing. Smash the skull, and the spell would end. A shape raced past him – Ildorae. Whatever the magic of the skull was, it had no effect on elves. Their old wounds did not haunt them.

There! There was the skull – and there was Talis, staggered, her hands clutching her belly over the arrow-wound that had ended her old life. Blood welled up between her fingers.

Strike now!

He raised Spellbreaker, and strength flowed into him from the blade such that he had never felt before.

Out of the smoke came Thurn, and Thurn's black spear like a thunderbolt. He thrust it at Alf, serpent-swift, before Alf could bring the sword down. The point of the spear caught Alf in the shoulder, but his dwarf-forged armour held. The blow was enough to stagger Alf, sending him stumbling. Thurn's features were visible through the smoke for an instant, his face a mask of fury, but then the Wilder grunted in pain and he too fell, toppling like a tall tree brought low by the axe.

Chopper had bitten deep, cleaving through Thurn's spine.

The hero of the Nine twitched in the mud, once, twice, and then lay still. His eyes stared up at Alf, but there was no life in them. Gundan, half blind, shouted at Alf, but he could not understand the words.

Alf brought Spellbreaker down on the skull and shattered it into a thousand fragments. The assault of the spell ceased. He spun around, trying to guess who had thrown the skull, but all was chaos. Some of the soldiers had retreated back up the slope towards the road and the body of the cavalry. Others had attacked the Wilder, or been attacked. Bodies lay pierced by many arrows, or torn apart by the walking dead. He could hear the sounds of fighting off to his left, by the lakeside. Wilder in huge numbers poured out of the woods, shrieking war cries. The two attendants of the Old Man of the Woods hauled their charge away to safety, his feet dangling in the water as they splashed through the shallows.

Gundan crawled towards Thurn's body. He knelt by his friend's side. Tears glittered on his bearded cheeks.

"Ah no, no. I couldn't see . . . I didn't mean to . . ." he muttered.

"Talis," said Alf. The child was Death. She had power over death. Surely she could heal her father.

A breeze blew over the lake and dispersed the smoke. Quickly it gathered strength to become a howling wind that snuffed out the remains of the fire. Overhead, a raven cawed, over and over, a meaningless animal noise of distress.

The child walked, trembling and unsteady, towards her father's body.

Beware! hissed the sword.

The world shattered.

The same blast that had destroyed Daeroch Nal in an eye blink struck the lakeside.

All was ablaze, a fury beyond imagining. The only thing that Alf could see was Spellbreaker, a black shape against the overwhelming light. The sword's counter-magic shielded him against the onslaught, but it was still like being caught in a raging river. The earth beneath him was boiled and blasted away, and he fell, buffeted this way and that by the torrent of anger. He clung to the sword like a drowning man clings to wreckage.

On and on it raged. He saw the world in snatched glimpses, the after-images of the blazing thunderbolt dancing in his vision. The lake exploding into steam. Soldiers blasted to ash on the wind in an instant. Death, the power within her so terrible that her skin seemed translucent, and he could see the skull beneath the child's face, see the thing that Lath had called back from the grey land.

He saw Gundan, but that was only an after-image, too, memory overlaid on ash.

Then he saw no more.

PART THREE

After the death of Lord Bone, the eight who yet lived gathered amid the ruins.

Lath, the orphan of the woods, was much afraid, for he thought that now the deed was done and evil defeated, his companions would each return to their homes. He asked if the company of the Nine was now broken.

"Nay," said Thurn, "here in the north my people dwell, and here I shall remain."

"Nay," said Blaise, "there is yet much to be done. For though Lord Bone is gone, his evil lingers on, above and below."

The Lammergeier replied, "I shall keep watch on those below, and no horror from the Pits shall pass while I guard the door."

"Aye, who but those who slew Lord Bone can meet this challenge?" asked Berys.

Answered the Princess Laerlyn. "'Tis plain that it is our duty to guard the city of Lord Bone from those who would use his works to work evil."

Then the dwarf Gundan laughed, and said: "I once dreamed of a warm bed, and good food, and a mountain for a roof. But if you are all intent on staying, I shall not be the one to break this friendship. When this quest began, nine of us swore an oath not to turn back or fail. Now there are but eight, and the quest is done. Let us swear a new oath to our common purpose!"

"To the Intercessors who guided us," prayed Jan, "may they bless this oath."

"To friendship!" cried the dwarf.

"To freedom," said Thurn.

"To wisdom," said Blaise.

"To the future," said Laerlyn.

"To brighter days," said Berys.

"To the Nine," said Lath.

Here ends the Song of the Nine, who brought an end to the evil of Necrad. I ask all who read this tale and whose hearts are gladdened by the wonders and exploits of the Nine whose deeds are recorded herein, remember in your prayers the poor sinner who wrote this book while he yet lives, and when he passes may the Intercessors to take his soul.

Sir Rhuel of the Eaveslands

CHAPTER THIRTY-TWO

T he piercing light of dawn woke Alf, the light and the whimper of the dreadworm as the sun scorched its wings. He stirred, and Ildorae hissed at him, warning him not to move. He was slumped over her, his arms around her waist, the two of them mounted on a single overburdened dreadworm.

He tried to speak, but his throat was thick with ash.

"Some of them escaped," said the elf. "Duna's horsemen. I don't know how many."

"What about the others?"

"What do you think? The Wilder called up a horror from the elder days. None of them – not even one of the Nine – could stand against her. None can, not in open battle."

"There was a spell-skull," said Alf, remembering the battle. "Someone had a skull. Who planted it? Was it you?"

"No. One of the soldiers – one of Duna's men, I guess, but it might have been one of Vond's knights. They must have carried it with them when they offered me to the Wilder." She glanced back at him. "I thought it was part of some plan to ambush Death. The skull was well chosen – it took her by surprise, and weakened her. She was not expecting such an attack. Did you not order it?"

"No." Alf closed his eyes. The skull had ruined everything.

"Was it the dwarf?"

Alf did not answer. He knew that it was important, that it was a matter that would be discussed in council. Whoever had thrown the skull – whoever had *commanded* it, for the poor wretch who actually carried the weapon was dead – had ended any chance of a truce with the Wilder. It would be all-out war now. Vond and the rest would obsess over this stratagem, this treachery. And Gundan would still be dead.

He pressed his forehead against the hard metal of Ildorae's shoulder armour. The chill of the upper airs in which the dreadworm flew made the armour bitterly cold.

"Thurn was a chieftain – there'll be funeral rites, and the As Gola will have to elect a new war-leader. That shall take a few days." Ildorae shifted in the saddle and pressed Spellbreaker's hilt into his hand. "Take this back."

"You keep it awhile," said Alf. He felt shattered. Every part of him ached, and his heart ached most of all. *Thurn is dead. Gundan's dead.* Disintegrated in that lightning bolt. Death had killed him.

"It let me call a dreadworm and carry you out of danger. It wouldn't let me fight with it." She glanced over her shoulder. "The sword told me to rescue you."

"There is no time to grieve, Lammergeier," said the sword. "There is no hope for peace any more. You must wield me in defence of the city now."

The dreadworm banked over the Charnel, angling to keep the sheltering necromiasma between it and the rising sun. It passed over the line of Stone Dragons and began to circle down in great lazy loops towards the city of Necrad.

Ildorae guided the dreadworm down towards the edge of the Liberties.

"I need to tell the council what happened," said Alf. "Land in the Garrison."

"You can bring the worm there yourself, mortal." The dreadworm landed on a Sanction rooftop near the city walls. Ancient statues of Witch Elves stood sentry, facing the north. Their faces had worn away, making them all featureless as wraiths. Ildorae slithered off the beast's back and stood beside the stone sentinels.

"You're leaving?" He didn't move to stop her.

"Here our paths diverge. If I go back to the citadel, they will put me in chains again." She pointed south. "If you want my counsel, Lammergeier, leave. Take the sword and whatever other treasures you can carry, and go south. We both did all we could to fulfil our shared quest, but we have failed. It is too late to stop Death. Your time here is done. Live out the few years left to you as you see fit." Ildorae threw the sword to Alf. "Topple the Lords of Summerswell, maybe. Put the cursed blade to good use."

"And what will you do?"

She shrugged. "I shall fight for my people and the city we built. Slay Death, if I can. If I cannot . . . well, in time, even Death may die. The mortal girl will perish and go to the Grey Lands with the rest of you. If I must wait for that, so be it."

With that, she was gone.

The worm lay down its head, exhausted. Alf kicked the beast in the flank and got it to flap slowly into the air, skimming along the rooftops of the Liberties and barely clearing the Garrison wall. It began to disintegrate in the air, strips of its hide peeling away, but it held together long enough to make it to the courtyard of the League fortress. Alf struggled out of the wreck. League guards – human and elven and dwarven, just like the old days – hurried up to help. He waved them away.

"What news from the north?" they asked him, and he just shook his head.

They escorted him through the crowd, up the steps to Lord Vond's palace. Alf wanted very much to cast himself down on the stone stair and never move again. Still, he let them lead him through the great doors of the fortress and down the long corridors. He felt himself sway, and gripped the sword for support.

"Sir Lammergeier! This way!" Threeday emerged from a side door. The Vatling nimbly extricated Alf from the honour guard, taking Alf's arm and escorting him through a maze of little chambers with the polished grace of a courtier. Threeday showed him to a small and humble room in the bowels of the palace, a nest of papers and broken furniture. He fished a stool out from under a pile of ledgers and gestured for Alf to sit.

"You seemed overwhelmed," said the Vatling. "And clearly in need of rest after your travails." From a cabinet, he fetched a bottle of wine and some food.

"The council," croaked Alf. "I need to talk to them."

"Of course," said the Vatling. "But rest a moment. Collect your strength. I surmise the parley did not go as hoped?"

"Gundan's dead. The Wilder are still coming."

Threeday lowered his head. "A dark day, indeed. As bad as any I have known."

A hero would offer some words of comfort. If Peir were here, he would have said something inspiring, something that would take the Vatling's fears and forge them into action. But there was nothing left in Alf. He stared at the floor, unseeing, unthinking.

Threeday stood. "I shall go fetch and Lord Vond, and send word to Master Blaise that you have returned. Rest here, my lord." The Vatling slipped away, leaving Alf in silence.

Bad times are coming, Jan had said, and something in Alf had rejoiced. Bad times meant monsters to fight, perils to brave. It meant honour and purpose, the Nine coming back together, a band of heroes closer than family. For all the horrors of the war, for all they'd suffered, those years had defined him. He hadn't been happy – there'd been little time for joy, although maybe that only made the snatches of merriment all the sweeter – but he had been complete. He'd known his purpose then with perfect clarity.

Now, he was adrift.

If the Wilder once more invaded the southland, if the Gulf of Tears was thronged with dragon-headed longboats again, then Alf would not hesitate in taking up his sword. To fight in the defence of Summerswell, of the Mulladales, of little Ersfel in the wooded valley – that he could do. The quest had been to save those lands, save his people. They'd sought to defeat Lord Bone, not conquer his city, not occupy his throne.

Why take up the sword in the defence of Necrad? To Alf, Necrad was rubble and dust and wraiths, slimy tunnels and endless dungeons, a cavalcade of spawned horrors. A monster to be contained, a burden to be carried. It was only since Jan sent him back here that he'd glimpsed another aspect to the dark city, and, even then, he could not be sure it was worth defending.

The thought of razing the place to the ground – of letting bright sunlight sear the Pits – surely that was the end of what the Nine had started, long ago?

"I hated them," said Spellbreaker, suddenly. "Both of them. The dwarf and the Wilder. Thurn took the Wilder from my master. They worshipped the Witch Elves; their spirits were supposed to be broken! They should have seen my wielder Acraist as a living god! But Thurn rallied the Wilder to fight against us. He taught them to rebel, and ruined them as a weapon for us. We could no longer rely on them – any of them might have been a secret adherent of Thurn. All my master could do was set them loose as a distraction, send small bands pillaging across the eastern provinces. Petty vandalism, with little effect on the greater war. But there were plans, Lammergeier, to send a host of Wilder to destroy Arshoth and the Eaveslands! Think on that! All your heroism in the Mulladales and the Crownland and still we would have put the lands of mortals to the torch – if not for Thurn's meddling."

Alf drew the sword and laid it on the table in front of him. He topped up his own glass, and splashed a little wine on the blade.

"And Gundan?" he said.

"Lord Bone sent my master Acraist to hunt the Nine down. We hunted you across all the land. By the stars, Lammergeier, you cannot grasp the depths of the hatred he held for you meddling fools. It sustained him, even when Lord Bone's spells could no longer keep his wraith bound to his rotting body. He lived to see you suffer, and I was to be the instrument of that suffering. It would have been glorious. But the Nine had grown too powerful for even my master to defeat in battle, so he decided to exhaust you first. The Oracle found you, and Acraist sent foe after foe to assault you. Do you remember the Barbed Hydra? The Giant of Leuthnos?"

"Gundan killed 'em."

"You and the dwarf were ruinous. You were all ruinous, in your way. But the others, we could have worn down. The wizard was always frail. The Changeling a mere child. Berys would have fled. Thurn, too, perhaps. Laerlyn was a spoiled princess, and her courage would have failed her. And then it would just have been the paladin." The sword spoke with a ghastly wistfulness as it contemplated killing Peir. "But you endured, you and Gundan. Curse you all."

"He'd have liked to have heard all that."

"He was a fool," said the sword, "and Thurn a fanatic. Mourn them if you must – but the battle is not done. You have not stopped Death. She still intends to attack Necrad. You missed one opportunity to strike her down. Pray that we have another."

"Who do you think threw that skull?" Alf said, hollowly. The skull had ruined everything.

"I have given that matter some thought," said the sword. "I thought at first that it was the dwarf's plan. The spell in the skull was well chosen: few incantations would have had such an effect on Death, but that one attacked wounds she carried in her mortal life. The dwarf was certainly wily enough to think of such a thing. But it was ill-timed. Whoever threw it waited until the dwarf was on the verge of bargaining Necrad away to the Wilder." The demon sword's eye glittered. "We have another foe, Lammergeier. An unseen hand that tugs at threads, arranges chance meetings, sets friend against friend."

"I'm not in the mood for riddles."

"I am but a sword, Lammergeier. I was made to slay, not to speak. What spirit and wit I possess is but an afterthought, a vestige of all the souls I have eaten and the spells woven into me. I am but a steward of my own body, appointed only to watch and wait until the moment I was forged for arrives, and I do not know what that moment is.

"But I have seen much of the world, on Acraist's hip or by your side. I watched as you wandered the wastes of Thal. I saw the ruins of the Old Kingdom, the sullen tombs of Haush and the drowned ruins of Minar Kul. I saw the Dwarflands when Acraist besieged them, and I saw the lands of your home. Oh, the wounds there have scabbed over, but I could still smell the bloodshed. War after war, carnage upon carnage. And, I think, the same unseen hand behind all of them." The sword's voice became a rasping whisper. "You ended my master's war, Lammergeier, but division and mistrust are the lot of mortals. You stood aside for twenty years after your victory, and rot crept back in. If you wish to bring peace and justice, wield me properly. Take power. Take responsibility."

"I'm not a leader."

"If that is true, then give me to one who has the courage to use me. But I know you, Lammergeier. You think of yourself as the farm boy from the Mulladales, the faithful follower. But you must be more than that, now. If you would prevent slaughter, Death must be defeated. Wield me!"

The Vatling returned, signalling his presence with a gelatinous approximation of a cough. "I have informed Lord Vond of what transpired – and of your exhaustion and sorrow. The council will convene as soon as possible. Princess Laerlyn and Master Blaise are invited to attend. I have taken the liberty of arranging a carriage to bring you home to rest."

*

Home. Home was his mansion in Necrad. Alf walked slowly up the path to the house's great front door, head bowed. Ghastly elven gargoyles watched him impassively, this brief gasp of mortal dust that swirled around their feet. Gundan was gone, and Alf would soon be gone, fallen to Death . . . or some other death, if there was a difference. He still had no clue about what the girl really was, but honestly, he'd never much understood half the things he'd killed. He knew the shape of things but not their meaning or purpose. He felt old – not tired, but brittle and drained, his chest hollow. Gundan was dead, and Thurn was dead. Berys had fled, and Jan and Lath had fucked off mystically, and Blaise . . . Blaise was Blaise. And Peir was dead, too, of course. At least Lae had come back.

The sword had told him to take charge. He wasn't the man to do that, he knew that in his bones. Alf was comfortable with a simple demarcation: good and evil. He'd fought on the side of good against evil. Evil was the side with the zombies and the wraiths and the ogres and the vatspawn and the blood-drinking vampires. Good was loyal friends, kindly elves, shining spirits, the villages and cities of his homeland. Good was the light against the darkness, and there'd once been a clear bright line between the two. A sharp divide, as if cleaved by a sharp sword. Like the songs told.

Now it was all muddied. All too confusing for a simple man.

A guard hailed him.

"My lord Lammergeier, you have a guest. She came from the Isle of Dawn with the elves."

One of Lae's people, Alf guessed. He nodded and passed by the sentry. The hallway beyond was a shambles. They'd sent masons to repair the damage inflicted by Spellbreaker, but they'd been called away to work on the city walls. *Or, not Lae's. Her brother's folk.* He stepped around the rubble and the discarded tools.

Gods, they'd been so close, back then. The Nine all together, all united. Their quest to the Isle of Dawn – that hadn't been the last time they were all together, they'd stayed together until the end, until Peir left them. But it was the last time they'd had time to just breathe, to sleep without setting watches. To laugh together about stupid things. After the isle, it was all fighting down the dark road to Necrad and victory.

It was Laerlyn who'd warned them that the elves had decided to stay out of the war. Her brother Maedos had sworn her to secrecy, she said, but she couldn't stand by. She'd warned Gundan and the rest of the Nine, choosing her friends and their kinfolk over her own brother. And that choice led to so much more – they'd taken the elf fleet, attacked Lord Bone's ships. Alf remembered Thurn scowling as he tried to work out how to ride a sea-serpent, or the water like glittering diamonds as it cascaded from Lath's flank as the Changeling breached the waves, having taken serpent-form himself.

And they'd kicked Maedos out of his own castle along the way, dragged the Isle of Dawn into the war. That had been more of an accident than anything else – Alf had got lost in the fighting-blindness, the red haze. He'd barely noticed who he was thumping. And Laerlyn only told him to stop after he'd thrown her brother over the side.

The songs never told it that way, though – same way the songs never spoke of the folly of the Lords of Summerswell, or the way the dwarves used bane-metal. The songs never spoke of the messy parts, the compromises and the arguments. They told of the Nine riding to battle on the backs of sea-serpents, but never the quarrels and bargains that came before. In the songs, it was always good against evil, the free folk against the hosts of Necrad, and you knew that however dark the tale got, there'd be light at the end. All would seem lost, then there'd be some last, desperate act of courage, a heroic stand or a twist of fate, and from that would spring victory unlooked for. There'd be no compromise, no lingering doubt.

You'd never get Vond's bloody council meetings in the songs.

Gundan had loved a good song. Thurn, too, maybe. Who could tell with the Wilder crouching at the edge of the firelight, like a morose scarecrow? Alf had seen the man smile maybe twice in his life, and now he never would again. Lost in thought, he barely noticed the grey-clad elf-maid who waited on a bench until she raised her head and looked at him.

Not an elf-maid.

Olva.

He saw her then, properly. She wore the ghost of his mother's face, the same way his father Tom stared out of the mirror these days. In his head, she was the gangly young maiden he'd left behind in Ersfel, half a life ago, and now all those years caught up with her in an instant, memory crashing into the present. He stared at her.

"Olva?" he said, unsure. They were not strangers, but their paths had long since diverged. She half rose from the bench, and then she must have seen the grief on his face, because she stepped forward and hugged him.

He held onto her for a long time, marvelling at the familiarity of it all. For a moment, the weight shifted from his frame, all thoughts of Death and the quest and duty melting away. Then Olva's hip brushed against Spellbreaker's hilt, and she jumped back as if stung.

"What's wrong?"

"Alf?" she whispered.

Alf nodded. "Why are you here? Why now, of all days?"

"My son – I have a son. His name's Derwyn. He went in search of you." Olva gaze flickered between Alf and the sword, and there was a look of revulsion in her face. Alf unbuckled the sword and flung it into the wreckage of his bedroom, where it landed with a squawk of protest among the rubble.

A dwarf Alf did not recognise peered out of a side room. "This is Torun," explained Olva, "she came with me from the Isle of Dawn." Torun emitted a high-pitched chirp of surprise, then ducked back. "That was Torun."

Alf smiled. "You travelled from Ersfel with a dwarf?" A memory of Gundan in those early days, before they'd even met Peir: the two of them lost in the Fossewood, looking for a rumoured treasure trove that turned out to be a midden.

"Some of the way," she said, and did not elaborate. "Please, I need your help."

He led her into another room that was less exploded. He sat her at a table and went to the adjoining pantry to fetch food, only to remember that he had nothing. The shelves were bare, except for a few empty glass jars in the shape of coiling worms. Delicate elven craftwork, and he'd broken two of them.

Awkwardly, he sat down opposite his sister. The room felt full of ghosts – not wraiths, but memories. There had been no table in the little cottage in Ersfel, and that whole house would have fitted into this one room of Alf's mansion with room to spare.

Alf did not know how to begin. The past was too big. He could not bridge twenty years with a few words. "I missed your wedding," he blurted out. "I'm sorry. Is your husband here, too?"

"He's dead, Alf. He's fifteen years gone."

"Ach. I'm sorry." It felt horribly inadequate.

"You didn't just miss my wedding. So many funerals, too. It's just us left. All the rest are in the ground. You never came home. Why did—"

"I was busy. The war. And after . . . I was needed here. I wanted to come back home, but I could not. I had my duty." He stared at the floor, unable to look her in the eye. "Your boy. Tell me of him."

She paused. "Derwyn. He's a lot like you. Idolises you. Always full of tales of the Nine and all your deeds. He's a good lad. He's . . . " Her voice broke for the first time. "I told him about you. I held off for as long as I could, but I had to tell him – and that night, he left home. He went on the Road, all alone."

Alf remembered leaving Ersfel himself, long ago. But he'd been lucky – he'd fallen in with a dwarven mercenary early on, a merry wretch with a big axe who'd shown him how to survive. He'd had a friend from the start.

A friend who was now dead.

He forced himself to listen to Olva's tale.

" . . . followed him to Highfield. He'd met a blood trader – Lyulf Martens of Arshoth. Do you know where he is?"

"I don't know the man." Alf wracked his brain, trying to recall. If Martens was involved in the blood trade, though, then presumably he worked for Berys at some remove. Where the hell was Berys when he needed her?

"Martens caught me, too. They wanted me and Der to get to you." She clutched his hand. "The elves rescued me from Martens, and . . . well, Princess Laerlyn rescued me from the elves, but he's still got Derwyn. You've got to find him, please."

"I will, Ol. I promise."

"I won't ask anything of you again," she said quietly, and somehow that hurt more than anything else.

"Ask for anything!" he shouted, springing to his feet. "Anything in the world! Anything in my power, and I'll give it! I'll find your boy! By all that's holy, Olva, I've missed you! Do you think I didn't want to go home? I did. I do. But it wasn't safe. I had enemies, Olva, things that would freeze your blood. You've no idea how hard we had to fight to stay alive, how close it all came to failure. There were times when I didn't think we had a chance. Each of the Nine, they saved my life a dozen times over. We barely survived, but we did. They hunted us across Summerland, up the Dwarfholt. Here in Necrad. Those were the worst days. You can't imagine . . . you don't *want* to imagine . . . " He stopped and looked at her. "Do you know what I clung to? How I endured? I told myself that as long as the Witch Elves and the monsters were here fighting me, then they weren't in Ersfel. I kept the darkness bottled up here. I told myself I was keeping you all safe at home—"

He caught himself. His sister was crying now, sobbing wildly, her shoulders shaking as her whole body convulsed. "What's wrong?"

She couldn't answer. She was laughing, too, but there was no mirth in it. She clasped her hands over her mouth and rocked back and forth. She pointed back towards his bedroom, back to where he'd thrown the sword.

"What's wrong?" he asked again, helplessly.

And Olva told him.

They came to the house by night.

Derwyn had been no more than a month old, a quiet baby even then. She'd stay up, some nights, just to listen to him breathe. The village women laughed at her, told her that she wouldn't be as precious about the next child, or the ones after that.

That night, she'd been awake, sitting by the fireside, Derwyn in a little basket by her feet. Galwyn was awake, too, bent over his desk, talking idly to her as he wrote by candlelight. A letter to some relative. He had talked about leaving Ersfel and going to his family lands in Arshoth. He'd told her that he could obtain some position there in his cousin's household. They would be safer there, he said, further away from the war. Protected behind the stone walls of a town, instead of out here in the wilds. But Olva had argued, saying that Ersfel was their home. They had land here, friends here, roots that ran deep.

And more, their marriage had been blessed by the Intercessors. She did not know why the holy spirits had matched a lowly farm girl with a young nobleman (even though Galwyn had laughingly protested he was only barely of noble blood, and that one had to go back half a dozen generations before you got to a *Lord* Forster), but they had chosen her and Galwyn to be wed, and to live here in Ersfel. That was what the village priest said, up in the holywood. They were chosen ones – not for some great quest, not for some mystical destiny, but to be happy. No, she said, they would live here in Ersfel. Soon, the war would end and there would be peace again.

She remembered watching Derwyn sleep. She remembered the scratching of Galwyn's quill on paper.

But she could never remember the Witch Elves entering the house. Had they burst through the door? Crept in the windows? The dogs had barked in the yard outside, but she'd paid no attention. They were just suddenly *there*, three of them. Two were unmasked, their elven faces unearthly in their beauty under the candle's glow, the dancing light picking out the details of their rune-marked armour, charmstones glimmering like stars in the dark.

The third, though, was a horror. His armour was battered and scored, marred with a dozen gashes, a dozen mortal wounds. He had been burned at some point, too, making him a hideous mockery of his compatriots' grandeur. Mercifully, the third elf's face was hidden behind a helm, but she could see – could never, ever, forget – his eyes burning like coals in the shadows behind the visor.

He carried the black sword.

"I seek the Nine," said Acraist the Wraith-Captain, "They were here a little while ago. Have they returned? Are they here now?"

A little while? It was years ago. Six years ago, Alf and his friends had taken refuge in Ersfel. It wasn't even the same house! They'd hidden in her parents' cottage, not here in the Forster house! Olva tried to speak, but her terror was too great.

A little while? What are a few years to an immortal?

And when she saw the blood on the black sword, she knew with terrible certainty that this was not the first house the Wraith-Captain had visited that night.

"Alf's not been back. They went away down the Road. I don't know, I swear!"

"The Oracle sent us here," said the Wraith-Captain. "We have travelled far in search of the Nine. For thy own sake, let this not be a wasted journey." He raised the black sword.

Galwyn grabbed the knife he'd used to trim his quill pen and rushed forward, the little knife held like a dagger. He hurled himself between the Wraith-Captain and his wife and child. It was a moment of great courage, the sort of heroism that the songs should sing about. Selfless, instinctive, pure.

The blade sword flickered, and he fell. The gush of his blood over the floor, almost black in the dim light, warm against Olva's bare feet. The little noise he made as he died, almost apologetic.

The Wraith-Captain stepped over Galwyn's body. He reached up and undid the mouth-guard of his awful helmet. He stooped and took the baby from his basket. Olva stood, frozen, the horror so complete that it filled her utterly, leaving no room for any other thought. She could not move. Could not breathe. Could not look away.

Acraist raised Derwyn to his lips. Jagged teeth bit deep, and blood welled out—

Olva lapsed into silence. All through the tale, she'd spoken as if it was an old story, someone else's nightmare all along. When the tears came, she briskly wiped them away.

"What happened?" asked Alf.

"I was never sure," Olva said quietly. "I looked up and he was gone. I don't know why. One moment, the wraith-knights were there, and the next it was just me and Der and ... and the body. Galwyn, dead at my feet. Butchered. I couldn't do anything. I picked up the baby, put my hand over the wound to hold in his blood. There was so much blood, Alf."

She looked up at him, as if pleading for him to make sense of it all.

How could he?

"My friend Jan," he said, haltingly, "was a priestess. She could call on the Intercessors for aid, in the war. They didn't always listen. And I've seen their works of late – they healed the son of Earl Duna – but they don't always help. I don't understand them either, Ol. And there are stranger things in the world, too." He shrugged, helplessly. Over the course of the Nine's adventures, he'd learned to ignore mystical experiences. Everything – prophecies, omens, spirits, portents, numinous manifestations – was for wiser heads to worry about, while Alf and Gundan hit things. He wished Jan were here to counsel his sister. "A miracle, I guess."

"I've always wondered ... why not Galwyn, too? Why me and Derwyn?"

"Thinking like that will ruin you," said Alf, automatically. He'd heard talk like that from soldiers who'd lost comrades in battle. It came down to luck in the melee; skill and strength and magic all counted, too, but you had to accept that fate was beyond your ken. Wizards could read the stars for lords and princes, but for most folk it was down to luck.

"Why?" Olva spat. "Why not demand answers?" She sighed. "I wondered about it for a long, long time. It felt like half a blessing. I didn't feel safe there – or anywhere – but Ersfel was the one place I knew where *something* had watched over me. I thought if I could keep Derwyn there ... We've got to find him. He's all I have left."

Alf shook his head. "I wish you'd stayed there. I liked the thought that you were safe."

"Why did you send Bor, then? We didn't need your money. You could have forgotten us."

Alf frowned. The name meant nothing to him. "Who's this Bor?"

"Your messenger. The man you sent. Bor the Rootless." Olva saw Alf's confusion, and her voice filled with panic. "Alf, he said you sent him. He said he met you at the Highfield fair, and you gave him money and a message for me! He swore that you gave him that quest! You sent him!"

Alf shook his head. "Olva, I swear I've never heard of this man in all my life."

CHAPTER THIRTY-THREE

Olva could not say which was stranger to her – the city, or her brother.

Alf walked ahead of her, grim and guarded. His thoughts seemed far away, and she felt like an unwanted distraction, a chore to be dealt with as efficiently as possible. The crowds parted before him as they hurried through the city.

She had not expected Necrad to be so crowded and lively, or to be full of so many half-familiar faces. As long as she ignored the necro-miasma overhead, or the eerie spires that seemed to writhe in the air as the mists swirled past them, she could convince herself this place was not so different from Highfield or Ellsport, and that reassured her. Then Alf would lead her down some side street, or some ghastly cathedral would loom beyond the possibility of concealment, and the city revealed its true face, as bad as any of the nightmare visions that had plagued her.

Alf hadn't sent Bor. Someone else had sent him. Someone else had plucked her son from safety. Some unseen hand had reached down and stolen Derwyn away, lured him into peril. Nowhere was safe. Nowhere was unsullied. The fear was at home here in Necrad; she envisaged it as a little goblin-thing, but here was a city of ghosts and goblins, and here the fear could gird itself, armour itself in unknown horrors.

The next corner nearly brought her back to familiar ground. Alf took her into a tavern that was not so different from Genny's ale-house, with the smell of beer and woodsmoke. Only half the patrons were cold-eyed dwarves, and the servant that waited on them had skin like frogspawn in a pond.

"I'm looking for Threeday," Alf told the creature. The Vatling gave a curt bow and turned to go, but Alf's hand shot out and grabbed the creature's wrist. His fingers sank a little way into the Vatling's flesh. "Bring a bottle of the dwarven stuff first."

A bottle of some spirit was duly produced. Alf studied it. "I can never pronounce its name. Gundan always ordered it for us." He poured a measure into his mug. "Do you want some?"

Olva shook her head. Alf reminded her suddenly of their father, in his last days, mourning the loss of his sons. An old and broken man, numb to the world. She had not known what to expect when she got to Necrad – the tales had Sir Aelfric as a great knight, Bor had described him as a grim monster-slayer – and those imaginings were mixed up with her memories of Alf as she'd last seen him, standing in the door of the barn, keeping watch against the dark. She had not expected to find him so wounded.

In the tales, the Nine had won the war. Alf, she saw, had only survived it.

A dwarf approached the table. "Sir Lammergeier? I must speak to you of Lord Gundan. There are rumours—"

"Gamling. Aye." Alf stood and brought the dwarf aside. They were too far away for her to hear her brother's words, but the dwarf's face flushed with anger. More dwarves gathered around, pressing in on Alf. At first they were angry, shouting at Alf and stamping their feet, but as Alf spoke, they grew still and silent. They muttered to each other in the dwarven tongue.

Olva watched Alf. If he had not sent the letter to Ersfel, who had? Some enemy of his? Princess Laerlyn had suggested that Alf's enemies might use Derwyn as a hostage, but then why not just come to little defenceless Ersfel and snatch him away? Had Bor lied to her about who sent him? Somehow, she couldn't believe that – for all his faults, Bor had seemed genuine in his belief that the Lammergeier had charged him with a quest.

Alf had grown irritated when she'd tried to talk to him last night, as though the mystery of the note was another burden he'd had to bear, as if she was trying to hang some irrelevant geegaw on a pack horse that was already overloaded. For him, it was an irrelevance; for her, it was like a stone in her shoe. Maybe Alf was right and it did not matter; however her son had started his journey, she had to find him before it ended.

"Where is the messenger now?" said a cold voice. Olva looked around in alarm, then realised it was Alf's sword who had spoken. He'd left the blade by her chair.

"The messenger – Bor," she stammered. "I last saw him in Ellsport."

"Another move in the game," mused the sword, its horrible voice making her skin crawl. "Why set your son on the Road to Necrad? Why do it in so indirect a manner? There is more than one unseen hand at work."

Olva pushed her chair away from the ghastly thing. The sword's gemstone eye stared at her.

"I remember that night," it said, and she froze. "I was not as *awake* then. I remember it, but only with difficulty. I suppose this is what it must be like to dream."

"The . . . the vampire knight wielded you."

"Acraist Wraith-Captain, the Hand of Bone. At the time, I thought it beneath me to murder peasant rabble. I was forged to bring ruin to greater things than your husband. Killing him was like gutting a rabbit."

"Galwyn was a good man. And brave."

"Perhaps." The sword laughed. "But courage and righteousness offer no protection against a blade. A good man dies as easily as an evil one, the brave soul as easily as the coward. The sword cares not who it cuts."

"Why . . . " began Olva, then she fell silent.

"Ask."

"Why did they not kill me? What stopped Acraist?"

The sword did not speak for a few moments, contemplating its answer.

"There was an Intercessor watching your house that night. Why it was there, I do not know, but it protected you."

An Intercessor, in her home? Olva's mind reeled. The priests said that the holy Intercessors watched over all the lands of mortals, true enough, but she'd always taken that to mean they watched over lords and princes and heroes, over cities and temples, not over little farmsteads in the Mulladales. Even though her marriage to Galwyn had been ordained by the spirits, there had always been a niggling doubt at the back of her mind that it was a mistake, somehow – that either the Intercessors had meant someone else, or the priests had misinterpreted the omens.

"Such spirits are hard to kill," continued the sword. "It took Acraist by surprise, and we retreated. Anyway, what would have been the point of battling a troublesome spirit? The Nine were not there. We had been led astray."

Alf returned and pulled Olva to her feet. "Come on. We can't wait here." Glancing around the bar, she saw dwarves everywhere, all glaring at Alf. "I came back unwounded, and Gundan came back dead. I told Gamling what happened, but he doesn't believe me. The dwarves are angry, angrier than I've seen them in a long, long time."

"Are we in danger?"

"No. No. Gamling's furious, and he'll demand trial by combat if he wants my head, but he's not going to come after me in the streets. Dwarves aren't underhanded like that." Alf snorted, then shook his head sadly. "Most aren't. Gundan, now, he'd have mugged me in an alleyway. His cousins still might. Come on, let's get you back home."

*

After they returned to Alf's house, Olva went looking for Torun. The building had a hundred rooms, and some had clearly not been entered in years. Dust lay thick upon the floors. In one room, she found a magnificent mirror with a frame of the same unearthly metal as the coins, and wondered at her reflection. The elf-garb she'd been given on the isle made her look like some adventurer, a Rootless wanderer who'd found good fortune on the Road. Then the light in the room changed, and she saw the pale face of a wraith in the room behind her, and she backed away. Alf had insisted the dead elves could not hurt her, and she prayed to the Intercessors that he was right.

The sword had said that an Intercessor had saved Derwyn, and she warmed herself with that thought, letting it drive away the fear for a little while. Maybe they were still watching over him, wherever he was.

Olva found the dwarf on the topmost level of the house, standing on a balcony that looked out over Necrad. Torun had found some string and a few shards of broken glass amid the rubble, and had strung up another star-trap – although surely no starlight could penetrate the clouds of the necromiasma. In the gloom, the lights of the city looked like dim little stars, and the resemblance was reinforced by the way Necrad's streets copied the constellations and sigils of the night sky. Olva's stomach twisted, and she suddenly felt upside down, as if the clouds above were the ocean, and the city was an inverted bowl hanging in the sky.

Alf's mansion was not too far from the edge of the Garrison, and from its upper floors she could see out over the wall to the city beyond. Stripped of its tattered mortal disguise, Necrad was indeed the city of Olva's nightmares, as if the elves of old had spied on her dreams and clothed them in marble and brass. The city was both forbidding and forbidden, a place where mortals should not trespass. The tombs – no, they weren't tombs, she reminded herself. Elves never died. They were palaces like this one, temples too, all so huge that the streets were canyons, narrow and airless. The pale light filtering through the necromiasma danced on the carven walls, greenish and obscured, as though they were underwater. Drowning in a city of the damned.

The Isle of Dawn had been enchanting, but a little faded, a little worn. The elves there laughed and sang, but all their songs were sad and world-weary. Necrad was cruel and uncaring, and if songs ever echoed down those eerie streets, she guessed they were the wailing of banshees. There was nothing faded about the city. It was scarred and broken in places, but she could feel a terrible, sinful thrill as she looked at Necrad as if she was spying on something forbidden. It was a nightmare city, beautiful as a poisonous serpent, cold as bone – but it was not *sad*. Anger ran through the stone like bile.

Torun gestured out of the window. "For thousands of years, this city was ruled by the Witch Elves. No human nor dwarf could have beheld this in all those many lifetimes. My people fought many wars against the Witch Elves, battling to hold the mountain passes against their armies, and in all that time we never came within sight of the city's outer walls. To see the city like this would have been unthinkable even thirty years ago. The world has changed in a heartbeat."

"Thirty years is hardly a heartbeat."

"For a human, maybe it's a long time. The oldest dwarves reach more than ten times that. And the elves are eternal." Torun sighed. "I envy them. So much time to learn and work. I've chased magic for thirty years, and learned nothing worthy of note. But now . . ." She turned and bowed to Olva. "You're in Necrad now, in the house of the Lammergeier. And while he is . . . not quite as I imagined him, he shall help you, and that's right and proper. But this was never my quest."

"What are you saying?"

"I'm not going far, and will still be at hand if you need me. But I've sought magic for years, and now here we are in the city of sorcery." She crossed the room and laid her hand on the damaged stone. Her little hand pushed into the crack, probing for the secrets beneath the marble. "The elves of old built Necrad to study the power of the stars. As above, so below – this city is the point of balance, the mid-point between the celestial firmament and the realms below. It's a tool, a mill for magic." Her fingers picked at the crumbling wall as she spoke. "Here is magic a dwarf might learn."

"I don't know how I can ever repay you," said Olva. "You saved my life in the Fossewood, and at sea. After Bor, I feared to trust anyone, but you were as good a travelling companion as I could have dreamed. I'm thankful the Intercessors set you in my path."

The dwarf bowed. "All the dwarves owe the Nine more than can be counted. If I had helped you, then it is only a small payment towards that mountain of debt. But I would ask a favour, if I may."

"Of course."

Torun pointed towards the centre of Necrad, where a dark tower rose taller than any of the other buildings. "That is the Wailing Tower, the sanctum of Master Blaise. The college in Summerswell would not teach me magic, nor would any of the hedge-schools or the wizards who graduated from there. It is whispered that Master Blaise takes apprentices, and that he is not beholden to Summerswell. Will you ask your brother to speak to Master Blaise on my behalf?"

"You should ask Alf yourself, but I'm sure he'll say yes. Whether he holds any sway over Blaise, I don't know." Blaise had taken refuge in Ersfel, too, that night – a sickly little wretch, like a sack of chicken bones. He'd slept in Olva's own bed, in fact. A distant memory of her blanket smelling like burned hair afterwards.

Torun bowed again. "If Blaise will not take me as a student, then . . . I'll find magic here, even if I have to dig for it. I swear I won't leave this city until I've mastered it."

"You're welcome to it. I want to be done with Necrad as soon as I can." *Find Derwyn, then the first ship south. Or sea-serpent. Or dragon. Failing all those, the Road.* The thought of walking back to

Summerswell, through the hellish lands of the Charnel and the mountains of the Dwarfholt, no longer seemed as unthinkable as it once had. She'd made it here; she'd make it home again.

A knock on the front door echoed through the empty house. Olva descended the stairs, the chill of the marble seeping through her elf-boots. Torun followed her, and Olva was both amused and heartened to see that the dwarf had found a crossbow somewhere in Alf's arsenal. "Just in case," said Torun.

The creature at the door was another of the Vatlings. It bowed and introduced itself as Threeday. It knew who Olva was without being told, which did not endear it to her. "Lady Forster, the greatest pleasure. Welcome to Necrad. I fear I must steal your brother away immediately."

"He's in here." She showed Threeday into the side room where Alf slept. He'd fallen asleep sitting in a chair, his hand resting on the sword. She'd often fallen asleep the same way by the fire, with Cu on her foot. The sword was more watchful than the dog – a red light flickered in its gemstone eye. Somehow, without speaking, it woke Alf.

"Threeday. You came," he said around a yawn. Olva went to the kitchen to brew some tea to wake him up properly.

"I was sent to fetch you to the council, Sir Lammergeier. I have a carriage waiting. I would not recommend walking – the dwarves are sick with grief. But first, I am told you were looking for me. How can I serve?"

"I'm looking for a fellow called Lyulf Martens. I'm guessing you know him."

"In passing. A merchant operating out of Ellsport. Arshoth stock, I believe, though you are all out of the same vat to my eyes."

"A blood trader," added Torun, shaking her crossbow for emphasis. The Vatling nodded.

"You might very well think that. I couldn't possibly comment. You are new to Necrad, mistress dwarf, so let me urge a little caution. It is dangerous to ask too much about those involved the trade, and even more perilous to meddle in their affairs."

"Would you give the same advice to me, Threeday?" rumbled Alf.

"To you I would say: speak to the Lady Berys."

"She's not around, though, is she? No one's heard from her in days. At council, you said she's fucked off south on some mysterious errand."

"I may," said Threeday, "have been misinformed on that topic."

Alf tapped Spellbreaker's tip on the ground, and the whole mansion quivered. "So, tell me of Martens."

The Vatling studied the stubs of its fingers – it had no fingernails, but mimicked the human gesture. "I know he once served Berys, and grew rich in her service. Of late, though, I have heard whispers that there is strife between the Lady's followers."

Alf scowled. "Is that where Berys has been all this time? Off putting the boot into some of her thieves?" He looked over at Olva. "She was lecturing me about how I shouldn't go looking for Lath, and how I'd make trouble if I went off kicking in doors. And all the while she's piling bodies in the gutter, is that it?"

"There has been bloodshed," said the Vatling, "but from what I can gather, it was Berys who had the worse of it."

Olva glanced back at Alf through the open door. A confused expression crossed his face, as if he was hurt that Berys had not called on him to help. Olva wondered how much of the slimy creature's tale was true. "Is Berys hurt?"

"I do not know. Some whisper that she has fled the city. Others say ... otherwise. Certainly, many of her followers have fled, or switched their allegiance. It is whispered that there shall soon be a new master in the underworld, and a wise man – or Vatling – would align themselves with this new power. I do not pry too much into things that do not concern me. But I am loyal above all to Necrad, and I do what seems best for the city. So please, lord, we must go to the council."

"Wait a moment." Alf hauled himself to his feet. He leaned on the sword for support. "Ol, I'm summoned to the council. I owe it to Gundan and Thurn to tell the tale of how they died. I don't know what's to be done, but Laerlyn and Blaise are clever. They'll guide us. And Threeday here," Alf tapped the sword again, making the house quake. "Threeday will find Lyulf Martens for me."

The Vatling gave Olva a sickly wave. "I shall make such investigations as I can."

"And then we'll get your boy back."

Alf took the sword and climbed into the carriage with the Vatling. Olva stood by the door, watching the crowds go by on the street outside. Twice on this journey she'd put her trust in another, and twice they'd failed her. Alf had made finding Derwyn sound so simple, so certain, that she wanted very much to trust him, to put it all in his hands and lie down and rest, just for a little while.

But she could not trust him, so she stayed there, watching the city prepare for war.

CHAPTER THIRTY-FOUR

"Let us begin," said Vond. The young lord was back at his place at the head of the table. His long-fingered hands were splayed out against the dark wood, as if assuring himself of its solidity. Servants had nailed the council table back together after Gundan had smashed it, a hasty repair covering up a mortal wound. A great snowdrift of papers sat in front of Vond, accounts of the state of the city's defences and other matters. A chill breeze blew through from the open window, rustling the pages.

"Our scouts have seen little sign of the Wilder. The lakeside at Bavduin—"

Alf interrupted Vond. "Shouldn't we wait for Blaise and Laerlyn?"

"While I am told that the princess has returned to the city, she has not yet made herself known to me. As for Master Blaise, I sent messengers to fetch him, and they were turned away at his tower. I am not minded to wait for the others of the Nine to stir themselves. The city is in the hands of this council, Sir Lammergeier. We cannot tarry."

Alf propped Spellbreaker against the empty chair next to him and sat. Blaise's seat was empty. So was Berys'. Only the Piteous Seat was occupied, and Threeday had his hands folded and his head bowed, as if praying he'd become invisible. Certainly, he carefully avoided meeting Alf's eye.

Along the table, Alf marked the Abbess Marit. To his surprise, she did not react when he entered, and seemed unmarked by her brief imprisonment. She whispered prayers with a beatific smile on her lined face. It made her look almost young.

Next to her were three fresh-faced knights he could not name, though two of them looked familiar. One was the image of Duna when he was young, and Alf guessed it was the earl's oldest boy, the one named for Alf. He was supposed to be down south. The second knight Alf had seen at some tourney or other. The third just looked annoyingly young. All three wore fine armour, laden with charm-stones and other magic. A gaggle of boys.

He glanced at the shields hanging behind them on the wall – a golden lion rampant on one, the next a white bird with Castle Duna and the arms of Erdys' father Lord Brychan. The third was a confus-ing mess that would take a herald to interpret, but Alf guessed the third lad was a minor noble of some obscure family, of much lesser stature than the other two.

One of them leaned over to his comrade and whispered loud enough for Alf to hear: "*That* is the Lammergeier? Well, he looks like a plucked vulture, I suppose."

Alf felt like a prisoner in the dock before a jury of children. "Who are these lads?"

"Knights of Summerswell, led by Sir Prelan. The first re-inforcements to arrive from the south – and likely the last before the Wilder reach us. Sir Prelan and his company rode at great speed through the Clawlands, making the journey from the Cleft of Ard to Necrad in ten days; in any other assembly, it would be a considered an astounding feat."

"The Intercessors said there would be hope unlooked for," mut-tered Marit.

The third knight reached across the table to Alf. "Beloved cousin, it is good to meet you—"

"Beloved cousin," scoffed Alf, "who the fuck are you?"

"Why, I am Eddard Forster, sir, and we are cousins by marriage. My own uncle Galwyn, Intercessors guard his soul, was wed to thy sister Olva." The lad preened, as if all that meant something. "It was only a few weeks ago that news of our family's connection to the noble Lammergeier became known, but I have always felt since I was a little boy that we had an unspoken bond, a kindred spirit, a—"

"Aye, aye." It unsettled Alf that people had connected the Lammergeier to Olva and Ersfel.

"As I said," continued Vond, "the lakeside was deserted. We sent the best soldiers in Necrad with you, Sir Lammergeier, outfitted with the finest treasures of the arsenal – what became of them?"

"I don't know. I didn't see. A few of Duna's men got away, I know that much."

"Does my father live?" asked Duna's boy. Young Sir Aelfric sounded utterly disinterested, as if asking about the weather. His doublet was embroidered with the image of a snowy white Lammergeier.

"I pray he got away," said Alf, "but I can't swear it."

"The House of Duna is blessed by the Intercessors," said Marit, "they will guard him."

Vond ignored the Abbess. "Sir Lammergeier, what happened at Bavduin?"

"The Wilder met with us under a sign of peace, as they promised. Thurn was there, Lath . . . and Thurn's daughter."

"The one who calls herself Death?" laughed Sir Prelan.

"Gundan bargained with Thurn, and had him talked into a sort of truce when it all went to shit. Then someone threw a spell-skull – the sort that opens old wounds."

"A curse of necrosis," supplied Threeday, quietly. "I believe there are a few in the city's arsenal, but not many."

"It was someone on our side, though I didn't see who threw it. The skull affected everyone, even *her*. The Wilder thought we'd played them falsely. They attacked us." He closed his eyes, and the memory of Gundan's death filled his mind once more. He tried to think back, to describe what had happened before the world shattered, but it was all a confusion of shouting. "Thurn . . . Gundan . . . they fought. Thurn was slain. The skull got broken, and she regained her power. She called down a thunderbolt." Alf tapped the hilt of Spellbreaker. "My sword shielded me. Others . . . they were incinerated. I saw Gundan die. She burned him to ash."

The dwarf Gamling slammed his fist into the broken table, making it creak alarmingly. "My cousin must be avenged! The Wilder girl must die!" Gamling wore a gold chain of office now, and the Dwarfholt banner hung above his seat. Through these subtle clues, Alf guessed that Gamling had been appointed the representative for the Dwarfholt.

"At the last council," hissed Abbess Marit, "I said just such a thing. And you conspired with Lord Gundan and the Lammergeier to take authority from Lord Vond. You assaulted me on the very steps of this citadel!"

A shouted argument broke out. Alf let the noise of the dispute wash over him. He stared at the gash in the table left by Gundan's axe.

Vond raised a hand for silence. "Now is not the time to discuss the errors of the last council. Death is quite literally coming for us all." He let out a little bark of almost hysterical laughter at his own jest, and his hand flew to his mouth to stifle it. "If the Wilder-host marched straight for Necrad, then they might be at our gates within three days. If they turn aside to strike at Castle Duna, that might delay them by another two or three days."

"My father's castle cannot be taken—" began young Aelfric, but old Aelfric just shook his head gravely and the boy fell silent.

"In any event, it seems we are heavily outnumbered. Thurn has drawn a great many Wilder clans together, and we have no idea of the full size of their host. Nor can we expect reinforcement from the

Dwarfholt or Summerswell in time. We must hold the city walls if we are to have any hope."

"The Intercessors promise help will arrive," proclaimed Marit. The young knights struggled to look suitably pious, even as Sir Aelfric the Younger nudged Sir Prelan. Alf rolled his eyes.

"We shall of course pray that we are worthy of Intercession," said Vond. Again, he fought for composure. He waved a hand, indicating that someone else should speak.

Alf forced himself to speak. "Thurn's dead. He was chieftain of the As Gola. There'll be a funeral lasting seven days. We have that much time." *I could fly north on a dreadworm. I could be there.*

Gamling snorted. "They're fools if they stop to mourn in the midst of war. I'll wager they're already on the march."

"If the spell-skulls work," suggested Threeday, "then that at least is some help."

"We'd need to get close enough to use the damn things," said Gamling. "And they're not going to agree to another parley."

"Master Blaise spoke of waking the Stone Dragons," said the Vatling. "Those weapons foiled the previous attempt to besiege Necrad."

"Master Blaise is less likely to bestir himself," said Vond, "than the Intercessors. He hides in his tower, emerging only to give dire warnings."

"I did not ride all the way from Summerswell to hide in a tower, or behind walls," declared Sir Prelan. "If the solution to holding the city is slaying this Changeling child before she can lay siege to us, then let us do it! We have cavalry; the Wilder do not. My fellow knights are well equipped with charmstones and enchanted weapons; the Wilder have sticks and spears. Let us sally forth and strike the head from the serpent." The boy's face was flush with excitement. Sir Prelan was of an age with Vond. Children trying to fight wars.

Alf shook his head. "In case you hadn't noticed, there's naught but mud out there beyond the walls. If we were another month into winter, then maybe the ground would bear your weight. But now, no – the Wilder will have sport using you for target practice while you wade through the mire."

Prelan snapped his fingers. "A map, please." One of his aides ran forward and unrolled a map of the terrain around Necrad across the table, hiding the scar left by the axe. The map was of recent make, with Necrad and all the surrounding lands neatly labelled in the tongue of Summerswell, and little League banners fluttering over the turrets of the city. It depicted Necrad as a city of straight streets and neat little houses, wisps of smoke rising from chimneys, even a little peasant working in the fields outside. A fiction drawn by those who'd never seen the north.

Sir Prelan gave Alf a pitying look. "I may be new to these lands, but I have an Aelfric in my company, just as the Peerless did. Your namesake, Aelfric son of Duna, rides by my side, and he knows the battlefield as well as any man." Prelan traced his finger along the line of the Road, past the stone dragon. "The Road north of Necrad is on a raised causeway, well above the Charnel. The Wilder will use that route, and no doubt the Changeling will be at their head. We sally forth along the Road and slay her, then fall back to the walls. And if we cannot make our retreat, so be it – better to die on the field with sword in hand than behind a wall. If we must perish, let it be an ending worthy of song!"

"It'll be a short bloody song – the ballad of the knights who got blasted to cinders!"

"You survived," spat Gamling. "She called down the lightning at Bavduin, too, you said, and yet here you are, Lammergeier. Not a mark on you."

"I have Spellbreaker."

"And still you failed," said Vond quietly. "For all your boasts about slaying monsters, you failed to rid us of this peril. Perhaps it is time for another hand to wield the blade, while the Lammergeier takes on another duty more suited to a man of his years. Sir Lammergeier, will you yield the sword to a champion of the council's choosing?"

Whether Vond meant to punish Alf for his disobedience, or if he held Alf responsible for what had happened at Bavduin, Alf could not say. But old shame gnawed at him. A rustic oaf, a farm boy without name or title – he had no place in this high council.

"The sword," continued Lord Vond, "is our best weapon against the Changeling – I propose that another wield it, one whose skill and vigour are unquestionable. Sir Prelan, maybe. What say you?"

"Do I get a say in this?" Spellbreaker's voice rang out in the council chamber. Abbess Marit made the sign against evil; the smile faded from Sir Prelan's face.

"Pay no attention to the spirit of the blade," said Vond. "It is known to be malicious. Sir Lammergeier, silence the sword."

Prelan stood. "I shall take the blade!"

Alf laid a hand on Spellbreaker's hilt. "You bloody well won't." He fought the instinct to cut the young wretch down to size. He could take the blade and show all of them, take all their scorn and condescension and their mealy mouthed, grudging praise and show them true power. He'd killed Lord Bone! He was one of the Nine – what had any of them done to compare? He fought the urge down, but his grip on the sword tightened.

"There would be no dishonour in it, cousin," said the Forster knight. "All of Summerswell knows you are the greatest living knight, the hero of the Nine. But there is a season to all things. What better symbol of renewal and hope could there be than passing such a symbol of past victories on to a new champion? Just as Sir Peir the Paladin entrusted the black sword to you, so you could pass it to another! A grand ceremony, to inspire the city defenders."

Alf lifted his sword and placed it heavily on the table in front of him, like a wall of iron.

"It's my sword," said Alf, "and it's a shit idea."

Vond stared coldly across the sword. "In my capacity as the

representative of the Lords of Summerswell, I order Aelfric Lammergeier, sworn knight of Summerswell, to yield the blade."

From outside, Alf heard the tap-tap of a wizard's staff on the tiled floor. The doors of the council chamber flew open of their own accord.

"Aelfric will do no such thing," declared a musical voice. "The Nine entrusted Spellbreaker to him and no other." Laerlyn strode into the council chamber and took a seat at Alf's side. Blaise followed her, but he remained standing, leaning on his staff.

"I bring word from the Erlking," said Laerlyn. "The elves will join in the defence of the city. I will have my brother send the warfleet from the Isle of Dawn."

"And what of Death?" asked Threeday.

In answer, Laerlyn placed the bow *Morthus* on the table, alongside Spellbreaker. "I swore an oath to watch over this city. I shall meet Death with death, and I am not afraid."

"Hope unlooked for!" proclaimed Marit.

"Hardly," grumbled Gamling. "You block the seas, denying us easy reinforcement from the south until the enemy is at our doorstep, then conveniently show up in the nick of time? What price will we pay for this rescue?"

Laerlyn glanced at Alf. "That's a matter for the Nine. For now, know that the Wood Elves join the League in the defence of Necrad. We shall stand with you against the eldest of terrors."

Snow had begun to fall while they were closeted in council, and now lay thick on the cold stone of the city as Alf and his friends walked down the great steps of the citadel. It felt to Alf like they were mourners at a secret funeral.

"I wish I had been there, Aelfric," said Laerlyn. "It saddens me to think that Gundan and I were at odds when he died."

"You weren't," said Alf. "He spoke fondly of you, before the end."

"Liar. Gundan never spoke fondly of anything except his axe and food. But he was my friend." Laerlyn glanced up at the dwarven guards on a nearby watchtower. "I remember when the dwarves first used bane-metal against the Witch Elves. Gundan was so afraid that I would be hurt, he fetched this huge tower-shield that would have been big even in Thurn's hands. He insisted on standing in front of me whenever they fired bane-metal bolts, in case one ricocheted. I once caught him going through my bedroll with his beard comb, in case a shard of metal might cut me in my sleep." She wiped away a tear. Alf put his arm across her shoulders. "Thurn, too. It's too much, too fast. You're all slipping away from me. Stop dying, damn you." She pressed her head against his chest.

"Death herself is on the march," intoned Blaise. The wizard stood off to the side, away from the other two. "None of us may escape the Grey Lands."

"At least we'll go together," muttered Alf. The thought that they might all perish side by side was oddly comforting.

Blaise tapped his staff on the steps, as if testing them to see if they were hollow. "Vond has clearly lost confidence in you, Aelfric. He will bring up another as representative of the League."

"Little prick," spat Alf. "I tried to do right by the boy when I came back, out of love for his father, but I won't be ordered about by a lad who's barely out of breeches."

"There's all of twenty years between you," said Laerlyn.

"Listen!" said Blaise. "With Berys and Gundan gone, that removes our dominance of the council. The Nine will no longer control—"

"That's what you're worried about?" shouted Alf. Death was all around them – their friends had fallen in battle, enemies were marching on their city, and they were running out of time – and yet Blaise was talking about the bloody council?

"Yes!" hissed Blaise. "I can concern myself with more than one thing at a time. I can mourn without wailing or getting drunk, and I can consider what will happen should we *succeed* as well as the consequences of failure. If we die, we die. If we live, we shall have lost our control of the council and Necrad."

"Who gives a damn?"

"We swore an oath, Aelfric," said Laerlyn, "to watch over the city. Blaise is not wholly wrong."

The wizard inclined his head. "Thank you, princess."

"You're not *right*, either, for pity's sake. You talk like my father's advisers, moving their little pieces around the board, anticipating distant futures that never come to pass. Stop thinking like an elf, Blaise. Be what you are."

"I and I alone decide what I am," snapped Blaise, "and if I choose to contemplate my future beyond the next three days, it is not a mark of disrespect for the fallen. Thurn fought for a cause that seemed equally hopeless, after all. This is our city."

Laerlyn took a few steps away from them. Her face seemed to shift, her head bowing slightly under the weight of an unseen crown. "You both know that my father's court was divided on the matter of Necrad and the Witch Elves. There are some in the Everwood who would see this city reduced to ash and its inhabitants slain or driven out."

"Aye, so you said."

"If you leave your defeated foes with only ash, then they have nothing left to live for but revenge. I will see Necrad preserved, Alf, but there are costs. I had to make promises. The blood trade must end, no matter what."

"That'll piss off Berys. And the Witch Elves."

"Let her be angry. It is the right thing to do." Laerlyn turned to Blaise. "The second price is this: you must yield up the Wailing Tower. The secrets of Lord Bone cannot be left in the care of one mortal man."

"Well, at least the Masters of the College Arcane have finally spoken. I have known for a long time that the College dares not open a book without permission from the Everwood, and I tire of tormenting the spies they send to me as students. Better that they challenge me openly, for I will not give up the Tower." Blaise turned and began to walk down the steps. Laerlyn sprang after him and caught his arm.

"They will come after you, Blaise. As the lustre of the Nine's legend fades, how will you hold the Tower? They will brand you a criminal, or a heretic. Why do you think I made sure Aelfric kept Spellbreaker? If one of Vond's knights held that sword, what would you do when they broke down your door?"

"I am not without recourse, even against that blade. But Aelfric wields it, and I do not believe that Aelfric would strike me down."

"Can we talk about something other than killing each other?" snapped Alf.

Blaise stood in silence for a long moment, as if deeply pondering the question, then offered, almost shyly: "I decoded the seal on the ninety-third volume of Lord Bone's spells."

There was another long moment of silence.

"Well then," said Alf.

"It was nice to meet your sister again," said Laerlyn, "if ill-timed."

"Aye, well," said Alf. "Her boy's got into trouble. I've set Threeday looking for him."

"Children," Laerlyn said in wonder, "children having children. You humans could fill the world in a century, if you could be at peace."

"What is the boy's name?" asked Blaise.

"Derwyn."

The wizard scratched a rune into the snow at their feet and muttered a few words of power. The snow melted, and the steam hung in the air for a few heartbeats before blowing away. "Inconclusive, but that means little. If divinations worked reliably here, none of us would be alive today. I shall try more potent spells from my tower if I have time."

"Find Berys, too, if you can," said Laerlyn. "There's too much left unsaid."

"We shall not see her again, I think." Blaise pointed his staff at Laerlyn. "May you have good fortune on the battlefield. I shall send what help I can, but until the city burns and Death takes me, I shall continue my research. If you bother me, I may disintegrate you. Good day."

Alf snapped his fingers. "Oh, my sister came here with a dwarf. She wants to study magic. She's cracked about it, Olva says. Will you take her as a prentice?"

"Dwarves can't do magic, Alf," laughed Laerlyn. "It's not in their nature."

Blaise arched an eyebrow. "Send her to my Tower, and I shall make use of her." He departed, leaning heavily on his staff.

Laerlyn watched him go. "His arrogance will be the death of him, Aelfric. If he refuses to give up his secrets, then suspicion will grow. Blaise is just the sort of person to try ill-conceived magical experiments. He'll drag us all down, I fear."

Alf sat down on the steps of the citadel. "This is it, isn't it? The end of the Nine. Half of us are dead or gone, and you're talking about bringing down Blaise and Berys. Even if they go quietly, they'll be gone. There'll be no more . . . us."

Laerlyn sat next to him and rested her head on his shoulder. "I know. Our fellowship is fading. My family warned me not to grow too close to mortals. There is never enough time. Not for merriment and joy, nor for great deeds and struggles – and certainly not to correct mistakes. Ends come quicker than you expect, and so much is left half done, or unsaid."

They rested in silence, and it struck Alf that all the fates of the fallen Nine were ignominious. Thurn, slain by misfortune. Lath, a mad traitor. Gundan, dead and not even a thimbleful of ash to bury. Jan, vanished from the world. Now Blaise and Berys, too – their legends soiled, their tales becoming grubby, sordid tales of obsession or greed. No wonder all the stories of heroes ended in hasty happily-ever-afters, and never spoke of what might happen after. The heroes put the world to rights, and then it all stayed right for ever.

Or death. That was the other good ending. A good death, to cut the hero down in their prime, and preserve them for ever at their moment of glory. Peir had died well.

Suddenly, the thought of facing Death again did not seem so dreadful. For all Laerlyn's promises of aid from the elves, for all the youthful strength of Sir Prelan and his knights, and for all the magic they could bring to bear, Alf still could not guess at their chances of defeating the child. At the very least, though, they could make it a good ending.

Laerlyn glanced back at the citadel behind them. "I will remain here, after you are all gone."

"Assuming we can stop Death."

"Assuming that. I will sit on the council with Vond, and Gamling, and the others, and watch over the city. I won't abandon my oath."

"There's a Witch Elf I met. Ildorae. It was her dagger you took. She tried to kill Lord Bone. Put her on the council, Lae. Someone should speak for the Witch Elves."

"Very well."

"And there's the elf lad I hurt when I went into the Liberties. I've been feeding him blood. I don't know what to do about that."

"I will be kind to him. Children are precious to the elves."

"And to the rest of us. Thurn went into death's kingdom to bring back his daughter." He sighed. "Whichever side wins, Lae, they'll tell stories about how they were the heroes. And they'll be right, too. We were lucky – we saw real darkness, and we knew we stood in the light. It's not always so clear."

"It was never clear, Aelfric, even then. You were just young." Laerlyn took his hand, their fingers interlacing. Her fingers were slim and perfect, his callused and bloodied. "Thank you for trying to make a peace with the Wilder."

"Didn't work, though."

"No. But you and Gundan tried, and I love you for it."

Alf felt he had to be honest. "Gundan wanted to keep the Wood

Elves out of Necrad. He was willing to bargain the city away rather than let your kin have it."

Laerlyn laughed. "I can love him and mourn him and want to strangle him all at once, Alf. I understood Gundan better than he knew. I was a Princess of the Everwood long before he became a general of the Dwarfholt." She released his hand. "Speaking of which – I must go. The Isle of Dawn must be called to war once more – and this time there'll be no need to throw my brother over any balconies. Take care of your sister, Aelfric. I'll be back soon to stand by your side."

"You think we can win?"

"Jan saw a darkness rising. She called us back together for a reason. Of course the Nine will triumph." Laerlyn embraced him, then climbed onto the back of her dragon. She raised her bow *Morthus* in salute. Alf lifted Spellbreaker in answer.

"*Morthus lae-necras I'unthuul amortha*," said the sword. "Before you ask."

"Prophecies," said Alf, "aren't worth shit."

CHAPTER THIRTY-FIVE

T hey waited, and the whole city waited with them.

Alf returned to the house. He talked about death in a way that Olva did not understand, as if death was a person he had met and fought before, an old friend he was eager to see again, but she didn't push for any more explanation. He was very much Sir Lammergeier that evening, a stranger to her, and her brother was very far away.

Threeday. Alf had said Threeday would find Derwyn. So Olva sat by that topmost window, watching and waiting. Carts bearing heavy loads of stone rolled by; soldiers marched north and citizens fled south. Slowly, slowly, the day wore on. In the sunless city, only the slow drip of the candle confirmed the day was passing. The Isle of Dawn had seemed timeless, but that had been tranquil and pleasant, a long lazy summer afternoon. Necrad's time was lying awake in the small hours before dawn, sick with nameless dread.

She complained to Alf. He grunted that war was mostly waiting the way adventuring was mostly walking. His response infuriated her, and she went back up to the seat by the window. Gloom deepened into night. Wraiths came crawling out of the cracks in the mortar, and she lit another candle to drive them away.

Olva sat there all night, sleepless, powerless. She had stared out at Necrad for many hours now, and she swore the city was toying with her. The general hideous outline of the place was unchanged, and the major landmarks like the Wailing Tower were fixed, but the streets seemed to subtly twist to reveal new incomprehensible architecture, new eerie vistas. She imagined that the stone of the buildings was not solid at all, but was instead the brittle carapaces of beetles, and that if she moved too suddenly, they would take flight. She found herself staring at windows and balconies, as if a twitching curtain might reveal her son's face.

Derwyn, she prayed, *where are you?*

The morning came. Torun left for Blaise's tower, promising that she would always be a stalwart friend, swearing that she would see Olva again soon. Olva watched the dwarf shuffle awkwardly down the street, head bowed, departing from her life as suddenly as she had entered it. The city swallowed her in its vastness.

They did not leave the mansion, but they could not hide from the city. Runners and heralds came to the door. None brought news of Derwyn; they spoke of Wilder hunting parties, of scouting reports and divinations. Lord Vond sent messengers to summon Aelfric to the walls, but Alf did not go. He sat with Olva, waiting for Threeday to return.

"Shouldn't we go out looking for him?"

"Everyone in this city knows me," said Alf. "I'd be a bull chasing a rat. I've put a dog on its trail, and when Threeday finds this Martens I'll step on him. But for now, we've got to wait."

The day wore on. Olva remembered the war in Ersfel, when her parents had huddled in their little hut, and there was talk of Wilder in the woods and Witch Elves in the air. Now, she was in a great mansion far from home, but the fear was the same.

She went out to the Garrison market. The storehouses were bare; the only food Olva had found was a little grain and some vegetables she did not recognise, so she threw them in a pottage. She and Alf ate in silence; her ribcage was full of fluttering fears, so she had no appetite, but Alf methodically demolished his portion.

The war began in the sky the next day. The canopy of the necromiasma that hung over the city twisted like a sail. Wild winds came howling from the north, heavy with snow and biting ice. This north wind was answered by a steady wind from the east, a spear of summer that made Olva think of the high seat atop the Isle of Dawn. The two winds clashed above the city, rending the clouds. The sudden change in the weather alarmed Alf; he grabbed his sword, as if attack might come at any moment. But the storm blew on, and no enemy appeared.

That evening she heard cheering from the streets outside. The harbour was suddenly full of green sails, and the white wakes of sea-serpents. As Laerlyn had promised, the elves of Dawn had come to the defence of the city.

A note came from Threeday. Alf handed it to Olva to read. It was full of indirection and equivocation, and mentioned no names at all, but the gist was that he was on the trail of the merchant in question, that he believed the precious cargo was in the city, and that he had the matter well in hand.

Alf went out that night. Where, he did not say. Olva guessed that he went up to the citadel, where Princess Laerlyn feasted with Lord Vond, and the crowds cheered the sight of the elven knights riding through the streets of Necrad. He came back hours later, a fresh bandage on his wrist. His breathing was laboured, and he fell asleep in his chair again. And he brought no news of Derwyn.

Squires from the citadel arrived an hour after dawn to help Alf don his armour. They laid out his dwarf-forged plate mail, his scabbard adorned with charmstones, his shield with the sign of the Lammergeier. Alf stood there as they dressed him in a doublet of elven-cloth, as they cut his beard and placed upon his head a visored helm. Derwyn had wanted to be a squire like that. The first outriders of the Wilder-host had been sighted the day before, the squires said.

"Then they've likely been here for days already," muttered Alf, "and there are plenty of ways into the Liberties and the Sanction. We'll be fighting to hold the Garrison walls within three days, I'll wager." He got up and tested the solidity of one of the recently mended doors, thumping it with his big fist. "I'd put you on a ship back to Ellsport, but I know you won't go. But there are safer places than this house. There's a hall under the citadel where they've put the League officials and wizards and the like – it's well guarded. I could get you in there."

"I'll stay here." In case Derwyn, miraculously, found his way here. In case Threeday came back.

"This is just the start of it," said Alf. "She hasn't been sighted. They'll just be trying us today, testing our resolve. But they don't know the elves are here, and that'll dismay 'em. But if I'm wrong, and things get bad – head to the Wailing Tower."

He called a dreadworm and flew north to the walls.

Olva watched from the balcony window in Alf's house in the Garrison, trying to make sense of what she saw. She'd brought Derwyn to the Highfield fair some years, and watched the tourney there. Even mock-battles like that were confusing – the tourney was fought over a wide stretch of fields, so all she'd seen were tiny figures on horseback away in the distance, too far away to tell what was going on. The battle for Necrad was much worse – she could not tell who was fighting, or where. The cityscape divided the battle up into vignettes, little miniature scenes of carnage framed by towers and palaces. From the balcony, she could see different scenes at once. There, in that alley, a trio of dwarves worked to close up an entrance to the underworld; she saw one dwarf take off his helmet, mop his brow and trade some jest with his companions. They seemed unperturbed by the chaos – but one street over, just out of sight, an undead creature shambled about, spear in hand, hunting for foes. A dead Wilder, resurrected by Death's magic. If it went left, it would find the dwarves in a moment. Olva watched, unable to breath, until the zombie turned right and vanished from her sight.

Distant fires erupted across the city, sometimes accompanied by a flash of magic, well inside the walls. Many of the fires were close to the Wailing Tower, a pillar against the clouds, and she hoped Torun was safe.

By dusk, that first Wilder assault was repulsed.

Olva heard Alf returning in the small hours of the night. By the time she came downstairs from her perch by the window, he was already asleep, lying on a bed that was covered in rubble. She put a blanket over him, then returned to her window. The city outside was full of terrors, but she felt a strange compulsion to watch. She felt like a misplaced tool, a pitchfork or a hammer that had been put on a shelf and forgotten about, bereft of point or purpose, invisible and overlooked. If she opened her mouth, all that would come out was a shriek. At least if she watched, she could bear witness to all the acts of courage and desperation and humanity that would otherwise go unremembered.

When she closed her eyes, she saw Derwyn. Saw him as he was back home, trailing after dreams, falling over his own feet when he should be attending to his chores. Saw him, rapt with attention, firelight dancing in his eyes, as she told him who his uncle was. She saw him as he was when she'd last seen him, falling to the ground as Martens' man clubbed him. Saw him as she imagined him, lying dead and pale in some dungeon in Necrad.

Better not to close her eyes. Better to keep staring out of that window.

Alf brought no news of Derywn.

And no word from Threeday.

*

The next day brought a blizzard like none Olva had seen before. The icy wind from the north cut through the necromiasma again, giving her a glimpse of huge thunderheads like grey cliffs hanging over the city. Snowdrifts choked the streets and turned everyone – elf and dwarf, human and Vatling, rich Garrison merchant and desperate denizen of the Liberties – into snow-mantled shades, all alike, mottled in greenish-white. Olva watched a company of dwarven soldiers fight their way through the drifts, their armour weighing them down. They struggled on, vanishing inch by inch into the green snow, until all that was left of them was a procession of spiked helmets slowly migrating north, and then she could see them no more.

She watched one of the few horses she'd seen in the city stumble in the snow. It fell down in the gutter outside Alf's mansion and would not get up again. One of its legs was twisted in such a way that Olva was certain the shinbone had snapped, and the animal would never rise again. The cart driver clambered down and tried to haul the poor animal back to its feet. When that failed, he whipped it, screaming at it to rise. Something snapped in Olva and she hurried downstairs. She burst out of the door and stormed down the pathway of the mansion, her elven-cloak billowing behind her. She seized the driver's arm and wrenched the whip from him.

"Be off with you!" she roared. The man fled.

She rummaged in Alf's cabinets and found a vial of the healing cordial that Torun had used. She poured some on the mare's leg and dribbled the rest into her mouth. The potion did little for the broken bone, but seemed to ease the creature's pain. She fetched the blanket from Alf's room and spread it out over the dying animal's steaming flank, and she sat and waited in the cold.

The city receded from her. She was distantly aware of the sounds of battle, of whistling arrows and shouts and the roar of beasts. She could hear the clash of sword and spear along the Garrison walls, the blaring of war-horns and the thunder of magic spells, but it was all too vast, too terrible for her. She sat with the horse's head in her lap, soothing her, listening to her laboured breathing.

"It's all right, girl. It's all right," she whispered. "Just rest."

The mare knew nothing of the Wilder, nothing of Necrad. Unlike everyone else in this cursed city, she had not heard the songs of the Nine, or the war against Lord Bone. For the horse, thought Olva, the world must be a terrible confusion, an uproar of suffering, dragged this way and that for reasons you cannot comprehend. What must the horse think of Necrad, of this landscape of hard stone and choking vapours? She did not understand why she had been brought so far from home to die. The beast's life was spent in harness, and she had never known anything else. Her fate was to serve and eventually to die according to the unknowable dictates of her masters.

A shadow passed over her. A dreadworm landed heavily on the street, and Alf nearly fell from it. He clutched his side, his fingers pressed over a gash in his armour. "It's all right," he gasped, "I just ran out of potions. One of the dead Wilder got her claws into me." He lifted his hand and swore at the sight of blood. "We're holding our own. It's bloody work up on the wall, Ol. For every one of ours, they lose five or six of theirs. I don't understand it." He shook his head. "Prelan and your cousin were keeping count of their kills. Prelan hit forty-odd, last I heard." He spat. "I need a cordial."

He drew Spellbreaker and slashed the head from the dreadworm before stumbling into the house, leaving red footprints in the snow. She heard him throwing furniture around inside as he searched for another cache of healing cordials.

He staggered out again, revived. He stopped by the horse.

"What happened?"

"The ice. She broke her leg."

The scrape of the sword leaving the scabbard. "I'll make it quick." And then he was gone again.

*

Olva left the mare's carcass on the road. She went into the house, and there on the table was a metal box containing another dozen bottles of healing cordial. Every one of them was a life, a mortal wound healed. She snatched them up, bundled them in her arms and walked out of the door of the mansion before her fear could follow her.

She followed the sound of fighting, and it brought her to one of the walls of the Garrison. When the Nine had divided up Necrad, they'd drawn the dividing lines along the streets, so the 'wall' was mostly made up of existing buildings, their doors and windows bricked up and the gaps between them filled in with rubble. These internal walls were far less secure than the outer walls of the city, even in disrepair, and it was here that the Wilder had pushed the hardest. Olva flinched as several arrows came arcing over the wall from the Liberties side, and pressed herself into the safety of a doorway until the volley was done.

A League soldier spotted her. "Get back to the citadel!" he roared, pointing back the way she'd come.

"I want to help. I have these!" She proffered the vials of cordial.

"Follow me."

He led here through the ruins, climbing over old rubble and fresh snowfall, and brought her to a long, low building. Lights burned behind the shattered glass of the stained windows. She entered through a gateway that reminded her of the tithing-gate in Ellsport, and discovered that the place was a hospital for the wounded and the dying. The injured lay on benches, and the room was filled with groans and gasps of pain, each soldier intent on his own suffering. All was overseen by an old priestess in a brown robe, who snapped instructions at the staff of the little hospital, most of whom were Vatlings. They moved about unhurriedly, undisturbed by the carnage or the priestess's demands that they hurry.

On seeing Olva, the old priestess apparently mistook her for a runner from the League citadel.

"I knew old Urien had squirrelled more of the stuff away," she crowed, snatching a vial from Olva's hands. "Be careful with it. We don't have enough to spare to ease the pain of mortal wounds." The old woman leaned in close. "And don't let those Vatling get their slimy hands on any. They'll steal it and sell it back to us!"

Olva did not bother correcting the priestess. She got to work, and there was plenty to be done. The few other human attendants were all many years younger than Olva, little more than children in some cases. They all seemed a little stunned, and Olva could imagine why. Necrad meant something very different to them; to her, it had always been a name out of nightmare, the dread city of evil, but for those too young to remember the war it was a city of opportunity, the place you went to seek your fortune. They'd come here looking for new lives, and suddenly they were in the midst of death. They were in need of guidance, and the old priestess offered only preaching and platitudes.

Olva offered practicality. She had them fetch more blankets and stoke fires, had some of them tearing sheets for bandages, had others move furniture around to create space where it was needed. She sent one running back to the citadel, and told the girl to say that Sir Aelfric Lammergeier demanded more healing cordials. And if the Citadel had none, they were to go to the Wailing Tower and ask for Torun. Olva hurled herself into the work; doing something was better than just watching.

Only the foot soldiers of the League and the volunteer defenders of the city came through the door. If a great knight was wounded despite whatever charmstones and magic armour he wore, then he would be taken back to the citadel immediately. The greatest knights had wizards in their retinue, too, to treat their wounds. Not for them the little makeshift hospital.

Some of those who came down off the walls were only lightly injured. Olva had dealt with many wounds – a farmhand who'd fallen from the roof and cracked his head on the stones, or one who'd been gored by the village bull, accidents with scythes and flails. And Derwyn, too, had been a medical text in one little body, demonstrating every possible scrape and bruise and fever. She could wash out a wound and bind it, and a splash of magic cordial ensured there would be no infection.

Those wounded more gravely – a dose of healing cordial might save one – but what about the next wounded soldier to come through the door? She had to judge which had the best prospects of survival. Horribly, she was able for it – on the farm, too, she'd had a sense for which calf would thrive and which would not, and had learned to put aside sentiment and look clear-eyed. But every time, she would wash away the blood, or remove a helmet, and see Derwyn's face. She knew that her son was not here, that he was in some hidden lair of Lyulf Martens', but still, every time there was that little spark of hope mixed with dread.

In the next room, she could hear the old priestess praying that the spirits descend and heal the wounded, barking orders to the Intercessors the same way she talked to the Vatlings, demanding they attended her.

"They harkened to her in Athar," whispered one of the attendants. "An Intercessor flew down at her call and healed the son of Earl Duna. They call him the Miracle Knight now, Idmaer Lackhand."

"Ah, he's the son of an earl," said another. "Of course the heavens rolled back for him. Not for the likes of us. And not here."

The priestess exhausted herself with unanswered prayers, and left the hospital to rest. Night fell over the city, and the fighting dwindled. A wounded soldier explained to Olva that the Wood Elves were night-sighted, and could put an arrow in the heart of a Wilder even in the dimmest glow of the necromiasma, so the Wilder retreated out of reach and took cover by night. Olva found that she resented the relief. When there was no time to rest, there was no time to worry. The silence would let her fear find her.

She need not have worried.

"The Lammergeier!" breathed one of the attendants in disbelief. Alf stood there, silhouetted in the doorway. A soldier tried to cheer, but it ended up a bloody cough.

"Is there news?"

Alf removed his helmet. His face was grim.

CHAPTER THIRTY-SIX

Alf knew what it was like to be hunted by a dark lord. This was different. Something was wrong.

The Wilder attack on Necrad was not what he'd anticipated. He had expected Death to be in the lead, like the Nine had led the assault on Necrad. He'd expected the rising darkness that Jan had warned him about, a shadow out of the north, Death swallowing the horizon. He'd expected a Wilder-host of the living and the dead at her back, the tribes commanded by heroes like Thurn. It was to have been like Daeroch Nal, like Bavduin – the all-consuming thunderbolt shattering the walls of the city.

Instead – the Wilder assault was piecemeal and uncoordinated. They had the advantage of numbers, and their initial attack had all the hallmarks of Thurn's leadership. Sneaking through the Liberties and taking the fight to the streets – Alf could almost hear Thurn's voice ordering that stratagem. Or, knowing Thurn, silently pointing at a map scratched in the dirt until everyone else caught up with his thought.

But after the first day, it all went wrong. The Wilder hurled themselves against the walls and were driven back again and again. They fought with fanatical courage, but courage against stone walls and magic weapons meant nothing. It reminded Alf of Lord Bone's war, when some of the Wilder tribes still worshipped the Witch Elves as gods. They'd fought the same way, desperate to please the divine, offering their deaths as a sacrifice, as proof of devotion.

From the other side, it was butchery.

"It's a stratagem," insisted Lord Vond, "a feint to lure us into squandering our strength on this first wave."

"She's waiting for a challenger," suggested Sir Prelan. "We should send a herald to discuss a time and place for a contest of champions."

"It is a magical rite," intoned one of the League wizards, who advised the council. (Blaise had locked himself in his tower, and showed no interest in the war raging on his doorstep.) "Just as true spell casters draw their magic from the stars, and Changelings from the earth, it follows that Death must draw power from death. Every one of her kinfolk who perishes makes her stronger."

"I saw the fallen she brought back at Bavduin," muttered Alf, "but the Wilder we've killed are staying mostly dead."

"She's mourning her father," said Laerlyn, softly. "Poor Thurn."

"She's already killed you all," cackled Spellbreaker, "and you're wandering the Grey Lands in denial, too stupid to realise what's happened."

Alf crossed over into the Liberties. The Garrison gate was sealed and barred, so he called a dreadworm. The worm was a scrawny specimen; he wondered if the storms that had battered the necromiasma had also damaged the dreadworm flock. Still, it bore him over the walls and into the Liberties.

As he flew, he saw smaller barricades in the streets. The different denizens – the Vatlings, the ogres, the elves – had each marked off a defensible portion of the district, little islands in the tide of invasion. The Vatlings had mostly fled into the Pits; the ogres looked to have been overrun, judging by the titanic corpses littering their enclave. He circled over the House of the Horned Serpent three times, then brought the dreadworm down to land in the courtyard, green snow crunching beneath its scaly belly.

Ildorae prowled from the shadows a few moments later, like an alley cat.

"I thought it was the withered dragon when I saw it first. Where is the Erlking's daughter?"

"Out looking for the rest of the Wilder."

"Then who commands the elven-host?"

"Her brother's here, too."

"Now I know the city is truly doomed, if Maedos Dawn-warden comes to tread upon the ruins. Never has he strayed so far from his fortress."

"It's quite the reunion. I may punch him in the face for old time's sake." Alf climbed down off the dreadworm. Ildorae shied away, staying well out of sword's reach. "How are things here?"

"My city is overrun by mortals. I have taught them once again to fear me – but where once I wielded a heart-seeking bow and a dagger forged by Korthalion himself, now I have only a spear I took from a dead Wilder."

"Lae said that you all can take shelter in the Garrison."

"How kind of you, to offer shelter in the place where the heaviest assault falls. They want to kill you more than they want to kill us, which amuses me." She brandished the spear, and ice gleamed on the tip. "And what price would the Wood Elves demand for their hospitality? To bind ourselves to life-trees perhaps? Do you not know it is unwise to eat or drink the food of the Everwood, lest you remain there for ever?"

"You know the Wilder tribes better than I do. On our side of the wall, we all thought Death would be here blasting the city to rubble by now. We were all set to make a last stand, but now . . . we're pressed in places, but I can't see the Wilder prevailing, not with the way they're fighting. What's changed?"

"The Old Man of the Woods is close. He, too, has left his hiding place in the deep forest, and dared come closer to Necrad than any of his line have in a thousand years. He whips his followers into madness. But of Death, I too have seen no sign." The flash of a wry smile in the moonlight. "Some would prefer that doom fell more swiftly if it is certain to fall."

"Aye." Distant shouts brought Alf's hand to his sword, but the clamour passed and silence returned. "The fear can be the worst thing. You carry it around with you." He'd carried the linnorm out of the Pits for two years. He'd carried the fear of losing the Nine around for ten times longer.

"That is mortal folly. Elves do not give up our lives to dreading what-might-be. Winter always follows summer, and summer rolls round again. We find joy in the moment. Look – I am *happily* killing Wilder, and I should be pleased indeed if I can put this spear through the Old Man." She shivered. "But Death? Death is something strange, and I do not know when she will come for us."

"Behold this wonder," said the sword, "an elf who discovers herself mortal."

Dawn, and Alf walked the north wall of Necrad. Two stone dragons flanked the northern gate, and the walls were fifty feet high. A walkway wide enough to be a great street in any mortal city ran atop the fortification. He nodded at the guards stationed here. There were few enough of them to guard the length of the battlements, but the Wilder had no easy way to scale the sheer wall. And if Death came, then a few men-at-arms would be of no use.

Off to the east was a line of low hills, fortified with towers and barricades against attack from the sea, and, beyond them, the grey shore. Twenty years ago, the knights of the Riverlands had charged across this part of the mudflats towards a breach in the city walls. Alf had watched their charge from those grim hills. He'd seen their banners flying high, heard their voices raised in song.

He'd watched as the stone dragons roared, and the gloom had

turned – briefly – to a stark and cruel brightness. The flower of the Riverland's chivalry, reduced to ash in a heartbeat. Then, he'd been down in the mud with the rest of the League army, hiding from the fire blasts and the shrieking dreadworms. Then, the city seemed impregnable, but he knew better. If the Nine could conquer Necrad, so could another.

Out of the greenish mist came horsemen, riding atop the wall. Lord Vond, Sir Prelan – and a company of elven knights, with Prince Maedos at the head, Laerlyn riding by his side. Alf lowered his head, hoping that the knights would not notice the device on his shield and ride on past, but Maedos called for the company to halt. They looked down at Alf from horseback.

"Hail, Aelfric Lammergeier," called the elf-lord. "Though we sing of the Nine, how many are left now? Mortals pass away, becoming legends if they are fortunate. I pray you will be remembered with honour."

"I've got a few years in me still," said Alf. "Welcome to Necrad, by the by. You weren't here last time, so you might not recognise the place."

You absolutely should antagonise him, whispered Spellbreaker, *it is a very wise idea.*

Alf peered over the wall. "This is about as high as that balcony in your castle, aye?"

To his disappointment, Maedos smiled. "Your sister was a more gracious guest than you, and more grateful, too, after I rescued her from a storm." Some of the knights laughed. "Have you found your missing kinsman?"

Vond frowned. "What is this matter?" Olva's cousin, the Forster knight, looked about in confusion, as if wondering if he'd gone missing and not noticed himself.

"None of your concern, lord," said Alf.

"Ho, Sir Lammergeier," said Prelan. "You promised us a monster, but it seems to me that I rode all the way here to hunt two-legged rats! If I just wanted to fight Wilder, I'd have visited Earl Duna's castle for Yule. Where is this sorceress?"

"Don't be so eager to meet Death, boy. All those charmstones won't protect you," snapped Alf.

"Enough!" hissed Vond. "We are all enemies of the one enemy, here. Tell me, my captains, what do you make of the field?" He pointed out over the Charnel. A few Wilder camps were visible amid the snow and mud, but they seemed too few to seriously threaten the city. The long causeway of the Road wound its way over the blasted lands, and there were more warbands marching along it. Straining his eyes, Alf could see birds in the distance. Messenger ravens, maybe, or Changelings in bird form. Or carrion eaters like vultures.

Young Aelfric sniffed. "Thanks to the elves, time is on our side. The seas are open again, and soon relief will come from Summerswell. The Wilder know this. They must either withdraw before our reinforcements arrive—"

"Or they all freeze in this bitter winter!" complained the Forster boy.

"Or they try one last assault to overwhelm us," said Sir Prelan. He dismounted and sprang up onto the battlements, brandishing his sword. It flashed in the sunlight as he waved it over his head, as if imagining some heroic last stand against the Wilder. Some concealed archer loosed a desultory arrow at the knight, but it fell well short of the wall.

"The Old Man of the Woods is out there," said Alf. "He's some sort of Wilder priest."

"My father once told me about him," said Duna's son. "Often, when the Wilder attacked our estates, it was at the behest of the Old Man. He and Thurn were opposed."

"Now that Thurn is gone, I'm guessing the Old Man's in charge," mused Alf. "Maybe if we slay him, Lae, then all this ends. I know a good huntress who'd help."

"Thurn's monster remains our chief concern," said Vond. "Not some priest. With the inner wall of the Garrison under siege, too, we are spread thin. If the Changeling creates a breach, all will be lost. We must strike her down quickly when she finally shows herself."

"Aelfric," said Laerlyn, "do you recall that little town west of the Fossewood named Crow Bridge?"

Alf wracked his brains. Crow Bridge ... that was soon after they'd left Ersfel, twenty-odd years ago. Blaise was still sick, barely able to walk, and they were all exhausted after the battle in the High Moors. The memories came back, alive and vibrant, like blood after picking a scab. "There was some ghost thing, wasn't there? And weapons couldn't hurt it, and it moved like the wind. Only Blaise's spells could hurt it, and Blaise could scarcely walk."

"So we each took a portion of the town to watch over," continued Laerlyn, "and Peir and Blaise waited in the market square at the middle on a fast horse. And when any of us saw the spectre, we would blow a hunting horn, and Peir would come racing—"

"With poor Blaise like a sack of grain on the back of the horse," finished Alf. "Took us three attempts before we got him there in time." He smiled at the memory. "And four before he actually banished the ghost, 'cos the third attempt, he threw up instead of casting the spell. And remember how Gundan took over a pub as his watch post, and got so drunk he forgot which end of the horn to use?"

"I see the stratagem," said Vond.

"About which end to use?" muttered a confused Eddard Forster.

"Sir Lammergeier, you will station yourself near the Wailing Tower. If you will not give up the sword, then we must keep you in reserve. When Thurn's daughter is sighted, you must fly like a demon and engage her in combat with the Spellbreaker."

"One last effort, Aelfric," said Laerlyn. "I shall be by your side. We shall face Death together."

*

He went back to the mansion to tell Olva, and found it empty. He followed her steps – a mortal woman in Wood-Elf garb was easy to spot in the Garrison – and found her helping in a house of healing near the district wall. He lingered in the doorway for a moment, watching her with pride. Her hands and face were smeared with gore, and she looked exhausted. Alf did not know this grown woman, this half-stranger who his little sister had become over many years, but it was good to see that she was a worthy soul.

It made it harder, too.

"I've got to go, Olva," he explained. "I'm on watch. As soon as Threeday finds your boy, I'll go and get him, or send those I trust to help."

In her eyes, he saw the same fear that gnawed at him. It was like the prickling in the air before a thunderbolt. He lied to her. "All will be well."

CHAPTER THIRTY-SEVEN

Olva slept in the hospice that night. Something about it reminded her of the shed in Ersfel. It was a ridiculous comparison on the face of it. One had been a ramshackle outbuilding with walls of turf and a roof of woven branches, and stank of pigs; now she lay in a palace of marble with a vaulted roof of gold, and the serenely cruel faces of Witch Elves and celestial monsters stared down at her. But it was crowded, too, with wounded bodies, and again Alf stood guard at the door.

The boy on the bench opposite her might have been Derwyn. She was no fool, so she knew she was being foolish. At some point, you had to let your child go and make their own way in the world, if that was what they wanted. You armed your child as best you could, with all the lessons you'd learned. But if there was one lesson she should have impressed better on Derwyn, it was that the world is cruel and uncertain, and nowhere is safe. No one is safe.

After you let them go, you had only the fear. Would they thrive, or perish? Alf had become the Lammergeier, but her other brothers had died on the Road. They left and never came home. She could barely remember their faces, some days, though as Derwyn got older he unwittingly embodied them. People froze at the age you knew them best. The Lammergeier was a middle-aged man, a great lord and hero, but Alf was her lanky older brother who tormented her and protected her. She could tell that it was true for him, too – his offers of protection and aid always had that slight veneer of exasperation. His mind was on other things, but he'd indulge his little sister with whatever little problem she brought to him. Like Derwyn was a toy doll she'd dropped in the woods. And no matter how Derwyn grew, he'd always be that wailing infant clutched to her breast, her hands sticky with blood, and his father's body cooling on the floor ...

"You! I know you!"

Olva looked up, blearily. She'd drifted into sleep, and now bony hands shook her awake. She blinked, and saw the old priestess kneeling by her side. "Come with me!" She dragged Olva out of the hospital. A cart waited outside, and two guards stood by it.

"What do you want of me?" asked Olva.

"My name is Marit. I am the abbess at Staffa." The old woman pulled herself painfully onto the cart. "I know you. I saw you in the waters. You seek your son. They have shown me."

The cart raced through the streets, back through the Garrison, and turned west, away from the harbour, until they came to a closed gate in the city walls. At a signal from Marit, the guards opened the gates a crack. "We've seen no Wilder tonight," one of them called, "but watch yourselves."

Out there was the Road that went south across the hellish landscape of the Charnel, down through the Clawlands to the Dwarfholt, past mile after mile of sucking mudflats, the pools glistening with a poisonous sheen. Unlike the streets in the city, where the snow had turned to slush, no traveller had come this way in days, and the snow was untouched. Through the mists, Olva saw a little chapel, scarcely larger than the village shrine in Ersfel. It stood all alone, well outside the city walls, on a little rise. It was absurdly tiny and humble compared to the gargantuan temples of Necrad; a little scrap of familiarity in the midst of this alien land.

"Come with me," said the priestess. Olva followed the priestess as they slogged through the snow towards the chapel. The old woman talked as they went, her words punctuated by gasping. "This was the first chapel in this cursed land, built by Jan after the siege. But the Intercessors never showed themselves here, nor anywhere else north of Necrad. Not until they came to me! At Athar, and again here."

The doors of the chapel had been hewed down. It had been looted, the holy sanctum torn open, its treasures stolen. Marit lit a candle, and the flame flickered in the cold wind. She cradled it with her body until it caught. The light revealed a simple painting of the Erlking blessing the first Lords on one wall; it had been defiled, and in its place was a wooden carving that had the proportions of a human, a child maybe, with a daub of white paint for a face. "Barbarians," spat Marit. "I went to the Lammergeier. I told him the church needed his strength. He did not listen, but they showed me the way. They will show you."

From her robes, she took out a simple wooden bowl and a vial of water. "This water was drawn from the sacred spring at Arshoth. The eldest daughter of the Erlking anointed the first priests with water from that spring, and revealed to them the truth of the Intercessors. Behold!"

She poured the water into the bowl. It splashed and rippled, the candlelight dancing crazily across the reflective surface. They waited, Olva scarcely daring to breath, as the water became still and mirror-smooth.

And then they were not alone in the little room. For a fleeting moment, Olva thought she glimpsed a pale face floating in the darkness. A feeling of security and purpose surrounded her, as if the little mud-walled chapel had been transfigured into a mighty tower of guard. The Abbess breathed a joyous prayer of thanks, and her face was transfigured, too, flooded with light and wisdom. The feeling of sublime grace left them quickly, a passing wave that lifted them oh so briefly out of the sorrow and filth of the mortal world.

"Look!" whispered Marit.

The water in the bowl began to move, to swirl, as if touched by invisible fingers. Lights churned in the depths, colours and shapes that became faint images.

Derwyn!

He lay in darkness, manacled to a stone wall by one arm. His other arm was exposed, and some fiend had carved sigils into his skin. Blood dripped from his ritual wounds into another arcane sigil drawn on the floor. So still and pale!

"Derwyn!" called Olva, "I'm here!"

He did not hear her – but something else did. A dark shape materialised, a stain on the world. It hunched over Derwyn, feeding on his blood. Red eyes stared back at Olva.

The befouled water began to steam; it splashed and leapt as if trying to escape the bowl. Olva's skin crawled as unseen hands pawed at her. The Abbess tipped out the bowl, spilling the water across the floor of the little sanctum, soaking Olva's boots. She lit another candle – this one pungently scented – and the air in the room cleared.

"There are other unseen things," whispered the Abbess, "unclean spirits and ghosts. Here in the north, they swarm thick as locusts, and blot out the light of heaven. But you have seen what you needed to see."

"Derwyn."

She knew where he was. The knowledge burned in her mind, as though a star had fallen from the heavens to mark the spot. He was across the city, and underground, but – miraculously, impossibly – she knew exactly where.

And she ran.

Through the gate, and through the Garrison streets, slipping and falling, she ran. Her elven garb became stained with green slush, her hands and knees scraped raw, but she ran. It was a waking nightmare, the ghastly city rising around her, hollow ruins like the bones of some primordial monster, hollow skulls and scrimshawed ribcages. The Wailing Tower was the one fixed landmark she knew — that, and the burning beacon in her mind.

She ran through another gate, into the Sanction. A guard grabbed her. She babbled at him, words spilling out in a chaotic flood, but she must have made some sense, for he pointed to a tall tower not far away. Perched on the roof like a living gargoyle was a dreadworm, coiled and hunched, its wings wrapped around its body.

She found an archway on the ground floor, the door staved in long ago, and beyond an elegant spiral staircase rising into darkness. More League solders stood at the archway, but they recognised her and saluted her. She ran on, scrambling up the steps. The tower was taller than any mortal building she'd ever seen, second only to Maedos' castle, and these steps were steeper than the precarious stair around Kairad Nal. Still, she ran on without cease. Wraiths shrieked and pawed at her, and she felt them adhering to her wounded hands like leeches. She shook them off and kept climbing.

At the top was a once great ballroom, now roofless and exposed. Snow had piled on the marble floor, and lay like a shroud on the toppled statues of Witch Elves. She found Alf sitting there all alone, save for the black sword propped by the wall. A glowing stone on the ground in front of him radiated warmth and a little ghostly light.

"Alf!" she gasped. "I've seen Derwyn. I've seen him." She pointed out over the city, towards the harbour, towards the place she *knew* he was trapped. She forced herself to back away from the edge of the building — the compulsion was so strong that she felt she might throw herself into the abyss if there was no other way to reach that spot.

"Sit down," he rumbled. How could she sit? How could she stay still? She had to force herself down. "Breathe slow. Drink this." He offered her a waterskin. "Tell me what happened."

"The Abbess from the hospital — Marit of Staffa — she brought me to this old chapel, and showed me a vision of Derwyn. He's here in Necrad, Alf, not a mile away."

"A vision," repeated Alf. He rolled the word around like it tasted foul. "And through Marit."

"I saw Derwyn," she insisted. "He was trapped in a prison like the one in Ellsport, I think – the sort of place Martens keeps people he's sending to the vampires. There was a wraith, and it was feeding on him. And his hand – there were sigils cut into his skin, drawn in blood."

"Ol, I'm not denying what you saw, but these things are always trouble. Half of 'em are metaphors", he said with wary distaste. He sighed, and that hesitation was a door thrown open for her fear to leap past all her defences, all her hopes, and strangle her spirit completely. "Here's what we'll do. I'm sworn to say up here and wait for the signal. But Laerlyn's on her way here soon. Tell her what you saw, and she'll help. She'll know what's best to do."

"He's dying, Alf." Her voice cracked. "He's dying and he's alone. We have to go now. I have to go. If you can't help me, I'll leave you to your duty and go alone. I thought . . . " She stood, terribly aware of the gulf between her and the Lammergeier. This man had once been her brother, but that was a lifetime ago, and long years had divided them. "It doesn't matter. I'll go to him."

She hoped Alf would leap up, like he had on that first night, and promise to come with her. That he'd cast aside everything to save her boy, ride to the rescue as a great hero should.

But he did not move. "I went off chasing Jan's vision, and it brought ruin. Gundan's dead, and Thurn, and a lot more are going to die," he said quietly, "I thought I could bring the Nine together, and that we'd win again. But the Nine are gone, and it has all gone wrong. All that's left to do is slay the monster, and that . . . that I can do. But until the monster shows herself, I've got to stay here." His shoulders slumped. "I'm sorry."

"Well," she said, "that's that then."

The gulf between them became a void, dark and silent as a starless night at the end of the world.

And in that void, the sword spoke.

"What were the sigils?"

"Shut up," said Alf. "It's not the time."

"What were the sigils, wielder? Hand me to her. Let me see them in her mind."

Alf did not move, but Olva darted across the room and took hold of Spellbreaker. Pain shot through her head, as if the sword had pierced her skull and was now cutting a furrow in her brain. The vision of Derwyn filled her mind again.

"The sign of the Horned Serpent," whispered Spellbreaker, "and sigils much like those on Lath's scroll. Wielder, take me. We must go."

"It feels," said Alf slowly, "like a lure. Like some foe wants the city left defenceless."

"Oh, precisely so, wielder. It is patently a trap. But the city's salvation is there. You must defeat the wielder, not the weapon."

CHAPTER THIRTY-EIGHT

T he dreadworm was aloft for only a few heartbeats before Olva
hammered on Alf's shoulder and shouted in his ear. "There,
there! Down there!" They were above the south-eastern Sanction, not
too far from the Garrison gate. No doubt he was in plain view of the
sentries there; no doubt reports about the Lammergeier abandoning
his post were already on their way to Vond.

They landed in an empty square, eerily beautiful in the necromiasmic glow. This portion of the city had avoided the worst of the
siege, and while every charmstone and relic had been scavenged, the
surviving palaces had a grandeur that had nothing to do with magic.
Images of ancient Witch Elf kings and queens loomed above the
plaza. Alf looked up, and saw a face that he had seen only a few days
before. A statue of Amerith stared down at him, seventy feet tall,
carved before Summerswell, before the Old Kingdom, before . . .
who knew? It was all made to humble those who entered the city. Alf
could imagine the fathers of the fathers of the Wilder that Ildorae
talked about coming here, heads bowed at the glory of the living
gods of Necrad. It touched him, too, even after all those years living
in the wreck of the city. He felt like a trespasser.

But he looked up at those statues, and allowed himself a moment of
pride. He was the Lammergeier, of the Nine who defeated Lord Bone.

He dismounted from the dreadworm and strode across the square, ice crunching under his boots. In the dead centre of the plaza, half hidden by the snow, was a ring of iron fifteen feet across – the rim of a shaft leading down into the Pits. It was a later addition to the plaza; Lord Bone had forged it, for wizard reasons. Tapping the magic or channeling it down into his monster-spawning vats or summoning demons. No doubt Blaise could talk about its ... Arcane Purpose, but all Alf needed to know was that it was a way down.

Dwarf-forged iron bars blocked the gate. An even more recent addition – these bars had been installed to keep the Pitspawn from spilling out onto the surface. Alf could even see where some enterprising but foolish scavengers had tried to cut through the bars, hoping to sneak down and find treasures below. Layer on layer, age on age.

Alf tasted the air. He rubbed the exposed walls of the shaft, feeling the grain of the stone. Regions of the labyrinth had their own qualities, their own ecologies. After fifteen years below, Alf knew them as his father had known the soil.

He drew Spellbreaker. "What do you reckon?"

"A spur off the northern Dwimmervaults," said the sword. "Little travelled. An intruder might go unnoticed for a little while, if quiet and subtle."

"Aye."

He swung the sword, and the bars exploded, sending sparks and chunks of red-hot iron tumbling down the shaft.

"Stay here," he told Olva. "I'll be back soon with the boy. If anything happens, get on the dreadworm – it'll fly you to the Wailing Tower. You'll be safe there."

"I'm coming with you," she said, clambering over the lip of the shaft.

"Olva. These are the Pits of Necrad. The darkest, deepest dungeon in all the lands. I'm damned if I'm letting my little sister go wandering down there."

"Alf, you will climb down and show me the way to my son, or I'll kick you in the face."

He grimaced. "All right. But listen: step where I step. Stay quiet. Don't touch anything."

The passageway below was ankle-deep in slime and icy water. Carved walls receded into the shadows east and west.

"It's dark," she said, hesitating to leave the little circle of light that filtered down the shaft.

He took her hand. "The sword lets me see. Just stay close."

He took a deep breath of stagnant air, let the darkness bathe his eyes. The world was ending up above, and he was in a desperate race against time, but still he stood there for a moment, drinking in the timeless silence of the dungeon. There were countless foes between him and his quarry, but he was in his element here. This was where he belonged.

"Which way?" he asked her.

East. East to the sea.

He killed three times before laying eyes on another human. The first killing was a swarm of bonebeetles, which came clattering out of the walls, drawn by the scent of his meat and the bone beneath. The things ate flesh, nested and laid eggs in marrow, and then wore the hollowed-out bones like shells. He smashed a skull, and the rest fled.

The second was cousin to a dreadworm, a thing of congealed slime and darkness. One cut from the sword was enough to mortally wound it; a second blow silenced it, but not before its death rattle echoed down the corridors.

Alf quickened his pace, hurrying down stairs and corridors. His sword-granted sight revealed piles of debris, the burned-out wreckage of storerooms and laboratories, ogre-dens still fetid even after all these years. Endless ossuaries, where the bones of dead mortals lay stacked, awaiting necromantic experiments that would now never be performed. The bones of the ancestors of the ancestors of the

Wilder, Thurn once told him. Carved images of elves and spirits stared down scornfully at him, but their cold grandeur was diminished by the pipes and arcane machinery that had been added later by Bone's servants.

Others had been here recently, he could tell. Patches of soot where the ceiling hung low, left by burning torches. Scrapes and scratches where someone had struggled to drag a handcart through a narrow arch. Chambers that had been disturbed, the wreckage pawed through for charmstones. The signs of mortal intrusion into the underworld grew more frequent as they went, telling Alf they were on the right trail. Archways on either side opened into other rooms, some no more than little cells, others vaulted halls or corridors winding away into the unknown. He'd wandered down here for half a lifetime, but even if he spent all of what time was left to him (and how much time was that, he wondered, with Death drawing ever closer to the city), he would still only know the smallest fraction of the Pits.

Better chance of ambush up ahead, he thought. Or the sword thought. It didn't matter. *But this spot's safe.*

"Stay here," he whispered to Olva, and he released her hand. He could see her clearly in the sword-granted sight, but she was utterly blind in this lightless part of the dungeon. He watched her for a second; she froze in place, barely daring to breathe. In her stillness, she reminded him of the statues in the plaza above.

"For how long?" she whispered.

"Let me scout out what's ahead," he lied, "I'll be back in a moment."

He picked his way through the maze. An unworthy thought rose in him: how simple it would be to keep walking, keep wandering, descend for ever and never return to the surface. Never to be drawn into the conflicts between his friends, fights he did not understand, sides he couldn't take. Never to grow old, but to walk into immortal legend, like Peir had—

LINNORM! warned the sword in his mind.

The beast erupted from a pile of rubble, jaws gaping, teeth sharp as knives, a triple ring of fangs about the red gullet, scales thick and razor-edged like the bones of cuttlefish. Mane matted with slime, tangled with spiderwebs. Incredibly fast despite the sheer bulk of the thing, a coiled serpent fifteen feet long leaping at him in ambush.

But the sword's warning was enough. Alf got enough of his shield into the linnorm's maw that the beast bit down on wood and steel, not flesh. It thrashed, its little clawed feet digging into the walls, trying to push Alf over or tear the shield from his grasp. The tail lashed like a whip, coiling around his right ankle to tug him off balance, but he shifted his stance, his weight, every muscle in his body straining with the effort. The edge of the shield slid down the linnorm's jaw, inch by inch, scale by scale, until Alf had the monster's neck pinned against the wall. Its jaws snapped at his face, but couldn't reach him; its long body thrashed, but couldn't find the leverage to overcome his strength. The monster's bloodshot eyes bulged as it realised its death was at hand.

A heartbeat to judge the moment. To find the artery, the wellspring of hot blood beneath scale and mane. Then the sword plunged deep, opening the linnorm's throat. He held the beast against the wall through all its death throes, and when it went still, he let it slip to the ground as quietly as he could.

"You could have warned me last time," said Alf.

"I sought another wielder then," said Spellbreaker, "now I see that you have some potential."

"I don't want your esteem."

"But you do need my aid, wielder, and one comes with the other."

"So – what sort of trap are we walking into?"

"Who taught Lath the spell used to call up Death? You found the scrolls down here in the Pit, but not the answer. But your nephew is being used as part of the same spell, or one very like it. I recognised the runes. The same hand is behind both schemes, wielder – one stratagem aimed at the conquest of Necrad, and the other aimed squarely at you."

"At me? Why not the rest of the Nine?"

"Don't you see? Misfortune found each of them. The paladin, the cleric, the dwarf, the barbarian – all gone. The thief, Berys, overthrown by her own followers, or so says the Vatling. Lath is broken by his exertions. Only two are left – the wizard, hiding in his tower, and you, here in the dark."

"You forgot Laerlyn."

"I assure you, wielder, I did not," it said, and a laugh ran down the blade.

The distant smell of saltwater told Alf he was coming close to the eastern edge of the city, and the harbour. Ahead was a doorway, and a man sat there, a crossbow across his lap. Alf pressed himself against the wall – it was pitch-dark, but if Alf had the magic to see, then so might this sentry. He watched and waited.

The sentry did not move. Not at all.

He crept closer. The man was dead, slumped in his chair, unseeing eyes for ever fixed down the corridor. At his side was a horn, to sound the alarm if he saw any foes approaching. And a crossbow, with an enchanted elf-bolt ready to be loosed.

"A heartseeking bolt," observed the sword. It sounded proud, almost paternal. Alf removed the bolt and snapped it.

The scavengers of the Pits would make short work of any corpses, so he must have died within the last few hours. Alf was mildly surprised nothing had found the body already. He touched the man's neck and found there was still warmth in the corpse. There were no visible wounds, no sign of blood. Searching, he plucked a tiny object from the man's skin, like pulling a tick. It had the shape of an insect, but it was made of the same eerie metal as the coins of Necrad. In its abdomen was an empty glass vial, smaller than a fingernail, and it had a wickedly sharp stinger. "Witch Elf work. I haven't seen one in years. We smashed the workshops where they made these in the war. Devilish things."

"They blackened the skies," said the sword, dreamily. "What good was all your armour then, dwarves, and your unbreakable walls?"

"Lath whistled up the wind, and blew all the little bastards away." Alf blew softly on the metal thing, and it tumbled off his fingertip. He crushed it with his boot. "I'd hoped never to see weapons like those again. So, someone else is here. Friend or foe?"

"An enemy of your enemy, at the least. A boon. This way has been prepared for you – someone wanted you to come to this door undetected."

Alf pressed his ear to the door guarded by the dead man. Beyond, he heard the sound of boxes being dragged across stone, the grunts and shouts of many men at work. A hidden warehouse, by the sounds of it.

"Be careful, you dogs," shouted a gruff Ellscoaster voice on the far side of the door, "those treasures are worth a lot more than any of your lives. Faster! Faster! Martens, where do you want these boxes?"

"Well, then," muttered Alf. "Time to go to work."

CHAPTER THIRTY-NINE

Olva waited in darkness so complete it seemed to leach her awareness from her body. She knew that her feet were cold and wet, that her back was pressed against the slimy wall, that her hands could feel the intricate lines of carved stone, but the back of her head rested against a cold metal pipe, but it was all so very remote. She knew Derwyn was close at hand, so close that she had to bite her lip to keep from crying out so he could hear her voice.

She heard a distant roar, and then an animal grunt of pain. She held her breath, hoping that it meant that Alf was coming back, but the echoes died away and he did not return.

To fend off the dark, she tried to imagine the future, but hopes slipped away from her. This was not despair, but a terrifying uncertainty, the certainty that she could not return to the life she had known. Alf would rescue Derwyn, but after that – down here, the thought of Ersfel seemed as unlikely and bizarre as any magic she'd glimpsed on the Isle of Dawn, or any horror out of Necrad. She had ridden on dragons and dreadworms, watched magic sunder the skies and walked in the presence of the Intercessors – could she go home to Genny Selcloth's tavern, or join the rest of the villagers listening to old Thala's haranguing sermons in the holywood?

Once, the outside world with all its horrors had reached into

Ersfel, and shattered her old life. She'd spent seventeen years rebuilding it, holding it together so Derwyn could have the life she'd wanted for him. Now it was all broken again, and she could not put their home back together the same way again even if she wanted to.

"If he dies tonight," whispered a voice in her ear, "your son will be remembered as a great hero." A woman's voice, throaty and low. Olva whirled around in the darkness, but there was no light to see, and her outstretched fingers brushed against only air and stone. The voice seemed to come from nowhere. "There are worse fates. I had a family, once, but I had to forget them. You have to cut yourself off from anything that can be used against you."

"Who are you?" whispered Olva.

"I'll understand if you want revenge. But understand that the enemy claimed your son as their tool before he was even conceived. They hurt you first, not me."

Light flared. It was only a little glow, a glimmering ember, but it was still bright enough to hurt Olva's eyes. She blinked, and saw that she was alone. The light came from a crystal globe, small enough to be held or concealed in her palm. And next to it was a knife.

Her knife. Olva's knife. The knife she'd carried from Ersfel, the knife Martens had taken from her. She had to pick it up to confirm that she was not dreaming, or mad, but it was solid and real in her hand.

She followed Alf's trail. It wasn't hard, now that she had her own light. Just go from bloodstain to bloodstain, corpse to corpse. She stepped over the spilled guts of a serpent-thing with hideous fangs, and past the body of a sentry that Alf must have frightened to death. Beyond the sentry was a door, and beyond the door . . .

Olva Forster beheld the wrath of the Lammergeier.

The door opened onto a balcony, from which twin staircases swept like wings to the floor below. She looked out over a cavernous chamber, its ceiling held aloft by ornamented pillars. Titanic statues of elf-maids bore globes the size of a man's head, but unlike the smaller crystal in her hand, the light from those larger globes flickered and faded and danced – in time with the movements of Spellbreaker. The dread sword drank the light from the room, so that every time the blade fell, the lights dimmed and blood sprayed.

Stacked around the room were wooden crates and chests and boxes, all arranged in a way that put her in mind of a storehouse in the week after harvest, packed to the rafters with all that was needful to survive the coming year. But this was no granary or warehouse; some of the boxes had burst, spilling silver and gems and other treasures.

All around, too, were foes. Many reminded her of Abran's crew; others were League guards. Most were human, but she saw other kinds, too – dwarves, Vatlings, ogres. Some of them had burst, too, spilling their entrails out across the floor.

Amid it all was the Lammergeier.

He was unhurried in his slaughter, but thorough. Olva remembered their father Long Tom reaping in the wheatfields, watching him swing the heavy scythe back and forth tirelessly for hours.

Alf killed like that.

His enemies hurled themselves at him, screaming battle-cries, and he cut them down. Spells flared, only to shatter against Spellbreaker's aegis. Ogres charged him, great brutes twice the size of a man, and he cut them down, hewing and chopping limbs like firewood. Other foes he dispatched without even making contact, blasts of force flinging bodies to break and burst against the pillars. They threw spell-skulls and he smashed them; hurled lightning bolts and he parried them; loosed heartseeking arrows at him, and he knocked them aside.

In the end, they tried to flee. One turned, then another, then there was a great rush, the last dozen or so running away from Alf towards the double doors at the far end of the hall. But to their horror they found these doors barred from the far side, and there was no escape.

They turned and saw the Lammergeier, and then they too perished, and the dreadful laughter of the black sword filled all the world.

Until there was only one left.

Lyulf Martens cowered against a wall, shaking so much that the silver amulets in his beard rang like bells. He fell to his knees, pressing his face to the floor, wailing theatrically. "I had no choice! The boy tumbled into my hands! Spare me, spare me, Lammergeier, and I shall make you wealthy beyond measure! I have friends, powerful friends!"

Olva sprang up from her hiding place and ran across the room, skirts trailing through the field of gore. "Where is he? Where is my son?" She found that she had the dagger in her hand, and all she could imagine was plunging it into Martens' heart, to add one more corpse to the piled carnage of her brother.

Alf intercepted her with his shield hand and drew her in, holding her back. "Keep your head," he ordered.

"The prisoner is here," said Martens, inching towards a smaller side door. "I kept him as I was commanded."

Alf released Olva and grabbed Martens instead, flinging him bodily towards the door. Martens sprawled on the ground, scrabbling and slipping in the blood, then dragged himself upright. "Mercy," he begged, and as he did so he made a curious gesture with his hands, and a sly expression crossed his face, like an actor breaking character for an instant.

Alf froze at the gesture, all his confidence and his grim intent leaking from him. He looked befuddled. "Open the door," he ordered. Martens had a key, but his hands shook so much that he could not find the lock. Alf shoved him aside and kicked the door open.

There lay Derwyn!

Dead? He was so still that she feared he was dead, but no, no, he was only unconscious. There was a sword lying on his breast, clutched in his left hand, and it rose and fell with his breathing. He was exhausted, sick maybe, but alive! Filthy, bedraggled, wounded, too – the marks of beatings, of cuts, wounds scabbed and fresh, and each injury horrified her anew, but he was still alive. She wasn't too late!

She rushed forward, only for Alf to thrust her back, his arm like a bar of steel. "Wait!" he hissed.

"I have to go to him!" Olva pleaded.

But it was Alf who advanced into the room, slowly, step by step. The sword Spellbreaker he held in front of him, ready to strike as if he feared unseen foes. He moved the blade cautiously, probing the empty air. Then, at last, Alf cast aside his shield and scooped Derwyn up, threading his left arm under Derwyn's shoulders and hoisting him up like he was carrying him home from the tavern. Derwyn stirred, his eyelids flickered and he groaned. He was alive!

Olva could bear it no more and she rushed forward, too, holding him so tightly she could feel every rib, every inch of him. She cradled his maimed hand, touched the old scar on his shoulder, and even that was bleeding again.

Alf glanced at Martens, who remained cowering by the door. Again, confusion creased Alf's face, then he shook his head. "Out," ordered Alf. "Back the way we came."

Between Alf and Olva, they began to carry Derwyn back across the hall, towards the stairs and the tunnels and the shaft and the waiting dreadworm and out into the cold air and the wide sea and – she dared to dream – escape.

"Wielder," cried the sword, "beware!", and at that moment, the double doors were flung open.

There stood Prince Maedos. His armour was chased in pearl and emerald, and the white tree of the Erlking was emblazoned on his breastplate, while his shield bore the image of the rising sun. He carried a silver sword, like a sliver of starlight.

Alf shrugged his left arm free, letting Olva take Derwyn's weight.

He raised Spellbreaker as the elf-lord approached. The two men glared at each other.

Martens rushed to the prince's side. No longer was he the snivelling coward of a moment ago; now, he was an aggrieved courtier, respectful but still demanding his due. "Your warning arrived too late, sire! There was not enough time to clear all my men from the hall before the Lammergeier struck! Is there to be recompense for this slaughter?"

"Thieves and blood traders, all. They deserved death. So do you, Lyulf Martens – I hold yours in my gift." The prince strode on as Martens crumpled to the ground, clawing at his throat. Ivy sprouted there. The same elf-curse that had afflicted Bor and Abran. Olva ignored the choking man and dragged Derwyn across the hall. The stairs seemed an eternity away. Behind her, Alf and Maedos traded barbs like stags clashing antlers.

"Maedos," shouted Alf. "What is this? What have you done?"

"My sister has a fondness for you, Lammergeier. For her, I tried to be gentle. You could have stayed away, and spared yourself this. You could have taken the church's offer. But here you remain – stupid, stubborn, and in possession of a treasure far beyond your station."

Alf snorted in fury. He struck at the prince with Spellbreaker, and Maedos parried the blow, though it nearly tore the silver sword from his hands. He danced out of reach of Alf.

"You and the rest of the Nine disturbed the designs of the Wise. Upstart troublemakers, wild beasts trampling the fences of my father's garden." Maedos glanced at Derwyn. "Behold the leash we made for you."

"A hostage," growled Alf.

"A troublesome one," said Maedos. "He nearly slipped away from us, you know, but he snared himself in Highfield. He'd heard tales of his uncle's glory, and wanted to see for himself. I fear he will be disappointed."

Alf struck again, driving the prince back. This time, his blow ripped the sword from Maedos' hand and sent it flying across the room. He spat at Maedos' feet. "I've naught to prove to the lad, and a better foe than you to defeat. I beat you already. Now if you want a second thrashing, you can wait until I'm done with Death."

"That victory does not belong to you," said Maedos, "it's meant for me. In truth, it was the Lord of Necrad who I was *meant* to defeat, but no matter. 'Tis known that only one blade can defeat Death, and I shall wield it. Give me Spellbreaker, and you may go."

"To hell with it," said Alf. "Enough nonsense. You want my sword, come and take it."

Maedos smiled. "It was never your sword, mortal."

A terrible strength flooded Derwyn, as if every sinew turned to steel. His face contorted, his lips drawing back from his teeth. With a twist, he flung Olva to the ground, then turned and leapt at Alf. He grabbed at Spellbreaker, the pair wrestling for control of the blade. Alf was the larger of the two, and the stronger, but then he staggered to the side, as the blade became unbearably heavy. Spellbreaker tore itself from his fingers and fell to the floor, the steel clattering on stone.

Derwyn scooped up the sword, and for him it was no burden at all. He swung it at Alf. The blast wave caught the Lammergeier, flinging him across the room to slam into a pillar with a hideous crack. He landed limp and unmoving. His head flopped to the side, and blood gushed from his mouth and nose. Olva rushed to him.

"Wielder?" said the sword, but it was not speaking to Alf.

Derwyn lifted Spellbreaker, and a shadow coiled around him, hung about him like a heavy mantle. His expression was one Derwyn had never worn in all his life – haughty and cruel.

Oh, by the Intercessors, Olva knew that expression.

He turned to Prince Maedos, raising the sword to strike, but the prince leapt back out of reach.

"Hold, Acraist!" he cried.

Derwyn – the thing that was in Derwyn – spoke with a terrible voice that would haunt Olva's nightmares henceforth. "We are sworn enemies, Prince of Dawn. The Oath of Amerith endures; I shall defy your House until doomsday." He took a step towards the prince.

Maedos held up his hand. A rune glowed on Derwyn's forehead, and he stopped.

"A geas?" said Acraist in that awful, tortured voice, as if every word scarred Derwyn's throat. "I wield *Spellbreaker*. No magic can hinder me."

"Break the spells then," laughed Maedos, "for it is magic – my father's magic – that bound your wraith to this mortal's frame. Break the spells, and cast yourself back into the howling void. We have both perished before, cousin – I would not be so quick to throw away this chance at life. And remember, I know the sigil used to bind you, so I can break it too with a word. Defy me, Acraist, and I shall *unmake* you."

As they spoke, Olva tried to revive Alf, but he lay insensible. She searched his clothing, guessing that he would carry a healing cordial or three with him. She found none. "Wake up, Alf," she whispered.

Acraist lowered Spellbreaker and rested its tip on the ground. He clasped his hands over the pommel. "What are your terms?"

"All know that the only blade that can defeat Death is the Spellbreaker. You will command the sword to serve me, truly and faithfully. I shall defeat Death, and return to Necrad as its champion and ruler in the Erlking's name. The first city shall belong to the elves once more, and my father's house shall rule over all the lands, north and south."

Olva crept over to where Lyulf Martens lay. The merchant's face was a hideous purple, his eyes bulging from his skull. He had managed to get two of his fingers in beneath the ivy collar, and the strangling vine had cut so deep into the flesh that Olva could see the whiteness of scraped bone. She could not tell if he was alive or dead, and did not much care. She ran her fingers over his richly embroidered coat, and found the hard shape of a metal flask in a hidden pocket.

"And if I do not serve?" said the sword. "If I turn on you in the midst of battle?"

"Then you will be locked away in a casket until you can be destroyed," replied Maedos. "In truth I do not need you – I can unmake Death with a word. You are but a trophy, a sign for others to see so they do not question my triumph."

Acraist looked at his hand – Derwyn's hand. "This body is mortal. You offer me thirty or forty years, and in exchange, you want dominion over all the lands for eternity?"

"I throw coins to a beggar as I ride to my coronation," snarled Maedos, then he composed himself. "Defy me, and there is nothing for you but the wraith-world – and should you ever find your way back to life, it will be in my father's kingdom. Amerith is gone; the Witch Elves are passing. The war between our people is over, and the wood has won. Now is the time to consider your place in eternity – and if the life of this body is short, then you of all people know there are ways of prolonging existence."

Acraist turned to look at Alf's unconscious form, at the blood that stained his face and neck. A terrible hunger rose in him. "My Oath is ended." He drove Spellbreaker into the floor, embedding the blade two inches deep.

"Wielder," pleaded Spellbreaker, "I was made to serve you. Lord Bone gave me to you. I was made for slaughter and destruction, not to be some elf-prince's trophy. Not to prop up the Erlking's reign. You must not abandon me."

But slowly, reluctantly, Acraist released his grip on the pommel, his fingers trailing across the black metal.

The Wraith-Captain stepped back. His head hung. "I yield the blade," said Acraist.

"Very well," snarled the sword, "let the spells be broken."

The city convulsed. The sword was a black pillar, an axle on which the whole world might spin, and now it came to a sudden, grinding halt. The lights in the hall leapt wildly, like candles in a hurricane, then faded, darkness filling the hall. Lyulf Martens gasped as the ivy choker released its grasp on his windpipe. Far below in the bowels of Necrad, ancient elven spells and Lord Bone's foul arcane machines alike flickered and failed.

And Derwyn fell, toppling to the ground, a young tree uprooted by a storm. The wraith of Acraist howled, and its shadowy limbs reached for the sword as if repenting of its choice, like a drowning man reaches for the shore. Then it was gone.

The darkness was complete. Olva clenched her fist tightly around the little light-globe she'd been given, not daring even to let a sliver of light escape. Her fingers were a faint reddish glimmer, and she wrapped a fold of her cloak around her hand. Only darkness now protected her from Maedos. With her other hand, she tore the healing potion from Martens' jacket.

She crawled towards where Alf had fallen, groping through the field of slaughter, climbing over corpses. Off somewhere in the void, the prince conjured a beam of light. He played it around, and Olva froze, pressing herself to the ground as it passed over her. Silver flashed in the shadows, and the prince darted over to retrieve his sword. Olva scrambled to Alf's side and lifted his head, splashing the cordial in his mouth, working his jaw so he did not choke. "Alf! Come on!" He began to stir.

Then the light found them, exposed and defenceless, prey caught in the open by a patient hunter.

CHAPTER FORTY

I t wasn't the first time Alf had opened his eyes and seen someone
about to stab him. There was that time early in the war, when
Wilder crept into the mercenary camp, and the only reason he'd
survived was because of Gundan's elephantine snoring. There'd
been hired assassins in the Crownland, a barmaid in Arden – and
now a prince.

He brought up his arm, catching the tip of the elf's sword on his
vambrace. He felt the blade skitter along his armour and slice deep
into his right bicep. The cordial that Olva had poured down his
gullet numbed some of the pain. He grabbed the prince's slim wrist
and tried to wrench the weapon from the elf, but Alf's strength failed
him, and Maedos tore himself free. He slashed at Alf again, and Alf
ducked aside, using the pillar to shield him from Maedos' assault.
Spellbreaker lay only a few feet away next to Derwyn's unconscious
form. Even with his right arm wounded, Spellbreaker would give
Alf a chance – but the prince saw the danger, too, and stepped back,
inviting Alf to lunge for the black blade.

If Alf had been younger, faster, he could have made that leap
before Maedos skewered him. Now, his age made it a trap.

Instead, Alf backed away, and took up a sword dropped by one of
Martens' guards. The feel of having a weapon in his hand heartened

him, even if it was in his left hand, even though it was but a common blade and not Spellbreaker. Already, though, he could feel the weight of the weapon; his strength was ebbing fast, each heartbeat sending a fresh gush of blood from his arm. He pulled the strap of his elbow-couter tight as he could, as a makeshift tourniquet. His right arm was still just short of unbearable agony, and he could feel blood pooling in the hollow of his elbow. He felt no fear, only a sense of grim inevitability, lava rolling out across the tortured earth, turning slow and grey but still moving.

He moved.

He pushed forward, hammering at his foe. Maedos was faster by far, fleet-footed and agile. Alf could land few blows, and those he did strike were easily blocked by the prince. In return, the silver blade flickered once, twice, thrice, and each time a thin spray of Alf's blood rained down on ground already awash with gore.

He advanced again, staggering, making a clumsy slash. Again, Maedos evaded it, and again, the silver sword struck. But in that moment, Alf pushed Maedos far enough away from the fallen Spellbreaker for Olva to rush forward and—

The prince spoke a word of power and a shock ran down Alf's arm. His borrowed sword cracked and shattered, and his strength deserted him. The magic overwhelmed him, making a mockery of whatever courage and hope he had left in him.

And in the same moment, the same motion, as if it was all part of some courtly dance, the elf-prince whirled across the room, and his heavy boot came down on Olva's hand just as she reached for Spellbreaker. Maedos kicked back with his heel, sending Spellbreaker spinning out of reach. He caught his breath for a moment, then advanced on Alf.

"Know this, Lammergeier: you are the last of the Nine. Even now, the wizard perishes at the hands of his apprentices. Mortals pass and are forgotten; all their works come to dust. But the reign of the elves is eternal. From the first dawn to the last, this world is ours."

A bow sang in the darkness.

Maedos fell, clutching his leg as an arrow pierced his thigh.

Berys stepped out of the shadows. Berys! She wore the same garb as when he'd last seen her, when she and Lath had fought in the Sanction, but she'd clearly been through many trials since then. "You're not the last of the Nine, Alf. Not yet." She nocked a second arrow to her bow and drew back the string. "This one's edged in elf-bane. Throw down your sword, or you'll feel its bite."

Maedos dropped the silver sword at his feet. He leaned against a pillar, taking the weight off his wounded leg. He stared defiantly at Berys, and clenched his fist. There was a hideous crunching noise. Alf looked around in confusion, and saw Lyulf Martens' head roll free as the ivy collar tightened until it cut bone. The merchant's corpse convulsed, then lay still. "He assured me you were dead, thief," said Maedos. "He betrayed you to me years ago."

"But even then, he served my cause. Thanks to him, every turn-coat and traitor in my service was exposed." She kicked aside the head of a thief that Alf had dismembered. "And thanks to him – and Alf – you're here now, and my prisoner."

Alf dragged himself upright, and Olva fetched the black sword for him to lean on. He waved her away, tried to tell her to go and attend to her boy, whatever his name was. In his present state, Alf was somewhat vague on who the boy was. Derwyn. The object of the quest.

I could not disobey Acraist, insisted the sword. It sounded like it was pleading. *But I held true to my oath. I freed the boy from possession. I kept you alive.*

"Barely," muttered Alf. "Berys," he groaned. "What's going on?"

"She used you, wielder," said the sword. "She knew Maedos had your nephew as bait in a trap. She knew Maedos was plotting against the Nine. She used you to draw the prince out of his fortress on the Isle of Dawn."

"But why, Berys? Is the blood trade worth all this?"

"The trade?" Berys' arm trembled as she kept her bow trained at Maedos. "No. No. It's . . . " The bow wavered. "What do the stories say happened to the Old Kingdom, Alf?"

"It was destroyed," said Alf, slowly. The relevance of the question eluded him. This was a question for Jan or Blaise, people who cared about ancient history, kings and nations and prophecies. The Old Kingdom was just a bunch of overgrown ruins down south. He and Berys had always been more interested in the question of how much treasure could be found in the tomb of the ancient kings. He struggled to remember what the priests taught. "They became corrupt through demon worship. They destroyed themselves."

"That's what the stories say, all right. You know who writes the stories? The elves. It's always been the elves, Alf. The Wood Elves. They tore down the Old Kingdom out of fear, and in its place they gave us lies. The Lords of Summerswell – those families owe their rank to the elves. The wizard's college only knows the magic that the elves permit. The church is theirs, too – the Erlking sent the Intercessors to watch us. We're *thralls*, Alf. They keep us in unseen servitude, and we live out our short little lives unaware of their deceits." There was a desperation in her voice he'd never heard before, not even in the war, mixed with the effort of keeping the great bow drawn. "There are a small few of us who fight against the Erlking's dominion. A few free folk, working in secret. Fighting since the Old Kingdom fell. We had to be careful. The elves have spies everywhere. Alf, *grab the bastard prince.*"

Alf put Spellbreaker to Maedos' throat, and took great satisfaction in doing so. Whatever else was going on around him in this whirlwind of plot and counterplot, traps and intrigues and prophecies and rituals, he was certain that Prince Maedos was a smug bastard who deserved to be thumped. Berys lowered her bow. She flexed her fingers. "Not as strong as I used to be," she admitted.

Olva knelt down by Derwyn. The boy's face was grey, his skin clammy. She pressed herself against him, spreading her elven-cloak over him to warm him. Absently, Alf dug around to see if he had any more healing potions. *The boy needs a healer*, he thought.

Berys continued. "I lost so many friends when I was young. I've been hiding from the elves all my life. Always running, always lying. Until . . . until I found you lot. Until the Nine."

"Why didn't you tell us any of this?" Alf tried to focus on what she was saying. His head was still ringing after Acraist gave him that knock. Acraist had been here. He shook his head like a dog, and it dislodged a gush of stringy blood from his ear, making him lightheaded. On the bright side, he could hear Berys a lot better now. He swayed on his feet, but he kept the point of the sword steady at Maedos' neck.

"I wish I could have. I wanted to. But Alf — we were travelling with a priestess of the Intercessors and the Erking's *daughter*. Because people who know all this *disappear*, Alf." Berys waved her hand at Olva and Derwyn. "Maedos would have killed you all to silence you. They will kill you if they can. I had to hide what I knew, to protect the Nine."

The prince shrugged, as if to say that killing mayfly mortals was of no concern. That was nearly enough for Alf to chop Maedos' head off, right then and there, but he swallowed his irritation. Berys was always an adept liar, and by her own confession she'd used Alf to butcher her treacherous minions — he wouldn't put it past her to have made all this up.

He tried to poke holes in her web. "The elves helped us in the war," said Alf. "They came to our aid by the end, even if we had to drag it out of them."

"Just enough to ensure a stalemate — they wanted the threat of Necrad to keep us fearful. While Summerswell lives in dread of the north, we'll never look south to the Everwood. That's where the real evil lies. But we ruined their plans when we killed Lord Bone and ended the threat. We had Necrad. This city changed everything. There's magic here that the Wood Elves don't possess. We could make allies, make plans, strengthen ourselves. This is the one place in all the world that the Erlking didn't have spies . . . except for Laerlyn."

That was too much for him. It was taking all their adventures together, all their friendship, and turning it into something ugly, something grubby and cruel. His friends had flaws, all of them – some he'd always known, some he'd seen too late. But not like this. "I can't believe that *Lae* is part of some . . . elven conspiracy against all mortals. No, she was always one of us – Berys, she warned my sister about Maedos. She took Olva off the Isle of Dawn."

"And brought your sister right to you, to push you into this snare. Lae is part of it, Alf, just like her brother. She has to be. And that's why I never tried to tell you any of this. Most people reject the truth. They prefer the stories of the kindly elves watching over us. The priests know. The nobles know. The wizards know. But they're content with scraps from the Erlking's table. Not me. There's going to be another war, Alf. A war against the Everwood. It's our last chance to break free."

"The uprising of the animals," mocked Prince Maedos, "beasts that have learned to talk. The elves are the firstborn, the inheritors of all creation. You will be put in your place, mortal. Your brief life will be full of suffering and—"

Alf punched the prince in the face, sending him sprawling.

"Sorry," he said to Berys. "But Gundan would have really wanted me to do that."

Chapter Forty-One

Olva sat and held her son's hand, and feared that he was dying. She had seen death before, after all. Not like Alf – for Alf, death was all thunderbolts and magic swords and fiery gouts of dragonsbreath; death was heroic last stands in battle. Death for Alf was sudden in its dealing and sudden in its coming. Death or glory, said the poets, but they lied – for Alf, death was glorious. Of all the Nine, it was Peir whose legend shone the brightest, and he was the first to die.

Olva knew death another way. Galwyn's death, with all its attendant horrors, was an intrusion of Alf's world into Ersfel. Galwyn's death was an exception. For the most part, she'd known other ways of dying. The slow, wasting, death of their parents, for example. Their father Long Tom had been the strongest man in the Mulladales when he was young, and had always prided himself on the might of his body. She had watched that body betray him, inch by inch, year by year. His hands had trembled (and she held Derywn's hand as it trembled), and his legs had failed him. Then his eyes, his teeth, his bladder. She would sit him out on a little stool on summer evenings, so Long Tom could feel the warmth on his face, and put a blanket over those withered legs to hide the pool of piss.

Alf never came home to that.

Their mother, Maya – her wits went before her body. She'd go wandering in the woods, looking for her vanished sons. Some days, she'd mistake Galwyn for one of Olva's brothers, and treat him like her own child. Other days, she wouldn't know Olva, or Long Tom, and she'd shriek at them to get out of her little cottage. The village children called her a witch, and whispered that she drank the earthpower and consorted with demons. Her spirit departing, leaving the living shell behind.

Alf never came home to that, either.

Nor the terrible uncertainty of Garn's fate, either. Waiting for answers that never came, looking to every stranger for news, no knowing when it was time to give up and call him dead, so you never started grieving and never really stopped, either.

Now Derwyn was dying.

She sat there. Berys and Alf and the prince talked about great matters, about secret wars and eternal dynasties and things being in thrall to other things, about the doom of the city and the saving of the world, and her world was dying in front of her. Despair swallowed her and turned her to stone; her fear had triumphed, breaking through her ribcage and climbing out into the world, becoming real. She had feared Derwyn would die, and Derwyn was dying.

And then, a wet nose pressed against her hand. A hound's muzzle snuffed at her, insistently shoving under her, forcing her to stand. She could see nothing, there was nothing there, but somehow, impossibly, she knew Cu was there, offering comfort and – more importantly – a push out of her frozen horror. Whether it was a memory or a visitation or some strange miracle, she did not know and in that moment it did not matter.

Berys spoke quickly. "I have a ship waiting. She's fast, and warded against the Erlking's spies. I've been preparing it for years. We bring the prince south. I've got friends there who have questions for him. We need to know which of the Lords are certain to oppose us, and which ones will switch sides when we rise. And there are other things, too, that only the Erlking's favoured son would know. The Wandering Companies, the Mists of Eavesland, the truth behind the church of the Intercessors – we'll break him on the wheel, or use elf-bane needles if we have to. Make him regret his immortality. Come on. We'll need you and your sword too, Alf."

Alf shook his head. "I've got to go back up, Berys. I've got to watch for Death."

"Oh, Alf," said Berys, sadly, "the city's lost. As soon as the seas opened, every merchant and noble in the Garrison made for their ships. Soon, there'll be no one left except the Liberties and those too poor or stupid to escape – and Blaise, for he won't leave his tower. He'll die there." She took out a little enchanted timepiece, a sundial orbited by a tiny sun. "We've got to go. Bring the prince."

"Aelfric." Olva spoke quietly. They didn't hear her.

"I'm not abandoning Necrad!" shouted Alf. "We swore an oath! The city's our responsibility, that's what we agreed."

"And you're going to fight Death? Like this?" Berys poked Alf in his wounded arm. "You're injured and exhausted. Even with the sword, you'd be going to your doom."

"There is no need to fight Death," said Spellbreaker. "Prince Maedos gave the resurrection spell to Lath. Therefore, he knows the sigil to undo the spell. With a word, he can banish Death."

Berys hesitated, then shook her head. "There's no time! Maedos isn't going to give up that sigil easily. He'd sooner see Necrad destroyed than let mortals rule it. Alf, we have to leave. The fight's in Summerswell now. The ship's waiting."

"Alf!" Olva stood. "We need your help. Derwyn needs you."

Berys drew close to Alf, whispering to him. Olva could not hear what the other woman was saying. The few snatches of their conversation that she caught meant nothing to her – they spoke of shared horrors during the war, people and places she'd never heard of, lords and kings. Alf argued back, shaking his head, but Olva couldn't wait for him. She lifted Derwyn – he was terrifyingly light, as if Acraist had hollowed him out – and began to trudge towards the stair and the darkness of the Pit. She had no idea how she'd get Derwyn up the shaft to the plaza and the waiting dreadworm, but she'd manage somehow.

She glanced over her shoulder. Her brother took a few hesitant steps, looking between her and Berys, and all her talk of quests and wars. Then Alf squared his shoulders and made his decision. He turned his back on Berys and hurried after Olva. He took the weight of Derwyn from her and slung the boy over his shoulder.

"Alf!" called Berys. "You're being a fool. The boy's dying. You know he is."

Alf kept walking.

"At least give me the sword!"

Alf kept walking.

Berys snarled in frustration, and nocked an arrow to her bow. Alf turned, raising the black sword to deflect any attack.

The double doors at the far end of the hall rattled, and they all heard the distinct gurgle of Threeday, saying: "I pray we are not too late, princess."

Olva would never forget what happened next. In the cold weeks to come, she would often brood upon it, wondering at the meaning of it all. She would speak to her counsellors, especially Ildorae, trying to fathom what each actor in that tableau had intended.

Alf refused to discuss that moment, afterwards, so she could never be certain.

The double doors swung wide. There was the Princess Laerlyn, in shining armour identical to Maedos, the dread bow *Morthus* in hand. Elven knights of Dawn flanked her, a dozen at least. There, too, was the Vatling. Olva would always remember catching his gaze from across the room, and seeing the shock on his face reflect her own.

For as the door swung wide, Prince Maedos leapt forward. With his wounded leg, he could never have covered the distance to the far end of the hall where the elves stood – not before he stumbled, or Berys struck him an arrow, or Alf caught him. Instead, he flung himself forwards with a wild look of triumph, past Berys, past Olva – leaping, with fluid elven grace, to impale himself on Alf's outstretched sword.

Spellbreaker took his life eagerly. The point of the blade cut through armour and bone, through the Prince of Dawn. Elven blood commingled with the mortal sea spilled by Alf. The prince gasped as the sword pierced his heart, but Olva heard the laughter of his wraith as it pulled free of the ruin of his body.

The elven guards cried out as they saw the Lammergeier slay the Prince of Dawn. Appalled and beyond measure, they surged forward. In the midst of them stood Laerlyn, and crystalline tears ran down her cheeks as she raised *Morthus*.

Later, she would learn about *Morthus*, the Executioner's Bow of the elven court; that it was made by the Erlking himself, and that its arrows had brought down giants and dragons in the elder days. That not even Spellbreaker could have deflected Laerlyn's arrow, had she loosed it.

But she did not. She hesitated.

Berys did not.

Berys aimed not at Alf and Olva, nor at the elves, but at a spot in the middle of the hall, amid the mighty pillars. Her arrow struck and blossomed into the false dawn of a fiery explosion. A wave of dust and heat and flying shards washed over Olva, and in the chaos she heard the crash of the hall's ceiling collapsing. All the lights went out again, but before they did she saw the thief Berys fleeing, and on the far side of all the falling rubble, the Princess Laerlyn, shining like a distant star.

Then darkness.

*

Alf seized her wrist and dragged her on. Up steps, through narrow passageways and echoing mazes. Onwards, onwards through the Pits of Necrad, while behind them the underworld cracked and convulsed and then finally became eerily quiet, the uproar settling into a watchful stillness, broken only by Alf's heavy breathing and the distant drip of water. She had dropped the lamp that Berys had given her, and could see nothing. She had to trust Alf to guide her.

The journey back seemed much longer than before.

"Do you know the way to go?" she whispered, and Alf considered the question for a long time before he answered.

"I do."

They came to the shaft. "Call the worm," ordered Alf. The dread-worm slithered to the lip of the shaft, and its hideous eyeless head extended down. It caught Derwyn in its maw and lifted his limp body up to the surface, while Alf took Olva by the waist and lifted her up so she could grab onto the broken iron grating and haul herself up. Alf climbed up himself, and she saw in the light that his left arm was badly wounded.

"Your poor hand!"

"It doesn't matter." He hauled Derwyn onto the back of the dreadworm. "On to the tower."

And even as they flew, the siege rolled on all around them. Beyond the necromiasma, dawn had broken over the seas, and shone upon the silent stone dragons that guarded the approaches to the city. Towards those dragons marched another host of Wilder, coming down the north Road.

In answer, the gates of Necrad opened, and Sir Prelan rode out upon the Road with a dozen other knights. Lances and spears crackled with the fell magic of Necrad, and their armour was encrusted with charmstones and talismans. Those knights knew they rode to their doom, but their charge would purchase time for the defenders to rally.

Dwarves still held the Garrison gate, and the wall, as they had held the Dwarfholt against Lord Bone's hordes for many years. They were far from home now, standing on stonework not made by their forefathers, and under the strange sky of Necrad instead of the tunnels of their home. But their kinsman had been slain by the Wilder, and they would have vengeance upon those who had failed him.

Beyond, the Liberties ran with blood. Bands of Wilder went from house to house, searching for the elves their ancestors had worshipped as gods. Sometimes, they found what they sought, and dragged some unlucky elf out to be butchered in the streets. More often, they found Ildorae's swift spear, or needle-darts of ice.

Olva knew none of this. Alf saw more, as he scanned the city with a practised eye, but there was yet one question that troubled him. There was death on the streets of Necrad, and on the walls, and at the north gate.

But Death herself had still not appeared.

The Wailing Tower defied the eye, an unnatural obscenity, a thorn in the skin of creation. It was too tall to stand, yet it stood; too great to be the work of mortal or Elvish hands, yet it existed. Only magic could have wrought it, and yet it was unutterably foul – an anti-wonder, a marker that declared there should be a limit to the ingenuity of magicians, that things could be conceived in the mind that should never be conjured into being. It rose, hundreds of feet of beetle-shell and cancerous gargoyle, twisting and writhing as if aware of its own monstrosity. Lesser towers and turrets protruded from it, and about a third of the way up were the broken remnants of an iron bridge that once spanned the gap between the tower and Lord Bone's temple. Now only the black pit remained of that vanished temple, a monument to the Nine. But the tower endured, and towards it they flew.

Alf guided the dreadworm to a balcony high on the north face.

He climbed down from the worm, and glanced over the balustrade to the black pit far below. "Climbed up here with Berys, long ago," he muttered. Gently, he lifted Derwyn down and carried him through a doorway into a comfortable study, the walls lined with bookshelves, stacked with curios and treasures from Necrad. Things with Vatling faces leered at Olva from their glass jars; near the window was a brass telescope and an orrery.

Alf laid Derwyn down on a table, sweeping the piled books and scrolls away. An inkwell splashed onto the polished wood of the floor, and Alf kicked it away into the corner. Olva sank into an overstuffed leather chair. Another door burst open, and Torun hurried into the room.

"Olva! Master Blaise foresaw your arrival."

"Did he now?" muttered Alf. "He and I need to have a long, long talk, when all this done." He raised his voice. "Blaise! Did you also foresee all this?" He waved his good arm out of the window, at the pillars of smoke that rose into the miasma above, at the distant battles.

Torun hugged Olva. The dwarf's hands were sticky with blood.

"Are you hurt?" asked Olva.

"No. No. It's just the other apprentices. They tried to attack Master Blaise. They're gone now."

Before Olva could ask Torun what had happened, a voice boomed from all around them. "Sir Aelfric of Mulladale, Knight of Summerswell, called by some Lammergeier. Keeper of the Spellbreaker! You come to my tower as the city trembles. The League has fled, the Nine are scattered! A prince of the Everwood is dead, and doom is at hand."

"Knock it off, Blaise," said Alf. Suddenly, the wizard was in the room with them, leaning over Derwyn. "I need your help."

"You shall have it." The wizard ran his thumb over Derwyn's forehead, as if brushing away a fleck of dirt. "We must be quick. Many of the city's defenders have already fled."

"Vond set me to watch for Death," said Alf, "otherwise I'd have been down in the thick of it."

"Death remains the great unknown." Blaise anointed Derwyn with a sweet-smelling oil.

"Can you heal him?" asked Olva.

Blaise's hood hid his face, but she could see his eyes glittering as he turned to her. "Olva Forster. There is much to be done this day. Your son has passed beyond the reach of any healing charm or potion I know. Perhaps the Intercessors might be able to draw him back across the threshold, but ... " The wizard paused. "There is no Intercession in Necrad. In the absence of the spirits, mortal cunning must suffice. I know a spell that can save your son. I must warn you: the magic is costly for all involved, and Derwyn will not return unchanged."

She nodded. "Aye. Whatever must be done."

"Aelfric," said the wizard, "a word in private."

"I've no secrets," said Alf, leaning on his sword.

"It is a matter for the Nine."

The wizard and the warrior withdrew into an adjoining room, leaving Olva to wait by Derwyn's side. She wanted to pray, but Berys' words rang in her ears. *The church is theirs, too.* Abbess Marit's vision had brought her right into Maedos' trap. All her time on the Isle of Dawn, all the prince's friendship: he'd been keeping her trapped until the moment was right to *use* her against Alf. Bor, too – everyone she'd met on the Road had taken her for a fool. Every smile had hidden fangs; every kind word was a trick.

She had been a fool. And now Derwyn lay dying on the slab. *He will not return unchanged.* What did that mean?

Torun fetched a bowl of water and washed the blood from her hands, which reminded Olva of their meeting in the Fossewood, all those weeks ago. Then, Olva had been overcome with horror after wounding one of Martens' soldiers in the ambush. Torun, though, was unfazed.

"What happened with the apprentices?"

"They were spies and assassins for the College of Wizardry in Summerswell," said Torun. "Master Blaise knew of their treachery, of course. They tried to sneak into his chambers during the night, but he was waiting for them. He drove them away. Now I'm his only apprentice." The dwarf swelled with pride. "You must see the library here. There are scrolls here written in the days when Necrad was first built, books by the greatest wizards of elves – and mortals, too. More than I dared dream. So much is locked away behind cyphers and sigils, though. Unravelling them will take years."

"Years in Necrad." Olva shuddered at the thought. "This place is monstrous."

"I think it's beautiful," said Torun.

Whether the study became a great ritual chamber, or Olva was too distracted to notice Torun escorting her to another room, she could not tell for sure. All became strange and dreamlike. Now Derwyn lay on a bier, and he was clad in a white winding cloth as though dead. Blaise stood nearby, a great leather-bound tome levitating in the air before him.

Alf came over and knelt by her side. "Blaise told me his plan. The daughter of a friend of mine – Thurn – she was injured, too, and Lath used a spell to save her. Blaise says we can use the same ritual to help Derwyn. To go into the Grey Land, and bring him back. The spell's perilous – I saw what it did to Thurn – so I'll go. I'll bring your boy back." He glanced behind him, looking out of the window over the city. Fires burned in the streets, and a noise like thunder rolled from the north gate. "I'll have to make it quick," Alf muttered.

"No." Olva rose. "I'll go. It's magic, Alf – it's not a matter of strength. I can do this." And as she spoke, she felt as she had in the heart of the Fossewood, as if her spirit was ready to soar free from her body. Almost eagerly, she stepped towards the wizard. Torun noticed her approach and hurried over to help Olva, anointing her brow with some foul-smelling oil.

"Wait," said Alf. He wrapped Olva's hand around the hilt of Spellbreaker, closing her fingers about the sword's grip. "Take it. I can't go with you, but this can. And . . . and if you have to, if you can't find him, tell the sword to break the spell and bring you back."

He stepped away. Blaise began to chant, a low, sonorous drone. Olva felt like she was back in her chair in her house at Ersfel. Two overlapping images of that cottage rose up in her mind – one warm and homely, Cu at her feet, the fire burning in the hearth. The sound of distant laughter up in the holywood as Derwyn bade farewell to his friends, and then the crunch of his footsteps on the path as he came home to her . . .

And the other that awful night, Galwyn's death, the pale faces and the black sword. Now, though, the sword was in her hands, and it drove the phantoms of memory away as the spell took hold.

CHAPTER FORTY-TWO

A lf watched Olva fall asleep, her head drooping to the side.
Blaise stood, still as a statue, impassive and unknowable. The
dwarf busied herself with Alf's wounds. She'd dug up another few
healing cordials, too, although Alf doubted they'd do much good.
He was probably more cordial than man at this point.

Still, could be worse. He looked down at Derwyn's grey face. In his
time, Alf had seen many dying men. Dead men, too. And undead
ones, for that matter. He knew all too well the pallor of death,
the stink of it. Olva's boy was among the dead, and Alf could not
imagine him returning. But he'd thought the same of Duna and
Erdys' boy, up in Athar, before the Intercessors saved him. And no
doubt Thurn had thought the same as he watched Talis sicken.

Out of the window he could see fighting at the north gate. He
couldn't make out details, only the clouds of dust and smoke, and the
flash of magic. South, and he couldn't see the League banners above
the citadel any more. Ships set sail from the harbour. The Garrison
had not fallen yet, but its masters had abandoned it.

He should be out there, hewing and hacking, but he felt like an
old man, brittle and broken. The battlefield was not for him, not
any more. Lammergeiers, he reflected, were birds of carrion anyway.
They showed up after the fight.

He wished he'd spoken to Thurn more, in the last years. The Wilder was the only one of the Nine to have children. Was he, then, the only one to have faith in their victory? All the rest of them had sworn to guard Necrad, to preserve what they had won – but that had held them in place, trapped them here. Fifteen years had passed, and they were all still playing the roles of their youth, rotting instead of changing. They'd all been unwilling to let the story of the Nine end.

There are only two endings to a story, after all.

A bird tapped at the glass. A raven.

Torun yelped in alarm. "I didn't know there were birds in Necrad," she said.

"There aren't birds in Necrad," said Alf.

He stepped out onto the balcony. The raven perched on a railing, so black it was a hole in the world. It was a young bird, sleek and healthy, not a feather out of place.

"You're not Lath," said Alf.

"I am not," said the bird, and its voice was that of a girl.

He sighed. "I wondered where you'd got to. I thought you'd be blasting Necrad to rubble."

"There is time enough for that. For seven days and nights, as befits a chieftain of the As Gola, I mourned my father. He taught me the old customs well, for he feared they would be forgotten. The Old Man would not wait. He said he had cast the runestones, and they said we had to go to Necrad. He broke the customs and led the Wilder away, so I mourned there alone, except for Lath – and his mind is broken. He speaks in riddles, and will not take human form again."

"Ach." Alf sagged against the railing. "Poor Lath. I failed him. And I'm sorry about your father."

"You promised a truce, and betrayed him. It was the dwarf who struck him down, and I have taken him, but I am not satisfied."

Lightning flashed in the raven's dark eyes. "I could claim you here and now."

"Aye," said Alf. "You're not a thing I can fight. I've slain many monsters, but you're not something I can defeat. If you want to take me as punishment for Thurn's death, so be it. I'd ask only that you wait a little while. I want to be there when they're done."

Talis the raven followed his gaze and hopped over to the window. The light of Blaise's magic reflected in the glass, like a shower of sparks. "They are in my domain! Who are they?"

"That's my sister Olva. She gave your father shelter, long ago. And her son. In truth, I've never even laid eyes on the boy before today. He came following the stories of the Nine, and got lost. He's dying."

"I followed my father," said Talis, "and offered to bring him back to the land of the living. He refused. He would not explain why."

"That's Thurn all right."

"I think that he feared me," said Talis. "I do not think I am what he thought I would be."

"I doubt that's it," said Alf. "But in truth, I don't know much. Take Derwyn there. I don't know a thing about him, save what Olva told me." He closed his eyes and rested his head against the cold marble. "But I've been thinking about what I'd say to him when I found him. See, I wandered into this life. I went off to seek my fortune with Gundan, thinking I'd earn a few coins as a mercenary. A place in the tournaments. Maybe, at most, a place in some great lord's household as a retainer. I never set out to be a hero, and I don't think I'm much of one. But I found good friends by chance, and those days were bright. I'd have them back again if I could. Even the worst day was sweet." He opened his eyes and stared down into the dark crater. "But time moves on, and life is brief. You can't live in the shadow of the past all the time. The old stories can guide you, but not all the way. You've got to push on, find something new. Otherwise . . . otherwise the world's just a tomb."

He looked at the raven. "I'd tell him all that. And I'll tell you all that, too. I don't care if they say you were once Death and you were the first human to ever walk the earth. You're Talis the daughter of Thurn now, and what that means is up to you."

The raven was silent for a long time. Then she said, "I will tell you a story."

Now, Death gathered to her the mightiest warriors of her people, and made them her warband. These she loved above all others. With Death, these companions chased and hunted the Endless, and none could stand against them in battle. When one fell, Death went into her shadowy kingdom on the borders of the world, and carried her companion back to the lands of the living. The elves had no such good fortune – when a mortal slew one, the elf's body would perish, and its spirit would remain in the world, haunting the land for ever. But Death knew spells to drive these troublesome spirits away into the wastes where they would trouble us no more. With the magic of Death, many victories were won by her company of heroes.

Now Death knew that the elves had fled south across the sea, and desired to pursue them unto the ends of the earth, saying: "To the sea! Fear not the wild waters, for I shall quell them with the power that is in me. Fear not the storm, for it is mine to command. We shall go beyond the lands we know, and fight until the Endless are ended. And should you perish in this endeavour, I will find you in the Grey Lands, and take you back to thy house of bone and blood so that you may fight on. You need not fear, for I am with you."

But her companions said, "You say we need not fear, but we fear for you. You are Death, but you are mortal, too. We look upon you, and we see that your hair has gone white as snow. Your eyes are no longer bright, your limbs no longer lithe. You can take any shape you desire, but always your back is hunched and you walk with a limp no matter how many legs you have. You can command the earthquake and shatter the sky with a spell, but the world is cracked and scarred enough already. And should you fall, who will find your spirit in the shadowlands? If you fall, who will bring us back? We have spent many years in your service, and fought for you in many strange lands. There are few enough years left to us, for we are not elves – and you cannot bring the spirit back to a house that has crumbled. We would live ere we meet you again. Let there be peace between Mortal and Elf; no more shall we fight them, and no more shall they try to imprison Death."

Death called her children cowards, and cursed them for balking at this last battle. She took on many forms, each more frightful than the last, but her companions would not relent. The host of death divided into three, each one led by one of her three captains, and they took their tribes off in different directions, north and south and west. And they all forbade that this story should ever be told, lest other men learned of their betrayal.

And Death, alone once more, looked upon the city of Necrad. She despaired, and when her mortal frame could no longer bear the burden, she walked into the wood and came to a place that had no name in the tongues of elf or mortal.

There, she cast herself down, and the leaves covered her, and a mound was raised over her grave.

"I will come back," said the raven, "in a little while. And then I shall see if I am still minded to take you." She turned her head towards the window and stared at Derwyn. "Or him. There is a darkness in him I do not like." She spread her wings.

"A word of warning," said Alf. "The spell that called you back – the Erlking made it. He can unmake it, too. Maedos was going to save the city by breaking the spell and destroying you. I'd stay away from the elves, if I were you."

The raven cocked her head as if considering Alf's warning, then she was gone, a dark shape spiralling upwards until she vanished in the necromiasma. A few of the dreadworms gave chase, and Alf watched their corpses plummet from the clouds and crash on rooftops across the Liberties. She was flying west, and at speed, leaving the city behind her.

*

Olva opened her eyes.

She hadn't moved an inch. She was still in the exact same spot, in Blaise's chamber, only everyone else had vanished – and the light had changed. It was a pale grey light, a ghost light that glimmered in the thin mist that had begun to roll in through the window. She stood, her knees complaining with the effort – she was a ghost now, how could her knees still hurt – and looked around the suddenly deserted room. Where Blaise and Torun had been a moment ago, there was no one, just empty air. On the table where Derwyn lay, there was the shadowy impression of the boy.

She crossed to the window and looked out over the city. It had changed, but it took her a moment to understand the nature of the change. All the damage inflicted by mortals was gone in this ghost-reflection. There was no trace of the Wilder's depredations, nor the scars left by the League's assault on the city during the war, nor even the works of Lord Bone. There was no huge crater in the plaza aside, no rubble left by his gargantuan palace, only a deep and still well. Stars shone in the depths. The great rune of the streets emanated from this central well. This was Necrad as it was thousands of years ago, she guessed, as the elves knew it.

She had called it monstrous, Torun had called it beautiful.

That's not it, thought Olva. Beauty meant little; the place was indeed beautiful in a ghastly, alien manner. It was not the pretty, tranquil beauty of the Isle of Dawn, nor the homely comforts of Ersfel. It was more akin to the beauty of staring into the night sky, or of standing before a raging torrent. It made her feel tiny, an insignificant little drop of blood and bone that for a moment flickered into consciousness. Necrad's sublime beauty battered her soul – but it was more than appearance. Appearance was part of it.

"It is honest," said the sword. "Necrad does not cloak itself in stories. It does not hide its monstrous nature. It is not a city for mortals, and never can be."

An honest monster. That was it. The city was honestly monstrous.

She would never feel safe here, be fooled into thinking she could trust anyone here. Necrad would never lull her into weakness, or let her think that evil had been driven from the world.

"I wasn't safe in Ersfel, either," she said to the sword. "I thought I was, but evil came anyway. You came anyway."

"My wielder brought me there. Now, I serve another," said the sword. "This is the borderland, between the earth and her domain. The elves are bound to the world. This is where they linger. You've got to go down to find him."

"Down," echoed Olva. "The Pits?"

"Just down," said the sword. "Take me with you." There was a plaintive note in its voice that she had not heard before. "He is far gone already, wielder. You will need to hurry."

The staircase of the Wailing Tower became a grassy hillside, sloping gently downwards. The mists of the Grey Land prevented Olva from seeing more than a few feet in any direction, but the smell and the feel of the air told her she had left Necrad far behind. She was not especially surprised when the familiar trees of the holywood at Ersfel loomed before her, their branches leafless and bare in a spectral winter. The grass underfoot crackled with frost.

The village was deserted. A ghost town without ghosts. Olva was the only spirit who walked there, through fields and woods she knew so well. Much of Ersfel was as she remembered it, but not all. She looked for the house she'd grown up in, the little cottage on the edge of the village in the shadow of the trees, for the barn where the Nine had sheltered after fleeing the High Moor. It was gone. She found only a void there, a swirling grey mist that seemed darker than the rest.

"I don't recognise this," she muttered to herself.

"These are not your memories," said the sword, "but his. Go down. Always down."

She came to the treelined path that wound around the foot of the hill. There lay the Forster lands, her home, the home she'd made with Galwyn, the safe little refuge where she'd lived all her life. A powerful desire to go there came over her, a warm weariness mixed with the expectancy of seeing home after a long journey. She would go there, and collapse into her seat by the fire, and fall asleep with Cu warming her toes.

Maybe Galwyn was there. If there were so many miracles in this strange world, why not another?

The sword became immensely heavy, wrenching her ghostly wrist. "Go down!" it insisted. "If you linger here, you will never have the strength to finish this quest!"

Olva turned from the way home and instead walked past the empty shade of Genny Selcloth's house, down the muddy slope of the river.

The terrain changed around her as she descended, a dreamlike shift, and now she was in a forest glade. A campsite – a fire burned, cold and colourless, and there were blankets and other supplies scattered about. A lone dwarf by the fire, trying to repair his battered old axe. When he saw Olva and the sword she bore, he laughed.

"Now there's a wonder indeed – Alf giving up that bloody sword." He hopped to his feet and bowed low. "Gundan, son of Gwalir, at your service. Not that I can serve you much, being dead and all. I'm only still around because Jan asked me to hang about a while." Gundan scratched his nose. "I must say, death's a lot less restful than I was led to expect. As many comings and goings as a knocking shop in Arden. I've met a bunch of friends here I haven't seen in years. A few lads from the Dwarfholt I used to know. Jan. Even big Thurn. He didn't stay, but we had a chance to talk, which was nice. And I thought I'd wait a spell for Alf, but there's no sign of him. Does you having his sword mean he's on his way, or he's not coming?"

"I don't know what's become of my brother," said Olva, "he went away to fight Death."

"Without the sword?" Gundan laughed. "I'm surprised he didn't beat you here with such foolishness. Who's going to keep an eye on the lunkhead without me, that's what I want to know?"

"Please, I'm looking for my son Derwyn. Have you seen him?"

"Tall lad? Looks a lot like Alf did before he got old and a few ogres hit him in the face, eh? I thought I saw a fellow like that, all right. And there's only one way he could have gone."

"Down," said the sword.

"Aye, down. I can show you the way . . . " said Gundan, suddenly reluctant.

"Please, if ever you loved Alf, help me."

"That's the thing about this place, miss. It's a slope, though it doesn't always look like one. Up top's the land of the living, and down below is, well. Not. And you can't go up the slope. You can't go back."

"Not without aid," rumbled the sword. "I have help in mind."

"Thought you might," muttered Gundan. "But listen to me, you fucking evil thing – it doesn't matter that I'm dead, and that you don't have an arse to kick. If you cross us, I shall fight my way out of the afterlife and come back just so I can fucking *ruin* you, aye?"

"Lead on, master dwarf," said the sword.

Gundan lingered a moment, surveying the memory of the campsite. "This was where we camped, the last night before we went up onto the High Moor. Peir and Jan and Blaise all jabbering about prophecies, and poor young Lath shaking and frothing at the mouth as he had magic visions. Berys looking like she wanted to bolt. Laerlyn talking about saving the world, and Thurn sitting over there with this grim look on his face like he was fit to kill us all. And me and Alf just here, wondering what the hell we'd got mixed up in." He scuffed the earth with one foot. "Ah, well," he muttered, "that was fun."

Then the dwarf led Olva down on the slope into the Grey Lands.

They passed into a bleak region, a barren hillside stripped bare of memories. No work of man or elf endured here; all was dark grass and broken stone, as it had been since the beginning. They were all alone in an empty land as far as Olva could see. There was no sun or moon in the sky, only thousands of stars. Most were very faint, but a small few burned brightly. As they walked, one kindled, flaring with an angry light.

"No bloody idea what that means," muttered Gundan. "But it's probably significant. Or symbolic, or something. Ask a bloody wizard." He sighed. "I don't know how much further I can go with you. I don't think dwarves go to the same end as you humans. Look."

Olva looked down and saw that Gundan's feet had sunk into the earth. Now he was wading through the grass.

"Keep going," said the dwarf. "Somewhere down below, there's a tower. I've seen it from afar. *She* dwells there, aye, but she's not there now. So, you go past the tower, and look for—"

"I will guide her," said the sword. "I can sense him."

"Right."

They walked on down the slope. Olva struggled to keep going. She leaned on Gundan more and more, even as he continued to sink slowly away into the ground, and the dwarf spoke as they walked.

"It wasn't all in vain. We stopped Lord Bone, didn't we? Turned back the dark, at least for a while? I remember them cheering at Karak's Bridge, when we brought down the Chieftain of the Marrow-Eaters? I remember Alf bringing the elf fleet to rescue us. All of us pretending we hadn't seen Jan sneaking over to Thurn's tent. The first few years after . . . "

Olva looked back and saw that he was gone.

She remembered what Torun had told her about the beliefs of the dwarves. "May Az judge your works fairly."

On down the slope. If the sword knew where it was going, it said no word. If there was a tower here in this desolation, Olva saw no sign of it. She kept her eyes fixed on one particular faint star that was somehow friendly to her. It was low down by the horizon, leading her onwards, and it twinkled and twirled and bounded in her vision, reminding her somehow of a playful dog. She followed that star as she descended.

She walked for a time that could not be measured, in a place that was not a place.

She walked as the keening wind blew through her, until she could count every one of her bones.

She walked as age caught her, and bent her, and withered her.

She walked as her skin flaked away, as her flesh rotted, as her bones grew thin, and dry, and cracked, and in the end crumbled into dust.

Until all that remained of her was a hand holding the sword.

Until she was not alone. Though she could not see him – how could she, when she had no eyes? – she would always know her son.

We have to turn back, she thought. *The land of the living is up there.* But the memory of her legs kept walking ahead, down and down and down the slope.

We've come too far, she thought, *I'm sorry. I failed you.*

No, came a thought, *there's still a chance. We must not give up.*

At the edge of the Grey Lands, there was a precipice, and on that precipice at the edge of the void, there wrestled two figures. Giants they were, alike in greatness, though one was foul and dark, the other bright and glorious. For many years they had wrestled there, neither wholly alive nor wholly dead, and perhaps they would have fought on there for many ages of the world, neither willing to relent.

But Olva Forster came to them, and raised the sword in token of her quest.

The young man who would be king of Necrad awoke, and there was an unearthly light upon his brow.

"Derwyn?" said Olva, and in the same moment, Alf said in wonder: "Peir?"

But it was Blaise who moved first, rushing to the young man's side, whispering urgently in his ear.

CHAPTER FORTY-THREE

This is a tale they tell on the streets of Necrad: the tale of the Return of the Uncrowned King.

Now the Widow returned from the Grey Lands, and looked upon her son, and lo! his wounds were healed. No mark of fang or arrow marred him. The Wizard Blaise fell as though stunned, his power exhausted by the spell he had wrought.

The Widow said, "Wake, my son, for you are renewed."

And the Uncrowned King of Necrad opened his eyes, and the Widow saw that it was not only her son Derwyn of Mulladale who lay there, for he had not returned from Death unchanged.

In him also was the wisdom and courage of Peir the Paladin, hero of the Nine.

"Too long have I slept," said the king, "and it seems to me I dreamt of death, and I have had my fill of it. Life is in me now, and there is much work to be done to rebuild this city so that it is fit for heroes. This is the first day of a new age, a time when all shall look to Necrad with hope and not dread."

He rose then, and saw the Wizard Blaise. "I have brought knowledge back with me, old friend. I know hidden signs and sigils to command the power of my city. Hark!" And he whispered to Blaise certain magic words that no living man had ever heard.

With these words, and with the blessing of the Uncrowned King, Blaise woke the defences of Necrad which had slumbered since the death of Lord Bone. The city groaned. Fissures opened in the streets and the necromiasma issued forth. The Pits opened, and chimeras and other monsters drove the invaders from the streets. Fire blazed in the throats of stone dragons. The Wilder were much dismayed, and they fled into the north, wailing they had lost Death and found Death all at once.

But one mortal alone returned from her land, and now he sits on the throne of Necrad, bright lord of the dark city.

Olva's new boots clattered on the marble floor of the hall outside the council chamber. The sound was too loud, and made her feel self-conscious. She dared to peek inside through a crack in the door. The new council had gathered; she recognised only a few people, like Alf and Threeday. Alf was sitting next to a Witch Elf. Her silver-white hair reminded Olva of the winter frost on the rooftops outside. She shivered.

"I've got no right to be in there," she said. She nervously pulled at the fine elven gown they'd made her wear, at the fur stole around her neck. The Widow Queen, they called her on the streets.

"You've as much right as any of them," said Torun. "I've been studying this city. I can't stop. And you know one thing I've learned. It's a wheel of destiny. All the constellations are reflected on the streets below, all fates are made here. It can lift you up or throw you down, exalt you or break you." She poked Olva's arm. "Right now, you've been lifted up. It may throw you down again one day. For your sake – and for his – stay up as long as you can."

Derwyn came down the hallway, Blaise at his side like a shadow. The two were deep in conversation, and she did not recognise the look on Derwyn's face. But when he saw her, he smiled, and he was her son again.

He gestured to the council door. "Shall we?"

It would be winter too, in Ersfel, the grey weeks after Yule. On the farm, she'd be worrying about the spring thaw, about the quality of the seed, about the health of the ewes. Now, she worried about the road through the Dwarfholt becoming passable again, about the state of the city's depleted granaries, about the danger they knew was coming.

She had found Derwyn, but they would never be safe again. Olva Forster gathered her courage and marched into the council chamber.

"Let us begin," she said.

The sound of the ringing church bells combined with Bor's hangover to drive spikes of brass through his skull. He stumbled down the alleyway and vomited copiously, which helped a little. The damned dog followed along, like a curse. It stood there and judged him while he puked his guts out.

He slumped against the wall. "Fuck me," he muttered.

Cu whined at him.

"Fuck you, too. Stupid dog. Go away. Go home." The beast had followed him all the way from Ellsport, from when he'd . . . "Go home!" he spat again. The dog didn't move.

"All right. All right. Breakfast." Bor hauled himself upright and dug in his pocket. It was empty. The pile of vomit – or, more accurately, the cheap dwarven booze that was now an intrinsic part of it – marked the last of his coin. He cursed again.

He could go north. There were rumours of war in the north again, and the whole League was moving, the great war machine shaking off the dust of twenty years. He'd seen columns of soldiers marching through the town on their way to the Cleft of Ard and the Dwarfholt. Knights, too, armour studded with charmstones, riding off to battle. A brave man, good with a sword, could earn a fortune there.

Bor vomited again, a dry heave. "Fuck that," he whispered to himself. Not north. Not Necrad. Something, anything else.

Suddenly, the dog began to bark frantically, a frenzy of yelping and shouting. "Shut up!" muttered Bor, clutching his head. The racket was the last thing he needed. "Shut up!"

The barking stopped abruptly, mid-yelp.

Silence. Bor looked about. The dog was gone. The alleyway empty.

Only it wasn't.

There was no one else in the alley, no one else in sight, but Bor somehow knew he was not alone. The sounds of the church bells and the clamour of the distant streets fell away, smothered by a blanket of crushing silence. Everything felt strange and wrong, as if he'd slipped out of the waking world and into a shadow realm. A terrible presence eclipsed the winter sun, swallowing its light. Fear took him, and he stumbled away, crawling through his own vomit, staggering – but slow, too slow.

The Lammergeier, he thought, *the Lammergeier has come to punish me!*

For an instant, he thought he beheld a shining figure standing over him, and then a blow struck him, sending him sprawling back into the mud – and back into the world. The sun was back in the sky, the noise of the town could be heard again. He lay there stunned, and Cu ran up to lick his face, urging him to get up.

But he could no more rise that he could fly.

An Intercessor passed, he thought, *and stopped to punish me for my sins*. The thought gave Bor a surprising amount of relief. There was justice in the land, in the end.

Presently, he heard footsteps approaching.

The story continues in . . .

Book TWO of Lands of the Firstborn

AFTERWORD

... and Barad-dûr would not have been destroyed but occupied ...

I was probably nine or ten when I read that line for the first time.
Tolkien is one of the threads that runs through much of my life – if
I hadn't gone to a Tolkien event at the local library, I might never
have discovered tabletop gaming, and that sends my life and career
off in some other direction entirely. A chance meeting, as they say
in Middle-earth.

Another point of origin – the *Heroes of the City* series pitch I wrote
for the *Dramasystem* RPG. Between hope and heroic mismanage-
ment, that's where this story resides.

Thanks, as always, to my editors Emily, Nadia and Bradley, agent
of legend John Jarrold, and all those sung and unsung on the pro-
duction team. And to those who read this book in any form, from
messy first draft to battered third-hand paperback bought in some
second-hand bookstore twenty years from now, thank you too.

extras

orbit

meet the author

Edel Ryder-Hanrahan

GARETH HANRAHAN's three-month break from computer programming to concentrate on writing has now lasted fifteen years and counting. He's written more gaming books than he can readily recall, by virtue of the alchemical transmutation of tea and guilt into words. He lives in Ireland with his wife and children. Follow him on Twitter at @mytholder.

Find out more about Gareth Hanrahan and other Orbit authors by registering for the free monthly newsletter at orbitbooks.net.

if you enjoyed
THE SWORD DEFIANT

look out for

THE LOST WAR
The Eidyn Saga: Book One

by

Justin Lee Anderson

Justin Lee Anderson's sensational epic fantasy debut follows an emissary for the king as he gathers a group of strangers and embarks on a dangerous quest across a war-torn land.

The war is over, but the beginnings of peace are delicate.

Demons continue to burn farmlands, violent mercenaries roam the wilds, and a plague is spreading. The country of Eidyn is on its knees.

In a society that fears and shuns him, Aranok is the first mage to be named King's Envoy. And his latest task is to restore an exiled foreign queen to her throne.

The band of allies he assembles each have their own unique skills. But they are strangers to each other, and at every step across the ravaged land, a new threat emerges, lies are revealed, and distrust threatens to destroy everything they are working for. Somehow, Aranok must bring his companions together and uncover the conspiracy that threatens the kingdom—before war returns to the realms again.

Chapter 1

Fuck.

The boy was going to get himself killed.

"Back off!"

Aranok put down his drink, leaned back and rubbed his dusty, mottled brown hands across his face and behind his neck. He was tired and sore. He wanted to sit here with Allandria, drink beer, take a hot bath, collapse into a soft, clean bed and feel her skin against his. The last thing he wanted was a fight. Not here.

They'd made it back to Haven. This was their territory, the new capital of Eidyn, the safest place in the kingdom—for what that was worth. He'd done enough fighting, enough killing. His shoulders ached and his back was stiff. He looked up at the darkening sky, spectacularly lit with pinks and oranges.

The wooden balcony of the Chain Pier Tavern jutted out

over the main door along the front length of the building. Aranok had thought it an optimistic idea by the landlord, considering Eidyn's usual weather, but there were about thirty patrons overlooking the main square with their beers, wines and whiskies.

Allandria looked at him from across the table, chin resting on her hand. He met her deep brown eyes, pleading with her to give him another option. She looked down at the boy arguing with the two thugs in front of the blacksmith's forge, then back at him. She shrugged, resigned, and tied back her hair.

Bollocks.

Aranok knocked back the last of his beer and clunked the empty tankard back on the table. As Allandria reached for her bow, he signalled to the serving girl.

"Two more." He gestured to their drinks. "I'll be back in a minute."

The girl furrowed her brow, confused.

He stood abruptly to overcome the stiffness of his muscles. The chair clattered against the wooden deck, drawing some attention. Aranok was used to being eyed with suspicion, but it still rankled. If they knew what they owed him—owed both of them…

He leaned on the rail, feeling the splintered, weather-beaten wood under his palms; breathing in the smoky, sweaty smell of the bar. Funny how welcome those odours were; he'd been away for so long. With a sigh, Aranok twisted and turned his hands, making the necessary gestures, vaulted over the banister and said, "*Gaoth*." Air burst from his palms, kicking up a cloud of dirt and cushioning his landing. Drinkers who had spilled out the front of the inn coughed, spluttered and raised hands in defence. A chorus of gasps and grumbles, but nobody dared complain. Instead, they watched.

Anticipating.

Fearing.

Aranok breathed deeply, stretching his arms, steeling himself as he passed the newly constructed stone well—one of many, he assumed, since the population had probably doubled recently. A lot of eyes were on him now. Maybe that was a good thing. Maybe they needed to see this.

As he approached the forge, Aranok sized up his task. One of the men was big, carrying a large, well-used sword. A club hung from his belt, but he looked slow and cumbersome, more a butcher than a soldier. The other was sleek, though—wiry. There was something ratlike about him. He stood well-balanced on the balls of his feet, dagger twitching eagerly. A thief most likely. Released from prison and pressed into the king's service? Surely not. Hells. Were they really this short of men? Was this what they'd bought with their blood?

"You've got the count of three to drop your weapons and move," the fat one wheezed. "King's orders."

"Go to Hell!" The boy's voice cracked. He backed a few steps toward the door. He couldn't be more than fifteen, defending his father's business with a pair of swords he'd probably made himself. His stance was clumsy, but he knew how to hold them. He'd had some training, if not any actual experience. Enough to make him think he could fight, not enough to win.

The rat rocked on his feet, the fingertips of his right hand frantically rubbing together. Any town guard could resolve this without blood. If it was just the fat one, he might manage it. But this man was dangerous.

Now or never.

"Can I help?" Aranok asked loudly enough for the whole square to hear.

All three swung to look at him. The thief's eyes ran him up and down. Aranok watched him instinctively look for pockets, coin purses, weapons—assess how quickly Aranok would move. He trusted the rat would underestimate him.

"Back away, *draoidh*!" snarled the butcher. The runes inscribed in Aranok's leather armour made it clear to anyone with even a passing awareness of magic what he was. *Draoidh* was generally spat as an insult, rarely welcoming. He understood the fear. People weren't comfortable with someone who could do things they couldn't. He only wore the armour when he knew it might be necessary. He couldn't remember the last day he'd gone without it.

"This is king's business. We've got a warrant," grunted the big man.

"May I see it?" Aranok asked calmly.

"I said piss off." He was getting tetchy now. Aranok began to wonder if he might have made things worse. It wouldn't be the first time.

He took a gentle step toward the man, palms open in a gesture of peace.

The rat smiled a confident grin, showing him the curved blade as if it were a jewel for sale. Aranok smiled pleasantly back at him and gestured to the balcony. The thief's face confirmed he was looking at the point of Allandria's arrow.

"Shit," the rat hissed. "Cargill. Cargill!"

"What?" Cargill barked grumpily back at him. The thief mimicked Aranok's gesture and the fat man also looked up. He spun around to face Aranok, raising his sword—half in threat, half in defence. Nobody likes an arrow trained on them. The boy took another step back—probably unsure who was on his side, if anyone.

"You'll swing for this," Cargill growled. "We've got orders from the king. Confiscate the stock of any business that can't pay taxes. The boy owes!"

"Surely his father owes?" Aranok asked.

"No, sir," the boy said quietly. "Father's dead. The war."

Aranok felt the words in his chest. "Your mother?"

The boy shook his head. His lips trembled until he pressed them together.

Damn it.

Aranok had seen a lot of death. He'd held friends as they bled out, watching their eyes turn dark; he'd stumbled over their mangled bodies, fighting for his life. Sometimes they cried out, or whimpered as he passed—clinging desperately to the notion they could still see tomorrow.

Bile rose in his gullet. He turned back to Cargill. Now it was a fight.

"If you close his business, how do you propose he pays his taxes?" Aranok struggled to maintain an even tone.

"I don't know," the thug answered. "Ask the king."

Aranok looked up the rocky crag toward Greytoun Castle. Rising out of the middle of Haven, it cast a shadow over half the town. "I will."

There was a hiss of air and a thud to Aranok's right. He turned to see an arrow embedded in the ground at the thief's feet. He must have crept a little closer than Allandria liked. The rat was lucky she'd given him a warning shot. Many didn't know she was there until they were dead. Eyes wide, he sidled back under the small canopy at the front of the forge.

Cargill fired into life, brandishing his sword high. "I'll cut your fucking head off right now if you don't walk away!" His bravado was fragile, though. He didn't know what Aranok could do—what his *draoidh* skill was. Aranok enjoyed the thought that, if he did, he'd only be more scared.

"Allandria!" he called over his shoulder.

"Aranok?"

"This gentleman says he's going to cut my head off."

"Already?" She laughed. "We just got here."

All eyes were on them now. The tavern was silent, the crowd an audience. People were flooding out into the square, drinks still in hand. Others stood in shop doors, careful not to stray too far from safety. Windows filled with shadows.

Cargill's bravado disappeared in the half-light. "You... you're... we're on the same side!"

"Can't say I'm on the side of stealing from orphans." Aranok stared hard into his eyes. Fear had taken the man.

"We've got a warrant." Cargill pulled a crumpled mess from his belt and waved it like a flag of surrender. Now he was keen to do the paperwork.

Perhaps they'd get out of this without a fight after all. Unusually, he was grateful for the embellishments of legend. He'd once heard a story about himself, in a Leet tavern, in which he killed three demons on his own. The downside was that every braggart and mercenary in the kingdom fancied a shot at him, which was why he tended to travel quietly—and anonymously. But now and again...

"How much does he owe?" Aranok asked.

"Eight crowns." Cargill proffered the warrant in evidence. Aranok took it, glancing up to see where the rat had got to. He was too near the wall for Aranok's liking. The boy was vulnerable.

"Out here," Aranok ordered. "Now."

"With that crazy bitch shooting at me?" he whined.

"Thül!" Cargill snapped.

Thül slunk back out into the open, watching the balcony. Sensible boy. Though if this went on much longer, Allandria might struggle to see clearly across the square. He needed to wrap it up.

The warrant was clear. The business owed eight crowns in unpaid taxes and was to be closed unless payment was made in full. Eight bloody crowns. Hardly a king's ransom—except it was.

Aranok looked up at the boy. "What can you pay?"

"I've got three..." he answered.

"You've got three or you can pay three?"

"I've got three, sir."

"And food?"

The boy shrugged.

"A bit."

"Why do you care?" Thül sneered. "Is he yours?"

Aranok closed the ground between them in two steps, grabbed the thief by the throat and squeezed—enough to hurt, not enough to suffocate him. He pulled the angular, dirty face toward his own. Rank breath escaping yellow teeth made Aranok recoil momentarily.

"Why do I care?" he growled.

The thief trembled. He'd definitely underestimated Aranok's speed.

"I care because I've spent a year fighting to protect him. I care because I've watched others die to protect him." He stabbed a finger toward the young blacksmith. "And his parents died protecting you, you piece of shit!"

There were smatterings of applause from somewhere. He released the rat, who dropped to his knees, dramatically gasping for air. Digging some coins out of his purse, Aranok turned to the boy.

"Here. Ten crowns as a deposit against future work for me. Deal?"

The boy looked at the gold coins, up at Aranok's face and back down again. "Really?"

"You any good?"

"Yes, sir." The boy nodded. "Did a lot of Father's work. Ran the business since he went away."

"How is business?"

"Slow," the boy answered quietly.

Aranok nodded. "So do we have a deal?" He thrust his hand toward the blacksmith again.

Nervously, the boy put down one sword and took the coins from Aranok's hand, tentatively, as though they might burn. He put the other sword down to take two coins from the pile in his left hand, looking to Aranok for reassurance. He clearly didn't like being defenceless. Aranok nodded. The boy turned to Cargill and slowly offered the hand with the bulk of the coins. Pleasingly, the thug looked to Aranok for approval. He nodded permission gravely. Cargill took the coins and gestured to Thül. They walked quickly back toward the castle, the thief looking up at Allandria as they passed underneath. She smiled and waved him off like an old friend.

Aranok clapped the boy on the shoulder and walked back toward the tavern, now very aware of being watched. It had cost him ten crowns to avoid a fight...and probably a lecture from the king. It was worth it. He really was tired. The crowd returned to life—most likely chattering in hushed tones about what they'd just seen. One man even offered a hand to shake as Aranok walked past; quite a gesture—to a *draoidh*. Aranok smiled and nodded politely but didn't take the hand. He shouldn't have to perform a grand, charitable act before people engaged with him.

The man looked surprised, smiled nervously and ran his hand through his hair, as if that had always been his intention.

Aranok felt a hand on his elbow. He turned to find the boy looking up at him, eyes glistening. "Thank you," he said. "I... thank you."

"What's your name?" Aranok asked. He tried to look comforting, but he could feel the heavy dark bags under his eyes.

"Vastin," the boy answered.

Aranok shook his hand.

"Congratulations, Vastin. You're the official blacksmith to the king's envoy."

Aranok righted his chair and dramatically slumped down opposite Allandria. The idiot was playing up the grumpy misanthrope because every eye on the top floor was watching him. He looked uncomfortable. Secretly, she was certain he enjoyed it.

Allandria raised an eyebrow. "Was that our drinking money, by any chance?"

"Some of it . . ." he answered, more wearily than necessary.

Despite his reluctance, Allandria knew part of him had enjoyed the confrontation—especially since it had ended bloodless. The man loved a good argument, if not a good fight—particularly one where he outsmarted his opponent. Not that she'd had any desire to kill the two thugs, but she would have, to save the boy. It was better that Aranok had been able to talk them down and pay them off.

"You could have brought my arrow back," she teased.

He looked down to where the arrow still stood, proudly embedded in the dirt. It was a powerful little memento of what had happened. Interesting that the boy had left it there too . . . maybe to remind people he had a new patron.

"Sorry." He smiled. "Forgot."

She returned the smile. "No, you didn't."

"You missed, by the way."

Allandria stuck out her tongue. "I couldn't decide who I wanted to shoot more, the greasy little one or the big head in the fancy armour." The infuriating bugger had an answer to everything. But for all his arrogance, she loved him. He'd looked better, certainly. The war had been kind to no one. His unkempt brown hair was flecked with grey now—even more so the straggly beard he'd grown in the wild. Leathery skin hid under a layer of road dust; green eyes were hooded and dark. But they still glinted with devilment when the two sparred.

"Excuse me…" The serving girl arrived with their drinks. She was a slight, blonde thing, hardly in her teens if Allandria guessed right. Were there any adults left? Aranok reached for his coin purse.

"No, sir." The girl stopped him, nervously putting the drinks on the table. "Pa says your money's no good here."

Aranok looked up at Allandria, incredulous. When they'd come in, he wasn't even certain they'd be served. *Draoidhs* sometimes weren't. Innkeepers worried they would put off other customers. She'd seen it more than once.

Aranok tossed down two coppers on the table. "Thank you, but tell your pa he'll get no special treatment from the king on my say-so, or anyone else's."

It was harsh to assume they were trying to curry favour with the king now they knew who he was. Allandria hoped that wasn't it. She still had faith in people, in human kindness. She'd seen enough of it in the last year. Still, she understood his bitterness.

"No, sir," the girl said. "Vastin's my friend. His folks were good people. We need more people like you. Pa says so."

"Doesn't seem many places want people like me…"

"Hey…" Allandria frowned at him. He was punishing the girl for other people's sins now. He looked back at her, his eyes tired, resentful. But he knew he was wrong.

"Way I see it"—the girl shifted from foot to foot, holding

one elbow protectively in her other hand—"you've no need of a blacksmith. A fletcher, maybe"—she glanced at Allandria—"but not a blacksmith. So I want more people like you."

Good for you, girl.

Allandria smiled at her. Aranok finally succumbed too.

"Thank you." He picked up the coins and held them out to her. "What's your name?"

"Amollari," she said quietly.

"Take them for yourself, Amollari, if not for your pa. Take them as an apology from a grumpy old man."

Grumpy was fair; *old* was harsh. He was barely forty—two years younger than Allandria.

Amollari lowered her head. "Pa'll be angry."

"I won't tell him if you don't," said Aranok.

Tentatively, the girl took the coins, slipping them into an apron pocket. She gave a rough little curtsy with a low "thank you" and turned to clear the empty mugs from a table back inside the tavern.

The girl was right. Aranok carried no weapons and his armour was well beyond the abilities of any common blacksmith to replicate or repair. He probably had no idea what he'd use the boy for.

Allandria raised the mug to her lips and felt beer wash over her tongue. It tasted of home and comfort, of warm fires and restful sleep. It really was good to be here.

"Balls." A crack resonated from Aranok's neck as he tilted his head first one way, then the other.

"What?" Allandria leaned back in her chair.

"I really wanted a night off."

"Isn't that what we're having?" She brandished her drink as evidence. "With our free beer?" She hoped the smile would cheer him. He was being pointlessly miserable.

Aranok rubbed his neck. "We have to see the king. He's being an arsehole."

A few ears pricked up at the nearest tables, but he hadn't said it loudly.

"It can't wait until tomorrow?" Allandria might have phrased it as a question, but she knew he'd be up all night thinking about it if they waited. "Of course it can't," she answered when he didn't. "Shall we go, then?"

"Let's finish these first," Aranok said, lifting his own mug.

"Well, rude not to, really."

Her warm bed seemed a lot further away than it had a few minutes ago.

if you enjoyed
THE SWORD DEFIANT

look out for

EMPIRE OF EXILES

Books of the Usurper: One

by

Erin M. Evans

Magic, mystery, and revolution collide in this fantasy epic where an unlikely team of mages, scribes, and archivists must band together to unearth a conspiracy that might topple their empire.

Twenty-three years ago, a duke with a grudge led a ruthless coup against the empire of Semilla, killing thousands. He failed. The duke was executed, a terrifyingly powerful sorcerer was imprisoned, and an unwilling princess disappeared. The empire moved on.

Now Quill, an apprentice scribe, arrives in the capital city believing he's on a simple errand for another pompous noble: fetch ancient artifacts from the magical Imperial Archives. He's always found his apprenticeship to a lawman to be dull work. But these aren't just any artifacts—these are the instruments of revolution, the banners under which the duke led his coup.

Just as the artifacts are unearthed, the city is shaken by a brutal murder that seems to have been caused by a weapon not seen since those dark days of rebellion. With Quill being the main witness to the murder and with no one in power believing his story, he must join with a young mage, a seasoned archivist, and a disillusioned investigator to find out the truth of the attack. And what they uncover will be the key to saving the empire—or destroying it.

Chapter One

Year Eight of the Reign of Empress Beneditta
The Imperial Archives
Arlabecca, the capital of the Imperial Federation of Semillan Protectorates
(Twenty-three years later)

Quill had been hoping, before he came to the Imperial Archives, when all this was just forms and plans and schedules, that Brother Karimo had been exaggerating. But here in the entry hall with the shouts of Primate Lamberto echoing over them, he had to agree: dealing with the Kirazzis made people uncommonly irrational.

Primate Lamberto's voice carried much farther than the head archivist's, but Quill could tell by the way his bellows kept cutting off abruptly that up in her office, the head archivist was giving as good as she got from the formidable primate. Brother Karimo kept looking anxiously up the stairs that led out of the enormous hall.

"I don't *think* she's going to throw us out," Quill said.

Karimo turned back to him and smiled. "You haven't met the head archivist before. It's still a possibility." He glanced once more at the stairs. "Better than when the Dowager Duchess Kirazzi died, though. No one's thrown a punch and I don't *think* anyone's set a fire."

"Saints and devils," Quill said, but Karimo turned back to the stairs.

Quill glanced over at the woman behind the reception desk, a pale, pretty archivist in robes of dark blue with a silver chain running from shoulder to shoulder. Her melting brown eyes fixed on the two scriveners of Parem waiting for their superior in a way that seemed somehow speculative and predatory. Quill gave her a little wave and she frowned.

"Are either of you facilitating those requests?" she demanded. "The Kirazzi ones?"

"Karimo is," Quill said, elbowing the other young man. Karimo jumped and Quill nodded toward the archivist with an expression full of meaning. Karimo often got the attentions of admirers—he was good-looking in a way that a half dozen protectorates would have claimed. Dark curls, golden skin, light, tapered eyes. Unfortunately for those admirers, Quill was usually the one who had to point his dearest friend toward them because he was never paying the least bit of attention.

Karimo followed Quill's gaze and shook his head with a faint smile. "Don't fraternize with clients."

"She's not a client," Quill pointed out.

"She's an *archivist*," Karimo said. Quill gave the young woman an apologetic sort of shrug, but she only continued her speculative study of Karimo.

"Anyway," Karimo went on, "you're the one interested in this place—you should stay."

"If it were up to me, in a heartbeat." The enormous doors to the Imperial Archives dominated the opposite wall, gleaming with their legendary opal mosaics. Symbols and representatives of every protectorate—every culture that shaped the Imperial Federation, every people whose wisdom and treasures had been safely gathered behind those doors—gleamed in a rainbow of shades.

Quill let his gaze drift between them: The elongated Alojan holding a bone flute. The Khirazji woman, adze and compass in hand, her braids picked out by iron banding. The Borsyan man, the curls of his pale, thick beard suggested by the undulating edge of the opals. The Orozhandi holding the horned skull of some ancestor, her own horned head tilted down as if in conversation. The Kuali with her shepherd's crook, the Beminat with a jaguar mask and axe, the Datongu with his ornate basket, the Ashtabari with tentacles clutching a variety of religious icons Quill didn't remember the meanings of. The Minseon man with a drawn bow, his hair sleek and eyes keen, who truly managed to look like Quill's next-eldest brother despite being made of rainbow stones.

A ring of palest white embraced the ten figures: the Salt Wall that surrounded Semilla. Beyond, the jagged edges of a changeling army bristled in more opals of red and green and brown, the force that had appeared as if from nowhere and destroyed all those nations from within, forcing them to flee to Semilla. Eyes and arms and teeth splayed from those strange figures—as if the fearsome shape-shifters were mid-transformation. Or maybe that was what they looked like when they weren't wearing someone else's face—Quill certainly had never seen such a creature, locked away as they were beyond the Salt Wall.

At the center, divided by the doors' split, stood the tenth figure: the Semillan emperor who had reigned during the Salt Wall's sealing, Eschellado, his face the imperial mask of gold instead of more opals.

All the imperial masks were beyond the doors. The archives held the treasures of ancient Semilla and all her protectorates, all those things carried away from the end of the old world that must be kept safe and sure. There was no end to the stories: Whole libraries rescued from kingdoms burning before the changeling army. Intact temples to dead gods. The proclamations of every emperor. The skin of a changeling queen. Diamonds as big as your head. Once, he had heard, a live mammoth, but that was madness—

"You're thinking about all the junk in there right now, aren't you?" Karimo teased.

"You're not even a little curious? I mean, the Kirazzi items aren't that interesting, but they can't stop you looking around while you're standing there. There's *certainly* a collection of Emperor Eschellado's notes about the formation of the protectorate government—if you try to convince me you don't want to see that, I'll call you out as a changeling."

Karimo shook his dark-curled head. "Eyes on the task, brother."

"I've got two eyes," Quill said. "I can do both. Just like you can make sure they find the Kirazzis' things, nice and tidy, *and* ask this girl out for a coffee."

"'Do not be slack in your own business but busy in others'.'"

"I cannot wait until you're through *The Precepts of Bekesa*

577

and on to some other way of lecturing me about how you can't have fun."

Karimo chuckled. But his gaze went up the stairs again.

It would be Karimo who stayed. Brother Karimo had been assisting Primate Lamberto for several years now and had the older man's trust. The primate was highly positioned within the Order of the Scriveners of Parem, the juridical order that managed most of Semilla's legal needs. The primate and his assistants traveled Semilla, spreading the strength and order of the imperial laws and assisting powerful and interesting clients. Assisting the primate was, in all, an excellent position, one Quill's parents found ideal for his station. Even if it didn't suit Quill very well.

Karimo, on the other hand, had his eyes always on the task: the client, the request, the complexities of the law, and the words that made those complexities solid and complete. He prized the duty of the Paremi in a way Quill had always found unsettling in others but somehow right and understandable from Karimo: *The law is what makes us more than beasts, more than the changelings, more than even just ourselves. The law keeps us safe.*

And if Karimo had given Quill a greater appreciation for their duties and their oath, Quill liked to think he'd managed to remind Karimo he could be dedicated and still live a life, deal with "clients" like people sometimes, and look up from his work.

Mostly. Karimo was still watching the staircase.

"Look, she keeps eyeing you," Quill started to say.

But then the door to the office above banged open, and the primate and the head archivist reappeared. Quill and Karimo shot to their feet. The archivist behind the desk only folded her arms over her chest.

The primate came to a stop before them. He was a big man, pale and paunchy, with a fluff of coiled gray hair looped up beneath his miter and half-hooded eyes. Unlike Quill and Karimo, he wore his robes of office instead of traveling robes, and decked in scarlet and gold finery, Primate Lamberto looked very imposing.

And very annoyed.

"The head archivist," he said, "has kindly acceded to our legal and approved requests. Finally."

The head archivist snorted from the foot of the stairs. Mireia del Atsina was an older woman, with a bridge of silver braids framing a narrow, tanned face that suggested at least a little Ronqu blood, and steady gray eyes that declared a Borsyan progenitor or two. She wore the same dark, crisp dress as the girl behind the desk, but hers was accented by a silver chain of office, weighted by the sigil of the imperial crown, a lacquered red cross in the middle of a stylized nest of live branches.

"Next time," she said, "get them approved *properly* and we don't have to do this."

Quill glanced at Karimo, who didn't meet his eye. The whole trip to Arlabecca, Primate Lamberto had been very clear that whatever Quill was used to, this request had its own set of expectations. This was a *highly discreet* undertaking, for a *very important client*, and so there would be *irregularities* that must be set aside because of *expediency and discretion*.

Such as the permissions, signed off not by the empress's secretary but by the Alojan noble consul, Lord Obigen.

"You don't need to bring it up," Primate Lamberto had assured Quill and Karimo. "In fact, until you are within the archives, you don't need to say a solitary word. Your help will please some very powerful people." He hadn't, Quill suspected, thought the issue with the permissions would come up as quickly as the entrance hall, necessitating the long, contentious conference with the head archivist.

"Who gets the bronzes?" the woman behind the desk called out.

Mireia shut her eyes. "Sit *down*, Zoifia."

"It's just a question—"

"Sit down!"

Primate Lamberto grimaced. "I see the Imperial Archives are as . . . *loose* with regard to decorum as ever."

The head archivist regarded him blandly. "Were you introduced to Archivist Kestustis, Most Reverend? She is one of the foremost experts on pre-Sealing cast-bronze works in the entire empire and the possessor of a very strong bronze affinity. When her services are available again, she will find your bronzes and identify them down to the mines their component metals were pulled from. She is twenty-two. The trade is, on occasion, she might offend someone's sense of decorum." Zoifia began to retort but Mireia raised a hand, silencing her. "I assume you're not loitering around yourself this time. Which of them are you leaving to spy?"

Lamberto drew back with a grimace. "Brother Karimo is very experienced, and I will thank you not to besmirch—"

"Most Reverend?" Karimo interrupted. Both Lamberto and Quill looked over at him, startled. Karimo did *not* interrupt the primate.

"If you please," Karimo went on, "I think you should leave Brother Sesquillio behind. He is very interested in the work of the archives—he's been saying so since we left the tower, you know—and beyond that . . ." Karimo faltered. "Beyond that, you have clients today and tomorrow which I know are difficult matters and which I would feel more comfortable being the one to help you prepare for."

"Or you could leave no one," the head archivist suggested, "and let us get on with our jobs." The primate did not so much as look at her, narrowed eyes on Karimo as if he were trying to find some sleight of hand in the words. Karimo only stared back.

Quill straightened, stinging a bit at the implication that he wasn't capable of scribing for one of Lamberto's clients alone. Besides, while the requests involved the archives, they *came* from the Kirazzi family, and if there were a more complicated client out there, Quill doubted Lamberto would take them on, wealthy or not.

But at the same time, oh how he wanted to lose this argument.

"With all due respect, brother," Quill began.

"Please." Karimo shot a look at Quill, bright with desperation. "Anyway, I think you'll enjoy this assignment. Is it all right, Most Reverend?"

Primate Lamberto studied his two assistants, puzzled, and Quill was certain Karimo's surprising suggestion would be cast aside like a mis-scribed contract.

"It will do," the primate said slowly. "Brother Sesquillio, you...you can accompany the head archivist back to her office. She will apprise you of the limitations the archives insist upon."

"Yes, Most Reverend," Quill said, scooping up his scribe kit and his ledger.

I'll explain later, Karimo mouthed as he passed.

"I'll see you tonight," Quill said, uncertain of what he'd just skimmed the edge of. The archives. The Kirazzis. Or just some tension between the primate and Karimo, some private battle. He glanced back down the stairs as he climbed them, but the other Paremi were already gone.

Whatever it was, Quill reminded himself, Karimo could solve his own problems.

And Quill would get to see the Imperial Archives.

Mireia led him to a room dominated by an enormous wooden desk, dark with age and heavily carved. The light slicing through three windows narrow enough to be arrow loops was somehow sufficient to fill the room and illuminate a wall covered with dark blue satin ropes hanging down from the ceiling, each labeled with a name in delicate script on a cream-colored tag.

"Sit," she said, gesturing at a pair of chairs. Quill did, as she came to stand behind the massive desk. "I assume Lamberto told you not to breathe a word with regard to what this is all about."

Quill made himself smile. "The Kirazzis merely wish to borrow some of their belongings back from the archives."

"Let's skip the things already written on the forms," Mireia said, "and go on to the truth. Which of the Kirazzis hired you?"

Had Primate Lamberto not said even that much? "I...I don't think they want their business aired."

"Let me make this simple: Is your client Ibramo Kirazzi?"

Quill frowned. The empress's consort, the son of Redolfo Kirazzi—but nobody, so far as Quill knew, who was associated with anything approaching mischief. In fact, he'd had the distinct impression that Ibramo Kirazzi held himself apart from anything his family did these days.

"No, no." Quill pulled out his notebook, flipped to the page where he'd written up what he needed to know, copied from the primate's notebook on the road. This had not been a client he or Karimo was allowed to sit down with, and Karimo had been the one to draw up the requests—but Quill had gotten the information down eventually.

"It's...the Duchess Kirazzi," he said. "The new one. I think that's his cousin?"

"And the newly crowned duchess wants the Flail of Khirazj? She thinks that's a good idea?"

It was a *terrible* idea, Quill was in full agreement on that much. When Redolfo Kirazzi had ridden against the previous emperor in his attempt to take the throne for the emperor's lost niece, the Grave-Spurned Princess—but really, as everyone knew, for himself—he had always carried the Flail of Khirazj, a symbol of the ancient god-kings the Kirazzi family descended from. A reminder he was greater than what he seemed, a challenge that he was greater than Semilla.

"I cannot say what the duchess thinks is a good idea, esinora," Quill said politely. But then he added, "I hear it's for a Salt-Sealing event. Something in the temple at Palace Sestina."

"And with it she requires..." Mireia lifted the requests and read from each page in turn. "One illuminated book, titled *The Maxims of Ab-Kharu*, bound forty years ago with Kirazzi crest on endpapers. One prosthetic arm"—she leveled a sharp gaze at Quill over the papers—"bone and hide, belonging to the late Djacopo Kirazzi. And two bronze statues of Khirazji queens, Bikoro dynasty: one with a headdress of three feathers, one with a scorpion crown. What sort of event is this?"

Quill frowned. His notes only had three items in dispute. Gods and devils, how had he missed one? Had Karimo folded in some other request by mistake? "Statues? Are you sure about those?"

"Am *I* sure?"

Quill shut the book, pushing down the edge of panic with the gesture. Of course Karimo hadn't made an error. Quill had been sloppy and missed an item. *Eyes on the task*, he thought. He could do this. Handling clients was what he was best at.

"It seems my notes are in error. I guess Brother Karimo was correct about my scribing." He smiled winningly at the head archivist. "But to be honest, being graced with a ducal title doesn't necessarily shower good sense on a person. We try not to pry into private matters," he added.

"Even with the Kirazzis?"

Quill took a deep breath and repeated Karimo's words. "The Kirazzi family have paid their debts to society. They make no more mischief than you or I. And legally, while the majority of the items seized in the forfeiture of Redolfo Kirazzi's effects are the possessions of the empire, the Flail of Khirazj remains joint property with the royal bloodline of that preexisting kingdom."

"I understand how the laws work," Mireia said wearily. "But you know as well as I do that the flail is a different beast."

Quill folded his hands. "The requests were approved."

"By Lord Obigen, who will sign any damned request given to him, if he thinks it takes him somewhere politically," Mireia said. "He wants his second wall. Probably wants Duchess Kirazzi to gift him the land around Sestina."

She sighed, then went to the long blue cords, taking three of them in her hands and considering. "While the primate is keen to pretend this is nothing at all, I'm sure the Paremi and the Kirazzi family understand that what you're asking for is akin to kicking a hornet's nest, midwinter," she said. "Maybe nothing, or maybe you're waking something that's going to hurt a lot of people."

"That isn't our intent," Quill said.

But he knew. Everyone knew, including the Kirazzis. No one talked about Redolfo Kirazzi with anything approaching practicality for fear they'd find themselves endorsing treason or worse. And there was no pretending these requests weren't peculiar—the flail, an old hand, and Lord Obigen—but would they be so peculiar from anyone else? A duty was a duty, and ultimately it wasn't Quill's place to say.

"I shall be out from underfoot as soon as possible, esinora."

She snorted. "You assume that because we are the Imperial Archives this is merely a matter of shuffling down a row of boxes and fetching what you want, don't you?"

Quill hesitated. "I don't dare imagine what the archives contain, esinora."

"Hmm," she said. "Sounds like you've heard stories. The mammoth?"

Quill hesitated. "That's *not* true, is it?"

"If it ever was, it's starved by now, but—this is the issue—I cannot say anything for sure. There are centuries of artifacts and writings and more in the archives, the treasures of no less than every Imperial Majesty, every king and queen and duke and warlord and reza and chief, every people that escaped the changelings. Not every Imperial Majesty allowed access. Not every Imperial Majesty had archivists. We are in the middle of a race which we were only allowed to begin halfway, and someone kept flinging pomegranates into our path. You want something from twenty-three years ago. Some of my archivists are still cataloguing things from the Salt-Sealing of the Wall."

Quill could not have hidden his shock, he felt sure. Almost a hundred years had passed since the Salt Wall had been completed. He wondered how much the Kirazzis *were* paying per day. "When...when do you expect to be caught up enough to find Redolfo Kirazzi's effects?"

"Oh, slam the shitting gates," Mireia said. "I'm not going to make you *wait*. They can stop and look—they do it all the time. I mean to say that you all are a nuisance, and you in particular are likely to be underfoot for an uncomfortably long time, but your primate wants his fingers in every pie and he has the right." She looked up, at last, from the three cords. "You never saw Ibramo Kirazzi? Swear it?"

Quill sat a little straighter. "No. Why? Why would it matter?"

Mireia nodded once and gave the center rope three sharp yanks. "I suppose it doesn't," she murmured, "since it's nothing to do with him."

It settled atop the uneasy feeling the strange request had already churned up in his stomach. Quill folded his hands on his knees and focused instead on how soon he would be within the fabled Imperial Archives.

＋・ーＥ◆Ｅ・ー＋

The official title given to Amadea Gintanas was "Archivist Superior of the Imperial Collections (South Wing)," which she felt was a great many words to say "a solver of problems."

Managing the archivists and collections housed in the southern portion of the Imperial Archives asked for many skills in service to many problems. Amadea spoke four languages, had a passing familiarity with six more, including several ancient ones from beyond the Wall, and was, specifically, the one you called when you needed Early Dynastic Khirazji translated. She knew how to preserve many treasures against time and the elements. She knew how to date clayware and basket weaves and stone carvings. She knew the faces of the Orozhandi skeleton saints and the names of the thirteen sage-riders of Min-Se and the forms of their dresses. She could level a worktable, repair a torn binding, and fix a Borsyan cold-magic panel without taking her fingertips off.

Amadea knew how to track the affinity patterns of her specialists, how to talk them down when their magic aligned and overtook them. She knew how to make a perfect cup of coffee, how to soothe a heartbreak or the crash that came when an alignment ended, a burst of anxiety or grief or shame that needed a kind word and a firm reminder that everything was all right.

Amadea Gintanas did not know what to do about the rabbit skull sitting on her desk.

"This is the *eighth* time this week he's pulled something like this." Radir, one of her newest generalists, stood opposite her desk. His dark, heavily lashed gaze was locked furiously on Amadea. "He put it under my worktable. I went to sit down and there's this...this *thing* snarling up at me."

Amadea considered the skull, the sharp points of its horns and the fierce arch of its teeth. In the cold-lamps, its shallow orbits glowed eerily, and the lacy bone of its narrow maxilla filled with shadows. A flash of gold traced the bone around the horns' bases—an Orozhandi ancestor gift, and a cheap one considering how faint the gold and how heavy the traces of glue. It wouldn't look friendly in the dark.

"Are you sure it didn't fall?" she said.

"From *where*?" Radir demanded. "You need to assign me elsewhere. I'm done."

Amadea folded her hands in front of her. "Where is Tunuk right now?"

Radir hesitated. "In the Bone Vault."

"Where he is not supposed to be left alone," she noted.

"He seemed fine." Radir rubbed the back of his neck. "He's not in alignment. Bone doesn't come into alignment for four more months."

"He's not in alignment," Amadea agreed, "and how very conscientious of you to keep track."

"Why do you need someone to keep an eye on him if he's not in alignment?"

Amadea smiled. "Because alignment raises the risks of a specialist being caught in an affinity spiral. It doesn't create the risks. You know this."

Radir shook his head. "He wasn't going to go for a walk just because I said so. He *hates* me. I want...I want to be here, but I don't know how to keep doing this. Maybe I'm not good enough. He keeps saying he wants you back."

That was when the bell on the wall started jangling. Amadea

pressed fingers to her right temple. "You might remind Tunuk that isn't going to happen."

Radir huffed out a breath and said, softer, "I'm worried he might spiral again just so you have to. I don't know how to stop that."

Amadea was beginning to worry about that too. "Tunuk knows that if he does any such thing, he will be sequestered," she said as she came around the desk. "Listen, he has a good heart, but Tunuk is prickly at his best. And a month out from a spiral, he is not at his best." Her own words tugged on Amadea's heart, flooded her thoughts with the memory of Tunuk, a month ago, huddled in the shadows, frozen in place by plaques of bone that clustered over his skin.

"Now, a month is long enough," she continued, telling herself, telling Radir, "that he can probably be left alone with the bones for a bit, and maybe he will appreciate the longer lead. But he needs you."

"He doesn't appreciate anything I do."

"He's not himself right now," Amadea reminded Radir. "And our job is to help the specialists when they can't help themselves. Which they don't always appreciate."

"It's a shit job," Radir said.

"Sometimes it is a *very* shit job. But someone needs to do it." She sighed. "Obviously, the Bone Vault isn't for you. I will work on finding you a replacement, but it will be a while, and right now, even if Tunuk can work alone for a bit, it can't be for long. I'll go talk to him. And if it keeps up, you'll come back to tell me."

The bell on the wall jangled again and she scooped up the rabbit skull. "Go. Take a walk. Buy some cakes or sit and have a coffee or go see that young woman you've been courting. I have to see what Mireia wants and then I'll go return this and talk to Tunuk."

Radir left, and Amadea followed, pausing to check her face

in the looking glass that hung over a shelf of figurines. Despite how careful she'd been, fixative gummed her olive temple and the dark streak of her right eyebrow. She licked the corner of her handkerchief and scrubbed at it, noticing as she did the new shaft of silver sprouting from her hairline. Amadea cursed under her breath and pinched the hair out.

You are entirely too old to be vain, she thought, mostly because she ought to hear it. Not because she believed it. She gave the remainder of her part a cursory examination for more traitors before smoothing her hair back down and heading out.

One-handed, Amadea opened the little tin in her pocket and pulled out a knob of scented beeswax. She warmed it in one hand as she walked. An archivist washed well before touching precious things, and old magics kept the archives cool and dry. Good for the artifacts, terrible for the skin. She studied her cracked cuticles a moment, rubbing the beeswax more firmly into them with a thumb, before swapping the skull to her other arm and the beeswax to the other hand.

Vain, vain, vain, she scolded herself as she glanced over the walkway's edge, through the ornate ironwork grating down at the archives floor below, to the archivists moving among the uncountable treasures collected there. When civilization had fled the changeling forces, they brought all manner of precious things to Semilla, and in their subjects, their materials, the names they bore, the shapes they made, lay a map to a world no one living had ever laid eyes on. Beyond the Salt Wall, the remains of those kingdoms and countries lay in ruins, but their traces were treasured and preserved in the Imperial Archives.

Amadea drew another deep breath, full of dust and past and promise, as she came to the foot of the iron stairs that wound down to the main floor. Sometimes it was a shit job, but mostly it was exactly where Amadea belonged.

"Did she call you?" Zoifia demanded as Amadea came into the entry hall, her voice rising and rising. "Do you know if she's giving Stavio my bronzes? Did you know there are Bikoro dynasty bronzes in there that no one's catalogued? I don't know them anyway, and *Stavio*—"

"Good afternoon to you, too. Who is it?"

"A queen consort and a queen regnant, and if they're Bikoro, I think—"

"I mean who is making the requests, not who are the statues." Amadea stopped and eyed Zoifia.

When Amadea had first come to the archives, she had envied the specialists. They had such clear and certain purposes. Not quite sorcerers out of stories, but born somewhere on the stairs to that platform of exaltation and madness, the specialists could connect with worked materials, "speaking" with bone and ink and metals and gems and more. Each material responded to its specialists, granting them information and even limited manipulation, but that skill ebbed and flowed. Sometimes the connection was so thin, so *off*, a specialist could only feel the soft, specific song of their material—*yes, I know this one*.

But when they came into the peak of their power, each turned to each and the magic became greedy and dangerous. A bronze specialist in full alignment could find a pin in a mud puddle, could repair an urn cast a thousand years ago, could even—for the most powerful affinities, at their very deepest depths—coax tin and copper and trace metals together, make something new like a sorcerer could. But each taste, each use, demanded more, and if the specialist wasn't careful, they would begin a spiral of magic that ended only when they were completely merged and entombed by their material, one forever more.

Needless to say, keeping track of alignments and keeping aligned specialists distracted were the greatest of Amadea's problems—and bronze was moving swiftly into alignment. She considered Zoifia's tapping fingers, that too-familiar manic note in her voice, even as she brushed aside anything that wasn't bronze.

"How are you feeling?" Amadea asked.

"I'm *fine*," Zoifia said, tossing her wild curls.

Sometimes Amadea thought it was the prayer of the specialists: I'm fine. *I have lost my sense of self to something inanimate, but* I'm fine. *I've been up all night eating glass and talking to bones, but* I'm fine. *I have smothered myself in gold and drawn trees up through the floorboards, but* I'm fine.

"Did you eat?" Amadea asked, trying to gauge the width of Zoifia's pupils, the color of the irises. She didn't see any bronze flecks there, which was good.

"You'd better hurry," Zoifia retorted. "Mireia wants you to handhold that Paremi. There was a fat old one who thought he could bluster his way in and a young handsome one who was stuffy as a scrivener in a melodrama, but they left. The other young one, a short one with the stupid name, went up with Mireia." She paused, bit her lip a moment. "It's Paremi," she said carefully. "But it's *for* the Kirazzis. You should know."

Amadea's chest squeezed tight around her breath, all her worries about Zoifia suddenly gone. "Oh," she said, and then: "Oh," again, as if that would make anything better.

All she could think of was the letter. *Please never doubt: My love and esteem for you have not changed. There is no force within the Wall that could change them, my darling.*

She cleared her throat. "Well. That's surprising. What do they want?"

"A bunch of junk. And the bronzes. Which, if Mireia gives them to Stavio—" Zoifia stopped herself that time. "I have to assume they said it wasn't Ibramo because Mireia is heartless to *me* but she wouldn't have called you, if it were him."

"It's not anyone but some Paremi," Amadea said. She wondered who had told Zoifia that Ibramo Kirazzi was anyone who mattered, and what exactly they had said.

But love is not enough to withstand the truth of our respective stations, and the dangers of my past are too great to bear. Wedding Beneditta could change all of that…

"I bet I could get someone else," Zoifia said. "Some other superior. It doesn't have to be you, right, so I'll go—"

"You have reception duty," Amadea said briskly, brushing the memory aside. "Thank you for your concern, Zoifia, and I'll be sure to remind Mireia you wish to be involved in finding the bronzes when you're up to it. Which is *not* today." She lifted the skull. "Could you keep this for me?"

Zoifia seemed to suddenly notice the horned rabbit skull. "Why do you have *that*?"

"Tunuk." And before Zoifia could be roused to any further kindness, Amadea swept through the entryway and up the stairs to Mireia del Atsina's offices.

Mireia sat at her desk, finishing a request for a specialist. In front of her was what must have been the Paremi—but he was so painfully young that for a moment Amadea couldn't accept that the venerable Paremi came in the form of boys with such guileless eyes. But there he sat, his black, shining hair shaved around his skull, with the top pulled back in an intricate knot at the crown. He smiled eagerly at Amadea, putting her in mind of a puppy. At least Zoifia hadn't destroyed his good mood.

"Amadea, this is Brother Sesquillio," Mireia said. "Quill, this is Amadea Gintanas, one of our superior generalists."

He leapt up from his seat, his dark, tapering eyes sparkling, and grabbed her hand. "Very nice to meet you. I'm so excited to be here."

"It's nice to meet you too." She folded her hands against her skirts, then added to Mireia, "Zoifia mentioned the Kirazzis made the request?"

"The duchess." Mireia handed over the requests to Amadea, eyes full of warning. "But what she's asking for is trouble. You're going to need Yinii, Tunuk, Bijan, and then Zoifia when she's back to herself."

Amadea flipped through the pages, saw the words "the Flail of Khirazj."

She caught her breath, a memory dragged up: *Redolfo, Ibramo's father, flail in hand, looming, looming. Lireana on the floor, on the carpet, the good Alojan carpet, and she's both a million miles away and close enough to hear the beads clink together as the flail swings, before Ibramo shouts—*

Amadea forced herself not to flinch, to ask, "The flail?"

"Apparently, we're not to inquire as to the Duchess Kirazzi's good sense," Mireia said dryly. "Also, Brother Sesquillio has been volunteered to help you, or possibly to make certain we comply to the primate's standards. Or possibly because the primate believes we will make off with the goods, and this one's going to stop us. At any rate, keep him busy so the primate doesn't bother me anymore."

"Right," Amadea said, though it was anything but. She flipped through the request documents as they walked back down into the entry hall. Nothing was ever all right when Redolfo Kirazzi was involved.

Ibramo looking at her, young and fragile, and it scares her. "He's gone to the tombs with her this time. He's going to do something—"

Amadea blew out a breath and the ghost of the memory before it could stir up anything more. A request was a request—what came of it was a question for the officials who reviewed them, not Amadea Gintanas. At the foot of the stairs, she turned and found the Paremi nearly on her heels. "Brother Sesquillio—"

"Quill, please," he said. "No need for formality if I'm helping you."

"Yes." Except there was no task she could think of that she'd be pleased to hand to this untrained young man—maybe someone had a ledger he could check. She considered the requests, calculated how long to find these things, how long she would have to keep this boy—this hostage, this spy—busy to keep peace between Mireia and the primate.

"Perhaps... a tour," she said slowly.

"Oh! That would be *wonderful.*" He grinned at her. "The head archivist made it sound like this would be a complicated endeavor. I'm so glad it means there's time to see everything."

Saints and devils, he was so *young.* She sighed. Tours of the archives weren't uncommon—there were public galleries and chapels, but if you had the influence and the interest, and Mireia wasn't annoyed, a tour of the rest of the archives could be arranged. Only, they were arranged months in advance and Amadea's thoughts were full of the many, many things she needed to take care of. Maybe she could find someone else to take him around.

"*Some* things," she corrected. She went to the reception desk and plucked up the rabbit skull. "This way." Amadea heaved one of the great doors open a crack, and she ushered Quill inside.

Amadea tucked the requests under her arm as she mapped the archives in her mind. She narrowed his tour down to the four areas connected to the Kirazzi requests. If Quill met the specialists, perhaps he'd trust them and not worry about hanging around, being in the way. She started up the iron stairs again: The Bone Vault first, where she could collect Tunuk.

Then Bijan's workshop. Then Yinii's library; it was close by, and the bronze rooms would be locked for another—

Amadea reached the top of the staircase and stopped. She looked back at Quill. "Did you see Zoifia at her desk?"

He looked startled. "The blond woman? No? Should I have?"

Amadea glanced back at the doors, then up to the third floor, where the bronze collections were. A flash of pale curls appeared between the railings, and Amadea cursed.

"Is something wrong?" Quill said.

"It will be fine," Amadea told him, striding toward the Bone Vault. "But someone else will need to handle your tour. Come with me quickly, please."

orbit

Follow us:

f /orbitbooksUS

/orbitbooks

/orbitbooks

Join our mailing list
to receive alerts on our
latest releases and deals.

orbitbooks.net

Enter our monthly
giveaway for the chance
to win some epic prizes.

orbitloot.com